F[illegible] whose novels have been Sunday Times best-[illegible] as the voice of young, med[illegible]
[illegible]
cottage in Oxfordshire. To find out more about her novels, visit Fiona's website at www.fionawalker.com

Praise for Fiona Walker:

'Romps along with plenty of self-deprecating wit'
Sunday Times

'A sizzling summer read of love, sex, passion and soaring temperatures'
Sun

'Walker has a nicely epigrammatic turn of phrase and she understands how love can make normally sensible adults behave like imbeciles'
Daily Express

'Romantic, intelligent, steamy and really rather wise'
Bookcase

'The bonkbusting read of the summer'
For Women

Also by Fiona Walker

Kiss Chase
Well Groomed
Snap Happy
Between Males
Lucy Talk
Lots of Love
Tongue in Cheek

Fiona Walker

FRENCH RELATIONS

First published in Great Britain in 1994 by Hodder & Stoughton
First published in paperback in 1995
A Coronet paperback
A division of Hodder Headline
This edition published in 2003

37

A CIP catalogue record for this title is available from the British Library

ISBN 978-0-340-63488-2

Typeset by Hewer Text Ltd, Edinburgh
Printed and bound in Great Britain by
Clays Ltd, St Ives plc

Hodder & Stoughton
A division of Hodder Headline
338 Euston Road
London NW1 3BH

For the Saint, the Genius, the Doctor, the Red-head
and both the Dotties

Prologue

'Ohmygod, I've forgotten my passport!'

Tash French bombed back out of Hampstead Underground's lift just as the doors were shutting, trapping her rucksack in its metal jaws with a dubious crunch and almost dislocating both of her shoulders as she was brought to an abrupt halt.

Freeing the tattered and shredded bag – which had halved in size – she was briefly accused of fare-dodging and searched for incendiary devices by an enthusiastic guard before bursting out on to Hampstead High Street to run home and collect the truant document. She'd put it out on the kitchen table so that she wouldn't forget it. She'd then covered it and the table in rubbish from her bag when searching for her luggage tags.

Fighting her way through the crowds of shoppers, she glanced at her watch. She was supposed to be checking in for her flight in three-quarters of an hour. She'd never make it. If only she hadn't got so engrossed in the daytime TV phone-in on restructuring and prioritising one's life through astrology to overcome shyness and skin problems, she wouldn't be this late.

She ran breathlessly down the High Street before darting to the left and along Old Brewery Mews, unaware that pairs of holey socks, shabby knickers and some decidedly antique bras were being scattered from a tear in the rucksack, leaving a paperchase trail of smalls behind her. As she dashed into Willoughby Road, she left the mews looking as if a hundred swinging singles about to set off on a day trip to Benidorm had conga-ed down its pavement.

With her nose in a fellow rope-hanger's armpit half an hour later, Tash was too tightly crammed into the corridor of a Piccadilly Line tube to look at her watch, but she knew she was cutting things finer than a Barbie doll's hair ribbon if she was going to make it to Heathrow in time. She was firmly wedged between the anonymous armpit – devoid of Right Guard for several days, Tash deduced – a thin-haired woman with a twitch who was sucking a Fisherman's Friend pungently and thrusting a *Daily Express* into the back of Tash's neck, and a little Indian who was reading on tip-toes over the thin woman's shoulder and listening to what sounded like a battery of tap-dancing centipedes marching along a metal sink unit on his personal stereo.

In a very black section of tunnel between Hyde Park Corner and Knightsbridge, the train came to a shuddering, hissing halt and the lights dipped on and off like a department store five minutes before closing time. The engine went eerily quiet. Someone muttered in a did-you-know voice about signal failures at Gloucester Road. Everyone ignored him – only maniacs, after all, conversed with strangers on public transport – and pretended to be engrossed in the posters overhead telling them not to fare-dodge. A drunk began reedily singing 'Underneath the Arches'. Still they didn't move.

A German couple were starting to have a heavily vowelled argument with the only recognisable words being 'Wictoria', 'Vestminster' and 'Lie-cest-er Sqverer'.

The did-you-know told them they were going the wrong way, but not to worry, just think – they were currently directly underneath Harrods.

'Ve did Harrods on Ved-nes-day,' snapped a German.

The Indian's centipedes continued on the drainer. The *Express* woman inserted another Fisherman's Friend. Still the train remained motionless.

Tash, reeling from the combined BO and lozenge fumes,

started to snivel into the armpit. She'd definitely never make her flight now.

In the depths of her patched-up rucksack, her alarm clock went off.

There turned out to be a bomb scare at South Kensington. All stations were to be evacuated.

Having been firmly smacked on the bottom by the electric ticket barriers before filing out of Knightsbridge Underground, Tash walked groggily into a convoy of heavily guarded Arabs who almost swept her like driftwood into a stretch Merc. She hastily extracted herself and jumped on to a bus.

Two stops later she jumped off. It was going the wrong way.

Whimpering in panic, she looked at her watch. Her check-in time had passed; the plane was due to take off in three-quarters of an hour. Risking her life, and that of a cycling courier who was talking on his mobile phone and reading a map at the same time, she shot across the road.

Once there, she ran after another bus and tripped over a Japanese tourist, flying gracefully into a striped Telecom tent and flattening the entire thing and the engineers inside.

'Sorry!' Tash muttered, disentangling herself from a web of Nikon straps and crushed BT employees.

She dived after the bus and threw herself on to the tailgate

The bus terminated at Chiswick because the driver wanted to have his regulation coffee break.

Tash wailed with frustration and looked around desperately for a glowing yellow rectangle above a black cab.

Traffic groaned past her in convoy, emitting great clouds of grimy exhaust fumes and strains of top forty hits. Occupied cabs threaded in and out of the choked lanes like fat beetles pushing their way through slow-moving ladybirds, their drivers' jaws constantly moving, occupants staring at the meters in silent horror, watching the numbers tick up like a jogger's stopwatch. Hundreds of unoccupied cabs seemed to be whizzing back towards central London. None passed Tash, stranded forlornly on the opposite side of the busy road.

In a few minutes' time she'd be able to see her plane rising up from the distant smoky horizon like a great metal phoenix. She threw down her rucksack and stamped on top of it in frustration, her eyes bleary with tears.

'Wanna lift, love?'

A Darth Vadar in black leathers straddling a throbbing ebony 800cc BMW which was big enough to fit a jacuzzi pillion on, had drawn up beside her and was looking at her through half a centimetre of tinted visor.

'Going to Heathrow?' he asked in a muffled voice.

Tash nodded doubtfully and peered through the smoked glass. All she could see was her own blotchy reflection – piggy-eyed and miserable. He was probably a mad rapist, she decided, intent on whisking her off to deepest Kew and torturing her in a hot-house.

'It's all right,' he lifted the visor and turned out to be about fifty, West Indian and in possession of a Mother Teresa smile. 'I work there. Look.' He pointed to a parking permit on his wind deflector. It said he was called Murray de Souza and was in Security Division 385.2b.

'Thanks, but I've missed my flight,' Tash shrugged miserably.

'Where you going?'

'Paris. De Gaulle,' Tash told him glumly. 'At least I was.'

Murray's mouth split into a toothy laugh. He had gold fillings, Tash noticed. It was like looking into a prospector's cellar.

'You didn't phone to check all the flights were running?'

Tash shook her head.

'Child, get on the bike.'

When Tash got to Heathrow – and miraculously, thanks to Murray's help, into the right terminal and up to the correct desk – she found that all the flights into Paris were running three hours late due to an air traffic control strike.

She then had to wait two hours by a rubber pot-plant and

three depressed-looking angel fish in the departure lounge before boarding her plane. It was only when she was finally shuffling along a huge plastic tube with her grouchy fellow passengers, towards the mouth of the tin bird, that she realised she'd left the house with the television waffling downstairs, the radio blaring upstairs, all the lights blazing, the answerphone switched off and a garden window open because one of the cats had developed a phobia about the cat-flap. She also had an unpleasant feeling that she'd left her keys in the front door.

'Er . . . do you mind awfully if I make a phone call?' she asked a make-up-enamelled stewardess apologetically.

As the 'Fasten Seat-belt' and 'No Smoking' signs pinged on and off overhead, Tash drifted in and out of a fitful dose. Every time blissful and silent incoherence descended, she slipped sideways on to the tense, annoyed shoulders of the passenger beside her – a large, middle-aged woman who had earlier announced herself from 'Cheam, dear', before plugging into the 'Easy Listening' music channel. Mrs Cheam was layered in pink acrylic and every perfume tester Duty Free had to offer.

Finding herself nose-to-shoulder with cérise and C'est La Vie!, Tash forced her motion-displaced body upright and tried to take an intense interest in the in-flight magazine instead.

As soon as they were airborne she lurched up the aisle during a hefty bout of turbulence and located a mercenary-looking card-phone. Using the last few pounds left on the credit limit of her plastic, she rang the next-door neighbours in Derrin Road to ask them to take her keys out of the door. The wife (who Tash had nicknamed Molly Toff-Cocktail because she was so short-fused) answered with a pert sniff that she'd done exactly that five minutes after Tash had left and did she know her underwear was spread all over Hampstead?

Feeling queasy, Tash wandered vaguely back to Mrs Cheam and the in-flight magazine.

Thoughts of Max kept flashing through her mind. These generally consisted of the most embarrassing things she'd ever done: returning from the loo in Langans on one of their first dates with her skirt tucked in her knickers; him catching her cleaning her contact lens case with his toothbrush or spraying Chanel Pour Homme liberally round the kitchen to hide the smell of two-day-old cat lit; laughing when he told her his old bag of a mother had been accused (mistakenly as it turned out) of shoplifting in Harrods.

Tash supposed she wasn't the most sympathetic of cohabiters. But she loved Max – beautiful, spoilt, charming, the antithesis of herself – so desperately that sometimes it expressed itself in odd ways.

He'd picked her up in the Café Bohème. Literally – a buckle of his beloved John Richmond jacket attaching itself to her tatty leather coat and lifting her off her seat as he'd brushed past, linking them together like a two-horse team. Trying to break free, Tash had looked into the most mischievous and merry grey eyes she'd ever encountered. Then a warm hand had covered hers and she'd almost passed out, the attraction was so sudden.

'Why bother?' With a gorgeous, crinkly smile Max had bent over her shoulder and, donkey blond hair mixing with her dark locks, tied their coats more securely together. 'My mother keeps telling me to get hitched to a beautiful girl.'

'I'm not sure I'm ready to get tied down,' she'd laughed, taking in the long sooty lashes and cleft chin shaped like the base of an apple.

They'd remained tethered together all evening, Max's friends joining her university cronies. As they'd chatted and tangled eyes – accidentally brushing hands, feet, elbows, knees and cheeks in the crowded bar – Tash had thought she'd explode with excitement, her stomach grinding bubbles of anticipation into her pelvis like a pepper-mill. Later, they'd eaten at Kettners, clumsy with exuberance, getting unstoppable giggles over the silliest of jokes.

Tash attended one lecture in the following six weeks.

Max claimed she was a revelation. He adored the fact that she had boundless energy, drank as much as him, always finished her meals with relish instead of treating each chip as an increase in dress-size, and didn't have to spend an hour taking her face off each time they went to bed. But, falling in love, Tash had no need to diet, wear make-up, sleep or sober up. Nor did she feel an urge to revise for her finals.

Trailing back from her last, gruelling exam, she'd found three huge new Samsonite suitcases and a pile of packing cases completely blocking the steps to her shared flat. Beside them read a note:

Come live with me, and be my love,
And we will some new pleasures prove,
Besides, there's piles of washing-up,
And the hall carpet could use a Hoov.

Inside, surrounded by red roses which matched his hay-fever red eyes, Max was smoking one cigarette after the other with shaking hands.

They'd been living together for nearly a year. Tash had moved from her squalid university digs into the large terraced house in Hampstead with dreams of breakfasting together on the patio, cordon bleu and Puccini in front of the fire, whole weekends spent in bed with nothing but fresh fruit and champagne.

Why did all her dreams revolve around food? she pondered, wishing she'd worn something with an elastic waist to fly in.

What Tash had discovered in Derrin Road, Hampstead was endless chaotic piles of sullied smalls and two enormous Australian cricketers called Graham and Mikey, who shared the rented house with Max.

('Kiwi!' Graham would cry, 'I'm a flaming New Zealander, not a beach bum whose granny was a pickpocket in Skittlefield, mate.')

Tash sank dreamily on to Mrs Cheam's sumptuous shoulder, locating a patch of White Linen, and thought back on her maiden over at the Derrin Road house, affectionately known as the H-oval.

It hadn't taken long to realise that her new home continually doubled as the club changing room. Webbed kit bags lined up outside the washing machine in the vague hope that their pungent contents would miraculously transfer themselves, clean and Persil-window-tested, into their owners' drawers. Take-away cartons and empty beer cans littered every surface until the house resembled a recycling depot. Loud music and strangers pervaded the H-oval twenty-four hours a day. Tash grew accustomed to finding comatose bodies on the sofas, floorspace, in the bath and once even in between her and Max in bed.

Tash occasionally harboured a resentful suspicion that Max adored his two team-mates far more than he did her. For a start, she reminded herself as Mrs Cheam swabbed her perspiring cleavage with an airline hot flannel, she couldn't hit a boundary six from a slow delivery looped with backspin. Nor could she do a convincing Richie Benaud impersonation.

When she'd moved into Derrin Road, Tash had been at the total adoration stage with Max. He was the first lover she had ever shared toothpaste and phone bills with. His spoilt, confident public charm, matched with intense private gentleness towards her, seldom failed to reduce Tash to a spun-dry jelly of love. She would hug his jumpers when he'd gone to work, walk miles out of her way to get his favourite breakfast cereal and feel warm and romantic when she found one of his hairs wrapped round the soap (although more often than not it belonged to Mikey, who was paranoid about going bald).

Torn between an inability to keep his hands off her and loyalty to his mates, Max had battled valiantly to secure them time alone together, apologising with a lop-sided smile every time three wingers trooped in with a video during a candlelit take-away. But not having him to herself had at times been agony. And being groped between mouthfuls of chop suey during a First Eleven gathering to watch *Basic Instinct* was embarrassing.

Things came to a head when Tash, having blown a week's wages on a wildly sexy outfit to please Max on his birthday, discovered on the night that his house-mate, Mikey, had whipped it from her wardrobe to wear to a tarts and vicars party. Instead of taking her side, Max had found the whole thing screamingly funny. He'd infuriated Tash further by claiming that Mikey had the legs for it – insinuating, Tash felt, that hers were like steel girders – and then suggesting she go as Terry Waite because she was tall and had big feet.

Tash extracted herself from Mrs Cheam's tense shoulder-pad once more and accepted a huge gin and tonic from an air stewardess. She smiled up at the pretty woman dreamily, her thoughts full of Max.

'I said here's your credit card back, madam,' the woman repeated irritably. 'Madam left it in the phone. It seems a call to Dubai has been charged to it since take-off. Did madam place that call?'

'Oh dear. No, I didn't.' Tash took back her card and handed the hostess a suddenly empty plastic tumbler in return. 'Do you think I could have another one of these, please?' she added weakly.

Halfway down her next drink, the Dubai call miraculously lost significance. A short spell of turbulence deposited the remainder of her drink over Mrs Cheam's handbag, but Tash was too wrapped up in nostalgia to notice. Oh, how she'd loved those first months at Derrin Road.

Although she and Max were seldom alone, their childish, hedonistic high spirits had been contagious. Night after night, the assembled Derrin Road revellers would stay up too late drinking whatever they could afford (usually the cheapest of enamel-stripping wine and lager) and playing a variety of competitions they made up from half-lost board games: Monogamyopoly, Strip Twister, Trivial Pervert, Draw-On-Your-Neighbour Pictionary and Snog Scruples. It was normally the gregarious Kiwi, Graham, who invented these, getting more and more creative until his games were totally unplayable.

Tash was great friends with enormous, curly-haired Graham who, extremely soft-hearted under his flippant exterior, mothered her mercilessly. Graham worked as an off-shore oil-driller, spending two months on-rig and two off. This meant that when Tash was out of work (which was more often than not) they would sit in the kitchen all day drinking pints of coffee and smoking packets of fags, gassing like a pair of old women and watching day-time TV.

Less accessible was the more image-conscious Mikey. The biggest earner of them all, working in the city, he regularly bailed the others out when the rent was due and more often than not bought in the household's enormous alcohol supply. He was also the tidiest. Max and Graham were hopelessly unhouse-trained, and mess followed Tash around like a gutter-press gang. Mikey was less of a lad and more of a womaniser, with a seemingly unending stream of Louisas, Samanthas and Gemmas leaving earrings in the bathroom, lipstick stains on the mugs and tantrums on the answerphone. He treated Tash like a slightly irritating child.

Looking back, Tash supposed she had behaved like one.

Unable to hold down any job for more than two weeks, she had countered feeling increasingly bored and isolated by entertaining the Derrin Road mob. Soon her chilli was notorious in North London and she had an alcoholic intake second only to Oliver Reed's. Her repertoire of blue jokes increased tenfold and Mikey started to complain that his girlfriends kept bumping into one another when they dropped in for a chat with her.

Then one night several months ago, Max had gently suggested she should try harder to find a decent job. It was only then that it occurred to Tash – three-quarters of the way down a bottle of Fitou at the time – that she wasn't the world's most dynamic partner. Her days consisted of sleeping off her hangover until it was time to get up for *Neighbours*, the *Daily Mail* quick crossword and riotous coffee with the Derrin Road stragglers.

Getting into his subject with increasing vigour, Max had gone on to point out that when he returned from work each evening he was greeted with an action-packed summary of Australian soap plots followed by long moans about Mikey helping himself to her butter from the fridge. She was corrupting Graham, he'd told her lightly, and now saw more of Max's cricketing and rugby gang than of him – *and* she kept making them coffee with his Nescafé.

Max had insisted that he was only telling her for her own good, she was far too bright, talented and zany to waste her life as she was. He wanted to see her where she belonged, emblazoned on the catalogues of all the greatest galleries in London.

Tash now suspected this 'talk' marked the first mildewed dots of rot appearing in their relationship. It had been the forerunner of a legion.

Determined to live up to his expectations, Tash had dug out her interview skirt and redoubled her efforts to find a job which she wouldn't get fed up with before her first coffee break. With a degree in fine art – or 'potato printing' as Max referred to it – she found a limited spectrum of choice. The eighties boom was over, and one needed a PhD in information technology to temp at a desk-top keyboard.

In the end, desperately broke, she lied through her teeth to a very flash local estate agent and got freelance work photographing split-level church conversions in Camden and mock Georgian houses in The Bishops Avenue, where even the garages were en suite. Her erratic fees just about got the rent in on time, although she had many sleepless nights poring over the *Hamlyn Guide To Photography*. She told everyone else that she was working as a freelance illustrator.

Max had initially been so pleased that he bought her a wildly expensive dinner in Suntory. Tash, not wanting to offend him by confessing that she hated Japanese food, had spent the entire night throwing up in the bathroom.

That night the wind changed and set Max's face in a habitual grimace.

More freelance work for a local newspaper followed. Tash swopped boozy lunches in Derrin Road for even sleazier ones in the Horse and Groom with her new-found hack friends. They made her laugh, were acerbically ambitious, knew everyone and bought enormous rounds. She loved them to bits.

Max, grumbling that he saw her even less than before she worked, booked tickets at the Coliseum to see *Tosca.*

Vapid from spending all afternoon at a drunken private viewing with the listings editor, Tash had fallen asleep in the tube on the way and ended up in Kennington. When she'd finally made her way back to the West End, Max had given the tickets to two students and was fuming by a railing.

She'd made it up to him afterwards by agreeing to play Seed-uction, Max's favourite game. He would go into a bar and sit nursing a drink; Tash would follow five minutes behind and, pretending not to know him, eye him up across the room, order a drink to be sent over and generally flirt till it hurt. Tash found these routines intensely embarrassing, especially as she was terribly short-sighted and often got the wrong man, which infuriated Max.

With a snowball of panic careering ever larger down to her stomach, she'd started to sense that the barely bridgeable gap between Max's idea of fun and her own was fast becoming a chasm.

Yet his continually scornful face had merely made her twice as determined to win back his approval.

At the far end of the plane, stewardesses had started to extract plastic shrink-wrapped breeze blocks from metal trolleys and deposit them on the fold-down tables in front of passengers. Tash mindlessly put the in-flight magazine into Mrs Cheam's damp handbag and cast her mind back two months.

Why, in this life of Beamish and board games till dawn at the H-oval, had everything turned so sour? she asked herself miserably.

Max, beautiful, friendly, laid-back Max with his crinkly smile and Jean Hughes Anglade looks had suddenly, almost over-night, gone off her. He found fault in everything she did. Her scatter-brained optimism, childish impulsiveness (she bought two cats, Boots and Poshpaws, not realising they were incon-tinent, misanthropic and hated one another) and her constant need for security seemed to irritate him beyond belief. He started suggesting she dye her hair blonde, wear red lipstick and invest in flat shoes because her favourite 'bimbo boots' made him nervous.

Tash had been terrified he was seeing someone else.

She'd decided to probe Graham and Mikey as subtly as possible about Max's fidelity. Tash's subtlety being non-existent, they had twigged immediately.

'Get outa here!' Graham's eyes had widened dramatically. 'Does Her Mag wear a g-string? Is the Pope a lesbian? Forget it, Tash, and make us a cuppa to get over the shock.'

Mikey had just raised an eyebrow and asked her if she'd been taking acid.

So Tash had read up on stress at work instead. Positive that Max's stress factor was at top rating, she started running him hot baths for his return from work, giving him nightly massages and cooking him low-fat, high-fibre meals.

'Do you think I'm pregnant?' he would snap from the confines of the bathroom, ensconced in Aroma-foam for the Modern Man.

'I'm not constipated,' he'd mumble, deep in a plate of lentil stodge (whatever Tash cooked, it always turned out looking like porridge).

To cheer her up, the Derrin Road mob had taken Tash out for a raucous Chinese. Max refused to go. Returning in the small hours, she'd discovered him curled round a bottle of vodka, asleep in her wardrobe. Coaxing him out, Tash had kissed his wet eyes with tearful apologies, stroking his hair like a child until he'd fallen asleep with his head in her lap. But the next day he'd refused to talk to her, staying out until the small hours to pay her back, coming in so drunk that he'd crashed out fully clothed on the sofa.

Tash, fearing rejection, hadn't dared confront Max and simply ask him outright what was the matter. Yet the harder she tried to please him, the more withdrawn he became. Finally, in despair, she'd persuaded herself that if she ignored the problem it would simply go away.

They just walked round one another for weeks on end. He stayed home at night, getting pissed with the team. She went out more and more with her hack friends and old university chums, spending too much money and feeling inadequate. She got into bed long after he'd fallen asleep and he got up long before she woke.

'Thank you.'

Tash stared without enthusiasm at the white plastic tray containing pale plastic cutlery and anaemic plastic food. Max could have fast-bowled eleven wickets with the salad roll, she thought wistfully.

While Mrs Cheam unplugged herself from 'Easy Listening' and tucked in, Tash studied the overhead gadgets thoughtfully, playing with the light and nearly blasting her eyebrows into her cleavage with the ventilating fan.

'You going to France for your hols, dear?' Mrs Cheam asked through a mouthful of ham and latex pancake.

Tash nodded, her own mouth occupied by rubberised asparagus tubing.

'Me too,' Mrs Cheam glowed over a thimble of champagne. 'I'm off for a jolly. I'll tell you this because you're sweet and somehow I'm sure you'll understand. Since my husband, Malcolm, died I haven't had much company, you see, dear.' She lowered her voice and cast a secretive eye over her shoulder. 'I'm going on a singles weekend.'

'Oh, yes?' Tash croaked, wondering fretfully why she personally looked like she'd understand.

'Yes,' Mrs Cheam looked excited. 'It's called the Queen's Club – Stopovers in Gay Paree for the Discreet Unattached Art Deco fan, they say. I saw it advertised in *Time Out*. Very reasonable price, dear.'

Tash choked on her trifle-in-a-tub, hoping her neighbour wasn't heading for a big surprise about Gay Paris.

'You meeting anyone you know?' Mrs Cheam continued blithely.

'My family,' Tash muttered with a heavy heart. 'My mother lives in France, you see.'

* * *

When her mother had phoned, Tash had just finished attempting to flatten her stomach with a few sit-ups in the kitchen. She'd got to five and cricked her neck so was raiding the fridge instead.

'Natasha . . . is that you, sweety?'

Tash had had her mouth full of potato salad.

'Mmmmph.'

'Tash? . . . Are you all right? The line's bloody awful.'

'Mmmph . . .' Chomp, chomp. 'Fine, Mummy. How's everything going? How's Pascal and Polly?'

'Pascal's in Zurich. Polly's super. Hardly speaks a word of English, though. Far from being bilingual she just sprouts Franglais all the time. Look, darling, I've had this simply splendid idea and you're not allowed to say no. If you had anything planned for July, sweetheart, cancel it.'

Tash's mother, Alexandra, was the product of a wild French mother and a somewhat unhinged British writer. Having divorced Tash's father, James French – a stuffy golf fanatic – eight years ago, Alexandra had gone on to marry the far more exotic Pascal d'Eblouir shortly afterwards.

'I've stopped being a half-French French and am going to become a French ex-French, darlings!' she'd announced brightly to her three astonished children. 'Granny's chuffed to bits because she says that your father still thinks Victor Hugo is an air-traffic control term.'

Tash had been devastated. France seemed further than Narnia. She'd never got on with her father, and saw her mother's desertion as personal.

Glamorous Pascal was one of the youngest sons of a powerful French shipping family and ten years Alexandra's junior. They now lived alternately in an enormous ultra-modern Parisian apartment, courtesy of d'Eblouir Inc, and a vast and wonderfully tumbledown manoir near Saumur in the Loire, which they had been trying to renovate for the seven years of their marriage. For six of those they had been joined by Pollyanna, their untamable offspring.

Standing in the Derrin Road kitchen, mindlessly dropping

potato salad over the tiled floor, it had suddenly dawned on Tash that she was being asked to spend the summer at the manoir with her disparate, feuding family and – oh no! –

'Do bring Max, darling. I'm dying to meet him. Sophia tells me no one's been allowed to see him yet . . . simply everyone's coming, even your uncle, Edward. None of us have seen the old rogue in over ten years. He's flying over from the States in July. Did you know—'

And, like a scurrilous gossip columnist phoning copy through for a last-minute deadline, she'd barely paused for breath as she launched into full anecdotal flood.

Sipping lukewarm airline coffee which tasted like infused cricket box, Tash remembered her mother's excited gossiping about the family.

A very lapsed Catholic meeting the promiscuous sixties head-on, Alexandra had produced three children from her first marriage – two of those with James French's permission. Later, with her second husband, came the addition of Polly. She loved them all with wholehearted, if unconventional, intensity. It clearly terrified her that, holed up in France and preoccupied with Pascal and Polly, she had drifted further and further from the thoughts of her grown-up children across the Channel. Summer visits were getting rarer. Tash's elder brother, the intractable Matty, referred to her simply as 'Mammon'.

Tash now realised that this family house party was Alexandra's attempt at a grand reconciliation.

She guiltily recalled how, a month ago, she had simply stopped listening to her mother in favour of thinking up a convincing excuse not to go.

'. . . and you will bring Max, won't you, darling? Promise?' Alexandra had repeated towards the end of her spiel. 'You can't keep him all to yourself.'

To Tash the thought of spending a whole summer with her entire weird and wonderful family was intimidating enough. The prospect of inflicting them, even for a week, on Max was doubly daunting. The idea of all that plus the current cold war which was going on between Max and herself had made the potato salad shift uncomfortably in her stomach.

'The thing is, Mummy,' her doodles had become more and more Pollockesque on the phone pad by this time, 'I'm absolutely stony broke at the moment. I can't afford not to work for that long. Cat food's hellishly expensive in England.'

'Pascal and I can let you have some money, darling. It's not a problem. Whatever happened to your shares?'

'I bought a car.' No need to mention that she'd already wrapped it round a lamp-post on the North Circular without insurance.

'Well, just let me know how much you need. I'll sort out your flight. All your expenses are covered at this end. I'll even send you some tog dosh.'

As teenagers, Tash and her sister had been given a monthly clothing allowance known as 'tog dosh'. Tash had spent most of it on cheap ra-ra skirts and boob tubes which she was far too fat for. Now she prayed for kaftans to make a reappearance on the cat-walks.

'Um . . . that's great, Mummy . . . just . . . great . . . but you see Max can't get much time off work, really. He's already got three weeks off for cricket tour in August.'

'Not a problem. He can just pop over for a weekend or something. Meet everyone.'

Tash had by now completely dead-headed an already dead busy lizzy. 'He could . . . yes . . . um . . .'

'You don't sound very keen, sweetheart.' Alexandra had paused, obviously thinking out a new tactic. 'Darling, we haven't seen you for simply *ages*. It would be just awful if you couldn't come.' Pause . . . more thought. 'Sophia and Ben are bringing little Lotty and the new baby – oh! And those glamorous friends of theirs, Hugo and Amanda – er – thing-amybob.'

Ah, veiled attack, Mother! Tash had almost passed out. Hugo Thingamybob – alias Hugo Beauchamp, best man at Sophia and Ben's wedding and object of all Tash's fantasies from eighteen to twenty-one (Max intervened at that point, although occasionally Tash had a relapse).

Her mother had continued the Paris-to-London blanket bombing on Tash's conscience, while all the time Tash secretly envisaged Hugo's divine face.

'Matty and Sally are bringing the children too,' Alexandra had enthused. Matty was Tash's politically correct elder brother. 'I haven't seen Tor since the christening. She'll have doubled in size no doubt—'

Off again. Tash had tried to concentrate, but dreamy images of Hugo Beauchamp kept floating past. Beautiful, insolent, spoilt but impossibly sexy Hugo. The potato salad performed several back flips until her mother snapped her out of her daze like a shot of adrenalin into a strained muscle.

'So how's the job, sweety?' Alexandra had suddenly asked, inadvertently terrifying Tash into absolute submission to her every whim.

'Great!' Tash had squeaked defensively.

'Still working for that glamorous art studio?'

'Oh yes, Mummy, quite.'

'Sophia tells me you got a commission for a book cover.'

Christ! Tash had clutched a drawer handle so hard it snapped off. Had she told her sister that? Sophia always made her lie out of paranoid inadequacy. What else had she told her?

'I'll post you the tickets a.s.a.p., Tash . . . Tash? . . . Natasha? . . . NATASHA!'

'Okay, Mummy, that'd be lovely.' Tash had finally conceded defeat with a worried sigh. 'I can't vouch for Max, though.'

By this time Graham had surfaced from one of his twenty-four-hour sleep-ins and was staggering round the kitchen bleary-eyed, looking for a clean mug.

'Look, I must go, Mummy, someone's at the door,' Tash had muttered, handing him one off the drainer.

Graham had raised his eyebrows and spooned three heaped teaspoons of coffee into the chipped Snoopy mug.

'Mmmm – yes, Mummy . . . I will . . . mmm . . . yes . . . okay . . .'

'Ding Dong!' Graham had said loudly, shooting her a wink.

'Yes . . . well, it's always sounded odd, Mummy. The batteries are running down.' Tash had aimed a kick at him but missed and stubbed her toe on the dresser instead.

'Okay . . . love you too. Give Polly and Pascal my love. Bye . . . bye.'

Afterwards, Tash had stood beside the phone for a long time, chewing her thumbnail in trepidation. Then a thought had struck her a pleasant blow on the chest.

Hugo Beauchamp! Well, well. She'd wandered distractedly past Graham, not hearing his offer of a cuppa, and drifted upstairs to do some more sit-ups in private.

Tash suddenly came to with her face buried deep in Mrs Cheam's pillowy stomach. Her eyes watered from Anaïs Anaïs. She'd just been dreaming about Max seducing a troop of cornflower-blue-eyed, all-American cheer-leaders.

Apologising profusely to Mrs Cheam, she ordered her third enormous gin and tonic and thumbed through the emergency instructions leaflet before opting for working out which passenger looked most like a terrorist.

Staring with critical suspicion at a very thin man who was nervously clutching a cheap briefcase, Tash mulled over her dream. It was one of many since their disastrous final 'talk' ten days ago.

Somehow there had never been an ideal time to ask Max about the holiday. He was either being unbearably ratty or ignoring her. She kept putting it off.

Surely a free trip to the Loire was the ideal pick-me-up for a flagging relationship? Tash had told herself whenever on the verge of broaching the subject with Max. Not with my family it isn't, her conscience had countered.

She'd told her mother that she'd fly out in the last week in June. It got to June the sixteenth and she still hadn't mentioned it to Max.

Graham was on-rig that week. Mikey had taken up weekend

residence in a flat in Covent Garden belonging to someone called Letitia. All the Derrin Road drunks had been temporarily evicted by Tash, who, in a moment of Taurean guilt-compensation, had located the vacuum and was attempting to find the carpet under a debris of cans and ashtrays. She and Max were for once alone and awake at the same time.

It had come out in an incoherent babble just as he was lifting his legs for her to tidy underneath them.

'My mother's having a summer house party in the Loire and we're invited – she's sent me the tickets – it's all expenses paid – you only have to come for the weekend she says – but, I mean you could stay for much longer . . . er . . . she's invited lots of family and friends – if you can take the time off, that is – not that you have to come at all if you don't want to . . . um . . . well?'

'Pardon?' Max had looked up from a copy of *Esquire*, somewhat perplexed.

'Er . . . do you want to come on holiday to France this summer?'

'Come and meet the folks sortofthing?' Max's slate eyes had been unreadable, his dark brows arched in two bemused bass clefs.

'Not exactly. My family aren't quite like that.' How could she explain to him that a holiday with the Borgias would probably be more appetising?

'I've never had the opportunity to find out,' he'd muttered, returning to *Esquire*.

'Well, now's your chance.' Because she didn't want him to come at all, Tash had sounded as if she were offering him a week in a Moss Side nudist colony.

The inevitability of Max's reaction hadn't stopped it hurting.

'Tash, I think we need to talk . . . I've been wanting to say something to you for ages now.'

'Oh,' she'd squeaked. Why did her voice sound like she had just emptied the vacuum bag into her mouth? She had stopped mid-tidy and sunk into a sofa, unfortunately on top of Poshpaws, who took great exception.

'Yes,' Max had sighed, hooking an ankle up on to his knee. 'In fact I get the distinct impression that you've been avoiding conversing with old Maximilian lately. I've been thinking seriously about flash cards.'

'Have you?' Tash had picked at a balding patch of her jeans. Like Mikey's head, she'd found herself thinking quite irrationally.

'Tash, look at me.'

Tash hated eye contact. It came from having odd eyes – one amber, one grey. She looked constantly as if she'd lost one tinted contact lens.

Turning in his direction, she'd held Max's steady gaze for an instant before settling for staring at his mouth.

'Tash, do you love me?'

'Yes . . . that is . . . yes.' Her voice had wavered, desperate not to sound clingy.

'You don't sound very sure.'

Oh, get it over with, Max. Tell me I'm fired.

'Oh, I am, I am!' She'd stared at that gorgeous mouth and wanted to weep. Then she'd noticed a cold sore and looked quickly away.

'Are you happy with things the way they are?' He'd moved in next to her on the sofa.

No, no – you don't love me any more. I have no self-confidence without you.

'Yes . . . well . . . it's a bit awkward with Mikey and Graham and stuff . . . but . . . you know . . .'

Why can't I express myself? Why, why, why?

'Well, I'm not.'

She'd chewed her lip and fought tears.

That had been her opening, she now realised. The chance for her to bow down gracefully had nudged her in the heart expectantly. She should have nobly taken her cue and suggested he keep Kate Bush while she took possession of Ry Cooder.

Instead she'd just croaked, 'Oh, yes?' staring glumly at his shoes until he was forced to plough on.

'It's everything, Tash, not just us. The job, London, the lads, everything.' He'd taken her hand, examining the paint stains and bitten nails which always smelt of white spirit or photographic fluids.

'Henry's bankrupt,' he'd announced finally.

His boss! Tash had looked at Max in horror. He'd once told her that Henry was the only man on earth he really admired.

'The receivers come in at the end of the week.'

'Christ . . . I'm so sorry.' Tash had squeezed his hand. 'What's he going to do?'

'He'll have to get a job working for someone else. His house is mortgaged up to the roof felt,' Max had told her sadly, 'and Sarah's expecting sprog three in August.'

There was a pause.

Tash, looking back, could only remember hearing one of the cats sharpening its claws on the stairs' carpet, nothing of Max's shattered expression.

'And you?' she'd finally managed to croak.

Max had let her hand go and stared out of the window. 'I'm . . . er . . . I'm thinking of going to the States.'

Tash had remained motionless, the pause button depressed on her pulses.

'Just for a bit. See how the land lies. Perhaps get a job there for a while . . . or just have a holiday. See Dad.'

Max's father lived in New York. Tash had always thought Max and he loathed one another.

'I really needed your support recently, Tash.' Max had measured his voice carefully for the final insult. 'But you've been too busy to notice. It seems you've got time for everyone else but me. I'm amazed you still bother to sleep here at night.'

Tash had been too aware of the truth in his words to disagree and too ashamed of herself to attempt the hopeless post-mortem of an apology.

The memory of that strained conversation where more was left unsaid than actually spoken, leaving silences so heavy that a mind-reader could have taken dictation, made Tash's eyes blur over. Turning away so that Mrs Cheam couldn't see, she blew her nose loudly on her hot flannel, inadvertently affording most of the plane a full view of her distress.

Yet, looking back, she was amazed at how calmly she'd taken Max's news, asking 'When are you going?', 'Have you got enough money?', 'What about Derrin Road?' She even thought to ask about the cricket tour. Anything to divert from the topic of their relationship and her culpability.

From that day on, Max's disapproving face was replaced by a martyred one. Tash had guiltily helped him prepare to go, dyeing all his shirts prison grey in the wash, losing his socks and ironing burns into his chinos. She'd even agreed to lend him her precious camera when he dropped heavy hints later that week.

Yet, right up until he left for JFK ten days later, nothing was said about their relationship. Max became more affectionate than in recent months, but his thoughts seemed somehow miles and miles away as if they'd been sent on ahead to wait in left luggage. It was as though he was putting his whole life on hold to step outside of it for a bit. Tash had an awful feeling that when he returned she would no longer be included.

Mikey and Graham had been equally perturbed.

'He owes me a grand,' Mikey had raged.

'Who's going to bat first?' wailed Graham.

Tash had hidden from them both, convinced that she was personally responsible. Escaping to France should have come as a relief, but the thought of her overwhelmingly self-confident family and the sneering beauty of Hugo Beauchamp waiting for her there made her mourn even more desperately for Max. The warm, gentle Max she'd let down and lost.

With ten minutes to landing, Tash desperately wanted to spruce up for whichever of her family had come to meet her – particularly if, by some complete and rather horrifying miracle, Hugo Beauchamp was with them.

Penned into a two-foot-square toilet cubicle, she realised that her reflection needed more than the contents of her soap-bag to revive it. In fact it was doubtful that the entire cosmetics department of Dickins and Jones could do much. The bags under her eyes looked like coal sacks, her hair was as greasy at the roots as it was frizzy at the ends and two giant spots had emerged in perfect symmetry on either side of her chin. She needed dark glasses, a hat and a yashmak. Instead she slapped on some spot-cover and a few hefty puffs of CoCo and meandered back to Mrs Cheam, who had swopped her scratchy scarf and enormous spiked brooch from right to left shoulders and was gibbering because a stewardess had accused her of trying to make off with the in-flight magazine.

Ears popping as they descended, Tash wished she had time for another gin and tonic.

2

Meanwhile, at Home Farm on the Holdham Estate in Worcestershire, Sophia Meredith was busily ramming a three-day-old flower arrangement down the waste disposal unit in her sumptuously oak-clad kitchen.

Provided Josh didn't throw up his Heinz babyfood Chicken Provençal, everything was running perfectly to schedule, Sophia told herself proudly. She glanced dubiously at her long-lashed, blond-haired boy. Who would imagine something so angelic could produce so much waste product? He wasn't taking to solids as well as his sister, Lotty, had. Three lots of Farley's Rusks had been returned on to his Beatrix Potter bib only that morning. But Josh remained sucking intently on a red plastic alphabet chain from Hamleys.

Sophia busied herself slinging out the contents of the fridge that would go off in their absence. Out flew the untouched M and S delicatessen tubs, all the Fortnum's goodies she'd bought last week, half a goose and the salmon she'd bought yesterday, before she and Ben had decided to eat out instead.

She'd half filled a black bin liner when it occurred to her that she could have offered the lot to Joan, the char, who was coming to collect the keys that afternoon.

'Drat it!' Sophia secured the top with string instead.

She glanced at the clock. Half one. Where was Ben? She'd specifically told him he had to be back in plenty of time for the arrival of his friends, Hugo and Amanda. *And* he had to take the dogs up to the Hall to stay with his parents. In fact, there were only two things marked as done on his list of *Things To Do* – both of those delegated to Ron the gardener that morning.

Tutting irritably, Sophia ticked off *Fridge* from her own list. As the unpleasant realisation that she'd just jettisoned the lunch she was due to give Hugo and Amanda dawned on Sophia, Paola, the smudge-eyed, coal-haired au pair, walked in with a sheepish-looking Lotty.

'As queek as I pack 'er clothes she ees unpack them,' Paola moaned.

'Want to take Noo Noo!' wailed Lotty.

At three, Charlotte Meredith was an exquisite ebony-haired mini-replica of her mother. She was also spoiled rotten. She was seemingly surgically attached to her 'Noo Noo', a grubby old cot blanket which no amount of Biotex could improve. In fact the current Noo Noo was a great advance on the previous one, an ancient pair of Granny B's support knickers fished out from who knows where. They had met a tragic end – or so Ben had told Lotty – at the hands of the Noo Noo Monster. Since then Lotty hadn't let her new Noo Noo out of her sight.

'You can only take Noo Noo if you let Paola pack your clothes,' Sophia sighed, lifting an eyebrow as she noticed her nanny's suede mini-skirt, donned no doubt in Hugo's honour.

'Want to take Hippo.' Lotty's mouth set into a concrete pout.

'You can take Hippo too – *if*—'

'Want to take Ted and Mugs and Mr Messy and Nelly and Flumps and—'

'You can take Noo Noo and Hippo and that's that!'

Lotty had her I'm-about-to-cry-until-you-give-in face on so Sophia added quickly, 'You can tell all the other toys about your holiday when you get back. Won't that be fun?'

Lotty looked speculative.

'I'm surprised you didn't want Puddles to come too,' Sophia added under her breath as she turned back to her list. Puddles was Lotty's Shetland pony.

'Daddy said no this morning.' Lotty wandered over to the French windows. 'Why are the doggies playing piggie-back?'

'Oh no!' yelped Sophia. 'Not again! Molly's in season.'

In the end Sophia took the dogs up to the Hall herself. She would have liked to walk across the estate to clear her head, but with four dogs plus their baskets and assorted paraphernalia she had to load them into the Range Rover instead.

Even driving up the back entrance to Holdham Hall she was, as always, struck by the sheer size and beauty of the place. Looking at the rows and rows of vast mullioned windows nestling in ivy-coated ornate stonework like rock pools in a seaweed-choked shore, she was shot through with pride. One day all this will be Ben's and mine, she thought triumphantly. With the medieval splendour of Holdham and its formal landscaped park set against a Cambridge-blue sky, nothing could so idyllically encapsulate Sophia's childhood dreams. It was the backdrop to the Barbara Cartland novels she had once devoured, the glossiest cover *Country Life* had ever had, Sophia's enchanted play-pen. And if she squinted, she could almost ignore the Visitors' Car Park sign beside the coach house.

As she swung the Range Rover into the Hall's gravel carriage sweep, Sophia cursed her mother for the umpteenth time that week for organising this stupid house party in France. What did her family care for Ben being Viscount Guarlford, soon to be twelfth Earl of Malvern? Did it matter to them that the locals idol-worshipped her? Glamorous Lady Guarlford, ex-model, perfect mother, society hostess – did you see her featured in *Hello!* last month? Gorgeous.

Daddy had been so pleased for her, Sophia reflected wistfully. He'd even sold his precious Cotmans to pay for the wedding. That wonderful reception in three vast marquees in the garden of Benedict House, her childhood home. Daddy and his marvellous second wife, Henrietta, running everything like clockwork. Mummy's side of the family kept to a minimum and hidden behind vast flower arrangements at the top table.

Except Cass that is. Sophia adored her aunt, who was her mother Alexandra's younger sister. In fact the assured presence of Cass was the one bright spot in this whole dismal holiday idea.

Sophia parked by a series of colourfully flowering tubs and let the dogs out of the back, keeping a firm hold of Molly's collar.

Bea, Ben's mother, came out of the house to welcome her.

'Hello, Sophie,' she barked brusquely. 'Here, let me help.'

Beatrice Meredith was a big woman – big-boned, big-bottomed and very big-voiced. Having herself been titled before marrying the current Earl, she had at first disapproved greatly of her eldest son's choice. Ben had no sense of form. Fine for a younger son to marry looks, but the heir to Holdham?

However, Bea now grudgingly conceded that her daughter-in-law had proved her worth over the past four years. Holdham's public image was up. They'd had more visitors flocking to the Hall this year than ever before in the hope of catching a glimpse of the elegant and famous young wife of handsome Viscount Guarlford. And visitors meant money to the flagging estate funds.

Sophia also seemed to produce healthy, good-looking children, which was all to the good. Bea hated to admit it of her own offspring, but the last generation of Merediths – except perhaps Ben – had been a pretty motley bunch. Bea would never fully approve of her eldest son's choice – and got Sophia's name wrong as often as possible to demonstrate this – but she'd learnt to endure the pink champagne and parquet brigade with just a twist of a withering smile. Lineage, after all, was what mattered.

Sophia, in turn, relished life at Holdham. She was happy to be cushioned away from the five a.m. starts of the modelling world, the paranoid vanity and acid bitchiness.

At first, marrying into such a closed, suspicious family with its rigid, unspoken rules was a nightmare which made the catty cat-walks seem Utopia by comparison. They'd all oozed unending, arrogant self-confidence and a distinctive disdain towards her.

But Sophia had her fair share of guts. Finding that her looks couldn't, as usual, propel her into distinction in this eccentric, cliquey circle, she tried new tactics in her determination to fulfil her dream and become lady of the manor, or Viscountess of impeccable manners. She pored over *Debrett's* and involved herself wholeheartedly in the West of England gentry.

Within weeks of her marriage she was sitting on committees for the World Wide Fund for Nature and Guidedogs for the Blind. She helped Bea organise fetes for the BFSS, coffee mornings for the National Trust, gymkhanas for the local hunt and balls for the Conservatives. All the time she was blissfully unaware that she was continually 'doing the wrong thing', serving up cucumber sandwiches and Kir at shooting lunches or wearing next to nothing to the Royal Yacht Squadron Ball in Cowes week (nearly causing William, Ben's father, to have his second stroke).

While Ben, in time-honoured tradition, was following Cirencester AC by on-the-job training to run the two-thousand-acre estate, Sophia helped Bea plan the summer open days at Holdham. She had never in her romantic dream anticipated the organisation and planning that went into opening a stately home to the public and maintaining its upkeep. Furniture and pictures had to be restored, gardens replanted. The public demanded tea rooms, toilets, a gift shop and tour guides. It all boiled down to money and more fund-raising events.

This is where Sophia finally slotted into the Holdham puzzle and made herself indispensable. She'd met and befriended a great many famous names throughout her modelling career. Through these contacts she organised hugely successful crowd- and money-pullers for Holdham: a celebrity murder weekend, a hot air balloon race and fashion show, an outdoor Shakespeare in the grounds and that unforgettable jousting weekend where a particularly auspicious chat-show host had lost his wig in front of several hundred spectators.

The green welly and gundog brigade had been agog. They couldn't approve. Four-hundred-year-old parkland being cut up by overexcited pop stars wielding ten foot poles on horseback. They couldn't disapprove either. All that money! The tapestries could be rehung, the coach house reroofed, Bea wouldn't have to sell her four-in-hand team to indulge her children. Camilla could come out to a proper ball instead of a boring drinks party and – whoopee! – they could get rid of bloody Fergus for a year in Australia to decide he wasn't a Buddhist of the Seventh Order of Hedonesia; that would ensure the youngest Meredith went to Christ Church to study agriculture and join the Bullers like his elder brother, Jonathan, *not* to grotty old Manchester to study Ancient Norse literature as he seemed wont to do. Eton really was getting too liberal for words.

So Sophia was at last accepted into the closed society she was in love with – albeit as 'the Noo Noo Noov'.

Yet Sophia's triumph meant nothing to her own family. The only titles Alexandra respected were embossed in well-worn gold on musty, leather-bound books that lined the walls of her tatty house in the Loire.

Always the dunce of the French family, Sophia had lacked the natural academic ability of her brother and didn't possess her sister's artistic flair. Whereas they could accumulate O and A levels without missing a single first team match, she had struggled and sweated over the simplest exercises, and only accumulated boyfriends. Despite having adorned the front cover of every glossy magazine and being linked with some of the most desirable men in the world by the age of twenty-six, Sophia was aware that to her cultivated, eloquent family she had never really achieved anything.

Only Tash looked up to her, she reflected bitterly. But poor old Tash was so lumpy and gormless. No, she wanted to dazzle her mother and all her vivid, articulate, multi-coloured house party with her new-found skills. If she had inspired the Meredith clan then surely she could capture the admiration of her own family?

She shared a quick jug of Pimms with Bea and her sisters-in-law, Camilla and Lucinda, in the long Holdham terrace. Bliss! It was so peaceful, with just the faint whirr of one of the gardeners mowing a distant lawn.

Suddenly Sophia groaned. Moving fast along the avenue of

limes in the distance was a red BMW. The light was dappling through the archway of trees on to its paintwork.

Would it go left or right at the park gates? She held her breath. Drat it! It went left. That meant it was heading for the farm. Hugo and Amanda, no doubt.

'I must go, Bea,' she announced, standing up. 'Thanks a million for the absolutely smashing drink.'

Bea winced. She wished her daughter-in-law wouldn't use such gushing vernacular.

'Do you want me to come over and help?' asked Camilla, her large, round face crimson. She'd had a massive crush on Hugo Beauchamp for as long as she could remember.

'No thanks, Milly.' Sophia glanced at her own reflection in a massive paned window. She looked like a cubist painting. Not bad though, she told herself with satisfaction. Thank God she'd changed out of jeans into her little Caroline Charles trouser suit. Amanda, though not exactly competition, was a very slick dresser.

As she bumped up the front driveway to the farm (must get that resurfaced, she noted), Sophia leaned forward and extracted Ben's Ray Bans from the glove compartment. Sunglasses always made her feel more in control. Gave her an edge. Besides, she hadn't reapplied her eye make-up in four hours.

'Darlings!' She stepped from the Range Rover as Hugo and Amanda appeared out of the glass doors to the left. 'So sorry I wasn't here when you arrived. Ben's mother insisted I stay for a drink.'

Lord, but Hugo was looking good, Sophia marvelled – better than ever. Tall, high-cheek-boned, with that thick, luscious tawny hair one just longed to run fingers through, and those wicked sapphire eyes . . .

'You're looking tired, Hugo,' she said smoothly, taking a sharp grip on herself. Hugo may be madly attractive – she had almost fallen for Ben's dearest chum herself on first meeting him – but he was also horribly conceited and, Sophia reminded herself, far too good at putting her down.

'Hello, darling.' Hugo smiled, Spode-blue eyes crinkling against the sun as he came forward to greet her. 'You look typically edible – such a shame Amanda's put me on a diet. We've been sitting in your conservatory admiring your Zen taste in greenery.'

The new conservatory had been finished last week but, as yet, Sophia had only bought one rather ugly rubber plant, which was gasping for life amid the paint fumes.

Sophia smiled feebly, then spotted Hugo's companion scuffing an expensive leather toe into a pot hole.

'Amanda, sweetheart!' Sophia enveloped the small, shoulder-padded woman in a scented hug. She hoped Givenchy was fighting off any smell of dog. 'You look absolutely wonderful.'

Drawing back, Sophia noticed that Amanda *did* actually look surprisingly good. The last time they'd all met, Amanda and Hugo had been on the verge of splitting up for about the fifth time. Amanda had been piggy-eyed, dirty-haired and foul-mouthed. Now, wearing a sparkling white business suit that nipped her waist to non-existence and displayed shapely brown legs at the end of a pencil-thin skirt, she looked every bit the powerful executive that could cut you dead with a single glance. Her hair was cropped to an inch and slicked back. Sleek and blonde, it emphasised her bold, ever critical, almond-shaped eyes.

'Hi, Sophia.' Amanda flashed a wary smile.

'You've cut off all your gorgeous hair!' Sophia lamented, guiding them into the house.

'How's the job? Has Paola given you any of her disgusting coffee yet?'

Amanda smiled to herself. Sophia liked to ask questions, considering it correct social form, but got bored by the answers. She had developed a way of avoiding them by asking how you were, then immediately saying something that prevented your telling her.

'Yes, she did.' Amanda followed Sophia into the vast sitting room, glancing around critically. Yuk! She'd bought two of those ghastly new Liberty chintzes to cover the chesterfields.

What was wrong with the old striped covers? Amanda wondered. They had reminded her of smoking dope and eating curry off her lap with Hugo and Ben during those nefarious weekends before Sophia and her little lists arrived. Ten to one the silly cow had written an itinerary for the trip and stuck it on to the fridge in the kitchen with one of those awful fake-food magnets she kept buying. Why did Sophia run everything like a military operation?

'The job's great,' she announced, sitting on an armchair to avoid the chintz. 'The chief exec had an apoplectic fit when I told him I was taking four weeks off. "But you've just come back from skiing!" he kept wailing – forgotten it was over a year ago. I've bribed the old shit by promising to bring him back a case of Pouilly Fumé.' Amanda paused, noticing that her hostess was still wearing a pair of very scratched sunglasses, which kept slipping off her nose. 'Have you got a headache, Sophia?'

'No!' Sophia, who was too vain to expose diffusing mascara, threw open the French windows and positioned herself in a shaft of sunlight. Realising she looked silly, she started haphazardly thinning the wisteria. Hugo's girlfriend could put someone on edge just by uncapping her pen, she reflected.

Amanda was top media planner at a glossy advertising agency with more initials in its title than members of staff. In some ways Sophia found her ludicrous. When she had first met her, Amanda had had a Vodafone permanently glued between power-dressed shoulder and Chanel earring. But she was an immensely charismatic woman – she had to be to keep the capricious Hugo in tow for so long (not that he hadn't strayed once or twice, the knowledge of which saved Sophia from feeling totally intimidated by the abrupt Amanda). For someone so slight, she acted more like a man. She swore like a trooper, could drink anyone under the table, was guaranteed to know someone in virtually every restaurant in London, regularly beat men twice her size at tennis and fought tooth and nail for her independence.

Despite all this, Sophia guessed that Hugo and Amanda remained unmarried through his choice, not hers. Amanda had her own flat on Chelsea Harbour and, because of her work, only stayed with Hugo at Haydown, his Berkshire pile, at weekends. As far as Sophia knew, Hugo very seldom bothered with London. Besides, she mused, he could have much more fun on his own (or rather not) at home during the week.

Hugo wandered back into the sitting room, having disappeared off for yet another pee. He'd taken cocaine with Amanda and some of her cronies last night. Bloody awful drug – it was playing havoc with his waterworks. Terrific sex though, he remembered, admiring Sophia's long curving body, almost hidden by her dreary suit. She'd started wearing such Women's Institute clothes since getting in with the Vulture, as Hugo called Ben's mother.

'Where's the old sod himself got to?' he asked, helping himself to a large scotch.

'If you mean Ben, he disappeared off with some Forestry Commission bloke at the crack of dawn and hasn't been seen since,' Sophia explained tersely. She'd decided there was a limit to the amount of time one could wear dark glasses indoors. 'How's Haydown? I must just check Paola's packed everything on the children's lists. Help yourself to a drink, Amanda.' And she was off.

'Do you think old Merrydeath's given Sophia a black eye?' Hugo asked Amanda after she'd gone. He studied a photo of the Eton team that had won the Princess Elizabeth cup at Henley ten years earlier. 'God, I look miserable. Chap behind me was a raving queer – had a gruesome pash on the cox.'

Amanda raised her eyebrows at Hugo, contemplating whether to continue the argument they'd been having in the car. Thinking better of it, she picked up a copy of *Tatler* from the coffee table. It fell open with broken-spined obedience on a spread of Sophia wrapped in velvet Dior with Holdham majestically in the background.

Ben rolled in at three, having taken the Forestry Commission man for some pub grub in the village.

A tall, rangy blond mid-fielder, he was the most wonderfully laid-back man Amanda knew. Whereas Hugo's insolent and bored indifference had a very volatile, almost childlike flipside, Ben was simply a gentle giant. What came across initially as the same arrogance as Hugo exuded was just his lazy, unconcerned manner. He was also the scruffiest individual you could care to meet.

After giving Amanda a kiss and searching every cupboard for his fags, which Sophia had tidied up, he sat down on a sofa, stretched his long legs out on the coffee table and started talking to Hugo about his passion, the estate.

'Marvellous chap that Les Edgecombe. Knew old man Millar when he was over at Mitcheldean. Suggested I replanted Wexcombe Copse with fir. Told him it's been a birch plantation for the best part of three centuries. Just said the bloody puritans hadn't a clue when it came to conifers.' He laughed. 'Christ, I'm parched. Beer?'

Hugo, who'd downed two enormous whiskies, fancied nothing better and went with Ben through to the kitchen.

'Don't s'pose I could help myself to a bowl of cereal or something?' he asked. 'I'm actually famished. No lunch. Sophia on another diet? By the way I've seen a terrific three-quarter bred in—'

Amanda, about to pursue them, heard Hugo start to talk horse and changed her mind. Hugo kept a yard of eventers in Berkshire, mostly for pleasure, but seemed to be getting more and more consumed by them. He played cricket and polo less, even skied less. Now it was bridles and bits, haynets and hunting from dawn to dusk. Ben, whose father kept his own pack, loved nothing more than a hard day to hounds and was only too happy to talk about God's noblest beast for hours on end. Amanda would rather talk about boiled potatoes and cabbage.

She decided to go and find Sophia, who'd only been glimpsed popping in and out clutching potties and cuddly toys for the past half-hour.

Having wandered upstairs (noticing yet more unfamiliar chintz and nick-nacks), Amanda went into a bedroom to find

Sophia supervising Paola cleaning up what looked like regurgitated babyfood.

'Chicken Provençal,' muttered Sophia through clenched teeth. 'Where the hell's Ben? He's so bloody unreliable.'

'In the kitchen with Hugo.' Amanda was staring at five enormous Louis Vuitton cases stacked neatly by the door.

'I suppose one of those is stuffed full of disposable nappies?' she observed.

But Sophia had stalked past her towards the stairs to bring Ben to heel.

'Those are just 'er clothes,' said Paola nodding at the cases. 'The cheeldren's things are in the nursery and Signor's is here.' By the bed was a grip bag no bigger than a satchel.

They set off in the overloaded Range Rover at four, by which time Sophia (who'd scheduled three-thirty on her list) was twitching noticeably.

She's very uptight, thought Amanda happily. Sophia normally oozed bovine motherhood and professional social skills.

They had chartered a flight from Staverton. Paola, who'd matched her suede mini with a skin-tight lycra body stocking, got car-sick within ten minutes and asked to have all the windows open. Sophia's hairdo instantly developed a heavily backcombed look and she assumed an even more murderous expression.

'A mate of mine's selling a bloody good nag in Boddington,' announced Hugo, who'd commandeered the front seat next to Ben so he didn't have to sit with 'the brats'. 'Don't s'pose there's any chance of a detour?'

Amanda joined Sophia in twitching. Sophia's chin moved forward an inch.

3

Tash waited ages at the revolving baggage-claim because she didn't recognise Mikey's canvas rucksack. She then threw it over her shoulder, nearly garrotting herself and several by-standers, and staggered with as fresh a smile as she could muster through the arrivals gate. Her eyes darted around the gallery of faces for a familiar one.

They were still darting round from a seat in the arrivals lounge twenty minutes later. They continued darting from the bureau de change and then from the cafeteria as she downed three espressos in forty-five minutes.

Eventually, fearing eye-strain or her contact lenses popping out from caffeine overdose, she picked her way through to the collection of telephone booths, which sprouted up from the centre of the lounge like a French Milton Keynes, and then attempted to shove some unfamiliar coins into a slot which kept spitting them out again.

She finally got through. It rang for ages at the other end. Tash watched a couple being reunited as more arrivals flooded in. They kissed so sensually. She was shot through with a sudden ache for Max.

Pascal answered.

'Pascal, it's Tash – Natasha.'

'Natasha, chérie! Comment ça va?'

'Fine . . . I mean bien, Pascal. Thing is I'm at the airport . . .'

'. . . Oui . . .'

'Well, no one else is. That is, no one's here to meet me.'

'You did not come weeth your – er – brother?'

'No – I flew. He's driving Sally and the kids. Should I have?'

'Er – c'est un problème. Tu es seule?'

'Yes, Pascal, I said I was seule.' She could imagine her stepfather puffing out his cheeks and looking desperately round for Alexandra. He must be sober. He could only speak English when he was drunk, which was mercifully most of the time.

'Depuis combien de temps es-tu là?'

'Sorry?'

'Attendes . . . Xandra! Xandra! . . . A téléphone! . . . Xandra! Il y a un appel téléphonique pour toi! Merde!' There was a long silence and several clunks. Tash noticed her reflection in the metal behind the operating instructions. The spots were getting bigger: she now looked as if she'd been bitten on the chin by a vampire. She shoved in another phone token.

'Natasha – allô—' Pascal panted. He'd obviously done a quick sprint round the manoir. 'Elle est absente pour le moment – er – look, you can – er – take a taxi? Yes? You understand?'

'Yes . . . I mean no! Pascal, I haven't enough money. It's over two hours' drive.'

'This ees good. À tout à l'heure, chérie!' And with that the phone went dead.

Bloody Pascal! Tash knew her stepfather well enough to realise that he understood English far better than he let on. Undoubtedly, on discovering that he was alone in the house, he couldn't face the drive to Paris and conveniently forgot how to use the future tense.

Two and a half hours later, Tash sat sweating in the back of a taxi, sliding from one end of the burning plastic seat to the other as the dusty Renault sped round hairpin bends and skirted sheer precipices with barely a pin-width to spare. Cheerfully oblivious of Tash's green face, the taxi driver had accompanied (flat tenor) the whole of Bon Jovi's greatest hits and was now starting on Queen's.

It was unbearably hot. What had been a grey, overcast day in London was a scorching and stuffy one just across the Channel. Ian McCaskill would have a field day with the warm front that was currently blast-furnacing Tash.

Her memory of where the manoir was, combined with confusion over 'gauche' and 'droite', got them lost several times. The sun was sinking in a red and orange shot-silk sky as she spotted the silhouetted shapes of the spiky medieval pilasters and the large dome of the bell-tower peeking up from behind a giant black oak wood to their droite . . . or was it gauche?

When the taxi crunched into the courtyard, scattering chickens, Alexandra d'Eblouir came rushing down the steps from her beautiful, decaying house followed by three overexcited spaniels and her daughter, Polly, who was dressed as a nurse.

Tash unglued her bottom from the seat and lurched out of the sweltering car.

Standing on the heavenly cool of the shaded cobbles, she looked at the slender woman approaching her. Her mother looked more glorious than ever. Even dressed in Pascal's jeans and a faded silk shirt, Alexandra was unspeakably stylish. Onyx eyes sparkling, her once scruffy nut-brown hair had been cut into the chicest of bobs which fell like a racehorse's paddock blanket on either side of her high round cheeks. She was also tanned the colour of milk chocolate.

'How long's the Loire been having a heat-wave, Mummy?' Tash laughed, surprised to find tears nudging her eyes.

'Oh, it's been frightful, darling,' replied Alexandra, gathering her into a big bear-hug.

'You've got the first sunny day in weeks. This tan's fresh from Dominica – Oh! Didn't I tell you? Pascal and I went there in May. I'm sure I sent you a postcard.' She smiled distractedly at the taxi driver, who was hanging round in the hope of getting paid.

'And you must be Max,' she murmured fondly, going up to kiss him on the cheek.

Tash raised her damp eyes to heaven and went to hug Polly, who pretended to shoot her with two fingers.

'Aghh! It's the killer nurse from Space-pod Gobbo!' Tash moaned, collapsing with much leg-wriggling on the cobbles.

André, the taxi driver, had always thought the English a dubious nationality. Today's activities merely confirmed his fears. After all, didn't they buy farmhouses in the most beautiful places in France, insist on calling them 'Valley View', then stick nets in the windows so they couldn't see out?

In the end, Tash was forced to use all but one hundred francs of her spending money to pay the irate driver; Alexandra had no cash on her and Pascal had temporarily disappeared (probably in the wine cellar improving his English, Tash decided).

Typical! thought Tash an hour and a half later.

She was sitting drinking her fourth glass of white wine in a vast oak-panelled room which was filled with enormous brightly painted ceramics. Her mother's taste, no doubt. The wine, instead of giving her a euphoric glow, had made her feel fractious and tetchy.

Typical! she thought again, curling her toes in annoyance and focusing on the most vulgar three-foot vase. Mother says I'll miss everyone if I come any later than June and I'm the first bloody one here!

'You bet there's no getting away till August, buster – you just wait and see,' she muttered as one of the spaniels jumped up beside her on the tatty crimson silk sofa. Tash scratched its nose and it thumped its stumpy tail appreciatively. She already missed the cats.

'That was Sophia on the phone,' announced Alexandra, breezing into the room with one earring missing. 'They're staying overnight in Paris then hiring two cars and driving down tomorrow.' She sat on a huge blue armchair. The spaniel immediately tore away from Tash and crash-landed on her knee.

'The Beauchamps are with them,' Alexandra added vaguely.

'They're not married, Mummy,' sighed Tash. 'She's Fraser-Roberts.'

'Who's Fraser? Is he coming instead of Max?'

'No, Mummy.' Tash smiled, despite her black mood. 'Hugo's Amanda is Amanda Fraser-Roberts. They never married. Don't you remember at Lotty's christening? Amanda wasn't there because they'd split up?'

'Let me think.' Alexandra put a finger to her nose thoughtfully. 'I remember Lotty pulled Sophia's hairpiece off and threw it at that fat vicar. And your brother arrived two hours late. Didn't Hugo give Lotty an engraved hip flask and cigarette box? Yes, he did. Bea Meredith was livid. I'm sure the reason Amanda wasn't there was because she had some meeting in London. There was a frightful row about it. They were both going to be God-awful-parents.'

'Oh well, they're not married anyway.' Tash sighed, wishing she hadn't brought the subject up.

She remembered Lotty's christening only too well. At the party afterwards, Hugo had thought she was one of the caterers. Tash hadn't enlightened him, having looked particularly lumpen and revolting that day.

Tash started to panic. The thought of being so close to Hugo Beauchamp had excited her to begin with. Now it terrified her.

'I'm glad you've grown your hair,' Alexandra broke into Tash's churning thoughts with cheerful disregard. 'It suits you, looks smashing.'

Tash had worn her hair as short as a boy's since her teens, in total contrast to Sophia's sleek black mane. It had suited her amazing slanting eyes and long neck. It hadn't, however, suited her bulk and height. Even taller than her model sister, she'd often at a distance been mistaken for an elder brother. Now she'd persevered in growing what Max called her 'outcrop' and it fell below her shoulders in thick, untidy waves.

'Thanks.' Tash's toes curled again. *Please don't talk about the way I look, Mother, please.* It was the one topic which Tash could not bear her family to discuss. They treated her appearance with the same sympathetic encouragement they would dyslexia.

'Did you buy any clothes with the tog dosh I sent you?' Alexandra asked evenly, regarding Tash's holey jeans and baggy red t-shirt with 'Australia' splashed across the front. Really, she reflected, Tash had hopeless dress sense. Adorable, but hopeless.

'Um . . . a few bits and pieces . . . you know.' *Nothing. Not even a few pairs of pants to replace my holey grey ones, Mother.*

'You've lost weight.'

'A bit.' *CHANGE THE SUBJECT, MOTHER!*

'Yes, quite a lot. I bet you'd fit into some of my stuff now. We'll have a rootle through later. It'll be fun. Pascal can give us his opinion. He loves fashion shows . . .'

God! Not that! Tash's toes touched the soles of her feet.

'. . . you'd look super in my red Moschino or the—'

'Where's Pascal?' *If you won't change the subject then I will.* Tash was painfully aware that she was being ungrateful to her mother, but it was a subject that made her back tighten and her temples squeeze inwards.

'Popped out – organising a little surprise for you.' Alexandra looked speculatively at her daughter. This wasn't as easy as she'd planned. If only she'd got a little more time, but as Tash had come so late she had to cram everything into twenty-four hours.

Alexandra sometimes felt she was the only one in the family who understood Tash. Her daughter's sense of melodrama was not so far from her own – Tash had the same strange, inverted vanity which had ruled Alexandra's childhood. She understood all the pain and misery Tash had suffered being brought up in a family where comparisons were inevitable. Clever, erudite, judicious Matty. Beautiful, ambitious, competitive Sophia. And Tash.

Darling Tash . . . gawky, shy, funny, intensely bright and talented but totally without drive. Alexandra could weep from loving her so much.

Sometimes, late at night, she admitted to her secret self that she probably loved Tash more than her other children.

She silently regarded her daughter sitting in awful studenty clothes, legs crossed under her, head down, picking away at a cushion. She wanted to rush over and give Tash a massive cuddle but knew that she'd shrug her off, embarrassed. At worst, Tash thought she was repulsive to everyone. And

Alexandra suspected that the black gloom her daughter was currently shooting out from beneath arched brows heralded an all-time low.

Alexandra realised that Tash minimised her looks because she felt there was no point in 'dressing a manky goose as pâté de foie gras' as she put it. But she wanted Tash to feel attractive even if she was still wearing her old jeans. She was, after all a vividly striking girl – that stunning face with those incredible eyes, the full sensual mouth and slightly upturned nose. She was overweight, but it was mostly how she stood – shoulders slumped, toes together, endless legs not shown off to their best advantage when bowed at the knees to make her the same height as everyone else.

She'd invited her early on purpose. 'Confidence bolstering,' she'd explained to Pascal. She knew how important it was that Tash met up with the rest of her family – particularly Sophia and Cass – on an equal footing.

'Will you stop staring at me, Mummy? You know what I look like. I've been around for twenty-three years.'

'Sorry, darling.' Alexandra had forgotten Tash was a real person for a moment. She had become a grand projet d'amélioration. 'I was just thinking how good you're looking, that's all.'

Tash felt bemused. Her mother was laying it on a bit thick. Perhaps she did look better. Oh dear. If this was 'good' then she must have looked simply awful before. She felt depressed again. And ravenously hungry.

'When's Max coming to stay?'

That old chestnut. Tash thought longingly of Death by Chocolate.

'I don't know. He's gone to visit his dad in the States.'

'Oh. How exciting. What does he do?'

'Lucian? I'm not sure exactly. Some sort of banker, I think. Like Dad.' Tash bit her lip, on the verge of dumping her awful guilt about Max.

There was a loud banging of doors and two voices could be heard speaking French somewhere in the back of the house.

'Ah, good!' Alexandra's face brightened. 'Here's Pascal. He's been creeping round all day avoiding your arrival. You know how useless he is at keeping secrets. He didn't want to spoil your surprise.'

Tash, deciding to keep her self-imposed troubles schtum, was intrigued.

In the kitchen they found Pascal with Jean, the toothless old lodge-keeper who 'managed the estate' (at eighty, it was all he could 'manage' to puff up to the house and back for an industrial-strength coffee with Pascal). They both looked exceptionally pleased with themselves.

'Natasha! Chérie!' Pascal always wore a vaguely distraught look, however relaxed he was. It was the enormous watery grey eyes set against the dark of his ruddy, tanned face with its giant Gallic nose. He also possessed a Byronic mane of wild, brown hair, making him look as if he'd just had a session of ECT.

'You are looking ver' beautiful.' He leant over and gave her a kiss. He smelt of expensive aftershave and French tobacco.

Really, Tash decided, all this flattery and white wine had made her feel odd. Not exactly ebullient – more butterflies-in-the-stomachish.

'Thanks. This is nice,' she said shyly, admiring a shiny silver espresso-maker. It was a strange kitchen – a kind of dried-flower Provençal meets Zanussi showroom.

Her mother was whispering with Pascal, who was puffing out his cheeks in characteristic fashion and saying something in French. Alexandra seemed to disagree. Pascal shook his head and took off his waxed jacket (in this heat – a waxed jacket? Tash was impressed. Even now it had got dark the manoir was like a hot-house). He poured himself a glass of cranberry red wine.

'Natasha?' Pascal gestured towards the bottle.

Should she? Why not?

'Please.'

He poured three more glasses. 'It ees my own grapes but malheureusement I do not make it. Tomorrow we see the vineyards and you meet my . . . er . . . neighbour, the—' he puffed his cheeks again, searching his mind for a word, 'the vine-maker!' He seemed to find this very amusing.

Tash adored Pascal – he was a very open, fun, passionate man. He could also be excessively moody but that was his hot-blooded and emotional French spirit, or so Alexandra said.

'We 'ave a dilemme.' Pascal pouted at Alexandra.

'Thing is, darling,' Alexandra looked at Tash through her lashes with a bewitching smile. 'Pascal thinks you won't be able to appreciate the true wonder of your surprise till morning – although that means he'll have to speak French all night or he'll give the game away. I think you'd like it now. Mmmm, sweetheart?'

Tash looked from Alexandra to Pascal, who shrugged his green cotton jersey shoulders. She looked at Jean. He grinned his gums at her. She slugged back some more wine. It was surprisingly tart.

Best to side with family at times like this, she decided finally, feeling the peaty heat of the wine ooze down. What did it matter anyway? Her mother's surprises were usually cloth and made her look fat.

'Okay . . . I'll . . . um . . . that is—' Tash noticed that Pascal's cheeks were inflating, 'I'll have it now, please.'

Alexandra looked delighted. Pascal started to pull his jacket on again.

'I'm sorry, Pascal,' Tash started. 'I mean please don't take offence if—'

'I put my jacket on because your surprise 'e 'ees outside,' said Pascal sulkily.

'Oh.'

They trooped into the muggy dark.

4

Outside, a large marble moon shed faint, steely light on to the cobbled yard, distorting its proportions into a dappled Expressionist film set.

A cool breeze brushed Tash's face, lifting her hair as she wandered unsteadily through the gloom. It was so peaceful. All she could hear above the muffled crunch of footsteps were insects snoring reedily in the hedges. If only the others weren't coming tomorrow, everything could be so lovely.

Pascal strode ahead, glass still in hand, to the tall peeling double doors that led to the stalls. Tash, hiccuping slightly as she followed, didn't notice a trailer hitched to the back of Pascal's jeep in the shadows nearby.

Inside, the big building was crow-black and echoed like a derelict chapel. Tash's nostrils were filled with the warm, dry smell of straw and a faint sting of dung.

From the pitch-dark stalls came an indignant snort.

Pascal fell over something that clattered loudly.

Another snort.

'Where's the switch?' laughed Alexandra, running her hands along the wall.

Tash fell over whatever Pascal had. The snort was followed this time by an enraged whinny.

Suddenly the musty stone building with its heavy wooden partitions and metal bars, its cluttered collection of buckets, empty haynets and bits of ancient apparatus covered in a thick layer of dust, was filled with raw neon light.

'It's a good job we had the old place re-wired for that party,' Alexandra prattled cheerfully.

'Where did all this mess come from?' She picked up a pre-war bucket.

Despite speaking no English, Jean, who was standing arthritically behind them, got the gist. Pascal's ancient odd-jobber had of late slackened the odd job to a refined artful dodge. Looking shifty, he muttered 'au vin' and, hissing through his gums, shuffled off towards the house.

But Tash wasn't taking any of this in. She was staring instead down the long aisle in the middle of the stalls towards the end of the building.

Something distinctly equine was staring irritably back.

Tash glanced at Alexandra and Pascal, who were side by side glowing at her.

'Viens,' offered Pascal, waggling his wine glass in the direction of the scowling four-legged inhabitant. 'Introduce yourself.'

Tash smiled weakly and walked towards the snorting newcomer.

A horse! Her mind was racing, trying to form itself into a coherent reaction. Why on *earth* are they giving *me* of all people a *horse*?

Hesitantly, she approached the big chestnut. It had a startling zigzag blaze and a nose as pink as a snooker ball. With another snort and a flash of white eye, the red horse backed off.

'Hello, old fellow.'

More eye-popping, this time with a touch of angry red nostril.

I knew it! Tash looked at the animal pleadingly and stretched out her hand. It stamped its hoof against the stone floor like a judge's hammer, pink snooker ball raised in a fierce challenge.

Alexandra appeared beside Tash and put her arm round her.

'Isn't he gorgeous?' she whispered as if they were in a library. 'Chestnut – like Samion. I knew you'd like a chestnut.'

Samion! Tash shuddered.

All the French children had been obsessed by ponymania from an early age. None more than Tash, who at eight went through the age-old stage dreaded by many a prep schoolteacher. Every story was about horses, every drawing of a pony, even maths seemed to add up four square.

The Frenches had been lucky. Benedict's ancient stable block was knocked into shape and three scruffy, Thelwellian ponies installed by their adoring father. James French even spent some unprecedented weekends away from the golf course to build them a little cross-country circuit around the paddocks and through the woods. Later, as a result of Sophia's whining, an all-weather menage and several glossy jumps appeared.

Very few children got the same opportunity as the Frenches. Few were less appreciative. The eldest of the children, Matty, would grudgingly lead his little sisters around the villages, but was keener on rugby and escaping the parental clutches for weekend drinking sessions and illicit cigarettes with his pals from boarding school.

Sophia only enjoyed competing and considered success to be in direct proportion to expenditure. To her, plodding along lanes or schooling in the paddocks was too nursery slope for words. All she really wanted to do was pound around show-grounds with her pony's bridle positively weighed down by streaming red satin rosettes. To her fellow competitors' (and particularly their mothers') surprise, she spent most summer Sundays doing just that.

Sophia was totally without nerves and hadn't much skill either. But she persuaded her doting father to buy her an amazing competition (or what Matty called 'push-button') pony – a half-Arab mare costing four hefty figures. The showy little bay, Harlot O'Hara, won everything; Sophia pot-hunted shamelessly, soon became a regular member of Pony Club teams and ostentatiously lorded it over Tash, who never seemed to win at all. All the local Jemimas, Emilys and Fionas alternatively loathed and sucked up to her. Their mothers just loathed her.

No one took any notice of Tash, pottering around in the background on fat, greedy Seamus.

Yet while Sophia whined for new jods and a flashy horsebox, Tash had patiently and privately battled with her crafty, stubborn grey gelding whose heart of gold wasn't quite as big as his stomach. Because he was such a difficult pony, she was forced to learn and adapt quickly. Barely noticed in her sister's lengthening shadow, Tash grew into a very capable rider. She was sensitive enough to appreciate that the plodding Connemara was never going to beat the fiery Harlot – Seamus simply hadn't the engine capacity – so they seldom competed, enjoying instead the quiet solitude of hacking, or the thrilling buzz of hunting. This maddened James French, who thought she was unspeakably wet.

But Tash, with the guileful ingenuity only shy children are capable of devising, had been competing on a private level the entire time.

During the summer vacs, Sophia was too lazy to school her costly pony at home, away from the glory. Tash, however, dragged herself up religiously (and often rattily) each morning to loosen Seamus's stiff rheumatic joints before the sun got too hot for him.

Only then would she sneakily tack up Harlot and, with a guilty heart in her throat, ride her to the thirty-acre field behind Downe's Copse, which wasn't overlooked by the house. There, to the grass-chewing curiosity of spectating cows, she would revel in the mare's supple obedience, teaching her moves in minutes which she had sweated over for hours with wily Seamus.

She now remembered with embarrassment the childish satisfaction she'd derived from the fact that the mare went so much better for her. The knowledge had kept her on a high for hours, rendering her father's scathing disdain into distant thunder.

Tash had lived in adrenalin-pumping fear of being found out. Yet no comment was ever made as Harlot – notoriously manic without exercise – grew more and more pliant even under Sophia's rudimentary aids. It was simply put down to an indiscernible improvement in the latter's riding.

In her more selfish moments, Tash now wished her secret morning excursions had been discovered. Wished the scornful, toffee-nosed Pony Club mothers and their carping offspring had found out just *why* 'Bashful French', as they christened her, wasn't interested in competing against her sister. But at the time she'd been too frightened of her father's reaction. James doted on Sophia, and Tash – seasoned against his sarcasm if not insulated from his wrath – had even then understood just how vital it was to Sophia to impress him. James French sulked if Tash let him down; he would bellow plaster from the walls and shatter Benedict's eighteenth-century glass from its leading if Sophia did. And Tash knew that her elder sister – for all the pretence at blithe indifference – would simply fall apart if her bluff was called.

Later, after the terrible events that followed, no one would have believed Tash anyway.

James French – as competitive as his elder daughter – had been as amazed as anyone that Sophia could work so little on her mare and still rake in the pots, while the feckless Tash – who was constantly grubby and smelt of horse – was such a failure. He was privately ashamed of Tash's low status on the gymkhana circuit and vented his resentment by ploughing more and more money into Sophia. No coach was too good, no saddle too expensive.

He barely seemed to notice when, however much Tash shortened her stirrups, her legs still seemed to dangle down to fat little Seamus' knees. Tash, who adored Seamus for all his faults, didn't want him to. Nor did Sophia, who feared that Tash would be bought a superior animal as a replacement.

But James had merely been biding his time, waiting to rattle his quieter daughter out of her dreamy complacency.

Coming back from her first, miserable term at boarding

school, Tash found her whiskery old friend sold on and in his place a huge chestnut gelding, barely broken in and with a vicious buck amongst his assortment of bad habits.

Samion.

James French, in his excitement that his golfing connections had paid off and produced an inexpensive new mount for his daughter, hadn't appreciated that a twelve-year-old girl on a sixteen-hand human-depositing machine was not a good idea. Tash was terrified of Samion. Samion knew it. Tash resented him for replacing lazy old Seamus. Samion didn't like her much either, thank you very much.

But the bolshy, irritable newcomer to the Frenches' yard didn't deserve such a short, painful life.

'He's lovely,' Tash forced herself to say. 'Yes, very like Samion.'

The big horse – and he was big, much higher than even Samion – stretched his pink nose towards her a fraction, then bared his teeth.

'Who've you borrowed him from?' Tash asked hopefully.

'Not borrowed,' corrected Pascal proudly. ''E ees yours. My fazer give 'im from 'es – er—'

'From his racing yard,' finished Alexandra, unable to contain her delight. 'His mother's a steeplechaser. He's a Selle Français colt, whatever that means.'

A colt! Tash felt slightly sick.

'Thank you,' she muttered through frozen lips, realising that her mother and Pascal mustn't realise how many painful memories their gesture had just exhumed. 'Thank you so much – it's – he's wonderful.'

'Pascal's father bred him for one of the boys to show-jump, but he was too much of a handful for him,' Alexandra went on excitedly. 'He's only a baby – five, I think. You can have him all summer and then take him back with you if you want. Or keep him here till you can afford to. Pascal can ride him round the vineyard.'

Tash had a sudden image of the tall copper horse disdainfully sitting down to a Chinese take-away in Derrin Road.

'At five he's not a colt, Mummy,' she muttered between clenched teeth, 'he's a fully fledged stallion.'

'Ees a bit . . . er . . . temperamental,' laughed Pascal as the chestnut stamped his hoof, 'but Xandra say you are ver' good rider.'

Oh Mother! If only you knew.

The young stallion had lost interest in them and was snatching sulkily at his haynet.

Tears stung Tash's eyes. They always did when she remembered. She had put Samion to the back of her mind for so long, tucked tightly away behind the worst of her guilty secrets. Desperate not to let her mother see how upset she was, she turned away, blinking furiously.

Pascal said something to Alexandra and they smiled indulgently at her, thinking how moved she was at their first 'confidence bolster' – much better than the antique oak bedhead they'd bought to placate Sophia.

'Let's go in and have another drink,' suggested Alexandra warmly. 'Pascal's promised to cook us something ambrosial.'

Tash found she'd lost her appetite.

Inside the kitchen the bottle of red wine was sitting empty on the huge scrubbed oak table and Jean was snoring blissfully with his mouth open.

Pascal just smiled and, with a shrug of his broad waxed shoulders, fetched some celebratory champagne.

'Pour le cheval rouge,' he puffed theatrically, broad thumbs enveloping the ripped gold foil.

As Jean woke with a groggy start, Tash shuddered in agonising recognition.

The sound of the cork's bulging flight from the bottle-neck was like the deadening shot of a humane killer.

5

'Look, Tom, look at all the boats!'

Matthew French simulated excitement to his seven-year-old son as they approached Cherbourg.

It was blisteringly hot. His eyes ached from the early morning sun and he felt slightly sick from the smell of diesel.

'Shall we go and find Tor and Sally?' he asked, hoping to get off deck.

'Five more minutes, Mashy, please?'

It was Tom's first trip on a boat and he'd been so excited. Matty didn't have the heart to deprive him of a moment's fun.

'Okay then.' Matty buried himself back in the *Guardian* and tried to concentrate on nuclear spillage rather than his potential gastric one.

'Will Granny Lexy be in Sherbet?'

'No,' Matty smiled, 'we're driving Audrey to where Lexy lives.'

'Brilliant!'

Audrey the Audi was their dilapidated and dirty white car. Matty, strongly disapproving of London pollution, rode a mountain bike from their Richmond home to work. But Sally, his wife, had insisted on having a car for the kids. At least it was lead-free.

'What's that boat's name?' Tom pointed to a rusty tug.

'Mabel,' grunted Matty, who was getting bored of the boat-christening game which had started in Dover.

'And that one?'

'La Baxter.'

Tom fell about in giggles. Mrs Baxter was his bullying old boot of a primary schoolteacher with whom Matty had regular and heated arguments.

'Mrs Baxter told Rodney Brown's mum that you were a Pinko,' Tom said, swinging from a bar of the bench Matty sat on. 'What is a Pinko, Mashy? Rodney Brown says it means we're from Russia. He said you're probably a ballet dancer or something.'

Matty laughed.

'Are you a ballet dancer, Mashy?' Tom stopped swinging and looked at him.

'Have you ever seen me in a tutu?'

Tom looked confused. 'Is that like Grandpa Plus-Four?'

Matty laughed again. Sally always referred to his father, James French, as 'Grandpa Plus-Four' because of his golfing gear.

'Not quite.' Matty picked Tom up and put him on his knee. 'I, my boy, am a socially aware independent documentary producer. Do you know what that means?'

Tom shook his head and played with the dial on Matty's diving watch.

'It means we're permanently broke and I'm having to do lots of boring work for the IPPA to support you, Tor and your mother until I get another commission.'

'What's the I-pee-I-pee-pee—'

'IPPA? It's a legislative nightmare.'

'What's leggilative mean?'

Sometimes Matty wished his son and heir didn't have quite such an enquiring mind.

'It's a kind of maths.' That would do for the time being.

'Plus-Four!' Tom went off into more giggles.

Actually, thought Matty, Old Bore Plus-Four could be very useful at the moment. He wished his thoughts didn't revolve around money so much. If only that deal with Channel Four hadn't folded. No. He wouldn't think about it.

But with ever greater struggles to keep up the mortgage repayments he couldn't help but think about it.

It would have been okay if they'd stayed in Holborn, he told himself – yes, so his old flat was grotty but it was so handy for Wardour Street, and the kids had loved going to Covent Garden and watching the acts or walking round Lincoln's Inn. Then again the house in Richmond was, as Sally frequently pointed out, a dream. A very, very expensive dream. And now, with a new baby on the way, he was continually fighting the guilty hope that he'd wake up.

Perhaps old Plus-Four would let him have five grand or so? he wondered. Just to tide him over. But Matty's conscience just wouldn't be able to cope with sponging off the self-satisfied old snob. Shooting and salmon, croquet and the Conservatives. Matty shuddered. Not to mention the fact that he was bound to rave on about Matty joining the family firm again. The old goat would just have to wait for one of Sophia's wailing brats to grow up. Or were they destined to be royalty? Perhaps old Tash would find herself a nice, boring city type to settle down with and produce executive sprogs.

'When's Nilly coming?' Tom was bored with his father staring into space.

'Oh.' Matty felt a stab of guilt. He hadn't really thought about it. 'I'll give him a ring when we get to Lexy's.'

Matty knew he really had to do something about Niall. He'd been too wrapped up in his own problems recently to do more than send his old friend a scrawled postcard asking him to join them in France. He'd heard nothing back. Each time he was on the verge of chasing Niall up, something urgent had cropped up, or he'd simply been too whacked from work to remember. Also, the Irish actor's agent and the film company he was currently under contract to were being maddeningly evasive, vetting all calls and refusing to give Niall's exact whereabouts; they were terrified that a tabloid invasion would provide Niall with even more bad publicity after the drinking rumours a couple of years ago.

Niall O'Shaughnessy, reeling from the recent break-up of his marriage, had buried himself in Nîmes, filming a terrible mini-series spin-off. He'd told Matty that he was only taking the work because his wife Lisette's parting shot had been to fill their house with crates of malt whisky bought with Niall's increasingly inflexible plastic. *I'm leaving you. I picked up your prescription at the off-licence to help you get over it, L xxx,* the accompanying note had read.

Bloody Lisette! Matty thought savagely of Niall's beautiful, bewitching and utterly poisonous wife, now languishing in the States with her rich, brattish lover. Poor, stupid, besotted Niall. Last of the great Irish romantics, sacrificing himself on such a lost cause. Yeats would be proud.

Matty knew he had to get his manic drinking partner out of the pit he'd dug himself into.

What would he do if Sally ran off with a brainless shit with tenners falling out of his silk-lined Armani pockets? Probably what Niall was undoubtedly doing now – drink himself to death.

'I'll try and call him when we get to your grandmother's,' Matty repeated absently to Tom, who was busily making unsympathetic farting noises by blowing into his elbow.

They were nearly docking. Strange, straw-coloured fortresses rose like medieval ruins on either side from the long sand flats. It was more like arriving in Tel Aviv than Cherbourg. Matty pulled his wits together.

'Come on, young Tomato,' he gathered his son up in a big hug. 'Let us save my wench from the clutches of the wicked Duty Free Shoppe.'

Sally drove the French leg of the journey. Having once bummed round Europe for six months in an ancient Beetle with some college mates, she was used to continental driving. As Sally had confessed to a friend before they set out, Matty was an appalling driver at the best of times. It was the one thing he wouldn't take criticism about. Let loose in France, he was quite capable of wiping out the last of the Frenches at the first *priorité à droite.*

They crawled out of Cherbourg behind a long line of cloned Vauxhall Cavaliers towing caravans advertising their resort mileage with plastic bunting hung between identikit floral curtains in the back windows. Sally glanced at her children in the back seat. Sweet, dumpy little Tor asleep with one blonde pigtail skew-whiff. Tom, bright-eyed, firing questions at poor Matty.

Matty always looked so tired these days, she noticed sadly. He shouldn't have taken that weekend barwork. He'd also totally given up writing his book. Once Sally had resented Matty's passion to write all the wrongs of the world in black and white. Now she longed to hear the muffled tapping and electric whirr of the word processor in the small hours.

She wished she'd had time to wash her hair. Even if they couldn't afford to buy new clothes at the moment, she could at least look clean. Matty's mother was so glamorous.

Despite this, Sally was looking forward to seeing Alexandra and Pascal again. They were such fun – and Matty badly needed the break. This was their first proper holiday since their honeymoon eight years ago. Even then, Matty had taken his camcorder round Ireland for some damn project which, as usual, never saw the light of day. Sally had spent more time with Matty's friends Niall and Lisette O'Shaughnessy than with her new husband.

They came to a halt at a railway crossing where a dusty train was unhurriedly pulling its mile-long industrial load past. Sally looked across at the tall, skinny, impossibly beautiful man slouched in the passenger seat beside her with a battered old Australian rancher's hat over his nose and odd socks propped up on the dashboard. Things had become increasingly tense between them lately, with arguments getting more and more heated and bitingly personal, a vent for angry despair at the lack of time and money. But he could still curdle her stomach with the merest wisp of a smile.

'You okay?' He lazily played with the loose tangle of blonde hair which had strayed free from her hurriedly pulled pony-tail. The sun streaming through the broken sun-roof made his hazel eyes deep, liquid gold.

> Man's love is of man's life a thing apart,
> 'Tis woman's whole existence.

'Fine,' she said, hastily putting Audrey into grumbling gear as a car beeped impatiently behind them. 'You get some sleep.'

6

Tash woke in a sweat, hanging half off the bed. Somehow, her sheet was over the other side of the room.

What had she been dreaming about? She squinted at the dial of her watch but her eyes wouldn't focus.

Her temples were throbbing. All those endless glasses of wine last night. She had a feeling that she'd done something acutely embarrassing. Had she cried? No, she didn't think so. Passed out cold? Possibly. Sung 'House of the Rising Sun' whilst standing on her head? Doubtful. She generally reserved that for rugby parties.

Her eyes were open enough to detect thin strips of cold, white light filtering through the shutters. She guessed it must be just after dawn.

I'll get up and go for a long walk as part of my new fitness regime, Tash resolved, and promptly fell asleep.

She was in the middle of Hampstead High Street, sitting on Samion, wearing nothing but her underwear and a pair of green wellies. He was spinning round and round, snorting.

'Stop it, Sam. Stop it . . . please, Sam . . . please! . . . No!' Her voice was thin and whiny, terror blotting out any authority.

A tractor was turning out of Willoughby Road. Samion hated tractors.

She jumped off and held his head like a clamp as she had so often in the lanes near Benedict House, her terror transmitting itself to him, totally unable to soothe him. He went up on his hind legs, lashing out.

Her bra seemed to have fallen off.

Hugo Beauchamp walked past just as the tractor was within feet of Samion and Tash. He stopped and stared.

'Aren't you my mother's cleaner?'

Tash dropped the reins and the panic-stricken chestnut galloped into Gayton Road. Hearing Samion's shod hooves clattering away from her, Tash sprinted through the sloping maze of streets.

In front of her stretched the Heath.

There were marquees and roped-off rings in the clearing where the Hampstead Fair was normally held. A loud-speaker was reciting French verbs in a distorted public school drawl.

'Je sois – tu sois – il soit – nous soyons – vous soyez – ils soient.'

Ahead of her was Sophia, beautiful in a lilac suit, holding Samion. His mane and tail were plaited now, flashy blue bandages enveloped his legs. Behind Sophia, Hugo had reappeared and was holding the lead-rein of a hairy bay pony on which both Ben and Lotty were sitting, smoking fags.

'Why aren't you wearing clothes?' asked Lotty petulantly.

Ben, Sophia and Hugo fell about.

'Your legs are very fat.' Lotty had a drag of her fag, eyes half-closed in boredom.

'Right, hop on,' ordered Sophia briskly, handing Tash Samion's reins. 'You're in the elementary jumping. Not that you'll be able to beat Ben and Lotty.'

Tash scrambled on Samion. He seemed enormous. She was so high up that all she could see was the top of Ben and Lotty's heads on the fat little pony.

She rode into the ring. Samion was twisting and letting out vicious bucks underneath her. She desperately wanted to cover her chest but had to cling on to the reins for dear life.

The bell rang. She pointed the plunging Samion at the first fence. It was less than a foot high. He refused and she fell off.

She burst into tears.

Her mother was running towards her, dressed in an outlandish sequinned rubber cat-suit.

'Mummy, Mummy, it's all that horse's fault,' Tash wailed. 'He's a monster. He's useless . . . just . . . useless.'

Suddenly her mother disappeared and in her place stood Matty with a television crew behind him. He was wearing his hair in dreadlocks and had a Socialist Worker t-shirt on and huge bell-bottomed pink corduroys.

'*No*, Natasha French,' he said as the cameras honed in on her within an inch of her face. She covered her chest with her arms. 'You've got to face up to your responsibilities. Stop being a spoilt baby. It's your fault. You killed Samion. You're a lazy, selfish, bad loser.'

Now she was alone in the Derrin Road sitting room, watching her face on the television. A close-up, blotchy and tear-stained, with a giant spot on the end of her nose. The picture then cut to Hugo, who was holding a furry microphone and wearing dark glasses.

'What a bloody attractive woman that is,' he said in his deep, drawling voice.

The doorbell was ringing.

Outside stood Hugo.

Without saying anything he bent his beautiful head and kissed her lips with exquisite gentleness.

'Tash, darling, wake up. It's half past ten.'

Tash squinted, unfolding her brain into reality. Alexandra was standing by her bed, holding out a mug of tea.

'You must have been tired last night. You're still wearing one shoe.'

'Drunk, Mummy,' Tash groped for her discarded sheet. 'I was drunk.'

'You certainly were,' Alexandra laughed, whisking towards the door. 'There's some breakfast downstairs. Sophia et al should be here around lunchtime.'

Tash sipped her tea and stretched out luxuriously, kicking off the offending shoe. She couldn't be bothered to worry about how she'd behaved last night. She was still feeling superbly warm and sexy from the memory of Hugo kissing her in her dream. What had happened before that? Something about Hampstead? Wasn't Matty in it? No matter. She closed her eyes and relived the kiss.

Her euphoria didn't last long.

When she staggered blinking into the kitchen, hoping for strong coffee, croissants and an English paper, she found instead half a grapefruit, Pascal and a partly assembled bridle.

'How does thees theeng work?' he groaned impatiently, trying to attach the headband to the bit.

'Here, let me. You need a cheekpiece.' Tash started rearranging the soft, thick straps of leather.

'You have – er – récupérer – er – recover from last night?'

'Eh? – yes. At least I think so. What did I do?'

'You sing "The House of" – er – quelque chose and do a head-stand. Then you burst into tears and faint.'

'Did I really? – God!'

'Alexandra, she say it ees my cooking.' Pascal sniffed.

'Yes, well I've got a very sensitive stomach.'

'Mmm.' Pascal was drumming his fingers on the table. 'I will get ze selle for your Selle.' He giggled, jumping up and striding out of the door.

Tash poured herself a cup of coffee with a shaking hand and wondered if Britain joining the EC had been quite such a bright idea.

Later, she stood staring over the wooden stall partition at her big chestnut gift horse's bared teeth, holding his 'selle' (which had turned out to be his saddle) in her arms. The copper horse stared back superciliously. Pascal had repeated his pedigree name several times, but other than knowing that it sounded something like unblocking a drain full of old gumboots, Tash hadn't a hope of pronouncing it.

'I shall call you The Snob, my French friend.'

He snorted back disdainfully.

It took a full quarter-hour to get him tacked up, avoiding

much biting and leg-kicking. Tash quickly started to despair. It was years since she'd got on a horse. She probably wouldn't be able to get her foot in the stirrup.

Sensing her apprehension, The Snob firmly towed her towards the light of the double doors with a demonic glint in his huge purple eyes.

Out in the yard Polly was sitting on the steps of the manoir dressed as an Indian squaw.

'How!' she said, giving Tash an Indian salute.

Tash felt too nervous to do anything but smile grimly.

'You've got a big cheval!' Polly cried.

'What? – oh yes.'

Snob was dancing round her now. The saddle seemed very high up. If she got the momentum up to go that far she'd probably go right over the other side. Tash studied the problem thoughtfully. Snob eyed her back with Gallic distaste.

He looked like a fox – ginger ears twitching, his tail flaxen at the ends like growing-out highlights.

Tash felt the stirrings of ponymania re-establish itself somewhere inside her.

'Okay, Snobby Fox.' No, that sounded naff. 'The Foxy Snob. I hereby christen this frog The Foxy Snob. Bless him and all who put a selle on him.' And with a deftness which surprised even herself, she hopped on.

Snob (although he was totally unaware that this was his new pseudonym) was highly annoyed at missing his usual fun when anybody tried to mount him. Deeply insulted, he let out a huge buck and deposited Tash on the cobbles below.

'Tu tombes!' cried Polly, giggling so much she fell off the step in simpatico.

Alexandra appeared through the doors behind Polly and dusted the now wailing little squaw down.

'How's it going, darling?' she called across to Tash.

'Just . . . terrific.' Tash rubbed her backside.

'Well, Pascal wants to take you round the vineyard in about an hour, okay, sweetheart?' She disappeared back into the house.

It took Tash precisely fifty-five minutes to get on Snob a second time. He tried every trick in the equine book. Spinning round in circles, presenting his pattes de derrière, his pattes de devant. He reared, bucked, bit, lashed out and even lay down. As his final coup de grâce he squashed Tash flat to the wall she was trying to mount him against. Pinning her there as unwilling captive, he rubbed his great red cheekbone affectionately against her shoulder.

It was only when Pascal came out into the yard and said he'd be ready in half an hour and why was she putting the horse away so soon, that Snob stood like an old bicycle while Tash mounted.

They bounced around the small railed schooling paddock for five minutes, disagreeing on everything. Tash wanted to walk, Snob to canter. Tash wanted to go left, Snob to go à droite. Then, deciding he was bored, he bucked Tash firmly on to terra firma once more before trotting round her, head held high, refusing to be caught.

When Tash finally rubbed the overexcited chestnut down in his stall she felt bruised, deflated and utterly humiliated.

She longed for a shower to wash off the dirt and sweat and to soothe her aching body. Instead she had to leap straight into Pascal's revving jeep and set off at breakneck speed to a load of boring old grapes and cellars.

On the outskirts of the estate they were forced, with a cloud of spinning dust, into a ditch as a red Peugeot pelted towards them. Climbing back into her seat and removing pieces of dashboard from her clothing, Tash glimpsed a split second of tortoiseshell hair and glinting dark glasses in the passing Peugeot. With a sickening lurch in her stomach, she knew for certain that it was Hugo Beauchamp.

7

Alexandra was delighted that Tash seemed to be having so much fun already.

Left alone in the house, she decided to phone her renegade brother, Eddie, in order to work out when to organise the welcoming party she'd decided to hold for his arrival.

Eddie didn't sound particularly pleased to hear from her. Alexandra felt rather hurt. He kept muttering about the fact that it was five in the morning in New York. Still, she reflected happily, at least the date was fixed – Friday, July the twenty-sixth. A Friday! What could be better for a party? *And* the day before an important equestrian event in the next village. Better and better! All the locals could come and spike each other's drinks.

She dashed up to her bedroom excitedly. For once she didn't mind that Polly had raided her make-up drawer and spread Rouge de CoCo lipstick all over the carpet.

Humming 'All You Need Is Love', she started flicking through her wardrobe, looking for things to put aside for Tash.

Money had never really mattered to Alexandra. You either had it or you didn't. She couldn't help reflecting, however, that one of the unexpected benefits of being married to someone as extraordinarily rich as darling Pascal was the exquisite beauty of the clothes one could buy.

Alexandra didn't buy a dress because it was Yves Saint Laurent couture costing ten thousand francs. She bought it because it was thick, heavy silk that felt like warm, oiled water on the skin and was the colour of a washed-up oyster shell.

She stared into space, misty-eyed, hugging a midnight-blue Ungaro jacket. After all, she mused, beauty was purely relative. She'd derived equal pleasure from a sunset over snowy Bayswater in her student days.

Polly trotted in doing a rain dance and stamping her feet. 'Bugger – sheet – bugger – sheet!' she chanted, waving a large chicken feather at Alexandra.

'Polly!' laughed Alexandra. 'Where did you learn language like that?'

'Tash say it to the cheval ce matin.' She waved the feather in the air. 'Maman, can I have a boyfriend, like Tashy has?'

'You've got a boyfriend, darling. You've got Michel.'

'Michel is en Paris.' Polly did a roly poly and landed on the Rouge de CoCo, her squaw dress around her ears.

'Well, Tash's boyfriend's in America.' Alexandra examined a long floral skirt.

'Can Tom be mon ami?' asked Polly, looking up at her from the floor.

'Tom, my darling little squidget, is your nephew.'

'Mon neveu? Oh la la!' Scrabbling up, she waved her feather around again. 'Bugger – sheet – bugger – sheet – bugger—' And she headed off to her tepee in the gardens.

Alexandra dreamily tried on a heavenly suit she'd bought because it was the colour of English holly berries.

Ten minutes later Polly was back, having discarded the lower half of her costume.

'Maman, there are people dans la cour.' She ran to the window. 'Un . . . two . . . three . . . quatre . . . cinq people,' she paused, 'and a dwarf.'

Alexandra burst out laughing. Polly had Rouge de CoCo all over her bottom.

'Let's go and see who they are, shall we?'

She took her daughter's hand and led her from the room.

Outside, Sophia was fanning herself with a copy of *Paris Match* and admiring the manoir. It had become somehow pokey in her mind's eye, compared with the vast dimensions of Holdham. In reality it was a beautiful house with its buttery stone walls, circular towers and creamy white shutters, snuggling into its squashy fur coat of wisteria and ivy like an ageing Hollywood grande dame.

'It's a fairytale palace!' shrieked Lotty, waving her Noo Noo and terrifying several chickens nearby.

'God, I need a drink.' Hugo stretched and looked about him. 'Nice place. Where's the gorgeous Alexandra?'

'Probably out, knowing this lot,' said Ben, lifting Josh's carrycot out of the boot of the hired Mercedes. 'They're gloriously untogether.'

Amanda was looking over a gate at the side of the house. Beyond it, an overgrown stretch of land that had once been a formal garden dropped away to reveal a spectacular view of the valley below. Acres and acres of woodland were patched with giant, ribbed fields of grapes. In a dip in the far distance were the tiny, sandy specks of a cluster of cottages. The village.

Oh, brother! It's not exactly London, is it? she thought glumly. How in hell am I going to survive the boredom? She kicked away a chicken with a ten-denier leg. Please, God, don't let Hugo near a horse. Please? All I want is a huge double bed and hours and hours of pure pleasure. Not necessarily with Hugo.

She turned round. Coming out of the house was the most incredible-looking woman. The sort who should be permanently draped over a chaise-longue in silk pyjamas, eating dewy grapes. Amanda blinked in disbelief. She was wearing the same red embroidered Lacroix suit Amanda had decided was too expensive to buy for the chief exec's cocktail do. In a farmyard!

'Hello, everyone. Sorry I'm so primped up. Do you think this would suit Tash?' Alexandra spun round.

'She'd never get into it,' said Sophia, then seeing her mother's hurt expression, she hurried on. 'How are you, Mummy? You look terrific.'

Amanda decided with satisfaction that Alexandra was much more attractive than her daughter. Sophia's features had the delicacy and perfect symmetry of other top models, needing make-up to give them substance. Alexandra d'Eblouir had a bolder, strikingly memorable face, full of warmth and character.

'It's love and money, darling. Does wonders for the hormones.' Alexandra laughed. 'Hello, Ben, sweetheart. Hi, Hugo – lovely to see you again.' She kissed them both. 'And you must be Amanda? Sophia told me you're wonderfully fit. You'll put us all to shame. Pascal's had the pool cleaned up for you.'

Alexandra, who'd got the impression Amanda was some sort of professional sportswoman, beamed at her. Amanda looked blankly back.

'Now, Polly.' Alexandra pulled her daughter away from Hugo, whom she was beating with her feather. 'If I can drag you away from the talent you seem to have spotted, this is Lotty. Take her to your tepee and show her your pale-face dolls.'

Lotty clung to Paola's leg and her Noo Noo.

'Want Wowla!' she muttered, pouting.

'Viens!' Polly, feeling her responsibility as a six- (and a quarter) year-old aunt, took little Lotty's hand. With their black hair and olive skin they looked like sisters. As they pottered off, Sophia stared with horror at Polly's bottom.

'Is that infectious, Mummy?' She pointed at what looked like a giant red rash.

'God, I hope not – I wouldn't have any lipsticks left.' Alexandra looked into the carry-cot. 'Isn't he angelic?' The Honourable Josh was asleep with his thumb in his mouth, swaddled in a blue towelling Babygro. 'What a little sweetheart. He's just like you, Ben.'

'Mercifully, Ben didn't throw up three times in the car,' muttered Hugo.

'I'll just show – Wowla, isn't it? – the children's rooms and then we can all have a massive drink,' Alexandra announced.

Ben was lifting the last of a huge selection of suitcases and baby apparatus from the boot.

'Oh, leave those, Ben.' Alexandra hooked his arm through hers, leading the way to the house. 'We can all bring them in later. I got Pascal to buy crates of Pimms especially for you. It's murder to get round here. Pascal won't touch it. He says it's worse than cough mixture.' She wandered through the big wooden doors.

Sophia stalked after them. She wanted desperately to unpack and sort everything out. Why did her mother live in such chaos?

They finally settled on the terrace which overlooked the wild garden Amanda had surveyed earlier.

'Pascal likes meadows,' Alexandra explained simply.

Insects danced in a shimmering haze above the bleached fur of grasses, and the distant valley dozed beneath a tracing paper mist of heat. The spaniels flopped down and panted under narrow strips of shadow cast by the balustrades, eyeing the newcomers hopefully.

Sophia was happily aware that she'd travelled better than the others. Amanda was looking hot and uncomfortable in her city clothes. Hugo had that impossibly sexy and seedy look of someone who'd just got out of bed and was heading for the percolator. Ben, as usual, looked like a down-and-out. She wished he'd get his hair cut, it was longer than her mother's.

'Place looks great,' Ben was saying cheerfully. 'Told Amanda last night she might be sleeping in a barn but you've done wonders since last year. Roof fixed?'

'Yes. Last October. It was simply awful when we first lived here.' Alexandra turned to Amanda. 'Every time it rained, Pascal and I would hare round with buckets, trying to catch drips. Once, when it rained non-stop for two weeks, we heaved the only dry mattress down to the cellar and stayed in bed, tight as two ticks for ten days. The locals thought we'd killed each other.'

'Don't you miss England?' Amanda asked her.

'God, no, darling! All those Victorian values. My mother is French – Etty. She's wonderful. Told me the facts of life by the time I was ten. Father tried to have her certified. The British are so twitched up about sex. It's a shame because they're such passionate lovers. The French love sex, love to buy presents, love wine, love food – all the things I adore, in fact. Have another drink.'

Amanda liked Alexandra on instinct. She didn't like many

women but Alexandra was so stylish yet unceremonious. She noticed that despite the nine-hundred-pound suit she didn't have any shoes on.

Sophia, in contrast, was horrified. Trust mother to talk about sex within ten minutes, she thought furiously. She'd be offering round a joint soon. There was no sign of lunch.

'When's Cass coming?' she asked tersely.

'In a week or so, I think. She's waiting for Marcus to break up. He's in some cricket match – Oh! And there's Ascot and Wimbledon. You know what she's like. By the way, I spoke to Eddie this morning. We're having a party for his arrival. You can help me organise it, darling.'

Sophia brightened. The manoir had great potential for a really jet-set do. Alexandra knew some amazing international names through Pascal. Then there were her own contacts. She could just see the write-up in Dempster. Pascal was so rich she needn't cut any corners.

'When?'

'Oh – last week in July, I think. I've written it down somewhere.'

Not much time. She'd have to pull her finger out.

'Leave it to me, Mummy.'

'Isn't it exciting about Eddie coming?' Alexandra purred enthusiastically. 'I honestly never thought I'd see him again.'

Hugo refilled his glass from the jug of Pimms. 'What does he do, this mysterious brother of yours?'

'Well, my dear, he took over Father's business in England in the seventies and it promptly went bust – so he upped sticks and moved to the States (more to escape from Father's wrath than anything else). Apparently he set up some sort of art gallery that flopped – Cass, my sister, knows more about it than I do. He came back in nineteen-eighty to borrow some dosh off Father. He looked like a camp Hell's Angel. Quite amazing. Father died of a heart attack while he was there – Cass still thinks it was the shock. So Eddie went back to the States without a penny. The old man left everything to the BFSS. Even Etty didn't see any of it.' She stroked the spaniel at her feet and smiled at them.

'What does he do now?' asked Amanda, noticing that Hugo's eyes had long since glazed over.

'Still in the art world. Some sort of dealer, I think. Probably still broke. We haven't had so much as a Christmas card till now. I tracked him down through Pascal's father and hounded him to come and stay.'

'And she virtually had to bribe Matty, I hear,' Sophia hissed to Ben under her breath.

Alexandra laughed, unfazed. 'Darling, you know that's not true.'

Ben looked up from trying to fathom *Paris Match*. 'So is the old devil coming to wave his union banner at us exploiters of manpower?'

Ben was in fact very fond of his impassioned and humanitarian brother-in-law, admiring his dedication. If Ben was ever to take his seat in the House of Lords he'd like to argue a point as lucidly as Matty French.

'Mmm – now, that's all very exciting.' Alexandra wiped spaniel slobber off her red skirt. 'He's bringing that gorgeous Irish actor – Niall . . . er . . .'

'O'Shaughnessy?' Hugo wondered.

'Yes, that's him. I think they're going down to fetch him from Nîmes before they come here. I can't remember.'

'Nice bloke, Niall.' Hugo stretched lazily. 'His brother's got a farm in Kildare – wonderful hunting country. Hasn't his wife just left him?'

'You know him?' asked Amanda. She'd seen Niall O'Shaughnessy in a couple of television plays. He was wildly attractive. There was something gloriously romantic about his untamed image and dishevelled good looks.

'I stayed with his brother for a few weeks point-to-pointing,' Hugo told Alexandra. 'We knocked back so much John Power one day we stripped down to the buff and swam in the Poulaphouca Reservoir. We were so plastered we didn't notice a bunch of American tourists were videoing the whole thing for Uncle Ern and the kids back home in Dakota. They thought it was one of those "cute" ancient Irish rituals. We charged them ten punts each.'

Ben laughed. 'That's typical Beauchamp. Remember that Eton Winchester rugby match where you told Whinney's they had to jog naked round School Yard in time-honoured tradition?'

'God, yes. Old Churchill caught them. He was furious that they'd gone the wrong way round the statue,' Hugo remembered.

'You were a bastard head boy.'

'I was a bastard full stop.' Hugo grinned, helping himself to another full glass of Pimms. 'They only made me head boy because my father was. And I was good at cricket.'

Amanda snorted pointedly, sighed and stretched out her legs. She secretly loved public school talk. It was amazing that after all these years it still made her back tingle.

At seventeen she'd been a swotty, overweight introvert buried in a suburban all-girl grammar school. Her father, lower middle class, hardworking and a believer that the only qualification women needed was in home economics, could only afford to send one child, her elder brother, to a fee-paying school for what he called a 'proper education'. As it turned out, Amanda took four A levels and went on to a first in economics at LSE. Her brother went to Stonehenge, took LSD and was now between jobs, working voluntarily at a re-hab centre in Birmingham. Amanda now recognised that his second-rate private school had been a stomping-ground for the snobbish, sports-mad middle classes. At the time, however, it was a gilded world of privilege and she'd endured crippling jealousy mixed with the first stabbing teenage angsts of lust. She'd developed huge crushes on her brother's conceited school friends, with their lazy, clipped voices, their holidays in Val d'Isère and their parents' lush houses in the home counties. She was also totally and numbingly intimidated by them.

They'd slept with her because there was nothing better around that night, and then forgotten her name afterwards. Amanda had vowed that one day she'd call the shots, shouting 'pull!' as they panted like eager Labradors beside her. Armed with a high-salary career, a rigorous exercise programme and a lap-top silicone chip on her shoulder, she'd embarked on sleeping her way to the toff. Now members of the old-boy network she loathed and loved wanted her because she scared them stiff and excited them beyond their wildest dreams of Nanny.

All except Hugo, that is. She doubted that she could ever scare Hugo. It was what kept her hooked. That and the fact that she still went weak at the knees to hear that drawling voice that was synonymous with first fifteens and dorm trooping. Right now, lounging in the sun with a childish grin on his face, listening to Ben drone on about farming, he seemed more unobtainable than ever. There was something utterly intoxicating yet thoroughly alienating about his narcissism.

'Find yourself a nice professional,' her mother had told her during their last phone conversation, the usual monologue. 'One of your own class. That Beach-hump chap'll never marry you, you know. His sort don't mix with ours. You're getting on. Don't you want kids? Your father and I are starting to get worried about you, you know. Julie Dean had her third last Tuesday – a little girl – did I tell you? She's two years younger than you.'

Amanda had spat lyrical about her career coming first, hating small children, and marriage being the last of her priorities. But it hadn't stopped her crying for hours afterwards.

The reality of her situation was beginning to wear through the veneer of euphemisms she so regularly reapplied to it. Insecurity had started to creep into her well-thumbed and meticulously prioritised agenda. She hadn't planned for the Caring Nineties, career motherhood and catalytic converted carry-cots. And she was reacting to her sudden insecurity as she always did when she took a blow to her self-esteem, by seeking a designer male distraction. A touch of jealousy might attract Hugo's wandering attention and gauge his affections. He was getting harder and harder to read these days, like Dostoyevsky.

Sophia was telling Alexandra about a visit to see her father, James.

'Henrietta's done the old drawing room out in pale green.

Remember how squalid it was? And they're extending the orangerie and turning it into an indoor swimming pool.'

'Paddling pool, you mean. That old shack is minute, darling, and riddled with rot.' Alexandra looked bored. 'Why can't they swim in the lake? We did.'

'You did.' Sophia sniffed disapprovingly and took a sip of her Pimms. 'Pa's trying to persuade Matty into the company again, he—'

Amanda stopped listening and slid out of her shoes. Thank God she'd nipped into the loo to take off her tights. The sun was heating them all to gas mark eight from a cobalt sky.

Hugo, sitting next to her, was now staring broodily out at the valley. His moods changed so quickly, one needed litmus paper to fathom them. Thick, tawny hair pushed back from his remote, watchful face, long lean body stretched out in front of him like a languishing puma, he was the ultimate in desirable, dangerous playthings. It wasn't fair that one man should have such presence. Why was it that after six years she still couldn't figure out what he was thinking? It was probably yet another reason she still kept coming back for more when she'd sworn to herself that she'd kicked the habit. She got so bored with everyone else.

She lifted a glossy brown leg and rubbed her foot against his thigh. He stroked it absent-mindedly, still staring into the distance, lost in thought.

Polly, still bottomless, bounded out of the garden with Lotty pottering behind, Noo Noo flapping as she tried frantically to keep up.

'Hello, darlings,' welcomed Alexandra, grateful of a diversion from her ex-husband's home-improvements. 'How many scalps have ye-um collected today?'

'We've been killing insects, Maman,' announced Polly, proudly brandishing a squashed beetle.

Really, thought Sophia, that child is completely wild.

'Bugger – sheet – bugger – sheet—' Lotty chanted brightly at her mother.

8

Michael Hennessy, teeth clenched around his pipe, handled the large Volvo through the Sussex lanes as if it were a Sherman tank.

'Need we go quite so fast, Michael?' asked Cassandra, his wife, whose hand kept slipping as she filled in the *Daily Telegraph* quick crossword. She only called her husband 'Michael' when she was annoyed, instead of the usual 'De-ah'. He seldom noticed.

'Got to push on, old thing.' Michael had developed a habit of speaking out of one side of his mouth as the other was continuously occupied by his pipe. 'We said eight for eight-thirty pre-dinner drinks.'

Cass glanced at the car clock. Six-fifteen – which meant that it was ten past. Michael always set his clocks five minutes fast. They had plenty of time. She supposed it would at least give her a chance for a nice leisurely bath before the guests arrived. Thank God she'd decided to get caterers in for this one. She was fed up with breaking her nails over the chopping board and missing half the gossip because she had her oven-mitts in the Aga.

She abandoned the crossword and leaned her straw hat back on the leather head-rest. It really had been a magnificent Henley. Granted, it had rained all the time and Michael's gammy hip had played him up, but their first year in the stewards' enclosure had made up for that.

'The boys aren't wildly keen on France,' Cass started cautiously, looking at Michael. 'Olly says he's got to write some thesis thing and Marcus said he couldn't possibly bring himself to go somewhere so "uncool" or some such word.'

'Hmmph.' Michael leaned on his horn as a lorry pulled out in front of them. 'Shame old Marcus wasn't in the Princess E. Still, at least he made the school cricket team for Lord's.'

'We've just got to get one of the boys to come with us, dear,' Cass pleaded. 'I promised Alex.'

'Can't Ol take a break from this thesis palaver, old girl?'

'Not really. It is his PhD, after all.'

'Stupid boy doesn't need a bloody PhD.' Michael waved an expressive, liver-spotted hand, veering across the road and sending a frantically wobbling cyclist into a ditch. 'I haven't even got a bloody degree and look how far I've got.'

'Yes, dear.' It was an age-old argument and didn't solve the problem in hand. Cass looked at her determined, explosive husband, panama tipped over his long nose, brass buttons on his blazer gleaming, old school tie at precisely ninety degrees – a military man, a sportsman and now a businessman. Cass privately and guiltily decided that a spell of university squalor might have done him the world of good. Instead, Michael was so intolerant of academics that he thought reading Melvyn Bragg was tantamount to communism.

'It's not as if Marcus has got A levels or anything this year,' she continued tentatively. 'He could easily give up two weeks of his summer hols. He'd only stay in bed otherwise.'

'Too bloody lazy by half. Needs a bit of discipline.' Michael overtook a tractor, narrowly missing an oncoming 2CV.

'Yes, dear. Perhaps if you bought him that car—'

'A car! At seventeen! He can wait till he's eighteen or buy his bloody own.'

'Yes, dear.'

Cass shut up and contemplated other forms of bribery for her beloved younger boy and optic apple.

They were driving through Hurstfield now. In the warm evening sunshine, The Old Rectory lurked – more sombre and distinguished than ever – under the long shadows of its cluster of sagging, ivy-clad outbuildings. From the strawberry-brick church beyond, a procession of earnest bell-pullers was heading on a well-worn path between their practice session and the Hare and Hounds.

'The grand old man of the village' was how Michael referred to his big, ugly Edwardian house. To him, there was nothing to rival sitting in the garden with the *Sunday Telegraph*, listening to the church bells and the hollow cracks of fours and sixes from the cricket pitch beyond the rhododendrons.

'That's odd.' Cass looked up as they swung into the immaculate raked gravel drive. 'Mrs Tyler must have left the windows open after she cleaned yesterday. I hope she remembered to turn the alarm on.'

When Michael switched off the engine, a loud, muffled thumping could be heard from inside the house.

'Sounds like the sort of bloody junk the boys listen to,' grunted Michael, jumping from the car.

Thump – thump – thumpety – thump – thump – thump.

'Oh, my God! I hope it's not squatters!' Cass followed her husband to the door.

'If it's those bloody New Age travellers claiming they're on a bloody ley-line again, I'll bloody—' Michael stopped hissing abruptly as they heard a terrifying, disembodied wail from within.

They crept inside.

The music was deafening. It came from the drawing room on the left.

Cass moved forward.

'Ssh!' Michael pushed her back against the wall.

Picking up a large, brass candlestick from the Pembroke table beside the phone, he edged towards the sitting-room door, back pressed against the striped wallpaper like an American cop.

'Everybody dance now! – *Aciiid!*' came another banshee wail from the drawing room. Cass held her breath.

Michael, pipe clenched between his teeth, pounced squarely into the doorway, candlestick aloft.

'JUST WHAT DO YOU THINK – *Marcus!*'

Darting behind Michael, Cass saw her younger son standing in the middle of their drawing room after what had obviously been a hefty bout of dancing. His shoulder-length curly bob was all over his face. His tatty REM t-shirt stuck to his bony chest. The music carried on thumping and thrashing around him.

'Hi, Dad – wotcha, Mum,' Marcus shouted over the din, circling a clenched fist in the air and wiggling his skinny hips. This was accompanied by much stamping of the enormous, unlaced trainers on his feet.

Michael marched over to the stereo and switched off the offending noise. Cass groped her way to a sofa for support and sank gratefully down on it.

'What are you doing at bloody home, giving your poor bloody mother such a fright?' Michael spluttered, positioning himself in front of the fireplace and puffing furiously on his now extinguished pipe. 'Why aren't you at bloody school?'

Marcus squinted his turned-down eyes at his father and paused for what seemed an interminable length of time. He got out a battered Marlboro soft pack from his trouser pocket and lit up.

The long pause had actually been to contemplate if his parents could stomach him rolling a spliff and deciding against it.

'Put that cigarette out!' snapped his mother.

'Wise decision, Marc, my man,' Marcus chuckled and carried on smoking.

'What?'

'Nuffink.' Marcus took a long drag, squinting from one parent to the other. 'Fing is . . . like . . . you're gonna love this . . .' He paused for effect, then forgot what he was saying.

Cass was wincing. Marcus was going through a fearfully class-conscious stage where all communication took place in a broad Cockney accent. One could have a ten-minute monologue from him and realise afterwards that all he'd really said was 'crucial' and 'happening', interspersed with 'um' and 'er'.

'Why are you wearing that wicked hat, Mum?' Marcus

wandered over to an armchair and slid into it rather than sitting down. He flicked his ash into a bowl of pot pourri.

'Never mind that!' bellowed Michael. 'Why are you at home?'

'I . . . er . . . got the sack, man. Y'know.'

'No, I DON'T know.'

'Excommunication.'

There was a long pause during which Marcus's eyes crossed so much that Cass thought they were going to spin around completely in their sockets.

'Are you trying to tell us you've been expelled, Marcus?' she finally managed to croak, casting a nervous eye towards Michael, whose face had turned the same angry red as his sunburnt bald patch.

'Yeah – that's it . . . ex-spelled. My spelling is no more. Get it? Ha ha, man.'

There was a shocked silence. The Hennessys' yellow Labrador, Enoch, chose this moment to crawl shakily out from behind Cass's sofa, deciding chaos had ended. He goosed Michael, which didn't help his composure.

'Why, Marcus?' Cass faltered. She wished she could ask Marcus for one of his cigarettes to calm her nerves. 'Why were you expelled?'

'Er.' Marcus scrunched up his sleepy eyes as if trying to remember. 'I . . . er . . . kind of organised this rave in Wiltsher's study . . . it was really happening . . . but we got raided, y'know.'

Michael had no idea what a 'rave' was and wasn't going to give his son the pleasure of asking. All he could splutter was, 'How could you . . . how *could* you . . . before the bloody cricket!'

'Yeah – the Head went on about that.' Marcus laughed. It was a wild, hiccuping laugh he'd cultivated with the Cockney accent.

Michael groped for his tobacco pouch and fought desperately to control his rage. If his blood pressure went up any higher, he'd need a valve in the top of his head. Unseeing, he started stuffing Olbas pastilles into the end of his pipe.

Brought up with the minimum of privilege between the wars,

seeing action in colonial Africa at nineteen, subsequently climbing first through the ranks of the Royal Navy and then – after injuries sustained in Korean water – battling his way into a top position in city investment broking, Michael didn't understand his children. Marcus had been given far more opportunities than himself, had far more back-up. Despite his mother's mollycoddling, he hadn't been spoilt; he had been made to work for everything he wanted, denied the more frivolous requests, sternly disciplined when he misbehaved. Yet he consistently let them down. Even as an eight-year-old boarder, he'd been sent home for putting Bond-it on the seat in the masters' lavatory. Marcus knew about as much of responsibility as Michael knew about needle-point.

Michael lit his pipe, which caramelised and fumed, spitting black froth. With as much dignity as he could muster, he cast it aside and glared at his son. Looking at Marcus's vacuous, smiling face, which hadn't a trace of shame, malice or embarrassment in it, his anger dissolved into despair.

'Couldn't you have stayed in school till we sorted all this bloody mess out?' He sighed gruffly.

'Nrrr . . . it was last week, man. You were away and that, y'know . . . I decided to cut my losses and get out.'

Michael stomped through to the answering machine in his study. As he guessed, there were several increasingly frantic messages from Marcus's headmaster. Looking out of the window and wondering which method of punishment was cruel enough, he noticed a white transit van turning into The Old Rectory driveway. It had *'Chez Vous'* italicised on the side.

'Caterers are here, old girl,' he called, turning wearily back to the drawing room. 'Go to your bloody room, Marcus, and wait for judgment. You shan't eat tonight, old boy.' That was petty, but then again he felt petty.

'Wicked.' Marcus heaved himself up from his sitting slouch to his standing one and meandered over to the stereo to flip out his tape.

'If I hear so much as ONE bloody note of that this evening, I'll . . . I'll . . .' Michael searched his mind for something suitably tyrannical. 'I'll get my barber to clip your whole bloody head on number one setting.'

For the first time that evening Marcus looked almost animated and bounded upstairs two at a time.

'I'll go and phone Parker,' Michael told his wife darkly, shutting himself in his study to ring Marcus's headmaster.

Cass hadn't moved from the sofa, hands clamped together, straw hat still in place.

Perhaps if Michael had been an Old Boy? She deliberated anxiously. Or hadn't been so competitive in the fathers' races on sports days?

She looked across at the collection of photographs of her children above the mantelpiece. Marcus looking so angelic at twelve; Oliver, smug and handsome in his graduation robes, and as a ravishing boy, hugging Enoch in the garden. They were beautiful children. She was so proud of them. Painfully proud. Above them, she saw her own reflection in the speckled old mirror which, with its burnished glow and majestic frame, she normally considered so flattering. A sad, middle-aged woman in a silly straw hat stared back.

Always considered prettier than her sister, with her cloud of black hair, round cheeks and upturned nose, Cass still had the mischievous delicacy of a cat licking the last of the cream from its paws. On a good day, with clever make-up and without a hangover, she could look thirty-five. On a day like today, a month away from her last diet, she looked every one of her fifty years (forty-eight to her friends). Making a mental note to apply some skin-food that night, she pulled her hat off and tidied her hair, drawing a deep, bolstering breath.

The doorbell rang and Enoch went into his usual frenzy of barking.

'Shut that bloody hound up – I'm on the bloody phone!'

Ignoring Michael's accompanying barks, Cass poured herself a stiff gin, barely graced with tonic, and led the caterers through to the kitchen. Normally she would have issued long and complicated instructions. This time she merely wandered back into the sitting room and sat down again.

This thing with Marcus, she mused. It was just a phase. He could go to a crammer in London after the summer – she'd ask Caroline Tudor-Wallis's advice. Perhaps Davies, Laing and Dick? Didn't one of the Whittaker boys go there? Michael could keep an eye on him from the flat in Holland Park. Yes, crammers were all the rage at the moment.

Feeling happier, she turned her mind to her sister. Poor Alex. At least Cass's children hadn't turned out like *that* bunch of ingénues. This phase of Marcus's was mild by comparison.

She didn't want to leave Marcus alone while they went to France. Who was to say he wouldn't have one of his 'raves' in The Old Rectory? Then again, exposure to Alex's Bohemian mob wouldn't do him much good – and there was Edward due to descend on them, too. Cass had grave doubts about her younger brother's sexuality. If he influenced Marcus at such an impressionable age, God alone knew how he'd turn out. And there was that alcoholic, Pascal, always hanging around in his underwear, swigging wine. He hadn't even got a proper job. Why Alexandra had married him Cass had no idea. Probably for the money.

She wished Michael would get off the phone so that she could call Caroline for a quick gripe. They wouldn't have a chance for a quiet chat with all the other guests there. If the caterers hadn't been around she could have asked Caroline to help her out in the kitchen for a few minutes, enabling a quick tête à tête.

'No joy, I'm afraid, old girl.' Michael appeared from the study, scratching his thinning hair. 'Chap says this is the last of a long line of trouble in that area – they had to punish someone.' He wouldn't worry his wife by telling her that Marcus had actually been caught in the possession of cannabis and it had taken Michael all his powers of persuasion to stop Parker informing the police.

'Oh dear.'

'Still – no use bloody crying over spilt whatsit and all that. I'm having a scotch in the bloody library. I think I'll ground him for the summer. Tell him he can forget about the car – you know the form. Run me a bloody bath will you, old girl.' He disappeared into the hallway.

Sighing, Cass felt that her husband was perhaps being a bit cruel to Marcus.

She wished that they'd stuck with the fortnight in the Italian Lakes rather than this ridiculous idea of Alex's. Michael was bound to get tense and ratty spending so long with a bunch of hippies. At least darling Sophia would be there. Cass adored boasting about her niece – such a perfect marriage.

Seeing things in a more positive light, Cass poured herself another gin, forgot to add tonic and walked upstairs to run Michael's bath.

From Marcus's room came the faintest of muffled thuds and an odd smell of bonfires.

9

Pascal screeched the jeep to a violent halt in the courtyard, nearly catapulting Tash through the windscreen.

'The others 'ave arrivé.' Pascal pointed to the large navy-blue Merc and a smaller, familiar-looking red Peugeot parked companionably on the cobbles.

Tash fell out of the jeep and tottered over to the other cars, clutching her head. She'd unexpectedly enjoyed meeting Anton Vignall, the burly little vigneron who ran the manoir's vineyard and who had flirted so outrageously with her – but need they have tried quite so many vintages? She couldn't get on with this spitting-out business and had swallowed most of what she'd tried.

She noticed that an enormous pile of suitcases by the Merc had been turned into a portaloo by the chickens.

'Oh dear.'

Then a sobering thought struck her. She must go and wash before Hugo saw her. He'd think she was a farm labourer or something.

'Come on, chérie. Let us say 'ello.' Pascal took her firmly by the arm and led her towards the house.

'Oh dear,' Tash said again.

Pascal, having fuelled his stepdaughter with plenty of Franco-Dutch courage, didn't want her ducking out. They'd had such a good time with his friend Anton that they hadn't had time to go into Tours and get Tash a new outfit, as he'd promised Alexandra.

Quand même, he decided, Tash looked sexy and alluring in her baggy t-shirt and those long, long legs in black jeans with clumpy jodhpur boots. Très naturelle, thought Pascal. Her face was already turning pink from the sun, freckles crowding her cheeks and nose. She reminded Pascal of a taller, more rounded version of her mother returning from a long evening's walk with the spaniels.

Inside, the house was cool and silent. Their footsteps echoed up into the high ceilings. They walked into the Blue Room – so called because Alexandra had filled it with all things blue, including a giant sky and cloud ceiling mural painted by Tash on a previous visit. The wall of French windows at the far end let in a blanket of yellow light, clashing with the cool cerulean.

A sharp, clipped woman's voice travelled through the doors as they walked towards them. Sophia's. Then a deep, throaty man's drawl. Tash stopped in her tracks. Hugo. Oh God! She'd forgotten just how fiercely she'd loved him. The intense pain of her crush. The frustrated tears and self-loathing.

She could see her sister's blond, haughty husband, Ben, lounging beside her mother. Hugo and Sophia must be around the corner. And Amanda, of course – how she'd childishly hated Amanda for having Hugo. I can't face them, she thought, I just can't face them.

But her mother had spotted Tash and Pascal.

'At last!' She leaned her head towards Pascal, accepting a long kiss. 'We'd given you up, darling. Isn't Anton fun?' she said to Tash, who was hiding behind Ben, trying to blend into the wisteria. 'Now, you know everyone of course, Tash. Pascal, this is Amanda Beauchamp, who's terribly athletic.' Amanda looked poker-faced. 'You've met Hugo before, I think.'

'Oui, allô, mon ami. Allô, Amanda, welcome to our 'ome.' Pascal kissed her on both cheeks. 'Allô, Ben. Ahh – the beautiful Sophia and Lotty.' The small, dark-haired girl on Sophia's lap looked horrified at the prospect of being kissed. 'Where is your leetle baby? 'E is asleep?'

'Yes, he's upstairs with the nanny,' simpered Sophia.

'Oh my God!' gasped Alexandra. 'I'd quite forgotten about

poor Wowla. Be a duck, Pascal, and ask her down for a drink. She's in the salle des chapeaux.'

'Mummy, we don't generally—' started Sophia.

'Don't be silly, darling,' Alexandra interrupted blithely. 'The poor thing must be parched. We can put Josh down here in the shade if you're worried.'

Pascal loped off cheerfully. Sophia crunched a lemon pip between clenched teeth.

Tash was still lurking near the wall. The only space left to sit was the bench next to Hugo. Even though he was ten feet away, her heart was hammering in her empty chest. She couldn't think straight – the wine had muddled her senses. All she could think was how glamorous they all looked. Like a scene from some ultra-expensive American mini-series one longed to step into. The only trouble was that in reality one looked so awful in comparison. She stared at her feet.

'Come and sit down, Tash,' urged her mother.

Tash shot a terrified look at Hugo, who was laughing with Ben about something. He was still utterly, hopelessly beautiful. Those laser-blue eyes, that exquisitely sculptured jaw-line and superior, slightly beaky nose. She was sixteen again, poring over love quizzes in magazines, pouncing on every horoscope, desperately insecure.

Alexandra sensed her discomfort. 'Have my chair – you'll get the sun. I'll pop in and get some more booze. Doesn't Tash look well, Sophia?'

Sophia had been thinking exactly the opposite. With masses of stringy hair covering Tash's face, all that was visible was a painfully out-of-condition body in awful, scruffy clothes. She'd look more at home in a cardboard box on the South Bank than the manoir. Ben looked positively tailored in comparison.

'Yes . . . you look . . . well, Tash. Thinner.'

'Thanks,' mumbled Tash. 'How are you? How did the balloon race go?' It was so unfair. Sophia looked as if she'd been exported from Champneys in tissue paper.

'Oh, absolutely terrific.' Sophia checked Ben wasn't listening. 'Bea was delighted. You should have come – I sent you a ticket.

Lots of names were there. The Le Bons, the Branaghs, Paula Yates and her scruffy chap, Jason Connery, Dylan Samuelson – didn't you have a crush on him?'

'Once, yes.' Nothing could reduce her to gauche teenager status quicker. She knew Sophia meant well. After all, wasn't she always trying to include her in the Merediths' high-glitz life?

In fact – as Tash's more critical subconscious had guessed years ago – Sophia would have been horrified if Tash had accepted. Inviting her little sister to celebrity events eased her guilty conscience but she relied on the fact that Tash always refused.

'It's lovely to see you again,' Tash said to Amanda, feeling two-faced. 'How are you? You look amazing,' she added sincerely. Amanda was relaxing like a sleek, blonde Siamese cat on the other side of Hugo.

Amanda was looking at Tash as if she'd found a slug taking a leak in her Pimms.

'I'm fine,' she murmured icily and turned round to talk to Ben.

Tash bit her lip.

At least Lotty liked her 'Nasha', who always played with her for hours without getting bored or telling her to go to bed. She crawled up on to Tash's knee and played with her hair.

'You smell like Puddles,' she complimented her aunt.

'Her pony,' explained Sophia sweetly, asking with a sly smile, 'how's the elusive Max? When's he arriving?'

'Um . . . well . . .'

Mercifully, at that point Alexandra and Pascal appeared, followed by Paola, who was clutching the sleeping Josh. Alexandra and Pascal were having another squabble in French. Tash heard her name and 'vêtements'. Didn't that mean clothes? Perhaps her mother was going to suggest she gave them all a fashion show?

'Here we are.' Alexandra put down two more enormous jugs of Pimms. 'Sit over there, Wowla. Next to Hugo. That's right. Top-ups all round I think, Pascal sweetheart. I'll get another couple of chairs. Isn't this fun?'

'We are out of food,' Pascal shrugged jovially, helping everyone to Pimms and himself to wine.

Sophia glowered into her glass. Trust mother to invite a houseful and forget to buy any food in. She was beginning to feel light-headed. She longed for a cup of tea.

'Pascal says we should kill a couple of chickens,' giggled Alexandra, returning with two blue chairs. 'But I think we should all go out for a slap-up meal.'

'Hear! Hear!' agreed Ben, who was famished.

'Good. I'll book a table at la Filature for ten,' Alexandra decided.

'But there's only seven of us,' Sophia pointed out, hoping her mother wasn't planning to include Paola and the children.

'Ten o'clock, darling,' laughed Alexandra.

Ben glanced at his watch. It was twenty past three. His stomach gave an indignant growl.

As their shadows creaked from north to east, the group chatted and gossiped with increasingly loosened tongues. All except Tash and Paola. The latter was aware of her employer's steely glances; as soon as Josh started bawling and looking nauseous she made her grateful getaway. Tash was not so lucky. She kept trying to include herself in conversations but couldn't think of anything to say. Even Lotty got bored with her and ran off to be an Indian again. Listening in to the others, she found herself chain-smoking and drinking too much Pimms. It mixed badly with the earlier wine and made her clumsy. When she got up to go to the loo she knocked over one of the jugs.

In the mirror above the hand-basin she was surprised to find her face looking pink, freckled and healthy. She had tan tide-marks where her t-shirt had covered her.

'So much for paling into insignificance,' she told her glowing reflection. Really, she had to pull herself together. She hadn't been this immature for years. She was shocked by the violent reaction her family had caused in her. Grouchy and tearful last night, painfully shy today. She felt horribly pubescent.

I'll go back and dazzle them with my acerbic wit and paradoxically gentle empathy, she decided purposefully.

Walking back on to the terrace, she fell over a spaniel.

Hugo glanced down at her as she sprawled on Sophia's handbag. It was the first time he'd looked her full in the face. His expression was dead-pan. Only the beautiful kingfisher-blue eyes betrayed his amused contempt.

Everyone was getting merrily well oiled. Ben thought he'd pass out from hunger. He kept helping himself to Pimms so that he could eat the fruit.

Tash watched Amanda, awed that anyone could possess so much self-confidence. The sensual blonde had cornered Pascal and was talking to him in a low voice, a seductive hint of a smile playing on her lips. Pascal had his cheeks puffed out to full capacity and an anxious, excited expression on his face. All the time Amanda's elegant little hand, with its massive opal ring on the third finger, was running up and down the back of Hugo's neck.

Tash glanced at her mother. She was deep in conversation with Ben and Hugo.

The focus of Amanda's attention had not, however, escaped Sophia's notice. She looked across and caught Tash's eye. One perfectly plucked eyebrow shot up towards her Alice band.

'Tash, darling,' Alexandra called out. 'Hugo and Ben are dying to have a gawp at your new horse. Why don't you take them to see him while I make us all a cup of tea?'

Sophia sighed audibly. Amanda groaned.

In the hazy drunkenness on the terrace, Tash had forgotten the humiliation of that morning with Foxy Snob, or the Poxy Slob as she'd later thought of him.

Together, she, Hugo and Ben walked down the steps into the garden and fought their way through the waist-high grass to the courtyard. Tash's head was spiralling groggily now. In the yard she fell over a suitcase, now almost covered with chicken deposits.

'Christ – Sophia'll hit the roof,' exclaimed Ben, staring at the soiled luggage. 'You okay, Tash?'

'Fine.'

Hugo decided that he'd never seen anyone as clumsy as Tash French. She was also completely ignoring him whilst asking Ben all sorts of innocuous and polite questions. He wondered if she was quite all there.

'He's in here,' muttered Tash, not taking her eyes off the ground. 'Hang on, I'll bring him out.' She scuttled inside. There was a clattering sound as she crashed into something.

Snob bit her twice as she put on his headcollar and caught her painfully on the shin with his hind leg.

He strutted like a King's Road poseur once she got him out into the sunshine. Holding his head and tail high, he showed off his flashy trot as he circled round her, neck arched, nostrils flared like two red trumpets.

'Now that's what I call a magnificent piece of merchandise,' whistled Hugo.

Snob let out a volley of snorts and reared up, coming to a halt four-square on the cobbles. Eyes boggling, he stared excitedly around him, taking an intense interest in a baby-buggy by the boot of the Merc.

Hugo admired the deep chest and well-shaped quarters.

'Nice outline. How does he jump?' he asked Tash, as if she was some inconsequential 'lad'.

'Like a stag.' *How should I know? It took me an hour to get on him.*

'Perfect build for an eventer. Lots of heart room,' admired Ben, appraising the chestnut. 'A stallion too. Imagine the stud fees if he went top class.'

'Wonderful legs,' observed Hugo.

Mine aren't bad, thought Tash. Infuriatingly, Snob didn't flinch when Hugo ran his hands down his limbs. Tash was astonished to find herself jealous of a horse.

'He's fiveish, isn't he?' Hugo asked Tash over his shoulder as he peered in Snob's uncomplaining mouth.

'Yes.' Why couldn't she be a little more animated? Crack the odd witty remark? For Christ's sake, she could joke with the whole of Max's rugby team and not blush. 'He's five,' she repeated uneasily.

Hugo came back to Ben's side. His face, which had been moody and still the entire afternoon, was now all smiles and laughter. It lit up his normally aloof beauty like a beacon. Tash felt her stomach disappear.

'I think, Benjamin, I've found my Badminton horse at last.' He grinned. 'I've never seen so much class in one nag.'

At that moment Snob snorted and gazed at Tash with his slightly suspicious, purply-brown eyes, as if seeing her for the first time. Then, sighing deeply, he rubbed his noble head with its odd streaky blaze affectionately against her shoulder and inserted his pink nose into her t-shirt.

She could have cried (half a glass more Pimms and she probably would have). *Thank you, God.* Her first minor breakthrough. A sign of trust.

Extracting Snob's nose, she pulled at his long ears and he scratched his whiskery muzzle against the roughness of her jeans' pocket as if to seal the friendship.

'Don't suppose there's any harm in making an offer to Pascal,' Ben was saying to Hugo.

Tash felt a hot flush of resentment creep up on her cheeks. How dare they treat her as if she weren't there? She wasn't some half-wit.

'He's mine,' muttered Tash, and then felt silly. It sounded so childish.

'Pardon?' Hugo looked as if one of the chickens had spoken.

'I mean he belongs to me, not Pascal. All his papers are in my name.' She spoke so quickly that she stumbled over her words. Hugo was looking her right in the eyes, a smile dancing on his lips. She stared at his t-shirt.

'All right then,' he said softly, his voice losing its usual dry boredom, 'I'd like to make you a really attractive offer for this chap. What would you say to—'

'No!' Snob had rubbed her shoulder. The gauntlet was down and that was that. 'He's not for sale,' she mumbled as firmly as she could in the direction of Hugo's chest.

'Listen, darling—' Hugo drawled easily.

Oh, that hurt. *Don't call me darling.*

'– that really is one spectacular animal and I don't honestly blame you for wanting to hold on to him. But with the money I'm willing to pay for him you could buy four horses.'

'I don't want a string,' muttered Tash, 'even if it's a quartet.'

Ben laughed, but Hugo's face had become deadly serious as he glanced from Tash to Snob.

'I mean it – I'll make you a fantastic offer for him.' He looked like a little boy staring at a solid gold BMX.

'And I m-m-mean it, I don't w-want to sell him.' A stutter, that's new; he's given me a stutter, thought Tash.

'Why ever not, Tash?' pitched in Ben, who had decided the conversation wasn't getting anywhere.

'He was a g-gift. From Pascal and my mother. I-I don't sell gifts.' She was trying to work out some drop-dead sarcastic remark about gift horses' mouths, but was too drunk. No doubt a perfect one would spring to mind that night in bed.

'Look,' Hugo sounded as if he were talking to a small child, 'that's very sweet of you.' He patently thought it was no such thing. 'But have you any idea of the cost of transporting a horse to England? The quarantine restrictions, the tax, the import paperwork to wade through? Then there's the fact he's a stallion.'

'Pascal says I can keep him here,' bleated Tash, trying to hold on to Snob, who was pirouetting around again. She was aware that she was really being pretty illogical. Selling Snob to Hugo would have been her dream come true that morning. Why did one affectionate rub make all the difference?

'That would be a complete fucking waste!' cried Hugo, getting seriously irritated. The girl was not only weird, she was stubborn. 'To keep this classy nag in a pokey barn all year waiting for some – girl' – he made 'girl' sound like 'monster with two heads' – 'to come and plod round the lanes when she's on holiday visiting Mummy for a week. This is a born competition horse, not some fat cob.'

Tash thought of Seamus and felt a burst of anger. Then she thought of Samion. Remembered crying by the ring-ropes because he'd humiliated her again, refusing to take him out on hacks because she was terrified of him, being scorned by Sophia and told off by her father because he thought she was being a 'lazy little cow'. Then she remembered the heady, intoxicating rush of pride from her first breakthrough. The unbeatable thrill of every piece of progress they made, however small. And the crippling injustice, the foul scheming, misunderstanding and unbearable lies at the end. Tash suddenly felt her much repressed spoilt, competitive streak grabbing her. Snob was her chance to prove something.

She looked at Hugo. God, he was beautiful. With a sickening mixture of pain and pleasure, she realised that she loved him as much as ever.

She'd had an exquisite fantasy when driving home from the vineyard with Pascal and letting her ego run away with her. She'd imagined Hugo standing by the little paddock, helping her school Snob into docile obedience. Then afterwards he had led her by the arm to one of the deserted out-buildings and kissed every inch of her body thoroughly. In the middle Amanda had walked in, outraged. Hugo had simply said, 'Piss off. It's Tash I love,' and carried on. At that point, Pascal had started asking her about the English property market.

Now she was being faced with reality. Hugo, twitching with exasperated animosity, was looking at her as if she were a toothless crone who had given him a bad tarot reading before his Common Entrance. Tash knew that she couldn't sell him Snob just for a brief honeyed thank-you. Snob was her trump card, her challenge. Her chance to prove her worth and make up for the awful mistakes of Samion. Much as she longed for Hugo's recognition, she knew that she had to do it the hard way. She owed it to Samion's memory and to her pride.

'No,' she said in a voice not nearly as calm as she thought it would be after such an epic decision-making process. 'I won't sell him, so you might as well stop asking.' She wished she could have thought of something a little less bald to say. Still, it would do. Turning on their heels, she and Snob left them both standing in the middle of the yard.

As soon as she got into the dusty stalls Tash burst into tears.

'You stupid fool,' she told herself glumly. 'Look what you've left yourself to do! Why oh why are you so pathetic?'

As if to illustrate her thoughts, Snob took a vicious nip at the shoulder he had earlier courted.

'Fucking little imbecile,' Hugo was spitting to Ben outside.

'No Selle,' chortled Ben.

'And you can fucking shut up.' Hugo stalked into the house.

Ben shrugged his shoulders and started collecting up the suitcases. He knew Hugo hated not getting what he wanted, but he normally charmed his way through eventually. Generally, he would have laughed with Ben and discussed tactics. He was really being unusually sulky over this.

Must want that horse very badly, thought Ben, very badly indeed.

10

Tash was dreading going out to dinner. She felt totally exhausted and her head was pounding. Another protracted drinking session filled with 'have-you-seen-Buffy-Armitage-lately?' was likely to trigger spots before the eyes and a unique rendition of 'Show Me the Way to go Home'.

Also, whatever she put on showed off the t-shirt tan marks she'd been so proud of earlier. She looked like an Australian builder. That made her think of Graham, and Graham made her think of Max, and thinking of Max made her stomach twist with guilt and her subconscious sing Joni Mitchell ballads.

Can you take me as I am – strung out on another man?

Would you take back me in the first place, more to the point?

She'd tried on everything her mother had laid out on the bed for her and felt suicidally depressed. The skirts wouldn't go over her hips or wouldn't do up. The tops made her look butch enough to star in *Prisoner Cell Block H.* In the end she plumped for a baggy cream silk shirt of her mother's, which at least hid her two-tone paintwork, and a short black skirt that showed off her long legs. The only problem was that she had to wear opaque tights to hide the bruises which Snob had inflicted. In the muggy heat, it felt as if she had three pairs of thermal long-johns on.

'You look like a waitress,' she told her penguin-like reflection. At least that would confuse Hugo.

* * *

But Hugo now knew exactly who she was.

Pacing round his and Amanda's circular room, which was in one of the manoir's turrets, he couldn't shut up about the chestnut horse.

'Quality horses are like gold dust these days,' he said, puffing irritably on a cigarette. 'If that nag were in England you'd have a mob on your hands. Instead I've got some soppy pony clubber who thinks she can train an animal of that calibre. He'll kill the stupid cow first.' He looked moodily out of the window, nearly giving a perching dove a heart attack.

'Tash French is hardly a pony clubber,' countered Amanda from the bed. 'She's in her twenties.' She liked nettling Hugo when he was being irascible.

'Doesn't stop her being fucking childish.' Hugo watched the dove flap frenziedly off to a tall maple.

'Hark who speaks.' Amanda stretched out naked on the antique bed-pane and started to meditate. She found it therapeutic before her callanetics work-out. Besides, she was fed up with Hugo raving on about sodding horses.

'It's not as if she could be that attached to the animal,' Hugo retorted. 'She's only had him for twenty-four hours for Chrissake.' He started pacing round again. 'I think she's got it in for me. You saw the way she ignores me.'

'You ignore her too.' Amanda pointed out, trying to focus her attention on her toes-through-to-knees. 'Everyone does.'

'Yes, but not on purpose,' snapped Hugo. 'She's just so wet. And there's something really spooky about her.'

'I think you're getting a bit carried away, Hugs. She's just shy,' knees-through-to-hips. 'Why don't you give her the benefit of your beguiling charm?'

'That fat cow? No way. I'd rather bang Ben's mother.' It had occurred to him to butter the girl up that night, but there was something really puzzling about Sophia's sister and her strange, mismatched eyes. Hugo was appalled to find himself unnerved by this clumsy, silent girl. She was the first woman who had ever had this effect on him. Even Amanda's snarls didn't induce this sort of skin-tightening. Why? When Tash French was such a drip?

'She'll change her mind once she's fallen off a few times.' Amanda sighed. Pelvis-through-to-abdomen. 'You wait and see.' Abdomen-back-to-pelvis. 'It's hours till we have to be ready. Come to bed.'

Sophia, despite having got the giggles earlier when tight, was not at her happiest.

'You must have left it in Paris, Ben.'

'Don't see how. Porters took down all the cases. Doubtful they'd have missed one.'

'Well, they bloody did.'

Sophia, who'd been furious on discovering her Louis Vuittons covered in chicken excrement, was doubly livid at finding the one containing all her underwear and casual clothes was missing.

'What am I supposed to do for four weeks? Trollop round the fields in Chanel with nothing underneath?'

Ben found the thought highly exciting.

'I'm not Mother,' Sophia continued furiously. 'I had enough of wandering round with my boobs hanging out when I was modelling full-time.'

'I'm sure Amanda'll lend you something, Sophs.'

'I can't wear someone else's *underwear*!' snapped Sophia, tightening the belt on her bathrobe.

'Well, I'll drive you into Tours tomorrow to get some. Buy you some jeans too if you like,' offered Ben, trying to pacify her.

Sophia's nostrils flared. She'd have to climb back into dirty knickers after her shower. She hated doing that.

'Go without,' Ben suggested hopefully.

Ignoring him, Sophia rinsed them out in the sink and hung them out of the window to dry.

Pascal and Alexandra were returning after walking the spaniels and calling in on Jean and his wife Valérie at the decrepit lodge house.

'You sink we will be togezer after so long?' Pascal turned his watery eyes on his wife. He was speaking English after three stiff brandies with Jean.

'Sans aucune doute,' smiled Alexandra, cupping his face in her hands. 'We'll be toasting each other to our graves.'

'Ah non. We, chérie, are without . . . er . . . mortality.' Pascal laughed. He paused, looking at the beautiful ornate house, tie-dyed cadmium in the dappled evening sun.

'Tash. She is strange girl.'

'Yes,' sighed Alexandra. 'I'm afraid she is.'

'I like 'er. She is fun. She remind me of you.'

'Do you really think so?'

'Oui. Except que . . . she is unhappy. Ver' unhappy.'

'I know.'

'She does not like Hugo.' He pronounced it 'ooogo'. 'Nor 'e like 'er. 'E was ver' rude to 'er at tea.'

'Poor Tash.' Alexandra picked a leaf out of Pascal's hair. 'I think, darling, she actually likes Ooogo far too much for her own good. He's a very attractive man.'

'You sink so?' Pascal puffed out his cheeks moodily.

Alexandra laughed. 'Yes. It's a shame he's so spoilt. It makes him so vile sometimes. Most of the time, in fact.' She paused, looking over Pascal's shoulder. 'Isn't that extraordinary? There's a pair of knickers hanging out of that window.'

'Eet's the salle orchidée.'

'I put Sophia and Ben in there.'

'Peut-être it is the flag of conquer en France.'

'I think, darling, that's a little too colonialist even for Ben.'

Tash was downstairs in the China Room ready to go ages before the others. She sat staring at the same ceramic monstrosities that she'd memorised, and quite probably thrown up into, the night before. Great yawns tugged at her mouth, and her eyelids, heavy with lassitude, seemed weighed down by dead man's coins.

After ten minutes she heard Ben and Hugo making their way across the hall towards her. Feeling like a criminal, but unable to face another cross-examination about selling Snob, she nipped through what had once been the servants' door and along a back corridor that led to the large, friendly kitchen.

'Ah, coffee. That'll wake me up.'

She studied the shiny espresso-maker doubtfully.

Five minutes and gallons of grainy froth later, she sat down with a cup of instant.

Paola came in, buckling under the weight of a box of tins.

'Here, let me help,' Tash offered. 'Poor Paola. It's not fair being left behind to babysit.' Privately, she wished she could swap places.

'I no mind.' They dumped the box on the surface and Paola looked round for a can-opener.

'Your mother very kind. She give me soup and cheese until I pop.'

Tash smiled. 'How are your family in Italy?'

'They good. My brother he go to the university in Milano now. My mother is very happyful.'

Tash sipped her coffee and watched Paola heating up a tin of lobster thermidor-flavoured babyfood. She had an image of the Hon. Josh ordering it from a velvet-covered menu before perusing the wine list.

Pascal came in through the back door, covered in straw.

'I go to feed your 'orse and 'e push me in 'es sheet,' he said moodily. 'Now I must 'ave a . . . douche . . . and there is no 'ot water.' The brown cheeks expanded.

'I'm sorry,' sympathised Tash, wondering why she always felt personally responsible for things that went wrong.

Pascal shrugged and took a giant carton of beer cans out of the fridge.

'Thees will keep the – 'ow you say – troops smiling.' He deposited a can in front of Tash before disappearing along the back corridor which had been her escape route earlier.

Tash offered it to Paola.

'Grazie.' The pretty Italian girl smiled at Tash, taking the can and hooking her nail under the ring-pull. So unlike her sister, she thought. 'So you have horse?'

'Yes,' sighed Tash, 'and a miserable bugger he is too.'

'I ride in Italia,' murmured Paola, spooning out lobster slop and swigging from her can simultaneously. 'I get my job with Her Ladyboat because I ride.' She paused, speculating on the fact that all the 'riding' involved had been clearing the dung up from the paddocks and leading a wailing Charlotte round on Puddle. 'Per'aps I can helping you?' She turned two enthusiastic brown eyes on Tash.

'Could you?' Tash's face lit up. 'I mean, will Sophia let you?'

'Her Ladyboat let me have time off sometimes. It will be fun. Per'aps –' ventured Paola, going pink, '– per'aps Signor Hugo will help us. He is very good horseman.' Paola secretly thought Signor Hugo all-man in more than just equine terms.

'Er . . . I doubt it,' muttered Tash, taking such a big gulp of coffee that it ran down her chin and on to her shirt. 'Damn!'

Paola helped her mop it off. Deciding the subject of Signor Hugo was out of bounds, she told Tash about Her Ladyboat's lack of knickers and they both fell about.

As Paola went off to feed Josh, Tash wandered outside to see Snob.

The moon was so bright it was as if FIFA had floodlit the manoir. Inside the stone outbuilding, Snob was standing sulkily in a corner of his stall. Tash leaned over the half-door and looked at him. He ignored her.

'I think you have a lot in common with Hugo Beauchamp, my French friend,' sighed Tash. 'Perhaps you would be better in his masterly hands . . . but I'm afraid you're stuck with grotty old me.'

Snob snorted and turned his dusty red hindquarters on her.

'And you think about as much of me as horny Hugo, don't you? Well, that will change, my boy. That will change.'

Twitching his blond tail, Snob let out a disrespectful fart.

Tash smiled ruefully and went back to look at the moon.

At ten past ten they still hadn't left.

Tash and Ben were sitting impatiently on the long sofa in the high entrance hall, chewing nails and tapping feet respectively. Ben was working his way through his third Mars Bar.

Hugo appeared briefly before heading off to chivvy Amanda who, unbeknown to him, was admiring the manoir's gymnasium with Pascal. In turn, Pascal was admiring Amanda's sleek legs in the shortest of Hervé Legère dresses.

Alexandra was trying to have a gossip with Sophia as she got ready. Without her luxurious Home Farm dressing room, Sophia was having major problems applying her make-up. There was only a dusty mirror on the small Louis XIV table. Moving the flower arrangement which had been in front of it had helped, but not a lot.

'The light in here's appalling, Mummy,' Sophia moaned. 'I could be applying lip-liner to my nose and not notice.'

'I think those old mirrors are wonderfully romantic,' sighed Alexandra, trying Sophia's base on her wrist. 'Imagine all the cherished mistresses that have gazed there before you, wondering if their lovers would visit them that night and look lovingly upon that same face they could see reflected.'

'Hmmph.' If her mother wasn't going to offer her any practical help, Sophia wished she'd leave her to get on with it. She pointedly screwed the lid back on her foundation.

'You always look gorgeous, darling.' Alexandra moved on to the eye-shadows. 'You couldn't not, even with lip-liner all over your face. Now tell me about Holdham and all the exciting things you've been up to . . .'

Ben was exercising his tapping legs and grumbling stomach up and down the hallway now. 'Bloody starving. Hope Sophs is going to get a shift on. Keeps complaining that she's forgotten to pack her exfoliager. Extraordinary things she puts on her face.' He came to a halt opposite Tash. 'Haven't got a cigarette, have you?'

Tash gave him a Camel and took one out for herself. 'I'm afraid I don't have a light.'

Ben rifled through his pockets and scratched his head. 'Hugs! – Hugs! Young lady here wants you to come and light her fire!'

Tash winced as Hugo appeared from a side room.

'Oh – it's you.' He tossed her his silver lighter. 'Haven't seen Amanda, have you?' he asked Ben.

It's pathetic, thought Tash. My chest feels full of hot air just holding his Zippo – what would I be like if I got to hold his zipper? She burst out laughing and received disdainful looks from Ben and Hugo.

When Amanda and Pascal appeared five minutes later, laughing at some private joke, Pascal looked like a poppy-eyed schoolboy.

Amanda glanced at Hugo for a reaction, but he was staring at a large painting of the manoir which dominated one of the whitewashed walls.

'This is bloody good. Wouldn't mind having one of Haydown like this. Who did it?'

'Tash,' replied Pascal. 'She give eet to us for our fourth anniversary.'

Hugo looked at Tash. Daring herself to hold his eyes, Tash saw that same gaze full of scornful amusement. Chastened, she looked away. What would she have to do to impress him?

'Where are the others?' asked Amanda, annoyed that her efforts to rouse Hugo from his current preoccupation had been in vain. She examined her watch. 'Shouldn't we be there by now?'

'I'll go and fetch them,' mumbled Tash, ricocheting off Ben in her hurry to get away.

'Graceful young thing, isn't she?' drawled Hugo in an undertone.

Tash found Sophia and Alexandra sitting on the bed in the Merediths' room. It was a large, feminine bedroom, covered in orchid murals and chintzes. Tash stopped in the doorway, taking in the heady mix of Givenchy and Arpège.

'I don't know,' Sophia was saying, 'it seems odd he's chosen now to go to the States. I haven't had a chance to speak with her about him. My guess is – oh, hello, Tash.' She was looking uncharacteristically shifty.

'The others were wondering how long you two would be?' Tash leaned against the door and it opened further, making her fall over. She wished she didn't feel so tired.

Alexandra glanced at her watch. 'God! Is it that late already? I haven't even changed.' She got up. 'Won't be a tick.' And she dashed out.

Tash had become so accustomed to her sister's bitchiness of late that she was surprised when Sophia linked arms with her in a big-sisterly fashion. It reminded her of a more gentle Sophia who had comforted her when she was teased for being fat at school or cuddled her when she had been afraid of the dark in the echoing Benedict House. A Sophia who had existed before the secret they'd shared for so long – never referring to it, barely daring to remember – had torn a great rift between them.

But tonight, malleable from booze and exhaustion, Tash tucked away the conspiracy of lies she'd so recently raked from the dingier corners of her mind. She just felt absurdly silly for building her sister up into someone so superior and distanced in her imagination.

'Come on, Fanny, let's face the menfolk,' Sophia giggled.

As very young children, Tash and Sophia had been nicknamed Fanny and Enid by Alexandra because they would babble on like two old women over a fence.

Tash laughed as they walked from the room.

'But, Fangs, before we go downstairs, tell me what's happened with old Max. There's no point keeping it bottled up – it only gets worse, believe me, I should know.' Sophia smiled softly. It lit up her beautiful face.

Ben had once said Sophia could turn icicles into puddles with one smile. Tash, desperate for reassurance about Max, as deferential to her sister as ever, was totally disarmed.

At ten-thirty, by which time Ben thought his stomach had inverted totally, they were finally ready for the off.

Hugo was aware that a huge amount of alcohol and no food had given him an urge to do something reckless. He longed to have a row with someone, preferably Sophia's sister, but that would probably piss off their lovely hostess. He settled instead for ignoring Amanda's attempts to get his back up.

Tash was half-asleep. The others were in roaring party spirit.

They all trooped outside to the cars and were in the middle of deciding who was to ride in which when an engine puttered loudly into earshot and a pair of headlamps bounced through the back gates and into the courtyard.

'Oh no,' groaned Ben. 'Who on earth visits at this time of night?'

There was a banging of car doors and the sound of Paul Simon being switched off the stereo before Matty and Sally emerged through the gloom.

'Sorry to turn up so late,' apologised Sally, kissing Alexandra. 'We had a change of plan.'

'It's just lovely to see you!' cried Alexandra, kissing Matty and making his hat fall off. 'You're just in time – we're all setting off to eat. Come along.'

'We can't,' said Matty regretfully. 'The kids are in the back, dead to the world. We've got to get them into bed.'

'Not to worry. Bring them in and we'll all have a quick drink,' Alexandra insisted. 'Isn't this fun?'

They never did get to the restaurant. Incapable of keeping a secret, Sally blurted news of her pregnancy within minutes and, as yet more baby equipment and colourful plastic toys invaded the hall, Pascal got out the champagne to celebrate. One quick drink turned into several, which took them rapidly towards midnight.

Ben's stomach reduced to postage stamp proportions. Noticing his distress, Sally foraged into her chaotic handbag and found him a battered Twix and half a tube of Smarties.

'I say, jolly kind,' Ben accepted the gifts gratefully, admiring Sally's rosy cheeks and playful green eyes. Sophia referred to her sister-in-law as Slapdash Sal, claiming Sally was a dreadful slob. But Ben privately thought she was rather charming, liking the fact that Sally was candid, witty and never wore a scrap of make-up.

Sophia, having earlier graced her brother with a chilly kiss on his cheek (noting two days' stubble and a light trace of mayonnaise), politely inquired as to why they were having another baby so soon after the last. Particularly as Tor was so – well – tricky.

'Of course, they say children born at home are always slower to develop,' Sophia told him loftily. 'Although it was frightfully popular in the seventies, wasn't it?'

Matty looked at her for a long time while she discreetly checked her reflection in the champagne cooler.

'I didn't get the last delivery on video,' he told her finally, his face completely dead-pan, 'so we're trying for another take – this time we thought we'd go for squatting in a tepid birth-tank, African tribal music in the background and getting the neighbours round to share a bong. You must come round for Guinness and veggie drumsticks when we show it.'

Sophia's eyes narrowed to two perfectly applied lines of kohl for a few seconds before she laughed shrilly and patted her brother gamely on his worn shirt-sleeve, determined not to rise. Turning sharply to Ben, who was now hooting at one of Sally's sardonic asides, she growled, 'Darling, *must* we hear you unwrapping choccies across the room?'

Ben's stomach let out a furious battery of growls.

'There's nothing for it,' announced Hugo. 'You'll have to kill those chickens, Pascal.'

'We're not quite that desperate,' Alexandra laughed. 'I'm sure I can prise something out of the freezer.'

They ate a strange combination of defrosted quiche, salmon mousse and pitta bread off their knees in the grand manoir drawing room, overlooked by Alexandra's collection of Picasso sketches and vast, colourful Miros. The anomaly pleased Matty. It was so wonderfully typical of his mother's lifestyle.

The champagne kept flowing as the conversation divided between smaller and smaller groups around the room.

Sally cornered Tash for a gossip. They often met up in London and Tash occasionally dashed across it to babysit as a favour when Sally forgot to book her regular sitter. Sally loved the fact that Tash, terminally disorganised, wore her clothes inside out and read the kids Jackie Collins at bedtime. Matty complained that his sister took down phone messages wrong and left the milk out.

Alexandra drifted around, picking up plates and then putting them all down again as she paused to chat to her guests.

Matty was talking to Pascal about British politics. Amanda, ignoring Sophia's monologue about Clinique's latest facial range, listened in.

'The cock-up they made of the poll tax is totally unforgivable,' Matty was saying, 'but if you compare it with the way in which the NHS is currently being bastardised it seems insignificant. A mate of mine was trying to research material for a documentary about the disparity surrounding waiting lists for organ transplants. He came up against this massive brick wall. What he did find out eventually was so hot that the Home Office put its cloven foot down and confiscated three years' work. Didn't leave him so much as a Post-it pad.'

'Your political censorship is ver' strong in England, no?' Pascal filled their glasses.

'Yes,' Matty agreed. 'But you have to look at *why* our censors are so heavy-handed. The public think that HM Gov is protecting their interests, but all the time it's covering up its own screaming raspberries. Who can trust a body of people who six weeks later allow their ad agency to approach the same production company which was raided by HO – asking them to produce five thirty-second commercials for guess who?'

Pascal laughed, although he really wasn't too sure what Matty was talking about. He spoke so fast and with a slight stutter which made him hard to understand. Something about advertising?

'Amanda work for a ver' big advertising company in London, n'est-ce pas?'

Amanda was smarting from Matty's comments. It was her company which had made the boob, triggering off a very laconic and ironic article in *Private Eye* which seemed to stare at her from tables in every restaurant in Soho for weeks afterwards. She had not been directly involved in the error but had felt the industry's sneers.

'Yes,' replied Amanda at her most guarded. She didn't want to launch an attack on Matty's opinions until she had his full measure. Instead she settled for her old tactic of bewitching the opposition. She gave him a direct-eyed smile. 'I'm afraid I am one of the unscrupulous media mob – but it doesn't stop me having an enormous amount of respect for what you're saying. Tell me, what are you working on at the moment?'

Listening carefully to Matty's reply so that she could comment on it afterwards, Amanda studied his undeniably attractive face. He was paler skinned than his mother and sisters but had inherited Alexandra's expressive hazel eyes, with a magnificent Roman nose, presumably from his father, giving him the guarded, alert nervousness of a wolfhound. But the feature that gave his face its magnetism was the wide, sensual mouth, forming its words carefully with flashes of white, slightly uneven teeth.

Yes, he was tempting all right, Amanda mused. But she guessed his passion was entirely wrapped up in the words he spoke. Make him the butt of jokes or flirt with him and he'd be lost and confused. She liked people to be aware of the games she played. Shooting a glance at Pascal, she gave him a barely perceivable wink before continuing to concentrate on Matty.

Sally, in a corner with Tash, noticed Matty trying to interest Pascal and the stylish little blonde in his Northern Ireland project. He always leaned forward and waved his arms around a lot with a rapt expression on his face when he was talking about his latest obsession.

'What's she like – Hugo's girlfriend?' Sally whispered conspiratorially to Tash.

'Very curt,' Tash whispered back. Amanda was talking now, listened to by Matty, Pascal and Ben. Tash wished she could resist the temptation to bitch, but it was so nice to have Sally on her side. Her tousled blonde sister-in-law was so receptive, gossipy and deliciously friendly, she could make a mother superior indiscreet.

'Has more high-powered contacts than an optician's warehouse – she's already asked Pascal to get hold of a fax,' Tash confided in a husky undertone. 'Sophia's convinced she'll start dictating letters to Paola between nappy changes.'

'Murder,' Sally rolled her eyes.

'But she's terribly bright,' Tash added quickly, feeling guilty, 'and when she turns on the charm even the walls lean in to listen.'

'Matty just looks terrified,' Sally giggled, glancing across the room. 'The only man here who has no apparent interest in her is Hugo.'

'Oh, he knows what she's up to,' sighed Tash, reddening. 'They both seem to enjoy riling each other.' She didn't want to talk about Hugo and Amanda's relationship. 'I thought you were bringing Niall O'Shaughnessy?'

Sally took a swig from her glass and nodded. 'He's holed himself up in Provence – Matty's been trying to contact him,' she explained. 'Apparently the poor love's in a pretty bad state.' She suddenly looked incredibly sad. 'His wife's left him, you know.'

'How awful. Didn't Matty meet Niall through her? – er – Lisette, isn't it?'

'Yes – she's a producer now. A good one. They were at the Beeb together years ago, before she killed her career on satellite. She's run off with some American high-flyer.' Sally paused thoughtfully. 'You never met them, did you?'

Tash shook her head.

'It's funny,' Sally lowered her voice. 'Our friend Amanda over there has a lot in common with Lisette. Same look, same manner. Uncanny really.'

'Oh dear,' Tash took a swig from her glass. 'Coming here might not be the best therapy for Niall, then?'

'No, it may not.' Looking bleak, Sally sank back on the sofa. 'Although from what I've gathered so far it might prove the most wonderful aversion therapy.' A wicked smile flashed past her pretty face. 'Did I tell you why we ended up arriving so late?'

Tash shook her head.

'Well, we were nearly here by lunchtime – but Matty, being Matty, wanted to divert past some bar in the middle of nowhere that's famed for its Resistance activities. Next thing we know—'

But Tash had stopped listening. Instead she sat with her glass frozen mid-way to her lips, unable to hear anything but the conversation that was going on to her right.

'– in America,' Sophia was saying to Hugo and her mother. 'Of course she blames herself. She told me she was too frightened to confront Max. Couldn't even ask him here until it was too late.'

'I think they had a row actually, darling,' Alexandra countered lightly, shooting a meaningful look at her daughter.

'That's not what she told me.' Sophia turned to Hugo. 'Can you imagine it? Not talking to someone for weeks? The whole thing sounds—'

'Tash?' Sally put her hand on Tash's arm. 'Are you all right, luvvie? You look like you've seen a host.' She indicated Pascal who was drunkenly trying to force a corkscrew into the screw-top of a bottle of brandy.

I should never, never have told her. Tash bit her lip in humiliation. *Now she's broadcasting my botched love-life to Hugo of all people.*

'I'm fine. Just tired. Sorry.' Tash forced herself to smile. 'How's the house in Richmond?'

They stayed up till nearly four. Tash wilted, but couldn't force herself to go to bed. She was feeling so paranoid by now that she was sure they'd all talk about her when she'd gone.

Sophia became increasingly bitchy. Alexandra played old sixties hits on the piano while Ben and Hugo duelled at poker, fags in mouths, eyes squinting against the smoke. Matty and Sally sat talking quietly on a sofa until Sally fell asleep on Matty's shoulder. Amanda continued engaging Pascal in deep conversations, mostly in French to exclude everyone else. Alexandra was too wrapped up in her mellifluous musical memories to notice.

Matty gave his younger sister a gentle squeeze.

'You okay? Poor Tash. You look bushed.'

Tash thought she'd cry if anyone else asked her if she was all right.

'Tell me about Niall,' she asked Matty. 'Tell me how you got to know each other so well?'

So Matty did. He talked of their wild, undisciplined years travelling around South East Asia and then later South America. Their pranks and parties. How Niall stopped Matty progressing from scared, lonely student to stuffy, isolated academic and showed him not to care less, but to do more. How to appreciate the wonders of 'Ma N', as Niall called the environment, and the grotesque atrocities and slow death man was inflicting on it. Most importantly of all, how Niall had taught him to trust other human beings and live, not shut himself away for ever with his books and a dream.

It was only half-way through Matty's heartfelt monologue that he realised he'd lost his audience. Tash had fallen asleep on his other shoulder.

'I must confess, I'm surprised at you, Mummy,' Sophia hiccuped slightly as she turned to her mother.

'Mmm?' Alexandra looked rather hazily back.

Checking that Tash was still snoozing, Sophia went on acidly, 'I mean, was giving Tash a horse such a bright idea? After what happened to Samion?'

'Well dear,' Alexandra shrugged regretfully, shutting the piano lid. 'You know we've never really got to the bottom of what *did* happen. Your father and I were skiing at the time, remember? And it was a long time ago.'

'Hmm.' Sophia glanced cautiously at Tash again. Her sister's lashes were so long that they stroked the sunburnt arches of her cheeks. She had a dark stain on her silk shirt (Galliano, Sophia recognised in amazement) and her skirt had rucked up to reveal endless legs with a ladder in the hip of her tights. Sophia felt her stomach curdle.

She knew she was clog-dancing on wafer-thin ice but resentment and irritation had been bubbling up inside her all day. She was utterly furious with her mother for buying a horse which reminded her so glaringly of her minor faux pas. Tash had totally overreacted at the time and Sophia had no wish to do yet more raking over hot coals. She'd lived so many years with the lie which she and Tash had concocted that, on the odd occasion she resurrected it, it had more or less become truth to her. She now felt fully vindicated in blaming her sister for what had happened to Samion. Buoyed up with booze, she also felt the pit-bull bite of indignation sink its jaws into her belly. How dare her mother so obviously favour Tash?

'I'm just saying that it might bring back painful memories for Tash, that's all,' she murmured, cocking her head caringly. 'She went right off riding after the – er – accident. She was always rather nervous of horses, you know.' Sophia sniffed pointedly. 'She might have preferred an antique bed-head.'

'Stop being a bitch, Sophia,' Matty's hiss was like a slashed tyre. 'You bloody well know what really happened.'

Sophia's face froze, her eyes glazing over like a dead fish. Matty had been in Australia that winter. He couldn't possibly know the truth. Unless . . .

Bristling with frightened hostility, Sophia shot Tash's face – horribly beautiful in its sleeping tranquillity – a look of barely concealed loathing.

She must have told him the whole sordid story. She'd promised not to breathe a word to a soul.

Totally oblivious, Tash sighed, snuggled into a cushion and mumbled, 'Your turn to switch the light off, Max.'

'Oh, I'm going to bed,' Matty sighed impatiently, getting up so quickly that Sally was tipped on to a disgruntled spaniel. He glared at Sophia before stalking from the room.

Hugo, who'd been listening in to the heated exchange, idly fingered three aces and a couple of kings and smiled to himself. He'd totally lost interest in the card game.

11

Like a majestic kiln, the manoir basked in sunshine, roasting its inhabitants under their greasy glaze of lowering sun-protection factors.

The morning after he'd arrived, Matty tried to contact Niall O'Shaughnessy. When several phone calls proved infuriatingly fruitless, he elected to drive down to Nîmes and search from there.

Leaving before he'd even had time to unpack, he kissed Sally and his children on the head and sent up clouds of dust from Audrey's balding tyres as he clattered the chewed gearbox from reverse to first and out of the courtyard.

Sally was left to be plagued by agonising images of Audrey and Matty wrapped around poplars.

When a brief call from a phone box crackled through to say that he was in Nîmes and would probably be away several days, she started worrying about the return journey instead.

By contrast, Sophia was privately hoping that her brother would get stuck in the longest traffic jam in history on his way back. Better still, receive a bump on the head from his sunroof caving in, and get amnesia.

Not only did he always treat her as if she was several IQ points short of double figures, but he'd also insinuated that he knew one of her closest guarded secrets. Preoccupied by organising the party for Eddie and then distracted by Ben's uncharacteristically debauched behaviour during the first few days of their visit (she blamed her mother), she didn't have much time to dwell on it. At least Tash was doing so badly with her new gift horse that Sophia's version of what had happened to Samion all those years ago seemed more authentic than the truth.

Amanda passed the scorching days in a foul mood, sulking between stormy rows with Hugo. Shrieking children seemed to thunder around her legs constantly, putting dead mice in her handbag, demanding to know what her rape alarm was, throwing up after meals and calling her 'Ammonia'. She'd phoned the office and been deeply insulted to be told that they were doing fine without her, that three of the creative team had been made redundant and that her yucca had died. Finally, she extracted her personal stereo and, teeth grinding, filled the tedious hours by sunbathing to *Carmina Burana* on auto-reverse.

The village bar was doing great business. Hugo spent hours there with Pascal and Ben, escaping Amanda's neurotic boredom and Alexandra's disorganised outings. The rest of the time he slept. In isolation. Amanda's argumentative attention-seeking drained him. He'd started telling bed-time headache stories.

Once or twice he broodily watched Sophia's dumb sister riding the chestnut stallion. The horse was stunning, brave as a lion and virtually unrideable. Hugo wanted him more and more.

On Wednesday, as a result of a drunken challenge, Ben fell off a first-floor balcony when completely plastered. The resulting X-rays showed that his ankle had sustained the finest of hairline fractures.

Comforting the stricken Sophia (who was actually livid) at the hospital while Ben was being plastered for a second, less convivial time, Hugo struck up quite a conversation.

In between leafing angrily through caterers' brochures and writing endless lists, Sophia started to tell him about the day Tash had broken her wrist out hunting. The same day her horse, Samion, had been destroyed.

The following afternoon, Tash limped into the manoir and nipped to the loo to examine her kneecap before the others could see her. It was like a black island on her all-too-white legs. Peering at it closely, she decided the huge bruise was shaped like Max's nose. At least it matched the one on her thigh, which was shaped like his ear. In the past few days she'd started quite a feature collection.

Things were not going exactly to plan with Snob. In fact they were going backwards – literally. He'd developed a habit of reversing sharply whenever she finally managed to get on him. He had now combined this with dropping his right shoulder and executing a perfect dressage pirouette which left Tash sniffing the earth like a diviner.

It was, decided Tash, a sad reflection on her original zealous determination to master the big red horse that she now only continued to tack him up each day for ritual humiliation because anything was preferable to a day spent in the company of her increasingly riotous family.

If Tash had hoped that her mother's energy levels would drop enough to allow any of them to bed before the dawn chorus, then she'd been mistaken.

In the past week, she'd used Snob as an excuse to avoid going to six churches, four vineyards, a monastery, two châteaux, a day trip to Angers and a boules match in the village from which Hugo and Ben had returned so drunk that they'd run over three chickens.

Covering up her knee, Tash decided to face the others.

It was the first day that they had all stayed in together, mainly to rest Ben's ankle. Normally in the morning Hugo, Ben and Pascal would slope off to the bar in the village while the others took the kids out. For the last couple of days Amanda had joined them. But today, with the white-hot sun beating down from a cloudless sky, they were all lounging around the pool.

Earlier, when bored, Hugo had come to watch her school Snob just as the fired up-stallion decided to rub her off on some overhanging branches.

'Admiring a horse chestnut, Tash? How apt,' he'd called. 'Just let me know when you've had enough.' Then he'd wandered off to talk to an ecstatic Paola, who was sitting with Josh in the shadow of an ancient gnarled oak.

After the first attempt to buy Snob, he'd taken to ignoring Tash completely, apart from making the odd bitchy aside about her grass-stained backside and stiff walk. 'Been Foxed again?'

Yet she had a forbidding feeling that he was biding his time and saving his big guns for a sudden ambush.

When Tash went outside they were all sitting in disparate stages of intoxication and undress, round a white table with an emerald-green parasol. The sunlight seeping through the green cloth made them look like glamorous aliens from *Star Trek* – perhaps Captain Kirk was about to pop out from behind a bush and ask Sophia for directions to the Clingons' camp?

In the pool, Tom was splashing water on Polly as she doggy-paddled widths, clinging on to a polystyrene board. Lotty was bobbing up and down in the shallow end, welded into a pink inflatable ring with a Nessy head. She looked like a day-glo life-buoy that had floated in from the Solent. Blonde little Tor was waddling round the edge in her nappy, picking cigarette butts off the paving stones and throwing them at the dogs.

'Don't do that, darling. They're trying to give up,' murmured Sally, whose blonde hair was bleaching in the sun as fast as her pale skin was reddening. 'Hi, Tash – come and join the underexposed and overdosed.'

Ben eased his plaster cast off the spare chair so that she could sit down. Tash quickly averted her eyes from Amanda, who was lounging away from the shade of the parasol, reading *Figaro*, in a red bikini that was more string than fabric. Her lithe, brown body shimmered under a layer of Piz Buin.

'We'll have some lunch soon, darling,' announced her mother, wearing a summer dress covered in red peonies that matched her burnt nose, yet still looking absurdly chic. 'But I can't be bothered to make it at the moment.' She stretched out her arms, inadvertently popping open the top button of the dress, and sighed contentedly.

''Ow is the Snog going?' asked Pascal, who was sporting dark glasses in order to gawp surreptitiously at Amanda.

'Er . . . Snob?' Tash shot a wary look at Hugo, but he was asleep, or at least pretending to be. He'd taken off his shirt. Oh, the beauty of that smooth, muscled chest.

'He's fine, a bit strung up at the moment, but he's got a lot kinder in the stable.' Tash smiled, hoping they couldn't see the yellowing bruises on her arms from Snob's little reminders of who was boss.

'This is good,' said Pascal, pouring her a marguerita. The cool, acid lime stung Tash's parched throat but made her feel refreshed.

'Paola's been a great help,' Tash told Sophia.

This was not strictly true. The Italian girl had in fact been using her excursions to the paddock as an excuse to sprawl out in the sun and plug straight into her personal stereo, cutting out the sound of Josh bawling and her boss calling. She was also terrified of Snob, refusing to come within gnashing distance and loudly applauding Tash every time she bravely clambered on the spiralling chestnut. But, with dwindling confidence over her ability, it was this bolstering encouragement Tash needed so much.

'You're very thick with Paola now, aren't you?' Sophia emerged from behind a battered Danielle Steel. She was wearing a pair of Christian Dior dark glasses which made her look like Dame Edna Everage.

Tash tried not to laugh, taking a massive gulp of drink, most of which went down her windpipe. 'Yes,' she coughed. 'I really like her. She's so selfless. She keeps insisting that she doesn't want to ride, saying she's happy just to watch.'

'That's because watching you fall off Snob is a lot funnier than doing it oneself,' murmured Hugo, not opening his eyes.

'I 'ave good news,' announced Pascal before anyone could react. 'I 'ave borrowed you an 'orse for Paola. 'E is 'orse of Anton. I will collect him ce soir.'

'Oh, thank you, Pascal – you're so gorgeous.' Tash kissed him on the cheek.

She thought he'd forgotten. Now she could take Snob out with Paola. Another horse might calm him. The one time she'd taken Snob for a hack he'd dumped her in a wood two miles from the manoir and trotted back without her. When she'd finally found her way back he was standing in the yard with a hurt 'what took you so long?' expression on his face.

The only problem was that Paola kept trying to persuade Tash to enlist Hugo's help. She might become even more insistent now. The idea made Tash's stomach heave with nerves.

'Aren't you hot in those jeans?' Sophia looked critically at Tash's ripped Levis. A second later, a massive splash of water flew over from the kids in the pool and drenched Tash's legs.

'Not now, she's not,' laughed Ben.

'You'll have to change, Tash,' ordered Sophia brusquely. 'Once that damp patch heats up it'll be like wearing a portable sauna.'

'Surely it'll just dry?' said Tash, who only had other jeans to get into or something microscopic of her mother's. The thought of exposing her large expanses of graceless pale flesh in front of all this slender, feline beauty made her shudder.

'Why don't you put on a cossie?' suggested Alexandra, waving her marguerita at Tash and depositing most of it on a spaniel. 'It's a shame to waste the sun.' She'd folded up the skirt of her sundress to expose a beautifully slender pair of tanned legs. Tash thought miserably of her own lard-coloured chops covered in purple blotches.

'My costume's in the wash,' she muttered quickly. 'Anyway, I want to ride again after lunch. There hardly seems any point in changing.'

'Here here,' agreed Sally, scratching the red stomach between her shorts and bikini top. 'I admire anyone who can cover up in this weather and still stay cool. Be a love, Pascal, and pass me the sun-block.'

'Eh?' Pascal had been staring at Amanda's glossy midriff.

Tash was actually aware that rivulets of sweat were working their way down her temples and that the backs of her knees were wetter than the pool-soaked fronts. She was sure that if she stood up she'd leave a great sweaty patch on the back of the seat.

'Come inside with me, Fangs, and I'll find you something to

wear,' urged Sophia, getting up in one lithe movement. 'Ben bought me a lovely new bikini in Tours last Wednesday that's adjustable, so you'll easily get into it. If not we can always turn one of your horrid pairs of jeans into hotpants.'

'Rather,' Ben smiled encouragingly.

Tash trailed inside behind Sophia.

'I don't know why Tash puts up with that sort of treatment,' remarked Sally, pulling a discreet face at Sophia's disappearing back.

'She's wet,' said Hugo, then added slyly, 'she needs to change into something dry,' before Alexandra could snap out of her daze.

'Not a bad body,' said Ben to Hugo as Tash slunk out to the poolside ten minutes later, hiding behind Sophia until she could sit down.

'For a wrestler.' Hugo opened one lazy eye.

Still, he had to admit it was a pleasant surprise. She was tall enough to carry the most wonderful lengthy, sloping curves without looking fat. Her long neck and slender waist detracted from the rather wide shoulders and hips. Her legs would be terrific, too, if they weren't covered in bruises and what looked like red grazes.

'You should be called Rash, Tash,' he murmured quietly to her and reclosed his eye.

Tash, not expecting to put so much flesh on display, hadn't shaved her legs for days and had been forced to scrape a dry razor over them in two minutes in Sophia and Ben's bathroom so that Sophia wouldn't see her Neanderthal black stubble. Even worse was that the tiny triangles of the bikini bottoms had refused to cover her pubic hair, so she'd been forced to rush back in and shave most of that off, too. It had left a horrible itching, plus lots of pubes in Sophia and Ben's bath, which now looked like it had been used to hose down a black Labrador.

Face burning, she sat with her legs firmly crossed and her arms welded to her sides because she couldn't remember when she'd last done her armpits. She couldn't breathe out in case her spare tyre popped out like Lotty's inflatable rubber ring.

'You'll have to put some work in on those t-shirt marks.' Sophia smiled at her creation with a Frankenstein glint in her eye.

'You look great, Tash,' Sally told her sincerely, 'and splendidly pale. I was that colour this morning.' She looked at Tash's pale legs enviously and fanned her sunburn with yesterday's copy of the *Sun*. 'There's a piece in here about Niall, *Another Niall in his Coffin.* Apparently Lisette is becoming quite a hot property in the States, thanks to her new lover – the silly cow's got the job of assistant producer on the new Zeilger pic. Not only that, but a big deal Niall had with MPM has just mysteriously fallen through. I remember him talking about it. He thought it was his big break – stardom and megabucks. His chance to win Lisette back. Poor sod.'

'I thought he didn't want to be a big star,' remarked Amanda, looking up from *Figaro* for the first time since Tash had arrived. 'Doesn't he have some hang-up about going into supermarkets?'

Sally laughed. 'I think he said that in some interview and has been plagued by it ever since. It's kind of true, though. The States have been after him for ages. They like his rugged, bad boy image. He says he just couldn't live up to it – when you meet him you'll see why. He's such a big Irish softy, far too open for his own good.'

'Surely that's exactly what Hollywood wants?' pointed out Amanda. 'It would be a breath of fresh air for them to get someone honest for a change. A Mickey Rourke image with a Jimmy Stewart personality.'

'Oh yes, he fits the bill all right,' Sally agreed, 'and the press certainly love him now – he's their hunky party animal, horribly mistreated by his fickle wife. But sooner or later they'd bitch him up. It'd destroy him. He can't hide behind Ray Bans and seven-foot minders like everyone else. The old fool'd tell them exactly how he's feeling and they'd turn it into alliterative headlines as big as their egos. Besides, he really does like going into Sainsbury's on a Saturday and only being bothered by the odd housewife saying "Has anyone ever told you that you look like Niall O'Shaughnessy?"'

'So why was he so keen on this MPM deal?' Amanda was rubbing more sun-cream into her arms and shoulders. The big opal ring slipped round and round her finger as her hand moved over the oiled skin.

'Because he's got it into his thick skull that if he's a superstar and every woman in the western world is lusting after his boxers then Lisette will too. Plus she's got expensive tastes and unfortunately Irish actors don't earn enough money to keep Lisantoinette in the manor house to which she'd like to become accustomed. Well, not if they're like Niall and keep taking badly paid theatre work because it's better than badly scripted TV or film work—' she stopped and stared at Tor, who was busy burying Lotty's Noo Noo. 'Sorry, I'll shut up. I'm rambling.'

'You really don't like Lisette, do you?' Hugo opened the blue eye again.

'I did,' Sally replied carefully. 'She was my best friend until she screwed up Niall.'

Oh Boy, thought Amanda. Niall O'Shaughnessy must be quite a catch to credit loyalty like that. I can't wait to meet him.

12

The group stayed beside the pool and feasted on a delicious lunch of melt-in-the-mouth tender charcuterie and an enormous Greek salad with feta cheese and black olives the size of walnuts.

Tash, at Sophia's insistence, had put sun-block on her tanned arms and face in order to let the rest of her pale body catch up. As a result, she kept getting great mouthfuls of Ambre Solaire and could hardly eat a thing.

Thinking she was pining for her London friends, Alexandra gave her some postcards to write home. They were an odd selection of prehistoric shots of seafronts complete with parked Ford Populars and women in knee-length skirted bathing dresses. Turning one over, she saw it had *Margate in July 1964* printed on the back.

'Aren't they fun?' giggled Alexandra. 'I found them in an old suitcase and have been dying to put them to good use.'

Tash wasn't exactly sure if giving them to her to write home with was of any use at all. What could she write? *My family are a complete bunch of weirdos. Have got horse with attitude, that makes two of us. Fancy complete bastard with beautiful girlfriend. Wish you were here. Tash.*

In the end she settled for telling her university friends, the Hampstead journalists and Graham and Mikey about the amount of alcohol they were shipping.

She had just started writing to her father when Amanda sat up from the sunbed she'd been hogging all day.

'Isn't that a car pulling up?'

She must have ears on elastic, thought Tash. All she could hear was Lotty wailing that Tom had hit her with his Transformer and she couldn't find her Noo Noo.

'I don't think so, darling,' replied Alexandra. 'You can probably just hear a tractor in one of the vineyards. When I was first here I couldn't get used to the silence, either. Every engine sounded like an F one-eleven on a bombing mission.'

The next minute a car door banged.

'There's definitely someone here,' squeaked Sophia, whipping off her shades and checking her reflection in them.

Tash wished she could put on a shirt to hide all her rippling flesh but there was only Hugo's sage green Paul Smith to hand, and she didn't think he'd be too delighted if she superglued it to her body with sun-block. She settled for putting Lotty on her knee instead, comforting the sobbing little girl and hiding her pale stomach at the same time. Such is the hypocrisy of vanity, she reflected sadly.

Pascal dashed off to welcome the new arrivals.

The debris of lunch was still heaped on the white table, collecting an orbiting cluster of flies. Clinging on to Tash by a single bikini strap, Lotty leaned across and polished off the contents of two wine glasses and a hunk of bread.

'Feel thick,' she snivelled, clambering back on to Tash and burping.

'Where the hell's Paola?' Sophia grumbled. 'She should be here to take the kids off our hands.'

'I think she took Josh for a walk,' Tash replied quickly, knowing that Paola had sloped up to her room with the walkabout phone to ring her boyfriend, Guido, in Italy.

'You'll probably be getting a ransom note any min – Christ!' Sally's face froze as she saw the three men appear round the side of the house.

Behind Pascal and Matty was a tall, hauntingly familiar man who didn't look a bit like the Niall she knew. Despite the breadth of his shoulders, he looked painfully thin. As they drew closer she could see his tanned face was pinched and drawn, his dark curls dishevelled and unwashed. Giant black smudges propped up his eyes, and a week's worth of scraggy beard covered his hollow cheeks.

For a moment Niall wavered, staring at Amanda, his face suddenly illuminated with hope like a dog seeing his master after weeks in kennels, then the expression dropped away and his face went blank.

Sally caught Matty's eye. His forehead was creased with worry and he shrugged despairingly.

As Pascal made introductions, Sally became increasingly aware that there was something dreadfully wrong with Niall. Not just his stunned misery. Something about the glazed, faraway look in his normally give-away eyes, the unnaturally wide pupils. He was being terribly polite – too polite. He hardly seemed to recognise her at all.

She looked pleadingly at Matty. He mouthed, 'I'll tell you later,' and went into the poolhouse to get more chairs. Niall had nicked one of Ben's fags and was lighting it with a shaking hand.

'So what have you been working on in Nîmes, Niall?' Sophia asked him brightly. Sally could have shot her.

'My blood to alcohol ratio, mostly.' His soft Irish voice had deepened; it rumbled languidly off his tongue without a flicker of expression in those clouded, milk-chocolate eyes.

'No, silly,' Sophia's ringing laugh could have cut through steel in comparison. 'I mean what have you been making?'

'Scenes.' A giant familiar smile crossed his scraggy, angular face but the eyes still weren't there. 'Lots and lots of scenes.' He laughed.

Sally wanted to cry.

'How exciting,' Alexandra chipped in. 'I used to long to be an actress but I could never be bothered to learn the lines – I once did Portia at school with the entire script copied up behind a pillar. My father thought I'd got my costume caught to it and that's why I spent all my time hopping round upstage.'

Niall laughed but he didn't seem to know when to stop. It just went on and on until tears poured down his face. Matty, coming back with two deckchairs, immediately dropped them and went to his side.

'Come on, you great oaf,' he chided softly, steering Niall away from the table. 'I think you need a rest. He's exhausted,' he told the others. 'Been working too hard. I'll take him inside to crash out for a bit.'

'Odd sense of humour,' Alexandra remarked after they'd gone, 'I didn't think it was that funny.'

The others were stunned. Was this the famous laid-back, friendly, wild boy O'Shaughnessy they'd heard so much about?

Muttering, 'Can you keep an eye on the kids, Tash?' Sally ran inside.

'Poor bastard,' Hugo shook his head. 'That's not the same bloke I met in Ireland. Must have been knocking it back to get in that state. Looked DTeed up to his eyeballs.'

Amanda had seen that look many times before in stressed-out colleagues in London. She knew it wasn't alcohol, but said nothing. Even in that state, Niall O'Shaughnessy had possessed more sex appeal than virtually any man she'd met.

Pascal had positioned himself so that his leg was brushing against hers. Moving away, she turned over and pretended to be asleep.

Sally waited in the hall for Matty.

'I've given him a couple of sleeping pills to zonk him out,' he said, coming downstairs. 'I'm sorry I stayed away so long. He'd got himself into some pretty deep shit down there, owed a lot of money to the wrong people. The stupid idiot had forgotten his car was hired and tried to sell it, so there were one or two angry gendarmes to be sorted out as well.'

Sally noticed Matty looked impossibly tired, his amber eyes ringed from lack of sleep.

'Is he going to be all right?' she asked, faltering. 'I mean he looks so awful – I had no idea Lisette's leaving had unhinged him quite that much. He's aged ten years.'

'It's nothing a few weeks' rest and talking his guts out won't cure,' said Matty, unable to look her in the eye.

'What is it, Matt?'

He stared at Tash's painting, taking in a huge breath as if about to say something and then letting it out again.

'Please tell me, Matty. It'll drive me insane with worry if I don't know.'

He turned his gentle, worried face to her. 'The crazy, dumb . . . *idiotic* fool's knocking back hard drugs like smarties. He was nearly dead when I found him.' He cupped Sally's face in his hand, wiping away the sprouting tears with his long, bony thumbs. 'He just didn't want to know me. Prising him away from his fucking coke spoon was like getting a starving Ethiopian out of Tesco's. Look, I'm sorry, you make sick jokes when you're trying not to cry.'

'Oh poor, poor Matty.' Sally hugged him. 'It'll be pure torture for him here. Can't we take him back to England?'

Matty shook his head. 'He's got to stay in the country till they've sorted out the car fiasco. Anyway, this place is paradise compared to the hell-hole he was in. He was sacked from the movie weeks ago. He's just been rattling round smashed out of his mind ever since.' He sighed, fighting back anger and frustration that had built up like an unexploded time-bomb.

'Has he . . . I mean . . . has he still got the stuff with him?'

Matty shrugged. 'He was so shifty about it to begin with – like a guilty kid. Then when I tried to make him stop he started getting violent. I had one hell of a struggle, and a couple of bottles thrown at me, just persuading him to come here – if I'd made him leave his stash behind I think he'd have decked me.' Matty rubbed exhausted red eyes. 'He's currently in the middle of what's known as a bender. Hardly eats or sleeps, talks mostly gibberish. Driving up here was murder – he kept trying to get out of the car on the péage.'

'Oh God.' Sally rested her head on Matty's chest. 'How are we going to stop the others from finding out?'

'We've just got to ride it through, tell them he's suffering from nervous exhaustion or something. Sooner or later his supply'll dry out and,' he gave a sad, rueful smile, 'I can't see Pascal popping down to the village with a shopping list. I just wish I knew more about this sort of thing. I mean does someone go cold turkey from cocaine?' He suddenly looked terribly tired again.

'Bloody Lisette. How could she do this to him?'

'She didn't know how much her leaving would affect him.' Matty shrugged. 'I mean we didn't know how bad he was, did we? Look at how easy-going he's always been – he's normally so bloody philosophical and optimistic it's maddening.'

'But will he ever be like that again?' wondered Sally sadly.

13

The new arrival didn't re-surface until dinner, which as usual was after midnight because Alexandra and Pascal had been distracted by a protracted visit to Pascal's vigneron, Anton Vignall. They'd returned hours later than promised, Pascal driving the jeep into the yard at such speed that he'd nearly taken himself, Alexandra, three spaniels, an ugly white horse in a trailer and three cases of Anton's special reserve straight up the stone steps and into the house without braking.

Niall appeared as they all finally sat down to roast duck, which smelt so good Ben nearly passed out.

Instead of being puffy and drowsy from the sleeping pills, Niall's eyes gleamed like two shining Maltesers from his smiling face. He was as lit up as a Guy on November the fifth.

'Before we go any further,' he announced, downing the glass of wine Pascal had given him in one, 'I feel I owe you all an apology for my behaviour earlier. Truth is, I was absolutely petrified out of my mind by my old friend Matty's driving. I haven't felt terror like that since my father – may the Lord bless his dear departed soul – thought he was going to miss the last race at Cork.'

As the meal progressed into the usual drunken round of anecdotes, Tash was painfully aware of Hugo's total contempt. Not once did those cool blue eyes flick in her direction, even when she cracked an almost funny cricketing joke about herself and Max only ever going out for a duck.

The arrival of Niall O'Shaughnessy had merely heightened her feelings of inadequacy. His handsome, craggy face was so famous yet she didn't know him at all, it filled her with crippling shudders of self-consciousness. Now Hugo was laughing with the newcomer, filling him in on scandalous gossip about mutual acquaintances and picking his brains about some Irish horse dealer. If only she had been immediately accepted into Hugo's élite alliance of Beautiful People like the tall, sparkling-eyed Irishman.

Niall wasn't at all how she'd expected him to be, either – Sally had made him sound so friendly and gentle, but Tash noticed that he never stopped helping himself to Pascal's wine and other people's cigarettes and bitching viciously about who she could only guess, judging from Matty and Sally's frozen faces, were his closest friends. He had cold, glazed eyes and there was something slightly bitter about the way he talked, a touch of acid in the deep, hypnotising voice. Tash couldn't think what all the idol worship was about – Sally's build-up, Sophia's stunning silk Galliano saved for his arrival and Amanda's rapt expression. Tash was in awe of his celebrity status and popularity, but she decided that she didn't like him nearly as much as she had expected to.

Reminding herself that Niall was terribly cut up about his wife, she tried to laugh at another of his backhanded jokes.

'You can't say that, Niall,' Matty was laughing too, but his words were edged with worry. 'Fritz wasn't even in Cannes – and anyway, what you're talking about is physically impossible.'

'And you should know, now, Matty French,' the melodic lilt of his voice and the dancing smile on his face didn't quite stop Niall from appearing bitchy.

Tash glanced at her brother for a reaction but Matty's face was a blank mask.

'This man. This wonderful boy here,' Niall slapped his hand so firmly on Matty's shoulder that his friend winced with pain, 'was such a repressed old train-spotter sexually when I met him that every erection psychoanalysed itself about its hang-up.' He pronounced it *op*. 'Nowadays even Cynthia Payne would have difficulty onderstanding his jokes.' He paused, his eyes sliding from side to side, drawing his audience in with a smile as charming as Mephistopheles. 'When we were in Peru the locals called Matty El Hechicero – the enchanter. Sure, they all thought he'd put a spell on their women to make them so in love with him. I told them that the magic was entirely in his tongue, so all the men would listen religiously to everything he said to gain a few tips. Now I don't think they quite onderstood what I meant when I said tongue.' He laughed and took a slug from Sophia's glass of wine.

'Wasn't it awkward taking your wife along with you on these travelling jaunts?' asked Alexandra, cheerfully oblivious of everyone else's furious glares.

Niall hadn't mentioned Lisette since Matty had found him in Nîmes. He looked into his glass for a long time. His silence was all the more apparent because of his complete lack of it all evening. Then, looking up at Alexandra, the briefest expression of confusion and pain could be glimpsed in his face before a smile cut it off.

'She didn't always come,' was all he said.

'Perhaps you needed some of Matty's Spanish language lessons,' Hugo said idly. He'd drunk over a bottle of special reserve.

'Shut up, Hugo,' hissed Matty.

'Have you heard about the party Alexandra's organising for her brother's arrival, Niall?' Sally chipped in quickly, her voice brittle with forced brightness. 'They've not seen each other for—'

'Be quiet a minute, angel,' interrupted Niall, not taking his eyes from Hugo. 'Now just what did you mean by that?'

'Look, I apologise, Niall.' Hugo looked genuinely appalled.' 'I'd take the piss out of Mother Teresa for wearing National Health specs if she were here. From belittling scorns do mighty oafs grow – I take it back unreservedly.'

Tash felt her stomach spin-dry the duck. If only she could think of things to say like that.

Niall was looking straight at Hugo, his expression unreadable.

'I just hope you washed your feet this morning, Beauchamp,'

he said eventually, a rueful smile lifting his sad face. 'After all, one of them's stuck firmly enough into your mouth for you to be able to taste every toe.' He laughed slightly wildly and turned his angular face to Alexandra. 'Now I want the beautiful Madame d'Eblouir to tell me all about this party.'

'Well really, darling, I'm leaving it all in Sophia's capable hands,' confessed Alexandra, 'She's such a professional at that sort of thing – you must get her to tell you all her super plans.' Across the table, Sophia smirked to hide her flattered excitement. 'I'll just phone round a few friends nearer the day.' Alexandra finished, smiling at him warmly.

Niall, barely taking in a word, wished he could sink into her arms and weep into that soft, flower-scattered chest. He dragged his eyes to Sophia. As they crossed past Hugo's girlfriend, he saw unveiled compassion. Hideous, churning bile rose in his throat. It took him all his power not to stare longingly back. But Amanda, whom he'd barely acknowledged all night, was too much for him to take right now. Close up, she didn't look much like Lisette at all; yet the same slender fragility, the cropped hair, slanting grey eyes and her undiluted sensuality unnerved him totally.

'So what are you organising, Sophia?' he asked Matty's sister shakily. No wonder she was a model, he thought, she looked like Hedy Lamarr.

A pair of enormous, strangely different eyes dropped from his detached appraisal and stared at the table. 'Er . . . I'm Tash – that's Sophia over there.'

Sophia was now peering at Niall with barely concealed venom, but Ben took her hand under the table and gave it a gentle squeeze.

'He's not himself, Sophs,' he said under his breath.

'Well, it's all taking shape very nicely,' Sophia chirruped in an artificially cheery voice. 'We've had a bit of a struggle compiling a guest list and getting the invitations printed out in time, but Pascal's brother, Philippe, has been simply super. Three hundred laminated cream envelopes flew through his franking machine along with the company stationery yesterday. I put a few feelers out and it looks like a perfect date to get a really fantastic number.' She couldn't resist adding: 'The Lloyd Webbers were going to have a do at Sydmonton but it's been cancelled.'

'I hardly think we're going to get the same crowd as them, darling,' laughed Alexandra. 'So far I've only invited Anton, Jean and Valérie and my friends the Rushvens.'

Sophia shot her mother a withering look and carried on. 'I thought a formal sit-down meal at first, but Hugo suggested we have a sort of medieval banquet to be in keeping with the manoir – roast whole pigs, hire some strolling players – we can make the long hall into the most wonderful minstrel's gallery, have all the caterers in costume and serve out mead from pewter jugs. I'm so excited,' she gave him the benefit of her most winning smile. 'I don't suppose I could persuade you to recite a Shakespeare speech or something? Mummy says Eddie used to adore going to Stratford. He'd be simply thrilled to see the great Niall O'Shaughnessy read from *A Midsummer Night's Dream* or – er – one of the other ones.'

'*The next thing then she waking looks upon*,' Niall recited in a low, melodious voice that seemed to draw music through the words like a cello,

> 'Be it on lion, bear, or wolf or bull.
> On meddling monkey or on busy ape,
> She shall pursue it with the soul of love;
> And ere I take this charm from off her sight—
> As I can take it with another herb—
> I'll make her render up her page to me.'

He stopped, lost in thought. If only he could take the spell from Lisette so easily – or cast one on her to make her love him again.

'That was lovely,' sighed Alexandra dreamily.

'Oh, *would* you read for us? Please?' Sophia asked enthusiastically; his beautiful deep voice had been mesmerising. 'What's that lovely speech about a willow growing aslant a brook?'

'It's Hamlet's mother,' explained Niall, 'telling her husband and a bloke called Laertes that her son's girlfriend – who incidentally is Laertes' little sister – has just topped herself.'

He was feeling really low now. If he didn't get away soon he'd be giving everyone a piece of the flower arrangement: 'There's rosemary, that's for remembrance,' and flinging himself in the swimming pool.

'I'm trying to work out what sort of band to hire,' Sophia was saying to Amanda and Sally. 'I mean a harpsichord isn't really very good to bop to if you're a rock star or one of the Planet Hollywood trio.'

Sally caught Tash's eye and tried not to giggle.

'I want to have a sound and light show set up in the cellar,' Sophia went on blithely. 'But Pascal thinks his wine collection will get stolen. I don't want a marquee – it'll detract from the theme.'

'She prefers dukes,' whispered Hugo to Niall.

'We could use one of the outbuildings,' suggested Alexandra. 'We've used the stalls before, but it's not really suitable for dancing – what about the old stone barn? It faces into the courtyard and has a hayloft that looks over it with a little gallery round the outside.' Her face suddenly lit up. 'We could do it up just like the Café de Paris used to look. Wouldn't that be such fun? So exciting!' She clasped her hands together with delight. 'I must go and make the coffee.' She then drifted out of the room, singing The Velvelettes' 'Needle in a Haystack'.

Hugo shook his head and laughed. 'I'm in love with your mother,' he told Sophia and Matty.

Tash pushed the remains of peaches in brandy round her bowl and wished she didn't feel jealous of everyone Hugo liked.

'You're a lucky bastard, Pascal.' Hugo turned to the poppy-eyed Frenchman, who was draining the last of the special reserve with a satisfied smack of his lips.

Amanda stiffened and glanced at Niall – she didn't want him to see Hugo anything but obsessed with her. But Niall was staring into space, clutching his fists together on the table in front of him. They were shaking, his knuckles white. His velvety brown eyes looked so dark they seemed all pupil.

Amanda decided she wanted him very badly. This man wasn't a spoilt little schoolboy, he was as deep as those haunting, heartbreaking eyes.

Aware that someone was watching him, he snapped out of his daze. This time she caught him off-guard. Groggy and dazed, he seemed incapable of tearing his eyes from hers.

'I love you,' he said quietly, his eyes fixed on Amanda, seeing her through layers of confusion. 'I love you so much it's killing me, so help me God.'

Conversations were petering out in hushed embarrassment around him, but Niall didn't seem to notice. Seeing emotion well up inside him like erupting lava, Amanda stiffened uncomfortably.

'My blood's neat battery acid,' he went on bitterly. 'I'm so eaten up by jealousy. Please come back to me, just to hold me for a bit? Please, Lis? I love you, I just—' He put his face in his hands, his great shoulders shaking.

Matty jumped to his feet and hurried round to Niall's chair.

'Was that a speech from your film?' Sophia hiccuped slightly, wondering if she wasn't really rather too drunk to try and smooth things over. 'I mean it's frightfully good and all that, but not terribly suitable for the party, really, no . . .' She trailed off, seeing everyone's horrified faces.

At that moment Alexandra reappeared, carrying a tray of coffee, singing 'Wonderful World'.

Niall pulled himself up, knocking over a glass of wine. 'Look, I'm fucking sorry,' he looked at Amanda. 'Christ! What a bloody idiot.' His chair crashed to the floor as he hurried from the room.

Matty ran after him.

Sally burst into tears and Tash put a comforting arm round her. Hugo whispered 'shit' to Amanda, who was smirking. Sophia cleared her throat pertly and Pascal puffed out his cheeks.

Ben scratched inside his plaster cast with a dessert fork.

'Oh dear,' gasped Alexandra. 'I didn't think my singing was that bad. Poor old Niall. Do you think I should take their coffee up, Sally?'

14

When Matty finally fell into bed hours later, he wrapped his arms round Sally and rested his head on her soft stomach.

Sally reached down and stroked the hair on the back of his neck.

'I thought you were asleep,' he whispered.

He could feel her shift slightly from side to side as she shook her head.

'I was too worried.' She gently massaged the knotted muscles on his neck. 'How is he?'

It took a long time for Matty to answer. He needed to feel Sally's security and warmth calming him before he could speak.

'Phenomenally screwed up,' he said finally. 'But I think talking's straightened him out a little.' He sighed into Sally's warm, sunburnt belly. 'He can't believe what he said to Amanda. I persuaded him not to get smashed again, so we drank half a bottle of brandy and talked about Lisette instead. She should never have said some of the things she did. His self-confidence is in tatters. He thinks it's all his fault.'

'I suppose she lashed out at him to make herself feel justified in swanning off,' said Sally. 'You know how she always thought she was right in an argument – she probably couldn't hack the fact that Niall hadn't actually done anything wrong.'

'Try telling that to Niall,' Matty sighed.

* * *

Hugo climbed off Amanda, dropping a kiss on one of her erect pink nipples.

'Christ, that was good,' he said, running his hands through his damp hair.

Amanda leaned across him and took a handful of tissues from the bedside table, smiling slyly.

'Don't tell me you were fantasising about our handsome host?' Hugo asked with a yawn.

Amanda stroked his muscled thigh absent-mindedly. 'Who needs to fantasise when they've got you?'

'Dear wayward Pascal certainly seems to get very hot under his t-shirt collar when you're around, my sweet.' Hugo turned on his side and dug his head into his pillow. 'Old a-niall-ated got pretty worked up tonight, too.'

'Is his wife very like me, then?' Amanda couldn't resist asking.

'You're better in bed,' murmured Hugo and fell asleep.

'Ben . . . Ben, your plaster cast's digging into my leg again.' Sophia was nearly falling off the bed in her attempt to avoid her skin being lacerated by Ben's injured foot.

'Mmm,' Ben shifted in his sleep and put his arm round her. 'Need to fetch the seedlings from Pocock.'

Tash couldn't sleep. Instead she lay restlessly awake, hazy with wine and badgered by confusion and guilt. She might not like Niall O'Shaughnessy but his problems made hers look so petty.

She had to face the fact that her crush on Hugo would never be reciprocated. He might make her abdomen tingle with longing and her chest tighten painfully but it was Max who made tears sting the backs of her eyes and her body ache for one of his bear hugs or butterfly kisses.

Muddled images of him fought for precedence in her head and embarrassing memories crowded in front of her eyes, waving accusing banners.

She remembered with an inward cringe that the first time Max had told her he loved her, she'd been so happy and flattered that she'd forgotten to say how much she loved him back. He'd sulked for days. Racking her brain she couldn't remember saying it at all in the last six months. Certainly not recently when she'd been scared of appearing desperate and clingy. Oh, poor, poor Max. She chewed her pillow in angst.

Hot tears of remorse were creeping out on to her bottom lashes and dropping on to her cheeks now. She sat up in bed, turned on the light and lit a cigarette. It tasted foul in her toothpasted mouth. She stubbed it out and got up.

Searching the bottom of the rucksack, she found the birthday card that she'd bought for him before leaving England. It had a Gustav Sheile on the front – a portrait of an old woman looking incredibly sad. There was no message inside. It wasn't his birthday until July the twelfth; she could get him a more cheerful card in Tours, or perhaps her mother would produce an ancient Easter Greetings card with a picture of Yoko Ono on the front?

She settled herself down at the rickety dressing table and found a biro in her bag. Looking at the blank, white rectangle made her eyes cloud over with tears again as she thought of all the things she could write. She blew her nose and only managed to write *Dear Max* before the pen ran out.

Of course, when she finally found another one it was a completely different colour. She'd lost inspiration. She lit another cigarette and allowed herself a small fantasy about Hugo coming in and comforting her patiently before ravishing her on the carpet.

Her head sprang upright. What was she doing? She was using Max as the basis for her horrid obsession about Hugo. He deserved better.

You deserve better than me, she wrote, *but I'm so hooked on you that I can't be selfless and let you slip away without telling you how much I love you.*

God, that sounded crap *and* clingy. She wished she had some Tipp-Ex.

I've been such a coward recently.

I think that you've stopped loving me. If I'm right then please don't worry because I guess I've come to accept it.

Her waterworks started again; she blinked frantically to see what she was writing.

But I can't help this terrible fear that it was all my fault for behaving so apaulingly – oh no, she'd spelt appallingly wrong. She scribbled it out and wrote *stupidly – In which case I'm writing not to justify myself but to apologise.*

Burying herself in repentant adverbs, Tash got thoroughly carried away. She painted him as a saint, herself as Cruella De Ville with Graham and Mikey in supporting roles as Jeremy Beadle and David Mellor. Soon she was two hundred words into a major contender for Mills and Boon publication.

I know you'll accuse me of bad copy-writing but you're a wonderful man: funny, intelligent, good-looking, generous, gentle, a terrific lover, a great listener and the best friend I've got – all this without the aid of a Thesaurus. If you ever need to word a lonely hearts ad, you know where to come. Only you won't – any woman would give her right arm for someone like you. If I could afford the postage I'd send mine, but I wouldn't be able to address the envelope without it anyway.

She'd run out of space on the card despite having used both sides and round the edge of what she'd already written. She read it back and winced. It sounded so contrived and sickly. She searched round desperately for something else to write on – her sketch pads were downstairs and she didn't want to wake everyone else in the house by clumping round searching for them. In the end she settled for a postcard of Frinton, 1965.

I need my right arm at the moment because I need to write I love you. And although we might be washed up, I want you to know that I'm desperately sorry I only added to your troubles with the job, and that you will always be the best thing that ever happened to me. I never merited someone as good as you and I truly hope that you end up with someone that does.

Blinking through her tears, Tash realised that she'd used up the entire postcard. Turning it over, she scrawled across the cloudless Frinton sky.

With all my love, apology and regret, Tash.

She sealed the envelope, addressed it care of Max's father and put all her remaining stamps on it because she didn't know the postage to America. Then she threw it on the pile with her postcards.

She felt totally purged, secure in the knowledge that in the morning she was bound to have a sober attack of nerves and rip it up. It sounded so crawling and final.

Tripping over her rucksack, Tash decided that if she just did nothing instead, everything would probably turn out all right. She could have a brief, passionate affair with Hugo, go on a crash diet and then return to Max and Derrin Road tanned, slim and confident.

She climbed contentedly into bed and fell asleep almost immediately to dream that there was a medieval banquet at Derrin Road and she was in the stocks wearing Sophia's bikini. Max was throwing tomatoes at her whilst in bed with Sharon Stone.

15

Cass walked into The Old Rectory's kitchen. After a quick look round, she sighed and walked out again. Bracing herself and taking a deep breath, she walked back in.

The sink was full of ketchup-encrusted plates, coffee-ringed mugs and bowls of half-eaten CoCo Pops. A pan of soup was congealing on the Aga alongside a greasy baking tray with a tea towel welded to it by bits of fish-finger. Empty beer cans littered the dirty marble surfaces like a shooting alley, and there was a distinctly odd smell lingering alongside that of burnt cooking.

'Marcus!'

No answer. She started to unload the dishwasher.

'Marcus!'

'Mmm – yeah?' A sort of guttural yelp from deep in the house.

'Marcus, come here.'

'Can't, Mum.'

'Why ever not?' The Crabtree and Evelyn lemon curd had been put, minus the lid, in the cutlery drawer.

'I'm on the bog.'

'Oh.' She wearily loaded the mess from the sink into the dishwasher, then realised that she'd only unloaded the bottom rack and now the dirties were muddled up with the cleans.

In the hall the grandfather clock asthmatically wheezed its way through ten chimes. She shouldn't have stayed in bed so long reading Joanna Trollope. But with Michael up at the crack of dawn to go sailing, it was heaven not to have to stagger downstairs to organise breakfast for once. Now, with Olly due at midday and her kitchen a shambles, she'd have to skip church. Because the new vicar wore a bomber jacket and was heavily into handing out hip prayer sheets and tambourines, Cass felt guiltily relieved.

Wistfully, she thought back on Sunday lunches when the kids were small. Their yelping excitement if they were having lamb and mint sauce, or chocolate mousse for pudding. Michael taking the boys out into the orchard to shoot air rifles afterwards. Then finally the parents' opportunity to creep off and read the Sunday papers while the children went to the Rumpus Room in the attic and played 'Starsky and Hutch' or 'Batman and Robin' or produced some awful play full of references to going to the toilet and 'titties' and 'willies', which she and Michael would have to sit through later. Michael invariably fell asleep.

Nowadays, Cass had to virtually blackmail the boys to come back to The Old Rectory on a Sunday. They hadn't all been together since Easter – and even then Olly had spent his entire time glued to Michael's word processor and Marcus had sloped off to some party in Devon with a bunch of long-haired, chain-smoking friends.

Cass had played on Olly's weak spots to get him back today. He needed to borrow some money and Cass had insisted she be allowed to read his thesis. She knew she wouldn't understand a word, but appreciated that he was at the stage where flattery meant more than constructive criticism. She also wanted to do a bit more of a sales job on Alexandra's house party.

She dumped a pan back in the sink mid-scour and wandered through to the hall to find Marcus. The downstairs toilet door was still firmly locked. And there was that funny smell again. She hoped it wasn't Enoch's flatulence. The charcoal biscuits had seemed to remedy that. She must buy some more air freshener.

As she walked back towards the kitchen, her eyes were drawn to the mantelpiece in the more formal of their two sitting rooms

– 'The Trophy Room' as Michael called it because of the large collection of family sporting cups and plates which covered the sideboards and shelves, and induced mutters and moans from Mrs Tyler every time they needed cleaning. All the cups won by Michael (mostly for cricket and tennis) were pushed to the front. The others had mainly belonged to Michael's father and were turned round so that the names and dates were hidden. In her more revengeful moments Mrs Tyler turned them back again.

On the mantelpiece were propped-up invitations to charity benefits and cocktail parties, rather too well spaced out. Cass noticed that three of them were for last month. She'd throw them out after Olly had left. On the right, leaning against a Staffordshire dog to hide the chip in it, was the thick, embossed card that had arrived from France yesterday. She picked it up and marvelled at the weight and texture. Tucked behind the dog was the letter from Sophia which had accompanied it. Cass unfolded the stiff cream paper and re-read Sophia's bold, round handwriting.

Darling Cass,

I know you don't need an invite to this, but I thought you'd like to see one – I've sent you the French version to fox your friends (terribly wicked I know, but such fun).

So far the hol is exactly what we expected. Mummy's a total darling but quite hopeless as a hostess (G and Ts before eleven, DIY washing etc). My poor Au Pair is expected to babysit five children. When she's not doing that she's sloping off with Tash (who's gone more peculiar than ever) – Josh and Lotty consequently feeling totally neglected.

Still, there are some rather exciting compensations. Matty has gone off to fetch Niall O'Shaughnessy – that très dishy Irish actor (should be good for a gawp). Also, the party looks like being a really super romp – lots of names, my dear. Even a possibility of a write-up in you-know-what. We're doing it as a medieval banquet (don't worry, costumes optional so you've finally got an excuse for that blue taffeta we saw in Belville Sassoon).

Anyway, must dash as have meeting with Pascal's wine merchant in ten mins (am NOT putting up with méthode champenoise). Do come over soon as would love the benefit of your good taste (plus help talking Pascal out of cutting corners). Love to all.
Sophia xxx.

Cass put the letter back behind the dog and felt a warm glow. Surely this was the key to getting the kids more enthusiastic? Lots of celebrities (Olly), free champagne (Marcus) and the whole thing set to a medieval theme (Olly again). She could dine off this for weeks and Caroline Tudor-Wallis would be as green as her family emeralds when she told her.

She glanced at the huge old carriage clock in the centre of the mantelpiece. Twenty-five past ten, which meant twenty-past. She'd better get the joint in or they wouldn't be eating until teatime. Michael had gone to check over a friend's new yacht at Chichester Harbour and was bound to return ravenous.

Back in the kitchen, Enoch was snoring in his bag by the Aga with the oven mitts on his head. He looked as if he was about to set off deer stalking. Considering he hadn't had his usual morning walk, the big yellow dog was unusually sleepy.

She threw the last of the beer cans into the bin and opened the fridge to get out the large shoulder of beef she'd prepared the night before.

That was odd, she was sure she'd put it in this fridge and not the one in the utility room – she kept that as an overflow for booze and dog food. She extracted a packet of breakfast cereal and a half-eaten sandwich left in there by Marcus and looked into the back of the fridge, but the meat definitely wasn't there.

She went into the utility room, which was almost entirely taken up with a mammoth deep-freeze and the glossy computerised washing machine that Michael had bought her for Christmas (of which she still could only work the short programme). The fridge was almost empty – she was sure it had been jam-packed with cans when she'd fed Enoch last night. There was no beef in there either. Where in heaven's name was it?

Back in the kitchen, Marcus was working his way through a punnet of strawberries originally destined for the fruit salad. He gave her a cross-eyed smile.

'You're up early.' Cass went into the larder in case she'd had a mental aberration and put it in there.

'I haven't been to bed yet, man.' Marcus threw a strawberry stalk at the sink and missed.

'I wish you'd clear up after yourself,' Cass said. 'And where on earth's the joint?'

Marcus looked shifty. Had his mother cottoned on to the fact he was smoking dope in the downstairs bog?

'I put it in the fridge last night and now it's not there,' Cass continued.

'Eh?' Did his mother keep her own private stash in the fridge?

'Today's lunch – beef. I can't find it.'

'Oh, yeah – I remember. There was a bit of an accident, y'know?'

Cass froze. 'What kind of accident?'

'Well, like, I was kind of watching this video in the ovver room and I came in for some grub. I must've left the fridge door open, y'know? 'Cos when I came back Eunuch' (Marcus insisted on calling Enoch 'Eunuch' since he'd had the op) 'was tucking into somefink – I, like, wondered what it was.' He lumbered over to the fridge and extracted a small, mangled lump of meat in a plastic bag. 'I got it off him and saved it for you. It might be all right, man, if you cut the chewed bit off, y'know.'

Cass opened her mouth to let out a scream of fury just as the phone on the wall beside her rang. She snatched it up, glaring at Marcus.

'Yes? I mean Cassandra Hennessy sp—'

'Hi, Ma.'

'Olly! Don't tell me you can't come?' She tried to catch hold of Marcus's collar as he wandered out with a Kiwi fruit but she missed.

'No, Ma. Can I bring a – er – friend today?' Olly blurted quickly.

Cass brightened. It was ages since Olly had wanted to bring anyone home. 'Of course, darling. What's she called?'

'Um – it's my flatmate, actually. He's called Ginger.' He sounded almost embarrassed.

Knowing Olly, this Ginger would be a bit of a lame duck in need of feeding up, mused Cass. He probably looked slightly odd and had disgusting table manners or something. A Buddhist perhaps? It was strange that someone as straitlaced and politely spoken as Olly attracted such peculiar friends. Cass supposed it was the penalty of being an academic. She'd have to defrost some chops in the microwave, but was almost certain she only had four in the freezer.

'Of course you can bring him, Olls. It'll give your father someone new to talk to.' She leaned back against the wall and listened to the church bells being drowned by the muffled thumping of Marcus's awful music starting up.

'Um . . . yes. Great – we'll be with you about twelve-thirty, then.' Olly coughed awkwardly.

'Super. I'm looking forward to it, darling.'

'Oh – one more thing, Ma. Ginger's a vegetarian.'

'Goody!' Cass cried, thinking of her chops.

'That's okay then?' Olly sounded bemused.

'Absolutely super. I'll see you later. Bye bye, darling.' She replaced the receiver and dashed off to have a dig through the freezer.

Lunch started off stickily. Michael, returning home desperate for a pee, discovered Marcus's stash hidden in a 35mm film pot in the downstairs loo, which he never normally used. The ensuing row was cut short by the arrival of Olly.

The Hennessys' elder son brought with him, not an Open University TV presenter lookalike in little round specs and brown corduroys, but a very good-looking tall red-haired man in a striped shirt and cream chinos. He was built like a polo player and had a wonderful upper-class drawl. Cass dashed off to powder her nose and spray on some more Rive Gauche at the first opportunity.

Olly himself was looking wonderful. Cass had expected him to be pale and drawn from weeks shut inside struggling over his thesis. Instead he was tanned and fit, wearing a navy blue t-shirt and white shorts which showed off his long, muscular brown legs. His short, brown hair was as sleek and glossy as an otter. Cass wished she'd invited Caroline Tudor-Wallis and her two daughters over to tea. They had often talked about how nice it would be if Olly paired up with Imogen or Daisy. Looking as he did now, they'd both be fighting over him.

Ginger said he was a trader in the city. An old school friend had introduced him to Olly. When he was looking for a flat-mate, that is, he added.

'Which school was this, Ginger?' Cass asked politely.

'Sherbourne.' Ginger grinned at her.

Olly had warned Ginger about his mother's question and answer routine. Ginger found it quite fun. Like a job interview. He noticed that Ol was jumping from foot to foot like a cat and drinking his sherry too quickly, despite the fact Ginger knew he hated the stuff. Really, Ol needed to loosen up.

'Do you have a girlfriend, Ginger?' Cass asked.

Olly nearly choked mid-swig.

'No, I'm afraid not,' said Ginger, giving Cass a straight-eyed stare which made her drop her eyes. He considered telling her that he preferred older women as a joke, but Ol's goaty father was lurking round within earshot, blithering on to no one in particular about boats.

'Well, that's a shame,' said Cass brightly. 'I suppose it's all the stress and late hours you traders go through. I used to watch *Capital City* every week. Tremendous fun, but I don't think I could do it.'

Ginger tried not to laugh. 'Yes, that's it. Still, having Ol in the flat's made a big difference. He makes a wonderful little house-wife – endless delicious meals, a sparkling clean bathroom. He even irons my shirts. I keep thinking I should be paying him.'

Olly shot Ginger a warning look. But Cass was delighted her son was proving so well brought-up. There was something that bothered her, however.

'Do you mean that you own the flat in Earl's Court, Ginger?'

'Yes, it was my father's, actually. He signed it over to me this April. That's why Ol doesn't have to pay rent any more.'

That really has blown it, thought Olly. Thanks Ginger, you great nerd, they're bound to twig now.

But Cass was so entranced, she hadn't noticed the implications of Olly not paying rent. 'What does your father do, Ginger?'

'He runs a publishing company – The Harcourt Group. Do you know it?'

Cass shook her head apologetically. 'Have you heard of them, dear?' She turned to her husband, who was lighting his pipe.

'Course I bloody have, old girl. Got shares in them – not many though, can't afford them. Bloody sound investment.' He turned two beady eyes on Ginger. He looked a fine sportsman. 'So your father works for old Lord Harcourt, does he? I've got a lot of respect for that man.'

'Ginger's father is Lord Harcourt, Pa,' said Olly.

Cass had to bolt out and put on the chops to stop herself jumping about. This was just the sort of friend she'd always wanted Olly to have – far more suitable than all the drippy types he'd hung around with at school. Between them they'd be a lethal combination where women were concerned. She could just see that flame-red head of hair beside Olly's dark one, handing him a ring from the pocket of his morning-suit waistcoat as Olly promised to have and hold the Honourable Georgina something, while she, Cass, sat in the front family pew, dabbing a damp eye.

Michael followed her in to fetch some ice-cubes for his second gin and tonic.

'Bloody good chap, that Harcourt boy. Used to row for Bath.'

He got ice on his pipe, leaning into the freezer compartment of the fridge. It steamed, like Popeye's when eating spinach, then went out.

Lunch went like a dream after that. Ginger even charmed Marcus into exclaiming 'crucial' and 'wicked' in between bouts of staring catatonically at his chops and veg.

Cass had made Ginger a huge vegetable pie and cauliflower cheese. He helped himself to thirds and flattered her shamelessly before asking Michael about his broking firm, a subject on which he was all too happy to splutter proudly away through dessert and coffee.

Michael was mid-way through a particularly mind-numbing monologue about an eighty-year-old dowager client of his who wanted only ten shares of anything she invested in. Cass had heard it many times before and could laugh in the right places in her sleep. When the phone went, she leapt gratefully up to answer it in the hall.

It was Alexandra.

'Cass, sweetheart. I can't speak for long, darling. Sophia, Sally and I are going to take the kids for a romp in the woods. The little ducks have been making wine all morning by squashing grapes into egg cups – so sweet. Where was I?'

'I'm not quite sure,' laughed Cass.

'Oh yes. I need to know when you're coming because this frightfully nice Scottish couple, the Gallaghers, have asked us for kitchen sups next Wednesday – I've never been there before, they live in this gloriously decrepit old abbey, I'm simply dying to have a squiz – anyway I don't think they realise quite how many of us there are. I need to know if you'll be here by then. I can't remember when you said.'

Cass sighed; she must have told Alexandra at least three times. 'We're arriving on the twelfth.'

'Oh – when's that?'

'Next Friday, Alex.'

'Hang on a minute, I'll write it down . . . the . . . twelfth. Friday . . . Niall Thingamybob arrived yesterday – he's absolutely divine, but terribly odd. Are you bringing the boys?'

'Just Marcus.'

'And the lads, old girl,' called Michael as he carried the coffee cups through the hall and into the kitchen. 'Ginger and I've just persuaded Ol to take a weekend off his bloody project thing for this party palaver.'

'Oh – Michael says Olly's coming the weekend Eddie arrives,'

Cass related to Alexandra, brimming with happiness. 'He's bringing a super mate of his, Ginger Harcourt. You know The Harcourt Group?'

'Never heard of it, darling. Pascal and I've bought Tash a horse. She's terribly pleased. Spends her whole day riding it round in circles. Oh, dear – pauvre petite Polly. It's only a graze, sweetheart. Here's Wowla – she'll give you a nice big plaster . . . what? . . . no, darling not like Ben-Ben's . . . Cass, are you still there?'

'Yes.' From where she was standing, Cass could see through to the dining room. Olly and Ginger seemed to be having an argument in hushed voices.

'When did you say the others were coming, darling? Sorry, I've forgotten.'

'The weekend of the party for Ed.'

Olly was banging his fist on the dining-room table now.

'Oh, yes. When's that?'

'The twenty-fifth through to the twenty-eighth.' How odd, Ginger was giving Olly a comforting hug. Men could be so much more physical these days without embarrassment. If only Michael had learnt to express himself like that. Mind you, reflected Cass, he'd then probably have been one of those smelly hippies in the sixties and she wouldn't have fancied him.

'. . . through . . . to . . . the . . . twenty . . . eighth. Right, I've got that. How exciting. I think Sophia wanted to have a word with you, hang on tight a tic.'

Olly and Ginger had moved away from the door. Cass watched Marcus lope through the hall from the library carrying the *News of the World*. He walked into the dining room and exclaimed '*wicked*, man' before walking out again and loping into the family sitting room instead.

Cass waited with the silent receiver pressed to her ear for another five minutes, listening to Michael noisily loading the dishwasher and the whispering voices from the dining room. She suspected Alex had forgotten about her. Just as she was about to hang up, a high-pitched voice at the other end said, 'Who's there?'

'This is Cass, who are you?'

'I'm Thomas Matthew Timothy French. You can call me Tomato if you like.'

'Hello, Tom. I'm your Great-Aunt Cassandra. Do you remember me?'

'No.'

'Oh . . . well, it doesn't matter.' Cass felt deeply hurt. The thank-you letter for his Christmas book token – which had arrived in March – must have been either written at gun point or forged by his mother.

'I'm coming to stay next week so you can see me then,' she told him tightly. 'Is your Grandmother around, Thomas?'

'Granny Lexy?'

'Yes. Could you fetch her for me? Or your Aunt Sophia?'

'Lexy has got into bed with Pastel again. She says you need a lot of sleep when you're old and Sofa's throwing things at Ben in the – er – in China. They just told me and Lotty to "bugger orff". Polly-aunty's cut her knee. There was lots and lots of blood all over the floor and walls and furniture – it was just like in *Predator*. Do you want to speak to my daddy? He's in the swimming pool with Nilly.'

'It's all right, Thomas,' Cass said quickly. 'Just tell them I said hello.'

'Okay. Can I wait and tell Sofa after she's stopped hitting Ben?'

'Yes, Tom.'

'Okay. Bye then, Big Aunt C.' And he put the phone down before she had a chance to respond.

16

The heatwave which was re-dressing the lush green velvets of the Loire in khaki camouflage gear continued beyond the weekend, despite Pascal's translation of a depressing radio forecast predicting storms. The scorching sun rose white and angry behind the oak wood on Monday morning, ready to bake the inhabitants of the manoir and not looking as though it was planning to lull beyond travelling from east to west.

Tash looked longingly through her window, scanning the horizon for a storm cloud, but only saw the vast uniform blue flag which signalled bare flesh and bruises to be on parade poolside, ten hundred hours.

She glanced at the letter to Max, still undecided about sending it. No post went from the village until that afternoon. She had put the stupid thing in the bin and taken it out again several times. If only she hadn't sealed it then she'd be able to re-read it, but she didn't have another envelope the right size and Sellotape stuck all over the flap would look awful.

In the end she wedged it into the frame of her mirror and climbed into her riding gear for a quick session of freshening up her war wounds. At least Paola had got the afternoon off. Pascal was driving Alexandra, Sophia, Sally and the children to Chartres, which meant that Tash and Paola could take Snob and Bouchon, as Anton's ewe-necked old gelding was called, for a long lazy ride into the valley.

Tash avoided walking within sight of the pool as she made

her way to the yard. Snob had been left in the field behind the stalls overnight in order to stretch his legs freely without getting eaten by flies. Tash was surprised to find him waiting at the gate and even more delighted when, instead of the usual nip, he gave her ribs an affectionate nudge as she clipped the lead rope to his headcollar.

He seemed remarkably clean considering his night out, Tash noticed. There was hardly a speck of dust on him for her to brush off. She revelled in the beauty of the glossy, lustrous coat covering hard, packed muscles. His three uneven white socks made him look like a drum majorette who'd dressed in a hurry.

Snob had developed a tragedian's art in equine dramatics when it came to being tacked up. But today he stood like a four-legged sofa for Tash. She felt a surge of pleasure. Was he beginning to trust her at last?

It was a critical morning for both of them: she'd decided to jump Snob for the first time. There were only a couple of old fencing poles balanced on wine casks which she and Paola had rigged up the night before, but these were easily sufficient for their first attempt.

As she and Snob jogged through the gate, she was slightly bewildered to find that the poles were resting on the ends of the casks, not the sides. It made the fences almost twice their intended height. However, she and Paola had fixed them up after sharing a bottle of wine in the kitchen and, with much giggling, had practised jumping them on foot. They must have left them like that.

Oh well, she'd work Snob in for a bit and then change them after one of the inevitable falling-off sessions, Tash decided.

Snob tried out a couple of hefty bucks, but Tash's leg muscles had developed enough during the last week to keep her gripping on. After a few close brushes with the fence and a sharp turn-and-shoulder-drop to the right hadn't succeeded in removing Tash, Snob settled sulkily into a working trot on the left rein.

He had a glorious long, bouncing stride. As she felt her confidence rise, Tash became less and less obsessed with which part of the paddock looked the softest to land on and found herself brimming with joy at the warmth of the sun on her back and the sweep of the valley appearing between those long red ears on every circuit. She changed reins and started Snob in his smooth canter. Instead of the usual mad dash for the trees, he actually responded to her command and stayed collected. Tash wanted to whoop with joy.

They rounded the corner at the top of the paddock. As the yard came back into view, Tash caught sight of Hugo helping Ben and a crate of beer out of the Merc. He was looking utterly breathtaking in nothing but sawn-off jeans and espadrilles, the breadth of his smooth back tanned the colour of caramel now.

Sensing her distraction, Snob swung round to the right and started heading full pelt for the nearer of the two jumps. Rendering himself airborne was the one thought in his red head.

'Stop, you idiot!' Tash frantically tried to pull him round to the left, but his mind was made up.

She desperately hung on to his mane and tried to stay with him as he set himself up for the fence . . . one-two-three-UP!

Snob soared over beautifully with literally feet to spare. This time Tash did whoop with joy.

There was no viciousness in the buck that Snob let out after landing, just pure exhilarated joy. Tash fell off all the same.

'Amazing jump, n'est-ce pas?' mocked Hugo, laughing over the paddock fence as she picked herself up from a fresh Tash-sized indent in the paddock's pitted earth. 'Only I managed to stay on this morning when he did that.'

'What?' Tash looked at him sharply, the clues starting to add unpleasantly up.

Hugo smiled his stomach-liquidising smile. But Tash's guts were churning angrily for quite another reason.

'What did you say?' Tash rubbed her aching hip and glared into his taunting eyes.

'You heard, darling,' Hugo grinned lazily. 'You see, your lovely mother said I was welcome to . . . er . . . school him for you, as long as I did it before you got up. I'm afraid I've let the chat out of the bag rather.' He turned away. 'It was supposed to be our little secret. Oops.' Still laughing, he walked into the house.

Tash was too furious to think of anything to shout at his beautifully tanned, departing back.

Ben, hopping after his friend, muttered an embarrassed 'Morning, Tash.'

Although she felt far too angry to get back on Snob, Tash couldn't face going back into the house or, worse still, skulking round hiding from the others and making it obvious to Hugo how upset she was. She put the two jumps back down to their minimum height and caught Snob, who'd found such a delicious patch of grass that for once he didn't see her coming.

As she rode him back round the paddock again with a calm authority she didn't feel, Tash began to doubt everything she thought she'd achieved in the past week. She'd been so sure that Snob's gradual, back-breaking taming was slowly coming within her grasp – still hours of sweat and swearing away, but drawing almost imperceptibly closer. Now she wasn't so sure. Beastly, loathsome Hugo. She indulged in a brief, exquisite image of tying him between two barrels and getting Snob to jump him. Blindfold.

At this point the impatient chestnut made a nifty detour into the fence on their left and rubbed her off.

She wearily climbed back on, feeling all her confidence and enthusiasm stay behind on the parched ground.

'Why am I the biggest idiot out, Snob?' she asked the twitching ears as they made their way in a beautiful, if unintentional, half pass down the centre.

Snob fought to get at a jump.

'I mean if Hugo keeps on schooling you, for whatever reason, you're bound to improve no end. It doesn't mean I have to sell you to him, does it?'

Sally was not sure if all the talking Niall had done on Friday night had helped him much at all.

Up in the oak-panelled room she and Matty were staying in, she kept breaking off from sorting out Tor's nappy-changing kit to check out of the window and see if he was still okay. He'd been floating on a lilo, burying his nose in *Gargantua et Pantagruel*, for over an hour. In the last ten minutes he'd been looking strangely lifeless.

Sally longed to find Matty and warn him, but she didn't dare in case he told her off for overreacting again.

Instead she stared glumly at a box of Pampers. Alexandra had planned a trip to Chartres for that afternoon, but with Niall in such an unpredictable state, Sally wasn't sure if she was doing the right thing to go. The fact that Matty was staying behind to keep him company should have been a comfort. Instead it twisted anxiety tighter in her stomach.

Over the past few days, Niall had withdrawn totally, only appearing at meal times to pick silently at Alexandra's delicious, if erratic, cooking before quickly disappearing, leaving a virtually full plate.

Yesterday, Sally had started to panic when she'd been unable to find him after returning from an afternoon walk with the kids.

'You were supposed to keep him by the pool!' she'd snapped at Matty.

'You can force a man to water, but you can't make him do the breaststroke,' Matty had said softly. 'Don't worry, Salls. He'll have taken himself off somewhere quiet to think. He needs time on his own.'

A faint sanctimonious hint of censure had laced Matty's words, which Sally picked up with indignant annoyance.

Then a terrible thought had struck her a direct hit in the chest. 'Supposing he's—' her voice had trembled '– gone off to do something stupid like trying to kill himself?'

Matty had told her she was overreacting, but to pacify her had helped look for Niall, his face set in Judge Jeffrey condescension.

In the end, they'd run him to ground sitting in the long grass under a tangled yew, in the middle of what had once been a formal topiary, ploughing through *Les Chemins de la Liberté* at an impressive rate of knots.

He'd looked up at Matty, his unusually bright eyes giving away how high he was.

'Your mother's got a fucking wonderful book collection.' Going back to the book, he'd read a page in about twenty seconds.

'How far have you got?' Sally had asked, noticing a discarded pile of books beside Niall's leg.

'*Iron in the Soul.*' Niall had looked up from the Sartre, then followed her gaze. 'Oh those. I read them all this morning. I cried all the way through *Le Grand Meaulnes*, and the Zola's so moving I kept throwing it across the garden in anger at the fucking misery of some of the poor bastards in it – I'll buy your mother another copy, Matt.'

'It's a first edition.' Matty had picked up the dog-eared book with a thoughtful smile.

Then he'd dragged Sally away and left his tall Irish friend to it.

Niall had always been an obsessive reader, Matty had pointed out to her slightly huffily on the way back to the house. This had to be a positive sign. She shouldn't try to smother Niall; he'd straighten himself out his own way.

The lecture had left Sally feeling itchy-skinned with irritation.

She wished she could be as sure as Matty that Niall's current behaviour was a good thing. Passing his room at three that morning on the way to the loo, she had heard a low moaning. She had pushed the door open and found Niall standing naked by his unshuttered window, tears streaming down his face. The cigarette in his hand was smoked down so far it had burnt his fingers.

'Oh poor, poor Niall,' she'd soothed, helping him into bed. He'd complied so meekly, like Tom when he needed comforting after a nightmare. 'Shhh, luvvie. It's all right. You mustn't, *mustn't* blame yourself. You were the most wonderful husband on earth, she just never knew how lucky she was. Shhh. Everything's going to be okay, I promise.'

'Huh?' Niall had looked up through drying tears. 'I don't understand.'

'It was all Lisette's fault.' She stroked his straggly hair. 'You'll get over her, honest. All wounds heal in time, however painful. You've just got to be patient. Matty and I are here to look after you now.'

Niall had looked at her incredulously. Then he started to laugh. He laughed so much that he clutched his stomach in pain and tears coursed down his cheeks yet again.

'Niall . . . shhh . . . Niall – are you all right?'

He was laughing so much he couldn't speak. Instead he'd just handed her, by way of explanation, a copy of *The Mayor of Casterbridge*, open at the last page.

When she'd told him about it afterwards, Matty had found the whole episode screamingly funny.

Sally listlessly gathered together two bibs and Tor's sick bowl for the trip.

Her relationship with Matty was very fragile at the moment. He was distancing himself more and more, treating Niall as his personal problem and taking his hurt frustration out on her. Animosity was starting to wriggle between them like an invisible harpy. And Sally knew that it was their financial problems which would soon erect the final coil of barbed wire down the centre of their mattress.

Searching through her suitcase for an aspirin earlier, she'd come across three final demands which had arrived the day before they set off for France and which she'd hidden from Matty in case he used them as an excuse not to go. If, however, they returned to Richmond to find the phone cut off and no electricity or gas, he'd be in an even more unforgiving black mood with her.

She'd carried them with her all morning, psyching herself to own up. But Matty was behaving so starchily she'd lost her nerve.

She also felt terribly tired. Her morning sickness, which had lasted hours, was camping down for a day-long siege on her empty stomach. Tor was teething and had kept them up all night, adding to Matty's ratty mood. And, she noticed with a sudden start, Niall *still* looked lifeless.

Sally bit her lip and pounded downstairs.

As she dashed out to the pool Alexandra's spaniels wound round her legs barking excitedly.

The lilo was empty. A swollen copy of *Gargantua et Pantagruel* bobbed beside it . . .

Pulling off her shoes and gasping for breath, Sally frantically scoured the tiled bottom of the pool for Niall.

'Sally, what *are* you doing?'

Spinning round, she saw Matty, his hand sheltering his eyes from the sun, looking at her in amusement. Beside him stood Niall – skinny and unkempt, but very alive – swigging from a can of 7-Up.

Sally muttered something about having hot feet and, fuming with herself, dabbled her toes in the cool, blue water for a few minutes. She was acutely aware that the overdue bills were burning a hole in her skirt pocket.

As soon as Matty disappeared inside for more drinks, she rushed to the overgrown kitchen garden and, ignoring Niall's bemused looks, buried them under some seeding cabbages.

Pascal rounded up the day-trippers at midday. They would stop for lunch on the way, he explained.

The children, used to being ignored, were acting up boisterously. Tom had grabbed a wailing Lotty's Noo Noo and was trying to encourage one of the spaniels to eat it. Polly refused to go unless she could wear her cowgirl outfit. Tor had fallen over in a dirt patch and looked like the Artful Dodger. She'd also buried one of her shoes. To cap it all, just as they were about to drive off in the overloaded jeep, Josh threw up his breakfast (liquidised luxury muesli with Greek yoghurt) all over Sophia's pink Nicole Farhi shirt.

Alexandra and Sally got the giggles.

After buttoning Josh into yet another spotless blue Babygro and herself into cream silk, Sophia tersely announced herself ready and they all set off at Pascal's usual reckless pelt.

From Snob's back, Tash watched the dusty jeep narrowly missing a gatepost. As it bounced in a cloud of dust along the cratered length of overgrown drive, she felt only relief that she wasn't going with them.

She knew she had to give Snob a rest before riding out with Paola, but couldn't face the poolside mob quite yet. Instead she settled for hosing and rubbing Snob down thoroughly in the yard and then sitting on a loose straw bale to clean his tack.

In actual fact the poolside mob had long since dispersed.

Ben, fed up with being confined to barracks, decided to go with Amanda and Hugo to the bar in the village for lunch. He sat on the long, sun-drenched terrace and waited for Amanda to return from fetching Hugo from the house.

The beauty of the golden valley in front of him could not make up for the increasing ache he felt in missing Holdham. He longed to be driving round his flat, stretching fields, surveying the ripening crops, stopping off every now and again to pop in on the farming tenants and discuss the harvest or share a cup of brick-red tea in a messy kitchen that smelled of roast beef and freshly baked bread.

He knew that in reality he'd be stuck at home with his aching ankle and Sophia's astronomical credit card bills, but even that would be preferable to where he was now. Sophia was so much more placid and loving away from her family. It seemed to Ben that since their arrival at his mother-in-law's house, Sophia had done nothing but snap at him and complain about Paola's dress sense.

Amanda was taking an awfully long time. Ben ate another blood orange from the big earthenware bowl on the table to ease his groaning stomach. It was lukewarm from the sun. Probably ninety-eight point four degrees Fahrenheit, thought Ben. A blood temperature blood orange. He chuckled to himself and looked around for something to scratch inside his cast with. If only Alexandra knitted like other women's mothers.

He was just having an experimental delve into the plaster cast with a wisteria twig when Amanda came out of the glass doors looking livid.

'Your bloody fucking friend's being a complete bastard.' She sat down huffily on the chair Ben was using as a footstool. Ben had to whip his cast away so fast that the twig broke off in his hand, leaving its painfully scratchy remains buried inside.

'What's he done now? – Ouch!' Ben tried to extract the twig with his finger and got that stuck too.

'I simply suggested he asked Niall along too, after all they're supposedly such great mates.' Amanda watched Ben agonisingly remove a reddened finger from his potted ankle. 'He said – and I quote, "If you fancy him so much, ask him yourself", which is completely overreacting. When I told him so in no uncertain terms – here,' she handed Ben a pen from beside a half-finished crossword on the table, 'he laughed at me and said that if Haydown were as transparent as my crush we'd have to stop throwing stones at each other.' She glared angrily at Hugo's espadrilles left by the table. Picking them up, she hurled them over the side of the low drop that separated the terrace wall from the garden.

'Don't quite understand the bit about throwing stones.' Ben could feel his ankle swelling up hotly as he poked around with the pen for the offending twig. 'Doesn't sound like Hugs to threaten a woman. Ahh!' He extracted one tiny leaf. 'Damn.'

'He was referring to people in glass houses,' snapped Amanda impatiently. 'Anyway, I told the sod that he could make his own way to the bloody bar. Are we going then?' She got up and stalked towards the steps that led down to the side of the courtyard.

'Well, actually the old leg's a bit painful at the minute.' The pen lid had come off inside his cast as well now. Ben felt as if the plaster was about to burst open like the Incredible Hulk's trousers under his ever-expanding foot.

'Don't be so wet, Ben.' Amanda smiled wickedly. 'After all, aren't you always telling us one of your forefathers – the fourth Earl wasn't it? – carried on fighting in the Battle of Naseby after his arm had been hacked off by the Roundheads?'

Ben sighed and hobbled with her to the red Peugeot. At least Amanda drank enough to keep up with him. A few ice cool beers would deaden the pain.

* * *

Watching them leave from an upstairs window, Hugo's eyes narrowed. Amanda's histrionics had thoroughly pissed him off. He had no intention of going to the bar. But she'd left him itching for a fight.

Dragging a match along a stone mullion to light his cigarette, he decided that the time had come to have a quiet word with Sophia's puddingy sister. After what Sophia had told him, getting Snob off the disaster-ridden Tash would be as easy as stealing a guide dog.

17

By one o'clock, Tash was drenched in sweat. The sun was more intense than ever. She'd tried sitting inside the stalls to rub neatsfoot oil into Snob's leather girth, which was stiff with dust, but it was so stuffy in there that she had been forced back out again. Now she was crouched on an upturned bucket in the smallest of shadows, cast by the eaves of the old grain store. Just the reins to do and she could go for a swim.

She'd heard the sound of the little red Peugeot setting off when she was settling Snob, and had later seen Niall and Matty heading off for a walk with two bottles of white wine and armfuls of grub. Paola had just appeared to say that she would be in her room writing to her parents, and to fetch her when Tash was ready to go.

Tash was secure in the knowledge that she had the place to herself for at least a couple of hours. The feeling was such bliss, and the longing to plunge into the pool for a long, cool soak so acute that she lingered over cleaning the reins until they were as slippery and supple as a leaping salmon, so as to make the pleasure of swimming all the greater through holding back.

She took the time to revel in the memory of jumping Snob. As soon as she had let him tackle the little jumps he had been set alight, bounding over them with such pleasure and so many bucks that Tash had laughed and whooped, staying on through every joyful plunge. She was aware that she'd had very little, if any, control over the situation but was sure that this would change in time. She'd found Snob's on-button, his delight in jumping. That was what mattered. It made a smile push at her sunburnt cheeks every time she thought about it. Locating the off-button could wait.

Inside, the house was so cool it made the sweat on her t-shirt feel like iced water. In her room, Tash put her gritty contact lenses into soak, then peeled off her clothes, throwing them into a heap in the corner. She half expected to see it steam. Her newly washed black bathing costume lay over the wooden towel rail. Next to it was Sophia's microscopic bikini. What the hell. No one was around and a one-piece would be sweltering in this heat. She put on the stringy bikini.

A huge new bruise had developed on her hip from that morning. This one was shaped like a love-heart. Wistfully, Tash looked across at the mirror for her letter to Max.

It had gone.

She looked on the floor around and behind her dressing table. It was nowhere to be seen. The postcards had gone too. That was that, then. Her mind had been made up for her. In a way, she was glad.

Leaning sideways to extract a towel from the rail, Tash caught sight of herself in the mirror. At first, all she noticed was how mucky and red her face was – she looked like a Swan Vesta. Then something occurred to her. There were no little rolls of flesh at the side of her bent waist, just a smooth, lightly tanned curve. She turned sideways. Her stomach was almost totally flat. She tensed it and had a tentative prod with her fingers. Instead of the usual soft dough, they came in contact with hard muscle. Shrieking with delight, she bounded downstairs to the pool and took a running leap into its welcoming, pale turquoise deep end.

When she surfaced, blinking, a minute later she saw, through her chlorine-stung eyes, a pair of brown legs by the table. She swam over to the side of the pool and, peeking over the tiled edge, squinted at the figure – it wasn't Ben, he was blond and had a white foot. This was brunette and buried behind a newspaper. But her myopic eyes could tell her no more. It must be Matty or Niall returned from their walk, Tash decided. She didn't want to draw attention to herself – although, God knows, her initial belly flop must have been pretty noticeable – so she quietly did a few lengths.

After six she was puffed out and dying to slob out on a sunbed with a cigarette.

She glanced back at the hazy figure. He hadn't moved an inch. Perhaps whoever it was was asleep? Why did her awful eyesight mean that she saw everything through a mist, like a Hollywood close-up with the camera lens coated thickly in Vaseline? She'd just have to brave it. As soon as she'd had her fag she could take a leaf out of Amanda's book and pretend to be asleep.

As she climbed inelegantly out of the pool and made her way over to the table, the man put down his paper and looked at her. Tash's clear focal range stopped at about six inches, but by the time she was just a few steps from the pool she knew it was Hugo. No one could mistake those broad, lean shoulders, that torso lightly quilted with muscles and the thick wavy hair which was the colour of autumn leaves. How could she have thought those beautiful long, hard legs belonged to anyone else?

Staring at the ground, she felt as huge and awkward as a bulldozer as she leaned over the table to grab a Camel from the packet, dripping water everywhere.

'Help yourself,' offered Hugo in an amused voice.

'Oh, God I'm sorry. I smoke Camel too.' Tash lit the soggy cigarette. It went out.

'We have something in common, then.' Hugo smiled, slowly getting up. 'How extraordinary.'

Tash desperately tried to get the cigarette lit again. It hissed damply and turned brown, but wouldn't light.

Hugo took it from her lips and threw it into a lilac bush.

'Disgusting habit,' he censured. 'I only do it to annoy Amanda. You have no excuse.'

He was standing very close to her. Tash could smell his aftershave, cool and spicy as a lime grove. His body blocked out the sun, casting a long cool shadow on her naked flesh.

Her stomach was squirming, her heart pounding so hard that her ribcage hurt. She backed towards the pool.

'Were you pissed off that I rode your horse?' Hugo asked softly, following her.

'Er . . . yes. No. I mean without asking, a bit annoyed maybe.' Tash backed away further.

With the sun behind it, his head was all shadow; she couldn't read his expression. Only his cobalt eyes sparkled in the gloom.

'I'm sorry. Your mother was so insistent.' He continued following her so that their bodies were less than a foot apart. 'She guessed you were having a few problems schooling him. All those bruises.' He brushed his fingers along the love-heart on her hip.

It was as if he'd touched her with live electrodes. Tash leapt back further.

'I'm doing all right.' Her throat felt full of sawdust.

'Oh, come on, darling,' his voice was like a kiss, 'I've seen you on that nag, or falling off it, rather. He's one hell of a handful for someone so –' his eyes ran down her body as slowly as dripping honey '– feminine. He's a remorseless bugger as well.' His sapphire gaze trapped hers, like a rabbit caught in headlights. 'I could fix you up with the most amazing grey gelding. Had him in my yard six months. He's as gentle as a puppy, armchair on four legs. Jumps anything.'

'I'm quite happy with Snob,' yelped Tash. If I say yes, will he kiss me? *No. Stop it, Tash. You must stand up for yourself.* But how can I, when my knees are turning into liquid pools on the ground?

'Are you really happy, Tash? You look so frightened on that horse.' Hugo's voice was so kind, so gentle. 'He needs someone that can tell him who's boss.'

'Like you, I suppose?' Tash mumbled, forcing her eyes free of his and finding the ground.

'You said it,' he moved forward again. Tash moved back. We'll be doing the Gay Gordon in a minute, she thought wildly.

'Sometimes when you get on a nag, you click,' Hugo went on. 'It hardly ever happens immediately, but when it does it makes your head spin.'

Tash knew she didn't want to hear this.

'This morning my head nearly span right off my shoulders,' he laughed, showing clean white teeth as straight as keys on a piano. 'Granted, the horse is green and he's been allowed to develop some fucking bad habits . . .'

Tash felt her over-pumped blood start to boil.

'. . . but we really clicked. I mean shit hot. He was going as quietly as an old Fell by the end.'

He put his hand under Tash's chin and gently pushed it upwards. He's going to kiss me, she thought, panicking. She felt faint with lust.

But he merely looked her in the eyes again and said, 'I know he could win Badminton with me on his back, Tash.' He leaned forward a fraction. Tash was up against the edge of the pool by now and couldn't budge. 'Can you honestly tell me that you've clicked at all with that horse?'

She was totally overcome by those hypnotic blue eyes. He was so close that she could feel the heat of his body on her bare skin. She had never even dared to dream of longing as intense as this.

'No,' she muttered.

'Then let me have him,' Hugo coaxed. 'Think of the horse. You'd be doing him a massive favour. If you don't like Tequila, I'll help you find the best quad in England.'

'No!' Tash howled, suddenly determined. 'No. I'm sorry, I know it sounds idiotic but I want Snob, not a winning machine someone prepared earlier, like a cake in Blue Peter. I need to prove that I can do it. I'm desperately sorry. I know you really want him. But you must understand—'

'Oh, I understand all right,' the soft voice was now as hard as a gunshot. 'I understand that you're a selfish little brat who thinks that because someone who knows something about "cute little gee gees" has pronounced yours a potential winner that means you personally can make him one. Let me tell you something, darling. You're going to wreck that horse just as you did Samion.'

Tash let out a terrified yelp.

'Oh yes.' A malicious smile flickered on Hugo's lips. 'Sophia's told me all about your last great equine love. Had to be destroyed, didn't he? All because you—'

Tash threw a slap across his face with all her might. It made her feet slip on the tiled edge of the pool and, flinging her burning hand behind her to break her fall, she encountered only cold water as she fell heavily into the swimming pool.

She surfaced, gasping for air, her lungs full of the chlorinated water. She was stinging all over from the impact of the pool surface on her skin. Her hair stuck heavily to her face as she frantically splashed her way to the far side of the pool and heaved her arms on to the edge, coughing out the water that was trapped in her throat.

Hugo was beside her in a flash.

As he leaned down, Tash thought he was going to help her out. Instead he grabbed her firmly by her sodden hair. She lost her grip on the side and was only saved from going under for another mouthful of pool water by Hugo yanking her head up. She screamed as his vicious tug made her scalp feel as if it was being torn from her skull.

'What are you doing?' she screamed, treading water frantically to stop the pulling on her head.

'Teaching you a lesson, little girl,' Hugo hissed. 'If you think you can cope in an adult's world you have to play by grown-up rules. Compris?'

Tash made a grab for the side and missed. Hugo was holding her at arm's length like a sheep about to be dipped.

'Please,' Tash pleaded. 'I'm sorry about Snob. But I promised myself I'd make up for what happened to Samion. I can't sell him to you, not now.' She frantically tried to tread water but Hugo was tugging her head back like a taut noose.

'What do you want to do?' he stormed in horrified amazement. 'Hope for better luck the next time? If not, never mind – third time lucky – Pascal might buy you a seaside donkey.'

'I made some horrible, unforgivable mistakes with Samion,' she sobbed, 'but you've got to understand it wasn't my fault – that he was put down – it was all a terrible, awful accident—' Great sobs heaved through her, making it almost impossible to speak. Hugo, pulling her hair out by the roots, was letting his arm drop lower so that her face was almost underwater.

'– Sophia—' Tash leaned her head back to avoid gulping more pool water, huge, terrified eyes pleading, '– hunting—' she was choking now, her lungs swilling with burning chlorine. Her arms flailed frantically against Hugo's grip.

'Oh dear, oh dear, oh dear,' Hugo laughed at her, letting her grab the side of the pool before releasing his grip. 'A little bit melodramatic, Natasha. You've been reading too many Pullein-Thompson novels. Is that what you get up to when you lurk around the house avoiding your own shadow? It just goes to show what a big kid you are. You've got one hell of a lot of growing up to do before anyone will be able to talk straight to you. One gets more scintillating conversation from Sophia's little brats.'

He got up and walked into the house, yelling over his shoulder as he went, 'I suppose I'll have to wait until you've turned that horse into a complete mess before you give up.'

Tash pulled herself furiously out of the pool and went over to the table where she smoked three of Hugo's cigarettes in a row. Then she felt sick, so she chucked the rest of the packet into the pool. Feeling dissatisfied with this, she followed suit with his newspaper, dark glasses and the recently retrieved espadrilles. Hugo was right, she thought, I am a big kid. That was what had hurt so much about what he had said – so much of it had been humiliatingly true. And she had thought he was coming on to her! She could kick her grotesque ego.

Poor, temperamental Snob, consigned to be ruined by her just as Samion had been. She was stabbed through with guilt. Hugo had made it sound as if she had signed his death warrant.

If only he knew the truth; she'd got so close to telling him that she shuddered. Hugo being the soul of indiscretion, the truth would have spread like measles in a prep school. And with Sophia constantly tapping into his conversations, as soon as she rumbled that their secret was out, Tash knew she'd have been torn apart by her sister's wrath.

Bloody, bloody Hugo. She threw his silver lighter in for good measure.

She then crept into the kitchen, making quite sure Hugo wasn't around, and crossly chomped her way through three enormous brie and turkey sandwiches. Then she scoffed the remainders of last night's pavlova and half a bar of cooking chocolate. Feeling slightly better, but hugely fat, she took a slug from the bottle of cooking wine that stood by the range. It was good. Far too good for cooking, decided Tash. She went back outside, taking it with her.

She worked her way through the wine, standing on the terrace and watching a tractor run up and down the golden grooves of a field deep in the valley. It was so muggy that there seemed to be no air left at all. No breeze stirred the leaves sparkling on the branches of the fruit trees that dotted the overgrown lawn. Storm flies gathered like suspended specks of dust frantically colliding in a schoolboy's physics experiment. Alexandra's spaniels sat panting underneath the chairs. The smell of frangipani fought with honeysuckle overpoweringly. Insects buzzed furiously inside the creepers that clung to the walls of the house. Tash could feel a glistening layer of sweat cover her body.

She took another swig at the bottle and, getting a mouthful of crystals, realised it was empty. It must be after two, later still perhaps. Amanda and Ben might be back soon. She didn't want them to find her pot-bellied on the terrace, wearing Sophia's bikini, with an empty bottle in her hand. Hugo had made her feel enough of a freak without them thinking of her as a kleptomaniac wino.

She tottered upstairs and showered away the sweat and grogginess with a blast of chilly, high-pressure water. As soon as she was dressed again, in clean jeans and her jodhpur boots, she could feel the moisture start creeping back out of her pores. She'd put on the t-shirt Mikey had given her for Christmas. It was cropped just below the bust and had 'Corking Sheila' on the front and 'Having a daggy day' on the back.

She longed for another drink, but didn't want to be standing on her head singing 'Waltzing Matilda' when the others got back, so decided instead to collect Paola and go for a hack before the storm broke.

Paola's room was at the top of one of the manoir's turrets. It interlinked with the nursery where Josh slept. Tash made her way up the circular staircase, passing the bathroom on the flight below. It smelt reassuringly of talc and apple soap. An empty laundry bag hung on the handle of the half-opened door to Lotty's little room next to it. Tash imagined Lotty placing her tiny pink shoes outside every night to be polished.

The door to Paola's room was ajar; sunlight streamed out of it on to the dusty boards of the shaded landing. Paola's transistor was blaring out a crackling Italian phone-in show. Tash caught her breath from the climb and pushed the door open.

They were in bed together.

Hugo and Paola, like two glamorous French lovers in a Hollywood saga, naked on an old brass bed with crumpled white linen, in an oak-boarded little turret room filled with sunlight. Tash's Vaseline-coated eyes opened wide in shock. Only this scene was far too explicit even for Hollywood.

Paola was on top of Hugo, smooth brown legs wrapped around him, her slender body moving feverishly back and forth as she let out little gasps of pleasure. Sweat ran in great rivulets down her back. Hugo, in contrast, was lying back without so much as a bead on his forehead, his hands behind his head. He looked like he was sunbathing. Neither noticed Tash frozen in the doorway, trembling with mortification. The radio started hissing 'C'mon Everybody'.

Tash wanted to laugh. No, she didn't, she wanted to cry.

She backed out of the room, pushing the door to and, creeping like grandma's footsteps, she made her way downstairs.

Once there she threw herself out of the back door and ran as fast as she could across the scorching courtyard. Bang into Matty and Niall returning from their walk.

'Tashy!' Matty caught her, then seeing her tear-stained face, 'Tash, what's the matter?'

'Hugo – I – um – nothing—' Tash hiccuped.

'Come on, I'm not leaving you like this.' Matty took her firmly by the arm. 'Niall will make us all a cup of coffee, won't you, old friend?'

Niall didn't look like he was up to making it into the house, let alone fathom out the mysteries of the espresso-maker.

'Sure I will.' He loped off, rather lop-sidedly, in the general direction of the kitchen.

Matty led Tash on to the terrace. Finding it totally devoid of shade, he took her through the echoing house and out on to the balustrade-flanked balcony on the other side. Here he sat her down in the shade of one of the emerald green parasols.

'Now tell me what's happened to make you so upset.' His voice had the detached kindness of a counsellor. 'Something about Hugo?'

Tash hiccuped again.

It was then that Matty noticed *The Times* floating in the swimming pool below them. Taking a closer look, he saw a pair of espadrilles bobbing in the shallow end. Wasn't that a pair of dark glasses that the filter machine at the bottom of the pool was trying to suck up? He looked at his sister with new-found respect.

'My God!' he laughed, 'You've pushed that shit Beauchamp in the pool!'

18

On Wednesday night, Alexandra took her party of house guests to eat with a local ex-patriot couple, the Gallaghers. Inside their baronial, desolate abbey, which made the manoir seem positively twee by comparison, the oddball Scottish duo laid on a spread so mouth-watering and varied that even the notorious pickers, Sophia and Amanda, greedily helped themselves to too much. The group chomped and chatted in the 'kitchen', which was actually ninety feet of flagstone refectory, with gnarled beams as thick as cedar trunks crossing a decaying vaulted ceiling like the upturned belly of a ship. As they revelled, overlooked by scores of disapproving stag-heads slain by Hamish Gallagher's flame-haired forefathers, the honey-smooth wine flowed so freely and the conversation so fluently that no one left until the small hours.

Consequently, the next morning a pin could be heard clattering to the floor in the manoir as everyone crawled round clutching their throbbing heads with evil tempers. A trip to the Loire river had been originally planned for the morning, but in the end the only excursion which took place was Pascal driving to the local pharmacy for more Alka Seltzer.

Niall knew he was losing his grip when he found himself crying his eyes out over a dubbed version of *The Waltons.*

He just couldn't face other people at the moment. He'd

stayed up long after they'd all returned from the hospitable Gallaghers last night and tried to sort out his pounding head.

Sitting on the little balcony of his room, smoking one cigarette after another to stop himself taking his last line of coke, had solved nothing. He'd tried harder than ever to put some of the blame for his misery on Lisette but couldn't; thinking about her made his temples throb and his eyes burn with self-loathing. Wracked with insomnia, he'd watched the sun come up beyond a distant field of vines, slowly filling the air with dewy warmth. He'd listened to the increasing babble of the dawn chorus with numb ears, not really focusing on it but unable to think of anything to stop the squeaking and screeching cacophony rattling his nerves until, finally, he was forced to go to bed and pull the covers over his ears.

There he had lain with every muscle in his body clenching and unclenching, his eyes wide open and his heart racing with adrenalin which wasn't induced by either drugs or thought. When he had finally dozed fitfully, his empty mind had been flooded with confused, overlapping dreams made up of incomprehensible, terrifying images and great rambling speeches he had to memorise but couldn't understand.

Then Hugo appeared first thing, demanding to know if he had a headache pill as no one else seemed to. Just as Niall was drifting to sleep again, Sally popped her head round the door, nappy in hand, to check he was okay. She seemed to think he was permanently on the verge of topping himself at the moment.

Giving up on the idea of dropping back off to try and sort out his nightmares, he made his unsteady way downstairs for a coffee. There the evergreen Alexandra pressurised him into eating an enormous breakfast of hot chocolate and great jam-covered hunks of warm bread, followed by heavily herbed local sausages cooked in an enormous fluffy omelette.

'You're far too thin, darling,' she smiled, helping him to piles of dry toast. 'When I was married to Matty's father, I refused to eat if I had a hangover, which was most of the time. But Pascal taught me to simply shovel it back until the dratted thing was gone – of course I put on bags of weight. Now I just eat a whole celery every morning, which seems to do the trick.'

Niall smiled weakly and said that he was going for a walk. As soon as he was out of the kitchen, he bolted to the nearest bush and threw up behind it, startling Jean, the idle handyman, who was sitting on a milk crate reading a seed catalogue.

Growling like an old dog and slyly glancing at Niall over his half-moons, Jean grumpily stubbed out his Gitane and pretended to examine the rampant ivy which grew up the kitchen walls like lumpy green leg-warmers. When Niall straightened shakily up, he came face to face with two suspicious eyes peering at him through the foliage.

'Ça va?' A Gitane packet was suddenly thrust out of a branch.

Aware that he was the object of fascinated scrutiny, Niall smiled as cheerfully as he could and shook his head. He felt too drained and sick to walk amongst the unbridled, lush wilderness of the damp, pungent garden. Nor could he face the friendly, babbling chaos of the kitchen. So, to Jean's bewilderment, he crawled at knee-level below the windows (steamed up by Alexandra's cooking) and slipped back into the house via an unlocked turret door. Then, hearing the clack of approaching sling-backs from one direction and the hissing of his hostess's frying from the other, he bolted through a familiar side door like a fox hearing the view halloo.

Here he lurked undetected, wiping tears away as Jim-Bob told Lizbeth that the kitten would be able to play for ever now it was in heaven. Sounds of activity rose to a frenzied burble in the house. Doors slammed, children wailed, heels clicked and echoed in the hall, voices drifted. Ben could be heard moaning about his hangover just outside the door.

'Going to call for Hughie – totally châteaued last night. Soph's bloody mother's just forced me to eat eight croissant soldiers.' His limping footsteps and the squeak of rubber from the bottom of his crutches trailed away.

The Waltons ended and a thin-lipped Frenchman started reading yesterday's racing results. Niall switched him off and walked over to the window-seat. The dam-bursting flood of adrenalin had only just stopped trickling away.

Pascal's library was a dark room, made gloomier by the smoky, overcast sky outside, still rumbling as Tuesday's storm orbited the valley. It was lined with heavy wood panelling set between ornate sills, mostly hidden by disorderly rows of books which leaned against one another like a sloppy regiment standing at ease. Two shelves were filled with the sombre maroon, dark green and navy backs of Pascal's first editions, the rest crammed with brighter, tattier lines of Alexandra's wildly multifarious, broken-spined paperbacks. Big gaps like missing teeth had appeared between them where Niall had raided for something to bury himself in.

He'd discovered this room on Sunday. It was quiet and dusty, littered with odd boxes of paperwork, piles of assorted junk and stacks of unhung paintings. The furniture, covered in white dust-sheets like slumbering, valuable ghosts – a Regency desk here, a Louis XV chair there – was shrouded and forgotten. It was clear from the festoons of cobwebs which hung undisturbed like a spidery sixties housing estate that no one had come in for months. Niall found refuge in the quiet, sombre room. After sating himself with reading he'd discovered an old black and white portable under some dusty hats and, tuning it in to the only station he could find, had slumped down day after day to a few snatched hours of dubbed American soaps and French current affairs. It blotted out the misery of needing Lisette, needing a fix and needing to scream and cry and break everything in sight. Only today it didn't.

Niall paced the dingy room like a convict. Everything he touched scalded him, his fingers drummed *prestissimo* against the sides of his legs, his stomach seemed to be climbing up and down the bars of his ribcage like a stressed gymnast.

A sudden rusty creak of long-unused pruners grated against his nerves, and he nearly jumped out of his skin as an inquisitive face appeared at the window and two wrinkled eyes squinted at him with almost botanical fascination.

Balanced on top of a rickety step-ladder, breathing heavily

from the effort of scaling it, Jean grinned toothlessly through the grimy glass and pushed the window inwards a crack.

'Ça va?' he wheezed, taking off his moleskin cap and scratching his bald head, before clutching the window frame as the ladder pitched left.

'Christ!' Niall muttered, rubbing his forehead in exasperation. Even the gardener was taking an interest in his sanity now. Deciding to take a walk after all, he turned on his heel and left Jean gaping at a slammed door.

Outside his mind cleared a little. He wandered to the edge of the garden and watched Matty's sister schooling a magnificent chestnut horse on the other side of the fence.

She was doing very well to control the headstrong animal, he noticed, calmly talking to it all the time and letting it have its head without allowing it to run away with her. Niall admired her gentle hands, long motionless legs and soothing voice, the way she calmly sat out the giant horse's playful bucks and head-shaking before taking him slowly down the little line of poles, ending up popping over the small makeshift jump at the end.

Grinning, Tash noticed him and let go of one rein just long enough to give him a small wave.

It was then Niall realised how hard she must have been working to keep the big stallion under control. In an instant, Snob shook his head violently, forcing the reins to slip through Tash's hand. By the time she'd gathered them up again, Snob was heading at full pelt towards the overhanging trees to Niall's right.

'Whoa, Snob! Steady – steady – whoa!'

Tash fought a hopeless battle to apply the brakes, but Snob, the bit firmly between his teeth, was intent on decapitating his rider on the nearest branch.

'Steer him towards the right!' Niall yelled, running to the fence.

'I can't!' Tash screamed back, as the snatching stallion nearly pulled her arms from their sockets. She ducked just in time to avoid the branches of an old, squat oak.

Undeterred, Snob headed at a thundering gallop towards a spindly, but none the less dangerous-looking hazel.

'Grab the rein by his bit!' Niall wailed, holding his breath helplessly as Snob ducked away from the hazel and decided on a more solid-looking cedar.

Doing as she was told, Tash ducked just in time to miss being knocked off by a thick, menacing branch.

But by now they were only a few strides away from the high post and rails with a straggly hedge behind it which separated the paddock from the garden. There was no use trying to stop, they were going far too fast.

Bile rising in his throat, Niall took in the size of the fence; the rails alone were at least five feet, but with the added width of the rambling, overgrown hedge it looked impossible to jump at their out-of-control gallop.

He sprang forward. 'Jump off him! Get off! Shit.' With a stunned groan, he noticed she had no crash helmet on.

Tash, however, clearly had other ideas.

Niall could only watch in powerless amazement as the tall rider suddenly pulled herself together. If the horse ran into the fence he could endure some horrific injuries. So she stuck tight and kicked him on.

But as Snob stood back to take off, he seemed to change his mind and hesitate. Legs flailing, he couldn't stop moving forward. His eyes suddenly rolled in terror.

Niall cursed in desperation. They were going to slide straight into the splintered timber.

With astonishing calm, Tash ignored him screaming for her to pull left. Only aware of Snob's feet sliding from under her, she gathered the nervous horse up, giving him confidence with an almighty push and an encouraging yell of 'GET OVER!'

He jumped it, scraping through the wide hedge and landing cleanly on the other side before careering round the overgrown garden, letting out a stream of ecstatic bucks which made Tash lose both her stirrups and cling on to his red mane for dear life.

Eventually, they came to a halt by the stone steps which led up to the kitchen door. Snob turned round to chew Tash's boot, his chest heaving, great snorts coming from his flared red nostrils.

Niall had been totally unnerved by the close shave. Dumbstruck, he stared at her laughing face as she stroked the horse's hot, damp neck, telling him how well he'd done. Hair everywhere, faded pink t-shirt slipping off one brown shoulder, she sat back and turned to him, the picture of relaxed confidence now. Niall was suddenly reminded of the girls his brother used to knock about with – wild, fearless Irish farm-girls who'd ridden since childhood and occasionally didn't make it beyond – breaking their necks during some childish dare-devil stunt, galloping bareback in midnight steeplechases or backing nutty yearlings ready for the sales.

'Wasn't he marvellous?' Tash called to Niall, shrouding her face from the sun with one hand so that Snob plunged his head down to snatch at grass, nearly shooting Tash out of the front door.

Something inside Niall snapped.

A magnum of bottled-up emotion swelling to be uncorked inside him, he walked towards her looking far more shaken than she was.

'Why the fuck haven't you got a hard hat to ride that animal?' he demanded furiously.

'Er—' Tash looked down at him, smile dropping like a popped balloon. 'I don't have one,' she mumbled nervously.

'Well, Pascal should have fucking given you one,' he stormed, catching hold of Snob's reins and glaring up at her. Unspoken anger and lack of sleep erupted to the surface like the great rush of a breaking oil well. People just got on his nerves at the moment.

'This horse isn't safe to ride,' he fumed. 'I'm surprised he hasn't broken every bone in your body by now.'

Snob, sensing Niall wasn't a fan, narrowed his eyes disdainfully and pulled back, lips snapping, ears flat to his neck.

'That's my problem,' Tash told Niall quietly, looking surprised and hurt.

'So it is, now.' Niall backed off slightly, trying to pull himself together. But his fists were still tightly clenched; finding a vent, the seething pressure of his pent-up rage had only just begun its release.

'So it's your problem if you break your back then, is it?' he continued, almost in a whisper. 'Your problem if your mother loses a daughter because the child's too vain to wear a hat? Your problem if that animal goes so potty that he bolts and really hurts someone – a kid, maybe?'

'Just a min—' Tash broke in, but Niall ignored her.

'What if Tom and Polly had been playing on the other side of that fence right now? Huh?' he raised his eyebrows accusingly. 'Or if your little stunt hadn't come off and that horse had damaged himself so much he had to be destroyed?'

Letting out a cry of anguish, Tash reeled back as if he'd hit her. Picking up on her panic, Snob half rose on to his hind legs, fighting to take off again.

'Strikes me,' Niall snapped bitterly, 'that you should stop being so fucking headstrong and enlist a decent bit of help.' Snob cannoned into him, and he just leapt out of the way in time.

Watching Tash calm the sweating, panicky chestnut, Niall's anger suddenly went flat on him.

'Look, I . . .' he trailed off, on the verge of offering her a hand himself. But he knew he wasn't up to it. Who needed a junky actor swigging from a bottle and bursting into tears instead of telling you to sit deeper? 'I'm sorry,' he finished lamely, squinting up at her stricken face. 'I've laid into you far too hard, angel – but I can't stand back and watch someone kill themself.'

'In that case,' Tash replied through gritted teeth as she gathered Snob up and turned him away, 'I suggest you don't look in the mirror.' And, loosing the reins a fraction, she and Snob thundered off across the garden.

Gibbering back in Pascal's study ten minutes later, Niall realised that he'd gone too far. But it was all too easy to see that now, reflecting in the peace of his temporary hideout, anger evaporating, guilt starting to wrap its all too familiar fingers around his conscience.

'Shit.' He sank his head into his hands in despair. He hardly knew the girl, but he'd bawled her out as if she were a stubborn younger sister.

He also felt bad that he'd snapped angrily at Ben and Pascal afterwards when they'd groggily asked him to join them for a medicinal drink in the village. Ben had staggered backwards with the impact of Niall's snarl on his hangover.

Then, to crown Niall's anguish, the sylph-like Amanda, wearing nothing but skin-tight cream shorts and a string vest, had crept up behind him as he stood brooding on the terrace, asking huskily if he wanted to come for a walk.

Caught off-guard, he'd swung round and stared at her. She had Lisette's level gaze – cool, assured, carnal – the same smooth brown skin and clipped-out hair, like a lithe, blonde greyhound. He'd been so tempted to say yes, to get her out of sight of the house and kiss her fragile, wanton mouth in despair. Then he'd been kicked in the stomach by the sour loathing of loss.

'Leave me alone,' he'd muttered without really thinking. 'Just sod off and leave me alone.'

It was only now, sitting alone with the cool glass of the window against his back and the distant sound of the children's high shrieks floating in, that he realised how insensitively and hurtfully he'd behaved all morning.

'There you are.' Matty walked unsteadily into the room. 'Fancy a quiet scotch by the pool? The others are taking the kids for a walk – rather them than me, my head's agony – except Hugo and Amanda, that is, who are having a furious row with each other, which makes a change. They weren't speaking last night.' He smiled, hungover eyes crinkling. 'So how 'bout it?'

Niall looked out at the darkening horizon. 'They'll be after getting caught in the rain,' he said mindlessly. He didn't want to inflict his black mood on Matty, but he badly needed a drink.

'What, Hugo and Amanda?' Matty's humouring was completely transparent. 'They're in the China Room breaking whatever Sophia and Ben left intact on Sunday. Really, my mother should glue her pottery down to the floor instead of gluing it together afterwards.' He laughed, flicking restlessly through some paintings which were leaning against a sheet-swathed commode. 'Christ, there's a Jack Yeats here – and a Lautrec sketch with coffee rings on it.'

'No, I mean the rest of them out walking.' Niall, three steps behind the conversation, heaved himself up. As he followed Matty through the house, the sound of Hugo and Amanda screaming at one another echoed into the hall. No breaking china, though.

'All you do when you're away from your fucking horses is sulk and get drunk.'

'I'm bored – I miss the dogs.'

'This is the first time we've been away together in over a year—'

'Exactly – they'll be off their food.'

'You're fucking facetious, Hugo!'

'I'm not fucking anyone,' Hugo hissed bitterly, 'as you well know.'

'I'm sure they won't mind a bit of rain,' rambled Matty, to cover up the din. 'I suppose Sophia might come rushing back holding Josh over her hairdo at the first roll of thunder, though.' He walked into the airy games room and extracted a bottle of Johnnie Walker Black Label from a small cupboard full of tennis balls. 'Pascal's secret supply. Actually, Sophia's pretty green at the moment – not ecologically, mind you – because Sally's persuaded Tash to do a painting of us and the kids.' He strode out on to the balcony and towards the steps that led down to the pool. 'It's ridiculous, really. Tash actually offered to paint Sophia's little monsters last week and old toffee nez wouldn't hear of it. Now she keeps ranting on about capturing Josh's long lashes in oils. Poor Tash'll be slapping paint on canvas all holiday as well as falling off that damned horse Mother bought her.' He settled under the green parasol and unscrewed the lid of the scotch. 'Shit, I've forgotten the glasses.'

'I'll get them,' offered Niall, keen to escape.

He'd had a sudden idea to stop himself feeling guilty about Matty's sister.

The big house had fallen silent when he walked back through

it. The China Room was deserted. Niall went into the kitchen to fetch a couple of tumblers and saw Hugo through the window, heading for the yard. He left the glasses on the table and bounded after him.

'Hugo!' He caught him up just as he was climbing into the red Peugeot.

'Hello,' Hugo smiled at him. 'Fancy coming for a drink? I need to recover my hearing somewhere quiet. Think Amanda's just ruptured one of my eardrums – don't know what's got into her today.'

Niall coughed awkwardly. 'Er, no thanks. Look, I need to ask you a favour, Hugo.'

'Fire away. If you want to borrow Amanda, feel free – I'll lend you my gum-shield.' Then seeing Niall's angry look, 'No, on second thoughts I take that back. What can I do for you?'

'It's Tash.'

'*Tash?*'

Seeing Hugo's amazed face, Niall remembered that – despite her furiously denying it – Matty was sure Tash had pushed Hugo in the pool on Sunday. Perhaps Hugo wasn't the best person to ask.

'No, forget it, sorry. Dumb idea.' He started to walk away.

'Wait!' Hugo called him back. 'Tell me what it is first. You never know.' He was going to add that Tash struck him as someone who needed a lot of favours but thought the better of it. Surely Niall couldn't actually be attracted to the little freak? he wondered.

'It's her horse. I think she's needing some help with it.'

'You're telling me,' Hugo laughed. 'She'd fall off a rocking horse with stabilisers. Don't tell me you want me to get up at dawn and secretly school him, because I'm telling you now I won't.'

'No,' said Niall, wondering why Hugo was so animated on the subject. 'I wondered if you'd give her some lessons.'

'*Lessons!*' Once again a dumbfounded look crossed Hugo's bronzed face.

'Not officially now,' Niall added quickly. 'Just help her out a bit. Show her where she's going wrong. Not so she'd know. Interested advice, you understand.'

Oh I'm interested all right, thought Hugo, but not in advice. Certainly not in helping Tash French in any capacity. Niall must be pretty thick-skinned not to realise that Hugo and Tash never spoke, avoided one another totally, in fact. She gave him the creeps.

'No. I'm sorry, old chum,' he said, starting up the car, 'but I've got more important things to do with my time than teaching schoolgirls to ride.'

The engine spluttered and died on him.

'Oh, come on!' wrangled Niall, a broad hand still on the roof of the car. 'Have you ever watched her? She's not bad at all and she's fucking brave. Sure, she just needs someone to give her a few tips. He's not an easy horse to ride – I bet he'd even give you a run for your travellers' cheques now.'

He has, thought Hugo. He didn't want anyone to know the battle he'd had with Tash's horse the morning he'd ridden him. But the pure power and talent he'd discovered, mixed with the exquisite smell of a challenge, had been manna to him.

'I'm not tutoring Tash French,' he repeated crossly.

This holiday had been a waste of time already. He was missing a huge chunk of the eventing calendar in order to patch up his and Amanda's tepid relationship at her insistence. Now she seemed to be even more tempestuous and wayward than ever in her desperation to rattle him, which, like the sight of an open nappy, only served to back Hugo further off. Ben was sulking because he'd crocked his ankle, Sophia was being a bitch and to cap it all her goofy sister had turned out to own the best horse he'd seen in years and was totally unwilling to sell it. He wasn't about to do her any favours. No, thank you.

This time the engine gave a throaty splutter and caught.

'Look,' persisted Niall, raising his voice over the sound of the car. 'Didn't you tell me last night you needed something to tax you? Tash seems a hard worker, she's not spoilt – she'd be a dream to teach. You could have great fun now.'

Hugo laughed dryly. He was about to say that he'd have more fun darning his underpants all week when an idea struck him.

Helping out Tash French could get her on his side. She wasn't about to sell the chestnut to him after he'd lost his temper and dunked her on Sunday. She certainly hadn't reacted well when he'd flirted with her; she'd backed off like a terrified animal.

Hugo reflected sourly on the fact that – although he found Tash disconcertingly odd – he'd taken Amanda's advice and forced himself to come on to her to try and persuade her to change her mind. It was strange but he'd found himself absurdly turned on by her trembling nervousness, her long, soft body and huge, unusual eyes. The fury he'd directed at her afterwards was not because she had turned him down but because yet again she'd made him feel out of control, his emotions running away with him like Snob did with her. He'd ended up screwing the all-too willing Paola, whom he didn't really fancy, as a result.

The episode had left a bad taste in his mouth and a feeling of being strangely one-down, not to mention a lot of sotto Italian he now had to dodge.

Yet if he helped Tash with Snob, he'd be taking command. He could make her trust his judgment implicitly, work her till her bones ached, until she was hugely grateful to him and yes, until Snob did improve. But all the time he'd be playing a careful, persuasive and relentless waiting game. Although he must help her, he must also make sure she was never totally confident on the big horse, always dependent on Hugo. If she ended up feeling completely obligated to Hugo, yet aware of the enormous task of keeping Snob, then surely she would willingly accept his generous offer of a replacement?

It was certainly a challenge. And a long shot. But, as he'd pretty much burnt all his bateaux and yet wanted the chestnut stallion more than ever, he'd give it a go.

'All right,' he said slowly. 'As a favour for an old mate, I'll do it.'

'Great!' laughed Niall, feeling better. At least he could stop worrying about Tash French for a while. And Hugo. He'd upset enough people today without dropping Hugo in it as well.

But now he'd got used to the idea, Hugo seemed genuinely pleased. Niall watched him drive grinning out of the yard and then waving out of the sunroof as he accelerated rapidly down the long, tree-lined drive. It was, as he'd thought, the challenge Hugo was looking for. He smiled warmly at a passing chicken.

He then set off back to Matty, chastising himself for getting a kick out of helping Tash. He'd been feeling so sorry for himself recently that all charity had gone out of the window. He'd become selfish and twisted. The trouble is, he reflected sadly, that I help people to get them off my conscience, not for their own sakes.

Pausing to light a cigarette by the rusting metal gate, he vowed that in future he'd concentrate on other people's feelings.

Walking back to the pool through the garden he caught sight of Amanda sitting forlornly on one of the swings which Pascal had rigged up for the kids. Under the shadow of the tall sycamore she'd lost the dangerous, incandescent glow of a replica Lisette trying to taunt and haunt him. She looked as small and vulnerable as a lonely child who'd been last to be picked for the lacrosse team again.

He walked over to her. She looked up at him defiantly, hiding her hurt pride under a cold, unfriendly gaze.

'Look, I'm really sorry about what I said earlier,' he said honestly. 'It's not fair to take out my black mood on you and I apologise.'

'That's okay,' Amanda replied flatly. She plainly didn't forgive him.

'I'll tell you what.' He felt a blob of rain ricochet off his nose. 'The others will be back soon. Let's you and I and Matty – who I happen to know is babysitting a bottle of scotch by the pool – go and hide somewhere inside and drink off our hangovers.'

He didn't really want her to come and suspected she would be too proud to accept anyway. He'd already broken his vow. He wondered how many Hail Marys a lapsed Catholic would have to say for being as two-faced as a bad penny?

Amanda glared at him for a minute and then smiled. 'I'd like that. I'd like it a lot.'

Niall decided God was not on his side today. Forget the Hail Marys, O'Shaughnessy my son, He was saying, you take your hollow offers and you just follow them through now.

Niall looked up at the sky, sighed, and winked dejectedly. He got a huge raindrop in the eye in return.

Matty, who'd grown increasingly concerned that Niall was taking so long to fetch two glasses, was further perturbed when he returned with Hugo's argumentative girlfriend and nothing to drink out of.

'What are we going to put the whisky into, Niall?' he asked, torn between amusement and worry.

'Into Amanda,' Niall said with a rather unsteady smile. 'And ourselves, of course.'

Amanda, staring idly at the warship-grey horizon, stopped brooding about Hugo's indifference and smiled to herself. She calculated that she could bed Niall O'Shaughnessy in twenty-four hours.

19

Friday morning, both in France and across the Channel in West Sussex, started with a steady, monotonous downpour.

In Hurstfield, great, gunmetal-grey eiderdowns massed on the horizon as Michael Hennessy crammed the Volvo boot with well-worn suitcases. The wind kept whipping the hood of his Gortex off so that now his bald head was glistening. Water was dripping down the back of his neck and creeping under the collar of his Tattersal checked shirt.

Cass came running out, holding the *Daily Telegraph* over her head.

'Have you put the green case in yet, Michael? I think I've packed the ferry tickets in it by mistake.'

Michael had painstakingly loaded the boot in precise order so that the weight and size of items were distributed evenly. It was a trick he'd learnt from his days in the army. The large, cumbersome green suitcase was neatly wedged in the centre-back of the boot under two grip bags, another suitcase, several blankets and a pile of sunhats.

After Michael had carefully extracted it, Cass remembered that the tickets were in the top drawer of the desk in the Trophy Room.

'Can you get Marcus to bring his bloody stuff out, old girl?' Michael called after her as she ran inside, the soggy *Telegraph* now affording little protection. 'We're rapidly running out of bloody room.'

Cass hated the feel of the house now that Enoch had gone to kennels; the kitchen seemed strangely cold and empty without him. A half-eaten Bonio lay forlornly by the Aga.

She quickly poured yet another cup of coffee for Marcus and took it up to his room. She'd started the long and arduous task of getting her son out of bed and packing his stuff at eight o'clock that morning. Michael was so punctilious about his planned set-off time – 'Ten hundred hours, old girl. On the dot.' – that she was quite sure he'd leave Marcus behind if he wasn't ready. So far she had taken Marcus up three cups of tea, a bowl of CoCo Pops and two cups of coffee. The last time she'd gone up he'd actually heaved himself out of bed and was wandering round his room in a pair of boxer shorts, looking almost awake.

She knocked on his door and walked in. Marcus was back in bed with his sock drawer on the duvet in front of him, sorting out piles of lurid, ill-matched pairs.

'Marcus, aren't you dressed yet?' Cass put the cup of coffee down on his bedside table and picked up the one he had let go cold.

'Yeah, man.' Marcus lifted up the duvet to reveal a grubby 'House of Love' t-shirt and a pair of flared jeans similar to the ones that Alexandra and Cass had worn in the sixties.

'Oh.' Cass looked around the room for a suitcase. The floor was carpeted wall-to-wall in crumpled clothes, which also upholstered every item of furniture. A huge rucksack lay by the bed. She peeked inside it. It was almost entirely filled with tapes and CDs.

'How near are you to being ready?' she asked hopefully, as Marcus squinted intently at a pair of red socks with 'Traffic' written on them. 'Your father wants to know.'

He gave the socks a thorough sniffing before throwing them into the rucksack.

'Nearly there, like, man.' Marcus discarded the sock drawer and heaved himself out of bed. He then started picking clothes off the floor and flinging them in the general direction of the rucksack, mostly missing.

'There's clean clothes in the wardrobe,' Cass pointed out, noticing a particularly squalid pair of yellow shorts hit their target.

'Only totally *un*happening gear, y'know?' Marcus dug around under the bed and withdrew a crumpled t-shirt.

Cass couldn't bear to watch. She'd bought him some lovely new shirts in M and S last week, none of which he liked. How could he prefer something made from J-cloth material with 'Johnny Fartpants' written on the front?

She went downstairs to find the tickets.

Sophia was on her third list that morning. She was sitting at the huge, old baronial desk in Pascal's office, looking out at the grey valley and chewing the end of a Mont Blanc thoughtfully.

She watched the progress of a huge raindrop speeding down the window-pane, then slowing as it linked into the network of the other little tributaries creeping towards the sill. She turned her attention back to the piece of white paper in front of her and wrote *Still Left To Arrange.* She then dotted the *i* neatly, then reformed the wonky *f*. Then she underlined it twice and looked at the window again.

She could see Niall wandering round in the garden in only his shirt sleeves. He was soaked through, his hair flattened to his head and his old jeans dark blue with wet. Eyebrows arching towards her hairline, Sophia watched him stop and stare out at the valley. The soggy book he was holding slipped from his fingers and dropped on to the flattened grass.

Really, Sophia mused, he might be a famous star but he's totally unhinged. She wished she hadn't sold the banquet to her friends quite so much on his being there.

She returned to her list and wrote: *disco (DJ, sound system, lighting), breakfast, wine waiters (use food caterers? or seperate firm?), caterers' costumes, outdoor lighting, strolling players, other entertainment?, hire long tables, cutlery (knives only) – no crockery needed, bouncers and car parkers?, somewhere to land helicopters.* Perhaps that was a little optimistic. She hadn't had replies from any of the real jet-setters yet. But it was early days. Perhaps they would need a landing strip for private planes? She wrote *field to park cars jets*. It looked good. She underlined it.

There seemed so much still to do and the night itself was only two weeks away. It was as if she had only just started. She had, however, been working non-stop for over a week to organise this party. She'd got all the invitations out, hired the caterers, discussed the menu so that it was authentically medieval, ordered the champagne (was a bottle and a half per head adequate?), located a company that made mead (it had to be shipped in from England, which Pascal had grumbled about). She had arranged the hire of goblets and seating, ordered hundreds of candles and ornate flower arrangements. She had even booked a band with a minstrel's harp, hurdy gurdy, fiddle, lute, psaltery and tenor madrigal singer. She never seemed to have stopped yet there was more to do than ever.

She added *construct stage for band* and *find spare bedding for drunken guests* to the bottom of the list.

Amanda sauntered into the study, looking bored and fed up in white jeans and one of Hugo's silk shirts.

'Not much to do around here when it's pissing down, is there?' she grumbled sourly, reading the list over Sophia's shoulder. 'Oh Boy. Shouldn't you add *charge entrance fee* and *hire portaloos*?'

Sophia chose to say nothing.

Amanda leaned against the desk. 'I wish someone would come to the village with me. Pascal's run out of vodka again.'

'It's only eleven o'clock,' Sophia lectured disapprovingly, adding *and rooms* to *bedding*. 'Can't you get Hugo to go with you?'

'We're not talking again. And besides, he's sitting by the back door waiting for the rain to stop like an unwalked dog. God knows why. What about *sick buckets*?'

'What are the others doing?' Sophia wished Amanda would go away. She couldn't concentrate with her moaning on and scrutinising every word she wrote.

'Well, Pascal and your mother have gone shopping – you've spelled *separate* wrong – they're taking Ben to see the doctor on the way for some reason.'

'His foot keeps swelling up,' said Sophia tautly. She'd got precious little sleep last night with Ben heaving his cast about like a dreaming footballer and muttering 'knitting needle' deliriously in his sleep.

'Matty and Sally are trying to hold the kids down for more than five minutes at a time so that your lumbering sister can draw them,' Amanda went on with a malicious smile, making a paper aeroplane out of an earlier list. 'One of the little terrors has already buried her pencil in a pot-plant.'

'Which one?' asked Sophia, who liked hearing about Matty's children misbehaving.

'Hart's Tongue Fern, I think.' Amanda gave up on the aeroplane and started leafing through Pascal's mail.

'Don't you ever wish you had your own baby, Amanda?' Sophia asked, turning to look at her kindly. 'You don't want to leave it too late, you know.' That would get rid of her, she thought smugly. Amanda's idea of babysitting was literally squashing them till they were quiet.

Amanda shivered. She'd had enough of screaming children on this holiday to put her off for life. 'Too much like hard work – I've only just got Hugo to say please and thank you. By the way, I saw Paola trying to teach Polly to change Josh's nappy. It was a scream – he had a Pampers on his head like a turban, wailing his little guts out.' That'll piss her off, thought Amanda in return. Sophia was getting horribly narcissistic and superior since she'd started organising this party.

'Did you? How sweet.' Sophia refused to rise. Instead she thought up another tactic. 'I'm glad you're here, actually, Amanda. Could you be an angel and make a few phone calls for me? My French is so rusty. I need to get a disco organised and sort out and hire some more bits and bobs. Just let me find the numbers.'

'God! There's Niall standing in the pouring rain,' exclaimed Amanda quickly. 'He'll get pneumonia. I'll go and fetch him inside.' She set off to the door. 'Oh, sorry about the phone calls, Sophia. Another time.' And she dashed off gratefully.

Sophia heaved a sigh of relief and returned to her list. Then, as she saw Amanda approaching Niall across the lawn, she remembered Polly and the nappy. She charged off to give the increasingly wayward Paola a piece of her mind.

Marcus had hidden his stash in the loose sole of his trainers, sticking it together again with Copydex, which he could unglue with lighter fuel in France. This had seemed to work ideally until he was in the duty free shop aboard the ferry. As he trailed round behind his mother, putting cartons of cigarettes in her basket as fast as she took them out again, the heel of his shoe started to work loose. He could hear it flopping down on the linoleum floor a fraction of a second before his foot made contact. It gradually came down more and more independently of the rest of his trainer. By the time he was in the perfume section, being gassed out by his mother trying samples on him because she had run out of space on herself, the sole of his shoe had virtually come off completely. He had to walk along with his left foot sliding along the ground.

Cass trotted off to the spirits section, basket swinging, head-scarf flapping. Marcus shuffled behind. A uniformed security guard was eyeing him suspiciously.

'Do you think they'd prefer scotch or gin?' his mother called out. 'Do hurry up, Marcus, and stop dawdling. Why are you walking with a limp?'

Marcus shrugged and mumbled something about a trolley wheel catching him. Mercifully, Cass was too wrapped up in deciding between Beefeater and Gordons to notice that there were no trolleys.

Marcus, by an amazing series of contortions, managed to preserve his cellophaned bundle within his rubber shoe until they reached the bar. This was not made any easier by the fact that his mother had given him both bags of duty free to carry, so he didn't have a hand free to reach down and pocket the little parcel. As soon as they sat down he could rescue it.

Cass searched the mass of seasick faces for Michael's. Ah! There he was. Having grabbed a table, Michael had saved one seat by putting his coat on it and was now having a tug of war with a young man – who was much bigger than him and had tattoos – for another. His pipe was clenched between his teeth more determinedly than ever. He knocked one of the drinks he had set down earlier with his elbow as he kept his furious grip on the metal legs.

'Come on, Marcus,' ordered Cass, grabbing her son's thin arm. 'I think someone needs rescuing from your father.'

As she propelled him across the room, ricocheting him off arms clutching mortgaged glasses of overpriced drinks to the accompaniment of wails of fury, Marcus felt the little lump of dope fall from his shoe. Looking round desperately, he saw it rolling across the patterned carpet to be speared firmly on the four-inch heel of a passing blonde. As his mother took the disputed seat and pushed him into it, Marcus watched his stash walk upstairs and into the Ladies.

Later, in Cherbourg, Wendy Bates from Croydon was totally horrified to find herself being interrogated for attempting to smuggle a small quantity of cannabis resin into France. She didn't know anything about it, honest, Monsieur, Wendy pleaded in a small voice. She and her mates had only come to France for the day to buy some wine and Camembert. She didn't have a clue how two ounces of wacky-backy had ended up on her shoe. It must have been planted, Monsieur.

The rain started to fall less heavily from midday. Small patches of lighter sky could be glimpsed trying to elbow their way between the heavy grey duvets, like wingers through a scrum. The strong wind was pushing the rumbling sky over towards Germany and leaving a blustery drizzle whipping the manoir.

By the time Alexandra and Pascal returned, loaded up with fresh supplies, the sky overhead was almost white and the skin-permeating dampness had all but abated.

Tash, fed up with only getting as far as drawing Tor's eyes or chin before the little girl had needed to use the potty or burst into tears because she was bored, helped her mother unload the jeep, assisted by Polly, who was dressed as a fireman. Delicious smells of freshly baked bread, ripe fruit and garlic sausages filled her nose. There was a whole side of smoked salmon and piles of unusual cheeses: veined, matured, goat's, smoked, with walnuts, port, Cointreau or herbs. Tash longed to take it all up to her room and have a wicked binge. She nearly passed out when she saw the huge box of chocolate-covered cherries.

'I know I bought some cherry chocs on Monday,' explained Alexandra, heaving out a bag full of fresh fish, 'but I think the children got at them. They'd all disappeared by Tuesday morning. Not that I mind, I just hope they didn't swallow the stones.' She put the bag haphazardly under her arm, depositing a king prawn on the cobbles.

Tash thought guiltily of the little pile of cherry stones on her dressing table. To hide her red cheeks, she buried herself in the back of the jeep, fetching out a huge chamber pot that weighed a ton. It was coated with paintings of plump, naked women draped provocatively over satin-covered four posters.

'Isn't it wonderful?' sighed Alexandra. 'Apparently, it originally came from a brothel in Angers frequented by the aristocracy. During the Revolution, the catins would lure members of the gentry into their boudoirs, then their maquereaux – pimps – would pop out from behind a curtain and grab the overexcited Count or whatever. Sometimes, or so the story goes, they got so carried away that they never got the poor aristo as far as the guillotine. They'd cut off his head there and then and put it in that chamber pot. Quite what they did with the body, I don't know.' She smiled happily at Tash. 'I'm going to give it to Cass and Michael.' She then wandered inside, depositing more king prawns, like Hansel's trail of breadcrumbs, in her wake.

They all lunched around the delectably overloaded kitchen table, watched with feverish intensity by a group of drooling spaniels. Ben, his freshly bandaged foot propped up on the chamber pot, ate three times as much as anybody else just in case his mother-in-law forgot dinner again.

Afterwards, the children were suitably distracted with a mountainous pile of Lego, an equally large amount of Play-do and a sulking Paola on the floor of one of the tattier, unrenovated rooms, while the adults drank strong and scalding coffee in the China Room.

It was still too cold to go out on to either of the terraces, but at least the wind had dropped. Small areas of blue were now patching the holes in the cloud. Out of the window Jean, Gitane clenched between his gums, could be seen staggering through the garden with an ancient pair of rusted secateurs and a length of rope. He'd often been glimpsed in a similar fashion since the house guests arrived, but in the garden nothing visibly changed.

Hugo was looking at Tash expectantly – when was she going to shuffle off to the yard? He was bored and wanted to start his plan of action.

Niall glanced at Hugo thoughtfully – would he bother to try and help Tash? He liked Hugo but, feeling more together than yesterday, was beginning to mistrust his motives.

Amanda was staring at Niall hopefully – had he responded to her charms yet? He was so wrapped up in himself it was hard to tell. Last night he'd been all over her, knocking back whisky and boring her rigid as he rambled on about Irish politics until he passed out on a sofa. Later, Matty had marched him off to bed with a sandwich, like a starch-capped matron. Today, she could have been stuffed and mounted and he'd barely afford her a cursory glance. Instead, she turned to wink at Pascal.

Flashing an oblique smile, Pascal observed Amanda with bemusement – why did the foxy Englishwoman blow hot and cold? He found her ver' attractive but preferred his dreamy, sexy Alexandra.

Sophia was considering Pascal calculatingly – would he stretch to the expense of a professional fireworks show?

Over the rim of his coffee cup, Matty watched Sophia's face intently – how could money and a title make his sister so different? She used to be much kinder, less narrow-minded.

Sally saw Matty's face harden and worried that he was thinking about money again. Why couldn't he swallow his pride and borrow some? They could pay it back eventually. And then there was the new baby . . .

Tash was gazing into space.

Alexandra in the meantime was telling everyone about the chamber pot. She had a strange feeling that no one was really listening. She hoped she wasn't becoming an attention grabber in her old age, but since organising this family gathering she was feeling more and more left out. It was as if everyone was taking off in a balloon without her, leaving her to watch from far below. There were so many complicated cross-currents that she couldn't quite latch on to, like trailing ropes just out of her reach.

Perhaps she was just being silly. After all, her plans seemed to be working. Tash was having a great time with her horse, and looking more and more gorgeous. She was tanned the colour of iced tea now; her strange, unpaired eyes stood out like expressive islands in her brown face. Sophia seemed content, too. Getting her to organise the party had been such a good idea. Now Alexandra just had to sort out Matty. Sally had confided that – although delighted – they were worried about the expense of another child. How could Alexandra help them out without Matty's stupid pride getting in the way? She would have to be very careful . . .

'Get out of the way, you bloody idiot!' Michael leaned on the horn as a confused-looking French lorry driver went up the verge – and nearly into a poplar – to miss him.

'I think it was his right of way, dear,' Cass pointed out calmly.

'Rubbish!' snapped Michael, 'bloody man couldn't drive.' He relit his pipe, steering with his knee. 'You all right back there, Marcus old boy?'

'Feel a bit sick, actually, man.' Marcus had gone green.

'Pass him back one of those plastic bags in the glove compartment, would you, old girl?' Michael turned left without checking for oncoming traffic, leaving a furious burst of Renault and Citroën horns behind him.

Marcus chucked up into a Millets bag. Not particularly happening.

* * *

When Tash rode into the paddock that afternoon she nearly fell off in shock to find Hugo sitting on one of the wine casks, smoking a cigarette. His dark glasses hid any expression on his face.

Tash started to panic. Panic because, despite his nastiness, she couldn't stop her heart beating faster than Toccata and Fugue when she saw him. And panic because she knew he despised her. What was he going to do? Drag her off Snob and burn holes in her jeans until she agreed to sell him? Taunt her every time she fell off? If only he knew that all he had to do was kiss her and tell her she was beautiful and she would melt like an ice cube in his pastis.

'Hello there.' He smiled lazily, showing a perfect set of white, even teeth. 'I've come to apologise.' He stood up.

Snob spooked backwards, rolling his eyes.

'S-sorry?' Tash hung on. She couldn't quite believe her ears.

'Exactly. Sorry and all that. I've been behaving very selfishly.' He walked up to Snob who flattened his ears before placidly letting him pat his red neck. 'I'd like to make it up to you, if I may.'

Tash looked down on him incredulously. Sitting on Snob so close to Hugo gave her a new perspective on him. The top of his head with its lustrous, wavy hair that flopped over his forehead was just level with her hands. She longed to hook a thick, shining curl around her finger. He'd probably bite it off. She must get a grip on herself.

'Er . . .' she was at a bit of a loss for what to say. Was he having her on? Since the pool episode he'd cut her dead at every opportunity.

'I'd like to give you a hand.' Hugo's dark glasses reflected the bustling clouds overhead like two weather maps. 'That is if you want me to.' He cleared his throat. 'Truth is, I'm pretty bored just sitting around getting slaughtered all day. I figure if you're not going to let me buy the horse, I can't sulk for ever about it.' He dropped the cigarette on to the damp grass and covered it with his shoe. 'Look, am I making any sense here?'

'Mmm,' Tash mumbled. Having never held a straight conversation with Hugo, she found his new-found openness confusing and almost embarrassing.

'So what would you like to do?' she asked eventually.

'Do? Oh yes, I see. Do.' Hugo looked across the paddock and into the distance. 'Well, it's up to you, really. Either I back off and leave you alone.' He wished he hadn't said that – she'd probably jump at the chance. 'Or,' he added quickly, 'I'll try to help you out. Give you the benefit of my experience. No ulterior motive – except that you'd be doing me a favour. I need something to do. I think I could give you a few good pointers to have more control and confidence. You see, your main problem is your seat – sorry, I'm off already.'

'No, please carry on.' Tash urged. Her mind was racing. She didn't really believe it – Hugo wanting to help her out just didn't ring true. Yet her wild, fantasising imagination was carrying itself away again. Hugo standing in the middle of the paddock in the lengthening evening shadows, watching her jump Snob and giving shouts of encouragement. Herself and Hugo sitting alone in the village bar until late at night, discussing Snob's problems over a vintage Pinot Blanc. Hugo catching her eye over dinner, sharing a secret joke.

'The trouble is you need to go back to basics before you can really help out the horse,' Hugo was saying. 'You may want to tell me to get lost but, honestly, an animal like that can sense lack of confidence and will play on it. If you didn't have so many problems in your technique, you'd find it much easier to control him.'

Tash wanted to be humble, but found her ego defending itself. 'I'm very out of practice,' she muttered, as Snob started to spook at a piece of flapping twine in the hedge.

'I know, I know,' Hugo tried not to be impatient with the silly cow.

'W-what do you suggest I do?' Like a ballerina doing spins, Tash tried to look at him as Snob leaped about.

'You could start by putting that horse away and tacking up Anton's.'

'But—' Tash objected. Sensing rejection, Snob stopped four-square and suddenly looked angelic.

'I said it was you who needed the work to start off with,' Hugo said, wondering why the hell he was doing this. He'd rather be screwing Amanda, but she was sulking and he had nothing better to do. He supposed that must be it.

Tash considered telling him to forget it, but she had to admit she needed his help. Paola seemed to have gone totally off the idea of riding and rapidly off Tash since her liaison with Hugo, and Tash couldn't say she was disappointed.

She knew that her progress with Snob was painfully slow on her own. With someone as experienced as Hugo to advise her, she could improve in leaps and bounds. Besides this was a chance in a million to get close to him. Perhaps not in the way she would ideally have wanted – she was laying herself open for some pretty serious humiliation – but anything was better than his complete contempt.

So she rode an enraged Snob back into the yard and put him away.

Two hours later, Tash thought she would explode in frustration, as she bounced round another circuit, staring at Bouchon's straggly white mane and lop ears. Her back and legs were aching to the very marrow of her rattling bones. She had lost radio contact with her bottom half an hour ago when she passed the pain threshold for the eighth time. Her head was sweating as the crash skull Pascal had bought her that morning became like a sauna with someone holding a watering can constantly over the coals. Even her eyes were sweating so much her contact lenses had to tread water.

'Don't hold on to his fucking mane!' screamed Hugo for the third time in a minute. He lit a cigarette and watched her coolly from the wine cask.

He's enjoying this, thought Tash angrily, trying not to cry. He's really bloody enjoying this. Well, I agreed to let him help, I'm not flaming well going to let him have the satisfaction of watching me fail. If he wants a battle of wills then he's going to get one.

For the past two hours – and to Tash it seemed like twenty – Hugo had made her do nothing but trot and canter round in circles at the end of a lunge line. To spice this up, he'd removed the stirrups and leathers from her saddle and knotted Bouchon's reins away from her reach. He'd then made Tash put her hands on her head, which left her arms screaming for relief and her shoulders stiffer than a Barbour that's been left outside for a year. Time after time she'd felt herself slipping off to meet the ground with a heavy thump. She was too stiff even to bounce.

Bouchon was pretty fed up, too. This was asking too much of an old, wise horse. He was bored and tired. Although they had stopped every now and again to give him a breather while Hugo made Tash touch her toes with opposite hands and get on and off without the stirrups, Bouchon was by now at the point of flaking. He wanted a good, long roll and a drink. Most of all he wanted . . .

Tash flew over his shoulders as the old horse came to a shuddering halt and dropped his head to graze. She landed painfully on her arm and lay on the ground getting her wind back, relishing not having to move for a moment or two.

'Get back on!' Hugo bellowed from behind her.

Bastard, thought Tash. At least this would exorcise her crush if anything would. But as she painfully got up and turned round to him, his beautiful, set face once again made her feel agonisingly in love. Have you got bad taste or what, she asked herself sadly.

'I think the horse has had enough,' she croaked unsteadily.

Bouchon was sweating as heavily as Tash. His ewe neck had turned dark grey, lathered in little kiss curls. His big drop belly was heaving and his lop ears more dejected than ever.

Tash felt simply awful that they'd put the poor old horse through this. He'd looked so happy when she'd tacked him up, having been pretty much ignored since he arrived at the manoir. Now he looked utterly miserable. She stroked and patted his neck softly and loosened his girth.

'You're right,' grunted Hugo, feeling like a shit. He never mistreated horses as a rule. Not honest ones. He'd been enjoying taking Tash French down a peg or two so much that he hadn't noticed how tired the old horse was getting.

'Yes, put him away,' he directed. He was about to suggest she tack up Snob again when he noticed the time on his watch. Had they really been at it for two hours? It seemed they'd only just started.

'Look,' he said walking over to Tash. He realised he'd have to justify himself a bit. 'I know I seem to be giving you hell, but it's honestly the only way. You'll see it working wonders if you stick with it for a few days, you've got a lot of potential. A lot.' He gave her a devastating smile.

A few days! Tash bit her lip. *Tell him to get lost, Tash, tell him.* But he says I've got a lot of potential, and that's coming from someone who told me I'd ruin Snob. *He's just doing it to make a fool out of you, Tash.* He's helping me. *He's laughing at you.* I love him.

'Thanks,' she mumbled, and she and Bouchon walked towards the yard like a pair of arthritic octogenarians.

Hugo made his way back to the house with rather mixed feelings. The fact Tash had actually thanked him for overworking her so much that she would be too stiff even to get out of bed tomorrow, made him smile. How stupid could you get? Yet when he'd told her she had potential he hadn't been lying, and that worried him. Niall was right when he said she was both brave and uncomplaining.

Hugo was torn. He could see Tash making a bloody good rider. Good enough to compete at a high level if she wanted to. She had natural balance and rhythm – he doubted he could have stayed on much longer than she did and he'd ridden all his life – and she was terrifically determined. But all this didn't stop him disliking her. She'd been a complete pain in the bum over the chestnut. He owed her no favours.

He smiled to himself as he walked into the hall. He was going to make Tash French work until her great long legs dropped off. Until she hated getting on Snob far more than she hated the idea of selling him to Hugo. She'd be grateful to get rid of him by the time he'd finished with her.

* * *

'I'm sure we should have gone left there, Michael.'

'Nonsense, old girl. If we'd gone bloody left we'd have ended up going back the bloody way we came.'

'I feel sick again, man.'

'Shut up, Marcus! Look at this sign, Michael. It says Angers fifty kilometres. We just came from there, dear.'

'So we did, old girl, so we bloody did. Hang on tight.'

'I don't think you're allowed to do a U-turn here, dear!'

'Holy shit – I'm gonna frow up again – Pass us anuver plastic bag, Mum.'

Edinburgh Woollen Mill this time. Marginally more happening than Millets.

'Look, Michael! Champegny-sur-Loire, eight kilometres to the right – RIGHT, DEAR, RIGHT!'

'Don't panic, old girl. I'm not deaf yet. What's that bloody frog doing?' Loud horn beep. 'Get off the bloody road, you moron!'

'If you insist on smoking, could you wind down your window, Marcus?'

Marcus wished for the hundredth time that day that he hadn't got expelled. This holiday was destined to be one of the least crucial things in his life.

'*They're here!* Quick, everybody, Cass and Michael are here.'

Alexandra rushed out into the courtyard then, waving at Cass and Michael in the Volvo, rushed back in again.

'I think she's probably gone quite mad,' Cass muttered to Michael, waving and smiling at her sister from behind the windscreen.

Alexandra reappeared clutching Polly, whose fireman helmet had slipped over her face, dragging an unenthusiastic Tom behind her.

As Cass and Michael got out of the car (Marcus felt too ill to move), Sophia appeared at the top of the steps like Princess Diana at a photo call, holding Josh, with Lotty at her feet. Behind her, Sally's dishevelled blonde head popped round the door and she waved at Cass before disappearing.

'Everyone's at sixes and sevens,' laughed Alexandra, coming forward to meet them. She gave Cass a warm hug. 'Let me look at you, my darling. Gosh, you're as perfectly turned out as ever. I don't know how you do it.'

'You're looking lovely yourself,' Cass had to admit, brushing imaginary creases out of her pleated navy skirt and wishing she'd left more time to diet.

'Michael—' Alexandra leaned forward to give the tall, angular man a kiss. He was so stiff-backed it was like kissing Nelson's Column. 'So nice to see you again, sweetheart. It's been ages.'

'Yes. Bloody long time.' Alexandra always made Michael feel rather idiotic. He resisted a temptation to wipe the kiss away, much as one would with an aged aunt.

'And who's this?' Alexandra pounced on the lurking figure in the back of the car. 'Marcus! My God, you've grown into a definite hunk. I love your hair.'

'Yo, Aunt Alex.'

'Are you all right? You look a bit peaky.'

'He gets car-sick,' explained Cass, wishing Marcus could be a little more presentable. He was smoking another cigarette now and had put on a very strange pair of circular-rimmed dark glasses.

'He needs a good stiff brandy to calm his stomach,' recommended Alexandra.

Marcus perked up and got out of the car, holding the two plastic bags away from him like time bombs.

Cass was about to object when Sophia arrived at her side and started saying hello.

Michael looked at Alexandra. 'I don't know if the old boy should really be drinking spirits at his—'

'And you, Michael, must be simply dying for a huge scotch.' Alexandra linked arms with him.

'Well, I wouldn't say no to a quick shot.'

'Super. Come on, Marcus, give those bags to Sophia to carry if you're feeling fragile, let's all go into the house and meet the others.' Alexandra led the way towards the steps.

'Nice old place this,' Michael said to her as they went inside.

'Cass tells me you're trying to do it up yourselves, bloody brave.' And he started on his long-winded story about The Old Rectory's dry rot.

Following behind at a safe distance, Cass walked slowly inside with Sophia.

'Really? I thought he was working on some Northern Ireland documentary.'

'Apparently not . . . can't get the backing or something,' Sophia whispered. 'No, Cass darling, they're totally broke. Sally was looking for a job when they found out she was pregnant,' Sophia dropped her voice even lower. 'Now one doesn't like to stir, but my guess is they've come over here to borrow money.'

'Never!' Cass whispered in conspiratorial surprise. 'Matty isn't like that, is he?'

'Why else visit Mummy for the first time since she remarried?' Sophia shrugged. 'I'm sure they can't afford a holiday at the moment.'

Cass supposed she had a point. 'Now, dear, you must tell me about this party – oh! But first I want to know about Tash – why in heaven's name did Alex give her a horse? I didn't think she was ever much good at riding. Not like you.'

Sophia smirked. 'Well, my darling . . .'

The Hennessys met up with the others over tea on the patio.

Cass was surprised to find Amanda Fraser-Roberts such a nice girl – Sophia had made her out to sound a fearful hanger-on. But Amanda was both attractive and attentive, sitting through Michael's twenty-minute description of the journey without looking bored once. She even asked questions, which to Cass was the height of politeness when listening to Michael.

She was less impressed by the arrogant Niall O'Shaughnessy. *Very* strange man. He didn't seem at all interested in talking about Ireland or about acting, subjects on which she tried to draw him out. He just slurped his tea noisily and then rudely went into a corner to smoke endless cigarettes with Pascal – the lecherous drunk had nearly caused a fight by kissing Michael on both cheeks – and a willing Marcus. Uttering his hellos, Ben limped over to join them, his foot trussed up in layers of bandages, having developed an allergy to his plaster cast. Cass couldn't hear what they were talking about, but was sure it wasn't suitable for Marcus's ears. They kept laughing raucously.

Instead, she focused her attention on Matty. He was looking too thin as ever. Sally should take more care of him, she reflected, envisaging their fridge full of boil-in-the-bags and half-empty tonic bottles.

Cass had never fully approved of Sally – she encouraged Matty in his strange political ideas: turning down well-paid jobs for idealistic reasons, supporting him in his refusal to join his father's company, sending Tom to a state school and making him play with dolls, dressing Tor up in dungarees. She remembered their wedding. Dreadful. A register office do, no religious blessing, Sally and Matty in jeans. All those awful, trendy friends of theirs dressed up like extras in *Doctor Who*. The reception held in a *pub* of all places, with loud music and jugs of beer. Cass shuddered at the thought.

Things hadn't changed much. Matty still looked like he needed a good night's sleep. Sally was scruffier than ever in an ancient Laura Ashley pinafore with nothing underneath and a floppy straw hat covering messy blonde hair in need of a wash. 'Sexy little thing,' Michael had once described her. Cass had given him very short shrift for that.

'So what have you been doing to the house in Richmond, Sally?' she asked, smiling charmingly.

'Living in it,' Sally smiled back with equal charm, ignoring Matty's kick under the table. 'No, I started off with great intentions,' she confessed, 'but so far I've only papered Tom's room and painted half of the downstairs loo. I only have to look at a colour chart before someone comes round demanding coffee or a guided tour. Matty's got three friends he met in Canada staying there at the moment. We've given them tins of Dulux and brushes and told them that their rent is a wall a week.' She giggled.

'But I thought it was virtually derelict,' countered Cass in surprise.

'It is,' Matty shrugged. 'But it's so huge it's difficult to know where to start, like the Forth Bridge. At least the fact it's terraced means that it won't fall down for the time being. The houses on either side hold it up.'

'But you can't live like that!' quacked Cass in a shocked voice. 'Think of the children.'

'They love it,' said Sally simply. 'Tom and his friends can scribble all over the walls without getting yelled at and Tor can bury whatever she likes in the garden.' She winked at Matty. 'We can have all the parties we want, can even invite Matty's friends because there aren't any carpets to stain or burn holes in. The best thing is that when we fight, Matty and I can fling everything in reach at each other without worrying about breakages – the mould provides a soft landing.' She grinned at Cass, enjoying winding her up.

'Plus the fact that it annoys the neighbours,' continued Matty. 'We've got an unbelievably pompous osteopath on the left. He sent us a letter requesting that we got the stairs carpeted because the noise of Sal charging upstairs was annoying his patients. So now we pretend to be having a screw next door to his waiting room every day. That or a blazing row with more expletives than a Jim Cartwright play.'

'He sent us another letter last week, demanding that we, quote, confine our marriage to outside office hours,' Sally laughed.

'He didn't!' Matty looked at her.

'I forgot to show you.' Sally apologised hastily, remembering that it was with the buried bills. 'It arrived by hand after you'd gone to work. I've kept it, though. It's at home.'

'Right,' Matty announced firmly. 'You know what this means, Salls. Plan B.'

'What's that?' asked Alexandra, pouring Sally another cup of tea, most of which went over her pinafore. She thought all this a tremendous hoot.

'After positioning myself beside the waiting-room wall and screaming accusations to Salls of infidelity with the overweight osteopath next door,' Matty explained, 'I murder her and the kids very loudly at about half-past ten, then put on my Leonard

Cohen tape and sob noisily for half an hour before doing myself in just as his eleven o'clock appointment arrives.'

'Don't you think murdering me's a bit of an overreaction, Matty?' Sally grumbled. 'Can't you just smack my bottom and make me repeat the commandment about not lying down with one's neighbouring osteopath fifty times?'

'Okay, Salls,' Matty sighed. 'If you say so. But we'll have to do it very loudly.'

Cass was too shocked to speak. No wonder Tom and Tor had turned out so bad-mannered. She was relieved to see Ben's handsome friend Hugo making his way towards them.

'Hello, darling.' Alexandra smiled dreamily up at Hugo. 'You're just in time for tea. Oh blast, the pot's empty again. I'll put the kettle on.'

'Don't bother on my account.' Hugo winked at her, glancing over at Ben nursing a quadruple brandy in the corner.

Cass noticed that Amanda didn't look up when Hugo appeared but carried on listening to Michael, who'd progressed on to the state of English cricket. She seemed remarkably interested in the subject.

'Hello, Hugo,' Cass smiled up at him. 'Remember me?' Really, she reflected, he made one feel quite girlish.

'Of course I do,' smiled Hugo, bending down to kiss her cheek and trying to think what her name was. 'How the devil are you?'

'Oh, very well.' Cass beamed. 'Tell me how you're getting on in the eventing world? Michael and I saw you at Badminton in May. You were doing *so* well. We were *so* sorry about the unfortunate mishap you had, quite dreadful and *so* embarras—'

'Thanks.' Hugo's face visored over as he cut her short and stalked off to the other table, ignoring Michael's outstretched arm and bellow of 'Hello again, old boy.'

Amanda looked up intently for the first time. This was interesting. Hugo hadn't said much about what had gone on at Badminton this year beyond a cursory reference to pulling out through injury, and Amanda, who'd been on a protracted trip to the agency's Philadelphia office, had never found out the exact details. She had a pretty shrewd idea, however, that it was much more serious than Hugo let on. He'd been on a short, explosive fuse for weeks afterwards, his grooms slinking round Haydown in constant, jittery fear of triggering his foul temper. All were banned from mentioning the B word, least of all to Amanda, whom they disliked because she couldn't remember their names and wrinkled her nose at the yard. If only she'd bothered to take more interest in Hugo's bloody horses.

'Yes, that *was* a shame, wasn't it?' she said to Cass lightly.

But Cass, feeling snubbed, had lost interest. She'd transferred her attention to drilling Sophia about the party. So Amanda was forced to listen to another of Michael's unstoppable dronings.

Tash appeared nearly half an hour later. Feeling guilty that Snob hadn't been exercised all day, she'd spent a gruelling hour lunging him. He had wrapped the long lunge rope round every tree in sight and nearly pulled Tash's arms out. Weakened by her earlier efforts and hardly able to stand, Tash had finally let go altogether and watched in despair as Snob broke free of the rope and cavorted happily around waiting for her to catch him.

She tottered on to the terrace, feeling ready to drop.

'There you are, darling – at last!' Alexandra beamed up at her. 'Sit down and have a nice drink.'

'Hello, Tash old thing,' Michael warbled before turning back to Amanda, who was by now bored stiffer than Tash's joints and staring unashamedly at Niall.

Cass showed about as much interest in Tash's arrival. She was far too intent on Sophia's guest list to say more than, 'You look tired, darling,' and give her niece a perfunctory kiss on the cheek. She did, however, notice Tash smelt distinctly of horse.

Alexandra caught Tash's hand, with a sly wink. '*Do* go and say hello to Marcus, darling, he's dying to see you again and looks frightfully dishy. Look, there's a seat next to him,' she nodded towards the far end of the terrace where Ben, Hugo and

Niall were all hooting with laughter. 'Pascal will give you a drink while you're over there.'

Tash smiled gratefully back and perched beside Marcus on a bench, as far away from Hugo's critical gaze as possible. Pascal instantly thrust an enormous brandy into her hands. 'Hair of the cheval that beet you, no?' he giggled. 'Hugo tell us how well you do, today.'

'Did he?' Tash caught Hugo's taunting blue eyes for a split second. Beside him, Ben was making daft farting noises as he tried not to laugh. On his other side, totally detached, Niall was staring at her with sun-narrowed eyes, a finger slowly trailing the rim of his glass.

Summoning her nerve, Tash took an invigorating gulp, shrugged and smiled at them all gamely.

'Hi, Marcus,' turning to her cousin, she kissed him on both cheeks.

'Yo, man.' He went pink. 'You're looking, like, well wicked, y'know.'

Marcus was surprisingly friendly, although he didn't seem up to much in the way of conversation. Tash mistakenly thought her cousin had taken a sudden interest in gardening when he suddenly started asking her if she'd done any '*Weed*ing' while she was in France, was the '*grass* ever cut here, man' and did she only "*smoke*" Camel?

'Oh!' she twigged finally, laughing. 'Matty usually has some,' she whispered. 'And I wouldn't put it past Pascal and Ben to have a stash. But I'd go carefully – Sophia and Amanda are dreadful gossips.'

'Crucial, Tash.' Marcus grinned, his eyes almost opening. 'You're a mate, man.'

Tash decided their relationship had certainly come a long way since the seven-year-old Marcus had floated a hugely embarrassed Tash's entire box of Tampax in the punch during Matty's eighteenth-birthday lunch.

Looking up, she suddenly realised Niall was still watching her. He had the curious expression of a psychiatrist silently and impassively observing his rambling patient. Tash smiled nervously but, lighting yet another cigarette, Niall didn't respond. Still staring, he now looked like an assassin watching videos of his prospective hit.

Swallowing hard, Tash wondered why he seemed to have taken against her. Had Sophia told Niall about Samion too?

20

Niall was so distracted as he dressed to go out that he sprayed pot pourri room freshener under his armpits and put on two pairs of socks without noticing.

Pascal had booked them all into a restaurant to celebrate the arrival of Cass, Michael and Marcus. Niall couldn't even remember who they were.

As his desire for oblivion subsided, Niall's mind was beginning to form itself into concerned coherence. He'd started to worry about the effect of his behaviour over the last week. It was making him increasingly twitchy and reclusive.

He wasn't sure what he'd said to Amanda when he was slaughtered last night, but Matty was pretty pissed off with him so it couldn't have been too bright. And Amanda had certainly cooed like a dove that's found the birdseed that morning when she brought him in from his vigil in the rain and poured coffee down him.

He mindlessly put on another pair of socks. Doing up the belt of his jeans, he realised he'd lost so much weight that he had to spear another hole with some nail scissors.

Niall had waited all day for his memory to come back but, between his eighth Johnnie Walker and waking up fully clothed on his bedroom floor that morning, the previous night was an obstinate blank.

He must have poured his guts out, he was sure of that, but what about? Christ, he was an idiot! He hoped Amanda was discreet. He couldn't bear the thought of all and sundry pitying him. As his ache for cocained insensibility had abated, the longing for Lisette had increased tenfold.

He was also feeling very uneasy about enlisting Hugo's help for Alexandra's daughter. He'd done it in a moment of deluded inspiration but was now doubting the wisdom of asking. The last thing Niall wanted was to get involved in other people's problems, but he felt more than a little responsible for Hugo appearing that afternoon looking positively elated, closely followed by Tash looking half dead. Hugo was capable of being bitingly cruel – he certainly didn't show much affection to Amanda – and Tash was obviously frightened by him; he seemed to exercise an odd sort of fascination over her. Niall had noticed it for the first time at lunch and then with more concern over tea – Tash had cowered away from Hugo like a chastised sheepdog when he was near, yet coveted him from a distance, her eyes drawn to him almost unwillingly over and over again.

Niall had watched in increasing horror, wondering why Hugo seemed to relish bitching her up so much. If he had it in for her – although Niall could see no reason why anyone should dislike Matty's quiet, amiable sister – then Niall's appeal was going to make Tash's life hell. With deadened enthusiasm, he knew he had to do something about it.

Thirteen was not a lucky number to have for dinner, Amanda reflected later. Everyone seemed unusually fraught. Matty had already had an argument with his mother over money on the way there, and was now laying into Sophia about her snobbish attitude. Amanda, who was sitting on his other side, expected to be next on his list of issues arising. His political fervency was mildly amusing in its naïveté, but she was in no mood to have an argument and thus draw attention to herself.

On Amanda's other side was Niall. She'd been particularly proud of her nifty manoeuvre to end up next to him but had been appalled when he'd called Hugo over to sit on his other side. They were now deep in conversation. What on earth did he think he was doing?

He'd behaved oddly earlier, too. He seemed to have no memory of how wonderfully flirtatious they'd been last night, almost getting off with each other in front of Matty's eyes.

Matty had not forgotten, however, and was now waiting maliciously on her left to move in for the attack. With Hugo on Niall's right the situation was potentially very dangerous indeed. Amanda's only solace was that she'd escaped the mind-numbing Michael, who was at the other end of the table inducing surreptitious yawns from Alexandra.

The fish course arrived in a flurry of twirled serviettes and kissed fingers. Amanda was peeved to notice that Niall had ordered the brandade de morne, which reeked of garlic. She picked irritably at her trout, finding imaginary bones. A waiter was flapping temperamentally behind Pascal, demanding to know who'd ordered crab. Pascal puffed out his cheeks and shrugged, spearing a langoustine.

Amanda suddenly stiffened as she heard Hugo say, 'You've got a fucking crush on her, haven't you?'

There was something odd about the way he said it. Not jealous, but amused. Looking across at him, she saw he was laughing. Bastard! She was not going to sit around to be made a fool of.

'Just what do you think you're saying?' she demanded, but her voice was drowned by Niall.

'I don't have a fucking crush on her – you should know I'm totally hung up on Lisette,' he hissed, almost wincing with the pain of saying it. Then he looked up at Hugo accusingly. 'I just want to know what you think you're playing at? I saw you out there today and you weren't giving her a hand. You were trying to humiliate her.'

Amanda shut her mouth and tried to work out what they were talking about. She and Hugo hadn't argued today.

'She needs to do a lot of groundwork,' drawled Hugo. 'I did it once – it's no great shakes. Why are you so protective of her if you supposedly don't give a damn, huh? Asking me to nursemaid her then getting all hot under the collar because my methods aren't quite BUPA approved? You care a lot more than you make out. Hung up on Lisette, my arse!'

'Fucking shut up, Hugo,' Niall breathed icily. 'Look, just forget I ever asked, now, all right?'

'No, it's not all right.' There was something frightening in Hugo's voice. A thin skin of boredom that hid a dangerous artery of anger. Amanda felt her heart beat faster in fear. This was the first time he'd got really worked up about her infidelity – and she hadn't exchanged more than eye-meets with Niall. What was he going to do to her?

'I'm not leaving a job half finished, Niall,' Hugo continued. 'Nanny taught me never to do that.' When he smiled there was a menacing look in his cool blue eyes.

'Why the fuck have you got it in for her?' Niall asked quietly. 'You might be an MEB, Hugo, but you behave like a vicious fucking bully with women.'

Amanda had to admire the way he stood up for her. Niall O'Shaughnessy was definitely worth the effort.

'Not all women,' Hugo was saying in a flat drawl. 'Just brainless bitches.'

Amanda's hackles rose for the attack, but at that point Matty leaned across to her and whispered, 'Why are you trying to screw up Niall?'

She was opening her mouth to let her anger finally take over when she heard Niall ask in a quiet voice, 'What has Tash French ever done to make you hate her so much?'

Amanda shut her mouth again and looked in shock across at Tash. She was sitting between Ben and Marcus, who were having a cryptic conversation about some Moroccan who cut Pascal's grass.

'But Pascal never has his grass cut, darling!' Alexandra called over to them.

Tash was suppressing a giggle, her messy, tousled hair falling over her sunburnt face as she caught Marcus's catatonic eye.

Amanda just stared at her unbelievingly. Why in Christ's name was Hugo so het up over *that*? Sure – he was pissed off with her over some horse, but that was last week. Amanda had forgotten about it until now. In fact, she'd hardly noticed the girl all holiday and now Hugo and Niall were arguing over her. It was totally ridiculous.

'Well?' Matty asked impatiently. 'The last thing that man needs is you dropping your Janet Regers every time he walks past.'

'Oh just shut the fuck up!' screamed Amanda, throwing her fork on to her plate.

Everyone around the table fell silent and looked at her.

Sophia coughed with practised social skill and then said brightly, 'Cass and I thought we might spend a day or two in Paris.' She looked at Pascal, who was still gawping at Amanda with his cheeks puffed to full expansion. 'Would you mind if we stay in the flat, Pascal?'

'Uh?' Pascal let his cheeks out slowly and looked at her. 'Non, chérie. I no mind.' He raised his eyebrows at Alexandra.

'What about you, Michael?' Alexandra smiled at her brother-in-law, trying to get another conversation moving a.s.a.p. 'Will you be staying on with us?'

'Excuse me, I'm going for a pee.' Amanda, looking murderous, stood up and pushed violently past Matty.

Choking in shock, Cass spluttered wine over Pascal's langoustines.

'Too bloody right,' barked Michael, totally oblivious of the undercurrents. 'Let the women get on with their shopping in peace. Thought I'd take old Marcus fishing.' Marcus looked horrified.

'Sophia tells me Ol's living with one of the Harcourt boys?' Ben winked at Marcus and turned to Cass.

'Yes, such a nice man and *so* attractive,' gushed Cass, dabbing a streaming eye. 'Used to go to Sherbourne. He's very big in the City now. Of course, you'll meet him when he comes to the party.'

'Which of Harcourt's offspring is he?' Hugo asked with his mouth full of red mullet.

'Ginger,' beamed Cass. 'He's got the most wonderful head of red hair.'

'I think the old bat's got a crush on him,' giggled Sally to Ben in an undertone.

'She won't get very far,' Ben whispered back, forking up Tash's untouched salmon. 'Ginger Harcourt's a raving queer.'

'This party's going to have more networking than your average fishing village,' Hugo muttered to Niall.

'You still haven't answered my question,' Niall replied quietly.

'Oh, that.' Hugo smiled across at Sally and took a long time eating a vine leaf.

'And?'

Hugo still wouldn't look at him. 'That's between me and Tash, right? As you declare no interest whatsoever in the girl you don't really need to know, n'est-ce pas? Tell me, Sally, does your husband always have that effect on women or is it just, as I suspect, that Amanda always has that effect on men?'

Leaving Sally to produce a suitably cutting reply, Niall watched Amanda walk back to their table, her glossy blonde hair slicked back to the narrow nape of her neck, bee-sting lips painted blood red. She was so fragile yet carnal, like an angry, waifish teenager determined to wind up her ageing parents. As she slid back into her seat, she stared across at Tash with unveiled contempt.

Niall followed her gaze. What was it about this tall, striking, gawky girl who was afraid of her own shadow, which made people react so violently?

Tash was politely listening to Marcus talking as monotonously as his father about 'the Acid Scene' and what it was like to 'trip' at a 'chilling rave' to really 'happening rhythms'. She listened and laughed without trying to butt in and hog the conversation as the rest of her family would. She suddenly reminded Niall of Matty when he'd first met him.

'So you *do* have a thing about Tash?' Amanda whispered in his ear. The heat of her breath sent a shiver down his spine.

Niall shook his head, unable to speak. He was disturbed by the way she could shoot his nerves through the ceiling without warning.

'Then why were you staring at her?' That same heat. Niall felt his shoulders jerk backwards as his spine tingled. Did he trust her enough to ask her why Hugo hated Matty's sister? He didn't even trust himself to speak at the moment.

'Do you want to go sky-high? I mean totally out of our minds?' Her voice was so soft he could hardly hear her, could just feel the warmth of her breath electrify the tiny hairs in his ear.

He couldn't look at her, instead he looked back across at Tash. She'd fallen asleep on Marcus's shoulder but no one seemed to have noticed except Marcus, who was helping himself to one of her cigarettes. Niall wanted to cry. Why? Because he saw himself in her? Because he wanted Amanda and not her? He could feel Lisette becoming a memory and he didn't want it that way. He desperately needed a fix.

'How do you mean?' he asked eventually. He could sense Matty staring at them but was too miserable to care.

'I've got enough for a couple of lines back at the house,' she purred.

Niall had this ridiculous image of Amanda as Nick O'Teen – a figure of evil used to stop kids smoking in the seventies. For a second he found himself repulsed by her. Then she put her small hand in his crotch and he felt himself overcome with horrifying, claustrophobic, pounding desire. Desire to get out of his skull and desire to screw her. It made him feel sick.

'How?' he whispered – his voice sounded unnatural, as if it didn't belong to him, thick and hoarse.

'I'll come to your room after Hugo's asleep,' Amanda muttered quickly and then turned to Ben. 'So what exactly did the doctor say about your ankle?'

She ignored Niall for the rest of the evening, leaving him to wrestle with his confused, raw-edged emotions over two more uneaten courses.

That night Sophia didn't hit Ben quite so much for tossing his bandaged ankle around like a fly swat. Tomorrow she and Cass would be going to Paris and she would start getting a few decent nights' sleep. She wondered where she would go first to look for a dress for the party. Yves Saint Laurent or Chanel?

Cass listened to Michael's snoring and wished they weren't quite so poor. If only Michael could pick up the tab for thirteen people at an expensive restaurant as Pascal had, without batting an eyelid. And, although she hated to admit it, Pascal was fearfully dishy – in a drunken, French sort of a way. Michael, bald and sturdy and very British, didn't have quite the same sex appeal. And the manoir was so huge and grand with so much more romance and history than The Old Rectory. Cass had an awful feeling that Alexandra had somehow gone one better than her again.

Resting her head on Pascal's sleeping chest, Alexandra wondered how she was going to help poor Matty. He was constantly ready to pounce on to his moral high horse every time she offered him money. She had to think of another method. How could she do something without him noticing?

Matty breathed in Sally's reassuringly feminine smell and wondered if he'd done the right thing. It was one thing trying to look after Niall's best interests, quite another deliberately fucking up his plans.

Feeling like a deranged female character in a Tennessee Williams play, Amanda twitched all night in total frustration. The first time she'd tried to get up, Hugo had woken up and she'd had to pretend to go to the loo. Then he'd stayed awake for hours going on about how hysterical Marcus Hennessy was, until he finally fell asleep mid-sentence.

The second time she'd been in the middle of fishing through her wash-bag for the powder compact she kept her coke in when he woke again.

'Get your diaphragm while you're at it, huh?' he'd said sleepily.

She'd frozen with fear; had he figured her out? Then she realised he'd just woken up feeling horny.

'I was getting out a painkiller, I think my period's coming,' she'd muttered. 'I'm not in the mood, Hugo.'

'Well, I fucking am. And you had your period ten days ago.'

Amanda didn't want an argument; it would put her in a bad frame of mind for getting high. She already had her diaphragm in, which would take a bit of explaining, but the thought of giving Hugo head at the moment made her go cold. So she'd gone into their bathroom again and pretended to put the stupid thing in.

'Why are you doing it in there?' Hugo had called.

Amanda had ignored him.

Their lovemaking was totally without enjoyment. Amanda just shut her eyes and pretended it was Niall.

Hugo had found himself imagining he was screwing Tash French. He wondered if she was a virgin. He'd make the little bitch scream in pain.

'Hugo, you're hurting me!'

'Good.'

Amanda would normally have kicked him off and given him hell, but she wanted to get to Niall so had stuck it out until Hugo came, which was mercifully quickly. He was in such a weird mood tonight it frightened her.

As soon as it was over, she'd gone to have a shower.

'Why the fuck can't you wait till the morning?' Hugo had snapped as she grabbed a towel off the rail.

'Because you repulse me. I want to wash you off my skin.' She'd banged the door shut.

When she came back out he was asleep. She'd waited for a while in the dark, listening to his breathing. It was deep and even. He was stretched out on the bed, the sheets kicked aside. Amanda had looked at his long, muscular brown body and suddenly felt ludicrously turned on. She must get over to Niall's room before she changed her mind. Hugo was just a spoilt playboy, Niall could be the real thing when she sorted him out. But first she had to trap him.

She'd wrapped herself in her white silk robe and grabbed the little compact before silently creeping from the room.

And now, ten minutes later, she was back again, lying furiously awake next to Hugo.

Niall had been dead to the world. He'd just mumbled, 'Lisette, I knew you'd come back to me,' before turning over and going back to sleep. The more she shook him, the less he had seemed to respond. Possibly worse still, she was sure someone was lurking in the shadows as she tiptoed back into their turret room.

Amanda grabbed a pillow and threw it across the room in frustration. Hugo didn't move.

'Hugo . . . HUGO!'

'Mmmm.'

'Wake up!'

'Fuck off.'

Amanda threw the other pillows across the room.

'If you want to throw the mattress, can you wait until morning?' asked Hugo and instantly fell asleep again.

That night, Tash woke over and over again from a heavy sleep with crippling cramps. Then she would clutch her searing, stabbing muscle in silent agony until the pain subsided and her exhausted body could drop back down the bottomless pit of disturbed sleep again.

The same dream was waiting for her each time.

She was running down the back staircase at Benedict House, her stomach landing three steps below her out-of-control legs. She jumped the last few stairs in one leap and clutched on to the rail as she spun along the lobby and into the breakfast room.

No one there, or in the adjoining kitchen.

She retraced her steps and flew up the small stairway to the green baize swing door that led to the main hall.

Her heart was racing; she could hear its frantic pounding in her ears, louder and louder, clouding her mind. She needed the loo but was too frightened to go.

From the library to her left came the sound of voices raised in anger. She stopped by the door and tried desperately to hold back her panting breath so that she could listen.

It was her parents arguing. One vicious insult flew in the wake of another, making no sense to her as she stood outside the door, her chest burning with the effort to keep quiet. They were talking about her, she was sure of it. They were saying what a disappointment she was, how much she'd let them down. She couldn't bear it.

She backed a few steps and felt fear clogging her senses with suffocating force. Suddenly her legs were racing again, slipping along the polished wooden floor of the hall as she skidded round and into the smaller of the two drawing rooms.

A couple were kissing on the sofa. The boy's hand was burrowing up the girl's skirt. From behind his rugby-shirted back and bull neck, she could make out the unmistakable black curtain of her sister's hair. She stopped and stared in fascinated horror.

'Get out, you little monster!' the girl screamed, her green eyes blazing with anger as she straightened her top and pushed the hand away.

She whimpered and tripped over in her scrabbling exit from the room. She really needed the loo badly now but had somehow forgotten where it was. She looked around the hall frantically. More doors than ever seemed to lead from it. Tall and imposing, they could all open to reveal the thing she was most terrified of, that she was running from.

But she had to try one, she had to be brave. Wasn't there a loo next to the dining room? Surely there was?

The door was stiff and took all her might to open. Inch by inch she eased its weight a little more towards her. Then, as she forced it just wide enough to get through, the hinges seemed to give and its heavy weight crashed on to the polished floorboards beside her, followed by piles and piles of golf clubs like giant Picastix clattering to the ground with a deafening series of clangs and clashes.

She leapt back. As the crashing subsided, no one appeared in the hall to tell her off. She listened in the ensuing silence for a little, waiting for a sound from somewhere, but none came, and her preoccupation with finding a toilet took over. She went to try the next door. It opened with a groan.

There was the lavatory, gleaming in welcome like an enamel bullfrog, its mouth open to catch flies. She moaned in relief. But the door wouldn't shut again behind her. It was stuck solid. She would have to pee within open view of the hall. She was too desperate not to and pulled down her jodhpurs in clumsy haste.

Then, just as she sat down to appease her bursting bladder, footsteps echoed rapidly down the hall towards her. She shrank in horror as her brother led a huge gaggle of whooping boys past the open doorway. They stopped and stared as she sat there hopelessly unable to move, her knickers round her blue ankle socks. Great cackles of adolescent male laughter surrounded her as she hid her face in her hands, bitterly ashamed.

'For God's sake,' her brother said in an angry, embarrassed voice, 'couldn't you even be bothered to shut the door? You're such a freak.' Behind him a boy with long hair and a faintly familiar, lop-sided smile took a photograph.

'Your sister's a total spastic, Matt,' yelled one of the pimply gang as they crowded away, still laughing.

There was no toilet paper, just a trace of tissue still clinging to the cardboard inner tube. She pulled up her jods – the stupid flies had broken so that they wouldn't do up – and ran as fast as her chubby legs would carry her through the huge front doors and into the pouring rain outside. Her burning face was cooled by the downpour as it mingled with the tears on her furiously blushing cheeks.

She darted between the high red walls of the house and the tall rhododendrons, into the garden on the left. There she ducked below the drawing-room windows as she stumbled along the gravel path beside the tennis lawn. She turned to dash across the long sweep of striped green to the narrow alleyway beside the potting sheds which led to the stables. As she started to run, she could see Samion being led out into the yard, his gait stiff with pain. Her view was partly obscured by the row of dying elms on the far side of the sheds but, as she got closer to the alleyway, she could make out Jack Fotheringham's sand-coloured Land Rover parked by the hay barn. A cry of panic caught in her throat like a giant hook tearing through her gullet; her legs nearly gave way under her.

She'd found what she was terrified of.

Jack Fotheringham was their vet. He'd come to destroy Samion. Her father hadn't been lying after all. Any minute now, a bullet would penetrate Samion's handsome chestnut head and he would fall to the ground like lead. Then he simply wouldn't be there any more. Her noble, fearless, red horse would have gone, leaving nothing behind but a heavy, immobile carcass. His old overcoat.

She had to stop them, she had to run faster, had to get there *now*. She couldn't scream, couldn't even breathe properly. Her eyes were blind with tears. She bolted across the rain-soaked lawn with her heart leaping from her stomach to her mouth like an uncontrollable, burning yo-yo. She was nearly in the alley-way now. Nearly there. She might just be in time to save him.

With a sudden lurch in her stomach, she felt herself falling, was aware of the thump of the ground pushing all the air from her lungs.

There was wet grass and mud in her mouth. She tried to struggle up but her ankle gave way under her. An agonising, scalding pain stabbed through it and seared its way up her leg, making her bite her lip till it bled.

Samion was going to die if she didn't get to him. She had to make it there, just had to. She dragged herself up but she couldn't focus. The garden was a haze of greens. It started spinning. She tried to blink but the ground was coming up to meet her again.

A single deadly shot cracked out, shattering the raindrops, splintering every tree, splitting the air like an axe through wood. Even though it wasn't aimed at her, she felt it thud into her chest with agonising accuracy.

Just before her head hit the muddy grass carpet below, her eyes focused for a fraction of a second. All she saw was a quick glimpse of the object that had brought her down. Sticking out of the lawn, now at an obtuse angle, was a white metal croquet hook left there from the previous summer.

* * *

The room was black and silent.

Tash felt her erratic, excited heartbeat settle as the painful cramp in her ankle subsided. Was she awake? Had she been dreaming about it again?

She couldn't be bothered to move to find out. But somehow, in the back of her mind, she was conscious that the nightmare wasn't quite as it had happened.

Niall had ten hours' deep, sound, uninterrupted sleep. The next morning he was sure he'd dreamt at one point that Lisette was trying to wake him up and he'd been too tired to make the effort. He could never remember his dreams clearly, though. Those sleeping pills Matty had insisted he take last night had really knocked him out.

21

Sophia and Cass, weighed down respectively by real and fake Louis Vuittons, set out for Paris the next morning.

Alexandra waved them off as they crackled and splashed along the damp drive in Ben's hire car. She then wandered back into her majestic, crumbling house to clear the wreckage of breakfast.

There was a strange stillness in the air, as if everyone were hiding in the cupboards, frantically working on some secret project. She paused for a moment in the doorway of the narrow corridor that led from the hall to the kitchen. But the only sound was from the washing machine gurgling greedily as it chewed its way through yet more towels and swimwear in one of the side rooms.

Alexandra sighed and faced the strewn table.

Sophia had left one of her lists behind with a large blob of honey on it. Alexandra wiped it off and, sucking her finger, read *fire-eater*, *snake-charmer*, *fortune-teller* and *strolling players* (underlined three times, that one). Without reading any more, she threw the list despondently away.

As she put the stack of uneaten dried toast back in the tin and screwed the wrong tops back on the jam pots, she reflected sadly that in all this excitement to produce the most glamorous and memorable party in years, the actual object of the celebration had been forgotten: the arrival of Eddie.

Alexandra remembered her difficult, gregarious younger

brother as a bright, immature child who got bullied at school; a moody teenager who wrote foul poetry about their despotic father which continually got rejected by *Granta*; and finally as an outrageous adult who wore pink chiffon shirts and had a crush on Joe Orton. Their mother Etty, in her vague way, had worshipped him – between affairs. Alexandra had adored him unconditionally and protected him fiercely. Even in Cass, clucking like a censorious old rooster, Eddie had inspired a strange sisterly devotion. But this hadn't been enough to counter the disapproval of the rest of the Buckingham family, who'd ostracised him with the savage reprisal of a defamed private club.

Escaping to the liberal, hanging-loose America of the sixties, Eddie had blotted out his agonising childhood in the only way he knew how, by turning his sequinned back on them all. His one return visit had been a disaster of leather and studs and bitchy vindictiveness.

Older, wiser, less uptight, perhaps he'd take them back. Alexandra knew his visit was vitally significant. And welcoming him with a fanfare of medieval trumpeters wasn't quite the subtle approach she'd had in mind. But, she reminded herself sadly, she'd let Sophia take everything out of her hands.

Her initial idea had been for a small, intimate gathering with mostly family and close friends, plus a few locals to spice things up. It now seemed that half the idle rich of Europe had been invited to watch an Interlude while sitting on the dais (sofa on the rickety gallery) in the draughty long hall and sup mead with a buxom wench in the buttery (kitchen). Alexandra found it all a bit ridiculous, especially as the manoir had been virtually rebuilt after a fire in the eighteenth century and retained precious little of its medieval roots. It wasn't exactly Hampton Court.

She'd now received acceptances from all over France and England, from Italy and Switzerland, Germany and Spain, even Miami and Martinique. She knew so few of the impressive names embossed on the top of these letters, and had a terrible feeling that Eddie would be totally overpowered, on arriving jet-lagged and a little wary, to be greeted by a host of drunken, famous faces belonging to people he'd never met before. Not to mention a lute-playing fire-eater and madrigal-singing bearded woman.

Alexandra sat down dismally by her half-eaten celery and started to peel off stringy strips, laying them over the salt cellar.

She had spent so long planning and plotting this holiday, and arm-bending her unenthusiastic family to come. Now she just felt rather lonely and left out.

In the long gallery, Michael scratched his angular chin and located the closest thing he could find to a desk under a dust-sheet. Sitting down, he took out a pen from his ratcatcher pocket and, snapping the nib up with a determined thumb, squinted along the length of the room.

He'd been given the job of organising a work-party to prepare the old barn and the dust-covered long gallery for entertaining.

Michael relished the prospect of such a taxing demand on his management skills.

He'd set to work almost immediately, demanding that Pascal and Jean rally help in the village while he drew up plans. But, although they had set off early that morning, muttering about the harvest taking up everyone's time, they had not yet re-turned. So Michael had to be content with laying down a few rough ideas.

He actually had no knowledge of conversion and renovation beyond putting up the odd shelf and fixing the occasional piece of loose guttering at The Old Rectory, but was sure that cleaning a rundown outbuilding, wiring it up for electricity and securing its staircase would present no problems. The long gallery was even easier – just needing a thorough cleaning. Pascal had muttered something ominous about death-watch beetle, but Michael had chosen to ignore such trivialities.

He relit his pipe and drew a sketchy outline of the room on graph paper. With the minstrel's gallery *here* and the audience *here*, there would be plenty of room for a few medieval sports at the end. Skittles and quoits perhaps? Did they have indoor cricket in Elizabethan times? he wondered. Bloody must have done. In which case – if he shifted the audience forward just a little more – there would be room for a good-sized game *here.*

Marcus took another drag on his spliff and sorted out his tapes again. He was indebted to his cred cousin Matty for giving him some excellent dope. In fact, Marcus decided, the whole holiday was beginning to look pretty wicked. He might not get the opportunity to visit Jim Morrison's grave, which was a bit of a downer, but at least his father had given up on the idea of fishing since he'd been asked to help with the party.

At first, the idea of a medieval banquet had made Marcus recoil in horror. What could be more naff and uncrucial? Not even a Women's Institute Tupperware bring-and-buy coffee morning in Marcus's eyes. But when Sophia had asked him, Marcus – the king of hard-core Garage-groove rhythms, chill-out boom and tuff techno sampling – to be the barn DJ, he had whooped 'Howzzzat!' and waited till the house was discreetly snoozing before creeping off to phone his best mate, Wiltsher.

Tip-toeing through unfamiliar corridors in the pitch dark had been a decidedly uncool experience, reflected Marcus. He'd been shit scared when he'd nearly bumped into the tiny blonde woman stealing along the turret staircase in her nightie at four in the morning (Marcus believed in ghosts since having his tarot cards read in Covent Garden) and even more agitated when he'd walked into a broom cupboard in the dark downstairs. But he'd finally located a phone and – after waking up a few pissed-off Londoners by misdialling – had got through to Wiltsher's house.

Admittedly, Pa Wiltsher was not too thrilled at being woken by Marcus in the small hours.

'Who? Aren't you the little bastard that got my son suspended?'

'No, man – I mean Mr W – I'm – er – group leader for the Duke of Edinburgh Award scheme. This is an emergency. Wiltsher needs to know a change of plan. I apologise for calling at such an uncool time but it's really urgent. The States need to know, like yesterday.'

Marcus – who had, he thought, pretty convincingly plagiarised the latest Jeffrey Archer – was probably the most unconvincing liar since George Washington, but Old Man Wiltsher had guzzled a third glass of port at his club that night so was in no mood to scrutinise.

Wiltsher Junior had taken the call downstairs. 'What the fuck do you want this time, Hennessy?'

'Your body and your system over here for the most buzzing rave since Savernake Forest, man.'

'Well pukka, dood!' Wiltsher was clearly impressed.

They'd gone on to make all the necessary arrangements. Wiltsher would get the sound system organised – he'd tell his father it was for a Duke of Edinburgh Award charity bash in France, or perhaps a Combined Cadet Force Allied European Unity Rally (Pa Wiltsher, who loathed Rees-Mogg, would approve of that). He'd also spread the word and possibly sell tickets (Wiltsher had an entrepreneurial streak). Meanwhile it was up to Marcus to get a really wicked light show (plenty of strobes for the trippers) and to provide some 'totally mind-blowing gear'.

Marcus was now rather perplexed as how quite to arrange the mind-blowing bit. Apart from tugging on the odd spliff procured by the Upper Sixth, Marcus was not too familiar with even the rudiments of supplying a full-blown 'rave' with drugs. He was not too keen on getting entangled with the Parisian underworld and you couldn't exactly mail order this sort of thing with the parents' credit cards. He had to think . . .

'You won't paint the bags under my eyes, will you, Tash?' Sally clung on to a furiously paddling Tor.

'You haven't got bags,' Tash told her, then groaned, realising she'd drawn Tor with three legs. 'Can you turn your head to the left a little, Tomato? Thanks.'

'How much longer is this going to go on for?' whined Tom, moving his head and his bleeping Nintendo in unison.

For most of the morning, Tash had been working on the first outlines for her painting of her brother's family in the airy Blue Room. Her progress was painstakingly slow because she was so stiff. At around ten they'd been joined by Niall, who'd now read nearly an inch of Sartre, pausing occasionally to watch Tash with narrowed eyes.

'Not much longer, Tom, I promise.' Tash darkened the shadow under the little boy's chin. Now she'd made him look as if he had a Middle-Eastern beard. If only she could concentrate. She stretched out her arms again to try and loosen her shoulders. They were agony.

'Have you finished?' drilled Tom hopefully, splatting a Martian with an electronic zap.

'Another five minutes,' Tash smiled apologetically.

'Will you play Murder in the Barn with me afterwards, Tash?'

'I can't.' She leaned back from the picture and looked at Sally's face. She'd definitely got the eyes but the nose was too long. 'I've got to ride in a minute.'

'Can I ride with you?' Tom's eyes lit up.

'Not today, Tomato,' lectured Matty, who didn't want his son hooked on any more expensive hobbies.

Matty was in a foul mood because Sally had cut his hair that morning whilst listening to Hugo and Amanda arguing in the next room. As a result he now looked like an extra from a Derek Jarman film. The fact that Tash had pencilled in some fake tresses on her sketch did not placate him.

'Surely you're too stiff to ride, Tash?' Sally glanced across at her with concern, just as Tash was trying to redraw her nose.

'Yes, she bloody is.' Niall looked up from his book and eyed her intently, his dark scraggy beard and dirty hair making him look like a menacing De Niro in a Scorsese film. 'Why don't you give it a miss today?'

Tash felt uncomfortable with Niall hanging around. She knew he was good company for Matty but he had a sort of black gloom which had infected them all and made the children fractious. He also seemed to take an intense interest in her progress with Snob, which she found awkward, especially since he'd slammed her down so priggishly the other day about not wearing a hard hat.

It was not a subject on which she was happy to dwell. The thought of another session with Hugo that afternoon was making more and more butterflies of dread and excitement flap against her aching stomach muscles.

'I'm fine,' she insisted, feeling flustered and giving Sally a nostril the size of Vesuvius. She found it totally impossible to look Niall in the eyes. He was so strange and intimidating.

'Don't look it to me,' Niall muttered into his Sartre.

'I might lead you round the paddock for a bit on Bouchon this evening if you like, Tom,' Tash offered, deliberately ignoring Niall's bossy comments.

'Brilliant! And then can we play Murder in the Barn?'

'If your Great-Uncle Michael isn't in there with his tape measure.' Tash thought glumly that she might be dead already by then, so Tom wouldn't have much to murder.

'That's amazingly good,' Niall whistled in awe as he walked behind her. 'You've got Matty totally right.' He studied the drawing closely. Tash felt herself instinctively leaning away from him. There was something decidedly manic about the glint in his hollowed, penetrating brown eyes.

'It's only the rough charcoal comp,' she muttered, wondering if he was trying to make it up to her for being so beastly about Snob. 'I've got to go away and play with it for a bit.' That sounded awful – like she was going to dance round it in an imaginary fairy glade.

Niall was looking at her as if she'd sprouted day-glo antennae and webbed purple feet.

'When will you need us for another sitting?' Sally asked, getting up and letting Tor waddle off as fast as her stout legs would carry her.

'Oh, not for a while, and then only one at a time.' Tash tried to get up and found she couldn't. Her leg muscles had jammed solid. 'Er – Sophia promised to get me some decent paints in Paris. I can't really do much more till then.' She made another abortive attempt to struggle up, and developed a crick in her neck.

'Are you all right, Tash?' Matty worriedly watched her stooping over her drawing board like Quasimodo after an aerobics session.

'Er, fine thanks. You go and get some lunch – I'll just clear up my paints and be with you in a minute.' The crick was joined by cramp in her left calf.

'Okay.' Matty shot a mock-horror glance at Sally.

'I tell you what now, I'll give you a massage,' suggested Niall kindly. 'That'll be getting you up and staggering around in no time.'

Oh no! thought Tash. No, no, no.

Tash hated massages more than anything else. The thought of those famous fingers pummelling her Araldited shoulders like an over-enthusiastic American drama student made her squirm.

'It's quite all right!' she yelped, managing to get to her knees, with much creaking of her dry muscles. 'I'll honestly be just fine in a minute.'

'Don't be daft,' ragged Sally. 'Niall gives the best massage in the world. You'll be able to make your friends wildly jealous. An O'Shaughnessy rub-down is a rare thing.' She winked at Tash and started to follow Matty out of the room.

Oh God! thought Tash. Most women would give all their worldly goods to be in my place now. I'd willingly swap for a gin and tonic and a tube of Deep Heat.

Any muscles that weren't taut before wound themselves into knots indefinable by the Boy Scouts' Manual the moment Niall's fingers touched Tash's shoulders.

'Christ, but you're tense,' Niall exclaimed. 'I'll swear it's like touching a stomach colic. Any minute now you'll explode.'

That made Tash virtually disintegrate from nerves. She couldn't stop herself shaking. She felt like an egg in a microwave. She was sure that at any moment Niall would wind his long fingers round her throat and throttle her. He was so unbalanced. He seemed to dislike humanity. Why not pick on her?

His bony thumbs started circling round the little tangle of

tissues at the bottom of her neck. Tash felt the top of her scalp freeze over and tighten unbearably.

'What did that sod Hugo make you do yesterday?' Niall asked in a soft voice.

He's trying to be kind, Tash told herself sensibly. But still no words would budge from her voice-box and her eyes assessed the distance between where she sat and the door.

'I have to confess I watched for a bit,' Niall was saying.

Tash tried to say 'Yes?' but it came out as a sort of throaty burp.

'Indeed I did.' Niall moved down to her lower shoulders, pushing the loose-necked t-shirt that she was wearing away with his fingers. Tash, despite feeling paranoid that she'd probably got spots on her back, couldn't help experiencing a slight buzz warming the length of her locked neck.

'He's not the easiest of guys to please, that Hugo Beauchamp, is he now?' Niall continued, trying to draw her out. But she said nothing.

Niall gently levered one side of her t-shirt over her shoulder and she shied away. She was as nervous as he was on an opening night.

'Sssh – relax, angel. I'm not going to hurt you now.' It was like reassuring a terrified, beaten animal. Whatever was going on between her and Hugo had screwed her up totally.

'Is that feeling a touch better, angel?'

'I . . .' Tash was beginning to feel quite strange under Niall's strong, kneading hands. Her back had started to sag inadvertently, her shoulders to droop in sublime pleasure. Don't let my brain go hazy, she prayed. I need my wits about me if he's going to try to attack me. But as Niall's slow circling loosened another agonising knot into relaxed submission, she couldn't help but let out a moan of relief. Perhaps he wasn't a homicidal misogynist after all.

She hung on to her t-shirt and wished she'd bothered putting on her bra. Not that it really mattered; she was beginning to feel too sleepy to care. Her head seemed to be getting too heavy for her shoulders, so she let her chin flop on to her collarbone, and sighed contentedly.

Niall's smooth, deep voice rambled on as his warm hands started spreading out across her back, easing away all the remaining tension like a warm bath.

In her soporific daze, Tash was reminded of a children's film she'd watched years ago with a wise old leprechaun telling stories to a crowd of eager faces. She wasn't really taking in what he was saying, just feeling the reassuring awareness of his voice.

'Now tell me what's going on between you and that Beach-bum fellow, huh?' Niall was probing insistently, worried by her silence.

But Tash wasn't listening. She was thinking of Max in their first weeks at Derrin Road, sitting behind her with his warm arms wrapped round her like a familiar cardigan, resting his chin on her shoulder, and herself just feeling the total security of being loved.

'You knew him before this holiday, didn't you?' Niall persisted.

Tash groaned out loud. Why had she sent him that pathetic letter? She'd made everything sound so horribly final. She longed to have him back. To turn round and find him here now where Matty's sad friend sat stroking her back. Her familiar, scruffy Max with his lop-sided smile, ready to cover her face in kisses and tell her she was being an idiot and he'd never stopped loving her at all.

'I 'clare, does he know something about you now?'

Instead, he could be reading her letter at this very moment on some Greyhound bus, enjoying the adventure of his life, laughing over her childish desperation and complete naïveté.

'Is that it, Tash?'

Tash felt a huge, ungainly hiccup jerk through her as her eyes started to plop out the inevitable tears.

In films women wept gracefully yet with passion. Why was it that she, Tash, could soak a whole roll of Andrex while her nose dribbled constantly and turned redder than a Victoria plum in August? All this accompanied by belching great hiccups and more whimpering than a locked-away dog.

She sniffed frantically and tried to pretend it was a sneeze.

Perhaps Niall wouldn't notice if she hid behind her hair. But his hands had slowed their gentle caressing almost to a standstill.

'Are you all right?' he asked, lifting his head and blinking unruly curls from his eyes.

'Fine!' trilled Tash in a forced, bright voice which sounded distinctly like Joyce Grenfell on the hockey pitch of St Trinian's during the bully-off.

But her horrible, unstoppable tears had decided to let the floodgates open the whole way at the slightest sound of sympathy. Another great shudder started tensing those slackened muscles again. A huge tear dropped off the end of her nose.

'Look at me, angel.' Niall started stroking her hair softly.

Tash hiccuped and sniffed simultaneously, which made her cough.

'I can't,' she spluttered feebly. 'Look, I'm really sorry. This is so pathetic.' A sob caught in her throat. 'I'll honestly be all right in a minute.' She wiped her running nose on her t-shirt and then realised how disgusting that must look. 'Oh God, I'm sorry!' she wailed.

'Hush, angel. You don't have to apologise to me, huh?' Niall turned her round so her head rested on his shoulder and continued stroking her hair like a child. 'Haven't I cried enough over the last week to justify other people here having a few sobs in return?'

'But it seems so rude,' sobbed Tash.

Another tear trickled its way down her cheek. She felt a complete and utter idiot blubbing away like a lovesick teenager in front of Niall O'Shaughnessy, famous Irish actor, heart-throb and now nanny.

'You were being so kind,' she apologised tearfully.

'It's all right.' Niall gave her shoulder a squeeze and Tash resisted an enormous urge to tear away and run as fast as she could to her room to thump her pillow in shame. She couldn't believe he was being so nice. She'd thought him hateful just half an hour ago.

'To be sure, if someone were to give me a gentle rub at the moment, I'd do exactly the same thing,' Niall reassured, ruffling her hair absent-mindedly. 'It happens when you're tense. You keep everything bottled up inside, then when you relax – whoosh, out it comes.'

'But—' Tash longed to say that her problems were so tiny and insignificant compared to his, but that sounded dreadful and opinionated. Instead, she had a huge sniff and realised she'd stopped crying almost as suddenly as she'd started. It was like a sudden downpour that has passed by the time you look out of the window again. She felt sillier than ever.

'I've stopped,' she mumbled, pulling away from his grasp and then feeling ungrateful. 'Thank you so much for being so considerate.' She turned round and stared indebtedly at his shirt button. There was a great damp patch on his checked chest. She hoped it wasn't from her nose.

'Don't mention it,' shrugged Niall.

'We'd better go to lunch,' she suggested, moving her eyes from the shirt button to the window.

The sun had shyly emerged, dipping everything in gold with a saffron lustre. Tash was immensely relieved that Niall hadn't asked her to tell him what had made her cry. It would be like moaning about a parking ticket to an innocent man on death row.

'Yes,' agreed Niall, not moving. It was strange, he thought. He'd been kind to her automatically, as one would comfort a child. Without thinking of himself for once. He found himself feeling almost human again.

The silence seemed to last for ever. A phone rang in the depths of the house. Tash wanted to say something in a great, shy dollop about being sorry she had misjudged him and that she hoped he would feel happier soon because Matty and Sally obviously loved him very much and he just had to learn to love himself. But even to her it sounded like a television evangelist on speed, so she kept her mouth closed. He was a famous star, everyone wanted to give him sympathy – it meant nothing. What really mattered was having his friends close to him to wait for the scars to heal.

She rubbed her wet, blotchy face with the back of her hand

and hiccuped with slightly less violence at embarrassed intervals. She wished he'd leave her alone for a minute so that she could blow her nose. Instead Niall leaned forward and gave her shoulder another reassuring squeeze.

'Sorry,' she sniffed again, not looking at him.

'Don't be,' Niall told her. 'Do you feel less like concrete, now?'

She nodded.

'I honestly wouldn't be riding this afternoon if I were you,' said Niall, trying and failing to get into her line of vision and look her in the eyes. 'Hugo'll drive you far too hard. Give yourself a day off, huh?' He wiped a huge tear from her sunburnt cheek.

Tash smiled weakly and shook her head. 'I can't,' she sighed, 'I promised myself.'

'Why?' Niall tried for one final time.

But as Tash opened her mouth to answer reluctantly, Sally popped her head round the door.

'Niall – your agent's on the phone.'

'Bob?' Niall looked up in horror.

''Fraid so. I told him you're not staying here but he's bloody insistent . . .' Sally paused as she saw Tash, hunched next to Niall with a tear-stained face. 'Er . . . I said I'd see if I could find you. Do you want to be out?'

'No,' Niall stood up. 'I've got to face the bugger sometime, it might as well be now.' He gave Tash's hair a final friendly rub.

'How on earth did he find you here?' Sally followed him out of the room.

'You don't know Bob,' Niall's voice faded away from Tash down the echoing hall. 'He could find a grain of Demerara sugar if it hid in the Sahara Desert.'

Tash sat for a while contemplating her embarrassment.

Logically, the best person in the house to cry in front of was Niall, for the very reasons he had pointed out. And he'd turned out to be so considerate and gentle it had changed her opinion of him as a selfish, murderous Irish weirdo. Yet she was still terribly shy of him. She just couldn't get over the hang-up of his familiar, pin-up face, his star status and his haunting, inconsistent misery.

To Tash the past few minutes had made the outlook of things somewhat worse if anything. She'd been about to tell him about Samion. Talk about telling the terminally ill about one's varicose veins. Thank God Sally had come in.

There was something seriously wrong with Niall O'Shaughnessy, she was sure of it. Something possibly even worse than Lisette leaving him or being sacked from the film. He was so thin and drawn, not like the tawny, romantic figure her friends had pulled out of *The Face* and stuck on their walls at college. He looked like a soul in grief.

Tash guessed Matty and Sally must know what it was. It made her feel impossibly inadequate and inferior about him. She was a total outsider in his life and her tears had been an intrusion. She knew that if someone was coming to terms with something like a terminal illness (Tash's vivid imagination refused to steer itself away from Aids) then people around you should behave as normally yet sensitively as possible. So, being Tash, she'd behaved like a selfish child in front of him. She longed to steal the last ten minutes back and comfort him instead.

'Do you want some lunch, Tash?' Sally reappeared at the door, a large blob of babyfood on her chambray shirt.

'Oh, yes, I suppose so.' Tash pulled herself up and found that, although her legs still felt like rusted Meccano, her back and shoulders were almost normal again.

'You and Niall having a heart-to-heart?' Sally asked casually as they walked towards the kitchen.

Sally didn't want Tash to think she was prying, but she'd noticed a slight change in Niall. He'd sounded quite together talking to his agent. Hardly anything really, but then again . . .

'Sort of,' Tash said non-committally, trying out her neck in a few twists. It didn't even creak.

'He's such a good listener,' Sally continued tentatively, trying to walk as slowly as possible to extend the time they were out of hearing-range of the kitchen. 'They called his caravan the Agony

Wagon on location for *The Plough and the Stars* adaptation because he was always on hand for advice and guidance – and a stiff dram of Bushmills.'

Tash smiled nervously and wondered why Sally was probing, but she felt too ashamed of her outburst with Niall to reply.

As they walked into the kitchen, Tash felt a nasty familiar lurch in her chest to see Hugo lounging next to the range dressed in old Levis and a black t-shirt with 'Jasper Condom' emblazoned across the front.

His long, Spode-blue eyes were undeniably hungover but they still retained plenty of their usual playful glint. He was drinking thick black coffee from a bowl and smoking a Gauloise Blonde. Why did she want to abandon all composure and leap on top of him every time she saw him?

Tash concentrated intently on piling up a plate with salad to avoid his mocking gaze.

Niall, back from his phone call, picked unhungrily at a green salad. He'd managed to placate Bob for the time being but – as his half-criminal, half-genius of an agent had pointed out with his usual bulldozer bluntness – Niall couldn't sit around licking his wounds for ever just because his 'oversexed wife had pushed off with a thick shit of a Yank'.

But Niall felt he needed a bit more time before he could face the outside world. Responsibility terrified him at the moment. Auditions, rehearsals, interviews, endless questions, industry gossip, press, camera crews and worse than all the gut-clenching fear of rejection – like he was fresh from LAMDA, a long shot, an Irish farm boy who might not make the grade. He'd been sacked for screwing up a picture; who wasn't to say he'd do it again? His career would be on trial when he got back and he felt he had no case for the defence.

He considered going back to Ireland and holing up there for a while. But there were so many memories of Lisette there, hiding around every corner, waiting to jump out and squeeze his heart till it bled. At least here was totally neutral territory.

But then there was Amanda. Niall threw his fork into his

salad bowl and looked up at the ceiling, oblivious of the others' surprised glances.

He supposed he'd responded to Amanda's attention pretty shabbily; he couldn't remember much of it, he'd been so unhinged. Yet she'd played along and that made her a dangerous temptation. Last night, if Matty hadn't intervened, Niall was certain he would have waited up for her like a schoolboy in a brothel, sick with fear but aching with hope that somehow his cowering self-loathing would be deadened.

She'd stayed out of his way all day. Even now at lunch she'd cried off to lie down with a headache. Niall knew it was his turn to make a move.

He glanced at Hugo, who was watching Tash with the impassive expression of a big cat lazily sizing up a distant fawn. He poisons everything he touches, Niall thought savagely. He's like a precocious, popular child who takes pleasure in testing how much he can hurt people.

Hugo caught him staring and grinned. Niall forced a smile in return and tucked his suspicions firmly away. He was trying to think up excuses to justify himself again. Amanda's come-on was flattering but it was no excuse to throw dirt in Hugo's face. He'd do better to concentrate on righting whatever he'd inflicted on Tash French by entreating Hugo's help.

Alexandra came into the room wafting a pair of red spotted boxer shorts around like a flag.

'Do these belong to anybody?' she asked the assembled company airily.

'Mine actually.' Ben looked somewhat pink as Alexandra passed over the flamboyant undies.

'They got in with Pascal's washing by mistake,' Alexandra explained. 'He only wears those revolting jockey short things. Has everyone had enough lunch?'

Everyone nodded, feeling a little like children in morning assembly. Sally wanted to ask if she could play the tambourine, but refrained.

Pascal, fresh from his 'nap' with Alexandra, loomed through the door. His poppy-blue eyes were sparkling more merrily than ever. He seemed blissfully unaware that his wife had just been discussing his choice in underwear.

'Oo is wanting to come wiv us to the river?' he asked enthusiastically.

'We can go for a nice walk and then have a picnic tea,' gushed Alexandra, sounding more like Margaret Rutherford than her usual sexy self.

Hugo wondered if she'd been playing teachers with Pascal during their 'nap'.

'Bloody good idea, Alex old girl,' warbled Michael. 'Go and find where your mother's put those bloody fishing rods, Marcus, there's a lad.'

Marcus groaned and sloped out to get the fishing tackle (via his personal stereo – he didn't want to have to listen to his father giving him the How To Cast lecture all afternoon).

Michael knew that Marcus didn't want to go fishing, but he was feeling pissed off because Pascal and Jean had returned from the village minus any workmen but with a definite Arôme de Public House wafting around them. He was too polite to take it out on his host so had decided to punish his errant son a little more.

'We'll come, too – it might cheer the skinhead up to have a paddle,' laughed Sally, who'd had too much wine at lunch.

Matty, broodily rubbing his stubbly head in the corner, shot his wife a withering look and returned to Duverger's *Party Politics and Pressure Groups*.

'Suppose I'd better give Josh and Lots an airing, although I'll need Paola to do the lifting,' muttered Ben, reaching for his crutch and nearly pronging a slumbering spaniel. 'I think she's got all the kids in one of the downstairs rooms. Tremendously maternal girl.' He dropped the crutch on to the stone floor with a clatter. 'Don't suppose someone could go and chivvy her into preparation for me?'

'I'll go,' offered Tash, grateful for the escape. 'I'll ride Snob this afternoon if that's all right, Mummy?' she added on her way out, not waiting for a reply. It was a tried and tested method. Her mother would have forgotten to raise an objection by the time she returned. As she walked away from the kitchen she heard Hugo telling Alexandra he thought he'd stay and help. So her fate was sealed. She was surprised to find herself feeling not sick but elated, her pulse fizzing excitedly.

Paola was looking far from maternal in the gym, sweating on the rowing machine to INXS, while Tom, in a towelling headband which obscured his vision almost totally, was chasing a screaming Polly round a huge weight-lifting apparatus, and Tor was happily hitting the sobbing Lotty – who was twice her size – with a soft-ball racquet. Meanwhile, Josh slept like a lamb in his carry-cot, which was balanced precariously on a long wooden bench.

'Er – Paola.' Tash had to raise her voice over the din.

'Si,' Paola looked up somewhat startled and turned off her transistor. She wiped her damp face with a towel.

'Ben wants you to get the kids ready to go out.' Tash removed the soft-ball racquet from Tor's remarkably strong grip and picked Lotty up to give her a cuddle. The little girl stopped sobbing and put her thumb in her mouth, rubbing her tears furiously away with her Noo Noo.

Paola stood up sulkily from the rowing machine and pulled her tight pink leotard back over her bottom. She muttered something distinctly bitter in Italian and walked over to the carry-cot.

'Is Signor Hugo coming?' She turned back hopefully.

'I don't think so,' Tash replied cautiously, aware that the Italian girl blamed her for the fact that Hugo was now completely ignoring her. Feeling terribly sorry for Paola, who was clearly having a rotten holiday, Tash longed to explain. But Paola, sullen mouth drooping like a wilting poppy, whipped up the carry-cot, grabbed Lotty from Tash, and stormed out of the room.

'She no like you, huh?' Polly, whose space-man costume was covered in raspberry jam, slid to a halt beside Tash.

Tom, panting in pursuit, did a killer rugby tackle on Tash's legs. Tor helped her brother to floor Tash with the aid of a second soft-ball racquet.

'It's all right, 'cos we like you, Tash,' Tom grinned, giving his aunt a Chinese burn while Tor practised a few backhands on her bottom. 'You're squishier than Wowla.'

'Thanks,' sighed Tash, as a jammy hand pummelled her shoulders with far less sensitivity than Niall had earlier.

When Tash went back to the kitchen, the others were trying to persuade Niall to go with them.

'It'll do you good,' Matty appealed lamely. He didn't like the thought of Niall alone in the house with Amanda while Hugo and Tash were distracted outside.

'Let him stay if he wants to,' argued Sally. She didn't understand why Matty was so keen on including Niall. She'd noticed an odd sort of bond building up between Niall and Tash. Strange as it might appear, Sally had a feeling it could help Niall a lot, take his mind off Lisette. She caught Matty's eye but he ignored it.

'Come on, Niall. We can take a bottle of plonk and carry on drinking by the river. Ben needs the company,' he urged.

'Thanks,' moaned Ben, thinking he was being insulted.

But, jaw set in a determined line, his eyes strangely distant, Niall wouldn't be persuaded.

'I'll stay with you then,' Matty offered.

'No!' Niall sounded unusually sharp. Noticing Matty's strained expression, he added jokingly, 'I just vant to be alone.'

Matty said nothing, venting his frustration instead by snapping at Sally to hurry up. He had a strong suspicion that even if he wanted it, being alone was the last thing Niall would experience that afternoon.

22

As the car engines faded into the distance, Niall waited in the silent hall, wavering on peaks and troughs of indecision. Through the window by the warped courtyard door, he watched Hugo and Tash walk across the courtyard, not talking. As Tash went towards the stalls on the left, Hugo walked over to the paddock rails and leaned against them, lighting a cigarette.

Niall studied the way he shook the match almost exaggeratedly out and tossed it behind him.

He'd be a wonderful character to play, he thought. That cocky self-assurance, the total lack of fear.

As he looked away, he caught sight of himself in the mirror opposite and stared in horror.

A scraggy old hippie stared back.

He was only thirty-two but he looked more like fifty. Niall rubbed his beard, hating it. He resembled a Central Park drop-out. He wasn't up to playing Hugo – what total egotism! In this state all he was fit for was a walk-on as a down-and-out in *The Bill*. Even then he'd probably fluff his lines. He was a mess.

He decided to go upstairs and shave the disgusting goaty thing off. Then, and only then, he'd be strong enough to go to Amanda and apologise for being such a total bum. She and Hugo might be on the rocks at the moment, but the last thing she needed was him sticking his dried-up oar in.

As he pushed open the door to his room an asphyxiating waft of familiar, caramel-sweet scent surrounded him. Fidji. The perfume Lisette wore. He was reminded so acutely of her that he felt the blood drain from his face and his pulse pound with crazy irregularity.

Then he caught his breath.

Lying on the bed, her naked body curled luxuriously around the old gilt-framed looking glass that had been hanging on the other side of the room, was Amanda.

The sunlight from the slats in the shuttered window was reflected so that it danced on her smooth, almost iridescent skin, streaking her body like a tiger. It touched the curve of her tanned belly and the tilt of her satiny breasts. Her blonde hair shimmered like a cornfield. She appeared carved from golden light – a tawny, carnal holograph.

In the centre of the mirror, like neat rows of salt ready for tequila slammers, were four lines of coke.

Even as he stood there – his mind racing with images of helping her into her clothes and telling her he was sorry, flushing the precious powder down the toilet – Niall knew all the time that he wouldn't be able to do any of it. He felt totally and utterly out of control.

When the others returned to the house, hours later, Tash was being lunged round the field on Snob. Hugo, at the other end of the rope, stood in the centre of the paddock, issuing instructions.

To Pascal, they looked the picture of a traditional British pastime. The scene reminded him of a book of John Betjeman poetry Alexandra had given him one anniversary. How did it go?

> It's awf'lly bad luck on Diana,
> Her ponies have swallowed their bits;
> She's fished down their throats with a spanner,
> And frightened them all into fits.

Pascal chuckled to himself. He'd recited that for weeks after Alexandra had translated 'spanner' for him.

'Isn't that wonderful?' enthused Alexandra, looking dreamily across at Hugo's circling bottom. Rather too dreamily, thought Pascal.

'So much for Hugo not liking poor old Tash,' Alexandra went on. 'He's being a complete love now.'

Pascal watched Tash's red, determined face as she bit her lip at something Hugo said. Pascal couldn't quite make out what it was, but the tone of voice had been clear enough. He looked across at his wife. She'd lost interest and was handing Polly the jar of dirty river water in which, somewhere, swam a microscopic minnow.

'Now don't put it in your wash-basin, darling. Remember what happened last time?'

'Oui, Maman.' The little girl dashed off, secretly planning to deposit the lot over Tom, who'd thrown a mud cake at her earlier.

Sally carried the sleeping Tor up to her room. Having wreaked havoc with the picnic, feeding one of the spaniels with three eclairs and a travel-sickness pill before biting Ben's good leg so hard it bled (pretty impressive for child with more gum than teeth, Matty had pointed out), Tor had conked out on Sally's knee for the rest of the afternoon.

She folded back the little rabbit-covered duvet and lay Tor down, starting to take off her muddy clothes. She contemplated putting a nappy on her – Tor's potty method being a pretty hit-and-miss affair – but decided against it.

Sally sighed and kissed the little girl on the head. She knew Tor was sometimes wickedly naughty and totally undisciplined. She was also far further behind than Tom had been at the same age, hardly saying more than the occasional 'glug' and getting about in a sort of drunken half-lurch, half-crawl. Matty had recently been heard muttering ominously about child psychologists and infant regression through over-maternal parenting. But Sally found Tor utterly sweet and darling the way she was. Matty could censure, Sophia and Cass could tut all they liked; Sally was going to let the Tor-nado tot develop in her own good time.

Switching on the baby alarm, she walked out of the room and across the tall, shadowy landing towards the stairs. She paused outside Niall's room and knocked on the door, longing to have a quick gossip and a moan about Matty. There was no answer. She popped her head round just in case, but Niall wasn't there.

The room was stuffy and stale with the shutters still closed. Sally went to open them and then the window, feeling a welcome rush of cool, fresh air numb her nostrils.

As she turned to leave, she noticed a large pale patch of wall above a threadbare slipper chair. Glancing around, she saw an old, yellowing mirror which was speckled with rust leaning at a dangerous angle against the taps on the sink. She picked it up to rehang it. The enamel basin was full of stubble. Thank God. Niall had shaved that dreadful load of goat hair off. He was definitely on the mend. She smiled to herself and stood on the groaning chair, finding the hook on the wall.

In the shaking reflection in front of her something shiny caught her eye. It was in the middle of the unmade-up bed over her shoulder. When she secured the string on the mirror's back to the hook, the glinting object disappeared from sight as the looking glass lay flat against the wall.

Knowing she was prying, but unable to stop herself, Sally went over to the bed and had a peek.

There, half obscured by Niall's towelling robe, was a huge opal ring cast in silver. The stone was nearly the size of a quail's egg. It was unmistakably Amanda's.

23

Without the glass-covering restraint of their wives, Ben and Michael allowed themselves to get rollickingly drunk that night. Pascal considered it only polite, as host, to join in, and even Hugo – notorious for remaining sober when parallel drinkers were crouched over the Armitage Shanks – started singing post-prandial Eric Clapton hits in a very slurred, very flat bass voice.

Tash tried hard to go off him for this, but, when he roped in Sally and Alexandra as a vocal backing group, with Pascal and Ben clanking away in bottle-bashing percussion, he was both screamingly funny and disconcertingly sexy.

The house-guests had gathered in the China Room after dinner, slumping in sofas to watch the show. Only Amanda refused to laugh, cradling an undrunk brandy in the corner, shooting out venomous looks as Hugo and his band became more and more raucous.

'Come on, Niall,' Hugo coaxed as he broke off to refill his glass. 'Join me in a duet.' His smile was unreadable – he could equally be being affable or mocking.

Niall – still high as the moon and wiping tears from his eyes – shook his head.

'To be sure, I've got a terrible voice, Hugo,' he waved Hugo away. 'When I sing, female cats in season turn up in droves.'

But Hugo refused to take no for an answer. Whispering in Alexandra's ear, he put his arm round Niall's shoulder and hauled him up. Ben and Pascal, cigarettes dangling from their lips, leaned back on their chairs to listen. Sally, her harmonising skills no longer needed, plumped down on a sofa between Matty and Michael, who was fast asleep and snoring reedily, pipe still in place as he lolled over the arm.

As Alexandra sat down at the piano, Sally turned to squeeze Matty's hand. He stiffened, his face set in an I-am-trying-to-enjoy-this smile. Sally had seen it before when he was being forced to endure one of Tom's school nativity plays or some trashy American film she'd persuaded him to see. His black gloom had been coming on all day, exacerbated by the trip to the river. He clearly thought them all too childish for words, and that Sally had let him down by making a spectacle of herself tonight.

As Niall and Hugo went into a huddle in the corner, Sally glanced at Amanda. Dressed in leather jeans and crisp white shirt tied under her small bust, blonde hair gleaming almost white from the sun, she looked strangely androgynous and hypnotisingly seductive. Although her face was bored and distanced and her red mouth drooped sulkily, her eyes were gleaming with mirth. She's enjoying this, Sally thought in horror.

She longed to tell Matty about the ring, but in his current mood, he'd explode. And she kept telling herself that it could have been just a one-off or that there was a completely innocent explanation, hoping that the more she repeated the idea, the more likely she was to believe it.

Her thoughts were broken by Marcus going into his hiccupy, whooping laugh over something Tash had said. They were huddled together on a red silk sofa beside the piano. With their long, gangly bodies, messy hair and tanned olive skin, the family resemblance was unmistakable. Sally had seen photographs of Matty looking almost the same as a student. But glancing at him again, his grey, glowering face could have been Heathcliff staring through the window at the Lintons' revelry.

Alexandra balanced her glass beside top E and struck a long, echoing chord. Ben and Pascal already had the giggles. Michael snorted and ground his teeth on his pipe in his sleep.

But, as Hugo and Niall started singing, all the room but them and the haunting, mellifluous piano, fell mute.

It's late in the evening; she's wond'ring what clothes to wear—
She puts on her make-up and brushes her long blonde hair.

'Gross!' Marcus groaned, pulling a face.

Pascal hushed him silent, a soppy smile playing on his face, his eyes watery with happiness.

– asks me, 'Do I look all right?'
And I say 'Yes – '

Amanda raised a quizzical eyebrow and tried to look bored. It certainly wasn't the most tuneful rendition of 'Wonderful Tonight', and, had Clapton been present, Amanda strongly suspected he would have sued. But inside she was bubbling over with excitement from the sexual frisson of the situation.

Playing with her glass so that her eyes just peeped over its glimmering rim, she caught Niall's eye and he winked. Hugo – thinking she was looking at him – gave a sort of Hooray sneer-cum-leer. Amanda found him revolting at the moment, but the unexpected attention was flattering. Nothing, she reflected, could compare to the heady, unexplored thrill of having a new, infinitely skilled, sexual partner. They say married men make the best lovers, she remembered happily. And boy, was Niall itchy after seven years' practise-making fidelity.

We go to a party, and everyone turns to see
This beautiful lady is walking around with me

Amanda suddenly stiffened. For, stretching to retrieve his glass from the piano, Niall started singing at just one person. And it wasn't her.

And then she asks me 'Do you feel all right?'

Tash turned puce with confusion as Niall folded his long body down on to the arm of the red silk sofa and took her hand.

It was an embarrassingly misjudged gesture, born of idiotic, looped kindness. Niall would never have done it when sober, but this didn't lessen the astonishment of the watching house guests or Tash's utter humiliation.

And I say, 'Yes, I feel wonderful tonight.'

Hugo's voice trailed off during the last line. He looked both irritated and uncomfortable. Sally hid a smile as she saw Amanda looking as if Elizabeth Arden's Flawless Finish had turned into a chilled mud pack, but the smile dropped when she noticed Matty glaring thunderously at Niall.

Niall launched on, unabashed.

It's time to go home now, and I've got an aching head

He grinned at Tash, giving her the ghost of a wink.

Hugo wavered uncertainly, his power over the situation slipping away. Then he suddenly seemed to make his mind up. Ramming Marcus up against a growling spaniel, he sat on Tash's other side.

– and she helps me to bed.

Alexandra, getting thoroughly carried away on the piano, put in a few flashy arpeggios. Mortified, Tash didn't know where to look as she felt Hugo's arm, warm, sinewy and dreamt-of, hooking around her shoulders. Horribly, her eyes caught Amanda's first – the look of mocking derision rapped long, red nails on her temples.

– as I turn out the light,
I say, 'My darling, you are wonderful tonight.'

At last it was over, with Ben and Pascal cheering, and Michael waking up to croak 'Bloody good show' to cover Tash's shuddering unease. Then Hugo – drunk to the point of near-humility – leaned forward to kiss her on the cheek. Flustered, Tash turned away and felt his warm, wet lips almost bite into her ear, scorching the side of her face. He immediately sprang up to get himself another drink, giving Alexandra a huge, far more indulgent, kiss on the way.

On her other side, Niall was watching Tash with his narrowed assassin-black eyes. She wanted to run as he leaned down and kissed her too, far more lightly and gently, on the forehead.

'I'm sorry, angel,' he suddenly caught her chin and held it up so that she was forced again to look into those wide, bottomless pupils. 'I'm so sorry.'

Turning away with hunched shoulders, he walked out of the room and upstairs. No one but Amanda saw him raise his eyebrows and blow a kiss as he passed her.

Lying in bed hours later, Tash, wracked with exhausted confusion, listened to the muffled sounds of merriment still siphoning up through the dusty house. She longed to sleep, but every time the lovely, gloopy swamp of blackness started pulling her down, the memory of the awful public duet shot her bolt upright again, her heart crashing like a crazed bluebottle against her ribs.

Sally and Matty could be heard coming upstairs now, arguing in taut, hushed voices, the words indistinguishable. A door banged, cutting them off like the switch on a radio.

Tash pummelled herself down into her pillow and tried to think of Max. But he was becoming a memory – faded and worn as an old photograph that's been hawked out of a wallet so many times for inspection, the face has started to fade away, replaced by the owner's rose-tinted imagination. In the darkness, Tash scrunched her eyes into two tightly wrinkled folds and covered them with her arm. But all she could see was a head of dull, donkey-blond hair and a bulbous nose. All his other features had disappeared. Instead, Hugo's scornful, cobalt eyes and – far more disturbing – Niall's wide, curly mouth formed a taunting, faintly ugly, photofit.

Deciding to get up and exorcise the image by digging out her photograph of Max, Tash fell asleep.

She was on the back of a huge motorbike careering along the motorway so fast that her ribcage and stomach seemed to be pressing against her backbone.

Who was driving the bike? She couldn't tell as she hung on to the leather jacket in front of her for dear life. Her fingers were freezing in the whipping wind. She was beginning to lose feeling in them. Soon she would let go altogether and fall backwards on to the tarmac of the fast lane.

They were crashing into cars now, sending them flying to either side as they carried on relentlessly. She recognised Matty's Audi and Pascal's jeep spinning away from the impact of the enormous bike.

Now they'd cut away from the motorway and accelerated at breakneck speed through an emerald and burgundy wood. She ducked away from the swooping branches, but one tore through her shirt and ripped it away, leaving her naked from the waist up. Another caught on to her leg and nearly pulled her off the bike. She clung on to the slippery leather jacket until she was just holding on with her fingernails, her body trailing behind the bike like a piece of fabric flying in the wind.

They came out of the wood and were roaring through Central London, weaving in and out of the stationary traffic. People pointed and jeered as they whizzed past Cambridge Circus and into Soho. In a noxious cloud of smouldering burnt rubber, they sped into a modern office building, sending screeching receptionists flying. Endless narrow corridors flew past as they smashed through swinging fire-doors.

They roared through a long boardroom to outraged cries and startled faces, then out the other side into a television studio, where they came to a shuddering halt which sent her flying into a vast, squishy bed in the middle of the set.

'At last!' screamed a voice distorted by a megaphone. It belonged to the director, who was wearing plus-fours and a checked flat cap with a red bobble on top. He looked suspiciously like her father at the nineteenth hole.

'Scene twenty-four, take one . . . and ACTION!' He still yelled through the megaphone although he was only a metre away.

She looked around in a panic. People with headphones and clipboards were creeping round behind the cameras, making hand signals at each other. Everyone was hushed and a camera on the left honed in on her with its red light glowing.

'Oh, I'm sorry!' she gulped. 'I'll get out of your way.' She clambered to get out of the bed.

'CUT!' screamed the director, moving the megaphone next to her ear. 'Look, honey. You're screwing up the scene. Niall's the star of the show here, not you. Just stay put and remember your lines, honey, *okay*?' He gave her a malicious smile through the metal cone. 'ACTION!'

She watched in horror as the motorcyclist lifted his black visor and took off his helmet.

It was Niall O'Shaughnessy, looking dishevelled and sexy, his handsome, famous face expressionless. He sighed with martyred professionalism and, taking off his leather jacket and boots, climbed into the bed. He glanced at her without interest as if she were a stranger. He was clearly disappointed.

The hushed silence seemed to intensify as he wearily started to undo his trousers.

'People are always falling in love with me,' he said calmly. 'It pisses me off but I have to put up with it. Life.' He unbuttoned the top of his shirt and then pulled it over his head.

He had the most glorious body. She stared, transfixed. He still had his socks on. They were white terry towelling but she was feeling too shaken to care.

'Now where do you want me to start?' he inquired in a bored voice.

She found she couldn't speak. The floor manager was waving furiously at her.

'Well – tell me, I haven't got all day,' Niall looked at his fingernails and buffed one on his Kermit the Frog underpants before checking them again. He gave her another uninterested look. 'Everyone has gone to a great deal of effort to make this possible for you. We've all got better things to do, you know. Now get on with it. What do you want?'

At that moment she found her voice.

'Nothing!' she cried. 'I don't want anything! I don't want you to feel sorry for me . . . go away! Please don't come on to me just because you pity me. It's humiliating and cruel. You don't know what it does to me . . . go away . . . just . . . go away!'

'Shhh, angel. It was just a dream.' The voice seemed to drift in from afar. Another world. 'Don't be getting yourself all upset now.'

Tash jerked her head up in a panic, suddenly awake. It was pitch dark. There was a heavy weight sitting on the bed next to her and someone was stroking her arm.

Her confused, half-asleep mind couldn't quite take the comforting signals in properly. She screamed.

'Sssh, calm yourself, angel. Do you want to go waking the whole house, now?'

The melodic Irish voice was unmistakable. Tash sat upright with a start and clashed foreheads with an anxiously creased brow.

'Ow – sorry,' she scrambled back on to her pillow, her heart trampolining off her stomach in shock.

Niall O'Shaughnessy was in her bedroom, sitting on Flumps the cuddly badger.

'Now, tell me. What was it you were dreaming about, angel?' he asked gently through the gloom.

'I – I can't remember.' She could feel the warmth of his hand on her arm. Her heart was beating faster than ever. In the sleeping silence of the house she was sure he would be able to hear its frantic thumping like a King Kong moth at a lighthouse window. The memory of her dream made her blush. She was glad it was so dark.

'H-h-how come you're here?' Her voice was so unsteady it sounded like she was sitting on a revving tractor.

'I couldn't sleep,' Niall said quietly. He seemed strangely elated. 'I was just embarking on an insomniac wander when I heard you shouting.'

Tash tried to remember what she'd shouted but couldn't. She prayed it wasn't too obvious what she'd been dreaming about.

Niall was wishing he'd thought up a more valid excuse for being over this side of the house. He'd actually been returning from a poolside rendezvous with Amanda. Outdoor sex and an almighty high had made him reel around the house unable to find his room. He hadn't actually heard Tash until opening the thick wooden door when mistaking it for his own.

Tash coughed uneasily to break the heavy silence which was hanging in the air like musty velvet drapes.

'Thank you for waking me up. I think I'll be all right now.'

She wanted him to go away. The embarrassment was killing her.

'You sure?' Niall didn't move. He felt alive and awake, buzzed through with the sort of electric charge which needed a vent. In this gloomy confessional, the longing to tell all, to purge his guilt, was almost unbearable.

Tash was too nervous to move. There was something odd about his overwrought tone. Why didn't he go? She suddenly wasn't sure if this was reality or not. She pinched herself hard to find out. She couldn't feel anything. She was still dreaming after all.

'Ouch!' cried Niall indignantly.

'Oh God, I'm sorry,' Tash said in a small voice.

'That's all right.' Niall rubbed his buttock and decided that perhaps Tash French wasn't the best person to confide in. 'I'd pinch a strange man if he was sitting on my bed.' He stood up. But then he stopped again, his black silhouette staring into space.

Tash shrunk under her sheet and decided to pretend to be asleep. Something told her that he was less likely to try and murder her if she was comatose. She tried to breathe deeply and evenly but ended up sounding like a dirty phone call.

Niall listened for a few minutes to Tash's soft breathing. It was almost a snore, he thought to himself fondly. Her tranquil wheezing just added to his opinion of her as a gentle, puppy-like little sister. She was the least threatening person in the house. He felt self-pity curdle in his stomach and the shame about what he was doing with Amanda stab through his chest.

He wandered aimlessly over to her window, falling over a chair on his way, and opened the shutters a crack. The window looked over the courtyard and the long straight drive which ran through the black wood to the village road. There was no moon and the ink-stained clouds overhead blotted out any stars.

'What am I doing with my life?' he breathed sadly, lighting one of Tash's cigarettes.

Tash snored even louder and wondered what on earth he was doing in her room. His life was too big an issue for her to tackle at the moment. She felt wide awake now and was starting to worry about Niall's mental stability again. She'd changed her mind about him being nice – he was still a self-pitying, fag-pinching, corridor-creeping, dream-trespassing weirdo.

Very, very silently, she groped for Flumps. She was too young to die.

Niall's thoughts were pounding around his head on fast forward. He wished Tash would wake up so that he could tell her about Lisette. Aware that he was recklessly careering towards really screwing up, he desperately needed to talk to someone. Matty was too moral to understand, too concerned about Niall's addiction to see the reasons behind it. Sally would just agree with whatever Niall said to jolly him along. And, despite such terrifying intimacy, he found Amanda impossible to talk to; it didn't take a psychologist to realise that she'd simply freak if he started banging on about still loving his wife.

Tash held her breath as she heard Niall say, 'Are you awake?'

She felt her lungs bursting as he turned from the window and looked into the room.

'Please wake up . . . Tash?'

Clutching Flumps tightly, feeling guilty as hell, she didn't answer.

He seemed to take for ever to walk across the room, muttering 'Shit' as he got his foot caught in her discarded clothes, then 'Fuck' as he mistook the wardrobe for the door to the landing.

The moment he was out of the door, Tash let out her lungs with a gasp and then wished with all her heart that she hadn't pretended to be asleep.

Flumps was jettisoned from the bed in remorse.

She buried her head miserably in a pillow and cheered herself up by indulging in an exquisite daydream that Hugo and Niall were fighting over her at the medieval banquet. She was sipping a tall glass of champagne and wearing sumptuous black velvet. No, she wasn't. She was leaning against a marble pillar and wearing a rich scarlet silk dress which clung to every curve of her miraculously slender and supple body.

Niall was screaming that he loved Tash more than life itself and would walk barefoot through the Gobi for her. Hugo yelled back that he would swim the Atlantic in a force nine gale with lead weights in his trunks for her. A *Daily Mail* reporter was jotting it all down in a spiral notepad and Sophia was looking furious (and wonderfully ugly in a grey nylon overall) in the corner of the room. Max was being refused entry by a huge bouncer at the front door.

'But I've come to tell Tash French that I love her more than David Gower. I'd bowl a hundred googlies in a row for her!' he screamed.

Then suddenly Tash's dress fell off, revealing her waist-high, grubby support knickers. Hugo and Niall both started laughing and saying what a brilliant joke it had been. Three photographers and Max's entire cricket team had appeared from nowhere.

Aunt Cass walked in dressed as the Queen of Hearts, carrying a wooden block. She was followed by Michael in wrinkled black tights, smoking a clay pipe from beneath his heavy black hood. He had a huge axe in his hand.

'Off with her head!' screamed Cass, setting the block down in front of Tash.

'Off with her head!' chorused the others.

Tash had fallen asleep again.

24

Woken early on Sunday morning by a chorus of hungry canine disapproval, Alexandra looked with increasing despair at the huge pile of washing from two days ago, then at the fur coats of dust muffling everything in the house. Finally, she steeled herself to go into the kitchen and face the debris of the night before.

It was all too much. Dolloping out dog food with one hand, she picked up the phone with the other and dialled through to the lodge.

Jean's wife, Valérie, came up to the house to help with the housework twice a week. When it was just Pascal, Alexandra and Polly staying in the manoir for a fraught-night at a time, Valérie's slow progress around the few rooms they inhabited, with a squeegee, a bucket of foam and all the latest gossip from the village, was ample. But with more rooms than ever before opened up for the guests, Alexandra's unique interpretation of housework simply wasn't up to it.

Even she couldn't help noticing that they kept running out of plates because the dishwasher hadn't been put on and that the spaniels' beds were looking fresher than the humans'. Smeary glasses and brimming ashtrays were congregating in picket lines on every surface. The overflowing freezer had packed up in frosty fatigue. With Cass and Sophia's dust-detecting fingers due back that day, something had to be done.

Although it was Sunday, a day traditionally preserved only for one's closest family and certainly not for work, Valérie excitedly insisted that she come up to the house for the morning, knowing that her employer would reward her loyalty with some fine wine and cheeses for Sunday lunch in the lodge. She was also dying to have a closer look at all les anglais, who had been the sole topic of conversation in the village for two weeks.

Alexandra found herself absurdly elated at the prospect of some company. It was ridiculous, really. She had a household full of family, yet they were behaving like shifty strangers towards her. And at least Valérie didn't refuse proudly if slipped the odd hundred-franc note.

As she sat at the table waiting for the kettle to boil, she pondered the problem of Matty. Dear, self-righteous, over-reacting Matty. She was still no further on in her attempt to make him solvent. She stared at the whitewashed walls for inspiration.

And then it came to her. She knew exactly how she was going to help him. Ingenious, Alexandra, my darling. How do you do it? It might be a bit tricky to organise but had that ever stopped her in the past? This could provide the best fun she'd had in ages.

She leapt up excitedly and went in search of her phone book, leaving the kettle whistling furiously on the hob behind her.

Michael found the kettle, still shrieking to itself, ten minutes later. There was just enough water in it for one cup of tea. He took the last cup from the hooks above the sink and went in search of a tea-bag.

Camomile, Rosehip, Nettle, Green Gunpowder (whatever *that* was), Apple, Fruits of the Forest, Cinnamon – the teas read like a character list of the fairies in *A Midsummer Night's Dream*. But no Typhoo or PG Tips. In the end, Michael settled for Lapsang Souchong, which sounded foreign without looking likely to cause delirium or indigestion. But when he opened the tin he was not confronted with a nice square bag but with a whole load of dried-up leaves.

All the teapots seemed to be full of the remains of previous tiffins. Michael looked around the kitchen hopelessly, wishing Cass were around to help. How did one go about cleaning out a teapot? He gave up and had a glass of orange juice.

The next minute he nearly had a heart attack as an old crone with a face the texture of neglected chamois leather carried a basket full of speckled ducks' eggs into the room.

She stood in front of the window, blotting out all of Michael's light, and made several bracing, bovine puffing noises as she got her breath back before nodding at Michael brusquely. There was a particularly hairy wart on the end of her damson nose, Michael noted, and her small, beady black eyes were dangerously close together underneath eyebrows which actually met in the middle. She'd brought with her a faint smell of tomcat.

He stared back in silent shock as she scratched her whiskery chin with stumpy, gnarled fingers, before rolling back her sleeves to reveal two muscular red arms which she buried in the sink.

Michael was perplexed. Was this some escaped loon from the village who'd been exposed to too much radiation from the local nuclear plant?

Mercifully, at that moment Pascal wandered into the kitchen in a striped cotton dressing-gown, blinking the sleep from his eyes. He smiled at Michael and then noticed the woman as she scrubbed with manly fervour at an encrusted casserole dish.

'Bonjour, Valérie! Ça va?' Pascal cried and, to Michael's amazement, planted two sloppy kisses on the old woman's cheeks. She was beaming like a pig with a truffle now.

They started gabbling in French. Michael – who prided himself on his broad knowledge and command of modern languages – didn't understand a word.

'Er . . . sorry to break up the parley, Pascal, old boy. I was wondering what the chances of organising this bloody work-party were today?' Michael butted in. He thought it was effing rude that they excluded him from the conversation. After all, he was a guest and – although the last thing he wanted was to be introduced to this fearful old hag – he felt that he at least merited some manners.

'Eh?' Pascal was not far enough into the day to take such a complicated sentence in.

'People to work on the barn.' Michael talked with the same painful slowness and enunciation that he had with each of the children's foreign exchanges from years gone by. Really, he reflected, the French should make more effort with languages as he had done.

'Ah, oui.' Pascal didn't exactly look ecstatic at the prospect. 'I weel speak to Valérie.'

Oh God, thought Michael. Don't tell me we're going to have *that* thing shifting tons of timber with a single hand and humping hundredweights of bricks up and down ladders.

But Pascal was finding out if Jean was free. Jean liked to go to visit the widow Drouhin on Sunday morning – although he pretended to his wife that it was his brother's family he visited so diligently.

'No, he's not with Claude today,' Valérie replied in French, wiping her hot face with a soapy hand and leaving lather on her cheek like a fluffy grey sideburn, 'he was snoring like an old bloodhound when I left the house. It is because he re-did all the fencing next to the top wood yesterday,' she added quickly.

'I thought he did that last week?' Pascal laughed.

They're at it again, thought Michael furiously. Speaking in a bloody foreign language.

He was about to deliver another haughty request when Ben and Hugo shambled in, looking tired and unshaven.

'Morning, Michael,' Ben croaked in a fragile voice. 'Morning, Pascal. Valérie.' He looked rather forlornly at the empty table. 'Alexandra not up yet?'

'She up one hour. I no know where she is,' Pascal shrugged. 'Valérie say she make English breakfast as a treat.'

Michael felt that anything prepared by Valérie was likely to have a high risk of being contaminated, but kept quiet because he was famished.

'You know, she rather reminds me of old Nanny Hogg.' Hugo regarded the old woman, who was wiping her dribbling purple nose on her apron and sniffing lustily. She gave Hugo an approving look and he backed off a little.

'Make us a cup of tea, Ben?' He sat down next to Michael and picked up the paper that was lying on the table. Michael had been trying to make sense of its French headline for the last five minutes.

'Damned horny woman, your minister for European affairs, Pascal.' Hugo looked at the front page photograph and started to read the article.

Show-off, thought Michael.

'Hugo.' He picked up his pipe purposefully and started to empty it. 'Need to enlist your help, old boy.'

'Mmm?' Hugo carried on reading.

'I've been given the job of doing up the barn for this bloody knees-up for Eddie. Need a bit of bloody brawn on my side, if you get my gist. Just for a couple of hours.'

'No can do.' Hugo got bored of the article and leafed through the paper. 'I'm taking young Tash for a ride. Very demanding young filly, Tash. You know the score, old chap.' He gave Michael a charming smile so that he couldn't quite tell if Hugo was making fun of him or not.

'That tea ready yet, Meredith?'

Ben was having considerable difficulty manoeuvring himself, his hangover and his crutches around the ample bulk of Valérie's derrière, but was far further on in making the tea than Michael had managed. Michael noticed that Hugo didn't offer to lift a finger to help.

'Why don't you have horoscopes in your paper, Pascal?' Hugo asked, lighting a cigarette.

'Don't tell me you've waded your way through the cartoon strips already, Hugo?' Sally wandered in, clutching Tor. 'Has anyone seen my husband?'

'Sounds like a West End farce,' Hugo mused, watching Ben sit down awkwardly, slopping tea on Michael's pipe tobacco. 'I think he went off with the vicar and three chorus girls. Pass us a couple of cups, Sally? There's a love.'

Sally wondered, as she took the freshly washed cups off the

drainer and held them away from Tor's grabbing paws, why people did so much for Hugo when he was so loathsome. It must be wonderful to be that attractive, she reflected, with everyone at your beck and call.

She handed the cups to him and he gave her a blue-eyed wink. I do not feel attracted to him, Sally told herself firmly as she stopped Tor hitting Hugo over the head with a wooden spoon. She determinedly thought of how spoilt he was compared to Matty. Anyway, Matty, when he was in evidence, was just as attractive.

'How are you this morning, Michael?' she inquired politely, then immediately regretted it as Michael launched into his construction and renovation plans.

'Amanda ees not up yet?' Pascal asked Hugo.

Hugo laughed dryly. 'Quite amazing. Amanda's gone green. She went out last night to be at one with the environment and she's now sleeping it off. Getting back to nature is a very exhausting process.' He poured himself a cup of tea with slightly too much care. 'Unfortunately, Amanda's shade of green is not really the environmentally friendly variety. It's more of an emerald hue, in fact.' He looked up at Sally, who had stopped listening to Michael and gone pale.

His cryptic patter had been a test to find out if any of them knew about Amanda's little fling. Sally had passed with flying lack of colour.

The others were totally bemused.

'What is thees green?' asked Pascal, leaning across Valérie to remove his bubbling coffee-maker from the range. 'Amanda is feeling ill?'

'Don't quite understand, Hugs,' queried Ben.

Hugo regarded them all for a moment and then stood up, his face blank.

Oh no, thought Sally. He's going to tell all. She couldn't really blame him, but knew it would have a devastating effect on Niall.

Since finding the ring, Sally had prayed that she was wrong. However ludicrous, she'd fooled herself that there was a perfectly logical explanation and hadn't even told Matty of her discovery. It was so unlike the Niall she knew to do something so completely stupid as screwing around with Hugo's wayward partner. Now that Hugo knew, the whole thing could escalate horribly.

But Hugo merely smiled philosophically and walked with almost calculated leisure to the door. Sally had to admire his cool.

'If you can't work it out for yourselves, then I'm damn well not going to tell you,' he said, and strolled out, leaving his tea untouched.

Michael saw the others staring at the door and quickly appropriated the cup. It tasted wonderfully British.

'What was that all about?' Ben turned a confused face on Sally, who was looking terribly relieved for some reason.

'I've no idea,' Sally gulped, standing up. 'I must go and find Matty.' She dashed out quickly, forgetting that Tor was under the table.

Valérie, who'd just broken enough eggs for all of them into the pan, hissed with exasperation and wiped the sweat from her forehead on the sleeve of her dress. Michael noticed great damp patches under her armpits and felt slightly queasy. Perhaps he'd just have muesli.

Hugo was waiting for Sally in the hallway. She didn't see him at first and was heading for the staircase when she heard a lazy drawl behind her.

'Any ideas?'

She spun round. 'What do you mean?'

'Oh, come on, darling. You know and I know. Who else . . . Matty?'

Sally shook her head.

Hugo was leaning against the wall, picking at a loose piece of plaster. In his dishevelled beauty with his shadowed jaw set, he looked the epitome of a passionately unhappy poet. He must be more cut up about it than he let on, thought Sally.

But when he looked up at her his gaze was steady and unemotional.

'Don't think I'm jealous,' he said quietly, 'although I'll admit it's not exactly terrific for my ego. She's done this sort of thing before – getting the hots for a pretty face or a famous name. But Niall's letting himself in for a lot of shit. It's not just her sympathetic shoulder she's luring him into her bed with.' A large crevice was appearing where he was digging into the plaster with an erratic finger. It was the only part of him that betrayed any feelings.

Sally froze. 'I don't understand.'

'I've seen it before, Sally,' Hugo said gently. 'A mate of Amanda's has no nostrils left – just one giant hole. There's a sniff echoing round this house with an Irish accent. And Niall doesn't suffer from hay-fever.'

'He's off it,' Sally said, trying to convince herself as much as Hugo. 'It was just for a couple of weeks while he was really low.'

'Oh, come on, he was so high yesterday we virtually had to scrape him off the frescoes. Talk about the shit hitting the overhead fan.'

'And you think Amanda's supplying him?' Sally asked quietly.

'Put it this way.' Hugo walked slowly over to her. 'I overheard a very interesting phone conversation between Amanda and a colleague of hers in Cannes. And there's not the sort of money they were talking about in advertising these days.' He looked down at her and put his hand on her shoulder. 'QED, it's not just Niall's body Amanda's screwing up.'

Sally's heart sank like a pint of mercury into her stomach.

'What are you going to do about it?' she asked cautiously.

'Nothing for the moment.' Hugo shrugged, removing his hand from her shoulder and running it through his hair. The action was strangely detached. 'I doubt talking to her would help, to be honest. She can be pretty single-minded when she's decided to get her teeth into somebody.'

'You must be able to do something,' Sally pleaded with him.

'I don't see why,' Hugo drawled. 'It's up to them to fuck up. I just don't want it getting out at the moment.' He paused thoughtfully. 'I've got other poissons to fry.'

It occurred to Sally that Hugo was being distinctly unhelpful.

His lover was being unfaithful under his perfectly formed nose and a supposed mate was digging his own grave with a small spoon, yet he was behaving like it was a minor irritation, a slight blow to his pride.

'Like Tash,' she spat accusingly.

Hugo laughed in mock amazement. 'Really, Sally dear, you must have to wipe your nose an awful lot. You're always poking it into things.'

Sally ignored him. 'Just what are you doing to her, Hugo?'

Hugo smiled non-committally and looked over her shoulder. He could assume a complete lack of interest which was totally infuriating. There was nothing to be read in those Gitane-blue eyes except their usual knowing gleam.

'Well?' Sally persisted.

'Oh dear.' Hugo rubbed a tanned thumb over his stubble and gave Sally a look which clearly stated that he couldn't be more bored if she were the fourth act of a Wagner opera.

'Well?' Sally repeated.

'What do you think we've been doing, my darling?' He grinned suddenly. 'Screwing like the end of the world's a week next Thursday, of course. Under that innocent façade, young Tash is a fiery little minx.' And with that, still grinning to himself, he turned and loped upstairs.

Niall, who'd been making rather precarious progress with his hangover in the opposite direction, stopped in his tracks. He stared at Hugo as he bounded past and tried to take in what he'd just heard.

Sally wandered unhappily across the hall, aiming for nowhere in particular. The door to Pascal's study was open. Glancing in, she caught sight of Alexandra with the phone wedged under her jaw, leafing through an old Heals catalogue.

'I appreciate it's Sunday, darling, but I know how horribly busy you are now you're so successful, and I wanted to catch you at home – you see, I need to ask you to do one of your absolute miracles . . . what? . . . has it really been that long? . . .' Alexandra kicked off a cream suede shoe and started scratching the proffered, speckled stomach of a spaniel with her narrow, brown foot. 'Yes, darling . . . in the Loire, Anjou. It's perfectly luscious, but it's not me I want you to do up, sweetheart. Much closer to home. Rich—' Suddenly Alexandra caught sight of Sally. 'Er – Rich – Richard. Yes, how is Richard? . . . Oh, Peter, sorry – you know how awful I am with names . . . Oh dear . . . with Janet Leopold, really? How extraordinary, I always thought she was gay . . .' Alexandra smiled at Sally, who was trying to mouth 'Would you like a coffee?'

She put her hand over the receiver and shook her head. 'Be a poppet, Sally, and close the door behind you. It's awfully chilly in here.'

As she felt the clunk of the heavy door hinges pull to, Sally speculatively concluded that Alexandra might find it a good deal warmer if she closed the three windows which were wide open in there.

'Richmond,' Alexandra hissed from behind the sound-proof thickness of four inches of solid oak door. 'Cancel everything, darling. I want you to perform one of your miracles in Richmond. Redecorate the whole house. I'm talking carte blanche – you can even rag roll the airing cupboard if you want. But one thing – it must be frightfully quick. You see, it's a surprise . . .'

Tash woke up at nine o'clock feeling absolutely ravenous – a sure sign that she was going to have a bad day keeping her complexes at bay.

She knew that she should go down and eat breakfast with the others but as soon as she caught sight of herself in the mirror she wanted to climb back into bed again.

I never have dishcloth skin in my dreams, she thought sadly. Here was herself, Tash French, with a lump of sleep hanging off her eyelashes and a long red crease across her cheek where she'd been lying too long on a crumpled bolster. Realistically speaking, someone who could never attract Hugo Beauchamp or get photographed laughing with Niall O'Shaughnessy.

She couldn't decide what to wear. Her hair looked awful.

New spots seemed to be growing on top of the old ones because there was no space left on her face. Her nose was peeling like old gloss paintwork and she'd pulled a muscle in her back riding yesterday, making her shoulders tilt at forty-five degrees.

She put on a pair of black jeans and took them off again. She scraped her hair back into a pony-tail and gave the mirror a smouldering look; she looked like a Russian shot-putter. She pulled on a skirt that her mother had given her and ripped it up the seam. She then worked her way through four more outfits, a French pleat and a graduated plait before finally sitting down on the end of her bed for a sob.

Just as she'd reached the Porky Pig face and dribbly nostrils stage there was the inevitable knock on the door.

'I'm not decent!' she wailed, having resorted to tears in only a pair of cheerful cherry-strewn knickers. She looked across at the brass door handle and held back a hiccup.

'Er . . . right. Me here. Ben that is,' came a muffled drone through the door. 'Want to come to the Sunday market?' She could hear the squeak of his rubber-based crutches on the polished floorboards.

On the verge of saying no, Tash had a sudden terrifying vision of being left alone in the house with Niall, Hugo and Amanda. It would be like walking around a Chanel boutique wearing nylon slacks and an anorak with only twenty pence in her pocket.

'Who's going?'

'Pascal, muggins here, Paola and the sprogs. Matty's driving Sally and their little monsters. Marcus might tag along too. 'Bout it, I think. Do you know, Tor tied my bandage round the kitchen table leg this morning? Nearly concussed myself on a pot of apricot confiture.'

Tash giggled. 'I'll come, if you can wait ten minutes.'

So, with her red blotches buried under concealer and her badly aligned body held together in faded denim shorts and the inevitable t-shirt, Tash squashed Max's Australian bush hat over her untamed hair and set off to Beaudîmes market in the back of Audrey the Audi.

25

About twenty kilometres from the manoir, Beaudîmes was a lively medieval Anjou village, famed for the quality of the rosé produced by its fiercely independent wine co-operative. During the Sunday market, this was sold from a stall set up on the back of a converted cattle truck in the most prominent position in the market square – just adjacent to the Café de Paris. The acerbic and fruity nectar was determinedly sipped from eight in the morning until midday by its hardened sellers without any apparent side effects.

From a table on the café's terrace (the patron accepted a case of wine in return for this temporary loss of his meubles), the collective members of the co-operative would closely scrutinise anyone giving their van more than a fleeting glance and then lay bets as to how much money they could persuade this person to part with. With much noisy camaraderie, they would take the potential purchaser under their wine-stained wings and invite him or her to join them in tasting the 'meilleur vin d' Anjou'. This would turn into several glasses which would inebriate the buyer sufficiently to purchase far more of the delicious brew than originally intended. The story went that the sellers even cleaned their teeth with rosé.

Ben, of course, was immediately hooked. With a lofty swing of his crutch, he stated his intention of amusing himself by beating these amateurs at their own game. Convinced that, despite the early hour, his hefty cooked breakfast ('More than these Frogs could stomach before noon') would soak up all the alcohol, he limped off to the van with an heroic deportment which generations of aristocratic in-breeding had honed to a finely turned peak. The collective faces of the members of the wine co-operative lit up as if a month of Sunday markets had all come at once.

Pascal shrugged and went off to a nearby stall where he was heard haggling enthusiastically with a thick-set, moustached man who looked like one of the Sicilian Mob. He returned a few minutes later with three huge padlocks.

'They are for my caves,' he explained to his bewildered charges. 'I do not want voleurs in wiz my wines at the party.'

The d'Eblouir house guests walked at a leisurely pace around the stall-lined square, squinting against the sun. Tom scuttled around picking up peas. Polly, dressed as a milkmaid, was given ten francs by an unwitting American tourist, causing Lotty to break into noisy, jealous sobs.

The market was like nothing Tash had seen before. Having kept herself firmly away from all the sight-seeing excursions which had set off from the manoir over the past two weeks, she was overcome by the whole occasion.

This, Pascal told her, was the biggest of the three weekly markets that were held in Beaudîmes, and Tash could well believe it.

The market spread out into little side streets like a great, multicoloured octopus stretching its cluttered tentacles. Every few minutes, another groaning Citroën van, looking as if it had never been washed in its life, would creak into the square, causing a commotion of horn beeps, shouting stall-holders and barking dogs, as it squeezed its way with neurosurgical accuracy through the displays of pungent ripe fruit and stacks of glinting copperware, high-rise piles of handbags and jigsaws of glistening fish. It would then park with a resounding wail of worn-down brake-pads and open up like a tatty doll's house to reveal yet more piles of irresistible goodies.

Sally was in ecstasy. She discovered a road entirely taken up with brocantes – local junk dealers selling anything from ancient agricultural oddities to 1950s table lamps or eighteenth-century cut-glass toothpick holders. She bounced about in front of Matty, clutching one item after another, pleading, 'Please, Matty. Please, please, *please*!' with increasing vigour and pitch. Any minute now, thought Tash, all the cut-glass toothpick holders were in danger of shattering, much as they would during a Kiri te Kanawa aria.

Marcus haggled over an oddly shaped clay pipe for a bit then gave up, moving along to squint at a stall sagging under sacks of pungent coffee beans.

It was only when Matty pointed out a tall, blond German buying a distinctly warped-looking mangle for the equivalent of eighty pounds that Sally finally agreed to move on.

Sulkily trailing behind her with a child on each hand, Matty worried about Niall left to his own devious vices back at the manoir while they were wandering through this glorified car-boot sale. He was annoyed with Sally, who suddenly seemed to be very bored with Niall's problems and changed the subject whenever it came up. Last night, Niall had acted like a has-been old soak, flirting with Tash, of all people. But when Matty had tried to discuss it with Sally in bed, she'd bolted to the loo, pleading morning sickness.

Tash hung behind the others, gazing around her. Wherever she looked was a buzz of rich, saturated colour and activity. She wished that she'd brought her sketch pad. Exquisite, characterful brown faces were gabbling with a curious animation that could only be French. Hands flailed around, gesticulating madly, while others poked through the different stalls' wares with critical, sunburnt fingers. They squeezed a peach here, prodded a sea bass there. One woman tested out the zip on a pair of trousers with such concentrated vigour that it came away from the fabric it was sewn to, still in full working order. With a sniff of displeasure, she put down the offending garment and moved on to the next stall.

There was a tremendous amount of repetition in what was actually being sold, Tash noticed. Two stalls away from the man boasting the best cotton shirts in Anjou was a display of identical shirts claiming to be hand-made by the vendor's grandmother in her tiny cottage near Richelieu.

It was food, however, which abounded. Everywhere she looked, Tash saw huge, mouth-watering piles of fresh produce ready to be tucked into a hefty basket and born off to an enormous, bustling farmhouse kitchen, where it was destined to become part of that most delicious of all feasts, the French Sunday lunch.

Tash, who hadn't had time to eat the breakfast she'd woken up so in need of, now felt her stomach cry out to try the stacks of sumptuously ripe pumpkins and peaches, the crisp, acid-green peas, artichokes and lettuce, the vivid, primary-coloured sweet peppers or the tangy little melons heavy with juice, that smelled of treacle and spice. There were displays of succulent herbed sausages, rich game pâtés and pungent goat's cheeses dripping with olive oil ready for passers-by to taste. Tash nearly passed out by a little trestle table loaded to groaning point with fruit tarts and custard cakes. Next to it, a dark-skinned girl in a floral dress straight out of Carmen prepared hot waffles with the sweetest of chocolate and hazelnut coverings. The smell was so divine, Tash dived for her purse in delirious joy.

After two chocolate waffles and a pistachio ice cream from the next stall along, Tash felt the size of a house. The others had disappeared out of sight, except for Ben, who was sitting at the little co-operative table saying 'when' slightly desperately.

At the next table, a tall blond man in cycling shorts and very dark glasses was sitting sipping a Ricard. He had the self-confident loucheness of someone who knows they look good – provided they check the fact every two minutes in the mirror. By his feet was a huge, hairy dog the colour of an old teddy bear except for dark smoke ears. It was enormous, the size of a well-built sheep, with a Beatles-style floppy fringe overhanging soulful, speckled brown eyes. It also possessed the biggest feet Tash had ever seen on a dog.

'He is very beautiful, no?' Paola appeared next to Tash, pushing a sleeping Josh in a Rolls-Royce of a baby-buggy.

'Yes, he's gorgeous. I'd love a dog like that.' Tash sighed

thoughtfully and wondered how Boots and Poshpaws were getting on. Graham and Mikey were bound to have forgotten to feed them and clean out their lit tray. She tried to imagine what returning to six weeks of unchanged cat lit would be like. Thankfully, this time her imagination failed her.

Paola was giggling, 'I no talk about the *dog*!' She opened her eyes wider and looked at Tash as if she were mad. 'I mean the *man*.'

She shot another longing gaze in the direction of the tall man, who was reading a magazine now and pouring water into his Ricard at the same time. Paola sighed in admiration at such manly ability.

'You will come and have a coffee with me, no?' She gave Tash a very poppy-eyed look of enthusiasm.

Tash felt far too blown-up to squeeze in a soup-thick espresso, but was immensely grateful that Paola was talking to her again. As she nodded in agreement, she wondered if she'd be expected to double-date with the dog. The Italian girl instantly handed over charge of Josh and Lotty to Tash before dashing over to commandeer the seat closest to Signor Perfect.

Because Paola was sitting nearest to the blond man, he was just out of her line of vision. This was a calculated manoeuvre, evolved from years of practice in Italian night spots. This way the blond man got the full benefit of her pretty profile and the long, glossy hair lying like a broad satin ribbon on the smoothest of brown backs. Meanwhile Tash was ordered in a low hiss to keep an eye on him and kick Paola if he looked at her. Not easy if you're trying to control a screaming baby and a toddler, added to which the object of scrutiny is wearing specs so dark it would be impossible to tell if he had one glass eye and a squint.

'He is not looking at me very often, Tash, no?' Paola hissed accusingly.

'Stop it, Lotty!' Tash removed Lotty from her knee, where she'd been persistently trying to force a sugar cube up one nostril. 'To be honest, Paola, I can't tell. The dog keeps looking at Ben, though.'

Ben was still at the corner table, surrounded by empty bottles and laughing co-operative members. He was singing rugby songs very loudly in a remarkably good bass voice, marred only by the fact that he was trying to simultaneously translate them into French for the benefit of his listeners. Most of this turned out to be German. His new friends shrugged at one another and offered him some more première cuvée.

'*Concentrate*, Tash.' Paola removed her scrunchy and ran her feminine little hand through her long dark hair, shaking it out luxuriously with a Lolita pout. 'Now. He look at me now?'

Tash thought that even if the man hadn't noticed Paola, he would have certainly become aware that there was a strange-looking individual with bad skin and a bush hat gawping at him from a corner table.

He'd called over a waiter and was ordering another Ricard in an undertone. Suddenly he looked across to their table and gave them the benefit of a gorgeous grin.

'He just smiled,' Tash whispered to Paola.

'At me, no?'

'I can't tell.' Then something occurred to Tash. 'Why would he smile at you when you've got your back to him?'

'Good point.' Paola stood up, looked slowly around at everything except her blond Adonis and stretched ostentatiously. 'We swap,' she hissed from the side of her mouth.

So they changed places, with Paola making a lot of fuss about sitting down, waving her mini-skirted bottom in the air as she moved her new chair sufficiently away from the table so that her legs weren't masked. She'd now donned some circular mirrored shades so that she and her prey were evenly matched, and gave Tash a running commentary as their sunglass-meets became more steamy.

'He look at me – this time a little longer. You will have to translate if he is coming over,' Paola said, 'I no speak any French.'

'I'm not too hot at it myself,' Tash pointed out, having a vision of herself acting as gooseberry interpreter with a French dictionary and a violin over a candlelit dinner à deux. 'Perhaps he speaks Italian.'

'He smile at me again,' Paola sighed dreamily. 'He is so – how you say – horned? And now he raise his glass at me.' She lifted her tiny espresso cup in return and looked lingeringly over her shades.

Tash took a large gulp of her coffee, leaving a frothy moustache on her upper lip, and felt faintly sick. The sun was strong enough now to make her skin sting. She squashed Max's hat further down on her head and thought of Hugo. She hoped he wasn't having a clandestine session with Snob while she was away playing Cupid.

'He come over, he come over!' giggled Paola. 'How am I saying "what is your name?" in French?'

'G'day girls.' A broad-shouldered shadow fell across their table. 'Mind if I join you?' The voice was unmistakably Australian.

'Sì, if you must,' Paola said nonchalantly, her dark glasses twinkling.

Tash was too embarrassed to speak. He must have been lapping up every word they had said about him in the past quarter of an hour. She inwardly cringed for poor Paola.

'You Australian or Kiwi?' twanged the blond heart-throb, settling two muscular thighs on the seat beside Tash and indicating her bush hat with a broad grin. He gave Paola a cursory nod.

'Neither,' Tash gulped, feeling absolutely rotten for Paola. 'I'm Tash – this is Paola. She's from Tuscany.'

'Tash is a beautiful name,' the man rumbled throatily as his dark glasses examined her legs, sun-streaked hair falling across his forehead. He extended a long muscular arm and, just as Tash was clumsily freeing her hand of Lotty's vice-like grip to shake his, he reached up and wiped a drop of pistachio ice cream from her chin with a warm finger.

'There,' he returned to his Ricard with a satisfied grin, 'now you're even more stunning.'

Oh Christ, Tash thought miserably. Poor Paola.

But the Italian girl was totally oblivious of the sympathy that was being transmitted to her across the table. She listened with besotted brown eyes hidden behind two black Perspex circles, pout firmly in place and a complete disregard of the fact Josh needed changing, as the tanned Australian told them his life story. This was a line of conversation that he was clearly not unpractised in pursuing.

He was called Todd Austin. His dog, a Briard, was called Rooter. Todd came from the east coast of Australia but had moved to France after uni to work as a marine biologist in the Côte d'Azur. There, he told them proudly, he'd 'swum, surfed, shagged and slept' until his contract ran out and was not renewed by the company he was working for.

Paola couldn't think why, and told him so. Tash could and kept quiet. She looked at Rooter. He looked back with a sad resignation.

'Of course, there were lots of openings available to me then.' Todd leaned back in his chair with his hands behind his head and a great deal of hairy armpit on display. 'Mostly female, y'know what I mean?'

Paola giggled. Tash felt even more nauseous. She watched Ben ricocheting off several tables as he limped into the café for a pee.

'But then I met these really great guys. Cyclists. I kind of hung out with them for a while – I guess they thought I was pretty wild, a daggy surf bum with a couple a thousand francs and two ounces of weed. Bought myself a bike and never looked back. I picked up Rooter in the Pyrenees while I was competing. He's my biggest fan.'

Rooter lifted one of his huge, manila paws and scratched despondently at a flea on his neck.

'You have been doing the Tour de France, no?' Paola eyed his bulging, glossy leg muscles with increasing excitement.

'Now you're talking my language!' A flashy smile swept across his bronzed face, aware now where admiration lay.

Tash, relieved that Paola had him hooked, noticed a large gap between his front teeth and thought of the Wife of Bath. A sure sign of promiscuity. Or was it good digestion? She could never remember.

'I couldn't devote enough time to training this year.' Todd was playing with his hooped earring and not quite catching Paola's eye through the two layers of tinted Perspex which separated them. 'I was stuck in a really intense relationship with this older woman. She was really possessive and demanding. It – er – it hurts me to talk about it.'

And he proceeded to relate every sordid detail, from her picking him up with a fifties Jaguar and seducing him in a sleazy hotel with Otis Redding drifting up from the smoky bar below, to the point where she held a knife to his throat and told him that if she couldn't have him then nobody could. Tash found herself wondering what Rooter was doing throughout all this excitement. Perhaps he was guarding Todd's puncture kit?

'But in the end she let me go. You see,' Todd took off his glasses for emphasis, revealing two sparkling grey-green eyes the colour of lichen, 'I taught her something about herself which gave her the strength to let go.' He looked deep into Paola's mirrored lenses for what seemed for ever. After a while, it occurred to Tash that he was actually looking at his own reflection. 'I taught her that making love is an art form – that women are the most sensual, most passionate sex and they deserve as much pleasure as men in bed.' His voice had dropped to a low, twangy croak. 'I taught her to love herself. You see, I adore women. All women – but especially the beautiful ones like you.' He leaned forward and removed Paola's dark glasses. 'And, phew! – are you beautiful.'

Despite chat-up lines as corny as a rambler's foot, he was the sort of man who could make one feel as if one was the only other person in the room. Which made everyone else feel like a standard lamp with the personality of an amoeba. If the flattery didn't get them, then the fact he loved his dog would. Contingency plan – smart.

Tash tried to impersonate a chair. Not that they'd have noticed if she was wearing her knickers on her head and wrestling with a seven-foot rubber plant. It was unusual for her not to be at least slightly attracted to anything half-way decent in terms of the male sex, but Todd Austin left her cold.

His monumental ego was so transparent. He also shaved his legs and waxed his chest.

'Tell me about yourself, Paola – no! Let me guess . . .'

Tash watched Ben limp back from the loo with his flies undone. Todd was telling Paola that she was obviously a giver with a golden heart who was taken advantage of too much. Paola was nodding sadly and shooting evil glances at Ben and the children.

Just as Tash was about to tactfully remove herself to change Josh, Rooter heaved a weary sigh and lay comfortably down on her feet. He looked up at her plaintively, willing her not to move, then pushed at her legs with his snout, demanding to be stroked. Tash tickled behind his ears absent-mindedly and tried not to think about Max.

Sally and Matty were waiting patiently for Pascal to finish choosing individual mushrooms from a huge boxful. He went about it with the same exacting perfectionism as a Booker prize-winner selects adjectives.

Sally watched Matty as he gazed into the distance, holding both the children's hands. There was no denying he was a wonderful father and a caring, sensitive husband, too. Yet he'd been so distracted recently, Sally was beginning to feel a huge distance yawn between them. He'd also just bitten her head off for buying armfuls of presents to take back to friends in London – even though she'd carefully ripped the zeros off the prices.

She realised she should tell him what she knew about Niall. But until he confided in *her* exactly how worried he was about his friend, Sally couldn't tell how he was going to react. She dreaded that he would blow up and storm off to be self-righteous, probably blaming her.

'I want a fram-bras ice lolly,' Tom whined for the hundredth time.

Tor glugged in agreement as she simultaneously rammed plastic sunglasses from a bargain bucket down her sundress.

'Ice creams rot your teeth,' Matty told them patiently, removing Tor's booty. 'If you promise to be good, I'll buy us all a bag of mixed nuts, how's that?'

Tom rolled his eyes despairingly and got out his Nintendo.

'And put that bloody thing away,' Matty snapped. 'I said half an hour a day.'

He turned to Sally, who was lost in thought, staring at an ugly watercolour of the Château de Saumur. He sounds just like his father, she thought sadly. He has absolutely no idea how alike they are.

'You coming?' Matty barked impatiently.

Nodding silently, Sally followed at a distance as he marched the grouchy children nut-wards. She was right not to tell him about Niall, she decided.

'Allô – Sally!' Pascal, loping towards a chilled meat-van now, waved from an aisle away. 'Nous viendrons bientôt, chérie – d'accord?'

'Okay,' Sally called in return. Then, spotting Polly trotting behind her father and bearing an ice-cream cone as if it were an Olympic torch, positively concertinaring under the weight of multi-flavoured balls, she lagged behind. Having checked Matty was still leading the kids in a Von Trappian crocodile, she nipped behind a restaurant board and doubled-back towards the ice-cream stall.

At the café, Ben had begun to turn faintly green. He kept swaying dangerously to either side but was helped back to ninety degrees by an eager work-worn brown hand, and encouraged to carry on counting out the money he owed the local co-operative for the wine he'd agreed to buy. Beside him, he seemed to have amassed a crate of virtually every vintage produced in the region. There appeared to be an awful lot of varieties for such a small area. And Ben had tried each and every one. Extensively. At length. Interspersed with a large amount of the local goat's cheese to freshen his palate. Now his palate was about as fresh as Michelangelo's after completing the Sistine Chapel.

'Feel a shquiffy,' he burped gently. 'Got to shoot a cat.' And he lumbered, limping, towards the café loos again, straight into the Ladies.

The members of the co-operative shrugged, licked their nicotine-stained thumbs, and counted their proceeds over a final glass of rosé.

Lurking beside a slumped sack of potatoes and adopting much the same posture, Marcus scratched his head and lit a fag. He was no further on in acquiring some 'happening gear' for the rave. No one seemed to be pushing anything around here except wheelbarrows. Flicking his ash into a crate of courgettes, he watched Sally creeping behind a fish van with several ice cream cones dripping on to her wrists. This morning had been a complete waste of time, he reflected. He should have stayed in bed all day as he'd planned.

Tash had been having the most wonderful fantasy about Hugo taking her back to England. It all got a bit complicated on the ferry because Niall popped up and threw himself overboard. Then, back at Hugo's yard, they found Amanda wearing a gingham pinny and fluffy slippers, cooking them both apple crumble. However, the fantasy soon got into full swing and they were just engaging in a rib-smashing clinch in the living compartment of his luxury horsebox when Pascal appeared at the café table with Sally, Matty and the kids. They were all weighed down with fresh supplies for the manoir. Even Tor was positively buckling under a bag of flageolet beans and a triple-choc ice cream. Matty was scowling broodily with an untouched cone of fraise dripping on to his hand.

'We are ready to go, no?' Pascal regarded Todd with interest. The tall Australian was expounding his theories on Derailleur gears to a riveted Paola. As soon as the Italian girl noticed Pascal, she dug Todd firmly in the ribs and winked.

Todd stood up, extending a brawny arm.

'G'day, mate – Todd Austin,' he grinned, towering over Pascal.

'Pascal d'Eblouir.' Pascal thrust out an amiable hand from under five sticks of bread.

Todd gave him a very firm handshake, sending a parcel of cheese flying.

While Matty, Sally and the kids grew increasingly red-faced and sweaty under the burden of shopping, Pascal, cheeks inflating with boredom, listened politely as the Australian trapped him in an intense gaze and launched into a monologue about cycling.

'It's all about commitment, you see – er – Pascal, mate,' he gave a broad grin and played with the colourful friendship strings on his wide wrists.

'Oui?' Pascal stifled a yawn.

Todd gave Rooter a pat and leaned forward. 'I sacrifice all my time and energy – even my love-life,' he paused dramatically to emphasise the loss. 'But top-level cycling eats money. As an independent I've gotta buy all my own equipment, not to mention digs and grub for my mate, Rooter and me. It's a tough sport for a one-man band up against professionals with team back-up and sponsorship.' Todd glanced at Paola, who was nodding encouragingly.

Tash, wondering what they were up to, wished she'd listened in earlier.

'We must be go—' Pascal started in vain.

'You see – er – Pascal, I – get off, Rooter – I'm looking for a job right now. There's a couple of big competitions coming up and I've got to a bit of a low tide-mark in my beer money – I mean finances. Er – Paola here said there might be some labour needed over at your place. Some sort of conversion job on a barn.'

'You want a job?' Pascal asked briskly.

'You're talking my language, mate!' Todd beamed at Pascal and then winked at Sally. He always found it useful to have as many women on his side as possible.

'Why you no say so earlier, instead of giving me all thees talk of bicyclettes?' Pascal puffed out his cheeks and sighed. Employing someone for the next couple of weeks might get Michael off his back. He blew out his cheeks and nodded. 'You've somewhere to stay in Beaudîmes?'

'Er – not really.' Todd scratched his head. 'I've been kipping on a mate's floor. It's not exactly the ideal set-up.' No need to admit that the patron of the cheap hotel he'd been staying at in exchange for bar work had found Todd in bed with his daughter and kicked him out. Todd had, in fact, spent the previous night in a derelict mill, using Rooter as a pillow.

'You come back wiv us then, we talk about thees over lunch,' Pascal nodded at him. 'Now where ees Marcus? We will be eating the lunch by moonlight if we leave any later.' He heaved up his shopping bags to get a better grip on them and looked around.

Marcus was thoughtfully sniffing a bunch of parsley at one of the few remaining stalls. It was nearly midday and most of the stall-holders had packed up as noisily as they had arrived and set off in throaty, rusty vehicles for their own lunches.

'Marcus! Nous partons!' Pascal marched off to his jeep.

That was where the problem became apparent. Not only were they taking Todd and Rooter back with them, but also enough food to feed the All Blacks for a week plus Todd's bicycles, backpack and saddlebags. Without Michael's packing expertise it was like fitting the Royal Philharmonic into a transit van. It was only after they had succeeded on the third attempt that it occurred to Tash something was missing.

She was wedged in the back of Matty's car between Marcus and a sack of potatoes with Tom on her knee.

'Er – Matty.'

'Mmmm?' Matty was grinding Audrey's gears and trying to see through the clutter of people and paraphernalia over his shoulder to reverse.

'I think Tor's just wet her nappy, man,' Marcus groaned.

'Don't worry about it, Marcus,' Sally murmured rather vaguely. She was doing her mascara in Matty's rear-view mirror, which she'd adjusted three days ago without his noticing since. She was also sitting on a wildly expensive silk scarf she'd bought for Alexandra while Matty was taking Tom to the loo.

'Matty!' Tash pleaded.

'Hang on a tic, love. I'm just doing an awkward manoeuvre.' There was a tremendous squeak of rubber against stone as Matty reversed alongside the pavement.

'Matty, we've forgotten Ben!' Tash blurted.

'Ohmygod!' Matty put on the brakes. He looked at Sally, who now had mascara all over her forehead. 'Could you pop out and fetch him, love? He'll just have to fit in somewhere.'

Sally opened the door, causing an AA map, a box of tissues and a half-eaten packet of digestive biscuits to fall out. She hastily whipped the scarf into an open bag of Pampers near the gear stick.

'Don't be long, Salls, I can't park here,' Matty called after her. There was a beep from an angry Peugeot behind. 'All right, keep your beret on!' he barked out of the window.

Sally was back in less than a minute.

'Matty, I think I'm going to need your help.'

'Why? Can't you find him? Are you sure he didn't go with Pascal, Tash?'

'Oh, he's here all right,' Sally giggled. 'The trouble is, he doesn't know it. Come and see.'

The Peugeot beeped even more frantically as Matty got out of Audrey to see what his wife was talking about. Tash, Marcus and the kids, who were too firmly lodged in the back to join them, stayed behind to blush as a torrent of French abuse was directed at Audrey and her GB sticker.

Ben had passed out cold at the table which he'd occupied all morning. His top half was splayed across the wine-stained expanse of wood in front of him, blond hair flopping into an ashtray, whilst his legs sprawled underneath at obtuse angles to one another.

Precariously stacked to his left were a large number of crates of local wine. Leaning against them, like two flying buttresses holding up a sagging wall, were Ben's crutches.

As Sally and Matty approached him they could hear a loud contented snoring, interrupted by the occasional belch. At even closer range he could be heard to be muttering 'genug, mein Freund' from time to time.

'What do you suppose he means?' Sally whispered.

'God knows.' Matty swung Ben's arm over his shoulder and started to take his snoring brother-in-law's weight, 'Let's get him out of here before anyone sniffs a rat. Supposing Sophia sees him like this? She and Cass – Christ, he's heavy – are coming back from Paris today.'

'Wisteria's a beautiful word – hic – isn't it?' Ben piped up before sinking back into incoherence.

They managed to push and shove him into the front seat of Audrey, leaving Sally to contort herself into the back. Ben's wine, however, had to be left in the hands of the café's proprietor, who was a shrewd businessman and charged them a bottle a day in rent.

Half an hour after Pascal had left, Audrey finally set off in the general direction of Le Manoir de Champegny with Tor wailing, Tom complaining and Ben's head lolling out of the window because he had become compos mentis enough to announce that he felt sick and wasn't herbaceous a nice word?

Tash, sitting on a rather peculiar lump in Audrey's rear upholstery and nursing a sulking Tom, prayed that her sister wouldn't be waiting at the house to witness Ben's après-dégustation disgrace.

26

It had been a frustrating morning for Hugo. He'd stayed at the manoir because he needed to get away from the sound of screaming children – a noise which set his teeth on edge. Other people's brats filled him with horror, and it was with considerable relief that he saw them all safely borne off for a few hours' wailing, nappy-wetting and throwing-up in the company of the Beaudîmes locals.

The fact Tash had gone with them was not wholly a bad thing. It gave him a chance to think up a few more gruelling exercises to put her off equine pursuits.

That neither Niall nor Amanda had gone was slightly more alarming, but Hugo was damned if he'd get wound up about it. Let them get on with it if they were going to; throwing cold water over a bitch on heat only stopped her from howling for as long as you were in view. He preferred to work up a sweat out jogging instead.

Snapping open a latch gate to the woods, he started pounding through a sea of dusty, crackling leaves, feeling his anger drum through the rhythm of his thudding feet.

This holiday, as well as being a waste of time, touched on Hugo's private failures with clinically cold fingers.

For one, his world was smaller than he'd thought. It was okay being a big name in the tightly knit community within which he existed, but experience had proved that one only had to step outside for a breath of fresh air to be hit by a force ten gale. He was a star on the equestrian circuit – writing a regular magazine column, filling in endless publicity questionnaires, presenting clinics and winning fat sponsorship deals, which meant the only uphill struggle he had in such an expensive sport were the hills he pounded his horses up to get them fit. But the fan mail that dropped regularly from the letterbox on to the dogs' heads was more often than not written on 'My Little Pony' paper in a preppy hand, and the odd weekend in London with Amanda and her media friends had shown him how relative his fame was. In London's power circus he was a nobody, ill versed in a quick thinking world where the men could judge your income to within a grand by the cut of your suit and the women wore wing mirrors because they were so terrified of being stabbed in the back. At first he'd enjoyed the thrill of it – he had, after all, been initially attracted to Amanda because she was so different from the big-bummed, Barboured yak-yaks in eventing who still lived with Mummy. But just as his sport was growing increasingly competitive, demanding and time-consuming, so was Amanda. He found less and less enthusiasm for London these days.

His time in the Loire had proved almost as agonising. Hugo had a thirst for challenge and he knew that the one which satisfied him lay in England, where the eventing season continued without him.

It was almost ironic that he was staying so close to Saumur, where he'd clinched such a glorious victory in an influential three-day event in April.

He'd come back from that with renewed determination to win one of the only events which had eluded him throughout his career. The Mitsubishi Trophy at Badminton, the most famous horse trials in England. His desire to win it had increased with each year that he'd come close enough to sniff victory, without being able to grasp it in his clenched first. Third, second, third again. The pattern had been infuriatingly repetitive. But not this year.

Hugo knew that, although this holiday was extremely tedious, it was also essential. No one here was involved in eventing. He could easily have taken a break with friends in Germany, America, Australia, France even, who could have talked, breathed, lived horse as much as he did. Fellow competitors and trainers would have welcomed him. It was one of the most endearing things about the sport with which he was involved: the fact that the people one competed against were also friends who would have welcomed Hugo's request to stay for a few weeks – even in the most rigorous period of the eventing calendar. But Hugo had been forced away from the sport he loved for very good reasons. His first bitter taste of failure had come on the grandest, most humiliating scale. Badminton three-day event. Final trial before the short-list for the World Championships were announced. Great timing, Beauchamp.

If it hadn't been for seeing Snob when he first came to the manoir, Hugo might seriously have settled for jacking in the sport completely, marrying Amanda and settling down to live in London during the summer and hunt during the winter. Now his mind was made up and his toes were curling for his breathing space to end. Instead of coming up against a force ten, here he'd walked into a vacuum.

Amanda had provided him with his second sting of failure. Theirs had always been a tempestuous relationship based on mutual distrust. She flirted regularly to get his attention, throwing herself into love affairs much as a child will fling itself on to the floor during a tantrum, unaware of how much it will hurt. Each time she had come back with eyes that hadn't slept for a week through worry, not sex, claiming they meant nothing. Each time he had taken her back, aware that he was a bastard to her, and that she didn't mean enough to him to make him want to change. He stayed with the relationship because it was convenient, slotting into both their busy schedules, and Amanda was too frightened of being labelled a career spinster to let go either. But if their six years were actually compressed into time spent together, he suspected it would read more like six months.

All Hugo's ferocious determination had been wrapped up in his sport, living a gypsy's life as he moved from one horse trials to another, with commitment always awarded the second's blue rosette. It suited him that Amanda, wrapped up in her job, often barely awarded him an air-vent in her Psion for months on end. And yet, the one time when he'd been vulnerable enough actually to need her without the condition that his horses came first, was the one time that she'd cashed in the blue chips on her shoulder and had an affair for its own sake, not just the effect it would have on him. She'd planted one of her elegant designer heels firmly on to his ego and pressed down hard.

But, as he jogged out into the bright sunshine and alongside a row of basketballer-tall sunflowers all staring east, Hugo knew that what he was feeling was nothing to the demons Niall had been battling with. Niall had told Hugo that it was as if his wife had died in his life but was still alive somewhere else. People would come up to him and say 'Lisette's really well' but he'd only be aware of the utter pain of her being totally out of his reach. Hugo felt nothing of that, although admittedly Amanda was still around, perfuming his room and using his razor in anticipation of her secret soirées. Officially they were still an item, the BC sell-by date carefully concealed from everyone else at the manoir. In a way, Hugo was relieved. The cracks in their relationship had only needed the smallest amount of time in the sun for it to crumble into dust.

Wiping the sweat from his forehead and hooking left towards the house, he suddenly realised that he didn't resent her being with Niall at all. In fact, because Niall was so fucked up, he'd even found himself wishing Amanda would leave the poor sod alone.

As he ducked under a broken fence, Hugo knew for certain that the reason it hurt so much was because, without horses and without Amanda, the only challenge he had left was getting the chestnut colt from Tash French, and that was like playing ping-pong with a five-year-old after five sets in Centre Court with Becker.

When he came back from his jog, he went straight to the pool, ready to dive in and have a long, cooling soak followed by a chance to stew things out in private.

Instead, he found Niall and Amanda spread out on sunbeds. Although they were over a foot apart and Michael Hennessy was lurking in a nearby deckchair listening to the World Service on a prehistoric transistor, there was something uncomfortable about the atmosphere.

Amanda, in the briefest of black bikini bottoms, looked as lean, blonde and gloriously healthy as a Burmese cat soaking in the sun on an ornate Asian rooftop. Niall, without his beard and with his long, rangy body turning the colour of seasoned cognac in the sun, was looking healthier than he had in weeks. He'd been transformed in the last few days and Hugo knew by whom. They looked a dynamic and formidable combination.

'Hello, darling.' Amanda turned her head a fraction of an inch towards him. 'I've been at Niall with the shears. What do you think?'

'Ah – Hugo. Joining us for a drink now, are you?' Niall was clearly sky-high, his eyes sparkling like iced coffee under a new haircut.

'Very pretty.' Hugo was aware that he was hot and clammy from jogging. He wanted to plunge straight into the pool's inviting pale blue surface, but Michael had spotted an ally against the whispering duo he'd been stuck with since escaping the formidable Valérie and her mottled red biceps.

'Hello, old boy,' he barked, looming between Hugo and the pool's edge. 'Been giving the old stamina a dipstick? Bloody good. How d'ya get on, huh?'

'Bloody fine, dear boy.' Hugo looked at the veined red face and bullet eyes squinting through a thin screen of pipe smoke. Please God, let me never end up an old fart, he prayed, and, peeling off his sweaty t-shirt, he handed it to Michael before diving in.

Later, Hugo went in search of Alexandra. A cup of coffee and a gossip with their hostess was bound to cheer him up. Alexandra made him laugh. If she were thirty years younger he'd suggest they spend the afternoon in bed.

But he found her glued to the end of a phone in Pascal's clutter-laden study. Three full cups of cold coffee sat on the desk beside her as she talked down the phone, waving her hands around and raising her eyebrows as frantically as if the person she was speaking to were in the same room.

She smiled at him and waved a page of printed fabric from a glossy interior design magazine under his nose.

'Hold on a minute, darling,' she told the receiver. 'What do you think of these?' She cocked her head to one side.

Hugo shrugged. Interior decor wasn't his thing. Haydown had remained pretty much the same since it was built in 1704.

'I thought so,' Alexandra sighed. She took the receiver off her shoulder, where it had been resting. 'Hi, Georgie? Yes, I've got a second opinion and he agrees it's grotesque. It looks like it'll have to be that antique chintz of yours and bugger the expense. Sage and cream, you say? Are you sure it's not a bit accountant's beige? It sounds frightfully dull, darling.' She looked at Hugo across the room. 'Oh, be an angel and pass me that fax would you, Hugo? Thanks.'

As Hugo handed over the piece of paper ripped from the facsimile next to Pascal's word processor, he noticed it had a quote for a hand-made kitchen on it.

Giving her a wink, he left her to it and sought sanctuary elsewhere. But one sight of Valérie's sturdy buttocks, clothed in purple Crimplene to match her varicose veins, as she leaned over a bucket and wrung out her mop in preparation for an industrial assault on the grimy floorboards of the hallway, sent him back out to the pool again.

Sitting next to Amanda and Niall, he was unpleasantly aware that his presence was about as round, green and hairy as a piece of fruit can get, but he wasn't about to skulk around the house like Tash. On the other hand, he certainly wasn't going to bare his feelings like some old hippie with rush-mat sandals and a cellar full of home-made spinach and fig wine, and tell them to get on with it because that was 'cool' by him. Let them worry about brazening it out in public.

To stop Michael claiming his batting average for death by boredom at one hundred, Hugo decided to pretend to go to sleep. Before he was mentally even half-way through the latest BHS advanced dressage test, he actually was.

Cass and Sophia arrived to find the house apparently deserted. The door to the courtyard was open, and three excited spaniels fell over each other in their enthusiasm to wag themselves into delirium as a welcoming party, but no humans followed.

'That's odd,' noted Sophia, looking around the courtyard. 'Pascal's jeep's missing. So is Matty's car.'

'Surely they haven't gone out to lunch?' Cass sniffed.

'And left the front door wide open?' Sophia opened the boot. 'I know this isn't exactly St John's Wood, but isn't that a bit trusting, even for Mummy?'

'Darling, you know and I know how much worse she's getting.' Cass leaned across to extract her battered case.

'Mind my Louis Féraud bags!' squawked Sophia. 'Oh, Ben can fetch these. I'm dying to freshen up.' She headed off to the house, steering wide circles around the slavering spaniels.

Following her, Cass smiled. Having gossiped and shopped solidly for twenty-four hours, she felt gloriously fresh. She and Sophia had spent the entire journey down the péage bitching about Alexandra's house guests, especially Amanda, Tash and Niall O'Shaughnessy. Being with Sophia also meant one skipped meals and slept in until almost midday. She felt thinner already.

The house wasn't deserted. Over the gentle rumbling of a distant washing machine, Sophia could just make out her mother's voice. It got louder as she approached the heavy door to Pascal's study, which was ajar. Her mother appeared to be talking to herself again.

As Sophia popped her head around, Alexandra saw her and waved.

'It's totally angelic of you to agree to do it at such short notice, Claudia darling. You're an absolute trump. Look, I must go, my daughter's just come back from Paris . . . yes, Sophia . . . all right, darling, I will . . . No, there's no need to worry about that – the Canadians are fully briefed so there'll be someone there to let you in, they sound *sweet.* Wednesday's fine. You've got a clear two weeks. Okay, sweety. Ciao.'

Putting the receiver back on its hook, Alexandra raised her hands above her head for a luxurious stretch.

'Hello, darling. Did you have a super time?' She got up to give Sophia a hug.

Sophia held her at arm's length in case her new Saint Laurent shirt got creased.

'Lovely, thank you, Mummy. Was that Claudia Dutton you were just talking to?'

'Yes – isn't she divine? She sends her love.'

'So she should. Ben and I have only just finished paying off her astronomical fees.' Sophia picked at an imaginary speck of dust on her silk skirt. 'You're not seriously thinking of employing her over here? I know she's good but you have to wait an age just for a consultation. It'll be even worse if she has to hop on a shuttle every time she wants to show you a new colour scheme.'

'So it will, perhaps you're right.' Alexandra led her daughter away from the room so that she couldn't see the extensive notes she'd been making all morning. She wanted to keep her project under her hat for the time being. 'Now you must show me absolutely everything that you've bought. Did you spend an utter bomb? Let's all go and have a coffee and tons of chocolate.' And, putting an arm around Sophia's waist, she all but skipped into the kitchen.

Fighting off three spaniels in the hall, Cass raised a quizzical eyebrow at her niece as she was marched past. Alexandra was behaving like a guilty mother who'd been caught wrapping up stocking fillers on Christmas Eve.

Too irritated to notice, Sophia dragged her heels like a child being towed around the Science Museum. 'Er – Mother. Do you think we could rally some help to get our bags out of the car first?' She still couldn't get the chicken droppings out of her Vuittons from the last time.

'Later, darling. First I've got to catch up on all your gossip.' Alexandra was already firing up the espresso-maker, pink in the face from her subterfuge.

Following behind, Cass was discreetly running the odd finger over the furniture with pleasant surprise. Perhaps she wouldn't need the powerful disinfectant she'd bought to clean out the toilet in the bathroom she and Michael shared with Niall O'Shaughnessy.

Pascal nearly drove straight into the back of the Merc with its boot open in the courtyard because he wasn't expecting it to be there.

'Great château.' Todd picked himself out from under the pile of baguettes which had fallen on him when Pascal braked. 'Don't you just love it, Rooter?'

Rooter panted enthusiastically and licked Lotty's face, which made her burst loudly into tears.

'Sophia and Cassandra 'ave return from Paris,' Pascal announced. 'Polly, take your niece to see 'er mother inside while we unload the shopping, huh?'

Polly nodded and climbed over her father and into the back of the jeep, from which she led the snivelling Lotty by the hand to the house.

Paola, remembering the ticking-off her employer had given her before leaving for Paris, muttered something about changing Josh, and, seizing his carry-cot, dashed after the two girls.

'I'll just check over my bikes, if that's okay?' Todd lifted his precious contraptions down from the roof with one brawny brown arm. 'The slightest jolt can set the gears out of alignment.'

By the time Pascal had sweated inside and out again on six separate occasions with shopping piled up under his chin, Todd announced his bikes fit and healthy and asked if he could help.

Meanwhile, in the China Room, Lotty had severely creased and dampened her mother's Saint Laurent shirt by crying, while Polly recounted the fact that they had travelled back with a huge yellow sheep and its owner, who had a funny accent and wore shorts that showed his willy.

Todd had been given a dramatic build-up. Cass was already

expecting a cross between Boy George and a member of the local Hell's Angels' chapter. Sophia had discreetly fluffed her hair up and licked her lips twice. Alexandra wondered if it was someone they had asked to stay and forgotten about. The description fitted a number of Pascal's friends.

It was then that Michael Hennessy walked in.

He briefly wondered why everyone was staring at him as though he was an alien, particularly in a certain area of his fawn Bermuda shorts. Dismissing it as women's innate peculiarity, he walked over to kiss his wife on the head.

'Hello, old girl. Thought I heard a bit of a bloody kerfuffle. Guessed it was you coming back.' He sank down heavily on a sofa and sighed. 'Cup of coffee would be bloody excellent. Hello, Sophia.'

'Ah – Michael!' Pascal appeared at the door, looking hot and exhausted. 'I 'ave found you an 'elper for your – er – construction. Voici Todd.'

Todd knew how to make an entrance. He walked in with a swing of his narrow lycra-covered hips and a slight swagger of his broad shoulders. His long, hairless legs glistened; the huge inverted triangle of his bulging chest was accentuated by the brightly coloured geometric patterns on his tight cycling shirt. Aware that the group in front of him was almost entirely made up of women, and attractive ones at that, Todd ran a hand through his sun-bleached hair and gave the wide, lazy grin of a self-styled Adonis before saying 'G'day'.

The room melted. Alexandra gawped at the god next to her husband and wondered if she was too old to have a toy boy. Sophia wished Ben would look after his body like that. Cass tried desperately to avert her eyes from the bulge in his shiny black shorts. Alexandra didn't bother.

Michael choked on the coffee his wife had passed to him without taking her eyes off the newcomer. The boy looked like a raving nancy, he fumed. All that tight stretchy stuff was a bit too bloody Brighton for Michael's liking. Still, at least he looked strong enough to do most of the physical work, unlike Marcus, who had the build of a pipe-cleaner. Michael didn't like the effect this boy was having on the girls, though. Cass had just put five spoonfuls of sugar in her coffee and was drinking it without noticing. As Pascal excused himself from the room to start lunch, Michael decided that it was up to him to take action.

'Bloody good to meet you, old boy.' He stood up and held out his hand. Instead of the limp, damp handshake he'd expected, Michael's bony fingers were nearly crushed to a pulp by a warm, dry grip.

'Great to meet you, too, mate. Which one of these lovely ladies belongs to you?'

'Er . . . yes, well.' Michael, noticing the women still had their eyes out on stalks, didn't want to get into long introductions. If Todd was going to work for him then there was no need for him to be on first-name terms with all the occupants of the manoir.

'That's my old girl over there,' he waved his hand in the general direction of Cass. 'Now let me show you around, old boy. Pascal explained the problem in hand? Bloody good. No time like the bloody present to size up the task and juggle with some bloody ideas.' He opened the door wider and waited for Todd to go through.

Todd decided he'd better humour the old boy – who was clearly dotty – for the time being. He did as Michael indicated. At least it gave the women the full benefit of his well-muscled behind, always a killer.

'Got a bloody tape measure on you?' Michael continued as he followed him out. 'No, don't suppose you have – no pockets on that bloody swim-suit thing. Don't worry, lad, I'll get you a bloody boiler suit. Been in the construction trade long?'

Back in the room, Sophia's eyes had misted over. 'What a charming man,' she croaked.

'Yes, he is rather smashing, isn't he?' Alexandra put down the chocolate that had melted in her hand while Todd had been in the room. 'Don't you think he's rather dishy, Cass?'

Cass, her cat's eyes strangely opaque, said nothing.

'You must admit he has a certain something, Cass?' Sophia tried to sound objective as she stroked Lotty's head. 'Speaking as a mother, I wouldn't mind if Josh ended up looking like that.'

But Cass wasn't listening. She was looking thunderous and stirring her coffee as vigorously as she would a lumpy cheese sauce. She could forgive Michael for not asking her how she got on in Paris – just. But there was no excuse for introducing her to that attractive young man as the 'old girl' with a dismissive shake of his hand. He made her feel like a dribbling, blue-rinsed crone on a commode. He could run his own baths for the rest of the holiday. She no longer felt guilty about the vast amounts of money she had spent in Paris, egged on by Sophia. In fact, it brought a malevolent little grin to her mouth. First thing tomorrow she was going to call Chloé and get them to send the full-length turquoise taffeta after all.

27

'Psst!'

'Did you hear something just then, Niall?' Amanda sat up from her sunbed. Next to her, Niall, his face under a towel, didn't stir.

'Pssssst!'

'I think your Lilo must be deflating, darling.' Hugo, who'd only just woken up, scratched his chest with a yawn.

'Pssst! You lot!'

'There's definitely someone in those bushes,' Amanda whispered.

Hugo looked in the direction of the noise. A hand was beckoning them over.

'Go and see what they want,' demanded Amanda.

'I think this is a job for a real man. Wake up, Niall.' Hugo threw a pebble at their sleeping companion.

'Huh?' Niall removed the towel and shaded his eyes from the sun with his forearm. 'Is lunch ready or something?'

'Hurry up!' urged the voice. 'Over here.'

'Oh, you go, Hugo.' Amanda removed the pebble from Niall's stomach ostentatiously.

Hugo got up sulkily and walked over to the offending shrub. When he got there he burst out laughing.

'What are you doing, Matty? Don't tell me the impassioned Valérie has made off with your trousers?'

'Don't be stupid, I'm wearing shorts. Listen, I don't want the others to see we're back. I need your help. Ben's passed out cold in the car.'

Hugo's face changed from amusement to concern. 'What's wrong with him?'

'Drunk,' Matty said. 'We've got to get him upstairs and sober him up. If Sophia sees him she'll blow her lid.' He darted back into the shadows as Cass's head appeared over the balcony above.

'Hello, everyone. Alex wants to know if you'd all like a pastis before lunch?' She regarded Hugo lurking next to the shrubbery with suspicion. She hoped he wasn't having a pee al fresco.

'That would be gorgeous.' Hugo smiled at her. 'Amanda will come in and fetch them, won't you, angel?'

Amanda glared at him for an instant and then nodded.

'Well, be sure to cover yourself up.' Cass looked disapprovingly at Amanda's bare torso. 'That peculiar Australian Pascal brought back is wandering round with a tape measure.' She almost added that she thought he was clocking up the value of the more easily removed objects in the house, but decided the comment would be wasted on them. Perhaps Todd would bop Michael over the head and make off with a couple of paintings. It would serve Michael right. She wandered back into the house deep in this pleasant thought.

As soon as she'd gone, Hugo and Niall followed Matty to the car.

It wasn't an easy task getting Ben upstairs without being noticed or overheard. Sally had a full-time job keeping the children quiet and hidden from view in one of the outbuildings while Tash and Marcus kept an eye out from the gate to the garden and the main door respectively. Twice they all had to dive for cover as voices drifted loudly out to them. A third time they had got Ben half-way across the courtyard when a huge shadow fell across them.

'What in Christ's name is that?' Hugo stared at an enormous, hairy dog that was grinning and panting at them with acute stupidity.

'Rooter,' whispered Matty, not bothering to illuminate further.

Thankfully, the outside door to the largest turret of the house was unlocked. The stairs were steep and dilapidated, made of unpolished elm which creaked more loudly than a giant's new shoes as they heaved the immobile cargo upwards. Niall, holding Ben's leg end, noticed that his bandage was stained pink and smelt strongly of wine.

Instead of taking Ben to his own bedroom, which stood the risk of being invaded by Sophia, they carried their slumbering, hiccuping load up to Hugo and Amanda's circular room, where they deposited him in the bath and turned on the shower attachment to the coldest setting.

As the first indignant splutters of coherence issued forth into the room, Matty leaned out of the window to give the others the all-clear, before returning to the sobering task ahead.

'We thought you 'ad got lost.' Pascal welcomed Tash and Marcus into the kitchen by handing them a bottle of pastis and a jug of water. 'Where are the others?' He looked at the empty space over their shoulders.

'Here and there.' Tash sank down into a chair, breathing in the wonderful aroma of peppered steaks hissing nearby in pungent red wine.

'Around, y'know,' Marcus illuminated, propping himself up against the nearest wall and looking vacant, jug held in his hand like a mug of tea.

'Lunch, he is almost prepared.' Pascal dipped his finger into the burnt copper pan he'd returned to stirring and tasted its contents. 'Formidable!' He kissed his fingers expressively. 'Your sister is back, Tash.' He nodded towards the door. 'In the China Room.'

Tash grabbed an apple from the fruit bowl and went through. Her mouth full and apple juice running down her chin, she walked into the room. Alexandra and Sophia were sitting in the window-seat surrounded by glasses, sweet papers and a cloak-like atmosphere of gossip.

Sophia, who was in the midst of complaining about Tash monopolising Hugo, abruptly shut up.

'Darling!' Alexandra greeted her happily. 'I've been watching you standing by the front door through this window. You've lost bags of weight, sweetheart. What were that lot doing carrying a body upstairs just now? It looked like Ben.'

'*What?*' Sophia glared at Tash accusingly.

'Um – er—' Tash frantically swallowed her mouthful of apple. 'Ben was tired so the others carried him upstairs for a siesta as a joke. He's just having a quick snooze.'

'I'll bet.' Sophia flounced from the room.

'Thanks, Mummy,' Tash sighed, giving her mother an apple-juice kiss on the cheek.

'Isn't that Australian boy divine?' Alexandra, blithely unaware of her gaffe, removed the bottle Tash was still clutching and poured her a large measure of pastis. 'Pascal's wildly jealous. Keeps mispronouncing his name Toad on purpose,' she giggled.

Tash hid a smile and picked up the water jug only to discover it was empty. Marcus had the full one. He'd probably made a bong out of it by now.

'Sit down, darling – have one of Pascal's fags.' Alexandra's eyes were shining with an obvious need to unload some red-hot scandal. She unwrapped a piece of nougat and fed it to a drooling spaniel. 'I must tell you *the* most exciting gossip . . .'

Tash took a Gauloise from the gleaming walnut table and folded herself into the window-seat next to her mother.

'Sophia is convinced,' Alexandra leaned forward, waving a lighter around and almost scorching off Tash's eyebrows, 'that Amanda has quite gone off Hugo.'

'Oh yes?' Attempting to look indifferent, Tash took a gulp of pastis, forgetting that it hadn't been watered. The combined effect of the concentrated alcoholic aniseed and the strong black tobacco in Pascal's cigarettes made her choke and her eyes stream.

'And she now suspects that Amanda is dallying with darling Niall,' Alexandra went on in an eager whisper. 'Sophia was dying to know if anything's come out into the open while she's been in Paris. I said I hadn't noticed a thing. Darling, are you all right?'

Tash was coughing and spluttering too much to speak. She tried to show that she was okay by waving her hand in the air. But her eyes were streaming so much that one of her contact lenses popped out.

'Here.' Alexandra carefully picked it off a cushion and handed it back to her. 'Look, I'm sorry, I didn't mean to upset you. Is it Hugo? Do you still have a crush on him, darling?'

Tash groaned in horror, choking even more as a result.

'But I thought you'd be pleased.' Alexandra patted her daughter's back until Tash nearly swallowed her tongue. 'It means you and Hugo can move a bit faster if you want.'

'What?' Tash spluttered in disbelief.

Alexandra was brimming with clandestine loyalty. 'Well, I have noticed you two seem to be spending a lot of time together, darling. And he's terribly dishy.'

Tash finally cleared her throat but found she was lost for words. She took another swig of pastis and just managed to hold it down. Hugo loathed her. How could her mother get things so totally wrong?

'I'm sorry, sweetheart.' Alexandra squeezed her hand, still smiling knowingly. 'Your rotten mother's being an indiscreet old bag again.' She started to stand up and then paused with her knees bent, as if perching on a diving board, staring out of the window. 'He's pretty – gosh, it's Niall.'

Tash followed her gaze, closing one eye so that she could focus.

Niall was walking out of the front door. He wavered for a few seconds, scratching his tousled, newly cut hair before changing his mind and wandering back in again.

'He looks so much better.' Alexandra's eyes widened. 'You know, I'm rather inclined to believe Sophia. The only time Pascal gets a trim is when he's got a crush on someone.' She craned her neck to see if he was coming through the hall but he seemed to have disappeared. Just out of sight, Sally was telling Tom off.

'Lexy doesn't want a frog in the house, Tomato.'

'But it's an experiment, Sally,' Tom retorted indignantly, 'to see if he'll turn into a prince if Polly-auntie kisses him. I showed it to Huge-oaf by the pool and he said it had worked for Ammonia.'

'Do you want another drink, darling?' Alexandra picked up the empty water jug.

Tash, straining to hear Sally's reply, shook her head. Surely Niall wasn't having an affair with Amanda? she thought sadly. She was so spiky and argumentative. And she had Hugo, who was a thousand times more attractive than Niall.

Alexandra and Sally nearly bumped heads at the door.

'Oh hi.' Sally looked fraught. 'Do you have any antiseptic? Sophia's just crowned Ben with a pair of Guccis.'

'I think there's some in my bathroom.' Alexandra laughed, pausing to admire Tom's frog.

Sally, wavering in the doorway, noticed Tash gazing out of the window like a Chekhov heroine about to express a desire to go to a Moscow cherry orchard dressed as a seagull. ''Lo, Tash. Are you all right, luvvie?'

'Fine,' Tash croaked, squinting at her with one eye. She felt oddly as if she'd been punched in the chest.

Sally, looking speculative, dashed after Alexandra.

'Is she okay?' her hushed inquiry echoed along the hallway.

'Not really, poor darling,' Alexandra replied in a stage whisper that could have registered in Spain. 'She's got this awful crush on Hugo, but refuses to talk about it.'

'Really?' Sally exclaimed with carefully measured surprise.

'Yes, darling. And the silly thing is that Hugo's obviously . . .'

Their voices drifted out of earshot. Tash winced. If her mother had set up a PA system around the house she wouldn't have got much better coverage.

She sat at the table and contemplated what to do. She should go and offer to help Pascal prepare lunch but she didn't have the energy to move. Putting her contact lens back in might not be a bad idea either. Instead she spread her arms out across the polished walnut and rested her forehead on its cool surface.

What would she do to be back at Derrin Road during the cold war now?

'You're not going to do the world a lot of good by doing that, now are you?'

She threw her head back to see a figure framed in the doorway. Closing one eye to bring it into focus, she realised it was Niall.

'Oh, sorry.'

'Don't be. Do what you want – my fault for disturbing you. And don't apologise all the time. Why do you want to be going round saying "sorry" for things you haven't done?'

'Sorry.' Tash looked out of the window feeling flustered. Had he overheard what her mother and Sally had been saying?

'Have you seen Amanda by any chance?'

She wanted to ask 'Why? What for?' and hated herself for it. She couldn't be jealous. Could she? She had no right.

Shaking her head, she stood up. 'I must go and see if Pascal needs any help.'

'He doesn't,' Niall came towards her. 'Sit down a minute, angel. I want to talk to you.'

Tash felt her heart swell into a huge hollow lump as she sat back down at the table.

'Tash, I'm going to ask you a question which you might feel is none of my business. If you don't want to answer then fine – I won't press you on it or ask you again. But if you answer me honestly and truthfully then it could be a massive weight off my mind.' He sighed and rubbed his forehead between his wide thumb and the rest of his fingers.

Tash glanced up quickly and had to look away. It had been all right before, when he'd had his beard. He'd hardly been recognisable: pale, scraggy, gaunt. Now he was appearing before her on the large screen in 3D Technicolor. It was horribly disconcerting. She'd liked the messed-up scruffball not the film star. Back to his old self, it was as if the big pussycat she'd wanted to cuddle a few days ago had turned out to be a lion after all.

'Tash, look at me.' His soft, melodic voice hadn't changed. 'Stop playing with that wrapper.'

'I thought you wanted to ask me a question, not study my body language,' she muttered. It was hard to look straight at someone with one contact lens. It seemed undignified.

'Okay. Here it is.' He took a deep breath. 'Are you having an affair with Hugo Beauchamp?'

She looked up at him sharply. Incredulously. One contact lens or not.

'Well?' His fingers were tapping on the table. The nails on his hands were bitten down so much it was like a mouse tap-dancing in woolly socks.

For an instant she longed to say yes. Imagined it really being true. A passionate, torrid affair with Hugo, kept secret until now. Until Niall, driven mad with jealousy because he'd privately fallen in love with her too, forced it out into the open.

The stupidity of her imagination, the ridiculousness of his suggestion made her want to laugh.

'No,' she shook her head. 'No, I'm not having an affair with him.'

Niall covered his face with his hands, leaned back in his chair and groaned. Nothing melodramatic, just a quiet, sad, introspective groan.

Tash felt an absurd sense of anti-climax. Somehow her imagination had not allowed for his having any other reaction except joy. Relief perhaps. But not regret.

'W-what is it?' Tash leaned forward to touch his arm but couldn't bring herself to. She didn't feel she had the right to be sympathetic when she didn't understand the depths of his misery.

He looked at her intently. There was something slightly manic in his expression; she'd noticed it before. His eyes were unusually bright; he didn't blink. She longed to say something to break the silence but the only word that would come into her head was 'lozenge'. She had no idea why. It was hardly applicable. The pause crept into gaping, hushed stillness before he spoke again.

'I'm screwing Amanda and I feel like a shit.' He spoke so quietly, so quickly that she could hardly make sense of it. 'I heard . . . today . . . I thought . . . thought that you and Hugo were sleeping together.' He'd stopped looking at her and was staring out of the window. 'Stupid really – idiotic, I know, but somehow it made me feel better. Eased the guilt. Bloody Catholic conscience. I guess I wanted an excuse – that she was being cheated on, that it was an eye for an eye – I don't know. Whatever. Admit it. I *needed* some sort of justification because I don't have the excuse that I love her.' He looked at Tash again with an almost desperate need for reassurance. 'Do you understand?'

She nodded. She didn't. She needed the loo. Her bad dreams had become reality.

'Since Lisette – that was my wife – since she pissed off, I've felt . . . I don't know . . . fucking inadequate, I suppose.' He threw his head back. 'God! That sound's so puerile. I've spoken better lines in two-for-a-penny farces in Home Counties rep. But you know what I'm trying to say, don't you? She made me feel so . . . so . . ., damn brilliant, successful, accomplished, I don't know – you name it. I was the hottest fucking property out. I was going to be a star, baby, and she was going to be there to tread the red carpets into the premières at my side, and say that she loved me even when I was a skinny walk-on with knees that shook so badly on-stage I had to wear leg braces at each performance. Tammy Wynette, eat your heart out.' He laughed bitterly and looked up at the ceiling.

Tash crossed her legs as quietly as possible to hold back her need for the loo. She was afraid that if she moved too much he might feel hurt. Like an audience coughing and eating crisps throughout 'to be or not to be . . .'

'But I didn't get there quickly enough, did I? So she pushed off. Have you got a cigarette on you, by chance?'

Tash fumbled for a packet in her jeans' seat pocket. They were squashed flat. He extracted one and straightened it out. 'It's warm,' he said vaguely and lit it. Tash crossed her legs the other way and wondered how long her bladder would last.

'You know, I've met more attractive women than Lisette. I've met more intelligent women than her. More gentle women.

You're more gentle.' He looked at her and she felt herself reddening. 'But I've never wanted any of them.'

She tried hard not to feel affronted. He wasn't being personal, after all.

Niall mistook her expression for disbelief. 'Seriously. Oh, I've wanted to screw the odd one or two but not wake up with their legs round my neck, if you know what I mean. Don't you find that odd in a man?'

Tash felt her blush deepen. Really, she wanted to say. I'm not the person to talk to about this sort of thing. My experience is very limited. A couple of drunken gropes at college and then Max.

She nodded.

'I don't want Amanda,' he continued sadly. 'I mean I do and I don't . . . God knows. I want her so fucking badly when she's there in front of me with that Japanese body of hers, not an inch of fat on her and skin like silk. She's got Lisette's eyes, you know? I've never met a woman with Lisette's eyes before. Cold and calculating as a jaguar but as deep as a fucking well.' The ash fell off his cigarette on to the table but he didn't notice. 'And guess what? Afterwards, she makes my flesh creep. After I've screwed her I can't get away from her fast enough. I want to scrub myself all over, throw up, anything . . . blot it out . . . forget it ever happened . . . swear to myself it won't again . . . until there I am, knocking at her door, lathering myself up into a teenage sweat, desperate for some more . . . more – But it isn't her, is it?' He looked at Tash so intently, it was almost as if she had asked the question. 'It's the kick. It's the fucking kick. I need her because she wants me, and because she gets me so out of my skull that I don't fucking care any more.' He put his head in his hands again. 'Not because I want her, Amanda . . . If she wasn't around I'd still want – want – want . . . I don't know. Something.'

He lapsed into silence for a minute. Tash wasn't sure if he was crying. She wanted so badly to rush round the table and give him a hug. It was so painfully inadequate it hurt, but it was all she knew how to do. Instead she sat and looked at him. Well, squinted at him with her good eye. His creased silk shirt over wide, forlorn shoulders. His thick coal hair touched with polished oak. The burning cigarette clenched between long, bony fingers tinged with nicotine. She'd been wrong. The star, close up, was still human. And eaten to the husk with a stark, hollow, self-destructive misery.

She crossed her legs back the other way.

He looked up at her again. Somehow she'd expected his beautiful, sad face to disintegrate behind his hands. It hadn't.

'It wouldn't help much, you having an affair with Hugo, now would it? Ease the guilt.' He forced a grin but his brown eyes retained their pain. 'Talking to you has, though. I knew it would. I knew you'd understand.'

Tash felt like a traitor. She didn't understand. Any misery she'd experienced was paddling in the shallows compared with his ten-score fathoms. Her heart went out to this sad, beautiful man.

Suddenly a memory seemed to strike him. He looked at her speculatively for a moment. 'If you're not having an affair with Hugo then he's certainly got some hold over you. What is it? What's eating him up? Why do you let him walk all over you?'

Tash was about to mumble that she let everyone walk all over her, but she bit it back.

'I . . . I . . . ' She couldn't say it. She couldn't say she fancied him. It was like quoting 'Just Seventeen' back at him after he'd recited Donne. She looked down at her hands.

'You love him.' Niall's eyes widened. 'That's it, isn't it? You're in love with Hugo Beauchamp!'

Did she love him, when her first reaction was to wail 'of course not!'? It was, after all, a pretty strong way to term it. *Love.* Wasn't love restricted to the beautiful people, dressed in Oxford bags and drifting down the Thames in a punt? It demoted the whole ethereal state a little in her estimation to realise that all love really consisted of was feeling slightly asthmatic and worrying in case you'd forgotten to put on deodorant when a certain person walked in the room. Admittedly, there had been the tear-sodden pillow and suicidally depressed, thickly scratched entries in her diary, proclaiming the utter desolation his beauty had wrought to her gastric system over lunch, or the mind-blowing way the line of his jaw had made her pour salt on her cornflakes at breakfast. But those were nursery rhymes compared to the impassioned sonnets of unrequited love by great poets. How did her crush on Hugo Beauchamp compare with Yeats's desperation over Maud Gonne?

'Oh, you poor, sweet fool.' Niall's milk-chocolate eyes filled with sympathy as he leaned forward and took her hand. He gave it a gentle squeeze, thoroughly crushing the contact lens that was resting in her palm.

Funny how the mind fails to think serene thoughts at moments of touching closeness with another human being. Tash could only think that, as she hadn't got a spare lens with her, she'd have to wear her specs – which made her look like Christopher Biggins in a wig – at the party. Hugo would never want her now. She burst into tears.

'Oh, my poor angel. You've thrown your seeds on stony ground there, haven't you now?' Niall patted her shoulder, not noticing the fragments of Perspex he left on her cotton t-shirt. 'What do you want to be doing a fool thing like falling in love with Hugo for?'

She snivelled and hiccuped for a bit but couldn't answer.

'He's not worth it, you know that, don't you? He's shallow and selfish with a permanently cricked neck from looking down too many cleavages.'

Tash started to cry louder. 'I – I'm sorry,' she wailed. 'I always seem to be doing this in front of you.'

Niall shook his head. 'There you go saying sorry again.' He sighed and started to play with a teaspoon Alexandra had left behind. 'Does he know how you feel about him?'

Tash shook her head. 'He – he—' she hiccuped, 'he always acted as if I was invisible until I got Snob.'

'That's your horse?'

She nodded. 'Now he pretends he's trying to help me but I know he really loathes me.' The relief of telling someone was palpably cathartic. A shudder in her throat made her cough.

Her nose had started to run. 'It's Snob he really wants but, because it's the only way to make him notice me, I let him treat me like dirt. I suppose it's because I'm so wet, I've never known how to attract men. I—' a series of ugly sobs stopped her midflow.

Niall handed her his handkerchief. It was crumpled white cotton, but clean and smelled faintly of washing powder.

Blowing her nose with the elegance of a foghorn, Tash thought how nice he was. Sally was right about him having the soggiest shoulder in the business.

'Now,' he said, looking at her red nose and tear-ridden eyes, 'you are not wet. You are in fact far less of a coward than all of us. Who else would put themselves through the hell you endure every day with Beauchamp? I wouldn't get on that horse of yours for anything. Well, almost . . .' He pulled her chin up so that she was forced to look at him. 'You might be a besotted idiot with more heart than sense, but you are not wet. For one, I'll bet there's nothing I can say that would persuade you Hugo isn't worth it, is there?'

Tash thought for a minute and then shook her head. Short of Niall taking her in his arms and telling her he'd kill Hugo if he ever laid a finger on her, there wasn't much, no.

'So I guess I'm going to have to make attracting him a little easier for you now, aren't I?'

Tash looked up at him in surprise.

'So that you can feel less guilty about Amanda?' she whispered, feeling awful. Why was she being so beastly when he'd been so nice? It was like Desperate from Basingstoke asking Clare Rayner how much she got paid.

Niall studied her for a long time. 'You could be right,' he said finally, 'but there are other reasons as well. You're a sweet girl, Tash, but you need to feel better about yourself. I think you'd find that if you had old Hugo dangling on a string you wouldn't want him any more. Don't shake your head, Tash, I mean it. At the moment he's bound to feel superior; he's holding a royal flush. Every time he walks out into that field he knows exactly how to make you feel small. What you need is to be able to fight the battle on equal terms. It's not as hard as you think, angel.' Niall smiled reassuringly.

'Oh but it is,' Tash said shakily, a freezing rope of dread creeping up her spine. 'You see, Hugo's not really shown all his cards yet.' She was muttering so quietly that Niall's face was almost touching hers in order to hear. 'He's got a trump ace up his sleeve – oh God, shut up, Tash.' She bit her lip.

Niall looked at her intently, making Tash quail. She couldn't tell him about Samion. She hadn't told a soul about that day, keeping the guilty conspiracy between herself and Sophia buried alongside her most shameful secrets. Hugo might think he knew the whole story, could hurt her intolerably with it, but the truth was far more wounding.

'What is it, Tash?' Niall coaxed, gently pushing back her hair. 'Do you think he's planning something?'

'No, it's – it's nothing, honestly I—' Tash tore away from the table, sending a chair spinning, and stumbled towards the hall.

'Tash, wait!'

Skidding on a piece of discarded nougat, Tash thudded into the door. When she tried to pull away, she found her t-shirt, pronged by a metal hook on the door frame, wanted to stay behind.

'Damned, bloody thing!' she wailed, tugging so furiously that the material started to shred. Another angry yank and it ripped six inches across the shoulder, leaving Tash tethered like a goat. Embarrassed frustration welled up inside her and she fought a sudden desperate urge to sob for her mother.

Niall calmly unhooked her and led her back to the table. Then, picking up her chair, he left her sitting like a chewed rag doll staring forlornly out of the window and returned to shut the door. Leaning against it, he watched her for a long time.

'You'd better tell me about it, Tash,' he ordered. 'Because, I'm telling you, you won't get any lunch until you do.'

Tash sniffed and watched Rooter cocking his leg on a tangled rose bush in the garden. It was humiliatingly like being in the headmaster's study. She didn't want to burden Niall with any more of her problems. And she wasn't at all sure talking about

Samion would help her, just thinking about him made tears shudder in her throat.

'I had this horse . . .' she began, intending to give him the abridged story. But a great hiccup of sadness wrenched through her chest and she put her face in her hands, biting at her palms to stop herself breaking down.

Soon the sound of pastis glugging from bottle to glass reached her over the hollow thudding in her ears. An overpowering sting of aniseed hit her nose as Niall forced the glass into her hand, followed by thick black fumes as he pressed her with a cigarette and inadvertently singed her fringe. Tash didn't feel like either but was grateful for his quiet sympathy.

'Well?' he asked softly a few minutes later.

'I can't tell you,' she whispered, 'it's too awful.'

But – gentle, persuasive and persistent – Niall slowly coaxed it out of her. Pascal called lunch twice. Rooter appeared like a furry eavesdropper, panting and grinning through the window with giant brown paws balanced on the ledge. Cass stalked in and out on the pretext of collecting her bag but really to listen in. Alexandra and Sally were heard wandering back downstairs, talking loudly about Tash's crush and Todd's bottom. Lunch got underway without them, clattering, clinking and slurping through the salmon and dill soup. But Tash talked on, quietly, tearfully – every now and then prompted by Niall to continue as she came to a faltering halt.

Niall was surprised by what he heard. Amazed by its simplicity and innocence – the lack of culpability on the part of anyone except the brash thoughtlessness of youth. It was a childhood episode buried in a time capsule and now, exhumed years later, it stood like an anachronistic mountain amongst Tash's other molehills of guilt. It was an awful, terrifying thing to have happened and she was certainly partly to blame. But watching her face as she spoke, Niall realised she'd carried the whole weight of responsibility into adulthood, never thinking to question it with full-grown judgment.

Ten years earlier, Sophia – desperate to impress a new boyfriend – had mounted the barely-able upper-sixth rugby hero on her sister's irascible chestnut for a day's hunting. Tash, laid low with flu, hadn't found out until late morning when her grandmother – whom Sophia had sworn to secrecy with a bottle of Gordon's – spilled the beans. Appalled, Tash had dragged herself outside with jeans hastily pulled on over her nighty.

By the time she'd caught up with the field on her bike, Samion was going berserk in amongst the hounds, the terrified boy on board clutching to his neck strap in tears. The hunt staff were furious. Two hounds had to be destroyed, a third would lose a leg and never work again. Sophia was seething and humiliated in front of tens of locals and her new – soon to be ex – boyfriend needed eighteen stitches in his beautifully chiselled forehead. But worst of all to Tash, all the hard work, the patience, the sweat and tears she had dedicated to calming Samion over the previous months had been swept away in less than an hour.

When she led him away from the field, he went totally, shockingly crazy. He was absolutely terrified, worked up into such a hot-headed mania that gaining any vestige of control was hopeless.

Then she did the stupidest thing. With the hunt staff barking at her and Sophia bawling at her that the horse was mad, needed destroying, must have been ruined through bad training, Tash suddenly made up her mind to prove them wrong. Rationality fled from her mind as did fear. Instead of hanging on to his head, soothing him, leading him round until he calmed down, Tash mounted. It was her chance to prove something, show she would succeed where no one else could. For a moment, Samion had perceptibly relaxed. He stopped throwing himself around, his head dropped and the heaving, panting blasts from his red nostrils slowly subsided, his trust in her implicit.

As Tash had looked up to her rapt audience in triumph, an ear-splitting shot had cracked through the stunned silence like a whiplash; one of the terriermen had taken a pot shot at a hare. In that instant, Samion suddenly seemed to lose his mind completely. One of the locals later described it as like watching a speared bull see a double-decker bus. Within seconds he'd taken off through the field, scattering hunt followers, narrowly missing mowing down a child strapped into a basket chair on a fat Shetland pony.

The MFH – a retired Wing Commander with a sense of the heroic – had caught up with the bolting chestnut and pulled Tash from the saddle, heaving her across his horse's withers like a bounty hunter's catch, breaking her wrist as he did so. He'd crowed long afterwards that he'd saved the gel's life. What he never mentioned was that he'd cost Samion his.

Riderless, Samion had pounded out on to the main road, slap into a follower's Land Rover, shattering his foreleg into splinters. His piercing shriek of pain had been heard two miles away. Half an hour later, he'd been destroyed.

'Sophia was terrified that if Daddy found out that she'd lent Samion to Will without asking me, he'd go ape,' Tash told Niall, twisting the empty cigarette packet between her fingers. 'You see, our parents were away – skiing I think, another attempt at a patch-up – Matty was supposed to be looking after us but he'd gone off with his cronies for the weekend – they were planning some trip to Australia. Daddy would have gone simply barmy if he'd known Will was staying at all – Sophia was sixteen and terribly pretty. Granny Etty was visiting at the time, too – Mummy's mother – but she wouldn't have noticed if Sophia had smuggled the entire first fifteen into her bedroom. Etty's a terrible rogue – she blamed all the empty gin bottles on the housekeeper when Mummy and Daddy got back.' Tash smiled sadly.

'Didn't any of the locals tell your parents what had really happened?'

Tash shook her head. 'Daddy doesn't really get on with the horse brigade. They rather looked down on him then – he was terribly competitive, a bit too corporate. Of course he met them occasionally – drinks and such – but they just commiserated about "the accident", made the right noises. It was quite easy to pretend I'd been hunting Samion that day.' Tash took a sharp breath, her face momentarily crumpling at mentioning his name. 'We sold the rest of the horses soon afterwards,' she continued in a whisper. 'Sophia went off riding – she started going out with some Minister's son around then I think—'

'And you?'

'You know what they say – the longer you leave it,' Tash shrugged, finishing off her pastis. 'Mummy bought me a puppy to get over it – a Jack Russell bitch called Lump.'

'Is she in Lon—'

'She's dead. Sophia ran her over on her first driving lesson.' Tash looked at Niall's appalled expression and raised her hand to his cheek with a smile. 'It's all right. It was a bad year. The rest of my adolescence – with the possible exception of my parents' divorce – was pretty good, really.'

Tash's stomach let out a hungry rumble. On cue, Sophia marched into the room. Behind her, Amanda lounged in the doorway, a white silk sarong knotted behind her long brown neck, the inevitable foxy smile curling her lips to hide her fury.

'We've saved you some ragoût but it'll be stone cold by now,' Sophia announced curtly, scanning the table. 'You pig, Tash. Don't tell me you've troughed all the nougat? I wanted some with my coffee. Hugo said to remind you about jumping Snob this afternoon, by the way. Oh, that's where that got to . . .' Her eyes narrowed critically as she eyed the empty bottle of pastis.

'Niall,' Amanda purred from the door. 'A word.' She raised her eyebrows into two crescents before gliding into the hall.

Niall patted Tash's hand absently. She could almost sense his thoughts slipping away.

'Don't worry, angel,' he told her, standing up, his eyes drifting towards the door. 'We'll sort something out. You've done me a lot of good, you know. Thank you.'

As he walked from the room, Sophia dropped down beside her sister and turned to her with glittering, expectant eyes.

'So?' she demanded in a sotto voice, linking her arm through Tash's. 'You were talking for ages. We were all laying bets in the kitchen as to what about. Matty's livid – he thinks it's his job to be the Relate counsellor around here. What did he tell you? Did he mention Amanda? Her nose is decidedly out of joint, too. Did he say why Lisette left him?'

Oh God, thought Tash. He's got so many problems of his own, so much grief to carry around, and I've been rambling on about Samion and Hugo.

She looked out at the garden with her lop-sided vision and reflected sadly that in only a few minutes she'd stopped loving Hugo half as much. If only Niall knew that he was well on the way to fulfilling his objective of making her see Hugo's shallowness, without even trying.

Sinking her head into her hands, she suddenly realised that the winded feeling that had knocked her ribs into her backbone when her mother was gossiping hadn't been because Hugo was now available. It was because Niall no longer was.

28

With less than a fortnight to go until the party, preparations started in earnest at the manoir. By mid-week, the halls were thick with brick-dust and paint fumes. Ancient Jean had taken to hiding in the vegetable store to avoid being press-ganged into Michael's work team.

Sally put her head round the door to the long gallery and sighed. Tom was holding the bottom of one of the two ladders on which a plank was resting to support Todd. The blond god was painting the ornate ceiling with a thick, gunky substance while Michael issued loud instructions from below.

'You've missed a bit to your bloody left, lad. That's the trick! Coffee break at eleven hundred hours.' He turned to Sally and removed the pipe from his mouth. 'Sally! Good to see you, dear girl. Come to lend a hand?'

'Er – 'fraid not, Michael.' Sally shrugged apologetically. 'I've come to collect Tom. Tash is having another sitting for our portrait.'

'Bloody shame,' puffed Michael sympathetically. 'Still, can't be helped. Another time.'

'Er . . . yes.' Sally went over to fetch Tom. 'Will you be all right up there without him, Todd?' she called up. 'You look a bit precarious.'

'I'll be just fine, Sally!' Todd yelled down, beaming. The height of the ladder afforded him a glorious view down her sun top.

Todd reflected that he'd quite enjoy working at the manoir if it weren't for the eccentric old twerp who seemed to be in charge of cleaning up and converting the long gallery and the stone barn in the courtyard. Michael was a complete pain in the proverbs, but Todd had learnt to butter the old boffer up a bit and feed him a few questions about sport or war. As soon as he was twittering on, Todd could get away with doing the minimum. In return, Pascal gave him a good wage, unlimited lager, freedom to use all the manoir's facilities and a comfortable bed. Couldn't be bad.

When Todd wasn't working, he divided his time between cycling, swimming and chatting up the more attractive women in the house, mostly Paola. He'd been given a room in the huge, airy attics. With no one else up there, it was easy at night for Paola to slip through the door that divided her turret from his landing without being heard.

'You fallen asleep up there, lad?' Michael bawled from below.

'No, sir,' Todd sighed. 'I was just thinking – who won the fifth test last year? You know, I can't remember.'

Michael suitably distracted, Todd leaned back and thought about the girls at the house. Paola was sexy and available, but there was no real sport in that and her fiery temper was taxing. What he really adored was the thrill of the kiss-chase. He'd studied everyone carefully over the past few days. There were only two women who were apparently totally impervious to his charms. One scared him a little; she was just a bit too bright to succumb to his technique. But the other was more hopeful; she had the dreamy, faraway look of a Madonna but the body of a high-class call girl. Todd just had to find a way in. The only problem was that she was so busy all the time. No wonder she was so fit. If he didn't know better from experience, he'd say she'd hardly noticed his presence.

Sally tried to stay still while Tash put the finishing touches to the painting. The way Tash had positioned them all gave her a good excuse to study Matty's face and see if it belied anything more than the slight boredom in his expression.

They'd stopped talking. They still discussed what the weather was going to do and whose turn it was to change Tor, but Matty no longer looked her in the eyes.

He'd found out about Niall and Amanda quite by accident. But instead of reacting as Sally would have expected, by throwing his weight about and storming up to Niall, demanding to know what the fuck he thought he was doing, he'd withdrawn into himself like a hedgehog caught in the glare of headlights. He had told Sally quietly and calmly that he thought it was time they left France. He'd then disappeared to the village bar to get deliberately drunk with Ben and Pascal, leaving Sally clutching the note she had tried to snatch out of his sight. It had fallen out of Tash's chaotic leather satchel and was written on stiff artists' paper in a huge loopy hand – crumpled up, unfinished and clearly never sent.

Dear Niall,

I'm going off to visit the Museum of the Horse in Saumur with my mother today but I wanted to thank you for the books before I go. I found them outside my door this morning. You should be locked up for being so kind. I'm sure they'll help a lot.

Please don't worry about my telling anyone about our conversation on Sunday, I wouldn't dream of it. You mustn't feel bad about what you are doing with Amanda. I feel bad all the time and it doesn't seem to help anyone.

I just hope you find happiness soon, whatever the outcome.

Thank you again for buying the books for me. I know I'll see you at dinner, but I thought it might be awkward if I said any—

No one could mistake Tash's huge handwriting, which covered a page in two sentences.

Sally supposed what had horrified Matty more than anything was the fact that Niall had confided in Tash and not him. Of all his family, Matty probably had the least time for Tash. He was infuriated by her inability to stand up for herself.

It was possible, Sally reflected, that Tash could have found out about Niall and Amanda by accident as she had. But as she was permanently losing her glasses and wandering round with her mind elsewhere at the moment, Sally suspected Tash could have walked through an orgy without noticing. She was certain that Niall had told Tash himself.

Useless at keeping a secret, Sally had agonised all week about whether or not to tell Matty about finding the ring in Niall's room. Last night, she'd finally confessed, secure in the knowledge that he now knew about the affair. Matty had exploded in drunken anger, simmering for hours afterwards with a severely gashed pride. He now blamed her entirely for letting things escalate as they had, believing that had she told him about Niall and Amanda earlier, he could have done something to stop such a ridiculous and dangerous affair. It had also redoubled his determination to return to England as soon as the ferry could be booked.

To cheer herself up, Sally had taken Audrey the Audi shopping that morning and bought a wildly expensive dress. Vindictively, she'd used Matty's business card – the only one on which they hadn't used up the credit limit.

But now Alexandra was refusing point-blank to let them go back to England. In fact she'd become quite hysterical in her demand that they stay the ten days till the party. Matty's withdrawn lethargy was no match for his mother's dramatic refusal. He'd agreed to stick it out. But he had become totally uncommunicative, disappearing off on walks for hours on end, burying himself in obscure books he loftily called 'research' or sitting in sulky silence for Tash's painting.

Sally looked at him again. He was staring at Tash in deep contemplation. She supposed this holiday had opened his eyes to his little sister. First she'd pushed Hugo Beauchamp in the pool, then stood up to his bullying 'lessons' and now Niall had chosen her to become his confidante.

But Sally doubted that Tash knew the full story. That Amanda was supplying Niall with more than just sex. She was sure Matty had no idea, having convinced himself that Niall didn't need him any more, that he had got over Lisette in a flash and that he was now looking fit and well because he was happy again. In reality he was lit up on coke all the time. To

Sally he looked like a bulb burning slightly too brightly. Sooner, rather than later, he was going to blow.

'Finished!' Tash announced with a sigh. 'That must go down in history as the fastest portrait I've ever done. Now you can't complain that it's taken ages, Tom.'

Unable to sleep, Tash had stayed up late last night working from her sketches. The energy and pace with which she had painted had given the portrait a strange sort of vitality which her work didn't normally have.

Perhaps that had to do with her passion to get on. All she wanted to do at the moment was be with Snob. She'd read and reread the books Niall had given her about developing a trust between horse and rider. And overcoming her fear of her horse was one step closer to winning Hugo.

'Right.' Matty got up and headed towards the door.

'Aren't you going to look at it, darling?' Sally asked with a nervous edge to her voice.

'Oh, yes.' Matty stood behind Tash and looked down. 'Yes. Very good,' he muttered brusquely and then walked out.

Tash tried hard not to look hurt.

'I'm sorry, Tash.' Sally pressed her hand against her cheek awkwardly and shrugged. 'He's a bit preoccupied at the—'

'Let me see it, let me see!' Tom leapt up and ran round behind Tash. 'That's brilliant. Can you do another one for my friend Rodney? Please, Tash, please.'

'I think Tash might like a break from painting for a while, Tomato.' Sally laughed, glad of the distraction, and looked down at the finished portrait.

What she saw took her breath away. It wasn't just the likeness that was uncanny. It was the emotion in the faces. They were almost caricatured in their reality. Tom looked bored and fidgety, Tor looked gorgeously cuddly and mischievous, Sally looked worried and pensive. Most disturbing of all, Tash had seen in Matty's face what a few minutes earlier she herself had been searching for: a painful, hurt, forlorn look of regret.

Tash hadn't painted a flattering, posed portrait of family bliss but a study of characters caught off-guard. It was hauntingly powerful. Sally didn't know whether to laugh or cry.

'It's phenomenal, Tash. Honestly. I . . .' She looked at Tash's bright, happy face and ran out of words. How could she say that the picture summed up the fact that her marriage seemed to be crumbling apart? 'Could you look after the kids a moment? I'm going to catch up with Matty.'

After she'd dashed out, Tash looked at the portrait despondently. She knew it was hurried but she'd actually thought it was quite good. Perhaps it wasn't how they saw themselves. It was astonishing how hurt people could be when they realised how an artist interpreted them. Max hadn't spoken to her for a week after she'd painted him. He'd thought she made him look like Art Garfunkel.

She started to pack up her things, removing a tube of crimson lake from Tor's grip and listening to Tom's boastful description of a painting he did at school.

'G'day, Natasha.'

She looked up to find Michael's work-mate lounging in the doorway, conveniently positioned in a shaft of sunlight, his boiler suit unzipped to reveal a broad expanse of bronzed chest and lycra.

'Hello . . . um—' she smiled brittlely, hoping he was just passing by on his way to fetch some turps or something.

'Todd.' The Australian sauntered into the room and stood over her. Tash felt her back tighten. He set her teeth on edge like a dishy sixth former who was about to make her feel as attractive as greying tuna.

He looked across at Tom, who was doing a hand-stand against the wall. 'Do me a favour, kid. Bugger off. And take your little sister with you.'

'Sally said I was to stay with Nash,' Tom said, looking as affronted as a seven-year-old can when they're upside down.

'I don't care. Piss off.'

Tom turned the right way up and carted an unwilling Tor away from Tash's shoes, which the little girl was painting burnt umber.

Tash looked at Todd in surprise. He clearly didn't like children.

'I didn't know you were an artist, Natasha.'

Was it her imagination, or was she being nearly asphyxiated by Kouros?

'Tash,' she muttered, 'call me Tash.'

'Streuth! That's corking!' He looked at her painting in awe.

She couldn't help burying a smile in her paintbrushes as she sorted them out. He sounded like an extra from a bad convict film. Any minute now Rolf Harris was going to appear from behind a sofa with a didgeridoo.

'Thanks.'

'I'm into photography myself,' he crooned, unable to keep the conversation away from himself for long. 'Mono shots of beautiful women. Not smut, you understand. I want to capture a woman's sensuality in the frame. So many women don't realise what incredible faces – and bodies – they have until they see a moody shot in black and white.' His eyes roamed over her body as he said this.

'I'm more black and blue,' she joked, beginning to clear up pieces of tissue.

'You'd look sensational if I photographed you,' he murmured in a low voice.

Tash twigged. He was chatting her up. The smooth one-liners she'd been hearing all week were being directed at her. Did that make her fourth or fifth on his hit-list, she wondered.

He'd stooped down on his haunches now to talk to her. 'You've got a stunning face, Natasha. I haven't been able to stop staring at your eyes all week, they're mesmerising.' He demonstrated this by staring into them for a bit.

Tash felt her mesmerising eyes begin to smart from his aftershave.

'Has anyone ever told you you have the most beautiful set of shoulders ever, Natasha?' His voice was intentionally low so that she had to lean forward to catch the end of his sentence.

'Er, not recently,' her voice sounded like Orville in comparison to his rumbling, husky drawl.

'Well, they should have done.' He looked at her as sincerely as an American evangelist asking for a million dollars during prime time.

'Natasha,' he rasped her name throatily.

'Yes?' She backed off a little, desperately trying not to laugh.

'Na*tasha*.' He stood up decisively, giving her a passing glance at his long, muscular legs bulging through the thin fabric of the boiler suit. 'I want to photograph you more than anything. I want to seduce you more than that, but I can guess you'd tell me to rack off so I'll put up with second best. The camera will make love to you, Natasha.' She opened her mouth to protest but he held his hand out. 'Please don't say anything now. Don't make up your mind until you've seen my portfolio and you know what I do is art and nothing dirty.' He leaned down and put a strong arm under her armpit to help her up. Tash sprung upright like Zebedee, aware that she hadn't changed her shirt since riding Snob.

Todd bent his long, strong neck and spoke into her ear. 'Now let's go up to my room, Natasha, and I'll show you my portfolio, huh?'

This time Tash couldn't help burst out laughing. She leaned against him and laughed till her ribs ached and tears poured down her face.

'Hey, hey, hey. Have you been smoking blow or something?' Todd didn't see the joke. He thought he'd been making headway faster than he'd hoped.

Tash howled afresh and clutched her diaphragm in pain. Todd put a protective brown arm around her, obviously thinking she was having a seizure of some kind.

'What's going on here, now?' A soft, melodic voice tinged with the faintest trace of anger came from the direction of the door.

Tash found that with Niall there she couldn't stop giggling. Like a nervous reaction. Her knees gave way and Todd supported her whole weight to stop her sliding to the floor.

'I think she's having some sort of fit, mate.' Todd actually sounded quite frightened.

Tash felt the giggles finally passing as she gasped for air and only had the odd relapse into uncontrollable, silent laughter. She stood up straight and cleared her throat but found she couldn't look at Niall or Todd. Every time she tried, she felt another attack grip her stomach. She kept her eyes glued to the floor instead.

'Michael's looking for you, Todd,' Niall snapped dismissively.

Todd ignored him, still keeping his arm round Tash.

'Are you all right now, Tash?' he oozed, sounding like a stricken relative at her deathbed, dying for a peek at the will.

Tash bit back another shudder of laughter and nodded.

'Hadn't you better go and find Michael, Todd?' Niall persisted. 'He's pretty pissed off.'

It sounded more like an order than a question.

Todd hesitated for an instant and then went, pushing past Niall roughly as he left the room. Niall went straight over to Tash.

'Are you okay, angel? What on earth was he doing to you?'

Now that Todd had gone, Tash didn't find anything remotely funny about the situation any more. She felt unbearably shy.

'He tried to chat me up and I got the giggles,' she muttered.

'You what?' Niall looked at her incredulously.

'He – um – he wants to take my photograph. He asked me up to his room to see his portfolio and I burst out laughing.' Tash thought it all sounded too silly and pre-pubescent for words. She wanted to appear mature, accomplished and deep in front of Niall, not a giggling schoolgirl.

'I certainly shouldn't be after letting him photograph you,' Niall told her icily. 'He'll have you draped across Pascal's jeep in a g-string before you know it.' He looked at her seriously.

Tash felt rebuffed. He was acting the father figure again. Perhaps that was how he'd seen her all along. She felt gauche and inadequate.

Suddenly a smile broke through the clouds on his face and he started to laugh. He put a hand on each of her shoulders and held her at arm's length so that he could look at her properly. She stared fixedly at the floor.

'You really are an incredible, incredible girl, Tash,' he laughed. 'Everyone else in the house is applying lipstick and perfume like mad over this man and you fall about when he gives you the coveted come-on.'

Tash shrugged and found her tongue was stuck. The feeling of his hands on her shoulders was making her almost faint. What wouldn't she give for an O'Shaughnessy massage now? She felt herself shrink away, embarrassed by the stifling desire to melt in his arms. It wasn't the pounding, suffocating lust she had felt with Hugo beside the pool but a desperate need to be caressed and hugged by those comforting, warm hands.

Niall let her go and turned away. She was paralysed with fear for an instant, certain that he had read her feelings and was acutely embarrassed by them. But he had simply spotted her painting propped up on the floor to dry.

He looked at it for a long time, deep in thought. Tash busied herself tidying up.

She'd finished packing away all her paints and sorting out the brushes to be cleaned long before he spoke. She fiddled with her glasses which she'd found under a pile of newspaper but was too vain to put them on. Without them she couldn't read the expression on his face.

He looked at her but said nothing and then looked at the painting again.

What seemed like minutes later, just as he opened his mouth to speak, Alexandra appeared in the doorway behind him.

'Tash, darling – gosh, that's good!' She looked at the painting for a bit and then turned back to her daughter. 'Can I have a quick word, sweety?'

Tash glanced at Niall and then nodded.

'I haven't interrupted anything, have I?' Alexandra looked from Tash to Niall rather excitedly.

'No, Mummy,' Tash sighed wearily, putting on her glasses. When would her mother stop overestimating her pulling powers?

'Good. Then we'll have a cup of coffee in the kitchen. I've got some rather smashing news.' She hooked her arm under her daughter's and looked at her enthusiastically. 'Good grief!' She stopped in her tracks and looked at Tash properly. 'Are you still wearing those awful specs? You had those at school. What's happened to your contact lenses?'

Tash glanced over her shoulders at Niall but he was still staring intently at the painting.

'I – er – lost one,' she lied.

'Oh, we'll have to buy you some more then.' Alexandra started leading Tash from the room. 'And some more frames. Those make you look like Benny Hill. By the way, have you seen that hunky Australian today? Both Sophia and Wowla have been dashing about like rabid dogs trying to find him, but he's either up a ladder or nowhere to be seen. Unlike Rooter. Pascal fell over him three times this morning and gave himself a black eye on the door-stopper the third time. Very undignified, the poor love. He's locked in the barn now – Rooter, not Pascal, that is. Pascal's lying in bed with an ice-pack, avoiding Sophia. Did you know she's asked the caterers to dance in a procession with the mead held aloft in clay jugs? They're threatening to pull out.'

Marcus was on a roll. Happening gear was crucial. That is, crucial gear was happening. Or something like that. He'd found a way of procuring his ravers with narcotic substances anyway.

After hours of deliberation and sniffing round the overgrown herb garden, smashed-up cabbage frames and a long line of tumbledown eighteenth-century hot-houses, Marcus had come to the conclusion that the manoir was not a cover-up for Pascal's drug-dealing empire. In fact, he had severe doubts as to whether Pascal had ever so much as tugged on a spliff. There was little evidence of it, and Marcus's own stash had begun to dwindle. His chances of finding anything in time for the imminent arrival of Wiltsher – and whoever his resourceful school-friend had invited – were seemingly bleak.

Marcus had even resorted to desperate measures and swiped some travellers' cheques from his father's flesh-tinted nylon money-belt while the old boffer was taking a bath. Slipping away from a tedious plod around the museum of decorative arts with Alexandra's posse, he'd cashed them in and hired a moped in Saumur before puttering precariously to Tours in his quest for low-life. Finding only a sixteenth-century cathedral, an aquarium and a lot of sagging, half-timbered houses straight out of the Brothers Grimm, he'd decided to go home. Unfortunately, the dusty red moped had croaked to a thirsty, paraffin-starved halt beside a nuclear power plant.

Watched closely by three security guards, a Rottweiler and the unblinking eye of a closed-circuit camera, Marcus had shambled as far as a nearby garage and phoned his father.

Michael had not been amused to find himself several gin and tonics up, trawling the Volvo around busy French trunk roads to search for his errant son, who had described himself as being stranded 'somewhere near Tours, man', before running out of change. Nor was Michael delighted when he'd finally spotted Marcus, slouching beside a death-trap motorcycle, smoking a cigarette and flicking the ash into a sand-bucket attached to a Super petrol-pump. In fact, he'd been positively spitting when he discovered that Marcus and the tinny red contraption belonged together for five contracted days, paid for by what Marcus vaguely described as 'car-washing money'.

Marcus had been taken out fishing two days running as a result, thwarting his plans to find a seedy criminal element in Angers or, desperation necessitating, the village bar.

And then Todd had winked a red eye in his direction. At first Marcus had avoided the Australian. He was, in Marcus's opinion, brain-numbingly unhappening, used Sun-In and had never heard of The Microdot Dropping Purple E Machine – currently Marcus's favourite band. But last night while they were chilling out to some of Marcus's grooves in the attic, Todd had mentioned a few local contacts which had uncrossed Marcus's eyes in excitement. Todd might look like the last surviving member of the Kagagoogoo fan club, but he had proved to be a pretty pukka dood underneath.

Marcus was now sitting on the steps of the manoir squinting down the drive through his sixties dark glasses, which were exact replicas of ones Lou Reed once wore. He was waiting for Wiltsher, who had phoned that morning to announce he'd got as far as Le Mans but the Dormobile had broken down.

Marcus hoped Wiltsher had found alternative transport. A Dormobile was acutely indie and Reading Rock Festival.

When he heard something which sounded like a Tiger Moth taking a nose dive in the distance, his hopes started to fade. Then Marcus caught sight of the dreaded article: Ivor The Tank Engine with an out-of-date tax disc, emitting a power station's worth of pollution from its exhaust pipe as it spluttered up the drive. As the Dormobile got closer, Marcus noticed it was painted baby pink with lime green flowers. It looked like one of his mother's tent dresses on wheels.

'You dood! What d'ya think of the Dorm Trooper, huh, man?' Wiltsher jumped out of the passenger seat and went into their complex hand-slapping and leg-waggling greeting routine. Marcus joined in but was staring the whole time at his friend's hair.

'Wiltsher, man, what is that on your head, like?'

'D'ya like it?' Wiltsher slouched his shoulders and grooved his head from side to side for a bit. 'Dreadlocks, man.'

Where Wiltsher had sported long, clean blond hair that flopped over his face like an Afghan hound when Marcus had last seen him, he now possessed a head of thick, wildly dishevelled dreadlocks the texture of dressing-gown cord.

'The old man's a bit cut up about it, man,' Wiltsher went on, 'but it's fucking happening to rave with. I dropped a tab before going to Ascension the other night, man, and I could've swore I was a Vileda Supermop all night, y'know?'

Marcus looked at his friend in jealous admiration.

'You got into Ascension, man?'

Wiltsher nodded proudly, his dreadlocks bobbing.

'You've dropped acid, man?'

Wiltsher smirked and swaggered. How was his friend going to sus that he'd spent the entire night chucking up Rolling Rock in the bogs before being thrown out by the bouncer he'd slipped unseen past earlier?

'Meet Algy, man.' Wiltsher turned round to introduce the Dormobile's driver.

Algy was even skinnier than Marcus and had long, greasy brown hair scraped into a pony-tail, a bum-fluff goatee beard and a Stonehenge 84 t-shirt on. He nodded at Marcus vacantly and carried on rolling a fag with three strands of tobacco in it.

'It's all right,' Wiltsher assured Marcus in a low voice. 'He went to Millfield. His father's the drummer with some geriatric sixties band – they did Isle of Wight sixty-nine – so we've got a really wicked sound system, man.'

Marcus nodded doubtfully. Algy looked like the sort of guy who fell in love with trees, but he had to trust Wiltsher's judgment on this one.

'Where's the rave happening, dood?' Wiltsher pushed his dreadlocks off his face. He was getting overheated with half a ton of shag-pile on his head in the late morning sun.

Marcus pointed out the stone barn. 'I'll show you it later and we'll set up the system, y'know,' he suggested, noticing how hot Wiltsher was looking. 'Right now, d'ya wanna go for a swim, man? Then we can play Sonic the Hedgehog.'

Wiltsher looked relieved. 'Crucial!' He looked across at Algy, who was eyeing up a nearby poplar. 'Swim, Alg?'

Algy looked nonplussed for a minute and then nodded.

'He doesn't say much, does he, man?' Marcus asked as they headed round the house towards the pool, with Algy following behind, picking poppies from beside the path.

'Nah, he's partially deaf from one of his Dad's gigs in seventy-two. They put his cot next to the main amp without realising. Then he had a funny turn after sniffing Mr Muscle Oven Cleaner in sixth form. Now he's got this addiction to Minty-Molar Mouthwash. It makes him a bit withdrawn, y'know. But at least he never has bad breath, man.'

There was a pause while Marcus took in the enormity of Algy's disturbed childhood.

'Er – Hennessy, man.' Wiltsher sounded distinctly awkward about something.

'Yeah, Wiltsher.'

'Don't suppose I could borrow a shower cap or su'thing, man? Er – to swim in, y'know? Only my coif goes well frizzy in chlorine.'

'Sure, man.'

'You what?' Tash looked at her mother in utter horror.

Alexandra busied herself pouring coffee, not looking at her daughter.

'I said I entered you for a class at the local agricultural show, sweetheart. It's a sort of hunter trial, I think, for novices. Ever so easy, darling. I thought you'd be pleased.' She looked at Tash pleadingly with huge amber eyes.

'You did?' Tash asked in an unnaturally even voice. She sank her head into her hands. 'I don't believe this,' she sighed.

'But, darling, you've been doing so well with your horse. I thought you'd be delighted to have a chance to show off how much you've brought him on. Just think how exciting it'll be if you win!' Alexandra clasped her hands together in anticipation.

'If I win?' Tash laughed nervously. 'Snob humiliating me in front of everybody? Winning doesn't come into it. Fatal injury does come to mind, though.'

'Don't be silly, dear.' Alexandra felt quite hurt that her daughter wasn't as delighted with the idea as she had been when Hugo suggested it. 'It'll be such a boost to your confidence.'

Tash looked at the ceiling in disbelief. So much for improving Snob to impress Hugo. She'd almost thought it was within her grasp this morning. Now she needed a miracle to get her out of this one. It was one thing controlling the hot-headed chestnut in the paddock here, quite another in front of a crowd of faces with all the unfamiliar sights and sounds of a big show. Perhaps she could paint Bouchon red?

'I've got Pascal to translate the dressage test for you.' Her mother handed over a piece of paper with Pascal's neat, loopy continental writing on it.

'Dressage test?' Tash said in a faint voice.

'Yes. It's ever so easy-peasy. The equivalent of a pre-novice in

England. The cross-country course has lots of alternative options and the show jumping's a cinch,' Alexandra babbled happily.

A thought occurred to Tash. She eyed her mother thoughtfully.

'How do you know all this, Mummy?' she asked suspiciously. 'You thought a martingale was a type of bird yesterday.'

'I – er – I asked someone.' Alexandra scratched her head awkwardly. 'Drink your coffee, darling. It's going cold.'

Tash sipped in silence for a moment, thinking desperately of a way to get out of this. The competition would be the day after the party. Surely she could think up some elaborate plan between now and then? She had over a week. But the only thing that sprung to mind was hiding. Hardly original.

This was Hugo's doing. She knew it. What better way of getting her to give him Snob? If she competed she was sure to make a total fool of herself and want to give up completely. If she chickened out, he would nobly deputise and show her exactly how to do it, proving without doubt that he should have had Snob all along.

She looked at the clock. It was half past eleven. Time for her arranged meeting with Hugo. She wanted to go out there and throttle him.

Instead he appeared at the outside door, kicking the dust from the soles of his boots as he walked in.

Tash looked at his beautifully shaped jaw and straight nose and tried harder than ever to feel cold loathing. She stared fixedly at his blue cotton t-shirt and lean chest and imagined thumping it a bit. She glanced quickly at the bulge in the groin of his 501s and imagined kicking it. She looked at his thick silk hair now tortoiseshell from the sun and imagined the feeling of it flopping cool and clean on to her naked chest . . . she was off again. Why, oh why, oh why did he do this to her?

She whipped off her glasses, aware that she looked like Nana Mouskouri.

'Hello, Hugo darling,' Alexandra greeted him brightly. 'Coffee?'

Hugo shook his head. He glanced at the sheet of paper in Tash's hand.

'Got the test then, Tash?' He smiled at her for her mother's sake, but she could detect a cruel amusement in his voice. 'It's really a bit of an insult entering a horse like Snob in a competition like this. But it's being run alongside much higher calibre classes so it should be of a better standard than most. We don't want to overface you – either of you – on your first competition, do we?'

Oh yes, you do. Tash flashed a split-second weak smile back at him.

Alexandra glowed, thinking how much Hugo had changed in the last three weeks. He seemed genuinely interested in helping Tash now. Quite unlike him, really. But then again, Tash was positively radiating health and vitality at the moment. Hugo, despite Tash's fervent denial, was more than a little smitten with her, she mused excitedly.

Watching the two go out towards the yard, Alexandra thought how tall, lean and glorious her daughter looked. Tash didn't have the stick-thin way of making clothes look good that her sister possessed, or the same self-confidence in her stride, but she would make a room full of people turn if she walked into it now. Alexandra's plan had worked. With her new-found confidence, Tash looked every bit as glamorous as the attractive man next to her.

Tash herself didn't feel any new-found confidence. In fact, if Alexandra did but know it, she felt about as confident as a sky diver in a bikini at twenty thousand feet.

She tacked Snob up with the dreadful feeling that today Hugo was going to show her that what they had been doing before was nursery school stuff.

The chestnut looked at her placidly with deep purple eyes and nudged her for Polos with a velvet soft muzzle. Perhaps the long early morning hack she had given him had worked off some of his more tempestuous energy. Tash could only hope so, Snob was notoriously good at looking as if butter wouldn't melt.

Hugo was drenched in sweat by the time he'd positioned the dressage markers around the carefully measured rectangle in the paddock. He stopped for a minute and leaned against the gate, wiping his forehead with his arm.

It had been his idea to change the time he gave Tash her lesson from late afternoon to just before lunch so that the sun would be at its most powerful. She was getting far too fit for his liking. For the last few days, she'd hardly been perspiring after the gruelling routine he'd put her through. Unlike Hugo, who was getting more and more out of condition as time went on. He was still in pretty good shape compared to the rest of the guests, but a couple of jogs a day was nothing compared to the work-outs he'd had at Haydown. With three top horses to keep at the peak of condition plus many more up and coming novices to school, he'd be constantly in the saddle if he were at home now. On top of that he'd run, play tennis and have regular sex. Here the tennis court was overgrown and Amanda had all but put up barbed wire and pressure pad alarms in their bed for the past week; she haughtily claimed she still shared his room only because of the en-suite bathroom.

Consequently, he'd decided to kill two birds with one boulder. He would step up the pressure on Tash and get fit at the same time. This afternoon he was going to give her the new routine. As well as three hours in the saddle each day, she was going to run five miles, swim twenty laps of the pool and do a set of exercises for competition riders he'd drawn up to get himself to the height of fitness for the Olympics in '88. That should snap the silly cow out of her complacency.

Smiling at Tash as she rode past him on Snob, Hugo shouted, 'Just loosen him up for a bit, will you?' and lit a cigarette. He was beginning to enjoy this.

29

'It's all right, Cass, they've gone,' Sophia called over her shoulder as she made her way down the steps from the balcony to the pool, wrapped in a saffron sari.

'I must apologise for Marcus's friends, Sophia. Rory Wiltsher used to be such a nice boy. I can't imagine what possessed him to think you were a Buddhist monk.' Cass followed her niece down the steps, weighed down by a tray of Pimms.

'Yes, well, I was a bit taken aback by that, admittedly. This sari is Thai silk, nothing like a Buddhist wrap,' Sophia sniffed, draping the controversial garment over the back of a sun-chair and lying down in her beautifully cut black Donna Karan swimsuit.

Cass set down the tray and mopped her face with a tissue from the pocket of her cotton dressing-gown. Noticing it had become covered with foundation she hastily shoved it back and started to pour out the drinks.

'It's the other one that I couldn't abide,' she confessed, handing Sophia a tall, cool drink before sitting down.

'Archy, was he called?' Sophia put on her Christian Dior sun specs and noticed that Amanda was lying on a recliner on the opposite side of the pool, reading a magazine. 'Move your chair a little closer so we won't be overheard,' she whispered to Cass, nodding in the direction of the other woman.

Cass moved. 'Algy, I think Marcus said. Looks a bit of a dodgy character. Apparently his father's a pop star. I think he might be a bit of a druggy, if you know what I mean.' Cass shot a quick look to check Amanda wasn't listening, but on closer inspection she was plugged into a Walkman.

'Surely not? You mean . . .'

'I mean marijuana, Sophia.'

'Never!'

'He *did* go to Millfield.'

'I see what you mean.' Sophia got out her sun-cream. 'But they do produce frightfully good polo players,' she added by way of compensation.

'It's a worry. I'm afraid he might lead Marcus astray. If only he had friends like Olly's.' Cass sighed dreamily. 'I can't wait for him to arrive. You'll be surprised at the change in him. He's positively hunky – he used to be built like Marcus, you know. But Michael says Hennessy men always start out a bit bandy.'

'Isn't he bringing a friend?' Sophia finished applying her Factor 4 and switched to a higher protection for her face and feet.

'Yes, Ginger.' Cass tried not to sound too dreamy as she applied her own Superdrug sun-cream, hastily covering the label with her hand. 'He's rather scrum.'

'Really?' Sophia finally lay back to soak in the sun and it promptly hid behind the only cloud in an otherwise true blue sky. 'Tell me, Cass. Do you think Matty and Sally have fallen out? I detect a rift.'

'Now that you come to mention it, yes. They have been apart a lot this week.' Cass dropped her voice and glanced around.

'I blame it on having kids when they're not financially secure.' Sophia adjusted her sunglasses. 'I mean to say, having another one now is madness.'

'Quite.' Cass nodded. 'Not that we can really help much with that little problem.'

'Absolutely not. It's up to Matty. He could go and join Daddy's company any time instead of dabbling in television. There's no money in it these days. Especially if you're a lefty. He has to stick with the Beeb and you know what they pay.'

'Quite.' Cass was feeling terribly sticky. It was a horribly close day. She got out the little battery-operated fan she'd bought in Paris. The batteries had run out.

'Still, I hope they're not trying to scrounge from Mummy. Here – use my Vogue. I know she wouldn't mind but it would be such cheek. Oh! Did I tell you I've finally located a group of strolling players, thank God!'

'Have you? How super.'

'Yes. Trouble is they come from Gloucestershire. Do the rounds there apparently, stately homes and what-not. I'm surprised I haven't heard from them through Holdham. I probably had a mailshot and threw it straight in the bin; one gets so many circulars.'

'Quite,' Cass put her cold glass of Pimms against a burning cheek. 'So how did you find out about them?'

'A friend of ours in England spotted them and thought they'd be just the thing. Phoned this morning. That's why I couldn't get out to have our little chat till now; I've been booking them. They don't have anything on next weekend so of course they were delighted.'

'Isn't it going to be fiendishly expensive flying them over?' asked Cass.

'Well, it took a bit of squaring with Pascal but, as I pointed out, you have to pay for authenticity. By the way, you must look at the list of RSVPs I got this morning. It just gets better and better.'

Cass took the list Sophia had removed from the slim-line briefcase in which she now kept all the party-planning details. She scanned it with her eyes on stalks. One set of names in particular made her draw in a sharp breath of delight.

'They haven't?'

'They have. Cousins to you-know-who, no less,' Sophia said smugly.

Just wait till I tell Caroline Tudor-Williams, thought Cass. Just wait.

'This is why it's imperative that we make sure none of the house party shows us up,' stressed Sophia. 'Can you imagine what it would be like if Hugo and Amanda start hurling champagne flutes or Mummy starts singing "All I Need is the Air that I Breathe" in front of *them*?' She looked at Cass over her Christian Diors. 'Michael can wave bye bye to the New Year's Honours List.'

'Quite,' Cass replied in a horrified voice, knowing that Michael had no chance of making it anyway.

'And then there's the matter of Niall.' Sophia lowered her voice yet further and looked over at Amanda. She put her hand on Cass's arm. 'I think I just might have spoken to the answer to *that* little problem this morning. She happens to be staying all alone in the Beverly Wilsher – her new lover's just walked out with his leading lady, you know. And my dear, she was frightfully pleased to be invited.'

Ben was feeling extremely undignified. As if it wasn't bad enough that his wife was still reminding him with digital reliability about his humiliating lack of control at the market the previous Sunday, she had now put him to work like some sort of group therapy exercise for Alcoholics Anonymous.

He was sitting in the shady morning room at the back of the house with his foot up on a wobbly stool, making paper flowers and being supervised by Polly, who was dressed as a nun. The stupid things were damn fiddly to make, and infuriatingly, Polly's output was about twice as fast and twice as neat as his own. He watched enviously as the six-year-old deftly secured the base of yet another perfectly symmetrical carnation and then back rather hopelessly at his own attempt. It looked like the creation of an outdated Ministry of Defence shredder.

He leaned back in his chair and wondered whether Polly would snitch on him if he poured himself another tiny splash of whisky.

'You no finish, frère Ben,' Polly looked at him indignantly. 'Nous avons beaucoup de fleurs à faire. I promise Sophia.' She put on an imploring expression and, picking up a finished flower, scrambled up on to his knee and hooked it behind his ear.

Ben made a big effort to smile warmly at her despite the fact she had just trodden on his bad foot. It wasn't her fault Sophia had roped her in as prison warder. Why did his wife want five hundred artificial flowers anyway? She had already ordered ten thousand francs worth of real ones from a top Parisian florist. Surely these home-made efforts would look quite atrocious in comparison? Her logic escaped him.

Pascal walked in, swinging a bottle of Chateau Grillet between finger and thumb, his black eye gleaming like smudged kohl.

'You will join me in a drink, Ben?' He sat down and took out the corkscrew he always carried in his trouser pocket. 'Everyone else ees, 'ow you say, preoccupied.'

Ben sighed with relief and was just about to accept rather too willingly when Polly jumped back off his lap, mercifully missing his bad foot this time, and ran across to her father.

'Non, papa.' She put her little hand over the neck of the bottle to stop him taking out the cork. 'Sophia a dit Ben must make des fleurs wiz me.' She beamed up at him brightly.

Pascal smiled across at Ben. 'Then he weel make them.'

Ben felt his composure start to desert him. Another crêpe paper dahlia and he'd need a bedpan and a blanket over his knees.

'And I weel 'elp you, ma petite chérie,' Pascal continued, 'while Ben and I share a bottle of medicinal wine. It ees good for his foot, you understand, mon ange.'

Ben shot Pascal a look of intense gratitude, forgetting that the pink flower behind his ear detracted from his nobility somewhat.

Half an hour later, with Polly happily adding to the huge pile of flowers in the centre of the room, Pascal and Ben had finished their first bottle, which was now on the table with an artificial tulip in its neck, and were well into embarking on a second. Ben now had several of the paper flowers behind each ear and Pascal had one hanging out of each of his breast pockets and another slotted in between two fly buttons.

They were laughing immoderately over a joke Pascal had thought up involving Cass Hennessy and a stuffed moose when Sophia walked in.

'Darling!' Ben threw out both his hands in an expansive gesture of welcome. 'Just the person we need. Pascal and I were thinking of going to the village bar for some grub but he's had the odd glass of wine and I can't drive with my leg.' So far he had succeeded in making a concerted effort not to slur his words but unfortunately failed to control a king-size burp. 'Pardon me, Shofs. You can run ush down there and we'll all have a nice shalad or shomething.' His effort was failing. He shut up and settled for smiling rather cross-eyed at her.

Sophia looked from Ben to Pascal with murder in her eyes. If they behaved like this before lunch what hope was there with a house full of VIPs and champagne on tap? She cleared her throat to speak her mind, but at that moment the orange sari decided to obey gravity and make a plunge for the marble floor below.

Pascal and Polly got the giggles. Ben appeared not to have noticed.

Clutching the flapping fabric furiously around her, Sophia thrust her chin in the air and regarded the pile of flowers in front of her with narrowed eyes.

'Really, Ben, I am not your chauffeur and besides you haven't done nearly enough of these yet.' She kicked one of his lumpy attempts at a tiger lily with a manicured toe. 'These are to go in the swimming pool, you know. Real flowers turn brown in seconds. There aren't enough here to fill a wash-basin. And even then it would look as though it were full of dead parrots.' She sighed and gave him a hurt look. 'Honestly, Ben. I ask you to do just one tiny thing to help unburden the load on my shoulders and you can't be bothered, can you? I'm going to have a shower.' She turned to make a dramatic exit, pausing only for a split second to uncoil her sari from the door handle when she was nearly garrotted.

Ben looked forlornly at his large workmanlike hands with their old scars and well-worn calluses. Cinderella would be pretty pissed off to find her prince preferred dry-stone walling to passing the port.

Seeing how miserable he was, Pascal patted the blond man's

back sympathetically and searched around for something to say in their mutual language.

Before he could speak, the silence was broken by what sounded like an army of petrol-driven chain-saws attacking a line of galvanised steel railings outside. As it increased, it became deeper and throatier, like machine-gun-fire ricocheting round a corrugated-iron aircraft hanger.

'Mon Dieu!' Pascal leapt up and ran to the window. When he got there his expression changed from concern to laughter.

Making their way along the overgrown, dusty path which led from the cave house to the manoir, were Marcus and Wiltsher on a bright red moped and a familiar rusty white Vespa.

'Arrête!' Pascal called out, but his voice was drowned beneath the deafening splutters of sixty cc of engine, tanked up to sound like eight hundred. He looked round the room for something to catch their attention. Gathering up a handful of paper flowers, he waited until they were almost parallel with the window before throwing them out. The multi-coloured blooms cascaded down on the lads' heads like a Hell's Angels' wedding reception.

Marcus put on his brakes, reducing the sound of his moped to a waspish drone. Wiltsher nearly ran into the back of his wobbling friend, but managed to swerve his Vespa and came to a halt with the aid of a nearby bush.

Marcus squinted up at the window. 'Morning, Pascal, man,' he whooped. 'This is my mate Wiltsher. Er – Aunt Alex said it'd be, like, all right, if we borrowed Valérie's moped for the afternoon, y'know,' he lied.

'Allô, boys,' Pascal grinned down at them, too tight to take in what Marcus had said. 'You are going to the village, by chance?' He puffed out his cheeks and raised his furry eyebrows hopefully.

'Yeah.' Marcus watched Wiltsher disentangle himself and the Vespa from the bush, leaving the wing-mirror and most of the reflector dangling behind. 'We've gotta, like, get some adapters. Do you want us to bring you somefink back?'

'Non, mon brave.' Pascal beckoned over his shoulder for Ben

to get up. 'I want you to wait there un moment. You can give Ben et moi a lift.' Grinning, he disappeared from sight.

Marcus looked at Wiltsher and rolled his eyes. 'Where d'you s'pose he got the, like, shiner, man?'

'Dunno.' Wiltsher gazed towards the house and removed a twig from his hair. 'Rough sex? . . . Hey – I told you the bikes were a sure-fire way of picking up chicks, man,' he smiled sweetly, twiddling a dreadlock and nodding as Pascal and Ben shambled from the house, covered in flowers and draped in fantastic garlands like Ophelia and King Lear at a Shakespeare reunion.

30

Amanda was damned if she was going to leave the pool before Cass and Sophia did, bored as she was. The duo clearly found her presence restricting. They were talking in hushed voices and casting conspiratorial looks in her direction. Amanda had subtly switched off her Walkman but had been able to hear nothing of their conversation above the lapping of the pool and the gentle whir of the cleaning machine patrolling its base.

As soon as the two women made their way inside, however, Amanda wrapped herself in a long silk shirt of Hugo's and went in search of something to alleviate the solitary tedium of the day.

Niall was being a touch too distracted for her liking. He'd certainly responded with frightening passion to her charms early on in their brief affair but the relationship hardly seemed to be going anywhere now. He was far too unpredictable for Amanda's satisfaction, almost unbalanced in his violent mood swings and intensity. One minute he was the laughing, laid-back star, the next a brooding, self-destructive heap of nerves. Instead of gradually relaxing and taking their relationship more seriously, he was becoming increasingly withdrawn. Most of the time he hardly seemed to notice she was there. Infuriatingly, this merely served to increase her determination to win him.

He'd never exactly confided in her but had, from time to time, briefly expressed loyalty so deep that she had longed for him to feel for her with the same passionate emotions that he wasted on his ex-wife. Fired by an artificial high that made him laugh and joke and talk slightly too fast but with awesome erudition, he would make love to her with such skilful measure and breathtaking tenderness that she would think about it for hours, letting every nerve ending in her body tingle and quiver in the memory long after the effects of the drug had worn off.

And yet Amanda sometimes thought that once he'd come back down he wouldn't be able to pick her out from an identity parade of Mongolian rice pickers.

Her one compensation was that Hugo, for all his apparent indolent boredom, was showing signs of being cut up. His bitchy asides and thickly spread irony had not gone unnoticed. Hugo's jokey pretence at inattention had always been a cover for a calculating mind. Niall's current abstraction, however, came painfully close to indifference.

She walked lazily through the garden, batting at the long grasses with a dried stick and decapitating poppies.

Looking up at a now unblemished sky as blue as the *Concise Oxford Dictionary*, she wondered how they were all coping without her at the office.

Thinking about returning to work made her feel surprisingly tight-throated, an emotional response she hadn't felt since her schooldays, recovering her uniform the day before term started. She had been working too hard too long. She was fed up with propping open her eyes in the office until she was rattling from excess caffeine and too many uppers. She hated returning to an empty flat night after night in creased clothes, heavy with the grime and sweat of another frantic day. The kick of success and a fat salary was increasingly difficult to balance with the desperation she felt that her personal life was the same as it had been six years earlier. Her relationship with Hugo was frighteningly shallow. She was destined to become an old self-maid married to a career that burnt you out by forty.

Amanda was so deep in thought that she didn't notice her heel sinking into something softer than the bullet-hard ground until the smell became overpowering. Those bloody dogs of

Alexandra's! Furiously, she ripped off the shoe and hurled it into the distance, followed by the other.

She only just stopped herself from crying and was amazed by the overpowering punch of emotion which hit her chest. Tears had become as rare in her life as days off in recent years. Now she longed to weep like a wife at the pit head. Worse still, she wanted to pack in her job.

Picking her way carefully on bare feet to the edge of the garden, she leaned against the only bit of fence where the hedge on the other side hadn't broken through.

Why had she agreed to come on this God-awful holiday? she wondered sourly. After so long without one she could have justified a beach house in Barbados, Mustique or Miami. Perhaps a five-star hotel in Bali or Rio. Why then, had she agreed so readily to stay with Sophia's oddball family?

A familiar drawl drew her attention to what was happening on the other side of the fence. At first she just saw Hugo, sitting on a barrel with one leg drawn up, a brown arm resting on it. He was squinting against the sun in profile to her. He looked both menacing and unbelievably attractive. Amanda felt an involuntary twinge of desire in her groin. He was a handsome bastard, but still a bastard, she told herself firmly.

Although she still found him intensely physically attractive, she was surprised to find herself thinking that it was a shame he was far less educated than Niall. He was bright but lazy. Whereas Niall absorbed literature, art, news, information on anything that interested him, like air, Hugo flipped through the odd Dick Francis, glanced at the headlines and fell asleep if there was no decent sports coverage.

His total absorption in his sport had once fascinated her. Here was a man who was tanned, muscular and capable of devoting his life to something, she'd thought. Why not me?

It suddenly occurred to Amanda why she'd come to France. Somewhere, buried in her subconscious mind had been the desire to have one last, full-pitch attempt to make Hugo pop the question he'd proved allergic to all these years. Now she could see her total misjudgement. With so many married couples in the house party and no horses to distract him, this holiday had seemed like the ideal nesting ground for a proposal. Instead, it had proved a catalyst to their break-up. As if someone had come along with a highlighter pen and stained 'mismatch' in dayglo yellow on their bedroom door.

Over the past few years, she'd carried on clinging to him despite their non-stop arguments because she was too drained by her job to find anyone more suitable. Compared to the grey, work-obsessed men in London, Hugo had been golden and vital, lit up with an energy that came from within himself not a bottle. He had been the one concrete thing she had in a disorientating world of variables. Ultimately, she supposed she'd hoped he would prove her escape hatch when she was bored and hollowed-out. He was rich and old-fashioned. One day she could leave London behind to have babies and keep setters with Hugo in the Home Counties. But now that she no longer wanted power and glory but to honour and obey, Hugo was further away from her grasp than ever. Looking at his beautiful, petulant face she saw nothing but an arrogant little boy. The rich, energetic, devoted husband had never really been there at all.

She half expected him to turn and look at her, aware that someone was watching him. Instead, he kept his eyes firmly glued on something just out of her sight.

'Get his bloody hocks engaged!' he yelled. 'How do you expect to have any semblance of control if he's constantly leaning on his forehand?'

'Sorry.' A voice called from the direction of his gaze.

Amanda stiffened. No one else said that word with the same regularity as 'Mind the gap' at Bank tube station. There was something intensely irritating about the deep, soft voice tinged with worry.

'How many times have I told you, you won't get him back by yanking at his mouth.' Hugo's voice was cold and critical. 'The lightest of contacts, Tash. As if you were holding out a bunch of flowers. That's right. Now feel your weight right down into your heels and bloody well use it.' He wiped his forehead and rolled his eyes in exasperation.

Amanda watched in fascination as Tash came into view perched on her enormous horse. The last time Amanda had seen Snob, he'd been writhing and spinning about like Marcus Hennessy acid dancing. Now, although his whole body burst with barely hidden verve and energy, he was moving in a beautifully controlled circle at a smooth, bouncing canter. His long red ears were pricked like antennae, occasionally twitching back as if listening to his rider for encouragement. Tash gave him plenty; Hugo appeared to be giving Tash none.

'All right, stop. I can't bear to watch any longer. Your back is about as straight as a Norwegian prawn and your elbows were flapping around like some middle-aged divorcee doing the Birdie Song.' He stood up and walked towards her. 'Those faults are curable, given time and, considering the speed you pick things up, the patience of several saints. However—' he paused to light a cigarette, leaving Tash trying to hold on to Snob, who'd relapsed and started pirouetting again, 'having a lower leg that looks like it's constantly trying to kick start a Harley is not helping the horse one bit. He'd be better off with a shop dummy on his back, to be quite honest.'

'Sorry . . . what do you suggest?' she mumbled.

Amanda noticed Tash never looked him in the eyes. She was astonished that the girl didn't argue, considering how incredibly she'd improved. She must be wet to let Hugo grind her down like that. He was playing one of his games, it was obvious. Now, she noticed, Tash was taking in Hugo's bullshit about fitness with wide, unblinking eyes.

If it had been Amanda out there, she was in no doubt that she would have rammed his packet of cigarettes down his languid, supercilious mouth. And yet watching him idly rubbing his neck and holding out his hand expressively as he described the importance of rider fitness in building a confident seat, she found herself absurdly turned on. His total superiority and self-confidence could not be more of a contrast to Niall's constant doubt and deliberation. She'd slept with her back to Hugo for days, refusing to let him have sex with her, wanting instead

Niall's strong, gentle hands and patient selflessness. And yet she missed the white-hot energy with which Hugo made love.

She watched him dismiss Tash with no more than a nod, staring after her with an unfathomable expression on his face.

While I'm trying to play nursemaid to Niall, mused Amanda, Hugo's acting Pyg-headed-malian to Tash, for some reason. Hardly his style but ironic all the same.

Quietly, so that he couldn't accuse her of spying and consequently feel superior, Amanda backed away from the fence and crept barefoot towards the house. She thought briefly of trying to find Niall but couldn't rustle the energy. She had to put on an act with him, curb her tongue and nurture his battered self-respect. It was all too much effort today. All she wanted at the moment was to be herself. And get laid.

Michael approached the stone barn with his usual stiff-backed limping gait, swinging a huge ring of rusted keys like Thomas More's jailer.

It astonished Todd, following behind, that someone so comparatively young could have all the external mannerisms of an old man. Michael couldn't be more than fifty-six or-seven, yet he puffed and procrastinated like a veteran of two wars, the General Strike and Cowdrey's first test century.

As Michael sorted through the bunch of medieval-looking keys for the one which opened the tall dusty doors, a strange snuffling came from inside, followed by what sounded like long claws scratching against the stone-flagged floor.

'What d'ya suppose that bloody is, lad?' Michael stiffened even more, if that were possible.

Todd shrugged, preoccupied with examining an ancient, luridly painted Dormobile that was parked in the courtyard.

'Rats,' he suggested vaguely. 'Pascal said he had some ruddy great buggers around.'

Michael cleared his throat nervously and sucked on his pipe until his red-veined cheeks almost disappeared.

'Perhaps we should get Jean to open this bloody thing,' he suggested quickly, 'we could be here all bloody afternoon finding the right key.' The scratching from within increased and Michael backed away a little.

'Fine by me. No worries.' Todd noticed Marcus and a couple of daggy-looking characters sauntering their way.

Christ! He remembered with a start that he'd meant to go to Tours and meet his contact. But with Michael watching him like a hawk with binoculars and the enigmatic Tash not watching him at all, Todd had been too preoccupied. Now that Marcus had his friends staying, he'd expect some sort of sample of the goods Todd had promised to supply him with. All Todd had was a couple of suppositories for constipation and half a bottle of Paracetamol. He'd have to improvise.

'Er – I'd better go and see what Rooter's up to, Mike mate,' he said quickly, starting to walk away before Michael had a chance to splutter. 'I haven't seen him all morning. I'll be back before you know it.' And he ran into the house without a backward glance.

Michael would have followed him on the double had it not been for the appearance of his youngest son at his side.

'Yo, Dad.' Marcus squinted at him. 'Are you gonna unlock the rave site, man? Pukka. Wiltsher, Alg and meself, we – like – wanna unload our gear and set up the sound system, y'know?'

Michael looked at him for a minute. 'I wish you would speak bloody English, old boy.' He scratched his bald patch and looked at the door. 'And how many times has your mother bloody told you I don't like being called bloody "Dad". *Father* will suffice, Marcus.'

'Cool, man.' Marcus hadn't taken in a word.

There was a furious snort from within the barn, followed by more frantic scratching. Michael stood transfixed for a moment, his pipe sliding out of his mouth without his noticing. There must be the biggest rat in the history of France inside, he pondered fearfully. Big enough to mutilate a whole host of pied pipers.

'I – er – I don't seem to have the right set of keys here, old boy.' Michael fought to adjust his voice so that he didn't sound like Aled Jones. 'I'd better get Jean to open this bloody thing.'

Marcus studied the keys in his father's shaking hands. 'Could it be the one marked "grange en pierre", man?' he suggested helpfully. 'Why don't you – like – try it out, Dad – I mean, man – and the guys and meself'll unload the motor, y'know?'

Michael stared at his son in shocked horror. It was nowadays very rare for Marcus actively to use his brain. Even less often did he come to a reasoned conclusion from his discoveries or make any intelligent suggestions. Michael should feel elated. Why then, did he want to throttle him and put his remains through a trouser press?

As Michael put the key into the cast-iron lock, a mournful groan came from behind the door, followed by desperate snuffling. That was no rat. It sounded huge. Probably a ferocious wild boar from the surrounding woods, locked in by mistake and demented with frustration and starvation.

Michael turned the key as slowly as he could, preparing to leap behind the sanctuary of the thick wooden door as soon as the lock gave.

Marcus appeared with a pile of coiled black cable weighing down his bony body to a low stoop.

'Get back, son!' hissed Michael. 'There's something inside!'

Marcus shrugged rather vacantly and stood behind a tub of geraniums.

As Michael let the door swing back inch by inch, there was an almighty, earth-shattering howl. Before he could start to dodge behind the door, a scrabbling, panting, hairy creature the size of a leopard had stretched to its full height and leapt at him, pinning Michael to the ground with enormous, heavy paws.

Michael screamed hysterically as he felt the creature's hot breath on his neck. It was so heavy and he was so terrified, he couldn't move. He tried to scream at Marcus for help but his throat had tightened too much to speak. As the animal started to lick his face frenziedly, Michael passed out.

Rooter wagged his tail ecstatically and covered his liberator with wet dog kisses. When Michael didn't respond, he gave up and bounded over to the group of three boys watching.

Marcus patted the huge, shaggy dog enthusiastically.

'Fucking happening dog, man.' Wiltsher looked from the sandy animal to Michael. 'That's the first time I've seen your father lost for words, Hennessy.'

'Yeah.' Marcus scratched his head and studied his unconscious parent lying on the cobbles. A worried-looking chicken was pecking nervously at Michael's thinning hair. 'Suppose he'd say he was bloody bowled over.'

They all stood in silence and watched Michael for a little longer. Algy rolled up another wafer-thin cigarette.

After five minutes they came to the conclusion that Michael had not, as suspected, had a heart attack. He seemed to be breathing normally, at one point even muttering, 'Fix me a drink, old girl,' so Marcus propped his head up on Wiltsher's Joe Bloggs sweatshirt and they carried on unloading the sound system.

Hugo came out of the shower feeling exhilarated, his skin buzzing from the powerful jets of cool water.

He wrapped a towel round his hips, shook his wet hair like a water spaniel and clipped his watch back on his wrist. Glancing in the mirror as he went out of the bathroom, he noticed that two days of not bothering to shave had left him looking like a Mexican bandit. He retraced his steps and started to lather his face.

Coming into the bedroom, Amanda thought she was alone. She stood for a long time looking undecidedly out of the window.

The room was as stuffy as a sauna. She'd thought only Provence baked its landscape into a hard, dry husk like this. Pascal was delighted because it meant he would have a bumper harvest of grapes. Everyone else was concentrating on turning their whitewashed British bodies brown.

Amanda normally loved the heat too, but today it was making her sluggish. Why had she come up here? She wondered. Oh, yes. To get her compact of precious, illegal powder and go to find Niall. She sat down on the bed and let her body fall back on to the cool, crisp sheets, looking sulkily up at the beamed ceiling. Why did he never bother to come and find her? she reflected bitterly. Why was this thing so bloody one-sided?

She turned her head to one side and looked at the framed sketch on the wall. It was a study of a nude, unfinished but signed. Egon Schiele. Niall would rattle on about it for hours if he saw it. Hugo hadn't even known who Schiele was when she'd pointed it out to him on first arriving.

'Stupid Kraut hasn't even bothered to finish it,' was all he'd said.

'He was Austrian!' Amanda had snapped in return.

Amanda smiled and looked back at the ceiling. If Niall wanted her so much, or his stupid fix for that matter, let him make the effort.

She rolled over on to her front and found her face buried in one of Hugo's discarded shirts. Typical Hugo, leaving his clothes strewn around wherever he happened to take them off. Lifting it up, she pressed it to her cheek and breathed in. It smelt hot and masculine. Suddenly, she felt weak with longing.

Hugo chased the last of the shaving foam down the sink with water and towelled his face. On the shelf in front of him was the bottle of aftershave Amanda had insisted on buying him in Paris. Hugo didn't approve of aftershave. People who wore it generally did so because they were effeminate or lower class or had raging BO. But when he had opened it to get a whiff, Hugo had been taken with the spicy, expensive scent. Now he took some in his cupped hands and felt the cool sting on his face as the valuable liquid splashed over it. He grinned at his tanned reflection. Six months ago, if he had known he was going to suffer catastrophic humiliation at Badminton and temporary ostracism from the sport, to end up teaching a novice to ride and wearing aftershave, he'd have cried.

He swung the towel round his neck and walked into the bedroom.

Lying face down on the bed, wearing a creased silk shirt, was Amanda. One arm was flung out to the side, clutching the old denim shirt he'd been wearing. The other was hanging limply from the side of the bed, her huge opal ring slipped down to her finger joint. Her slim brown legs dangled from the end of the bed, rising up in a luscious curve to her well-shaped behind.

Hugo looked at her thoughtfully. She looked rumpled and sexy, the normally sleek blonde hair ruffled, the French manicure on her long, square nails beginning to chip.

She groaned and slowly turned over on to her back, covering her eyes with her arm without noticing him.

Hugo took in the parted lips and long expanse of bare midriff in front of him.

If only she were always this relaxed, he found himself thinking, if she took less effort with her appearance she'd look ten times better. More natural. More crumpled. Sexier. Like Tash.

Tash! He started in surprise. What on earth was he thinking about? Tash was a mess. She wore nothing but jeans and her hair was like a bird's nest. She wasn't attractive. He'd better get a grip on himself.

He turned away and cast around for a pair of clean boxers. But before he realised it he found himself staring at Amanda again. Looking at her spreadeagled brown body was an incredible turn-on.

How would she react if he asked her for a screw? he wondered. Would she spit in his face and go running to Niall with a smug grin?

He dropped the towel on the floor and deliberated. With her arm over her eyes and hair, Amanda could have been anyone. Hugo was appalled to find himself imagining it was Tash French lying there, soft and wanton. He closed his eyes to make the image go away but it wouldn't. Not thinking about what he was doing, he stooped down to drop a slow kiss on the inside of her calf.

Amanda felt her heart leap in hope and fear. She lifted her arm and looked down the length of her body to the man standing at the end of the bed.

Naked and glorious, his freshly washed skin glistening with golden health, there was Hugo. As he dropped another kiss on to the inside of her leg, Amanda felt her stomach grind with anticipation.

She looked at the thick, streaked hair and the broad brown shoulders and knew he was still a complete stranger to her. He always would be. The thought made her feel faint with excited, exploding lust.

Hugo didn't look at her at all. Instead, he continued his slow progress up her legs with his lips. As he knelt down, still kissing between her knees, he slid his hands up the outside of her legs and under her bikini bottoms. Gently hooking his thumbs under their fragile straps, he slowly slipped them down her thighs and, lifting his head, let them drop to the floor.

Still he didn't look at her. Amanda felt as if she was spying on their lovemaking from afar, her body squirming and flaming with voyeuristic pleasure, desperately turned-on yet not wanting to be found out. She suppressed a moan as Hugo's lips pressed with measured timing on the inside of her thighs over and over again, his tongue flicking unbearably lightly on her hot skin. He was teasing her, frustrating her until she screamed out with an urgent, desperate need to have him inside her.

She reached down and touched his hair. It was silky and squeaky from the shower. She let the clean, cool strands slip between her nails and the flesh of her fingers.

His tongue was drawing out delicate, intricate patterns on the soft, downy skin between her thigh and her pubic hair now. It took her breath away. She felt her fingers tighten on his hair until her nails bit into the palms of her hand but she could do nothing about it. Her whole body was beginning to disappear into one concentrated area of pleasure. She could feel nothing except the intense electric beat between her legs.

Hugo's tongue dipped into her and drew a line upwards. It began circling in strong, gentle sweeps, shooting delicious stabs of heat to every nerve ending. Amanda's feet started to buzz numbly as static pulsed down her veins. The circles became faster, more rhythmic. Totally without control, she felt her hands let go of Hugo's hair and clutch wildly at the sheets. As she felt the first rippling waves of an orgasm course through her pelvis, Hugo moved up her body in one fluid action and was inside her.

The result was almost more than Amanda could bear. She was held on the verge of ecstasy, great waves of vibrating pleasure rushing through her without let-up or end. His thrusts were so forceful that they moved up the bed together, pulling sheets, clothes and pillows with them, until her head was pressed up painfully against the wall behind. She could feel the heat of his body sink through her skin and into her lungs. His breath was coming in short, sharp bursts. Every muscle was tensed and strained beneath his glistening brown skin. She tried to look at his face but her eyes wouldn't concentrate, couldn't focus. She closed them on the world and let her whole self be lost as the final burst of thrilling warmth shuddered through her.

When Hugo came he cried out, but not in pleasure. It was a strange, angry, excited shout of victory. Then he let his head drop on to her shoulder before rolling off her and on to his back.

Amanda opened her eyes in shock and stared at him. Did he say what she thought he said? Surely not. She was imagining it. It was too far-fetched. Too Ealing comedy.

Her body lay saturated in lazy contentment, still echoing the buzz of pleasure she had just experienced, but her mind churned with disturbed anxiety.

'Hugo?'

'What now?'

It was like breaking the spell. As soon as they spoke, reality clumped in wearing size eleven Doc Martens to trample over her enjoyment. Hugo was Hugo. He had been for the past six years. Why should he change now?

'What did you scream when you came?'

'Oh, for Christ's sake!' Hugo sat up and scratched his head, not looking at her.

'Tell me!' She played with a piece of sheet, folding it over and over between her fingers.

'Nothing.' He stood up and started to wander around the room looking for his clothes.

'Yes, you did!'

'Well, I don't know.' He pulled on a pair of striped boxers only to discover they were back to front. 'Do you have to be so pedantic, even after a screw? One doesn't exactly catalogue these things in the heat of the moment. I probably said "Oh Boy" or "Christ" or something. Are you planning to put it in your diary for future reference?'

'You said someone's name.' Amanda sat up and watched him pull on a pair of blue chinos.

'Okay, I said "Amanda". Is that supposed to prove that I love you or something?'

'It wasn't my name.'

'Wasn't it?' Hugo asked without interest. He carried on selecting a white t-shirt from the pile of clean washing on the chair.

'No it wasn't, Hugo!' Amanda felt her temper snap. She'd laid herself open, unable to control the lust she felt for him. He'd seemed to want her so badly, want to satisfy her more than himself for once. How could he just switch off like this?

A thought struck her. She'd been turned on by his distance, by a feeling that she was anonymous, a spectator. Was that because he had been thinking about someone else all along?

'Who were you fantasising about, Hugo?' she hissed.

He hooked his arms into the t-shirt, pulling it over his head without answering.

'Who was I supposed to be?'

He looked at her. It was like being regarded by a bored, slightly irritated teacher.

'I should have imagined it would be you, dearest, that would be doing the fantasising,' his voice was as emotionless as his face. 'Lover boy couldn't get it up today, I take it?'

'You bastard!' She snatched a bowl of scented wooden spheres from the bedside table and hurled it at him. He ducked and they crash-landed against the tall chest of drawers, bouncing like hailstones on to the floor. 'Niall's ten times the lover you are. And he has more compassion and more brains than you'll ever have.'

'Then I suggest you pop along and talk to him about Proust

for a bit.' Hugo pushed the rest of the clean clothes off the chair and sat down to pull on his shoes.

'Yes! I fucking well will.' She jumped up and started to dress furiously, ripping a pair of silk knickers in her haste. 'I only let you screw me out of pity,' she said through her teeth. 'You've been missing out lately. Don't want you getting frustrated.'

'How considerate of you.' Hugo sat back and watched her. 'Niall's teaching you some manners at last. Sweet of him, I must write him a thank-you card.'

'Bastard, bastard, bastard,' Amanda hissed under her breath. How could he be so conceited, so difficult to hurt? He knew how badly she'd wanted him, he must have done.

As she walked to the door, Hugo put out his foot to stop her.

'Aren't you forgetting something, dearest?' He smiled at her, his blue eyes glinting with mirth. 'You've got to take Niall his sweeties or he won't play with you.' He nodded towards her wash-bag on the chest of drawers. It was where she kept her compact.

Amanda paused, willing herself to hit him but unable to conjure the nerve. Painfully, ironically he had a point. If she was going to give up the idea of waiting and run to Niall after such a short time, she couldn't go empty-handed. Yet to take the coke in front of Hugo was to admit that their relationship was based on supply and demand. The debasement would be crucifying.

Taking a deep breath and not looking at him, she walked to her wash-bag. What did one more humiliation count?

The compact wasn't there. She looked on top of the chest and on the floor around it. Nothing. She took the bag and emptied the contents on to the bed. Razors, Tampax, her massage mit, assorted face creams and body lotions. No compact.

Furiously, she turned to Hugo.

'What have you done with it?'

He grinned at her. 'You're not accusing me, surely?'

'Yes, you bastard. Now stop pretending to be a retard and give me my fucking compact back!'

'Poor Amanda.' Hugo stretched out, laughing. 'Can't you and Niall powder your noses?'

'This isn't funny, Hugo. Just give it back.'

Hugo looked at her seriously. 'I haven't touched your fucking compact, honey. Whoever has, however, is obviously doing you a favour. I suggest you straighten yourself out while you've got the chance.' He stood up so that he was facing her, his nose practically touching hers. 'You were always a mess emotionally, but screwing up Niall is just being a selfish bitch. He can't handle it right now. Back off.' And turning on his heel, he walked to the door.

'You bloody back off!' Amanda screamed. 'How dare you go around telling me what to do with my life when you're playing around with Tash French? You superior fucking hypocrite! You . . .'

But her words fell on nothing but polished wood. Hugo had gone, slamming the door behind him.

Amanda took a sharp intake of breath through her nose and refused to succumb to tears. Hugo had left behind him the erotic, lingering tang of his aftershave. She'd loved it when she bought it. Now it made her feel sick.

Suddenly she looked in panic at the contents of her wash-bag scattered across the bed. If Hugo hadn't taken her compact then who had?

She was disturbed by a knock on the door. Hugo back to apologise? No, he wouldn't knock. Oh God! Was it Niall? What would she say? Make or break time had come earlier than she'd planned.

But it was just Sophia, cancelling out the subtle traces of Hugo's scent with an overpowering cloud of Givenchy.

'Do you marinade in that stuff overnight or something?' Amanda spat.

'What?' Sophia smiled at her radiantly, taking in Amanda's pale face and dirty hair. It was a wonder that Niall saw anything in her, she thought smugly.

'What do you want?' Amanda didn't care if she was being rude. She felt rude.

'I was just wondering. You haven't seen my shower cap, have you? Only I was about to have a quick douche and it appears to be missing.'

'I think,' Amanda concluded slowly, 'that there's a toiletry thief on the premises.'

31

Michael was vaguely aware of the sun on his face. He thought himself to be bobbing lightly on a tufted turquoise sea, protected by the high, gleaming white cliff-faces of a semi-circular bay.

The next moment he heard a twanging, slightly amused enquiry.

'You all right down there, mate?' Todd stooped over him, his shadow turning the red behind Michael's closed eyelids to grey. 'Taking a kip?'

'No, I'm bloody not,' Michael spluttered groggily, opening his eyes a fraction and squinting up at him. 'Aghh!'

He scrambled back against the solid wall of the barn as he saw Rooter staring at him, tongue lolling from one side of his grinning mouth, shaggy tail rotating, brown eyes rolling with evil canine mirth.

'Get that bloody beast away from me!' Michael yelped.

Todd straightened up at a dilatory pace and called Rooter back. The big dog shambled away from Michael and threaded his scraggy muzzle between his master's arm and hip, panting brainlessly.

Marcus and Wiltsher, cigarettes dangling from their mouths, chose this moment to troop past carrying a huge sticker-coated loudspeaker between them. Algy followed carrying a two-plug adapter and a tatty roll of carpet.

'Your Dad's come round, Hennessy man.' Wiltsher nodded at Michael and nearly ignited his dreadlocks.

'Yo, Father, man,' Marcus greeted him from beneath his baseball cap. 'We thought, like, you were a gonner.'

Michael grabbed his pipe from the cobbles, tapped it out and – with as much dignity as he could muster – got stiffly to his feet.

'Right,' he barked, determined to regain authority. 'Always close my eyes when I'm thinking hard. Just mapped out a way to shore up that bloody balcony at the back.' He limped stiffly into the barn.

'Wow,' Algy croaked, shaking his head in disbelief. 'A meditating crusty. Like, wow.' Still shaking his head, he wandered into the barn.

Todd and Marcus gazed after them in amazement. It was the first time Algy had spoken.

Sally finally found Matty sitting in the old study. It was the dark, sombre room which Niall had turned into his sanctuary earlier on in the holiday. Signs of his presence were still littered around: a brimming ashtray here, a half-finished book there. On the desk where Niall had propped his feet day after day watching junk television stood five empty whisky glasses like unwashed milk bottles awaiting collection.

Matty was perched on the windowsill, his chin resting on his knees as he stared unseeing out of the window.

Sally stood in the shadows, feeling like an intruder, waiting for him to turn around. Breaking the silence seemed harder than cracking through ice on a skating rink. It summed up the current state of their marriage: they'd gone beyond skating on thin ice, now it was a barrier between them.

She'd come dutifully to apologise, but instead felt hot anger leaping inside her. He could be so outrageously self-pitying at times.

Not looking at her, Matty raised his chin from his knees and rested the back of his head against the window frame.

'Come here,' he said quietly.

She walked over to the window and stood a few feet from

him. He put out his arm and took hold of the skirt of her old denim sundress, tugging her gently closer.

'Sally, I . . .' He looked out of the window and swallowed, as if the pain of what he was about to say was too much to bear. Suddenly he blurted out, 'You don't have to keep on doing this, you know.'

Sally stiffened. 'Doing what, Matt?'

He blinked hard and carried on looking fixedly out of the window.

'I appreciate your loyalty more than anything, you must know that.' He was still holding on to her skirt, his hand shaking. 'I can see how difficult it must be for you, how torn you are. I mean it would have been much easier for you to make the . . . to make the . . . break,' the word caught in his throat and he paused, biting his lip, 'before you found out about the baby, but you must understand that I never wanted – I don't want – you to feel tied to a commitment simply because convention dictates.'

There was another pause while Sally tried to take in the logic of what he was saying. He could be so extreme and irrational in his conclusions, sulking for hours about the most trivial things.

'I'm sorry, Matty, I don't understand what you're telling me.'

'I'm letting you off the hook, Sals,' he let go of her skirt and covered his mouth with his hand. 'I can see what a selfish, b-bloody-minded sod I've been recently, keeping you tied to the kitchen sinking ship. The job, the house in Richmond, my idiot p-projects – one failure on top of another – and all the time I've expected you to be there with your beautiful, sympathetic face and your never-ending patience. I didn't see it running out before it was too late. Once we got here it suddenly struck me. I looked at you and saw nothing but all the disillusions that have built up over the years staring back at me and then—'

'Matty, I—' Sally started in disbelief.

'Wait, Sals. Let me finish, please.' Matty took hold of her hand with his own trembling one. 'And then I realised that I've messed everything up. I p-promised you a whole load of things I've never come up with. I somehow thought that if we kept muddling on for just a year more and six months on top of that and then just another month – or two – or three, I'd finally do something I could really feel satisfied about. Something that wasn't messed about and compromised in the edit suites until my credit at the end became an industry joke.'

Matty got up and started pacing the room, beginning to ramble.

'I think – I guess I became so obsessed that our relationship simply didn't figure in the equation at all. I somehow thought I could keep you happy just by giving you that hollow tomb of a house to rattle round in and by scraping together enough money at the end of the month to pay for the b-bloody thing.' He gave a high, bitter laugh of self-reproach.

Sally sometimes felt that working through the complexities of Matty's mind was like solving a riddle in a different language with only an out-of-date phrase book for help. Where other people had lows, Matty had bottomless pits. Once his neurosis had been triggered, it could ricochet for hours.

'I've been working so bloody hard that I haven't had any time left for myself,' he continued before she could speak. 'I even had the nerve to resent you and the kids for taking away my freedom. It was just b-bloody ironic that I was actually doing it in a desperate attempt to keep hold of our marriage. I saw another baby as an albatross around my neck,' he laughed bitterly. 'It was only when I stood back that I realised you were the one who was trapped and miserable. Stuck in a huge, cold house expecting a baby you didn't want.'

'But I do want this baby, Matt!' Sally cried out, unable to bear his complete misjudgment any longer.

'Only because it's there inside you!' Matty yelled back. 'Can you honestly say that you would have wanted to bring another child into our marriage intentionally?'

Sally thought about this. The baby was such a reality now it was difficult to think back to the days of dread leading up to the discovery that she was pregnant again.

'No,' she answered eventually. 'No, I wouldn't.'

When Sally had held the positive blue strip of paper confirming her suspicions, she had sat down amongst a sea of mess and clutter in their Richmond kitchen and cried. It wasn't that she didn't want a baby, she would willingly bear Matty a whole kindergarten full of amber-eyed children. It was that she had known being pregnant would merely force Matty further and further away from her.

'You could have been free, we both could.' Matty clutched her hand again, his eyes glued to the floor. 'I'd already guessed you were going to go eventually. I resented that baby like hell but half of me was nastily, calculatingly pleased because it meant you would stay with me a little longer. Now I can't let you sacrifice your life like that.' Sinking back on to the sill, he let go of her hand and wiped away the tears that were slowly creeping from her eyes. 'You don't have to feel guilty, Sals. Christ! I find myself hard enough to live with.'

'Oh Matt!' Sally leaned forward and put her arms around him, resting her chin on his head.

His hair smelt of the cheap apple shampoo she'd bought before they left England. It reminded her of walking around Boots the Chemist preoccupied with worry about Matty until someone had pointed out that Tor was busy shoving cuticle cream under her jumper. She'd guessed then that, rattling with nervous exhaustion, he was on the verge of a breakdown, had hoped that the holiday would help. Instead, it had triggered off his insecurity.

She lay a hand on his shaking shoulder, but his back tightened and he shrugged her away.

'Matty, believe me,' she said firmly, aware that he was barely listening. 'I'd live in a tent and eat baked beans on toast for the rest of my life if that's what staying married to you meant—'

'Mashy! Sally!' Tom ran in and threw himself at them. 'I'm bored and Tor's just been sick. She's eaten three worms and most of Sofa's sun-cream.'

'Shit!' Matty pushed Sally to one side and ran from the room. Tom skipped happily after him.

Groaning in despair, Sally stood in the gloom for a minute, unable to think of anything but the fact that she hadn't told

Matty how she felt, incensed that Tom had rushed in just at the critical moment.

'What am I thinking of?' She caught her breath in horror and flew from the room to find Tor.

'The amp output goes into here, man.'

'No, you tit, it plugs in here. Look.'

Marcus and Wiltsher both looked.

In front of them was a mountain of interwoven loudspeakers and cables. The task had looked simple when they'd started to connect one to the other. Now the whole thing had taken on Krypton Factor intelligence test proportions. It was the flight deck of the Enterprise after the Clingons had zapped it with their intergalactic nuclear-powered laser catapults. A mess.

'Don't suppose there's any chance of a hand here, Algy, man?' Wiltsher looked round hopefully but Algy was still meditating on his tie-dyed rush mat. Rooter sat next to him with a helpful paw on the skinny boy's crossed leg. Their doleful, catatonic expressions matched.

'He's been like that since we started, y'know, Wiltsher?'

'He's concentrating his inner Karma on the sound system to create a force field of positive and happening energy around it, y'know?'

'You'd think he'd tell us how to put it together first, man.' Marcus took another swig of his Grolsch.

Todd came in through the door, winding a long extension cable from the house, followed by Michael with a clipboard.

'I got you some power, guys, so you can have a sound check,' Todd called out, unravelling the cable around Algy and Rooter.

'Wicked!' Wiltsher tossed his dreadlocks and waggled his hips around for effect.

'You've got five bloody minutes.' Michael whipped out a tape measure and handed it to Todd. 'After that, Todd will need the sockets for the power drill and the electric sander. Measure up these bloody walls, lad. I'll just pop inside to check with Pascal when the bloody timber's arriving.'

'Straight to the drinks cabinet,' Todd muttered under his breath after Michael had gone.

'Hey, Marcus,' he strolled over to where the boy was examining an adapter as if it were a Rubik's cube. 'I've gotcha some gear, kid. Here's a free sample.' He handed over a tiny plastic bag of white powder.

'What is it, man?'

'Coke, kid.'

Marcus gulped and held it out as if it were plastic explosive.

'Um – er – thanks, man.' He looked nervously at Wiltsher. If he admitted he'd rather Todd had procured him some dried banana skins then his friend would accuse him of being unhappening.

Wiltsher's eyes were out on stalks. His only knowledge of coke came from watching *Saint Elmo's Fire*, where Demi Moore was playing an addict. That was enough to put him off. He was a committed Demi fan and was heartbroken to see her with a dribbly nose.

'Like it's really generous of you and that, man,' Marcus mumbled, 'but coke's well yuppie y'know. Totally uncrucial in the acid scene. Totally eighties, y'see what I'm saying?'

Wiltsher nodded enthusiastically in agreement. 'Totally eighties, man.'

Todd shrugged. 'Well, if you don't want it.' He took it back. 'No worries.'

'I'll have it!' Algy was off his meditation mat and beside Todd like a shot.

Todd looked into the rather wild, red-rimmed eyes. 'Sorry, squirt. Marcus is the customer,' he said decisively.

Marcus cleared his throat.

'Well, man, like,' he started cautiously, 'if Algy wants to try the gear that's fine by me. I'm, like, totally spaced already. Tripping, y'know.'

'Me too!' gulped Wiltsher. 'Totally bombed, man.'

Todd reluctantly handed the bag of powder to Algy and settled himself against a wall.

'Are you going to try out this heap of junk or what, kid?'

Marcus looked at the stack of loudspeakers dubiously. 'Er – sure, man. Wiltsher, pass us that garage funk bee bop spliced sample tape, man.'

'You mean *Here's What I Call Club Music Three*, Hennessy?'

'Just pass it over, dood.'

'Okay, keep your square hairdo on.' Wiltsher passed over the tape.

Marcus slotted it in and pushed the final plug into the socket strip with a flourish. Nothing happened.

'Algy, your system's fucked, man.' Marcus laughed his high-pitched, hiccuping laugh.

'You have to switch the power input on first.' Algy kicked Rooter off his mat and resumed his lotus position, beginning to spread the fine white powder expertly on the back of his hand.

'Where's that?' Marcus looked at the rows and rows of switches and circuitry in front of him.

But Algy, giggling like a schoolgirl with an Ann Summers catalogue, was back on his apex flight in an astral plane to never-never land. 'Great,' sighed Wiltsher. 'He's the only one who knows how to work this stuff, man.'

Tash listened to the rhythmic munching as Snob worked his way through his haynet. She couldn't bear to go back to the house just yet. Everything was such a muddle in her mind. She wanted to spend a few satisfying hours tidying it out and putting everything neatly back into drawers and cupboards but she didn't know where to start.

Snob turned round, still chewing, and looked at her quizzically. He didn't like being watched while he ate, he'd made that clear over his cubes when he'd nose-butted her out of his stall. Now he looked sulkily resigned.

Tash had read the books Niall had given her from cover to cover and was sticking to their advice diligently. One said to build a relationship with one's horse out of as well as in, the saddle. *Treat him like your best friend*, it read between large glossy pics of children clearing three-feet fences on ponies with long eyelashes, *confide in him and never allow him to feel neglected and lonely.*

So Tash had been dropping in to see Snob every ten minutes like an unwelcome neighbour shouting 'Coo-ee!' and holding out an empty sugar bowl as a feeble excuse while the occupants of the house tried unsuccessfully to hide behind the hat-stand. Not that Snob could exactly hide. He just sighed mournfully and ignored her.

The book also told you to take your horse out for walks like a dog, showing him that you weren't frightened of the things he spooked at. *Be Mum to him.*

Snob was having none of that. He knew better than Tash that a plastic bag caught in a hedge was actually an axe-wielding equine murderer cleverly disguised. Similarly, he was far too sensible to allow Tash to persuade him that a passing high-bodied tractor from the vines with a flashing orange light on top wasn't several thousand horse-eating Martians kerb-crawling in their flying saucer in the hope of spotting their din-dins.

Tash felt their relationship needed work. And a small miracle.

Snob got bored with his haynet so turned to his water bowl and breathed into it heavily, causing bubbles to disperse noisily around his nose like a child with a straw. He soon got bored with that too and deigned to come and rest his head on her shoulder with a resigned sigh.

'Oh, Snob, what am I going to do with myself, huh?' Tash scratched his muzzle, feeling the heat of his breath on her hand. 'I'm so confused.' Moving her hand to his twitching red ear, she quietly started to babble to him about her problems.

She was so engrossed that she didn't notice that someone had walked into the building and was quietly watching her from the cover of the shadows.

Tor made a miraculous recovery on being offered a bowl of blancmange in front of the television. With the aid of a tub of triple fudge ice cream, Tom was persuaded to join her.

Sally dodged Alexandra, who was for some reason intent on a conversation about building societies and the cost of British mortgages these days, and then niftily dispatched Sophia's attempt to get her to make paper flowers. Finally, she got Matty alone.

They were in the room next to the one in which Tor and Tom were watching television. The noise of a trigger-happy French cop dispatching a few Parisian criminals ricocheted through to them, accompanied by blood-curdling sound effects and a running commentary by Tom. It wasn't exactly conducive to a heart-to-heart.

'Matty, you've got to let me tell my side of the story,' she began nervously.

'Why?' Matty sat curled up in an armchair, every limb folded in on itself in an attempt to protect himself from what he didn't want to hear. He looked like a chastened greyhound. 'I appreciate you need to air your frustrations, Sals,' he went on, 'but, with all respect to your feelings, is there any point in prolonging the agony further? I know I've been an idiotic bastard but p-picking over all the sordid details isn't going to help. I can't defend myself if you scream at me. You'll just get a sore throat.'

'Well, I'm going to scream at you anyway.' Sally sat down opposite him. 'You're right. You have been an idiot, but not for the reasons you think . . .'

Tash had just got to the bit about wanting Hugo to whisk her off into a nearby wood and undress her with his teeth whilst reciting Catullus when a startled Snob threw his head back, clouting her on the ear, and stared at the opposite end of the stalls.

Tash nearly went through the roof in embarrassed fright when she saw a figure standing behind the last partition. Without new contact lenses, she couldn't tell who it was.

Please let it be Jean, she prayed. The only English he understood was 'Drink?'

'Hello . . . who's there?' Her voice was up in top register again. Why was it she had an uncanny knack of hitting a perfect vibrato top C on occasions like this?

'Hello there.' The figure walked towards her through the gloom. Under the neon light his hair shone like jet. She was fixed by two huge Cadbury-brown eyes. 'I came to seek you out to tell you something. A couple of things, actually.'

Snob had the nerve to whicker affectionately as Niall extended an arm to pat him.

'Yes?' Tash tried to sound businesslike. She actually sounded like a Smurf.

'Yes. So I did now.' He gave her a big relaxed grin and leaned back against the wooden stall. 'One. I think your painting of Matty, Sally and the kids is utterly fucking fantastic.'

Tash felt her face colouring and fumbled round for something to say. Of course, the last thing that came to mind was a simple thank-you.

'I did it ever so quickly. It's not very polished,' she mumbled, fiddling with her ring.

'That's as maybe. It's still the best thing I've ever seen.' He noticed one of the books he had given her, lying with its spine bent back on itself on an upturned bucket, and suddenly looked shifty and nervous, like a guilty lover staring at the bunch of flowers he'd brought home when late from work again. 'The other thing I've come to say – well, it's an apology really. You see, Tash, it was me that asked Hugo to give you those lessons. I thought it would help. I had no idea what he had in mind or I wouldn't have asked him.'

'You put him up to it?' Tash gasped in horror, looking up at him.

He nodded. 'I felt a complete sod when I found out. I hadn't the guts to tell you. I guess I gave you those books to ease my conscience, but it didn't.'

Niall couldn't bear to look at the hurt in her face. Her lip trembled but she bit it hard and looked away from him.

'Listen, angel,' he moved towards her. 'Before you tell me what you think of me – and you have every right – let me try and make it up to you. You see . . .'

Marcus pressed a few more buttons and gave up. He lit a Marlboro and looked despondently at Wiltsher. Wiltsher looked despondently back through his dreadlocks.

'It doesn't work, man. The apparatus isn't, like, performing, y'know.'

'Yeah.'

Todd looked down from the hayloft, his arms spanning a rail with the tape measure. 'You guys aren't giving up, are you?' he asked with a pencil in his mouth.

'A few technical hitches, man,' Marcus called up. 'We'll have them ironed out by Friday.'

'Sure,' Todd laughed. 'You can borrow my personal stereo if you get really desperate. Everyone can take turns.'

Wiltsher fiddled with a dreadlock. 'Do you suppose he thought that was funny, Hennessy?'

Marcus nodded sadly. 'It's Rooter I feel sorry for, man.'

Michael strolled in purposefully and surveyed the scene. 'Not got it bloody going yet, old boy?'

'It's totally unhappening, Dad man. Won't work, y'know.'

'Father,' corrected Michael and peered at the hi-tech equipment, chewing his pipe thoughtfully. 'You tried pressing this bloody button marked power?' He leaned forward and pushed it.

Suddenly the whole toppling, high-rise pile of speakers and laser screens exploded into deafening, blinding life. There was an almighty, ear-splitting shriek of feedback which made the old barn groan to its foundations, accompanied by a loud buzzing like an army of locusts in the loudspeakers. This was followed by what sounded like the agonised cries of animals being clubbed to death to a drum-beat. The music had started.

Marcus and Wiltsher whooped with joy and started gyrating with loose hips, stamping feet and flailing arms. Michael covered his ears. Todd clung on to the balcony, which was shaking dangerously under the noise. Rooter howled and ran out whimpering. Algy burst into tears.

Without warning, and with a deafening explosion that sent Michael diving for cover screaming, 'The Gerries have landed!' the music stopped, leaving in its place ear-ringing silence and a powerful smell of burning electrics.

* * *

'You've been an idiot because you're so crazily hung up on this idea that you have to *prove* something to me,' Sally continued, laughing and crying at the same time.

'I said don't rub it in, Sals,' Matty sighed, looking up at her with sad, self-destructive eyes. 'I know.'

Sally was fighting a losing battle to make it clear to him that he was totally wrong. 'Can't you see I'm not rubbing it in? What I'm trying to say is—'

'Sally, Mashy! The telly's stopped working!' Tom bombed in from the next room and skidded to a halt in front of her.

'Bloody, bloody hell!' Sally looked up in despair.

'Thank you, Tom.' Matty stood up and walked to the door. He turned back to Sally. 'We'll sort this out later. I know you want to bawl me out, I just don't think I can handle it at the moment, okay?' And he was gone.

Tom looked up at Sally nervously. 'Why was Mashy crying, Sally?'

She turned her face away so that he couldn't see she was crying too.

'Is something I've done?' Tom's voice quivered and he clutched hold of her skirt.

Sally laughed sadly. 'You're very alike, you and your father. Very alike.' She looked down at him and smiled through her tears.

Tom hugged her legs even though he didn't understand. He was certain that it must have been something he'd done. She would have told him otherwise.

Alexandra echoed past the door on her heels, pausing to look in.

'Silly old trip switch has gone,' she smiled at them. 'I'm just popping down to the cellar to turn it on again. Sophia's furious. She was in the middle of faxing an invitation to Princess Margaret.'

Niall was just about to explain to Tash that he needed to tell her the truth because he valued her friendship and honesty when the lights went out. In the first few seconds the stalls were plunged into complete darkness as their eyes fought to adjust to the change. Snob let out a furious whinny and crashed his hooves against his door.

'Oh no!' Tash whispered shakily, 'I hope he doesn't hurt himself – ssh darling, it's okay—' her voice changed to a deep, gentle murmur as she sought to calm the frightened animal.

Niall listened in silence. She was so soft and sensitive. So selfless. He could smell her next to him, a faint, comforting mix of soap, suntan oil and fly-repellent. He wanted to curl up into a tight ball, far away from everyone, and listen to that voice reassuring him that everything would be all right. She was like a quiet little sister, always willing to listen and understand.

In the darkness, keeping her voice as steady as she could, Tash let the tears roll. Hugo had offered to give her lessons for no other reason than he'd been asked as a favour for a mate and even then he'd used the opportunity to his advantage. She'd dreamily imagined he was challenging her to some sort of duel when all he'd been doing was making her suffer for wasting his time.

And Niall. Niall had befriended her because he felt guilty. Rambling on about her problems to him must have just added to the load, like a stray dog attaching itself to a kind-hearted soul with an allergy to fur and feathers.

Hot tears were stinging on her dusty cheeks. She knew now for certain that what she'd dreaded had finally happened. Slowly, almost unknowingly, she'd started to fall in love with Niall.

She wished he'd go away. She was painfully aware of him still standing close to her. As her tear-filled eyes started to distinguish shapes again, she saw that Snob wasn't frightened at all. He was back at his haynet, pulling out long strands and letting them dangle from his snapping lips before finally dropping them to the floor. She stopped soothing him and stood in silence, willing Niall to go.

'Tash, I want you to understand something.' His voice made her shrink away. 'I know I've made a mess of trying to help you but that is what I was trying to do. Help. I used to be quite good at it, you know. I don't know what's happened – I . . .' His voice trailed off.

'You really don't have to bother,' Tash's voice was arch and stiff with tears. 'I'm not a charity case.' Her nose was dribbling like a stout keg but she didn't dare sniff in case he twigged she was crying.

'Oh, for Christ's sake, Tash—'

The lights came back on with a hum of neon. The atmosphere changed instantly from an intimate confessional to a bright, dusty farm building. Niall shut up and looked at Tash's back. She ducked her head. Her hair was typically falling out of its pony-tail. She had grass stains on her bottom. He suddenly found himself longing to touch both.

'You heard what the girl said, Niall,' a sharp voice snapped from the door.

Niall spun round. Amanda was standing in the doorway, dressed in a slinky crimson cut-away top and black chiffon Bermudas. Her eyes flashed dangerously, outlined with heavy black kohl, her small, pert mouth was painted cardinal red and her blonde hair was scraped back in a thick black turban. She looked ravishing, terrifying and like a witch, thought Niall.

Amanda shook slightly as she stood facing them, fragile and erotic and furiously angry. Niall wanted to run. He glanced at Tash but she hadn't turned round, her shoulders were hunched miserably.

'Well?' Amanda tapped a high-shod foot impatiently. 'Are you going to take me out to lunch or had you forgotten?'

Niall wasn't sure he'd ever mentioned taking her out to lunch. It was the last thing he wanted at the moment. He needed to explain himself to Tash. But Amanda looked dangerously explosive and in no mood to be argued with. He couldn't hide from her for ever.

Giving Tash a soft pat on the back, which she flinched from, he walked sadly towards the eye-watering light outside.

Alexandra washed the dirt of the cellar from her hands in the basin in her bedroom. Polly sat on the bed, swinging her legs and watching her through long, sooty lashes. Her wimple had slipped jauntily over one eye.

'Sophia say I no dress as a cowgirl for ze party, maman. She say I must dress as a milkmaid.'

'Does she dear? That's nice.' Alexandra looked out of the window as Niall and someone wearing a turban got into the Merc. It was, she noticed on closer inspection, the little blonde girl with the sharp tongue. Alexandra couldn't understand what someone as sensitive as Niall was doing with Amanda Fraser-Roberts. Perhaps she was nicer than Alexandra had thought. They hadn't spoken much. Come to think of it, Alexandra reflected, she hadn't spoken to anyone very much over the past few days. She'd spent her time starting conversations like soufflés, over and over again, only to find they went flat on her.

She saw Matty run out to the Merc carrying an old rucksack. He stooped to talk to Niall through the window. They seemed to be arguing about something, but eventually Niall nodded and Matty flung his rucksack into the boot and climbed into the back of the car. Where was he off to? she wondered. Why didn't anyone tell her anything any more? And why was that tarmac roller coming up the drive?

Everyone seemed to be preoccupied. Sophia and Cass were constantly talking in low voices, immediately changing the subject to the weather or knitting patterns when she came within earshot. Tash was always with her horse. Matty hid himself away in far corners and talked in monosyllables and Sally was permanently looking for him or having a crisis with the kids. Even Pascal – slyly avoiding his turns to cook – kept dragging the men off to the bar in the village.

She'd even resorted to going down and chatting to boring old Michael earlier that morning, until he'd told her she was getting in the way. She felt like the only girl without a partner at a May ball. People looked at her with pity in their eyes but didn't want to get lumbered – they were far too busy having fun.

She was just wondering what Wowla was doing and if she perhaps needed company when the phone rang.

'Allô . . . oh, hello – yes I do speak English.' She lay front-down on the bed and cuddled Polly to her. 'Yes? Who did you say? Sorry, darling, the line's bloody frightful – Margaret what? Yes? Oh Christ – I mean gosh. Yes, it's very nice of you to call, Your Royal Highn – no, that's quite all right, I'm sure she'll understand. Of course I'll pass the message on, ma'am.'

32

Sally spent the following few days on auto-pilot. Somehow, she put up a semblance of normality, but inside she was falling apart.

At meals, she found the food in her mouth harder to swallow than wood chips. The children's demands gave her migraines that left her screaming in silent agony. Conversation terrified her; she couldn't concentrate long enough on a question to answer, her mouth just spewed out nonsense like a chewed tape, but no one seemed to notice, or pretended not to. The heat left her drained and blistered, fighting a constant desire to pack her bags and follow Matty.

But she had no idea where he had gone. All he'd left was a flimsy little note saying he needed time to think.

She phoned the house in Richmond almost hourly, but the Canadian house-sitters said he hadn't been back. Each time she rang, it sounded as though the house was being demolished in the background. Sally was sure she'd heard electric drills and the noise of someone hammering, but the Canadians assured her it was road-works.

She'd tried calling as many of their friends in London as she could get hold of but none of them had seen Matty. She'd even called her despotic father-in-law, only to be told snootily by the housekeeper that the Frenches were abroad and they didn't wish to be contacted.

Keeping up a semblance of cheery calm to the others was

murder. She'd told them that one of Matty's projects was breaking at long last, necessitating his immediate return to London. His absence, overshadowed by the approaching party, was barely commented upon. Only Niall had figured out the truth – Matty had fed him a completely different story. The old Niall would have held Sally together and pulled his heart out to find Matty. But he was so distracted and careworn at the moment, he could barely raise the energy to give her a hug, just sitting with her for hours on end, pausing occasionally to look up from Zola and shuffle through a few lines of small talk much as a night nurse checks a pulse and tucks in sheets at half-hour intervals.

Now he had shot off to take a call from his agent, leaving Sally hugging her thoughts in the solitude of Pascal's gloomy study. She could hear her mother-in-law asking in a loud stage whisper if Niall thought Sally would like to come out shopping to cheer her up. Sally didn't hear the reply but, as Alexandra's heels started clicking away, guessed he'd shaken his head.

Strangely, Alexandra seemed the most concerned by Matty's disappearance. But her constant, anxious inquiries whether Matty was in the Richmond house made Sally ache for him all the more.

Recently, preoccupied by her pregnancy, Sally had neglected to provide the constant reassurance Matty needed. He'd been feeling low about his career and money, but all she'd talked about when he came back to collapse after a late-night bar shift was nappies, morning sickness, the cost of ecological loo-cleaner, a feature on Woman's Hour about single mothers' support groups, how bored she'd been all day, the Hoover breaking down, Niall's split-up and bills. He, being Matty, had put two and two together to make a three point three recurring nightmare.

Sally actually spent most of her time in their tatty Richmond home gassing over cheap wine to her friends, reading magazines and idly sifting through wallpaper samples. She told him these things because she felt guilty; she wanted to appear more domestic. She'd come across as a bored, whingeing housewife.

And, as ever when she was low, she'd given herself little shopping treats to cheer herself up, spending money they didn't have, which merely put the clocks forward on the time-bomb.

Sitting on the sill of the dingy study where Matty had delivered his idiotic blow just a few days earlier, she watched as two burly workmen slowly erected a pagoda complete with bunting and medieval coats of arms above the terrace which overlooked the pool. Sophia and Cass stood by in a Chanel suit and Marks and Spencer shirt-waister. Sophia was talking into a flip-backed mobile phone. Cass, with a pair of tortoiseshell spectacles balanced on the end of her retroussé nose, was flicking through a set of menu cards. She looked like an efficient, self-important PA.

Sally would have found the whole scene ridiculous if she didn't feel so utterly miserable.

Somewhere in the house, Michael could be heard yelling at Todd. 'Right a bit, lad. Left a bit. I said bloody left!'

A lorry had just arrived bearing casks and casks of mead. Pascal had hidden in the cellar and poor Tash was trying to supervise where to put them. Alexandra had gone shopping. Ben and Hugo had been playing cards in the kitchen since breakfast.

The heavy beat of house music was throbbing from the stone barn in the courtyard. In the field beyond, Tash's horse was thundering up and down squealing over the fence at the constant trail of people, deliveries and equipment which went by. Rooter, thoroughly overexcited, could be heard barking an echoing bass reply from inside the vegetable shed.

All around her there was a hubbub of noise and activity, but Sally couldn't even raise the energy to wash her filthy hair. The party wasn't until tomorrow. Matty might come back by then.

She leaned back and closed her eyes.

'Sally, the video's ended. There wasn't much blood.' Tom came in and sat on the sill beside her, looking let-down. Polly stood next to him, gazing with concentrated concern into Sally's face. She had her nurse costume on. Sally longed to ask for a shot of morphine.

'Where's Tor?' She cleared her throat and attempted a smile. Defying gravity had never been so hard.

'Asleep.' Tom kicked Polly. She retaliated with a right hook. 'What's two thousand four hundred kilometres long and purple?'

'Sorry?' Sally rubbed her forehead. Tom was always asking questions. It got on her nerves at the moment.

'The grape wall of China.'

He and Polly burst into giggles.

Sally looked at them blankly.

'Is Mashy coming back for the party?' Tom looked at her bravely, hiding his concern under an adult expression. He looked so like Matty that Sally had to close her eyes.

'I don't know. He'll have to see if he can get away. He's ever so busy.'

'Why is he busy, Sally?' Tom persisted.

In the distance Sally could hear the machine gun rattling of Marcus and his crony returning on the little red moped. There was another engine too, drowned out by the throaty bike at first, but growing gradually louder. It stopped, giving way to the thumping of music again, but was followed by the banging of car doors.

Sally leapt up, her heart pounding, and ran to the front door, slipping on the freshly polished floors. This time, surely, it had to be Matty. She dashed on to the steps, trembling with hope and fear, looking frantically around the clutter of cars – including Audrey with her dents and rust patches, the trucks and workmen's vans – searching for the newcomer.

A man with a shock of red hair was unloading something from the boot of a yellow sports car and handing it to a tall, dark-haired guy. The second man had his back to her, and for a second Sally's breath caught in her throat with excitement before her heart plummeted to her bare feet. He was too broad to be Matty. When he turned round she saw the Hennessys' elder son, Oliver, grinning up at her. He waved but Sally was too disappointed to respond.

Feeling more dejected than ever, she turned and walked

slowly back into the house, almost knocked sideways as Cass Hennessy bolted the other way to welcome her son, pearls and shirt-waister flapping.

'Niall?'

Crouched over the phone, rubbing his chin in his cupped hand, brow pleated like one of Cass Hennessy's navy blue skirts, Niall didn't respond.

When Amanda crept up behind him, sliding her small hands inside the back of his t-shirt and round to his chest, he jumped as if she'd slipped a stocking round his throat, spinning around so violently, Amanda at first thought he'd given her a bloody nose.

'What the fuck?' Eyes streaming, she clutched her nose and backed off.

'Christ, I'm sorry, angel.' Niall looked at her with a start. 'Did I hurt you?' he bent forward to examine her stinging face. 'I was totally lost in thought.'

'I'm fine,' Amanda snapped sulkily. Fighting to hide her prickly anger, she glumly asked him what his call had been about.

Looking shifty, Niall didn't answer. At the far end of the hall, Sally shot through the front door and up the stairs.

'Well?'

'Er, nothing.' Chewing his lip, Niall steered Amanda out of Sally's earshot. 'Look, Amanda, I think we need to do some talking.'

'Okay.' Amanda's yellow eyes gleamed. 'Hugo's five thousand francs up and won't stop playing until he's lost the lot. Let's go to bed.'

'No!' Niall backed away from her and hit his head on an overhead beam.

The itchy resentment Amanda had built up over the past few days finally snapped.

'Just because we can't go through our lines together, is that it?' she snarled. 'Now I've run out of your beloved cuff snuff, you don't want to know, do you? Can't you get it up without it?'

'Of course not,' Niall hushed her, coming forward. 'Shh, angel, I just want to—'

'So why are you spending day and fucking night with Sally?' Amanda carried on, her voice rising like chalk on blackboard. 'Avoiding me totally—'

They were edging dangerously close to the kitchen. Niall could hear Pascal uncapping another round of beers. A husky Australian twang told him Todd had joined them.

Amanda, used to arguing hammer and tongs with Hugo, could hurl the most lacerating of abuse without flinching. Excited by their ability to hurt, they usually took their rows to bed. Niall, who hid from confrontation like a dog on bonfire night, was simply appalled by her vitriol.

'The moment Matty's back's turned, you're all over her, aren't you?' Amanda wailed. 'Lumpy Tash didn't want to know about your problems, so you pick on the only other wet cow in the house. You should be working in a fucking dairy, milking human kindness straight from the bovine teat.'

'Amanda, shh.' Niall tried to take her hand, but she snatched it away, grazing his wrist with her nails.

'Well, I don't give a fuck any more.' Amanda hissed, long earrings swinging like whips against her throat as she spoke. 'Whatever was between us is over – consider yourself sacked as the love interest in this movie, darling. I get more interest from my current accou—'

'For Christ's sake, Amanda, keep your voice—' Niall shut up as a shadow fell over them.

It was Todd, loping along the small lobby that led from the kitchen, grinning amiably. He was wearing nothing but a pair of his tightest day-glo cycling shorts, quilted brown stomach gleaming in the half-light, flip-flops clacking on the polished floor.

'Put a lid on it, you guys,' he joked, raising two blond eyebrows good-naturedly. 'Michael Hennessy thought he was picking up *The Archers* on his radio.'

Bristling, Amanda shot Todd the most withering of sneers and started to stalk away. Entering the hall, she paused and looked back at Niall, her face agonisingly like Lisette's – huge, pitiless eyes taunting him, her cherub's mouth curled in an inverted circumflex.

'And you're a lousy screw. For a man who uses his head all the time,' she laughed with mock bitterness, 'you don't give much. Get a sex life, Niall.' If she'd been holding a gun, she would have blown away the smoke with a satisfied smile before turning away.

'Crazy Sheila,' shrugged Todd. 'Great bum, but crazy. Beer?'

Shaking his head, Niall stared up at the ceiling, strung with spiders' hammocks.

She'd said exactly what he wanted her to say – what he was about to admit himself – that their hopeless, doomed fling was over. The relief was tremendous. But the guilt still echoed on, like Amanda's footsteps clattering away from him. He'd let down yet another house guest.

Upstairs in her room, Amanda tried and failed to meditate. Instead, she did fifty sit-ups and then settled down to wolf one of Hugo's family-sized Galaxy bars.

What really hurt wasn't the fact that Niall and she hadn't worked out – she'd guessed early on that she was probably too impatient to cope with his three-hundred-and-sixty-degree mood-swings or ride out his current depression. However desirable, he simply wasn't strong enough for her. Yet she had gambled the last tattered shreds of her relationship with Hugo on it working out at least long enough to get her back to England. Plus the added incentive of rubbing Hugo's nose thoroughly out of joint. Instead, the affair had blown up in her face before she'd heard it ticking.

She'd lied about him being a lousy lover – he'd been breathtaking. But Amanda, smarting from her kicked pride, had really wanted to hurt him. Niall hadn't once opened up to her about his wife, or shown that extraordinary tenderness which made Sally blush purple and Matty stop arguing mid-sentence. More appalling still, it seemed from what Amanda had espied that he'd been showing both to Tash French – she of the ripped jeans, tangled hair and idiotic smile. She who Hugo pretended to hate. She who – even when Amanda was dressed in her highest stacks with hair spiked to its limits – made her feel like a dwarf.

Biting into the chocolate bar so angrily that she gave herself a mouth full of tin foil, Amanda decided that, while still wanting to settle down and fill her company's crèche, she no longer wanted a man as a sleeping partner on the deal.

In the lodge, a crack team of chefs was creating feather-light vol-au-vent cases in the ancient dusty range which belched out wood smoke like a twenty-a-day housewife.

Marcus and Wiltsher, covered in flour and translating the instructions on the ready-made puff pastry packet with the aid of a pocket dictionary, paused between batches and sat down at the messy table.

Plugged with a four-pack of Special Brew and a 'herbal' cigarette, Jean snored with porcine relish on his rocking chair beside the ancient stove, a copy of Wiltsher's *Biguns* slipping from his gnarled fingers. Valérie – oblivious of the culinary endeavours taking place in her private domain – had taken the Vespa out shopping for a pair of comfortable sling-backs to wear with her musty best dress at tomorrow's party, unaware that the wing-mirror was now attached with Wiltsher's chewing-gum.

Marcus clutched the cuff of his Stussy sweatshirt sleeve in one hand and brushed the sea of paper and debris off the table's scattered surface.

'Wait a minute, man!' cried Wiltsher. 'You've just swept off the, like, secret ingredient.' He leaned down and retrieved a cube of dark brown resin wrapped in tin foil.

'Ah, yes. The *truffle*, man,' Marcus grinned. 'My Ma told me she had a penchant for truffle this morning. I don't s'pose she's tasted any quite like this before, y'know.' He swallowed a hiccupy laugh.

'Well, Moroccan truffle has a flavour that's quite alone.' Wiltsher put the cube back on the table. 'I'm told even the pigs don't like it, man, y'know.'

'Oh, no, Wilt.' Marcus located a Marlboro coated in flour. 'I think they find it quite arresting, man.'

Snorting for air in his sleep, like a deep-sea diver bubbling up to the surface from ten fathoms, Jean let *Biguns* slip on to the disgruntled head of his wife's Shih Tzu.

'So, man – did Algy manage to get the ethanol from the village pharmacie?' Marcus lit his cigarette with a sniff.

Wiltsher nodded. 'Yeah – he told them it was for his spots, but,' he dropped his voice and glanced at the slumbering Jean, 'like, we won't get time to spike the punch, man – the rave's gonna like be a full-time spinning job, y'know.'

'S'okay,' Marcus grinned knowingly. 'I've asked me bruvver and his carroty mate to, like, do the honours. I've given him a list of fings to make Aunt Lex's party mondo crucial.'

'Howcum, man?' Wiltsher's eyebrows disappeared behind his dreadlocks. 'You said your brother was as square as Surf Automatic.'

'Oh,' Marcus waved his arms with expansive dismissal, 'let's just say I reminded him of a certain incident that took place in the dining room of Ma's last, like, cheesy Sunday lunch, man.'

'He knows *what*?' Ginger laughed.

'The little squirt spotted us snogging at Ma's that Sunday,' Olly sighed. 'He's given me a list, look.'

Ginger laughed even more as he read the spiky scrawls on a battered envelope.

'Dreadful handwriting – *Spike drinks, hide bog roll, pass round hash vol-au-vents, plug Pa's pipe baccy with dope.* The boy's spelling is appalling.' Ginger looked genuinely shocked. 'I thought he went to school on the Hill?'

'He did.'

'Well, it's slipped down it – subsidence, probably.' Ginger cast the list aside and unpacked his toothbrush. 'Still, you've got to admit he's got a vivid imagination.'

'But we can't actually do these things, Gin.' Olly followed him through to the small bathroom next door.

'Why ever not?' asked Ginger, his mouth already full of Colgate.

'Ma would never forgive me.'

'I expect she'd be far less willing to forgive the revelation Marcus is planning if we don't carry out his dastardly demands.' Ginger's blue eyes sparkled with mirth as he started to rinse his mouth under the tap.

'Don't do that, the water might be dodgy,' Olly snapped, starting to shift pickily through the assorted toiletries Alexandra had laid out for her house guests.

'Anyway,' Ginger carried on lapping up water like a thirsty puppy, 'I think it might be rather fun.'

'Christ.' Olly picked up a small packet from a china bowl of mini-soaps. 'My Aunt's even provided condoms.'

'Shall we test one out?' Ginger towelled his mouth and eyed Olly mischievously.

A wall of approaching perfume almost sent Olly into the shower in fright.

'Test what?' asked a cheerful voice and Cass whisked in, having just applied three layers of pressed powder and half a bottle of Rive Gauche for Ginger's benefit. 'Settling in all right, boys? Found everything you need?'

'Everything.' Ginger gave her a devastating, toothpaste-ad smile.

'Super.' Cass felt three layers of pressed powder fail to conceal a menopausal blush. 'Drinks on the terrace whenever you're ready, boys.' And she whisked back out again.

'We'll just unpack a few things first,' Ginger called after her, taking the condoms from Olly's shaking hand and walking slowly back towards the bedroom.

33

The morning of the party brought the first rain the valley had seen in almost two weeks. The parched ground drank it in like a tramp let loose in an off-licence. The dust became a thin layer of mud in less than an hour, turning every path beside the house into a skating rink.

After the third delivery man had slipped and dropped his load, Alexandra insisted that everything should be brought in through the house regardless of the clean floors. They would, she announced airily, just have to lay down newspaper.

Sophia stood in the courtyard, feeling as grey as the formidable sky. She looked up at it, ignoring the great droplets of rain impairing her vision and washing away her make-up. The weather forecast hadn't even mentioned rain. How dare it! she fumed. It was so bloody unfair.

She cornered Jean, who was walking round with a tool kit looking important and trying to avoid Michael.

'Il fera beau cet après-midi et ce soir, non?' she asked hopefully.

Jean scratched his sandpaper chin and sucked his teeth, surveying the horizon thoughtfully. He then licked his gnarled finger and held it up to the wind, mumbling under his breath. Finally, he walked to one of the wooden outbuildings and examined the grains of a slat of wood minutely, picking at it with his Opinel knife and giving it a sniff.

He turned to Sophia and assumed an expression containing

the wisdom of years of working outdoors with the seasons as friends and enemies, a man at one with the elements.

'Je ne sais pas,' he hissed gruffly, nodding knowingly at the sky. 'Peut-être oui, peut-être non. Eh alors!' And with a sigh he picked up his tool kit, which clanked ominously as if it could be full of bottles, and walked round the back of the barn.

Sophia clutched her Dryzabone tighter round her and looked across at a lanky French youth battling to hook a string of multicoloured lights and bunting which stretched across the courtyard on to some guttering. The little flags were being whipped violently upwards by the squall, causing the drenched boy to hang on to his ladder for dear life.

'No, not there!' Sophia shouted irritably. 'I said they were to hang across the entrance. I want them *all* moved *at once*.' And with that she hunched her shoulders and went to see if Ben had sorted out what had happened to the hired goblets yet.

Cass offered Ginger another biscuit with a warm smile.

'Don't tempt me, Mrs Hennessy,' Ginger laughed, creasing his pale blue eyes at her. 'I'd be like a tank if you were my mother. Not that I'd mind,' he added in a low voice.

'*Do* call me Cass,' Cass glowed at him.

Olly coughed and his mother looked round. He raised his eyes at the plate of biscuits and she handed it to him quickly, immediately turning back to Ginger.

'You haven't met my niece – Alexandra's daughter – Tash yet, have you, Ginger dear?' She put her head on one side charmingly. 'She ate early with the children last night.'

Ginger brushed some crumbs from his lap and crossed his legs. 'I don't believe I've had that pleasure, no.'

'You'll adore her – she's quite, er, stunning,' Cass enthused, feeling wonderfully martyred at doing Alexandra such a favour, 'far prettier than I was at her age, I'm afraid.' Perhaps that was pushing it a bit far, she wondered.

'Surely not.' Ginger's blue eyes burrowed deeply and sincerely into hers. 'I bet you left a trail of broken hearts behind you, Cass.'

Olly caught Ginger's eye behind his mother's back and creased his forehead sceptically. Ginger gave him a split-second wink.

Cass was blushing furiously. She pushed the plunger on the cafétiere so hard it made a sound like a large fart.

'Did you sleep well?' She handed Ginger a cup of coffee. 'I'm sorry you both had to share a room. Alexandra's awful housekeeper spent most of yesterday swigging calvados in the kitchen when she was supposed to be cleaning out guest rooms.'

Ginger caught Olly's eye again. 'We both slept very well, thank you.'

'It's lovely to have someone so uncomplaining around,' smiled Cass, 'but don't worry, I've seen to it that you've got a room of your own tonight.' She leaned forward and patted Ginger on the knee. 'I know what you young lads are like at parties.'

Olly nearly choked on his biscuit. What was his mother up to? he wondered anxiously. For a woman who thought the sun shone out of Mary Whitehouse's thermals, she was behaving like the madame of a brothel.

Cass heard the sound of an approaching engine. 'I'll just go and check if that's my brother Eddie. Excuse me.' She beamed at Ginger again and skipped out of the room like Bambi in a twinset and pearls.

Olly looked out of the window. 'I doubt it's my uncle,' he said, pouring himself a cup of coffee as his mother had forgotten him, 'he doesn't usually travel by cattle truck.'

'Who's that?' Ginger stared at a pair of endless legs in tatty jeans crossing the courtyard.

'My cousin.'

'Oh?' Ginger eeked several excited syllables out of the word. 'He looks like a young Byron – all that glorious hair.'

'Natasha doesn't limp,' Olly smiled smugly.

'Oh.' Ginger wrinkled his nose with disappointment. 'She's the one your mother wants me to make?'

Olly laughed. 'Tash is sweet – incurably scruffy and trodden-upon – but she could drink you under the table.'

'I like her already. But she needs a lick of paint.'

They watched Tash reappear from a pair of tall double doors leading a pirouetting chestnut horse.

'Her bone structure is superb – the face is almost Linda Evangelista if you squint,' Ginger mused. 'You know, I quite fancy taking your mother's advice.'

'What?' Olly looked at him in horror. He knew Ginger was occasionally prone to crushes on glamorous older women, but his cousin was neither.

'I think it would be quite fun to make Tash,' Ginger paused, grinning, 'over.'

Unaware of her audience, Tash supervised Snob being loaded into Anton's horsebox. It took all her powers of persuasion and several teeth marks on her arms to get him up the ramp and inside. Once ensconced, he looked at her with enormous, hurt brown eyes, mortally offended that she was shoving him off somewhere.

'It's for your own good, you great idiot,' she told him, avoiding a crafty swipe from his near hind as she closed the partition. 'You'd hate it tonight with all the noise and people next door.' She secured the bolt and gave his ears an affectionate pull. 'This way you can get a good night's sleep before your big day. Unlike me,' she sighed, as Snob turned his head away from her deep in a sulk. She longed more than anything to be going with him and escaping from the day and night ahead.

As the old cattle truck swung its way out of the courtyard, narrowly missing a head-on collision with an incoming florist's van, she wished Anton hadn't turned up quite so early to collect Snob and Bouchon. She'd only taken Snob through the dressage test for tomorrow's event once, and even then he'd done most of it on two legs or backwards. They were hopelessly unprepared for a competition, as Hugo pointed out with great satisfaction every day. Her only hope was that, if it carried on raining like this, the ground would be too slippery and the event would be called off.

Tash pointed out the main door to a well-dressed woman

clutching a huge flower arrangement which was taller than she was.

She had barely had any time or energy to think about the party that evening. Now, with Snob gone and a constant bustle of preparation and activity around her, Tash began to realise the sheer scale of things. This wasn't a family do she had to endure, quietly trying to blend into a convenient corner. This was a full-scale banquet and dance, with enough food being carried into the manoir by high-nosed caterers to feed Henry VIII's court for a month.

She peeped into the stone barn.

Gaggles of public schoolboys with bobs, baggy jeans wrinkling over mammoth trainers and synthetic bomber jackets in lurid colours sliding off shoulders, were standing about smoking and swigging from cans. A few flawless-skinned girls with stringy hair, dangling pendants and vast Doc Martens were sitting on straw bales eyeing up the boys, and each other, critically.

Clusters of them had been arriving at the house over the past couple of days, carrying whistles, dummies and tubs of Vapo-rub. At first, Alexandra had thought it was some outward bound school trip that had somehow got misrouted to the manoir instead of the local activity centre, and she'd tried helpfully to redirect them. It soon became clear, however, that they were in the right place. Some of them asked for Hennessy or Wiltsher by name. Most of them just asked for the 'rave' and produced glossy postcard-sized flyers, designed like a sixties *Dr Who* title sequence, announcing that the 'Whacko Château Dance Orgasmatron' would be taking place at Manoir de Champegny on the twenty-sixth of July.

Wiltsher had done his marketing and publicity work well.

Tash noticed an incongruous figure in the middle of the assorted group of slouching ravers. Wearing his usual skin-tight cycling shorts, a Surfers Do It Upside Down t-shirt, dark glasses and more highlights in his hair than ever, was Todd.

Quite unexpectedly, Todd had proved a great hit with the pubescent party-goers, far surpassing Marcus and Wiltsher in his organisational abilities and crucial kudos. When Pascal had refused point-blank to put up the teenage influx, Todd had rallied to and arranged for them to sleep in one of the empty outbuildings, locating blankets, bed rolls and Gaz stoves. Strutting around with his hip-swinging walk, Rooter at his side, he produced bread and booze (and Tash suspected a large amount of other substances) at an alarming rate. The ravers loved him, despite his gold neck chain and penchant for Duran Duran's early work.

Each night Todd took his pick of the female ravers who asked to feel his muscles and his shaved legs. And each morning the sound of Paola's Italian temper could be heard reverberating around the valley, making the grapes fall from their vines and Rooter run howling under the nearest table.

Tash was about to move away when there was a hush in the barn. Todd was fiddling with some cables on the balcony's lighting bar. In the DJ's console, which had been built on a platform between the wall of speakers at the far end, Marcus and Wiltsher stood wearing headphones; Wiltsher's were stretched to capacity over his hairdo.

They fiddled with a few knobs importantly and Marcus whooped into the microphone, 'Prepare to rave, Lunar Ecstasy trippers!' Or something like that. Tash couldn't be sure, it was lost in the feedback. Wiltsher stuck his thumbs up at Todd and the neon working lights went out.

Suddenly the barn was awash with shimmering, pulsing lights and the deafening hollow boom of a Techno-acid beat. The ground shook under Tash's feet and pain stabbed her eardrums. Lights of every colour and description whirled and spun, flashed and flickered around the old barn, refracting off the dust which hung in the air and making the whole place seem full of multicoloured, suspended metal particles. Lasers jabbed their blade-like pinions of light into the gloom. Strobes fragmented everyone's movements into jagged, unnatural jerks.

It was like an old flickering movie, coloured in by a child using a jumbo-shade set of pens, thought Tash. She held her breath.

For all his waffle and procrastination, Michael had done a wonderful job on the barn. The main floor was kept clear for dancing, with straw bales and scrubbed tables skirting it. The hayloft above, now braced and secure, looked breathtaking. More bales were placed around the balconies, which ran to each side of the building. At the back was a long trestle bar where two disapproving female caterers were unloading hundreds of small, plastic bottles of Evian.

One effect in particular cast a spell over the old barn, turning it into the sleaziest, moodiest of night-clubs. Swathes and swathes of white parachute silk were hanging from the walls. This was backlit with the faintest of ultra-violet, which made the walls appear to be made of light, without illuminating the bulk of dingy building at all. Marcus had told his father the effect would be naff. It wasn't. It was sensational.

'Sure, that's a wonderful sight to behold.'

Tash felt her back tingle and turned round to face Niall. He was wearing a tatty old oilskin and faded jeans. His hair was covered with tiny droplets of rain like a layer of fine white net. He hunched his back to the wind and shivered.

'I wouldn't like to see one of those youngsters drop a lit cigarette in there, though,' he added, assessing the burnability of the contents.

As he looked past her into the building, Tash dropped her head and followed his gaze, no longer seeing the mesmerising lights in front of her. She was furious to find herself swamped with suffocating shyness.

They'd hardly spoken since the power cut. He spent most of his time with Sally, now that Matty was back in London editing some film. Monopolised by Snob and Hugo's exhausting exercise routine, Tash had only seen him at meal times. She'd hoped that by being preoccupied, her embarrassing crush would die down. She'd taken to bolting her food and fleeing, her stomach writhing with indigestion and desire.

It's no good, she thought hopelessly. I love him, I love him, I love him.

'Look – er – Tash.' The pause before her name made her wince. Had he forgotten it already? 'Would you do me a favour?'

Tash looked up at him excitedly but couldn't hold those soft brown eyes for more than a split second. She shrugged and nodded, unable to speak for hope. He wanted her to do him a favour. No one else but '– er – Tash'. It wasn't much but it counted.

'Would you look after Sally for a few hours?' Niall was almost shouting to be heard over the din from the barn. 'Just check she's all right every now and again. Take the kids off her hands if she's looking tired.'

Tash nodded, hiding her disappointment. In her imagination's deluded, quick-thinking scenario, he'd been about to ask her to accompany him to the potting shed with a can of squirty cream.

'Are you going somewhere?' she asked, suddenly terrified that he wouldn't be at the party.

'What?' He couldn't hear her. He bent down so that he was closer.

She leaned forward and spoke the question into his ear. Her voice shook. The smell of him and the warmth of his skin made her face burn. Soon he would go. She might never see him again except on television, in the cinema or a magazine feature, covered in Olympian ring-marks on someone's coffee table. He would be relegated to star status again. Suddenly every tiny, precious moment she was next to Niall, the all-too-human man who cried, made mistakes and got blind drunk, had to be made the most of. They were all she had left.

He nodded in answer to her question. 'I'm going to meet Matty,' he spoke into her ear, burning it numb with excitement and freezing her shoulder. 'It means driving to Paris. We probably won't make the party. It depends on the traffic.'

She felt her heart begin to beat again as he drew away.

He turned to leave and then looked at her again. She kept her eyes firmly on the wet cobbles.

'And one other thing. Don't be telling Sally about this just yet, huh?'

With that he was gone. Tash looked up to the funereal sky and groaned aloud.

'Why're you standing here in the rain, Natasha?'

She felt a warm hand slip around her shoulders and nearly passed out under an asphyxiating cloud of aftershave.

'Here,' Todd crooned into her ear, almost chewing it off, 'come with me and I'll rub you dry with a towel.'

'Go bungee jump off a cliff, Todd,' Tash snapped, running into the house.

Niall tried to drive Audrey, read the map and control his racing mind all at the same time. The windscreen wiper on his side didn't work, meaning he had to lean over to see. It was giving him backache, but that was nothing compared to the pain he was feeling inside.

He was intensely relieved that Amanda and he were finally washed up, but felt bloody awful about the state he'd left her in. He'd hoped, cowardly and idealistically, that she'd go back to Hugo. She hadn't. She hated both of them and crawled round the house like an injured vixen, biting and snarling at anything that moved, particularly Sally.

That irritated him. Sally was simply falling apart. Anyone could see that.

Matty had phoned Niall yesterday – pretending to be his agent, the devious shit. If only he'd seen how Sally's face lit up when the phone rang. Every time it rang.

He claimed, in typical Matty style, that he'd just got back to Richmond and found the house crawling with poofs and paintbrushes.

'How's Sally?' he'd added before Niall could speak, not sounding like Matty this time, but like Imelda Marcos asking after the Filipinos, hoping against hope that they'd put out flags a mile high saying, 'Welcome Home, Mel!'

And well he should, Niall fumed. The insensitive idiot, doing a bunk and hiding himself as tightly from his responsibilities as he could. Because he always bottled things up, Matty got the wrong end of the stick more times than an apprentice juggler.

Niall had fought his temper with iron control and told Matty to fly back at once, booking the flight himself and phoning back to tell him the times. Matty had been terrified and desperate to know what had happened, imagining the worst. An accident – Tom, Tor, Sally. Niall had hung up on him.

He hated leaving Sally in the state she was in, tonight of all nights, but at least Tash was looking after her.

On thinking about Tash, Niall lost concentration entirely and nearly drove into a ditch. He braked hard and Audrey skidded to a halt. There was a furious beep behind. Niall rested his head on the wheel. Jesus, but he needed a fix!

The driver behind leaned a fist on his horn and held it there. Niall put Audrey into first and lurched forward into the driving rain.

Tash hated him now, he knew it. She was the one good thing about the past few weeks; a sweet, sensitive girl willing to listen and not judge and he'd trodden all over her like the insensitive Irish prima donna he was. She avoided him so studiously now, refusing to look at him when he tried to catch her eye. Niall was surprised to realise that it pained him far more than his guilt over Amanda.

He suddenly saw himself holding Tash in his arms and kissing her beautiful, quivering mouth with such exquisite pleasure that he nearly hit an oncoming juggernaut. He cursed himself for the thought. What did a beautiful, talented girl like Tash want with an embittered old fool like himself? She'd laugh in his face.

Then he remembered her earlier that day, standing by the barn so deep in thought his heart had gone out to her with – was it love? Please God, no. He'd loved Lisette, that had felt nothing like this.

'Oh Lord, help me!' he whispered, catching sight of himself in the rear-view mirror. 'Niall O'Shaughnessy, if you're not the greatest damn fool on God's earth. The great pursuer of lost causes. And herself in love with Hugo Beauchamp! You've about as much chance as a randy tadpole in the North Sea.'

He pulled haphazardly into a lay-by and sank his head in his hands.

He had no idea how long he'd been sitting there when a determined finger tapped on the window. The winder had broken, so Niall opened the door.

A keen, shiny face with an accountant's moustache and left-to-right haircut peered in at him.

'Bloody awful weather. Hope you don't mind but the wife and I were having our lunch in the car behind – the Astra with the caravan – there, you see? Terrific bargain. Frimley Campers if you're ever passing. Ask for Tony. As I say, we were just tucking into our thon and mayonnaise sarndvich, oh la la, and the wife says to me, "Tony, love" – she still calls me love. Eight years of marriage, not bad, eh? – "Tony, love," she says, "Isn't that that Niall O'Shaughnessy in the car in front?" and I says, "You know, Bunny" – that's my nickname for her, her real name's Beverley, actually – "Bunny," I says, "you might just be right, I'll just pop and ask," I says. So here I—'

Lunch! It suddenly occurred to Niall it was lunchtime. Matty's plane was coming in at two. The routes out of Paris would be as congested as a perfume tester's nose because of the Parisians' vacances. He had to get a move on if he was going to get there and back in time for the party.

Niall was quite certain that Hugo was planning tonight to take Tash to bed. The thought made him flinch as if hit, his knuckles clenched white on the door handle. He couldn't possibly leave them alone together at a time like this.

'– am. Tony Dawkins the name. Pleased to meet you. The wife and I've seen all your films.'

'I think you've made a mistake.' Niall banged the door on the enthusiastic red-faced man, nearly crunching his outstretched arm in the process, and started Audrey with a furious roar of outraged clutch.

34

Polly dashed into the house in front of her mother, clutching a host of brightly coloured carrier bags which trailed on the ground behind her short, racing legs.

Following behind her daughter, Alexandra ignored the rain and stopped to watch the swarm of bustling workers around her. A crew of men was clearing out the choked gutters around the courtyard. Another was erecting a covered walk-way between the courtyard entrance to the house and the barn where the disco had been set up. Alexandra listened to the muffled thumping from within, dreamily recalling her Chelsea days.

'Mummy, what are you doing standing there in the damp?' Sophia squelched over in green wellies. 'All your bags are getting wet. Here, let me.' She took her mother's shopping and steered her towards the door. 'Everything's going swimmingly – ha ha – drat this b-awful weather.' She got inside and pulled off her boots and dripping coat.

'Yes, isn't it simply grotty.' Alexandra noticed the hall was now full of lush, crisp flower arrangements. They rose up in great banks of colour from every corner like a funeral parlour. Along the stone hand-rail on the main sweep of stair, ivy and dog roses trailed exotically as if they grew from the very fabric of the house. With the huge old, yellowing chandelier now dug out of storage, cleaned and restored to its former brilliance, and every item of furniture gleaming, the place was transformed.

'Do you like it?' Sophia looked at her proudly.

Alexandra wasn't sure if she did. Eddie wouldn't care if he walked into a pig shed as long as there was Jack Daniels and a comfortable bed waiting for him. None of this was for his benefit, she reflected sadly.

'You've given the old place quite a new lease of life, darling,' she said carefully. 'But isn't arriving in the courtyard with all the chickens and cars going to be a bit of a let-down?' she queried.

'Oh, no one's going to arrive in the courtyard, Mummy,' Sophia laughed, 'don't be so silly! No, come and see our surprise. It's rather splendid.'

She led Alexandra to the tall double doors at the far end of the hall and heaved her weight against the stiff hinges.

When open, which they seldom were, they led to the grand stone-flagged entrance hall, now never used, which in turn opened out on to what was originally the front lawns. Once landscaped into well-drained hectares of green carpet, these were now nettle beds and wild meadow. Running through the middle was a pot-holed driveway, lined with ancient bollarded poplars that seemed to stretch away for ever to form the main approach to the manoir. No one had driven up it for years. It was a much further diversion than the back entrance and cost a fortune in upkeep. The impressive set of wrought-iron gates were now padlocked, rusted together and overgrown with grass and nettles.

Alexandra had images of guests in designer ball gowns and bespoke evening dress climbing over them. Even if the old gates were forced open, the pitted driveway would destroy most cars' suspensions before they got a quarter of the way up it.

'Is this going to take long, darling?' She watched her daughter still struggling with the double doors. 'Only I want to speak to Tash before everything gets too hectic.'

'They opened earlier,' Sophia spoke through gritted teeth. 'I . . . don't seem to be . . . able to . . . ah!' The doors finally swung apart with an ancestral groan.

Alexandra stared through them in disbelief. The entrance hall was as spotless as an operating theatre. The chequered black and white marble floor, which she had only ever known as sludge brown and darker sludge brown, was a clearly defined chess-board. Even the panelled walls shone with a rich lustre which looked like years of impregnated beeswax rather than a rush job. Sophia had unearthed a huge white marble statue of a winged angel kissing a voluptuous reclining woman and had it moved so that it now dominated the high-ceilinged area.

'Wasn't that in the topiary?' Alexandra asked weakly.

'This is where we're going to welcome the guests,' announced Sophia, walking purposefully towards the heaviest, oldest door in the house – original oak, nearly a foot thick in places and studded with lethal-looking ironwork like an S and M victim.

'We don't usually welcome guests formally, darling.' Alexandra followed Sophia across the hall. 'It's such a bind, especially if poor Pascal has to speak English. And anyway with the drive in the state it is, don't you think it would be better to . . .'

As the ancient door swung open, Alexandra was for once totally lost for words.

In front of her were still acres and acres of rustling, poppy-strewn grassland stretching as far as the woods on the grey, misty horizon. That much hadn't changed. But in the middle of it, straight as a book spine, was a new line of tarmac, black with rain. Even the windswept poplars seemed to be standing to attention like wet guardsmen wearing green busbies.

Sophia started pointing out an area to the left where the grass had been mown for parking but Alexandra was too overawed to listen. Any minute now she expected a gilt carriage drawn by two dappled greys to appear along the newly laid drive with Cinders inside, clutching her invitation. Nothing, it seemed, was beyond Sophia's aspirational party planning.

'Darling, when was all this done?' she gasped in horror. 'I must be going mad but I didn't notice a thing. Pascal hasn't even mentioned it.'

'He wanted it to be a surprise, in fact he was going to show you himself tonight when the floodlights are up, but I'm so excited I couldn't hold on a moment longer.' Sophia looked triumphant. 'We had to wait till you were out every time and frantically call the team in. But that took far too long; they'd only done half by yesterday lunchtime, so we took a gamble that you wouldn't hear with all the other racket going on. Pascal says no one ever comes round here anyway.'

'It must have cost a bomb,' blurted Alexandra, thinking of all the money she was soaking into Matty and Sally's house at that very moment.

Sophia smirked but said nothing. The only way she could get Pascal to agree to it had been by persuading him that her mother would be over the moon.

The manoir from this side looked out of this world, she mused. Guests driving up the long sweep and seeing it for the first time – the floodlights giving the honeyed stone a magical glow and the tall towers and turrets reaching for ever into the night – would hold their breath in amazement. It wasn't on Holdham's grand scale, but Sophia felt she had done more than her fair share to turn a rickety old mausoleum into a fairytale castle. She had hoped for a little more from her mother than a dazed expression.

'I must press on,' she announced eventually, deciding Alexandra just needed a little more time to let the effect sink in. 'I've got to chase up the strolling players. They were supposed to arrive by minibus half an hour ago. And the lute player! Oh my God, I meant to arrange for them to pick him up from the station on their way. Someone else will just have to do it . . .' Still talking to herself, she padded off on socked feet, clutching her clipboard check-list to her fevered brow.

Ben, Hugo and Pascal were holed up in an attic, escaping from the activity and demands below. With a crate of bottled beer stolen from the barn, a pile of assorted grub and a pack of cards, they were ready for the long siege before the party.

'Need a fourth, really,' muttered Ben, dealing out another hand, blond hair flopping over his eyes, cigarette burning between his lips. 'Shame old Niall buggered off this morning. Any idea where he's gone, Hugs?'

Hugo took up his cards and glanced at them quickly. He threw a pile of hundred-franc notes into the centre of the rickety table and took a swig from his bottle before looking at Ben. 'Escaping from Amanda, I shouldn't wonder. She's given up bitching us both up and is trying for the sympathy vote at the moment. She'll be kissing babies next. I'd keep a close guard on Josh, Ben. Amanda's lethal when she gets broody.'

Pascal equalled Hugo's bet and put his cards face down on the table. 'Myself, I do not know why you are so unpleasant to Amanda, 'Ugo.' His watery eyes twinkled kindly but were serious. 'If you do not love 'er, why did you bring 'er 'ere?'

Ben laid his bet with a rustle of crumpled banknotes while Hugo drummed his fingers on the table.

'It's Amanda who's been screwing around, Pascal.' Hugo looked at him in disbelief and threw another pile of notes on the table. 'Raise you five hundred.' He flashed his teeth at Pascal without warmth.

'Er, wonder if we ought to go down and see if the coast's clear yet?' Ben ventured nervously, taking a huge gulp from Hugo's beer by mistake.

'From the moment you arrive, you treat 'er like she ees not there,' continued Pascal, ignoring Ben's plea. 'There is no wonder she look elsewhere for attention.' He carefully placed five more notes on the table, not taking his eyes from Hugo.

Hugo lit a cigarette, clicking the lighter shut with an angry snap. 'Look, if you want me to put a word in you only have to ask, instead of doing the Dr Ruth act. You haven't followed the betting yet, Ben.' He lifted his bottle to his lips and, finding it empty, stood up to get another.

'Count me out.' Ben tossed his cards in front of him and glanced across at Pascal anxiously.

Pascal's cheeks were at full expansion, but he chose not to take the argument further.

Playing the rest of the card game in silence, Hugo lost over two thousand francs.

He felt exceptionally pissed off that the Frenchman had censured him. Pascal had a nerve to dictate so bloody pugnaciously and pompously, he fumed. Hugo had accepted Amanda's defection more graciously than he'd ever thought possible. He'd surprised even himself with the lassitude her infidelity had inspired.

Poor Amanda, he mulled without compassion, if she had intended to shock him into remorseful attendance, her plan had produced the opposite effect. If she had intended to win Niall for good then the result was even worse.

'Niall has a lost puppy complex,' he'd told Tash earlier that day. 'He loves bitches.'

Tash hadn't laughed.

Already in a bad mood, Hugo had then told her nastily that the reason she couldn't get a balanced riding position was because her bum was too fat.

Hugo's current state of flux was beginning to needle him. He was becoming aware of an unpleasantly unfamiliar emotion oscillating noisily in the back of his mind at all times. An obsession that had grown inside him like a disease over the past few weeks, hiding its symptoms under the guise of something else, something more recognisable. It had taken hold of him before he could fight it. Now that he was totally under its grip, beginning to suffer the full force of bitter-sweet addiction, he was at a loss as to what to do.

And he'd thought it was the horse he wanted.

Draining his bottle and staring through the rain-flecked window at the windswept horizon, he decided the only way to get through that night was to get blind drunk.

Ben shuffled the cards quietly with his shoulders hunched, like a corporal smoking in the trenches. The ace of spades fell to the ground.

'Shit!' Hugo stared at the card in horror. He was as superstitious as any competitive rider. The ace meant only one thing. Tonight was doomed.

As Tash sat with Sally she became increasingly fidgety. Their conversation had long since dwindled into the odd spurt of effort on Tash's part: a gabbled comment about the children here, a tentative remark on the weather there. Her desperation to lighten the tense atmosphere became such that she kept forgetting what she was talking about half-way through a sentence. Her small talk was fast becoming microscopic.

'Are you sure he didn't mention Matty?' Sally cut across Tash rambling nervously about the party.

'Er . . . no. I told you, I haven't seen Niall all day.' Tash wished she wasn't such a hopeless liar.

She looked past Sally at Tom, who was playing Monopoly with Rooter and Tor, throwing their die for them and fixing it so that he now owned more property than Donald Trump.

More minutes creaked past. With the evening drawing ever closer, the party preparations were growing increasingly fraught.

From the sanctuary of the old study, Tash caught glimpses of caterers dashing past the door clutching long foil-covered trays. The noise of chattering workmen in the main gallery across the hall had long since died and was now replaced by the mournful, disjointed notes of the medieval ensemble tuning up.

Outside, the rain had all but abated, leaving the strange, fragmented horizontal light as the evening sun tried to break through the thinning clouds. The landscape, although still damp and blustery, now sparkled like a cheap Christmas card.

Sophia's sharp, cool voice could be heard ringing through the house as she administered period costumes to all the hired staff.

Tash wondered if she could ask to borrow one. She was totally unprepared. Nothing in her wardrobe was suitable – everything decent was dirty and crumpled on the floor of her room.

'Will you play dive-bombing the sofa with me, Tash?' Tom, bored of wiping the floor with his financially inept opponents, came over to Tash's side and tugged appealingly on her shirt tails.

'Er . . .' Tash wished Tom's enthusiasm was a little more muted.

Soon he would be packed off to the nursery with the other under-tens, where Paola had been ordered to create a rival party for the children before putting them to bed early and guarding their rooms for the rest of the night. Poor Paola, who'd sloped off to Tours earlier that week for a haircut and a new clingfilm outfit, had not been amused. In fact her red eyes that day made Sally look like an Optrex advert in comparison.

Tash was reluctantly preparing for her first undignified crash-landing on the none too sturdy antique chaise when rescue came in the guise of Alexandra hawking several bulging carriers into the room. Tash eyed these rope-handled saviours with untold relief.

'Darling, at last!' Alexandra dropped the bags in the middle of the room and collapsed on the chaise just as Tash started to run towards it. This resulted in a quick sideways manoeuvre, depositing Tash next to her mother in an unintentionally matriarch-and-loving-offspring pose straight out of *Little Women*.

Alexandra, deeply touched, gave her daughter's shoulders a motherly squeeze, accompanied by the jangling of her heavy pewter bangles.

'I've been looking for you for ages,' she beamed with watery eyes, and stroked Tash's tangled tendrils. 'Polly and I have just had a deliciously wicked shop.'

She turned round to Sally, who was gazing abstractedly through the window. 'I've been terribly naughty, Sally darling, and bought you a little something to cheer you up. I know Matty hates me giving either of you pressies but I couldn't resist it. You've been looking so tired recently.' She leaned down and extracted the largest of her packages from its brown paper wrapping.

It was the painting Tash had done of Matty, Sally and the kids, now framed in the most exquisitely simple thick carved ash.

'Here.' Alexandra handed it to the gaping, gulping Sally. 'It'll go perfectly with your staircase in Richmond now that it's been stripped.'

'But the staircase hasn't been . . .' Sally started to protest but was too lost in the picture in front of her to swallow the lump in her throat and continue. She hadn't been able to look at the painting since Matty left. Now, set in its new, heavy frame, it was like staring at a group of strangers. Had she really thought they looked miserable when she first saw it? Now all she could see was a family. A close, scruffy, laughing, fighting, relaxed, happy family. The painting blurred in front of her eyes.

Tash looked at her mother in astonishment. The portrait was different. Very different. As it now stood the general mood was sickeningly like an old *The Good Life* repeat. Her eyes narrowed. Someone had made her brother's family look as if they were three-parts cut.

'It was Pascal,' Alexandra hissed guiltily out of the corner of her mouth, shooting a beaming smile at Sally.

When Matty and Sally had seemed so horrified at the original attempt, Tash herself had done some reworking. But after a sleepless night with her glasses slipping off the end of her nose as she crouched over four unnaturally smiling, linseed-oiled faces, adding a twinkle to every eye, Tash detested the thing more than anything she'd ever done. The turps had given her a headache and she'd wrecked her only decent tights by kneeling in yellow ochre. She'd finally hidden the still wet canvas amongst the cobwebs, dead insects and pen lids behind her chest of drawers. Her mother must have unstuck it from its lacy resting place, borrowed Polly's junior paint set and immortalised it for every passing Richmond dinner-party guest to remark on the dissimilarity. Tash fought an urge to jump through it like a clown through a paper hoop.

But Sally seemed delighted. Her eyes brimmed over with tears and she laughed out loud (rather demonically, Tash thought, like Rochester's wife).

'What stupid blind fools we are!' she smiled through her tears at Tor, who waddled over in her usual four-legged baby elephant gait and bit her mother's leg. Thankfully, her few teeth left only the faintest of red marks on Sally's skin and she merely seemed enchanted by her daughter's novel method of making an impression.

'Now, darling,' Alexandra began to hand Tash rain-dampened plastic bags to examine. 'I realised you had absolutely nothing to wear for the big day so Polly and I simply dashed around Saumur doing the dirty on the plastic.'

Tash felt an exhilarating tremor of anticipation and relief. Her mother's unending generosity usually made her feel embarrassed and guilt-stricken, but this evening it was manna from heaven to her vacuous wardrobe.

'But, Mummy, these are breeches . . .' Tash mumbled rather obviously as she examined the contents of the first bag.

Further discoveries proved equally startling. Inside a large, luxuriously stiff box which filled her with excited premonitions of moth-wing silk was a pair of ludicrously expensive long leather boots. They smelt of money and craftsmanship. They were also a size too small.

Tash could barely bring herself to continue as a silk stock, a beautifully tailored black jacket, a back protector built like a straitjacket, leather gloves, a hand-stitched riding crop, cotton dressage shirt and other assorted equestrian paraphernalia came tumbling out of their neat wrappings.

As the final bag was emptied, Tash forced herself to look up at her mother, unable to speak. She smiled dutifully and swallowed the familiar tightness that was again welling in her throat and chest. It was not her mother's fault, after all, that her presents merely served to increase Tash's fear that tomorrow she would be humiliated. Who could hope to blend into the rustic poles with a pair of brand-new two-thousand-franc boots on? How was her mother to know that looking like a professional by sporting all the right – and unused – gear would only draw attention to Tash's amateur riding as Snob carted her round the course and deposited her on the disapproving fence judges? She would look like a spoilt rich kid who thought she could buy talent. Which, when she came to think about it, was what Hugo had told her she was.

Alexandra, mistaking Tash's silence for rapturous gratitude, wiped a contented mascara smudge away and scratched Rooter's extended nose. From behind a nearby chair there was a low, resentful growl from one of the spaniels; they'd been keeping a very low profile since the arrival of the usurping – and sexually suspect – Rooter.

'Oh! One more thing, I almost forgot.' Alexandra delved into her handbag and eventually located a small package. 'I realise that you wouldn't want me to buy you anything to wear tonight, darling, so I haven't. My little efforts at getting you into anything of mine have failed – no, don't argue, sweetheart – it was rude and bossy of me to try. You have every right to wear what you want. And I'm sure you'll look ravishing. But I got these out of the bank just in case you wanted to borrow them. Please don't feel obligated on my account. But they are rather smashing. Pascal gave them to me for our first anniversary.'

She handed the package to Tash. It was a small, slightly battered leather box. Inside was an odd-shaped twist of metal, edged with translucent plastic. It looked revolting.

'Oh bother, I've given you the wrong box.' Alexandra snatched it back. 'That's Matty's old retaining brace. He was such a little monster about using it, I've kept it for sentimental reasons. Silly really. The places I used to find that thing hidden were extraordinary. Your father suggested buying a metal detector. Hang on.'

As she fished around and finally emptied the contents of her bag in order to find the correct item, Tash and Sally's eyes widened in bewildered awe. No wonder Alexandra looked as if she was planning an overnight stay every time she took her bag shopping. Inside was a collection of keepsakes that would rival the British Museum. An old baby boot, a tatty exercise book, several loose and dog-eared photographs, a toy car, an Observer's book of horses which Tash had written all over aged six, even a mangy piece of fur Sophia had hawked around once, much as Lotty did now with her Noo Noo.

Tash felt the tightness in her throat start to seriously endanger her breathing. She had no idea her mother was so attached to the past.

Sally, seeing her struggling to get a grip on herself, gave her hand a quick squeeze.

'Here!' Alexandra held another small box aloft. This one was covered in rich damson velvet and had the frightening aura of containing something priceless.

Tash opened the strong clasp of the box. It was as if she were looking into two naked flames. Inside glimmered a pair of earrings consisting of huge, simply cut diamonds set in a cluster of tiny yellow stones to form teardrops, like two slivers of the sun.

'Kerist.' Sally was the first to recover. 'Now I know why diamonds are measured in carats. I bet you could see in the dark with those.'

'Aren't they gorgeous?' Alexandra started to repack her bag before Tor could eat or bury its strewn contents. 'They're twenty-one carats each. One of them was even larger and Pascal had a third of it made into a brooch but I lost that in Paris. Since then he's made me keep these in the bank.'

'I can't possibly wear them then, Mummy,' Tash protested. 'They're far too valuable.'

'Don't be silly, darling.' Alexandra looked fondly at a picture of Sophia on her potty before tossing it back in her bag. 'They were made to be worn. Tonight's the perfect time to give them an airing.'

'But—'

'No buts.' Alexandra stood up to make her escape before Tash tried to hand them back. 'I'm wearing my rubies so I can't use them, sweetheart. Besides, it was Pascal's idea in the first place,' she lied, 'and he'd be terribly upset if you don't wear them. Which reminds me, I must have a word with him. I forgot to pick up his tux from the cleaners . . .' And with a final jangle of bracelets, she was off, leaving a baby dummy, a lipstick and three chewed-looking home-made birthday cards on the floor behind her.

'She's so lovely,' sighed Sally, picking up the painting again. 'You know, I'd quite forgotten how good this is.' She paused for a moment, brushing her blonde hair back off her face to examine it closer. 'I wonder if Matty will get here in time for the party.'

Tash looked at her in surprise but Sally just grinned.

'I believe I'm quite looking forward to tonight,' she declared. 'I'd better distract these sprogs and tart up. I'll take the portrait of Dorian Gray with me.' She gave a cryptic wink and, humming 'Heat Wave', somehow manoeuvred Tom, Tor and the portrait out of the room in a flash.

Tash caught Rooter's eye and shook her head sadly.

'Ah – the old dear said we'd find you here.'

Olly Hennessy appeared through the door wearing a bowler hat and weighed down with piles of clothes. He was followed by a dishy red-haired man carrying what appeared to be Sophia's professional make-up case with a tray of food balanced on top, a Sobranie Black Russian dangling from his curly lips.

'Hi, gorgeous cuz.' Olly dropped his pile on the floor and kissed both Tash's cheeks. 'You've been hiding from us. This is Ginger.' He nodded towards his friend, who was eyeing Tash as if she were a blank canvas.

'His other-persuasion half.' Ginger looked up and gave her a devastating smile. 'We've been raiding wardrobes in your honour.' He winked, ignoring Olly's warning look.

'Oh yes?' Tash laughed incredulously, liking his sparkling blue eyes and merry smile. 'I'm sorry I sloped off to bed before meeting you last night,' she apologised.

'I should hope so,' Ginger chastised, plucking the cigarette from his lips and stepping back to resume his blank-canvas scrutiny of her face. 'You'd be infinitely preferable to sit opposite than Ol's excruciating brother – pretty as he might be, he eats like a waste disposal unit with a Marlboro continually on the go.' He narrowed his eyes thoughtfully through the Sobranie smoke. 'That gorgeous skin could definitely take green, don't you agree, Ol?'

Baffled, Tash looked at her cousin. She'd always liked Olly's shy, comforting charm, which could warm a room like sunlight through a window. About a year ago, she and Max had accidentally bumped into him in Soho. Persuaded by Tash, Olly had come with them to eat at Won Kee's before meeting his friends in a club. Max, sulking, had whispered 'complete faggot' into Tash's ear each time her reserved cousin changed the subject from beer and sport to art or old movies. Tash had nearly died of embarrassment, finally shooting three pork balls into Max's lap to shut him up.

'Tash, darling . . .' Taking the tray from Ginger, Olly sat on the arm of her sofa, tucking his feet under a cushion beside her and cocking his head coyly. 'Ginger and I wondered if we might borrow you for a bit.' He tipped his bowler up and smiled hedgily. 'Are you busy?'

'No,' Tash smiled, watching in bewilderment as Olly's friend unhooked a mirror from the wall. 'I suppose I'll have to get changed soon, but that won't take long.'

'Exactly my thoughts,' Ginger agreed, setting the mirror down on a table. 'In fact, at a rough estimate I'd say we've only got half an hour with your sister's tart bucket.' He collapsed on Tash's other side. 'She's happily distracted with a blocked drain at the moment. What do you think of this?' Popping his cigarette in Tash's mouth for safekeeping, he extracted a beaded bra top from Olly's pile and held it up.

Still bewildered, Tash nodded. It was flagrantly daring. Almost entirely made of silk chiffon, the emerald and jet beading was hand-sewn to curl and twist around the curves of the tailored top, finally twining around the black-green velvet of its halter neck like a jewelled snake.

'It's lovely,' she shrugged, wondering if Ginger was planning to dress in drag. She glanced at Olly but he merely grinned silently, tipping the bowler back over his eyes.

'Right, darling.' Bending down, Ginger started to sort out the piles in front of him, casually adding over his shoulder. 'Take your clothes off.'

'And have a vol au vent,' added Olly with a wink.

Up in his attic room, Todd gave his hair a final blasting of Ultimate Hold and admired the result. His blond mane, newly cropped above the ears and at the nape of the neck was scraped back from his face. One rigid tendril dropped meanly over his forehead. His grey-green eyes twinkled out of a slightly enhanced suntan, thanks to Clinique's Bronzing Gel for Men. Two days' stubble shadowed the strong line of his chin. He was sporting his closest fitting, shiniest cycling shorts.

He took the stopper off a new bottle of Kouros and covered his face and neck. He then shrugged on the baggy white jacket he'd bought with the proceeds of a deal with young Hennessy.

Turning back to the mirror, he liked what he saw. The effect was somewhere between Don Johnson and Dolph Lündgren. He thrust out his chin and gave his reflection a sultry come-on, pulling up his collars like a Raymond Chandler hero.

He then splashed on some more Kouros for good measure and started to sort out his merchandise for the night's profiteering.

His supplier hadn't let him down. Todd decided happily that he'd have more nibbles on offer tonight than the caterers. And there was one particular elixir he intended to administer personally.

Strapping on his bum-bag, he removed the foil-wrapped parcel he'd marked earlier and kissed it before dropping it in his inside pocket.

The smell of Kouros seemed to have faded again so he emptied the remainder of the bottle into his hands and ran it over his now rigid hair before settling down for a quiet smoke.

There was a timid knock on the door. Todd groaned and looked at his travel clock. Six forty-five. Paola had been giving him earache all day, demanding that he keep her company that night. He wasn't up to another onslaught of Italian illogic.

On the other side of the door, glancing behind her nervously, was Amanda.

She felt like a gibbering wreck.

Half-way through making up her face that evening, she'd become too angry to carry on and had taken a cold shower to calm down. As a result, supposedly waterproof eye make-up had pot-holed its way into her pores and made her look like a miner. She'd painstakingly removed that with cream, only to leave the lid off and spill the lot on the white Ben de Lisi she was going to wear that night. The final straw had been discovering that Hugo had hung a smelly jumper next to her black velvet – the only other suitable dress she had with her – covering it with red horse-hair and a faint pong of quadruped. She now had nothing to wear and a face the texture of a pumice stone. Her only consolation was that she'd carefully unpicked the zip of Hugo's dress trousers and hidden it.

Todd seemed to be taking an age to answer the door, but the faint strains of Bryan Adams told her that he was in situ. There was also a strong smell of aftershave lingering in the air.

Perhaps he was in the shower, thought Amanda, clutching her bathrobe tighter round her. Would he think she was trying to pick him up, creeping to his door dressed like this? He wasn't really her type. Too thick-skinned and colonial. And the dog was a turn-off. Hugo had several dogs but they didn't drool on one's Salvatore Ferragamo shoes or goose one's Janet Regers. She'd even caught Rooter having a pee against a deckchair yesterday. She'd later engineered it so that Sophia sat there and at least derived a certain pleasure from that.

She considered going back downstairs, but needed something to help her get through the party too much, so she tapped again.

'What d'you want this time?' Todd swung open the door and looked surprised.

Amanda was nearly knocked sideways by Kouros. Her freshly cleansed eyes started to smart under the fumes and she coughed.

'Well, g'day.' Todd lounged against the door-frame like a macho room-freshener.

'Todd.' She nodded curtly, leaning back to find a pocket of uncontaminated air. 'I hear we can do some business together.'

A slow smile spread across Todd's handsome face and he beckoned for her to enter. Inside, the room was more brightly lit than a Japanese department store.

'You look as jacked off as a 'roo with Bali belly,' Todd purred gently. 'Joe Blakes, huh?'

Amanda looked blank.

He examined her peeling nose and the deep groves under her eyes. 'You should use a decent moisturiser. The sun's a bitch on English skin.'

'I didn't come here for beauty tips, thanks,' Amanda snapped, trying to avoid her reflection in the numerous mirrors that were hanging around the room. She reflected sourly that perhaps she should have slapped on some Flawless Finish before coming up.

At the far end of the low-ceilinged dorm was an area cordoned off by folding screens. Behind it, like cranes over the Docklands skyline, were several photographers' lights on tripods, protected by foil umbrellas.

Amanda regarded them without interest and tried to work out a subtle way of broaching the subject of what exactly it was she required and whether he'd accept a travellers' cheque. Todd came and stood so close to her she could feel his chest rubbing against her shoulder and was once again enveloped in Kouros.

'I see you're admiring my equipment,' he crooned into her ear. 'I say you need to take care of your skin because you're a beautiful woman, Amelia. I adore beautiful women. Sensual women like you. That's because to an artist there is nothing more perfect as a subject.'

Amanda raised an enquiring eyebrow and looked up at him. Two mossy eyes sparkled back and he flashed the gap between his very white teeth at her.

'I'd love to take your photograph, Amelia. The moment I first set eyes on you I thought, streuth! Is that woman photogenic! Your eyes are mesmerising. The camera would just adore you.'

Amanda felt her lip curl as she blinked in disbelief.

'If you want what I think you want,' Todd went on, 'then there's more Ice than a Siberian snowman in this powder pouch,' he indicated his bum-bag with a suggestive smirk. ''S'cheap, I'm robbing myself, but that's the sort of guy I am.' He dropped his voice to a rumble. 'Has anyone ever told you you've got the most beautiful shoulders?'

'Shoulders? . . . Shoulders?' Amanda laughed coldly. 'Go shag a wallaby, sport.' And, pulling the cord of her gown tighter, she marched from the room.

'No worries.' Todd shrugged and settled back down to finish his smoke.

That was twice in one day, he mulled glumly. He didn't like to think of his technique failing.

'They're all the same, these business execs, Todd mate,' he told his smouldering reflection. 'Substitute pills for sex because it takes less time. Probably frigid, too.'

Still, he mused as he smoothed his cycling shorts, he'd never had a career woman before.

'I'm ever so grateful, Ginger. But I'm really not sure if it's going to be *me.*' Despite Olly and Ginger's ludicrous flattery, Tash was getting colder feet than a Norwegian pot-holer.

'Is the child a fool?' Ginger asked with camp mock-temperament, a comb clenched between his teeth, fluffing Tash's hair like a deranged Nicky Clarke.

'You look terrific, Tash,' Olly assured, tucking into a vol au vent and admiring Ginger's handiwork. He'd been sitting upside down on the sofa with his long legs hooked over the back for almost an hour and was looking both flushed and Oriental, his pink cheeks pushing his eyes diagonal.

'Absolutely the horniest thing I've ever seen.' Ginger removed a lip pencil from behind his ear and added a little more definition to Tash's already Rubenesque Cupid's bow.

'Yes, truly luscious, my sweet,' agreed Olly, doing a backward roll off the sofa. 'Have another vol au vent, Tash – the black bits are truffle.' He reeled towards her, tapping his bowler back into place.

Ginger pulled the last few wisps of hair across Tash's left eye before spinning her round to face the mirror.

Tash was both amazed and appalled that the person looking back from the dusty mirror which Olly held up precariously, was in fact herself. The only reason she knew that was because of the odd eyes that were squinting out from beneath sweeping, mascara-ed lashes.

'Christ,' she whistled in awe.

Beneath the stunning bra top Ginger had prised her into was a long expanse of brown midriff leading to a sensationally foxy black skirt made from asymmetric layers of featherweight chiffon which skimmed her hips, making them look wonderfully narrow. This ended just above her knees, where shiny black silk stockings seemed to make her legs go on for ever into dreamy suede shoes with high Louis heels. Her face was made up like young Bardot's with a dramatic lick of liquid eyeliner and sweeping lashes, her hair piled loosely on top of her head with long twisting tendrils curling round her forehead. It made her neck appear endless.

'I should be touting for rough trade on Rue St Denis,' she scoffed, embarrassed at staring at herself for so long.

'Shut up and put these on your lugs,' ordered Ginger softly, handing her the earrings.

Tash hooked them on with shaking hands. They lit up her skin like two candles. The effect was breathtaking.

'Wow!' Olly grinned, nearly dropping the mirror on Rooter, who was also transfixed.

'One last thing.' Ginger dived behind the sofa and produced a jacket the colour of a Bollinger bottle. 'Shimmy into this, honey.'

Tash shrugged herself into it. There was something wildly sensual about the feel of the oyster satin lining the moment it touched her skin. The dark green jacket was huge on her, but so exquisitely tailored that it smacked of the oversized, slightly androgynous look which had stalked the cat-walks that spring, contrasting with the sensuous, gauzy top absurdly well.

The butterflies that had been emerging from their chrysalises in Tash's stomach suddenly decided to go back to bed.

'So, what do you think?' Ginger started to throw tubes of make-up with the wrong tops on back into Sophia's box.

'I like the jacket.' Tash fingered the soft fabric. It was silk or very light wool. 'Is it Armani?'

'C and A,' lied Olly, smiling at her with crossed eyes. 'You've got a marvellous figure, Tash. You're so fit. And you must be over six foot in those shoes.'

Tash hunched her shoulders at this thought and sagged slightly at the knees. No one would talk to her. Men were intimidated by tall women. Max, all six-one of him, had once told her his ideal woman was about five-three and size eight. They'd been in bed at the time. Tash had nicked the duvet all night, sulked and suggested he bought built-up shoes.

She wobbled on her heels as far as her packet of fags and nearly set her seductive wisps alight with Olly's matches.

'I'm not sure if I can . . .'

'Has anyone seen Michael?' Cass breezed into the room, swathed in full-length baby-blue taffeta with a nipped-in waist and frilly décolleté.

'Michael who?' Ginger flashed her a ravishing smile and reached for a Black Russian.

Olly, swallowing hard, whipped off his bowler and flattened his hair.

'How do you think Tash looks, Mother?' he asked nervously.

'Very nice, Tash.' Cass glanced at her and nodded dismissively. 'You see, I've run his bath and . . .'

She did a double-take.

'Good God!' Her eyes nearly popped out of their Lancôme pearlised blue eye shadow (or 'Smurf shit' as Marcus called it) as she stared at Tash.

'Doesn't she look beautiful?' sighed Ginger proudly.

Seeing his mother, eyes narrowed to two blue strips, opening her mouth to deliver a cutting reply, Olly rammed the tray under her chin. 'Have a vol au vent, Mother,' he ventured sweetly.

'I can't possibly—' snapped Cass, barely able to breathe in her dress as it was. Then, taking a look at the tray, she changed her mind. 'Well, just the one. Mmmm, delicious. Truffles. Where did you get these from?'

'Marcus—' started Ginger.

'The caterers,' Olly cut across him. 'We persuaded them to let us have a tray for the family. Hosts are always too busy welcoming people early on to have a nibble.'

'How thoughtful of you, boys.' Cass dabbed her lips with a lace hanky and returned her attention to Tash. 'Shouldn't you button that jacket up?' she asked, batting her lashes pointedly at Tash's bare stomach. 'It's still quite chilly out.'

She plainly wanted to say a lot more, but didn't wish to appear bitchy in front of Ginger. After all, it was she who had suggested that he and Tash get together in the first place. She was now bitterly regretting it, having had no idea that Tash would somehow transform herself tonight from stable girl to Moulin Rouge chorus one.

Gulping under her aunt's clinical blue gaze, Tash's butterflies jumped back out and started a formation flap team on her bare patches. Goose-bumps were huddling together for warmth on her skin.

'I'll just pop in and see how Sally's doing,' she explained, twisting both ankles as she backed towards the door on unfamiliar heels. 'You look lovely, by the way, Cass,' she added dutifully.

'Thank you, dear.' Cass gave Tash a steely look, flickering the briefest of smiles.

'That child is very odd,' she sighed kindly as soon as Tash was out of earshot.

'Quite. Have another,' coaxed Ginger, offering Cass the tray of vol au vents.

'Perhaps I will, Ginger, thank you.' Cass was rather addicted to the little pastries. They had an odd, earthy flavour she couldn't quite place. And they were very moreish.

'I must say, Mrs Hennessy, you look quite stunning tonight.' Ginger hovered, his blue eyes taking far too long to rake up and down Cass's blue taffeta. 'Doesn't she, Olly?'

Olly cleared his throat. 'Er . . . yes. Very chic, Mother.'

Silenced by her bridge work getting to grips with a particularly large lump of 'truffle', Cass went pink and beamed back at Ginger, rather frustrated that she couldn't breeze, 'It's just a little frock Chloé dashed off for me at the last minute.'

'There you bloody are, old girl.' Michael walked stiffly into the room and gave his wife an affectionate kiss without removing the pipe from his mouth. 'My bloody bath's gone cold. We'll never be ready at this bloody rate. You pressed my dress-shirt yet?'

'Yes, dear.' Cass could have thumped him. Instead, she

helped herself to another vol au vent before whisking from the room with a rustle of taffeta.

As the Hennessys made their way through the hall, Olly and Ginger heard Cass ask Michael, 'Do you like my dress, dear?'

Michael was heard to respond, 'Course I bloody do, you silly old trout. I said what a bloody nice frock it was at the last golf-club bollock.'

After which there was a short, tense pause followed by the unmistakable sound of a hand-crafted pipe being snapped in two.

Ginger looked at Olly. 'Right, we'd better get changed before putting phase B into action.' He glanced at the tray of vol au vents, now half-empty. 'I give her about an hour before it starts to take effect.'

35

Amanda clipped on the second pearl earring and brushed a few more red hairs from her velvet bodice. She was pleased that she'd ended up wearing her black after all. It suited her mood.

The dress clung like a sable vine along the length of her body to mid-calf, where it fanned into a dramatic, sweeping fish-tail. The demure, tailored front was in direct contrast to the back of the dress, which plunged almost to the buttocks, showing a seductive expanse of bronzed shoulder blade. With her blonde hair and the addition of several thick ropes of pearls, Amanda felt she appeared suitably merry widow. She looked both enigmatically sexy and dangerous, which was exactly how she felt.

She went into the bathroom and added a final coat of Starlet Scarlet to her lips, before applying the several Elastoplasts to her toes which were needed to endure a night balanced on four inches of lethal leather.

Hugo wandered into the room just as she was fastening her stockings and uttering curses as the awkward clips split yet another fingernail. She sucked her wounded index and shot him an evil look.

'Hello, darling.' He swayed slightly in the doorway and squinted across at her. 'You're looking very Vincent Price. It reminds me of a film I once saw. Don't tell me, you want a Dalmatian fur stole for Christmas?'

He was carrying a bottle of scotch, which he tossed on to the bed before starting to undress.

Amanda froze. If he thought they were going to have a screw then he had one loose.

'You're drunk.' She started to ease herself into the crippling shoes.

'What an acute observation. Must come from all those chums in Betty Ford.'

He was down to his boxers now. Over the past week he'd been on some sort of fitness campaign, Amanda remembered. The effect was not lost on her. He was looking sensationally raunchy. More lean and muscular than ever, his eyes not quite focusing, his thick hair tousled.

'I'd like a drink please,' Amanda demanded, furious that he could still do this to her.

'Sure.'

Hugo discarded his boxers and walked into the bathroom to collect a tooth mug. On his way out he turned on the shower. Amanda shivered at the thought of what he had in mind: her stripping off and joining him under the warm jets. Then she remembered what her make-up had done last time and thought better of it.

He poured out several fingers of Black Label and brought it over. That spicy smell again, tinged with cigarette smoke and alcohol. She should have been repulsed. Instead, her senses reeled deliriously.

As he looked down at her, she felt her head tip back involuntarily, demanding to be kissed. Her fingers wrapped round his as she took the glass.

'You've smudged your lipstick,' he whispered, wiping it carefully away. 'There. I'm taking a shower.' And, seemingly about as interested in her as a Born Again at a bar mitzvah, he walked into the bathroom and closed the door.

Amanda angrily threw back the scotch in one and headed towards the door, catching her heel on the edge of the loose carpet as she walked. Stooping to free it, she could hear Hugo belting out 'Mad Dogs and Englishmen' in the shower.

'The louse.'

She stalked back into the room to collect the bottle of scotch, then smirked as the thought of the current state of his trousers struck her afresh. On her way out, she scooped up his best cuff-links and dropped them into a bowl of scented pine cones.

While Michael was in his bath, Cass popped in to check on Olly and Ginger. Ginger was doing up Olly's bow tie for him, which Cass thought very sweet, although Michael had spent hours teaching him how to do it for himself in his teens.

Olly went positively pink when he saw her. And well he might, thought Cass, for he was looking utterly dishy in his penguins. Ginger was looking quite ravishing, too, she noticed. Cass always thought coloured bow ties and cummerbunds a touch common but Ginger's sapphire ones exactly matched his eyes.

'The girls won't know what's hit them tonight,' she gushed, straightening Olly's collar and brushing down his shoulders. 'You'll have to fight them off.'

'Exactly my thoughts, Mrs Hennessy,' Ginger said in a measured voice, grinning at Olly.

'*Cass*, remember,' Cass beamed. 'You must have a dance with little Tash's gorgeous sister, Sophia, later. I just *know* you've got bags in common.'

'One old bag in particular,' muttered Olly, after she'd gone to check on Marcus.

'I don't know.' Ginger patted his cheek. 'I think your mother's rather a goer.'

Olly looked at him in shock. 'Oedipus had nothing on you.'

'Never watch Bond movies, myself.' Ginger turned back to the mirror.

As luck would have it, Marcus was in his room for once.

As was Wiltsher, buried in the sleeping bag he occupied on the floor, refusing to be talked out of it. All there was to prove that the immobile lump zipped firmly into the quilted nylon sack was actually human was the odd sad grunt from its depths.

'What on earth's the matter with him?' Cass asked Marcus, who was sitting forlornly on the bed looking crestfallen.

Marcus was dressed in his most mind-blowingly happening gear: a pair of voluminous red denim jeans in which the bum seemed to come somewhere behind the knees, a baggy 'Day Tripper' t-shirt which changed colour as his body heated up, a black quilted bomber-jacket and the inevitable trainers. On his head was a back-to-front baseball hat; a toy whistle was swinging from a bootlace around his scrawny neck. Cass thought he looked awful.

'He won't come out, man,' Marcus mumbled.

'I can see that, and don't call me man, I'm your mother.'

'C'mon, Wiltsher, you great cheesy girl,' Marcus pleaded.

There was a grunt from within that could have been 'no'. It could have been a tip for the three-thirty at Newbury. Cass found it hard to tell under all that thermal insulation.

'Why won't he come out?' she asked, looking around the room. There was that funny smell again, she noted. Like bonfires.

The place was littered with beer cans and dirty underwear. She automatically started to tidy up.

'He's washed his hair, y'know,' explained Marcus, as if that was the most obvious reason in the world for self-confinement in a sleeping bag.

'So?' Cass picked up a pair of underpants and held them at arm's length.

'So his dreadlocks have gone freak, man. Like, he looks kind of Jackson Five, y'know?' Marcus sniffed sadly.

'Oh, honestly!' Cass marched over to the motionless lump and spoke slowly and clearly to what she assumed was the head end. 'Look, this is Marcus's mother here. Can you hear me?'

Another groan.

'Of course he can hear you, man – I mean Mother, man.' Marcus opened another can.

'Good.' Cass moved forward a fraction. 'Look here, you're going to have a far more rotten time if you spend the night inside that thing when everyone else is having fun. And all because your hair won't go right? When you look back on today in years to come, you'll be ashamed that something so petty stopped you having the night of your life. There was once an occasion when Marcus's father and I were invited to dine with the Cadburys. Well, I was trying this new hair tint out at the time – not that I have grey hairs, you understand, it was more of a lowlight in fact – and—'

'All right, man, I surrender.' Wiltsher appeared out of the opposite end to the one Cass was speaking to.

She looked at him in amazement.

Where he'd sported a mass of fat rats' tails earlier that day was now a coiffure of nuclear mushroom proportions. A frizzy blond cloud extended at an even eight inches all over his head like Co Co the clown. Underneath it all, a sad little face peeked out like a poodle after a clip and blow-dry at the pooch parlour.

Cass bit back her smile and cast around for a solution. She'd once had a disastrous perm that had finished up with her resembling an electrified Cleo Lane.

'Wait there!' she ordered and dashed back to her room.

There was a lot of swearing coming from the direction of Hugo and Amanda's turret as she passed it. Another tiff, no doubt. She went straight into her bathroom where Michael was loofahing his back, his contingency pipe firmly wedged between his false teeth.

'I say, old girl, steady on!' he exclaimed in shock as she leaned past him and extracted her conditioner.

Cass ignored him and went back to Marcus's room, narrowly missing being bowled out by a pair of rolled-up dress-trousers which came flying from the shouting turret.

'The bitch!' screamed the voice behind the tossed trews.

Cass gathered up her billowing skirt and ran the rest of the way.

Wiltsher was mercifully still debagged. He meekly complied as Cass sat him down on the dressing-table stool and started to coat the fluff with Coconut and Avocado for Naturally Flyaway. Wiltsher wished his hair would do just that. Baldness was preferable to bouffant. It took the entire bottle of conditioner before Wiltsher's tresses discovered gravity again. Cass dragged the limp mass back into a pony-tail and allowed him to look.

'Rigsby,' hooted Marcus, clutching his stomach.

It was true that Wiltsher now looked like a greasy spiv, but that beat Diana Ross. He was absurdly pleased and offered Cass a pre-rolled spliff from his Fungus the Bogeyman tin in return.

'No thank you, I only have the odd menthol.' She found the offer touching. She prided herself on the fact she got on so well with Marcus's friends. 'I couldn't touch one of those unfiltered Woodbine things before my first G and T.'

Sophia hopped round her room, letting hysteria fight an open battle with fury. Tonight of all nights, the cosmetics thief had struck again. This time, her entire colour co-ordinated, carefully labelled and meticulously assembled collection had been looted in one foul swoop.

She moaned afresh and banged her fists on the wall in frustration. The first guests would be arriving in just under an hour. How could she possibly greet them without her face on? She might as well appear naked except for gumboots and a woolly hat. These were *her* people. All the contacts she had built up over years at the top of her profession, plus a few she would have liked to have made. Stars of stage and screen. The rich and the super-rich. Even, no, she couldn't think about it, even royalty. Had she gathered them all together to be humiliated?

'I'm sorry about the paper bag, ma'am, but one had one's face lifted today and I'm not talking cosmetic surgery.'

Where was Ben? Sophia started to whimper. She'd angrily dispatched him to find her make-up case half an hour ago, gibbering with fury at his beer-breath and total lack of support throughout the afternoon. She could feel a migraine coming on. That was all she needed. It was all Ben's fault.

She caught sight of her angry, pinched little face in the mirror and recoiled in shock.

Maybe he was downstairs having a drink with the boys right now to teach her a lesson, she chewed. He could have instigated the whole thing, in fact. Perhaps he'd hidden her face to spite her toffee nose.

Sophia flopped down on to the bed, stabbed in the chest with sudden guilt.

Poor Ben had limped round forlornly, missing out on all the fun because of his ankle, and all she'd done was tear more strips off him than she ever had when waxing her legs. She'd bossed and booted him. All but made him sign the pledge.

It was because she'd been tense about the party, she told herself. She was never this bad at Holdham. Organising things calmed her there, stopped her from getting bored, made her feel indispensable. Here, it brought out the worst of her spoilt snobbery and awareness that she wasn't quite from the correct drawer.

Oh poor, poor Ben. So typically he'd never once complained. Just escaped into a bottle and a daydream.

She sat down on the bed and started to cry. Great sobs shuddered through her as she gathered Ben's pyjamas to her chest and snivelled into them.

'It's all right, Sophs. I've got it.'

Ben, now on one crutch, loped through the door. She looked up at him through bleary eyes and wailed. Then hiccuped. Then wailed again.

'There, there.' Ben patted her rather hopelessly.

'It's right here, look.' He held up the case for her to see. 'Found it in the study of all places.'

She howled afresh.

Ben cleared his throat and shifted his weight awkwardly.

Sophia raised her bedraggled face. 'I' – hic – 'I – hang on.' She blew her nose and quickly checked her reflection in the mirror. Horrific, but what did it matter? 'I really' – hic – 'really love you, Ben,' another wail, 'I just want you to' – hic – 'know that,' snivel.

Ben looked at his wife incredulously. She was red-faced and puffy-eyed. Her nose looked like a polished Cox's orange pippin and was dribbling slightly. Her shoulders were hunched like a collie in the rain under her dressing-gown. He'd never seen her look more beautiful.

'Love you too, Sophs,' he mumbled.

'Oh, do you?' She looked up at him as if he'd just told her he was pregnant. More sobbing, then an enormous bear-hug ensued.

Ben settled back to watch her get ready, feeling like a new man. She was a pain in the rear, there was no denying it, but he wouldn't swap her for all the tea in Fortnum's. And she still loved him! So ya boo to the Vulture saying she only wanted a title and if you called her *Great Expectations* she'd be happy enough.

'I don't believe it!' A frenzied, furious moan from the depths of her make-up case. 'Some – some utter – utter *piggy* person has been at my make-up. It's a total and utter mess. I can't use this. There's green correction powder everywhere. Ben. Ben, *do something*!'

'Pascal darling, I'm worried about Eddie. He hasn't telephoned.' Alexandra turned round so that her husband could do up the zip on her dress.

''E will come. Do not worry, chérie. Voilà!'

Alexandra turned round and smoothed down the crimson dress.

'Magnifique!' Pascal sighed in awe and looked at her with huge, glistening grey eyes.

'But he should be in France by now. He said he'd phone from the airport before they hired a car.'

'Ze plane, 'e was peut-être – delayed.' Pascal fastened the diamond and ruby necklace around his wife's elegant throat. 'And the phones at Orly are a cauchemar, you know.'

'Maybe.' Alexandra fastened on the matching bracelet and earrings before turning back to Pascal and pulling him close by his collars.

He smiled at her and bent his head to kiss her. Wiping the red lipstick from his lips, Alexandra laid her head against his chest. He smelt of expensive cologne and Gauloise.

'You know Sophia wants us to welcome the guests tonight, darling?' she ventured cautiously.

'Oui.' Alexandra could feel him shrug.

'You don't mind?'

He took her face between his beautiful hands and lifted it so that she was looking at him.

'For you, chérie, I would welcome Jean-Marie Le Pen into our house.'

'Oh,' Alexandra gulped happily, 'what a lovely thing to say.'

Tash tottered without much control in the general direction of her room, feeling more air-headed than ever. She seemed to have lost all co-ordination.

Perhaps it was oxygen starvation as a result of high heels, she pondered hazily. The air was bound to be very thin at this height.

Whoops! She ricocheted off a suit of armour. Where had that come from? She studied it thoughtfully. Some comedian had put her beloved bush hat on top of its metal head and a geranium was sticking out from its visored mouth. Suddenly, Tash found it hysterically funny.

She clutched her stomach and leaned against the wall, overcome with giggles.

'Psst! Ben, is that you?'

For a moment, Tash thought it was the suit of armour speaking and nearly fainted. Then she realised the voice was coming from behind the half-open door to the east turret. Whoever was hiding there couldn't have very good hearing, she thought, scrunching up her face in concentration. Lightheadedness was replaced by the sensation that her head had been removed completely.

'No,' she eventually declared, exchanging a knowing glance with her armoured friend.

The voice sighed irritably, 'Who is it then?'

A familiar drawl.

'Me,' explained Tash, smoothing down her jacket nervously.

'Oh, for Christ's sake! Is that Sally?'

Tash reeled. Was it her imagination, or could she see a glimpse of hairy leg protruding from the doorway?

'No.'

This was not exactly their most scintillating conversation, she decided.

'Tash!'

Hugo sounded relieved. A black-sleeved arm beckoned her over. She blew a kiss at the armour and teetered towards the door, her heart pounding against the constricting top.

He was standing on the landing to his turret room wearing his tux, dress-shirt, bow tie, socks, the lot. He looked as utterly desirable as ever. Except for one thing. He seemed to have forgotten to put on his trousers.

Tash stared at the long, muscular brown legs – object of many a wild fantasy – and began to giggle. This time she couldn't stop. She pointed in silent, ecstatic mirth at his bare chops and leaned against the curving banister, gasping for breath between guffaws.

Hugo, trying to keep his composure, was furious. He had not called her over for an amusing peep show.

'Look,' he fumed angrily, 'are you any good at sewing?'

With an almighty effort of will-power, Tash swallowed down the giggles and looked at him with happy, shining eyes.

'I shouldn't think you'd need my help, Hugo,' she smiled. 'After all, you've had enough practice with wild oats to do raglan sleeves and box pleating by now.' She blinked, astonished at herself.

Hugo was amazed, too. In the gloom of the walkway, he hadn't looked at her properly until now. Tash always looked the same, he thought. Scruffy and unkempt, as though she'd pulled on the clothes nearest her bed. It was what made her totally unique amongst the women he knew, whose bank balances stood in direct inverse proportion to their appearances.

At first, Hugo had found Tash's lack of vanity unfeminine and irritating. Later he'd grown almost to respect it. Almost. Not like it, he'd told himself firmly. It gave her a familiarity – like an old pair of moleskins one didn't look forward to wearing so much as know they were comfortable and fitted well. You could get them dirty and put them through hell in the sure and certain knowledge that they'd serve another two years' wear.

But tonight Tash was as far removed from a pair of moleskins as Sophia Loren was from a Pacamac. Wavering in front of him, her large, mismatched eyes gleaming with an unusual light, she looked simply amazing.

Hugo was astonished to find himself feeling terrified. It was like looking at a Raphael painting that dragged one's eye further and further in until one was lost for ever.

He pulled himself together and cleared his throat, aware that he was looking pretty silly, gawping at her in his smalls.

'Look, I need someone to sew the zip back in my trousers. It appears to have fallen out.' It also appeared to be missing but he'd save that until later.

'I'm afraid if I mended it, you'd probably spend the night with draughty drawers and severed scanties.' Tash smiled vacantly and looked dreamily up at the ceiling.

She felt distinctly odd. She blinked again and forced herself to concentrate on Hugo's face. With the extra height from her heels, their eyes were level. She felt herself yet again begin to shrink and lose her way under his cool blue gaze. How dare he look so ludicrously handsome with just blue and white striped boxers and a pair of black socks on his lower half? Max would just look ridiculously sweet. Even Niall might lose a bit of dignity. Suddenly Hugo didn't seem remotely ludicrous. Just every bit as unattainable as ever.

'Um, hang on there.' Her eyes found the shifting sands of the floor with intense relief. 'I'll go and see what I can rustle up.' She considered doing a Wonder Woman spin but thankfully was half-way to her mother's room before the thought really registered.

'You could 'ave borrow my spare suit.' Pascal cut through his wife's delirious babbling over Tash's get-up a few minutes later. 'But I am wearing eet as Alexandra have forget to collect mine. I 'ave 'owever a pair of black trousers which – er—'

'Might pass at a glance,' Alexandra finished for him, determined to have another bash at Tash. 'I mean, darling, I feel like crying. You look totally, totally gorgeous. So sexy too! I never thought—'

'Mummy, *please*—' Tash groaned, easing off a shoe and rubbing her numb toes.

'Yes, I know, sweetheart, your silly mother's overdoing it again. But I mean it, darling. Honestly I do. It's just so—'

'Voilà!' Pascal emerged from his dressing room carrying a pair of very smart trousers.

Thank God her stepfather had such classic taste in clothes, thought Tash. Hugo was bound to be pleased with her quick-witted initiative. He might even compliment her for once. He hadn't over her outfit. She was surprised how much that hurt. He could bawl at her all week for getting a move wrong with Snob, or not being able to keep up with him on one of their uncompaniable runs, and she would hardly flinch. It was what he didn't say which still gnawed at her self-esteem. She couldn't help herself, she reflected sadly. Whenever she was close to him she forgot everything but a desperate, slavish need to please.

'Oh, Pascal, you're an angel!' Tash laughed in delight and kissed him on both puffed cheeks, not noticing him eyeing her earrings suspiciously. 'Thank you. I'll see you both downstairs.' At the door she felt a burst of emotion and turned round. 'And thank you, Mummy, for everything. You're truly lovely.'

Tears stung her eyes at this point so she curled her painful toes and clattered off. She was getting maudlin now. It must have been that vol au vent. She was suffering food poisoning. She ought to warn Sophia before all the guests went down.

Instead she took off her shoes and scampered back to the east turret. The door to Hugo's room was closed. She could hear sounds of Hugo moving around inside but somehow couldn't get the nerve together to knock on the door. She hovered outside for a bit gathering courage. Taking a deep breath, she re-donned her clogs, rapped and walked in.

He was fixing his cuff-links by the chest of drawers – inexplicably scattered with pine cones – and glanced round at her through sooty lashes and tousled hair. Tash's stomach descended chiffon-wards and then trampolined back into her throat.

'I borrowed you these.' She held out the trousers.

Being in his room was overpowering. It smelt of him, it felt of him. There, crumpled in the middle of the room, was the huge bed. It seemed to grow as she looked at it like an inflating Hovercraft.

He came over and took the trousers from her outstretched arm. His fingers accidentally brushed against her wrist and she backed away, terrified of the electric shocks that were shooting up her arm.

'Thanks,' Hugo said, unfolding the black bundle. She always flinched from him, he thought. She'd done it that time he came on to her by the pool. It had angered him then. Now he just felt sad.

As he hooked one foot into the trousers, she made to leave.

'No, stay,' he found himself saying.

Tash hovered awkwardly by the door.

The trousers were mercifully the right length, although too wide round the waist. Hugo threaded a belt through them and covered it with his cummerbund.

Watching him, Tash allowed herself a quick fantasy that they shared this room and studying him dress was a lazy, everyday pleasure after hours of lounging and laughing in that huge, messy bed.

'Cigarette?' Hugo had finished dressing and was now observing her stare into space with mild amusement.

'Thanks.' Tash's hand shook when he lit the quivering fag. He had to cover it with his own to steady it. Her arm went completely numb this time.

Hugo reluctantly backed off and considered his next move. She was jumpy as a newly weaned foal. Looking at her filled him with self-contempt. Here she was, beautiful, desirable, infinitely more exciting than anyone he was likely to meet that night. And yet she was frightened of him. He'd made sure of that.

She was watching him as if he was about to sprout fangs and make a lunge for her jugular. Hugo looked wistfully at her long, swan neck.

Tash backed off further and fell over Amanda's briefcase.

She was wearing stockings on her long, slim legs. Glimpsing a length of brown thigh when she fell over sent Hugo's blood pressure through the roof.

'I like your hair.' He watched her pick herself up.

'Thanks,' she mumbled, not looking at him

'Yes, it suits you like that.'

The carefully positioned tendrils had actually flopped over her face when she fell. Tash blew out sharply to get them out of her face and ended up doing a raspberry.

He didn't seem to notice. He was still staring at her.

'Are you nervous about tomorrow?' Hugo decided to try another tack.

'Er – not really,' Tash lied. She was damned if she was going to tell him how terrified she was.

So that was it, she realised with a shudder. He'd make her stay so that he could have another go at persuading her to sell Snob. Hence the compliment. A little soft-soaping before the big blow. You'll look a fool, Tash. Everyone will laugh at you. Face it, he'd be much better off with me.

Suddenly, the thought of hanging around to hear Hugo discuss the shortcomings of her riding technique was more than she could bear.

'The guests will be arriving soon,' she said as brightly as she could muster – about five watts. 'I'm going to change.' Turning on her heel, and nearly snapping it off, she scarpered.

'Damn!' Hugo ran his hand through his hair and looked up at the ceiling in despair.

Back in her room, Tash sat on her bed with burning cheeks. How utterly dumb could you get? How can you get changed if you look like Julian Clary's Christmas tree already?

She caught sight of her sultry reflection and groaned.

'You're not me,' she told the glamour-puss staring back at her. 'You're a minxy goer with more balls than Wimbledon's centre court.'

She fished about in her still half-unpacked rucksack without much hope. There was a surfeit of odd socks, grey bras and creased t-shirts, but no subdued little ball gown suitable for a formal banquet for several hundred surfaced. She dug around in the bottom, wondering if she'd bothered to pack her faded little black smock dress (or 'the bin liner' as Max had nicknamed it). She hadn't, but her hands came to rest on something even more familiar. Soft as Snob's muzzle and as frayed and chewed as Lotty's Noo Noo.

She took out the keepsake which she'd guiltily removed from Max's wardrobe and packed at the last minute to keep her company.

They were his most valued possession and probably his oldest. He'd refused to take them to the States because he was afraid of losing them. Even when Tash first met Max, they'd been on their last legs, literally. Now they were all but legless.

They were a pair of old Levi 501s – although the amount of denim left in them was minimal. For what wasn't hole or tatty patch was laddered like old raffia. One entire leg was made up of stringy horizontals, held together only by the seam. The other was almost as bald, with the denim that still remained as thin as muslin. At the top, the fly was still miraculously intact – although almost white with age – but the bum had given way years ago and was patched on the inside with one half in spotted red hanky and the other in green and blue paisley, now itself beginning to fray. One rear pocket had dropped off, leaving an unfaded darker blue, as if a painting had once hung there. Two of the belt loops had also disappeared and kilt pins did the job for them. The thick black leather belt attached to them was almost as prehistoric as the jeans themselves. It was as floppy and pliable as old rope and had held together suitcases and broken exhausts the world over.

Tash loved these jeans almost as much as Max did. They were an extension of him. They'd seen it all: wine, women and every rugby party-going. The battered armour of a crusader, far more war-torn than the gleaming pile of ironwork which was standing on the landing.

Unable to resist the urge, Tash released the suction of the

crippling shoes on her feet, dragged off her stockings and suspenders in one foul swoop and unzipped the floaty skirt.

As she stood poised to climb into her beloved old friends, she noticed that she was still wearing the only pair of knickers she'd had clean that morning – dyed pink in the wash, held together by a very wimpy-looking thread on one side and a safety pin on the other and with a picture of a fat mouse on the front. Discarding them without a second thought, she stepped into one stringy leg of Max's jeans.

There was a knock on the door.

'Wait a minute!' she screeched, frantically pulling them up and buttoning up the flies.

'Come in!'

Silence.

'I said come in!'

Still silence.

Muttering under her breath, Tash scuttled to the door and stood behind it as she let it swing open a fraction.

There was no one there, just an empty, flower-laden landing with a suit of armour dressed like Paul Hogan performing Carmen staring at her from the far side. She ventured out and glanced around but, apart from the distant sounds of activity downstairs, nothing stirred.

As she backed into her room again, her heel brushed an envelope marked 'Tash' under the balding Persian rug on the floor. She didn't notice.

Returning to her mirror, she stared at her reflection. The top half was a pouting, wanton sex-bomb. The bottom half was Tash.

Walking to her sink, she washed her face, then loosened her hair free from its pins and shook it out.

Back at the mirror she was almost back to normal. Better than usual, but recognisably Tash. Having her hair up had made it cloud in voluminous waves around her face. The waterproof mascara still remained as did a smoky definition on her upper lids and at the outer corners of her eyes, making them look huge.

She did up her belt. When she'd last borrowed the hallowed jeans – causing a huge row in Derrin Road because Max had blamed Mikey for the resulting curry stains – she hadn't been able to do up the top notch. Now, even with the belt done up as tightly as it would go, the jeans dropped to her hips, showing her flat, brown midriff, the inward curve of her waist and a hint of belly button. The sexy top and designer jacket contrasted ridiculously well.

The tattered trousers didn't cover much, though, Tash noticed. The entire length of her brown legs was pretty much on show to anyone who bothered looking and – although her bum and crotch were well covered – she was aware of a definite, not unpleasurable draught. The whole rig-out was unexpectedly sultry. The just-got-out-of-bed look, spiced a little. Now this was Tash.

'Welcome back, chick,' she told her reflection. 'Stick with me.'

Filled with a fresh, exhilarating self-confidence, she pulled on her beloved bimbo boots and ventured downstairs to greet the first arrivals.

36

'Fuck!' Niall looked at his watch and banged his fist against the steering-wheel in frustration.

Ahead of him, a queue of camper vans and cars with Parisian number plates packed full of families, beach balls, granny's walking frame and three weeks' worth of disposable nappies stretched as far as the eye could see, idling along the straight, straight Roman road.

'Relax.' Matty looked for an unchewed piece of fingernail, far from practising what he preached.

He didn't know why Niall was in such a hurry to get back. He personally needed this time more than anything. Needed to digest what Niall had told him on their way out of Paris, to work out what he could say to Sally.

'Shit, shit, shit, shit, *shit*!' Niall hissed, his back hunched over the wheel as a white Peugeot 205 nipped out behind them and cruised past about eight holidaymakers during a minuscule gap in the oncoming traffic. Niall swung out behind him to have a look and nearly went head-on into a Brit coming the other way. The Brit's passenger leaned out of the window and yelled abuse which he was mercifully travelling too fast for them to catch.

Niall, his forehead quilted in tension, muttered 'Fucking, wanking great motherfucker of an arsehole' and similar pleasantries under his breath.

'Probably only wanted an autograph,' smiled Matty, and was rewarded with the radio on at full blast. Since it had been tuned to Radio Four in England, they got an earful of shrieking interference.

Matty leaned forward to turn it off and nearly had his face smashed against the dashboard as Audrey's brakes shuddered them to a sudden halt. Lighting a cigarette, Niall hadn't noticed the traffic in front stopping.

'Why do you want to get back for this buttock-licking bash so quickly anyway?' Matty sat back and rubbed his chin. 'I thought you said you'd rather be photographed for the Sunday rags exiting Stringfellow's on the arm of Prince Edward than be seen dead at Sophia's thrash.'

Niall ignored him.

'It's only just past eight,' Matty continued, opening his carton of duty-free fags as Niall plainly wasn't going to offer him one of his. 'They'll have hardly started uncorking the champagne. Bun fights and networking at nine, marriage break-ups and embarrassing displays of social climbing at ten. First patch of vomit spotted at eleven. The discovery of nude titillation in the pool and wife-swapping in the orangerie isn't scheduled till midnight, you know. Plenty of time.'

'Oh, fucking shut up!' Niall snapped, trying to wind down the driver's window without success. Audrey's ashtrays were full so he flicked his half-smoked butt towards Matty's window and missed.

'Thanks.' Matty fished around on the floor for the burning end. 'You've just doubled the value of my car. The interior light and heating system fixed in one throw.'

Niall wished again he hadn't offered to drive. He badly needed a drink.

'Look, what's eating you?' Matty located the butt and tossed it out. 'For Christ's sake, Niall, spit it out and do us both a favour. I'm seriously worried for my life here. Trying to kill yourself in Audrey isn't too bright an idea. Think of the obits: *Talented Irish actor found mangled in clapped-out banger with unknown documentary producer once compared to Nick Bloomfield.* Hardly James Dean. Even Jayne Mansfield had a better head for publicity.'

Niall's face at last split into the old smile. 'That's sick, Matty French.'

'Your driving does that to a man,' Matty groaned. 'Motion displacement's in the bag compared to this.'

Niall lit another cigarette, Matty grabbing the wheel at the vital moment.

'So what in God's name's up?'

Niall ground Audrey's gears and glanced across at his friend.

'Your sister's going to be seduced by that letch, Beauchamp, tonight.'

'What, Sophia? Come on, Niall. I know you've got a vivid imagination but – I mean to say she's far too keen on being the next Countess Malvern or whatever to jeopardise—'

'Not Sophia!' howled Niall.

There was another silence while Audrey's engine clanked and clattered ominously.

'He's going to seduce Tash,' Niall hissed quietly.

'Tash? *Tash?*'

The thought seemed ludicrous to Matty. It was as if the fact that she was even his sister had escaped his notice until now. If Niall hadn't been trying to turn left, he'd have punched him.

'Well, good on her,' Matty laughed eventually. 'I suppose it's been on the cards.'

'What do you mean?' asked Niall, shocked.

'Well, they've been spending so much time together. Even taking early morning jogs and cardiofunking in the courtyard. Do you know my mother actually thought that was a trendy sort of cardigan – cardiofunking. Sally told me. Anyway, Tash was always destined to end up with a shit like Beauchamp. She's far too sentimental and kind-hearted, pathetically willing to please. It used to drive my bastard of a father mad. He was a sod to her, really. Typical she'd end up with someone just the same.'

Niall counted to ten, slowly, and managed to contain his anger. Just.

'Can't you see,' his voice trembled but Audrey's engine hid that, 'can't you see that he'll just use her and leave her – sentimentality, kind heart and all – absolutely destroyed?'

Matty looked at Niall's set profile in total bemusement. He couldn't see what possible interest his friend could have in his sister's ill-fated love-life.

'So what exactly are you planning to stop this liaison?' he asked humouringly.

'I don't know at the moment. I'll be working that one out when I get there.' Niall rubbed his forehead and sighed despondently. 'It might be too late.'

37

At nine-thirty that night French time, three-thirty p.m. in East Coast USA, Eddie Buckingham attempted to phone through to the manoir from JFK, New York. He wanted to tell his sister that his flight had been delayed. He also needed to prepare her for another couple of clangers which were due to be dropped on – or in on – her.

Three to be exact, he mulled, glancing through a cloud of Henry Winterman smoke at his companions. Human ones.

It was not the first time he had tried dialling Alexandra's number. The pressure pads on the phone were beginning to get a well-worn look about them. In fact, Eddie had lost count of the hours he'd spent in the corner of the first-class departure lounge listening to various alien tones beeping and bipping through the handset.

He lit another slim cigar and waited patiently for the series of loud pips rattling through his ears to stop. These were followed by a muffled recording of a female French voice babbling a message which sounded something like the tannoy at Clapham Junction. She kindly repeated it at about twice the speed of sound – and probably backwards for all he could tell – before the phone went dead.

Sighing, Eddie gave up.

The fault on the plane had finally been located and remedied. Judging by the time it had taken, Eddie suspected both wings had been replaced and the interior repainted. In Germany. He went back to his three companions, shaking his head.

'No luck,' he shrugged.

They looked up at him with strained, dehydrated eyes which had suffered too much airport coffee and too little sleep.

Eddie squeezed the hand of his lover and felt a smile unzip his lips. His life-force. So strong. So utterly magnificent. Clichés like 'the best thing that's ever happened to me' sprang from his lips whenever he talked of their relationship which – according to his oldest friends – was incessantly. Strange then, he reflected, that he'd put off telling his sister about his new partner until the last minute. The thought of it had made him uptight all week. Now he had a terrible feeling that he'd left it too late.

'Hey, Eddie.' His hand was pressed to the most beautiful lips he knew.

A nearby woman, whose face had been lifted into her Californian tidal-wave hair, shot them a disapproving look under her hitched-up eyelids. Used to the reaction, Eddie ignored it.

'Don't let yourself get so uptight, huh?' the voice purred on. 'They'll love me, I'll charm the pantyhose off of them. Or should that be knickers?'

Eddie looked down at those shining, wicked eyes so full of life, and all his fears dissolved like a soluble headache pill to his neuralgia.

'I suppose we'd better board,' suggested another English voice behind them, a cultured baritone.

Eddie turned to his friend Lucian Merriot and nodded.

The tall, dapper man smoothed back his sleek peppered mane and stood up, the creases falling from his immaculately tailored chalk-stripe within seconds. Only Lucian would contemplate travelling red-eye wearing a Savile Row wool worsted and a pink silk tie, thought Eddie fondly.

That was another reason for needing to get through to Alexandra, he reminded himself. It was one thing turning up – a day late – with a new, controversial lover on your arm. But to be followed in by an old chum and his son was presumptuous even by his standards.

'Sure.' Eddie gathered up his jacket and waited for the others to finish collecting together their litter.

Lucian had polished off one too many bourbons and was trying to zip up his grip-bag with the luggage tag. His son helped him, laughing.

Merriot Junior was a good-looking boy, thought Eddie. Much like his father when Eddie had met him in those first weeks in Manhattan. Two ex-patriot Brits feeling isolated and out-of-step with this huge, cosmopolitan city. Even though Eddie had long since moved to the East Village and become one of the familiar eccentric figures which graced its seedy diners and alternative hang-outs, while Lucian had stayed in Manhattan frequenting power-house restaurants and exclusive bars, whilst putting the fear of God into Wall Street every time he got out his calculator, they had remained firm friends. A paradoxical couple when they met up – alternately on each other's stomping ground – but nonetheless drawn to each other if for no other reason than to keep the faint, guilty loyalty they had to Queen and country, to old school ties, cricket teas and Marmite soldiers.

Lucian could be brutally reactionary – he had outlandish political opinions, a legendary short temper and couldn't 'abide those fucking queers you hang around with, Eddie'. And yet he had been the first person Eddie had told about his new relationship. In turn, Lucian had confessed to Eddie that he was terrified of his wayward son's impending visit.

'Haven't seen the boy for years,' he'd admitted. 'He was an absolute brat as a kid. And he's the spitting image of his damned mother.'

Merriot's son, Max, had come along to the most recent of Lucian and Eddie's patriotic lunches. He was staying with his father at the end of a back-pack and bean-tin holiday which, it seemed to Eddie, only the young were capable of enduring. Lucian – hopeless at knowing how to react to him – had suggested they meet in McDonald's. By the time Eddie had arrived, a single-breasted Prince of Wales check and a scuffed leather flying jacket were sitting side by side at a plastic table, simply howling with laughter.

Seeing them together, Eddie had felt an absurd sort of bond with this urbane man who had thus far been a bi-annual scribble in his appointments diary and a good source of financial support when the gallery blipped into the red.

When it had transpired that Max Merriot was a friend of Eddie's niece, Tash, a chance to repay some degree of the debt had presented itself. As things turned out, his being in New York that week couldn't be better.

'I had a letter from old Tash a couple of days ago, didn't I, Dad?' Max had cocked an eyebrow amiably.

Lucian, clearing his throat, had said nothing.

'Yeah, Tash and I go way back,' Max had continued. 'Great laugh. So what's her mother like – sounds quite a character?'

'Alexandra?' Eddie had given a brief synopsis of his sister's life, culminating in her marriage to the sinfully rich, incurably lazy and impossibly charming Pascal d'Eblouir.

'However, I know most of this second-hand,' Eddie had confessed. 'From my other sister, Cass. Alexandra lives such a glitzy life – we haven't really kept in contact.'

He neglected to mention that he'd actually severed links when she was married to the priggish James French.

'She sounds great!' Max's eyes had lit up. 'Tash never said,' he whistled. 'The d'Eblouirs are quite a heavy family in France. Christ, I'd love to meet the old girl – and see Tash again, of course. Darling Tash, she's totally – well – unique.' His brows furled tragically. 'We had a bit of a – um – *thing* at one time, you know.'

He'd sighed with deep regret, making Eddie sense a profound sadness.

Lucian, however, had cleared his throat once more – almost, Eddie had mused afterwards, as if stifling a laugh. The paternal empathy clearly had a way to go yet.

Moving them on to one of his favourite wine bars, Eddie had insisted that they must both join him and his partner in flying to France for Alexandra's party. Max, it turned out, had theoretically been invited anyway. And Lucian – with his dapper charm and international reputation – would go down a storm.

Might even meet wife five, they had joked around the table after a third bottle of West Coast champagne.

Now, delayed and dampened by sobriety, the idea was not so hot. In fact, thinking about it, Eddie was filled with an icy chill. He hadn't seen his sisters or their broods for over a decade. He had never even met the youngest children, nor Alexandra's new husband – although ironically Lucian knew Pascal from years back. Worse still, he was bringing with him three uninvited guests. One of whom, at least, was certain to rock the ark Alexandra had set up to welcome him with. It might even capsize under the excess cargo.

'Eddie, you ready?' A warm arm linked through his and steered him towards the departure gate.

'Have a nice flight!' the blonde hostess chimed as she returned their boarding pass stubs to Eddie's partner. 'Hope you and your father have a great vacation!'

His brow pleated with worry and irritation, Eddie stormed on to the plane.

38

It was a crisp, blustery night lit by a wimpish moon that dashed between clouds like a flasher hiding behind Hampstead Heath bushes. The spitting rain earlier that day had washed all the mugginess out of the air and scoured the dust from every stone and cobble.

Lit by the newly erected floodlights, the manoir looked as if it had been dipped in gilt, framed against the fast-moving, splash-dyed navy sky, with deep, saturated yellow lights glowing a welcoming beacon from every ornate window. The tatty, merrily worn old house had been resurrected to its former glory for the night to become an enchanted château. Already Alexandra had been asked by an elusive and very dashing Hollywood director if the manoir could be made available for location work.

'I'll commission the script yesterday. Glenn would just *die* for a chance to act in a place like this, Alexandra, honey.'

Beyond the cool, mono entrance hall, the manoir was fast becoming a teeming throng of dinner jackets and clashing, competing haute couture. Voices shrieked over the clinking of glasses, splitting the air and drowning delicate strains of harpsichord. The banked flowers brought out florid adjectives of praise, plus a few handkerchiefs to mop hay-fevered brows. Huge candles flickered in the dingier corners, lighting up beautiful, characterful, laughing, arguing, flirting faces alike.

Sophia, glancing in on them, was glowing like a beacon of

perfectly made-up joy as she stood proudly by Ben welcoming guests. In her classic cream Chanel and a six-string choker which must have emptied the Pacific of pearls, she was being flooded with compliments like nectar gilding the lily. She hadn't felt so deliciously heady since her wedding day.

'How sweet of you to say so.' She crinkled her eyes at a dashing Arab who was wearing dark glasses and a tea towel on his head. '*Do* go through and get a glass of punch – it's awfully good.'

The sheikh flounced off, his tea towel flapping.

'Doesn't drink, Sophs,' Ben hissed out of the side of his mouth. 'Religion, you know.'

'Oh.' Sophia felt piqued. 'I knew that.'

She slipped behind the marble statue and picked up her concealed goblet, hastily downing another astringent mouthful.

But even the arrival of Jean and Valérie, looking like Gene Hackman and Bella Umberg after the wind had changed during a girning competition, couldn't dampen her excitement. They were wearing their Sunday bests, which had probably been bought during the German occupation. Valérie was even wearing a hat. Jean's stiff black trousers had their creases down the sides and were two inches too short.

Alexandra, unbelievably touched, told them they looked charming.

Sophia caught a whiff of Jean's cologne and needed another swig of punch before she could feel her nose again.

Peeping out from behind the statue, she suddenly spotted a cloud of wild hair and indecently ripped jeans causing a stir in the main hall.

Sophia stiffened.

At first she thought it was some wild modelling friend, looking horribly Vivienne Westwood and being chatted up by two of London's MEBs. Her jaw dropped when the tall girl turned round.

Her long thumbs slotted through two belt loops, lovely face animated and laughing, Tash was revealed to her view.

How dare she? Sophia fumed. How *dare* she? *And* she was

wearing their mother's diamonds. Alexandra must have lent them to her. How selfish! As elder daughter she should have had first refusal.

At that point, Sophia was diverted by the entrance of a recently engaged brat packer and her Kennedy clan fiancé. They posed while the photographer from *Hello!* simpered behind a zoom lens. Emerging from behind the statue at exactly the right second, Sophia was snapped being kissed on both cheeks by two of the most vogue sets of lips in Hollywood.

A few guests had mistakenly arrived in doublet and hose or farthingale and bum roll. Some, thinking the theme even later, appeared sporting a combination of liberty bodice, multi-stack powdered wig and lacy fan. One man came dressed as a gorilla. He was a leading gossip columnist from a British daily and, after several glasses of punch, was pointed in the direction of the barn, from which he never reappeared.

Thanks to Sophia practically breaking Pascal's arm through half-Nelson twisting, there was an unending flow of vintage champagne, mead and the potent pink punch.

Conversation soon broadened from the light and frothy to the wickedly acid. Sotto voices poisoned jewelled ears, while painted eyelashes batted coyly in the direction of the slander victims. A multitude of languages flattered, gossiped, bitched, joked and boasted throughout the house. Guests listening slyly in on each others' conversations longed for a headset and an interpreter. And all the time glasses were snatched from trays and eleven per cent proof came to rest in the gourmet-lined stomachs of the idle rich, loosening those healthy red tongues yet further.

Caterers dressed in white livery passed through the assembly bearing silver salvers of drinks and appetisers with professional arrogance, capable of homing in on an empty glass without swivelling their deadpan eyes left or right.

Weaving between both guests and caterers came a host of entertainers, whom Sophia had hired for the night. A man on stilts juggled with knives while a snake-charmer dressed as a court jester wrapped his boa around the diamond-encrusted necks of giggling, gasping or squealing women and told lewd jokes in Italian.

The fire-eater had his ardour dampened when a waggish joker, hooting loudly, emptied a bottle of bubbly over his sticks. Thinking of his fee, the fire-eater calmly got out another set and was promptly rewarded with a glass of punch on his kindling flames. The blaze that ensued nearly took his eyebrows off and burnt cleanly through a flimsy shawl nearby. The fiery punch was certainly going down a bomb; surgical high spirits had been up to a little spiking.

Amidst the rustling taffeta and swarming DJs in the long gallery, guests were taking turns at playing medieval sports. Whistle and pipe clenched between his teeth, Michael Hennessy was revelling in his role as referee. Instead of allowing the bigger names to get away with cheating, as Sophia had instructed, he bellowed and bawled at socialites whose only company had been yes-men for months. Finding the whole experience rather novel, many eagerly queued excitedly for more.

'Sorry, Ivana, old girl – can't bloody allow you to get away with that. Back of the bloody queue.'

On the stage area at the far end, a sinewy man dressed in leopard-skin trunks was bashing nails into a plank of wood with different parts of his body as a prelude to the first of the strolling players' interludes.

He was accompanied by the twanging, reedy medieval ensemble who were swigging mead, smoking fags and looking generally far more Muddy Waters meets The Doors than madrigal pluckers. The lute player was already tight. Having earlier travelled from Saumur station in the plumber's van, he was mistaken on arrival for the sub-contracted poultry chef. It was only when faced with a crate of unstuffed pheasant and partridge that the shy little man had wailed an hysterical, tearful explanation. He'd been given several glasses of brandy to calm him down and now wouldn't know a lute from a capon.

Tash and Sally were avoiding welcoming guests by hiding behind a tall potted cheese plant, and celeb-spotting through the vegetation like a pair of David Bellamys. Sally had commandeered a bottle of bubbly.

A pair of group-hopping carousers ambled up to introduce themselves. One – a renegade cousin of Ben's called Jamie Shrewsbury – was clearly wired, his bow tie already undone, curly blond hair falling on to his pink face in a dishevelled cherubic forelock.

''Lo, Tash,' he gave her a wet kiss on the mouth, lurching slightly. 'You look celestial, my dear. May I have permission to fondle you on the dance-floor later?'

He turned to kiss Sally, who hastily fluffed up her hair and let a bootlace strap slide off her brown shoulder.

Tash blinked disbelievingly. Jamie – for ever in the tabloids for letting down the blue-bloods – had totally ignored her on the few occasions they'd met before.

'I'm Raoul,' a husky voice tickled the downy hair by Tash's ear and a pair of sparkling eyes drifted up and down her body with the practised appraisal of a Christie's valuer.

'Hello, Raoul.' Tash took in the very white capped teeth and conker-brown skin.

The caps flashed an inch from her nose and she felt a light tug on the bottle she was holding.

'May I?'

Raoul clasped a warm hand over hers. Still gazing into her eyes, he slowly and deliberately drew her grip towards his face, swallowing a long mouthful of champagne from the neck of the bottle.

'You're terribly pretty.' Raoul wiped his grinning mouth with the back of his hand. He had red lipstick on one cheek and his eyes weren't quite focusing. 'I wonder if I might—'

'Christ, Raoul, look! It's Frisby Gillespie.' Jamie towed his friend towards a balding man who was fishing a canapé out of his giggling girlfriend's cleavage.

Feeling flustered, Tash checked to see if parts of her which shouldn't be were hanging out.

'He fancies you because you're novel and sexy,' Sally explained, laughing as she took the bottle. 'How many people would dare to come to one of these dos in jeans?'

'But—'

'My God, Tash. Is that Mick Jagger talking to your mother?'

Following Sally's gaze, Tash giggled and shook her head. 'That's Monsieur Ducruet – runs the village bar.'

'Oh,' Sally sighed, gazing around her. It was such an eclectic mix – jet-set mingling happily with locals and family friends. 'Tash, look at that!'

Jean – sipping pastis nervously in a corner – was being monopolised by a blonde in a Rodeo Drive cat-suit who was convinced that he must be a sinfully rich old French landowner. Wiping his red face with a huge linen handkerchief, he cast anxiously around for his wife. Valérie, fighting her way back from the gallery with a brimming cup of punch, looked furious.

'I *love* your style.' A gay art critic with a shaved head and leather trousers stroked Tash's bum, making her jump. 'I must say Sophia has some stunning friends. Are you a nob or a slob?'

Before Tash could answer, he was cooeed by an untamed Baronet's son whose obscure sculptures, made from human waste, were currently selling for thousands in Japan.

Glancing at her sister, it suddenly dawned on Tash what the art critic had meant. Through her marriage, Sophia had mixed a unique blend of new, brash money, glamour and glitz with old titled bloodlines. It was an irresistible cocktail for a party. Commoners – even the super-rich – secretly loved to clash jaws with the aristocracy, but hated freezing in a dilapidated mausoleum of a bygone age where there was no money for decent booze or grub and one froze to death because the windows rattled and the roof leaked all over the musty tapestries. In the same way, the increasingly skint upper classes didn't mind digging out their paste replicas of grandmother's emerald and pearl choker for an all-expenses-paid binge with a few rock stars and entrepreneurs, provided one of their own was behind it somewhere.

Tash admired the way Sophia welcomed each individual with sublime social professionalism. While her mother and Pascal did all the wrong things, laughing them off with characteristic bonhomie, Sophia was ultimately accomplished at hautesse hospitality, making everyone feel like the guest of honour.

This is what she does best, thought Tash. What she wanted all along. She's sweated and toiled to reinvent herself as the model society hostess rather than the society hostess who was a model.

'Pretty formidable, isn't she?' Sally seemed to read Tash's thoughts.

Tash nodded. The gulf between siblings had never seemed wider. And yet, Tash realised, if you really want something badly enough you have to go out and find it with your teeth gritted.

She scanned the hall for Hugo then stopped herself, laughing out loud at her absurd afflatus.

Sally gave her an odd look. 'I hope Matty comes back soon,' she sighed.

And Niall, Tash agreed silently. She needed his warmth and profundity, his reassuring presence in the house. An over-speculative, irrational fellow nut. She took a swig of champagne instead.

In the banqueting hall, Ginger and Olly were queuing at a long, white-clothed table, inching closer to liveried waiters ladling out fruity punch from two crystal bowls.

At the far end, Amanda was being handed a cup of the pungent pink brew. Downing it in one, she glanced around anxiously. She hardly knew a soul. Hugo was completely blanking her out, like a teenager meeting his ex at a barn dance, too proud to be conciliatory in front of his mates. She knew she should feel victorious and assuaged at having finally cut the strings, but instead she felt desperately insecure and alone and – for the first time in years – crippled with shyness. Having always felt gloriously superior to Sophia, she was staggered by the names pulled in for this party, realising that Ben's vacuous wife must have a phone book which read like *Who's Who*.

'What's the delay?' Ginger yawned idly, winking at a pretty waiter.

Olly shrugged, gazing around for someone to wink at in retaliation. Spotting only Michael Winner and David Frost, he gave up and watched the front of the queue with interest as a lissom blonde grabbed the punch ladle and helped herself to another spilling glass before picking her way through the yakking crowd like a heron stalking around a field of geese.

As the queue started to shorten again, Ginger extracted a litre of ethanol-laced Smirnoff Silver Label from his fifties dinner jacket and began to unscrew the top.

'What are you doing?' Olly laughed in amazement.

'Following out your brother's dastardly instructions.' Ginger edged behind a fat German industrialist and glanced over each of his broad shoulders. 'Now, when I say *go*, cause a distraction.'

'What?'

'Do something to divert everyone's attention for a few seconds.'

'Like wha – oh, great, that's all we need.' Rolling his eyes, Olly watched his mother bearing down on them.

Like a walking boys' portaloo tent in her billowing blue gown, Cass Hennessy wafted across the room, pursued by Pascal's vigneron, Anton, with his black hair slicked back and his several chins propped up on a stiff stand-up collar. He was holding out a slightly bent red rose.

Cass waved him off and went straight to her son's side.

'There you both are.' She twinkled her eyes at Ginger, before turning to Olly. 'Your father wants you to fetch his tobacco from our bedroom.'

'Vous voulez, monsieur?'

Olly looked up to see the waiter holding out a glass of punch to him.

'Oh, yes – thanks.' He took an enormous slug and handed it back, looking nervously over his shoulder. Ginger was holding the vodka alongside his thigh like a Guardsman's rifle.

'You come wiz me to look at les étoiles, Cassandra.' Anton was breathing garlic into Cass's cleavage.

'No, thank you, Anton.' Cass backed into Olly just as Ginger hissed '*Go*,' into his ear.

'What, now?' Olly gulped apprehensively.

'But I weel keep you warm, mon ange.' Anton was waggling his limp rose flirtatiously.

'Quickly.' Ginger raised two urgent red eyebrows at Olly. The queue was beginning to buckle as the waiter held out the refilled glass.

'Oh God,' Olly groaned under his breath, 'here goes.'

He turned to Anton, who was now pinning Cass up against the fat German.

'Leave my mother alone, you onerous rogue!' he bellowed with what he hoped was Hamlet-like angst. 'She's a married woman. Just because she's got her tits hanging out and a bit of slap on, it doesn't make her an adulteress ready for the rank sweat of an enseamed bed.'

'Eh?' Anton's eyes bulged in astonishment.

The waiter, who was still holding out Olly's glass, eyed Cass with interest. She had turned purple, her painted mouth completely disappearing into a puckered crater. Meanwhile a litre of spiked vodka glugged into his unwatched bowl.

Thinking fast, Olly took back his punch glass and thanked the waiter. Then, removing Anton's wilting rose and crying 'Dead for a ducat!' he upturned the brimming punch over the Frenchman's head.

But Anton, an agile adulterer with years of practice dodging blows, side-stepped neatly so that the sticky pink liquid gushed on to the fat German industrialist's pot belly.

'Oooeeeich – Mein Gott!'

'Ooops.' Olly handed the rose to the shrieking German. 'Thou wretched, rash, intruding fool, farewell.' Shooting Ginger a brief, martyred wink, he loped towards the door.

As the waiter, gibbering with Gallic apologies, started to mop the fat German's dripping cummerbund, further diversion was caused by his even fatter Frau starting to yell accusations at Cass. Taking back his rose, Anton developed uncontrollable giggles.

During the resulting disharmony, Ginger finished emptying the bottle he was carrying into the punch bowl, turning away to avoid the powerful fumes rising from it. Then, seeing Cass gearing up to give the German's Frau a handbagging, he gathered her arm under his and muttered 'punch drunk', into the fat German's ear before steering her away from the mêlée.

'Olly's rather overprotective of me, I'm afraid.' Cass cleared her throat uncomfortably as the German, goose-stepped by his wife, was marched past them and out of the room.

Ginger smiled down at Cass with a twinkle of his blue eyes. 'Emotional people are so much more rewarding than easy-going types,' he murmured lightly.

'So true, Ginger.' Cass smiled stiffly.

'And Olly is intensely artistic.' Ginger steered Cass towards one of the floor-to-ceiling windows which formed a recess in the panelled wall.

They sat down on the lumpy window-seats, from which he could keep an eye on Olly talking to an older couple at the opposite end of the room.

'Olly?' Cass laughed lightly, inwardly smarting from her son's recent remarks. 'I'm afraid Olly was born with his father's pragmatism. Michael was far more interested in sport than women when I met him. A confirmed bachelor. Of course he's ten years older than me,' she added quickly.

'I can imagine.' Ginger rested his head against the window and watched lazily as Olly slipped from the room. 'Did you marry young? You hardly look old enough to have grown-up children.'

'Well, of course when I was a girl, to be unmarried at twenty-three was to be left on the shelf.' Cass went pink with pride. She suddenly noticed Amanda lurking malevolently in the shadow of the gallery beside them.

'You're still such an attractive woman.' Ginger smiled at her warmly. 'In your prime. These days beautiful, mature women are the ultimate commodity as desirable lovers.'

'Thank you, Ginger dear.' Cass thought the conversation was getting a bit risqué. She dropped her voice to a whisper. 'I think Sophia's little friend, Amanda, has been very let down this week. Would you be an absolute angel and give her a couple of dances later, Ginger? I'm sure a smooth talker like you could cheer her up.'

'If you want me to, Cass, then I will. But on one condition,' he leaned forward and spoke into her ear, 'for every dance with her, I can claim two with you.'

'Oh, how nice,' Cass said in a strangled voice.

'I am thinking, what is jolie femme doing with only a child to talk to?' A waft of garlic and red wine announced the arrival of Anton and his wilting rose. 'I say to myself, I say "Anton – there is a woman who is wanting the conversation of an adult, not a schoolboy. There is a woman who is needing a man." So 'ere 'e is!' Showing a lot of gold teeth, he laughed immoderately and kissed Cass's hand with a gallant flourish.

Smiling, Ginger gave Cass a blue-eyed wink and moved away to find Olly, who was no doubt currently engaged in removing every three-ply loo roll from the house at Marcus's request.

The barn was literally pulsating. Hundreds of sweat-drenched teenagers, their thin arms flailing, hips stabbing the moist air around them, feet stamping the ground like frenzied revolutionaries, gripped whistles between their teeth and blew a shrieking percussion to the thudding beat. Lasers, slashing though the gloom, oscillated on entangled groups of limbs. Pony-tails whipped against Vaporub-smeared faces, jaws chewed gum with goat-like tempo, pausing occasionally to tug at an Evian bottle like a calf at a teat.

Marcus started a twelve-inch garage funk mix spinning, unhooked his headphones and went to find Todd. The grinning Australian was upstairs, helping out behind the bar.

'Todd, my man!' Marcus screeched and went into his intricate hand-shake and foot-stamping routine. Todd opened a Grolsch and watched him. Under the strobe lighting he looked like some sort of rabid stick insect trying to get a spider out of its underwear.

Half-way through Marcus's routine, a dopey-looking youth with a scarf tied around his head and a bomber jacket slipping off his shoulders loped up to Todd.

'I'd like some pills, please,' he shouted over the din.

Todd nodded and, checking Marcus hadn't finished, took the kid by the shoulders into a dimly lit corner.

'Right, mate,' he said, opening his bum-bag. 'I've got pink pills, white pills, yellow pills. I've got wopping great red pills, wicked little square pills, mauve pills that'll make your eyes pop out, these little babies here – blue pills – not for the faint-hearted and, the pièce de résistance, these here devilish little two-toners. What'll it be, sport?'

'Er,' the kid swallowed. 'A Holsten Pils, please.' He nodded towards the bar.

After he'd given the terrified kid his bottle – scaring him further by de-capping it with his teeth, an old party trick – Todd went back to Marcus, who had taken off his baseball cap to scratch his head and was now looking as if he had no idea what he was doing upstairs at all.

'What's cooking, mate?'

Marcus winced. 'You said you were gonna get us – like – a tab, man, y'know.'

'Oh, yeah.' Todd fished in his bag again. 'You sure you're up to this, sport? These things can make you feel pretty crook.'

'It's all right, man, I dunnit loadsa times before, y'know.' Marcus put on a suitably hard face while Todd handed over the tiny tablet. 'Er—' he examined it myopically, 'like – what d'ya do wiv it, man? This isn't my usual brand, y'know.'

Shaking his head, Todd bounced downstairs and out into the courtyard. Standing on the cool cobbles, letting the biting breeze dry the sweat on his forehead, he looked up at the gusting sky and the thin sliver of a moon. Then, patting the special package in his inside jacket pocket, he squared his muscular shoulders purposefully and strode inside the main house.

Todd finally picked up the scent in the long gallery. There, standing resplendent in his shiny cycling shorts, he watched in astonishment at what he assumed to be a bizarre English ritual. Some sort of courtly dance was taking place with women wearing dresses in varying shades of regurgitated fruit cocktail pirouetting around monochrome men, hands held aloft with dreams of having the daintiest fan and biggest codpiece.

The contrast between this and the frenzied, wanton writhing in the barn couldn't be greater.

In their midst, Tash, doing a duty dance with her stepfather, was tripping happily over her own feet, moving in the opposite direction to everyone else and laughing till the tears poured down her face. She was also, Todd noted with approval, wearing jeans.

Pascal, far from looking embarrassed by his ward, had irrepressible giggles, and kept doubling up, especially when they passed Sophia, who was glaring poker-faced at them over Michael's shoulder.

Michael himself – possibly as a result of his gammy leg, probably as a result of the unusual blend of pipe tobacco Ginger had just mixed into his battered leather pouch – was swaying rather dramatically, almost entirely supported by Sophia, with a faraway expression on his usually set features.

Alexandra was having an animated discussion with Hugo, with whom she was whirling round, pausing only to perform the intricacies of the dance: more arm-flinging, a few delicate steps and a quick circular promenade – as chaotic as queues at King's Cross station. Cass, pressed to Anton's frilly satin chest with her nose trapped somewhere in his large red bow tie, was obviously finding conversation impossible. Instead, she issued frenzied hand signals every time they passed her husband. Michael waved back like an enthusiastic pipe-smoking schoolboy.

Sitting alone at a squat oak table, gnawing at a long red nail, was Amanda. Apart from Anton and a German industrialist with a stained stomach, no one had asked her to dance. Hugo, meanwhile, had only come off the floor to drain glasses whilst swapping blondes. Amanda felt utterly desperate. If she didn't dance soon, someone would erect a trellis beside her.

Todd went over to the medieval ensemble, who were winding up the dance with a raucous hurdy gurdy and mandolin rift battle. He put in a request for something more mellow.

No, they didn't know 'The Power of Love', but they'd see what they could do, monsieur. He must be a pop star, sniffed the harpist disapprovingly.

Swigging a few more goblets of mead, the band launched into a medieval slow number. Smooching being kept to a minimum in the period that most of their material was written, it was actually a funeral dirge, but no one seemed to notice and couples started to drift on to the floor for a cheek-to-cheek shuffle. The lute player – now barely conscious – was playing at a completely different rhythm to his companions. The result sounded like Deepest Purple meets Hendrix in the summer of 1469.

Todd made a beeline for Tash, who was now standing chatting with Pascal and her mother. His plot was foiled, however, by Amanda – quick as a homing missile – with a one-liner that even Todd was impressed by.

'Dance with me or your dog dies.'

Todd danced.

Retreating behind a pillar to cool off with a revitalising swig of punch, Sophia watched her mother foisting Tash on Hugo for a dance.

Good old Mummy, she pondered happily. Mrs Worthington ignores advice again.

Tash looked terrified, her laughter dissolving into a frozen, wary face.

Sophia's smug grin spluttered into her punch as she caught sight of Tash's top beneath the beautiful green jacket. It was from Dolce and Gabbana's latest collection. Sophia had just bought an identical one in Paris. Her watering eyes narrowed.

How on earth could her sister afford it? she thought murderously. At least it couldn't be hers; Tash was at least two dress-sizes larger.

'You weel dance wiz me, Sophia, non?' Pascal, prodded by Alexandra, pounced on Sophia gallantly. 'I no like to see you wizout personne to dance with.'

'Er – yes, well actually I was planning to sit this one out—'

Too late. Sophia was already pressed against a stubbly puffed cheek.

'Don't you sink your mozer looks beautiful tonight?' Pascal asked dreamily, winking at Alexandra as they swayed past.

Tash was suffocating with lust as she moved around the room as lightly as she could. Not easy on inebriated feet. Her head was as light as air compared to sozzled legs which disobeyed her commands and trod on Hugo's polished shoes so often that he'd stopped saying 'ouch' and started holding her at arm's length.

'Oops,' she whispered blithely as she felt compressed toe under her boots.

Hugo ignored her.

He's hating this, thought Tash. But still she couldn't feel miserable. Champagne bubbles seemed to be bursting in every corpuscle of her body, especially between her legs. Oh, weak, besotted, befuddled woman, she reproached herself happily. This might be as close as we get all night. I'm bloody well going to make the best of it. She breathed in Hugo's spicy scent and leaned a little closer. Feeling the cool silk of his cummerbund against her stomach, she shivered luxuriously.

You're horribly drunk. I don't care, I'm having the time of my life. People actually want to talk to me. I've been chatted up by attractive, self-confident men, I've cracked jokes with American heiresses and gossiped with top models. And now I'm dancing with the man I love. *And playing with his hair.* Oh my God!

'Sorry.' She snatched her hand away and put it back on his shoulder. How could she let herself get carried away like that?

'You've changed your outfit,' he muttered brusquely.

Tash looked up at him hopefully, but he was squinting across the room, his face unfriendly.

'Yes.'

'It's a shame.' Hugo flickered a glacial smile. 'It was the first time I've seen you looking remotely presentable.'

Tash felt her face burn.

Hugo's senses were reeling. He was wrestling with a ghastly

urge to whisk Tash away from the dance floor, mixed with the unpleasant need still to hurt her.

She was so gorgeously, deliriously drunk, her eyes shining and a smile dancing constant attendance on her enticing lips. Yet, even when tight, she remained as baffling as ever to him. Clumsier, sweeter, but still distant and nervy, giving out conflicting signals. If he moved forward, she moved back. If he held her away from him, she cuddled up like a sensual child. Pouncing on her was too perilous a temptation. Hugo recalled vividly how she'd bolted from his room earlier that evening.

Better by far to get this dance over and carry on as he'd intended – getting out of his skull and chatting up beautiful, shallow women who laughed at his jokes.

'Tash and 'Ugo. They look ver' good togezer.' Pascal spun Sophia from one side of the room to the other in a flamboyant tango.

'He looks bored stiff.' Sophia glanced at them dismissively, concentrating on not tripping over her skirt.

Tash, Sophia decided, had dressed like a tramp on purpose. Hugo looked embarrassed, and no wonder.

'I sink they will be lovers.' Pascal, ignoring the beat, twisted Sophia back and forth as if he were playing a spirited game of swingball.

'How ridiculous!' Sophia's hairpiece had become attached to Pascal's cuff-link but she was too appalled at his last comment to notice. 'Really, you French have one-track minds. No wonder Mummy's not wearing a bra.'

Eyes narrowed, Olly watched his mother being propelled around the room with the lower half of Ginger's body. Behind them, Pascal was whisking Sophia round in very *King and I* fashion, ramming into couples like dodgems. They crashed into Cass but she didn't even glance up, her pink cheek firmly glued to Ginger's freckled one.

Olly decided he needed another drink – either to imbibe or to empty into Ginger's trousers before dropping in a flaming match.

But, as he launched his way across the dance floor, his attention was caught by a smell so acute that he gave a short, sharp sneeze like a Jack Russell entering a smoke-filled pub. Glancing round for the source of the chemical pollution, Olly saw a small minxy face with smarting kohl and a wrinkled nose. Rolling her eyes, she mouthed 'help' from underneath the manly clutches of a white linen armpit.

Olly followed the armpit up and tapped a padded white shoulder.

'Yeah?' Todd surfaced slowly from snuffling Amanda's crew cut.

'Excuse me,' Olly smiled politely, 'but would you mind awfully if I take over the pleasure?'

Todd shrugged sulkily. 'Sure – go ahead.' He reluctantly released his grip on Amanda's small velvet bottom, gave her a brief flash of his steamiest smile and then, switching it off like a dropped torch, gazed around the room for Tash.

'Thank you.' Olly stepped forward as the band launched into another dirge.

'My pleasure, mate,' Todd said vaguely, watching Tash dancing with Hugo. Although they were swaying almost a foot apart, he had a feeling that the air between them would burn through wood. Then he nearly jumped out of his skin.

Shooting Amanda a ghost of a wink, Olly had gathered Todd into his arms. 'Now, shall I lead?'

'Hey – rack off, you great poofter!' Todd gulped, fighting free and backing into three couples in his haste to bolt to the bar.

Laughing in delight, Amanda kissed Olly's hand.

'Thank you.'

Smiling back, Olly shivered excitedly. She was very Vita Sackville-West and seriously, sexily androgynous. He knew Ginger mustn't be introduced.

'I would dance with you,' he apologised, 'but basically I'm really, really bad.'

'Come and have a drink, then,' Amanda offered, anxious not to be left alone again.

Noticing that his mother was now stroking Ginger's collar in a way that definitely wasn't trying to brush away dandruff, Olly nodded and steered Amanda towards a circulating waiter.

Cass, having been interrupted mid-squeeze with Anton to waltz with Ginger, was trying not to enjoy herself too much. She was a middle-aged housewife. Let that not be forgotten, she told herself firmly. Ginger danced beautifully, she decided dreamily. He had much better rhythm than Michael, and didn't lead as if he were driving a tractor through a rain-logged ploughed field. He had very sensual hands, too.

'You remind me of Joan Collins, Cass,' he smiled down at her. 'She's been my idol since I was old enough to . . . well, since I was a boy, really.'

Cass flushed crimson with delight and held her tummy in. *Tonight I have no children. Tonight I am a mature, sophisticated and sexual woman in her prime. Adored by young men wishing to learn about life and love.*

She hadn't drunk more than two glasses of champagne all night but suddenly felt as high as cumulus.

Tonight I have no stretch marks or cellulite. I am a rose in full bloom. I am free. Thank you, Royal Jelly.

She giggled happily and rested her cheek on Ginger's chest.

'Christ, my mother's wasted.' Olly shook his head in disbelief and turned away.

Amanda didn't appear to have heard. She was staring fixedly across the room.

'Seen someone you know?' Olly looked at Amanda curiously.

He liked her. She looked like a classy designer dyke and had a bitter-sweet tongue, constantly keeping him laughing with sour comments and dry, witty sarcasm.

Followed her gaze, Olly saw a figure amongst a group of film types. Small, sharp-featured and lean as a whippet, dressed in a crotch-length second skin of black silk crêpe, was one of the most carnal-looking women he had ever seen. She was scanning the room with huge, tormented eyes, completely ignoring the animated monologue of the tall, bald man beside her. With a whistle, Olly recognised him as a Hollywood actor-turned-director, Paul Monro, a famous playboy and recluse, noted for treating the press only marginally worse than he treated women.

'A friend of yours?' Olly asked. Possibly her sister, he wondered. Or an ex-lover.

But Amanda shook her head. 'We've never met. But I've a pretty good idea who she is.' She smiled at Olly foxily. 'I've a notion she and I will be firm friends before tonight's out.'

Intrigued, Olly looked back at the woman in the slinky dress. Monro was saying something into her ear. Spinning around, she slapped him across the face, quite hard. Rubbing his cheek, he laughed at her. But instead of walking away, she downed her drink in one and studied the room miserably again.

'Shall we get some food?' Amanda asked, draining her glass and standing up.

Glancing to the far end of the gallery, Olly saw his father beaming smiles and waving frantically at him like a mother at a prep school sports' day. He turned back to Amanda and shook his head. 'I think my Pa wants a word.'

Amanda shrugged and kissed him on the cheek. 'Ciao, then.'

And, spinning her empty glass between finger and thumb, she walked towards the ballroom without a second look at Monro's carnal friend.

Seeing six stumps, two balls and endless glossy, bouncing cleavages, Michael was beginning to feel very odd indeed. When Olly wandered over to humour his father over a quick duel at table skittles, Michael felt unusually emotional as well.

'Damn good shot,' he croaked fondly, trying to slap his son on the back. He ended up cuffing his own ear, but didn't appear to notice. 'Bloody accurate.'

'You feeling all right, Pa?' Olly swallowed awkwardly, hoping Ginger hadn't overplayed the proportion of skunk-to-tobacco. 'Only I haven't started playing yet.'

Michael's kind smile dissolved into giggles and, as he cackled and honked, Olly was suddenly reminded of Marcus. The physical similarity was unmistakable – huge, goofy grin and half-closed red eyes.

'Never bloody better,' Michael hooted, tears beginning to course down his face. He went to take a sip of his drink and, sniggering madly, poured it Leonard Rossiter style, straight down Olly's jacket. Screaming with laughter, he bent double and toppled over.

'Oh Christ,' Olly groaned. 'Here, let's get you somewhere quiet, Pa.' He hooked his father's thin arm over his shoulder and heaved him up, half carrying him towards the door.

'Could do with a bloody lie-down, yes.' Michael stopped giggling and sagged against Olly's side. 'Tell your bloody mother I feel like a bath.'

'Yes, Pa.' Olly tried to get his father moving again.

'Have a bloody nap first, though,' Michael sniffed, slowly straightening up and taking off his jacket; he dropped it on the floor before beginning to undo his flies.

'Pa!' Grabbing his father, Olly dragged him from the room.

'You know I love your bloody mother, don't you?' Michael sighed tearfully, straining to see Cass over his son's shoulder and almost bringing them both down.

The hall was teeming with guests. It would be impossible to get to the staircase in less than twenty minutes. As Michael began to snivel, Olly gazed around hopelessly.

Coming the other way, his hand gripped blue by his wife, the fat German industrialist pointed at Olly's drenched jacket and let out a snort of delight. Olly ignored them.

'Ma loves you too, Pa.' He tried a door to their left. The room was dark and empty. He groped for a light switch.

'Then I wish she wouldn't bloody flirt with schoolboys.' Michael began to cry with huge, croaking sobs. 'Makes a chap feel bloody geriatric.'

As they stumbled into the room, Michael passed out.

In the ballroom, Amanda inserted herself in the queue for food next to an obnoxious American gossip columnist called Larry Saltzman. He was even shorter than she was and had a face like a subsiding burial mound, but claimed to know everybody remotely connected to 'the business'.

Neatly side-stepping his sweaty little hands, which continually slithered towards her velvet bottom, Amanda worked her way down the queue for entrées with him. The food was out of this world, with trays and trays of mouth-watering delights looking more like art exhibits than edible delicacies. Amanda asked for stuffed vine-leaves and Greek salad. It seemed appropriate for the tragedy she hoped to create in Niall's life. Next to her, Larry had heaps of everything until his pudgy wrist was buckling under the weight of his plate, his thumb soaked in salad oil and garnish.

There were tables set up all along the terrace beside the ballroom, but most people chose to stand and eat to avoid the excruciating table-hoppers who preyed on the unsuspecting with an empty chair in their ranks. Larry Saltzman proved to be one of these. The little American dragged Amanda with him as he gushed, 'Hi there, Mel, long time no see!' and, 'Who you screwing now, Rob, you lucky SOB!' followed by, 'Well, wha'd'ya know, Emma, they let you out for good behaviour, honey? I thought you were allergic to it!' and, 'Jane, angel, you look younger than ever – and I can hardly see the scars!'

At last Amanda got what she wanted. 'Of course, you've met Lisette and Paul, haven't you, Amy? The village's hottest couple. This must be an all-time record for you, Paul sweetheart, three weeks, is it? The press are getting bored. I can hear the sound of lawyers sharpening their pencils for a settlement from my hotel suite. What are you gonna go for, Lisette, honey? The Palm Beach mansion or the Hawaii hole-up, the choice is yours!'

'Fuck off, Saltzman.' Paul eyed Amanda with interest, a practised appraisal which burnt holes in her black velvet and made her legs quiver. 'I'm Paul Monro.' He held out his hand to her. Despite looking older and balder than the air-brushed photographs of him which graced endless women's glossies, he was undeniably sexy.

'I know. Amanda Fraser-Roberts.' She shook it firmly. This

wasn't the time to flirt, tempting as it was. Instead, she looked from the playboy legend to Lisette, waiting for an introduction.

Saltzman was now rabbiting on about an actress who was turned down for the lead in a current movie because she'd been so drunk she'd slept with the wrong producer to get the part. Paul was smouldering at Amanda from behind a litre of mead. Lisette was looking as if someone had put battery acid in her salmon mousse. Clearly no one was going to introduce them formally.

'You're Lisette O'Shaughnessy, aren't you?' Amanda skewered an olive and looked at her.

'Why do you use my married name?' Lisette eyed her suspiciously. If this woman was a friend of Saltzman she was probably press wanting a new angle on her break-up with Niall. She certainly looked hard-nosed enough to be paparazzi. Sophia obviously hadn't a strict enough door policy; British hacks were easily capable of forging invitations. Saltzman was harmless enough but the UK gutter press could take her to pieces. Her career was in detritus as it was.

'Have we met?' she snapped.

'No.' Amanda sucked her fork, watching Lisette through narrowed eyes. 'But I think we have a lot in common.'

'Oh yes?' *Oh no.* A young hopeful wanting a break, hanging on Saltzman's oversize shirt-tails to get an introduction or two. It was an age-old method of infiltrating Hollywood. It seldom worked. Lisette conveniently forgot she herself got in that way.

'Yes.' Amanda looked at the pinched little face and hard eyes. Had Niall actually thought they looked the same? She might have better legs but I could give her a good five years, she thought. 'We in fact have some*one* in common.'

'Really?' *Boring.* This woman was getting seriously on Lisette's already tranqued nerves. Was she going to dig up some mutual school chum to smooth her path? Too gross.

'Yes.' And fuck off yourself, thought Amanda. Uptight cow. 'He's scruffy, dissipated, sensitive, opinionated and Irish. He talks in his sleep and has a mole on the inside of his – hang on – left thigh.' She popped the olive in her mouth with a smile. Niall had used her as a surrogate wife and pharmacist rolled into one. Now she was going to thoroughly enjoy ripping him apart.

'I'm going for a pee.' Lisette turned to Paul, who was exchanging lingering eye-meets with a nearby redhead. She handed Saltzman her barely touched plate and jerked her head at Amanda, indicating for her to follow.

'But I haven't told you about her affair with a Greek fish-monger who told her he was Onassis's long-lost son!' wailed Saltzman, who hadn't stopped talking, his mouth full of seafood.

'Another lifetime.' Amanda handed him her plate as well and followed Lisette.

Saltzman shrugged and started to finish what Amanda had left. *Luscious Lisette in Lesbian Loo Liaison.* It had a pleasant colonial ring to it, he mused. The English were obsessed by toilets and closets. He'd sell it anonymously to that nice Australian magnate he'd met earlier. That way he'd protect his reputation in the States.

These British bitches were all the same, he reflected sourly, spearing a cube of feta cheese. Boarding school hang-ups, those good old days in the shower after lacrosse, old bean. Smiling to himself, Saltzman spotted an old acquaintance.

'Liz, honey! You're half the woman you were. Can I have a quote now your jaw's been unwired?'

39

Drifting from group to group in the hallway, ears alert for late arrivals or early leavers, smile beaming on and off like a smuggler's flashlight, Sophia saw Lisette O'Shaughnessy talking to Amanda in a gloomy recess beside the staircase.

She watched for a moment or two over the rim of her punch cup. Both women were talking with stiff-jawed restraint, like mothers supporting rival school teams on the touch line. Lisette's eyes raked the room over Amanda's bare brown shoulder and, when Amanda glanced around, she had the satisfied grin of a cat that's just deposited a mangled chaffinch at the feet of an ornithologist.

Unable to resist a moment longer, Sophia whisked over to the two women, giving the snake-charmer a wide berth en route. The whiskery little man was currently wrapping his muscular boa around the sinewy brown neck of the rock star-turned actor, Huey Jonson. Sophia glanced longingly over her shoulder. She'd had a crush on dark, swarthy Huey since her teens. The Latin-looking New Yorker had held his guitar at suggestive angles across her dormitory walls for years. Even now, with a pot belly, face-lift, Grecianed hair and a permanent room at Betty Ford, he still left Sophia tongue-tied whenever she met him.

'Lisette, darling, *so* glad you could come.' Sophia kissed the cloud of Fidgi on either side of Lisette's hollow cheeks. 'I see you've met Amanda – I bet you two girls have got loads in common.'

'Don't stir, Sophia.' Amanda nudged her away with her eyes.

Sophia pretended to ignore her. 'Yes, everyone's commented on how similar you are. In fact . . .'

As she opened her mouth to tell Sophia to piss off, Amanda was saved the trouble by the appearance of Huey Jonson, oozing Latin charm and the smell of poppers as he ran a beautifully manicured finger along Sophia's breastbone and down the length of her arm before taking her hand and kissing it, his eyes constantly smouldering into her cleavage.

'Oh,' Sophia squawked, caught between horror and excitement.

'Lady Guarlford.' He smiled his most sultry Latin smile, lifting a plucked, vaselined eyebrow. 'Enchanté.'

'Gosh.' Sophia coloured. 'Mr Jons – I mean, Huey. So glad you could come.'

'Wouldn't miss it for the world, your ladyship.' Huey's blue contact lenses twinkled, hiding completely dilated, drugged-out pupils. 'I wonder if I could request the pleasure of a dance to thank you for your kind invitation?'

'But of course.' Sophia went even more puce and glanced at Ben, who was nose-to-nose with Hugo, as he had been for the past half-hour, discussing crop rotation. 'It's just through here.' She pointed the way to the long gallery where the medieval band had just restarted.

'Er, I can't do that fancy stuff, your Ladyship.' Huey winked a surgically lifted, mascara-ed eye suggestively. 'I heard there was a disco somewhere.'

'Oh.' Sophia listened to the flagellating pulse that was currently thumping from the barn and wondered if her Chanel was up to it. But Huey was frightfully – well – Latin, she reflected.

'Why not?' she smiled, leading the way to the courtyard.

'What on earth?' Ginger watched with wide, amused eyes and an open mouth as Sophia and Huey shimmied past. 'But he's the biggest quee—' Realising he was with Cass and not Olly, he abruptly shut up.

'Oh – it's him.' Cass followed his gaze excitedly, her mouth disappearing with disapproval. 'Yes, Olly's a fan of his too – terrible slob, always being exposed by the *Mail* for getting squiffy at Jerry Hall's barbecues.'

Ginger's mouth curled thoughtfully, then he caught sight of Olly chatting to the snake-charmer. Olly had a large wet stain on his jacket and his usually sleek hair was on end. Their eyes met and for a brief moment Olly glared. Then he batted his eyes towards Huey Jonson, gave a quick wink and turned away.

'Yes, I think Olly met him at Piano Bar once,' Ginger mused happily.

In the chattering banqueting hall, Hugo was talking to a ravishingly pretty tall woman with acres of blonde corkscrews cascading down her back. Watching them through her glass, Tash felt a hard bullet of jealousy puncture one lung. The blonde honked a snorting, artificial laugh and laid a delicate hand on his arm. Tash winced, resisting the temptation to bolt across and remove it with some giant pliers.

'Are you all right?' The man with the tomato-red jacket and sandy eyelashes who'd been telling an impervious Tash a long and complicated anecdote, eyed her closely.

'Er – fine.' Tash smiled brightly at him. God, she'd forgotten his name again. He must have told her about eight times. 'I say – have you got a cigarette I could scab?'

'Sure.' He got out a packet of Cartier and took out two, lighting them both with an expensive gold lighter before handing Tash one. The gesture made her want to do a quick Bette Davis impersonation.

She took another swig of champagne and glanced across at Hugo again. He was looking in her direction. For a fraction of a second, their eyes met.

For once the blood didn't drain from Tash's face and her knees didn't sag. Beaming, she shot him a wink before quickly looking away. Really, she should go and eat something to soak up the booze she'd shipped.

The sandy man had been joined by another couple and was introducing them. So many names, thought Tash giddily.

One of them, an alternative comedian, looked suicidal.

'Don't ask me to tell a joke,' he snarled, as Tash kissed him hello.

Half listening to them name swapping and dropping, she looked across at Hugo again. But he'd gone, as had the blonde. She felt a cold drip of fear run down her backbone.

'Are you coming to see the strolling players in action?' The sandy-haired man put his hand on her shoulder.

He had a lovely, crinkly smile, like Max, Tash noticed dreamily.

'Should be good for a laugh,' he encouraged, sounding just like Max too.

She shook her head, suddenly deciding he was incredibly boring. 'I think I'll get something to eat.'

'I'll come too.'

'Please don't,' Tash insisted. 'I'm a terribly messy eater.'

She skipped her way over to Sally, who was turning to stone with boredom among a group of assorted socialites.

Sally's face lit up with relief as Tash plucked her out.

'Wonderful social mix Sophia's got here,' she laughed as they walked together to the ballroom, where the clatter and clink of plates mixed with gossiping voices. 'The self-obsessed and the obsessed with the self-obsessed. Your mother's friends are lovely though. Have you met Danielle, the mad Parisian painter? She's been trying to persuade Jean to pose in the nude all evening. Valérie's got a calculator out and is discussing rates.' She was smiling happily, her face flushed from drink.

'The last time I saw Jean he was following one of Sophia's modelling friends round like a devoted puppy,' giggled Tash.

They were in the hall now. A pop star had appropriated the harpsichord and was banging out his latest hit to the groans of the crowd nearby.

'Too many bloody oiks!' bellowed a hog-like woman dripping in paste diamonds.

Tash scanned the room for Hugo. Spotting only a tomato jacket closing from the left and Raoul beckoning from the staircase, she towed her sister-in-law towards safety.

In the ballroom the buffet, at right angles to the starter, was already laid for the main course. Tash and Sally started queuing there straight away.

'I thought Matty might have come back for the party,' Sally suddenly blurted, nodding to a caterer who offered her salmon poached in wine and honey.

'Yes.' Tash studied her face for signs of impending tears; a wobbling lip or shuddering hiccup. But Sally merely looked slightly miffed.

'He is a fool,' she shrugged, 'missing all this great grub. Niall gone to fetch him, has he?'

'Yes.' Tash was eyeing the food. 'I mean no.'

'Oh, Tash,' Sally laughed, instantly happy. 'You're a useless liar. You couldn't be calculating if you had a silicone chip implant.'

'So people keep telling me,' Tash sighed, waiting for a liveried waiter to carve delicate slivers of crimson roast beef, her stomach groaning happily in anticipation.

Turning away to find a table, she saw the blonde Hugo had been talking to. She was sitting in a large group by one of the doors, picking her way through a green salad. Tash contorted her neck to see who else was there and felt floods of relief warming her toes when she didn't see Hugo.

'You've spilled half your food, Tash,' Sally laughed, righting Tash's plate, which was at forty-five degrees. 'Look, there are the Gallaghers – let's go and say hello.'

'I'll just get a drink,' Tash called after her. 'Be with you in a minute.'

No longer remotely hungry, she put her plate down on an empty table and collected a glass of champagne from a circulating waiter.

'You're a model, aren't you?' A wild-looking man with uncombed black hair and tomato and basil soup spilled down his shirt cornered her.

'No, I'm real,' Tash laughed, wandering past him towards the Gallaghers.

She had barely taken two steps before an ageing beauty with too much rouge pounced on her with an outstretched claw.

'You look just like your mozer! I'm Véronique Délon. Please to meet my 'usband, Henri, and my son Xavier. We live in ze apartment above Pascal en Paris. I 'ave seen your picture but I never knew you would be as jolie en personne.' She proceeded to rattle on in barely comprehensible English about how lovely Alexandra and Pascal were. Meanwhile, Henri and Xavier shone rosy-cheeked grins at Tash and nodded enthusiastically.

Tash listened politely. It was impossible to do anything *but* listen. Her glass seemed to drain by itself. She grabbed another from a passing tray but that emptied remarkably quickly too. Excusing herself, she went to fetch another from the trestle table in the banqueting hall. Her face felt like a three-bar electric fire. Imagining it was all Véronique's flattery, Tash decided she must cool off. She couldn't remember quite what she was supposed to be doing in here anyway.

Tottering through the house, she was shocked to find herself wanting to stick her tongue out, do a cartwheel and scream 'I'd rather be in Croydon!'

Instead, she went out on to the balcony overlooking the pool. A few couples were cooling off from dancing, talking in hushed voices as they looked out to the horizon like characters from a fifties romantic film. From the French doors further along the balcony, the sound of the strolling players starting their second interlude could be heard: overt British drama school diction and long pauses to drag out laughs.

Tash held up her face to the breeze and smelt a distant tang of bonfire.

Out on the jet and gun-metal horizon, the clouds were chugging their murky, nebulous way eastwards, indistinct charcoal clusters against the kohl sky. Dim stars appeared in their wake, like pin-pricks in an unlit big top. Multicoloured strings of light bulbs and bunting were buffeted overhead by a punchy breeze. The medieval music sounded more discordant and out of time from outside, muffled by carried voices, rustling dresses and the monotone thudding from the distant barn. The harpsichord in the hall joined the brouhaha as it launched enthusiastically into Handel.

A drunk swaying from the balcony rail gestured Tash over, but she smiled and shook her head, weaving down the steps to the lapping, blossom-filled pool. Sophia's floating paper flora was a soggy mass of papier mâché in places, the dye bleached away by chlorine. The flowers had mostly congregated at the edges of the pool, clogging up the filters and leaving an expanse of rippling water in the middle reflecting the spilt Quink sky with its watery moon. Later the pool would be illuminated by the light in the deep end to stop drunken guests stumbling in, but for now it was a subdued flowery well.

Tash sighed happily and sank into a sunlounger. Such a wonderful night, feeling so utterly and totally unhampered and languid. The calm before the storm. Tomorrow . . . no, if she thought about that her content would dissolve like a sugar cube in the mouth, leaving behind only sweet guilt.

She finished the last drop of champagne and tried to balance her glass on the white table beside her. Missing by inches, the glass shattered on the concrete below.

'You're pished, Tash old love,' she told herself sanctimoniously, 'and we know why, don't we?'

Her face still burned despite the cool gusts which were whipping the pagoda on the terrace above. She took off her jacket and tossed it on to a nearby chair. That missed too.

She'd been working herself up to it all night, she realised. All the booze was some wayward attempt at Dutch courage. Courage to do the impossible, to lay the ghost once and for all – to seduce Hugo.

Tash snickered out loud at the preposterous idea and reached for her glass, which of course wasn't there. It would be the perfect kill or cure, as Niall had advised, she mused. Envisaging how Hugo would react, she giggled again.

A twig cracked behind her. For a moment her head spun hopefully as she swivelled round on her hips to see who it was.

Parallel to her eyes was a pair of Immac-smooth, muscular legs, an expanse of shiny black lycra and what looked like a crushed walnut nestling underneath a bum-bag. When she looked up, a gap-toothed Pearl Drop smile nearly blinded her.

'What's a beautiful girl like you doing alone in a place like this?' Todd, with his usual original turn of phrase, took in the halter-neck top and openings in the jeans with an even wider enamelled grin.

'Trying to stay that way,' Tash smiled sweetly. 'Alone.'

It was a while before Todd took this in. With a laugh he pushed her legs – choosing the holiest bits and lingering over them – gently to one side and sat beside her on the sunlounger. Once there he played with the frays in her jeans, smiling bawdily.

Those close-together eyes have a certain magnetic power, Tash thought mindlessly. Advise caution, Captain. Proceed at your peril – on your own hedonism be it.

'Be a darling and fetch me a glass of champagne, Todd,' she murmured, deciding to do the Bette Davis impersonation after all.

Todd's smile didn't flicker, his eyes stayed tuned into hers. Tash decided her remote control wasn't working.

'Go away,' she tried the more direct approach, but it came out as 'Galway', which wasn't much use.

Todd ignored her.

'I've got something better than alcohol.' He reached into the inside pocket of his jacket. 'Far better.'

Oh God! thought Tash in a mental yelp.

'I'm not taking any of those hallushina – hallanusiagen – any of those mind-bending pills!' She sprang upright.

'Calm down, darling.' Todd touched her cheek and she jumped to the back of the chair again. 'It's more of a relaxant. Makes you feel good. Heightens your senses.'

He produced a small red pill. Tash regarded it much as she would a cockroach on her toothbrush.

'I don't want my senses heightened,' she argued. 'They're high enough as it is.'

'Hey, relax. Why are you so uptight?' Todd sneaked his hand through a fray and stroked her leg.

Tash swallowed hard. She didn't trust her co-ordination to make a run for it. She'd probably head straight along the diving board. Anyway, his hand was doing rather sensational things to those heightened senses.

But as Todd started lecturing about her lack of maturity and trust, her denial of inner sensuality, Tash felt instantly turned off. Couldn't he appreciate that she could only take in one-word sentences at the moment?

'I'm really thirsty, Todd.' 'Thirsty' came out as 'thirty' but at least it shut him up.

'What?' He looked at her closely. 'Oh right – gotcha. I'll get you that champagne. Don't go away, beauty!'

He sprinted off with a wobble of crushed walnut.

As soon as he was out of sight, Tash tried to make her escape. But the sunlounger wanted to come with her.

It seemed the worst of the frays in Max's jeans had become embedded in the slats. She tugged at them furiously, ripping the jeans even further until almost all of one buttock was feeling the chill night air, but still she remained twinned to an inanimate piece of moulded plastic. Tash considered taking the jeans off and making a run for it, but remembered she had no knickers on. Sophia would never forgive her for flashing in front of her entire address book.

Todd must have travelled by Concorde because he was back within seconds.

'What's up?' He watched her struggling and admired the exposed buttock, firm as a peach.

'Seem – to – have – got – stuck.' Tash gritted her teeth and freed the last strand.

She started to back towards the steps. Todd followed, still grinning menacingly.

'Your champagne,' he held out the glass.

'Thanks.' Tash downed it nervously and backed into a bush.

'Ugh – it's flat!' She looked at the glass. There were peculiar red dregs in the bottom.

'Ohmygod!' she clutched her throat in Agatha-Christian horror. 'What have you given me?'

Sally polished off the last of the Armagnac whipped cream from her dessert and patted her belly.

'That's the best you'll have for a while, French junior,' she told the baby within.

'I'm sorry?' Hamish Gallagher looked at her over his half-moon spectacles.

'Nothing.' Sally smiled and scanned the room.

What she saw made her freeze.

For there, chic, sleek and dangerous, was Lisette O'Shaughnessy. Thinner than ever, her golden skin stretched like Lycra over unfleshed bones, wrinkling slightly at the joints, she'd acquired the hungry, slavishly healthy look of a Beverly Hills jogger. But it was still the old Lisette. She was also looking black as a thundercloud.

'Excuse me.' Sally smiled at the Gallaghers and made her way over.

'Sally!' Lisette saw her approaching and pounced forward, emaciated arms outstretched, a cigarette clenched between two bony, red-nailed fingers. 'Christ, you look good, you bitch!' She pressed her angled jaw against Sally's cheek and kissed the air noisily.

'Hello, Lisette.' Close up, Sally saw she had huge, black circles under her eyes and a web of narrow lines around her mouth where none had been before. 'How are you?'

'Fantastic! Never been better!' Lisette was quivering with tension. She drew Sally away from the group she was with, hissing, 'Where's that bastard husband of mine? I'll kill the fucker when I see him. No good SOB shit.' Lisette was notorious for owing the swear-pot the most amount of money whenever they'd all met up, but her savage ferocity made Sally flinch.

'I think we need to talk.' She rubbed Lisette's arm gently. Great tears were welling in those beautifully made-up cat's eyes. 'Come on, we'll find a quiet spot and I'll explain what I can.'

* * *

Nipping upstairs, Olly tried to soak the sticky punch stain out of his jacket lapel. He then laboriously blow-dried it with Ginger's Clairol. But the sweet-smelling stain just set like caramel and started to bleach the dark fabric a dirty shade of pink.

Olly sat down on the bed and sighed hopelessly. He was having a lousy night. Having drunk nothing for over an hour, he felt exhausted.

Leaning back, he picked a short ginger hair from the pillow and groaned. He knew that it would be pointless trying to prise Ginger from his mother – seeing that he'd made Olly jealous, the precocious redhead would simply behave twice as badly. He was only doing it to wind Olly up because they'd had a dreadful row about what colour to paint the flat's sitting room the day they'd set out for France. If Olly waggled a colour-chart in front of Ginger's nose, he'd probably drop Cass like a cricketer with a hundred-yard catch. But Olly was far too stubborn to let him get away with turquoise and gold stippled borders.

He heaved himself off the bed and peered at his reflection in the uncurtained windows. His penguins looked awful without the jacket – the crumpled white shirt emphasising his rounded shoulders and thick waist. And his cummerbund was done up with a nappy pin. He'd have to change.

Then Olly hit upon an idea.

Creeping up to the attic, he listened for a few seconds at Todd's door. Hearing nothing, he covered his nose with his hand and nipped inside. Digging into one of the Australian's panniers, Olly extracted a pair of shiny black cycling shorts and a leather photographer's waistcoat. Then, without a second glance, he ran downstairs. Hidden in his wash-bag was a jaunty Georgie Girl peaked cap. It was very Village People and very, very Ginger.

Putting on his favourite Edith Piaf tape, Olly grabbed the tape recorder and his shower-gel, and locked himself in the bathroom.

Michael woke with a start and found himself on a silk-covered chair in the deserted dining room. Something was licking his ankle.

Looking down in terror, he saw a spaniel slobbering devotedly over his best socks. He slowly registered several half-chewed bones, two thudding tails and a mangled squeaky toy next to them. Kicking the spaniel away, he looked around for his jacket. His head was pounding.

'Bloody thing's missing,' he muttered hoarsely. 'Bad show to mingle without the full penguin uniform.' But it seemed he had no choice.

He scratched his bald patch for a moment and wondered how he had ended up in with the dogs of all places. But, other than the fact he felt close to death, no immediate solution presented itself.

'Bloody Cass should be looking after a man when he's a bit harry tired,' he told a sympathetic spaniel. 'Damn woman must be bloody drunk.'

He found his rather unsteady feet and went into the hall. The place was swarming with guests, sardined together in a screaming, gossiping mass. Models squeezed past each other to press their hollow cheeks against those of self-satisfied men fleshed out with salient riches. Caterers fought to get through the crowd without dropping their loaded trays. Loud men bellowed conversations across several heads, and shrieking Hoorays balanced glasses on statues and threw food at one another.

Michael stood in the doorway, letting out the spaniels and a delighted Rooter without noticing, and wondered if he was up to it. His throat was parched. He had to get to a glass of water.

Then, like a walrus in fuchsia Crimplene and a fussy pill box hat, Valérie appeared in front of him.

'Vous avez mal à la gorge, monsieur?' she held a bricklayer's hand up to his forehead.

Michael nodded his head, too terrified to speak.

'Venez avec moi. On ira chercher un verre d'eau.'

Michael watched her solid, retreating backside and followed as meekly as a small boy.

40

'Just went outside for a slash,' hooted one of Ben's chinless friends as he passed by. 'Huge queues at the loo – no bogroll.'

'Couple out there in full-flung battle – think it's your sister-in-law, Ben,' honked his wife.

They disappeared into the crowd like Edwardian explorers heading into deepest Venezuela.

Ben looked at Hugo and scratched his head.

'Wonder who Sally's laying into now? One sniff of a fur coat and she's looking round for a biodegradable soap box,' he guffawed, now at the pitch of inebriation where his own jokes rendered him speechless for minutes at a time.

Hugo didn't laugh. He'd been drinking steadily for hours. Yet the funnier Ben thought himself, the less entertaining Hugo found his own predicament.

Amanda was clearly being poisonous. Mutual friends were cutting him dead, but he hardly noticed. It was Tash French, occasionally flicking her eyes over him with the nervy enmity of a young dog eyeing a grouchy old house-cat, that made him feel torn through with a fierce longing. And he knew he could do nothing about it.

He pulled another brimming glass from a tray as a waiter minced through the French windows.

'Going to get some air. See what all the fuss is about.' Ben, now recovered from his giggles, staggered in the direction of the pool balcony.

Hugo followed, running one hand hopelessly through his hair.

'You dirty rotten brute. You think you can get anything you bloody want with your revolting, mind-bending substances.'

Tash – her senses heightened to the peak of anger – threw another swing-chair cushion at Todd.

Her co-ordination was totally decimated, as was her timing. She missed by feet and the striped bolster went belly-flopping into the pool.

'Has anyone ever told you you're beaut when you're angry?' Todd laughed, opening his arms and walking towards her.

'Has anyone told you you're a scheming, low-down nerd with chat-up lines as predictable as the Speaking Clock?' This came out totally slurred but Tash felt she'd got her point across.

Todd didn't. He enveloped her in a great, slobbery hug.

'Ugh! You need fumigating!' Tash wailed, gagging under the neural anaesthetic of his aftershave.

'Doesn't that feel good?' Todd breathed into her ear.

Tash's responses were now amplified to such a degree that it was like standing sideways in a wind tunnel. She shuddered in revulsion, but he had her trapped like a match in a bulldog clip, the air squeezed from her lungs, her arms pegged to her sides. She tried to think fast, but in her present state it was like asking Pavarotti to do a backflip.

'Streuth, you've got a horny body,' Todd gasped, kissing her neck like an overexcited Hoover.

'Get off!' shrieked Tash, and suddenly found her mouth full of Todd's roaming tongue. 'Ughmophiglereeuch!' She tried to bite it but Todd took this for the height of aroused passion and delved further.

Tash, seriously fearing for her tonsils, put her hands around Todd and groped for the buckle of his bum-bag.

Todd moaned in nerdish nirvana.

Mustering command of her senses, she fumbled around

trying to undo the complicated contraption while Todd, mercifully giving up on her mouth, attached his suckers on to her chest. Finally the bum-bag was free. With a whoop of elated relief, Tash lifted it in the air and threw it towards the pool.

Stumbling on to the balcony with champagne flutes askew, Hugo and Ben arrived just in time to see what looked like a large leather slug entering the shallow end's calm surface with a decisive plop.

'It must be a hobby of hers,' Hugo took in the scene remarkably calmly, 'throwing other people's possessions into swimming pools.'

Todd, at first too heavily in the throes of passion to take in the lob of André Agassi accuracy, gradually realised what had happened.

Surfacing for air from Tash's halter-neck, he realised that the curious shifting movement around his crotch had not in fact been the earth moving, but his bum-bag *re*moving. He looked from his cycling shorts to Tash and finally to the pool.

'You wha—?' he lifted his hand to his slicked hair in dismay before running to the lapping, floral edge and looking over.

For a while, the bum-bag floated like a poisoned fish, small brightly coloured pills filtering out of the half-open zip and bobbing around like exotic skimming insects. And then, with an obscenely scatological burble, it sank like a brick.

Todd turned back to Tash. Her heightened senses were now affording her an enhanced sense of humour. She was screeching with relish, clutching her bare brown stomach and pummelling the ground with her feet in delight.

'You've just thrown thousands of francs in there, you bitch!' Todd was so angry he was barely able to speak. 'You stupid, stupid cow! You—'

'It was the craving, hungry, yearning itch, Todd.' Tash laughed through her jubilant tears. 'I was a slave to desire. Whatever you gave me, it took away all control. I was ravenous for you,' she started to dance around the pool happily, 'wanted to rip the clothes from your body and just melt in the hot, burning, steamy, stifling, scorching juice of ecstasy.'

Gasping with hazy hyperbole, she came to a halt at the diving board and began to walk along it. She felt so totally turned-on. Rampant and wilful. She no longer cared what Todd had given her. It was wonderful.

'Christ, what've I done?' Todd muttered, watching her.

Ben was laughing so much, he had to cross his legs. He leaned against the balcony for support and let the tears pour down his face. He grabbed his ribs and gasped for air. Eventually, he slid slowly to the ground where he lay in a crumpled, vibrating heap of mirth, muttering, 'What's happened to her? What in God's wonderful bloody name's happened to her?'

Hugo, nailed to the ground in rigid shock, watched a scantily dressed Tash pirouetting on the diving board with her hands flitting elegantly through the air like a bombed Margot Fontaine.

He couldn't believe his eyes, he couldn't believe his ears, he couldn't believe his luck.

Todd looked as if he was crying as he stood dejectedly by the pool watching multicoloured capsules rise to the surface like champagne bubbles. He covered his face with his hands and shook his head.

Tash began to sing 'For Those in Peril on the Sea', for once in perfect pitch. She accompanied this with a few more pirouettes and a couple of high kicks. The diving board wobbled dramatically. She stood bolt upright in surprise before starting to pitch to the left.

With a horrified start, Hugo threw himself into action.

As he flew down the steps three at a time, Tash seemed to lean in slow motion first to one side and then the other like a silver birch in a gale. Hugo shouted at Todd to do something, but the Australian was too pole-axed about his synchronised swimming pills to hear.

Hugo sprinted around the side of the pool, knowing he was too late.

Skidding to a halt at the rear of the diving board, he moaned in consternation as Tash spun round. But instead of plunging into the cluttered water, she merely stood facing him with a goofy grin. Then, somewhat unsteadily, she weaved along the diving board and on to terra firma.

Hugo, gasping for breath from a mixture of panic and running, put his hands on his knees and looked up at her.

'Are you all right?' She bent down to his level and turned her head on one side with a concerned expression on her face.

He nodded, looking into her over-bright eyes, at right angles to his.

'Good.' She smiled sweetly before keeling over.

In the narrow pantry that ran alongside the kitchen, the caterers had stored the long trays of pre-prepared food, breakfast kedgeree and uncooked ingredients which would be called upon throughout the evening to keep the tables in the ballroom fully stocked.

It was cool, dark and airy. The unlit store had remained silent and undisturbed for most of the evening.

Rooter pushed open the door with his long, wiry nose and inhaled deeply and contentedly. Unlike his master, he was definitely in luck. With a quick check over his shoulder and a wag of his shaggy tail, he plodded in undetected.

Through a satisfied fog, Michael looked up at Valérie's broad, manly shoulders and red-veined face, which was blotting out the searing light bulb's attack on his brow.

What a wonderful bloody woman, he thought vaguely.

She felt his forehead with her large, capable hand and tutted disapprovingly. Reaching across him so that his face was swamped in the huge, heavy cushion of her right breast, she plumped the pillows behind his head.

Leaning back, she muttered something under her breath, shook her head and, with her grey bun bobbing, went out of the room.

Michael snuggled down into the bed and sighed with the sad,

tragic sigh of a devout hypochondriac. He wondered for an instant whose bed it was. Certainly not his own. It didn't matter, he decided groggily. He was ill, feverish, feeling bloody squiffy, in fact. And he was in capable hands. He had a vague feeling Valérie had carried him in. The thought was rather exciting. A fireman's lift over those Atlas shoulders. Michael found himself giggling like a schoolboy.

Puffing back into the room, Valérie sat down on the bed beside him. Lifting his head to the other glorious cushion, she pressed a glass to his lips. Brandy. It burnt his throat and put a fire in his chest. When he'd finished the entire glass, she kept him pressed against her voluptuous breast with her hand on his cheek, crumpling his ear and squeezing his mouth open like a snapdragon. Michael felt quite happy clamped there, protected and smothered by this magnificently maternal, wholesome woman.

The brandy had given him strength. He felt alive, invigorated. The fog hadn't so much cleared, but now he could discern shapes through it. And, as Valérie stripped down to her thermals and clambered in beside him, he decided they were bloody marvellous.

Sophia came out of the barn a tattered and torn woman, her hairpiece dangling from one kirby grip.

As she leaned against a vibrating outbuilding for support, her ears rang and buzzed like a busy switchboard. Her aching eyes fought to readjust from the strobes – it was as if a hundred panda cars had just arrived in the courtyard, blue lights spinning. Her chest heaved from the overexertion of trying to keep up with Huey pogoing and stamping around the heaving dance floor.

That terrible, hellish building was worse than Oxford Street on Christmas Eve, she decided shakily.

Sophia had felt like a Fabergé egg launched into a pin-ball machine. It had taken her minutes of panic to find the door in the laser-stabbed pitch blackness. She'd thought she'd suffocate, if she wasn't trampled to death first.

Among the mass of writhing bodies and spinning, flashing lights, she'd spotted two close chums' daughters bopping frenziedly, blonde pony-tails flying, cigarettes and beer cans held overhead to prevent them being crushed. One had been wearing what looked like a bicycle inner-tube stretched inadequately over her torso, the other was attached by the mouth to a lanky bean-pole with no top on his sweaty, skinny chest and a child's dummy hanging from a thong around his neck.

More dreadful still, Marcus had cornered Sophia by the doors, his baseball hat lop-sided, and a wild, maniacal look on his face. She couldn't be sure, because the background noise had been so overpowering, but she was almost certain he'd screamed that she was a pineapple pavlova before disappearing into the swarming crowd.

Sophia straightened her tangled hair and mopped the perspiration from her brow. Her legs felt almost too weak to move, but she knew she owed it to her guests to be scintillating and sparkling a few hours longer.

Feeling years older than when she had glided so gracefully to the barn minutes before, she gathered up her crumpled cream skirt and staggered towards the house, passing teenagers throwing up into terracotta tubs of geraniums and necking against walls, with arms up to the tattoos in each others' clothes.

A lit-up couple with both hands on each other and one eye on the lookout for their respective partners, tried a few doors at the less crowded end of the main hall. Most were locked but one opened to their preoccupied twist.

It was Pascal's study, until then in darkness. In the shaft of light which fell across the dingy dusty room, a woman's stricken face was illuminated. As she turned, aghast, the tears on her cheeks shone brightly.

The pretty blonde woman sitting beside her put a protective arm around her sobbing friend.

'Do you mind?' She looked up at the couple who were now standing transfixed in the doorway.

The crying woman was staring at the man with ill-concealed hatred.

'Get out, Paul, you bastard. Go give her crabs too, why don't you?' she screamed, picking up a book from the table in front of her and hurling it at him.

Paul Monro and his red-haired companion backed rapidly out of the room and shut the door just in time to hear the hard thud of Eliot's collected works make contact with the other side.

'Who was she?' Paul's redhead edged away from him, unable to keep her eyes away from his zipper, behind which apparently lay a host of creepy crawlies. She just hated creepy crawlies. Thinking about it made her itch all over.

'Lisette Norton, latest Hollywood flop,' Paul scoffed. 'Slept with a few big men and thought she could make movies. She couldn't even make a virgin quarterback.' Realising this reflected badly on himself, he added quickly, 'She was dumped by Niall O'Shaughnessy, of course. She's probably strung out 'cos he hasn't shown yet.'

'Is Niall O'Shaughnessy coming?' The girl brightened. 'I'm just going to mend my face.' With another wary glance at Paul's nethers, she clattered off on pin-prick heels.

Wishing he'd worn his toupée, Paul headed back into the throng with both eyes roaming.

Tash gradually became aware that she was sitting in a sun-lounger, not – as she'd thought – flying over Derrin Road on Pegasus, watching Max sunbathing nude in the garden.

Totally disorientated, she looked up at the sky, now pebble-dashed with stars, and felt her body ebb and flow as if it were bobbing on a Lilo. Shooting currents of electricity were tap-dancing on her nerve-endings. Her head seemed tiny, like a hairy hazelnut balanced on top of her never-ending body. Her limbs were buzzing with an un-familiar heat as if waiting to jump up and whisk her off somewhere.

'Do you want some coffee?' The voice was gruffer than usual, but still so painfully familiar. Tash's heart threw itself into her throat with garrotting results.

Trying to sit up slowly, she found her torso was stapled to the plastic chair like a lead weight. She tried again and this time sprang upright like a trodden-on rake, leaving her senses reeling behind on the headrest.

'Thanks.' She took the cup from Hugo's outstretched arm but couldn't work out what to do with it.

Glancing at Hugo's face, Tash saw it was full of worry and affection. She stared incredulously. As far as she was aware, this one wasn't in his repertoire of facial expressions.

So that's it, she realised happily. I'm dreaming.

'Careful, you'll burn your hand,' Hugo warned, nodding at the cup.

'Oh yes.' Now that he'd pointed it out, the cup was scalding. Tash looked around in a panic for somewhere to put it and ended up handing it back.

'Here.' He leaned forward and held it gently to her lips.

She could taste strong, continental coffee and smell Hugo's warm, spicy body. Dreams were remarkable things, she decided. Smellyvision in the comfort of your own bed.

'Better?' Hugo took away the cup and looked at her again.

'Mmm, lovely.' Tash nodded.

She still felt as if she was plugged into a mains socket, but at least her co-ordination had returned. Looking around, she suddenly noticed that they were beside the pool.

Perhaps I fell in and drowned, she pondered.

Todd probably murdered her for soaking his merchandise. That was it: she wasn't dreaming, she was dead. Not a bad heaven for an agnostic.

'Where's Todd?' This theory needed testing.

Hugo's face hardened. 'Why do you want to know?'

That was helpful.

'No reason. I just thought he was here.'

'If you must know, I took him into the kitchen when I went to make your coffee. He—'

'You made my coffee?' Tash laughed in delight.

It was the nicest thing he'd ever done for her. A cup of coffee. She should treasure it. Whipping back the cup, she examined its murky contents lovingly.

'Of course I bloody did. You weren't up to boiling a kettle and doing Gareth Hunt impersonations.'

Hugo decided she was acting very oddly indeed. He'd assumed she was just pissed, but she was talking and moving normally.

What a nice dream, thought Tash. Positively her best. She contemplated what she should do next. That was the lovely thing about dreams. One could do what one liked without feeling intimidated or guilty.

She watched Hugo's mouth as he asked her if she was feeling all right. Having been kissed by it so many times in her other dreams, she knew every insolent curve; the way it showed a line of white teeth when it smiled and an entire mouthful, fillings and all, when it shouted.

She willed it to come towards her. It didn't. She sulkily handed him back the coffee

Hugo was horrified to find himself feeling as shy as a twelve-year-old virgin at a Young Farmers' barn dance watching a bouncing cleavage. He'd engineered this so that they'd be alone together. He'd waited for Tash to come round like a lurcher by a rabbit hole, patient and calculating, with the intent purpose of taking advantage.

But now he was here, with her half-focused eyes looking at his mouth in a way that made every hair on his spine quiver with excitement, he hadn't the guts to move. For the first time in his life he was unsure of himself.

Tash gave up willing and looked up at the sky again. It was quite still now, a wide speckled blanket.

Hugo was sitting motionless beside her, deep in thought.

Turning to face him, Tash mustered courage. It's now or never, she told herself and slowly let her fingers drift to the soft hollow beneath his ear, dropping it down to where the tanned neck dipped into a crisp white collar. His detached, Delft-blue eyes gave nothing away, half-hidden behind the silky tortoise-shell hair she'd wanted to stroke since her teens.

Tash tilted her head upwards and saw a look of complete surprise register on Hugo's face. Then, in an instant, his mouth was moving towards hers, too.

As their lips met and sparks shuttled through Tash's nerve-ends, a bellowing voice hiccuped from the balcony.

'You doing all right now, Tash darling? Managed to dump that idiot, Todd. So I've brought us all some shampoo.'

Spinning round, Tash saw Ben lurching his way towards them, a bottle of champagne swinging between the fingers of one hand, three glasses in the other.

How dare he be in my dream! she thought furiously.

And then it dawned on her.

She felt the warmth of Hugo's hand under hers and saw the turmoil and confusion on his face. Instantly, she felt the chilly plastic of the seat against her bare buttock and shivered as a chilly gust nipped at her back.

Looking down, she noticed her exposed arms were covered with goose bumps.

'Nobody dreams goose bumps,' she said faintly, picking her crumpled jacket from the ground and wrapping it around her shoulders.

41

Popping into her own loo in a vague hope of finding some paper still intact on its roll, Alexandra was amazed to find Todd rifling through her bathroom cabinet.

'Darling – are you all right?' she asked cautiously as Todd shot a box of depilatories across the room in surprise.

'I – er,' Todd gulped, bending down to retrieve the stray box, his pockets rattling ominously, '– I was just looking for an aspirin – got a bit of a crook head.'

Alexandra watched him thoughtfully. His red-rimmed eyes did look a bit crossed, and he was lurching around the floor like a sea-sick gull perching on a cross-channel funnel.

'You poor sweetheart.' She stooped over him, full of concern. 'Here, let me find you one. Gosh, you do look peaky. I know what'll make you feel better – go and lie down on our bed for a few minutes, if you like.'

Todd looked confused. 'You mean?'

'Make yourself at home, sweety.' Alexandra waved her hand vaguely as she searched through the half-empty cabinet. 'I'm sure we had far more than this in here – Pascal's such a hypochondriac, I always buy in bulk. Oh dear, will Junior Disprin do?'

Glancing over her shoulder, she saw that Todd had scuttled out of the room. The poor darling must be feeling truly grotty.

'Just crash out, darling,' she called through to the bedroom. 'I'll dissolve these in water and then I'll be straight through to pamper you.' Then, remembering the bed was strewn with Pascal's trousers and her old sundress, she added, 'Just drop those clothes on the floor.'

Creeping towards the landing door, Todd stopped in his tracks. She wanted him to strip. He couldn't believe his luck. A quick shag-stop with his luscious hostess was just what he needed to cheer him up.

He almost skipped around the sumptuous four-poster as he kicked off his espadrilles and slicked back his stiff hair.

'I'm afraid I'm terribly rusty at this sort of thing,' Alexandra laughed, tipping a glass of disclosing tablets down the sink and making sure she put two Junior Disprin in this time. 'I haven't played nurse in ages.'

Almost whooping with delight, Todd hooked his jacket over a balding slipper chair, making sure none of his pilfered pharmaceuticals dropped from the pockets, then plumped himself down on the bed. He loved dressing up – and older women were always so grateful.

'I hope you've got some protection,' Alexandra called, hoping Todd had paid up on his medical insurance. 'It would be just terrible if you caught something nasty, darling.'

Todd sat bolt upright. His rubbers had been in his bum-bag. Alexandra must have some sort of infection. He'd caught most of them at one time or another, and took far fewer risks nowadays. But the image of his hostess dressed up as a nurse had thoroughly over-excited him. There wasn't a single episode of *The Young Doctors* he'd missed as a child.

He looked on the d'Eblouirs' bedside cabinet, but apart from photographs of gap-toothed grinning children on ponies and mouldering geriatrics in wicker chairs, there were no condoms. Todd peeked into the top drawer, examined a frilly bra with excitement, then quickly shut it again. It was hopeless – Alexandra was far too old to need condoms and Pascal was a Catholic, wasn't he? Todd briefly considered going without, but guessed Alexandra would notice.

'Won't be a second, darling. I'm just having a pee,' Alexandra called out, leaving the bathroom door ajar.

Todd decided there wasn't a second to lose. Rolling out of bed, he ricocheted off the furniture in his haste to exit the room and bolt to the attic. He galloped up a back turret in order to avoid bumping into Paola, who was babysitting the children, then crept along the corridor to his room. Pulling out the contents of one of his photography cases, he located his family-sized pack of rubbers and, as luck would have it, a new bottle of Kouros. Emptying half of it down the front of his t-shirt, he applied a squirt more gel-spray to his hair and pounded downstairs.

Falling back through what he took to be Alexandra's door, Todd grinned. The connecting bathroom door was shut now. The only light in the soft-scented room was a gleaming, lagoon-like reflection from the multicoloured ropes of lights in the courtyard and a narrow strip of neon blue rising like dry ice from beneath the door.

Listening to the light, mournful voice of Alexandra singing 'Je Ne Regrette Rien', Todd dropped his shorts, peeled off his t-shirt, and clambered into bed.

'And you won't, darling,' he murmured happily, groping in the bedside drawer for the frilly knickers and feeling something cool and metallic instead.

Excitement churning in his groin, he drew out a pair of silver handcuffs.

'Now this is my kind of lady,' Todd whistled, clicking the cuffs around his wrist.

'I have no idea where he got to, darling,' Alexandra laughed as she joined Pascal and Anton in the bustling China Room. 'One minute he was lying close to death on the bed, with his pockets crammed full of my Royal Jelly tablets, the next there was nothing but a pair of espadrilles and an awful reek of Kouros – Oh my God!' She clasped her hand over her mouth and started to laugh. 'You don't imagine he thought I was going to seduce him, do you?'

Pascal shook his head and caressed his wife's red silk thigh. 'No, ma chérie. If 'e saught zat, 'e would have padlock 'imself to ze bed.'

Anton, translating frantically, choked over his eighth glass of mead and raised his bristly eyebrows at the gaping-mouthed Jean. But the gesture was lost as Jean, half draining his employer's glass of punch, hiccuped mildly and sank into the ample cleavage of a nearby redhead.

'Do you mind?' shrilled an arch West Coast voice. 'Just who d'you think you are?'

''E ees the younger brozer of Serge Gainsbourg, mon ange.' Anton winked a heavy eyelid.

'Really?' The redhead raised a thin eyebrow thoughtfully and, patting Jean's bald little head, had another sip of her champagne.

The atmosphere was electric. Tash couldn't look at Hugo. Hugo couldn't look at Tash.

Ben, however, felt wonderful. Being the centre of attention was a bit of a novelty. He could hold forth on any topic of his choice – and after several vats of champagne there were many – without being told to shut up. But why, he mused, when they didn't take their eyes off him, weren't his audience listening to a word he said?

'Saw three purple rhinoceros in Oxford bags fly past just now,' he exclaimed, to prove his point.

Tash nodded seriously and Hugo just looked blankly at him. The latter was opening and shutting the lid of his lighter with irritating regularity. Flick, snap, flick, snap. It was driving Ben mad.

'Amanda seems pretty cheesed-off, Hugo,' he murmured, draining the bottle into his own glass. Hugo and Tash hadn't touched theirs.

'Yes?' Hugo looked at him without really taking in what he was saying.

'Been a bit icy this hols. Used to be far more fun.' Ben raised his eyebrows and sighed, scratching his head. 'Remember those days when . . .'

Tash, sitting beside Hugo on the sunlounger, was facing Ben, who'd commandeered a deckchair for his fireside reminiscences, crutch leaning against it like a trusty crook. Her heart was skipping around in her chest and she fought an urge to fling herself into the pool to cool down. Her cheeks were still blazing and a churning ball squirmed excitedly in the pit of her stomach. She felt deliriously irresponsible.

While Ben was twittering on about some weekend in Amsterdam, she swivelled her eyes to the right.

Hugo was resting his elbows on his knees, his glass in one hand, lighter in the other, head down so that his thick hair fell over his guarded features. He'd unbuttoned the stiff collar of his shirt and undone his bow tie, which was hanging loose around his throat. As the wind lifted his forelock, Tash noticed that he was biting his thumbnail and looking bored stiff.

Then he glanced up at her and, just for a second, uncertainty and bewilderment flitted across his face before the visor snapped down.

Her mind made up, Tash turned back to Ben and pretended to listen.

Hot embarrassment and peppery mischief scorched her cheeks as she slipped her hand underneath the tails of Hugo's jacket and touched the warm cotton covering his back.

Hugo stiffened in shock.

Still staring at Ben, Tash unhurriedly let her nails trace the even bumps of Hugo's spine through the soft fabric.

'And then there was that time in the Gambia,' Ben chortled, producing another bottle of champagne from inside his jacket and starting to rip open the foil. 'Do you remember, Hugs? We stripped down to the raw and lurked in bushes, waiting to jump out on coachloads of tourists who'd read too many Wilbur Smiths—'

Tash smiled and drew figures of eight on the hard muscle at the base of Hugo's back. She pressed her thumb hard into the dip at the very bottom of his spine and felt him squirm.

'– got b-awful sunburn and Hesketh had a rash on his bat for months—'

Beside her, Hugo gulped his champagne nervously but didn't turn.

Thoroughly enjoying herself, Tash sank her fingers gently under his belt where his shirt was rucked up and came into contact with hot, smooth skin. Flicking her nails, she felt it tremble.

As she slid her hand up the inside of his shirt, feeling the warm length of his sleek, taut back, Ben popped the champagne cork.

Hugo jumped as if he'd been shot.

'You all right, Hugs?' Ben leaned forward to fill his glass.

'Fine,' Hugo snapped.

'Well, as I was saying . . .'

While she sipped champagne, Tash's fingers drifted down Hugo's side and round to his chest, feeling the hammering beat behind his ribs. She traced the taut muscle of his stomach, dropping her hand below his belly to brush idly against the first tufts of hair before sliding her fingers away.

Hugo was shivering from head to foot as if he were freezing cold.

Inside the warm fug of his shirt, Tash's palm massaged each side of his rigid spine and loosened the clenched muscles on his shoulders.

Then she realised Ben had stopped talking. He was looking at them both with a curious expression on his face. Her hand instantly stopped its exploration and she dragged her mind back to her brother-in-law.

'I *said* have either of you two got a cigarette?' he repeated. 'Am I that boring?' He had his hurt-beagle expression on. It was impossible not to feel sorry for him.

'Of course not, Ben.' Tash hastily removed her hand from Hugo's shirt. 'You were saying about the Dordogne?'

'I can't remember. Quite lost my train of thought.' He still looked put out. 'What about that cigarette, huh?'

'Here.' Hugo got out a packet of Camel from his jacket pocket and offered him one.

He turned to Tash. His expression was unsmiling and wary, but the Cambridge-blue eyes seared into her face.

Taking a cigarette, Tash realised with a rush of satisfaction that he simply didn't know how to read the situation. For the first time ever, she'd really rattled him.

'Course, badgers are an absolute bugger if they set up a den in your best covert,' Ben was saying as Hugo lit his cigarette for him. 'Had some of the little Trojans in Connolt's Hollow last year . . .'

Hugo's hand shook when he held out his lighter for Tash. She covered it with her own and leaned forward. Their eyes met on a level.

Ben cleared his throat loudly and Tash snapped the Zippo lid shut, releasing Hugo's hand and turning back to him.

'. . . course, gassing them isn't the answer,' Ben droned on, 'end up with a load of bearded weirdos pitching tents on your crops and hurling lentil loaf through your eighteenth-century glass . . .'

Tash stretched luxuriously and slid closer to Hugo. Their sides connected and she pressed herself softly against him, as malleable as putty. She could feel the warmth of his body and the violent crashing of his heart even through the layers of clothes separating them.

'. . . then of course there's baiting, which is even worse. Archie Russell ended up with three middle-aged women chained to his Bentley because his gamekeeper was bumping off their furry friends on the sly. Bloody townies simply don't—' hic '– pardon me – understand that . . .'

Stifling a laugh, Tash curled her ankle round Hugo's so that the length of their legs touched. He shifted slightly and she suddenly felt a firm, warm hand on her thigh.

She tried to concentrate on studying Ben's face. He had very long ears, she noticed.

Letting her hand creep up the back of Hugo's neck, Tash found herself curling her fingers into his hair. As she skimmed the hollows behind his ears and the short, bristly stubble above, his head yielded towards her stroke.

Ben gave them another odd look and Tash whipped her hand away.

'Doesn't it?' he repeated, like an impatient teacher.

'Oh, yes!' Tash agreed.

Ben smiled and continued.

'Quite . . . which of course gave old Stafford his third heart attack and bloody nearly did for him. Ma Stafford blamed it entirely on—'

'Ben!' interrupted an hysterical shriek from the balcony.

Looking over his shoulder, Ben saw his distraught wife waving frantically at him.

'Sophs old love! Come and join us. Having a wonderful chinwag down here.'

Tash felt Hugo hold his breath.

'Ben, I need you *here* this instant,' Sophia screamed. 'That horrid Australian's revolting dog has eaten nearly all the food, Cass is smooching on the dance floor with someone young enough to be her son – and Michael's nowhere to be seen, there's no toilet roll *anywhere*, Jean's passed out cold in the middle of the China Room and everyone's just stepping over him, and when I told Mummy and Pascal that I thought we should organise some adults to supervise the barn they *laughed* at me.' At this point she burst into noisy sobs.

'Sophs!' Ben leapt up, tossing his cigarette away and loping up the steps towards her without his crutch. He enveloped her in a huge bear-hug.

'It's just getting so out of hand, Ben,' she whimpered. 'Couples are going upstairs and not coming back down again. Some of the caterers are refusing to work because people keep throwing things at them. The snake-charmer's lost his python . . .' her string of grievances could be heard retreating into the depths of the pagoda.

Hugo and Tash were alone, side by side on the sunlounger. Neither of them moved or spoke. The only sound was the distant thudding of the barn, the louder chatter from the house and the lapping of the pool.

Tash, hardly daring to breathe, was suddenly uncertain what to do next.

At that moment, someone in the house switched on the light in the deep end of the pool. The water beside them was illuminated into a bright blue rectangle, chequered with glistening white lines.

Tash jumped up nervously and walked to the tall rhododendron hedge, wrapping her arms around herself in an uneasy hug. The champagne-induced euphoria and buzz from whatever Todd had given her started to drain away like sand through a sieve. She suddenly felt horribly, coldly sober and as if she were plummeting head first towards a marble floor.

Hugo was standing behind her. She could feel the heat of his body inches away, see his shadow eclipsing hers on the hedge in front.

'Tash . . .'

Rubbing her forehead with her fingers, she turned and looked at his beautifully cruel face. She remembered Niall telling her on the day of the market that it was Hugo who'd always held the cards, that if she once had him dangling on a string, she'd stop wanting him so much.

Tash wavered. She needed Niall here now, hiding in the rhododendron, linked up walkie-talkie to a plug in her ear, telling her what to do.

'Come here.' Hugo took the lapels of her jacket and pulled Tash towards him. She was shaking all over, but desperate not to let him wrest back control over the situation.

'Wait, Hugo.' She lifted her fingers to his lips and suddenly felt her nerves drop away like thawing icicles. Thinking fast, she ran an evaluating eye down his body.

'What are you doing?' Hugo sounded cross.

'I think it's time I tore you off a strip or two,' Tash smiled, dropping her hand to his chest.

One by one, she unfastened the small ebony studs of his shirt and then removed his gold cuff-links. Totally nonplussed, Hugo held up his wrists as if showing Nanny that his hands were clean.

Unbuttoning his braces so that they twanged upwards like bungee elastic, Tash lifted both shirt and jacket over his shoulders, and they landed heavily on the paving stones.

Hugo stood in front of her naked to the waist, his glorious

sinewy chest and broad shoulders shimmering from the light of the pool. He looked cold, perplexed and excited.

Unhurriedly, Tash dropped her hands to his belt and began to unbuckle it.

Groaning under his breath, Hugo leaned forward so that his face was in her neck. Then, without warning, the repressed, ferocious lust which had coiled up inside him seemed to snap. Grabbing Tash by the throat and pulling her towards him, he started kissing her hungrily, savagely, almost angrily.

'Hugo, stop—'

Tash felt his teeth cut into her lips and his tongue stab into her mouth. She struggled frantically to escape but the length of his body was pressed against hers, lean and brutal. His hands began creeping up inside her jacket with spiteful force. Long, powerful fingers wrapped themselves around her neck like a vice.

'Stop it!' she screamed, ramming her knee upwards so that Hugo recoiled in pain.

Breathing in sharp rasps, Hugo looked at her in disbelief, too furious to speak. Finally, raising two scornful eyebrows, he laughed bitterly.

'You're fucking mixed up, little girl.' His eyes mocked her as of old. 'I suggest you go and tease someone your own age, because here it won't rub.'

As he turned to pick up his jacket, Tash was shot through with a terrifying, cold-blooded anger unlike any she'd ever experienced.

Niall was right all along, she fumed. Hugo was shallow and selfish, with the sensitivity of a Jack Russell attached to a leg.

She remembered him lying beneath Paola like a reclining Buddha, recalled Sophia bitching that the reason Amanda had stayed with Hugo so long was because twenty-minute sex was easy to schedule into her packed diary. Hugo's idea of foreplay, decided Tash furiously, would be turning off the light.

'And I suggest you improve your lousy technique,' she said quietly, fingering her bruised mouth.

'Wha—?' For an awful moment, Tash thought he was going

to hit her, but instead he just stood in stunned silence, shirt in hand.

'You've set out to screw me one way or another all holiday, Hugo,' she hissed, 'and tonight – forgive my presumption – I decided I'd join in.' She stomped up to him indignantly. 'You see, just now – partly deranged through some revolting substance Todd fed me and partly due to inherited insanity – I found you irresistible.' She pulled her chin back into her neck and rolled her eyes tragically. 'But – strange as it may seem to you, and I'm sure it will – I rather enjoyed the idea of participating.' Getting into her swing, Tash resurrected Bette Davis once more. 'Quite extraordinary, I know. I might have guessed that a man who spends most of his life with horses would bite the back of my neck and bulldoze in as if I were some sort of two-legged sperm bank.'

Feeling drained, Tash plumped down on to the sunlounger to the sound of ripping jeans. Mustering dignity, she gazed into Hugo's astonished face.

'Look, I'm sorry.' Her anger evaporated and Bette instantly swanned back to her trailer. 'You're a gorgeous man, Hugo – quick, talented, brave as a lion. For a long and very childish time, I thought I was in love with you. I apologise. I'm sure you're a wonderful lover.' It's just that I've stopped wanting to find out, she added silently.

Hugo looked like an angry shark, who'd opened his mouth for attack only to discover he'd forgotten to put his false teeth in. He stared at her for a long time, his face alternating between arrogance, fury and hurt like someone undecidedly flipping channels on a TV.

Then his mouth curled into a wide, almost gracious smile and he laughed again. This time with genuine delight.

'You really are something bloody else.' He shrugged on his shirt and began tucking it into his trousers.

He glanced around for the studs but they'd bounced into the cracks between paving stones or disappeared under the rhododendron. He glanced at her again, still grinning, and straightened up.

'Come here,' he said again. This time he wasn't making a lunge; he was just standing watching her.

Perhaps the bit about him being a great lover was going a fraction too far, Tash wondered uneasily.

'Please?' He raised his eyebrows and tried to look endearing. It was quite impossible, given his face. He looked like an indignant piranha.

Tash stood up, felt a draught and abruptly sat down again. The rip in the seat of her jeans had become dangerously X-rated.

Squatting down on his haunches, Hugo reached out and held her face with his hands. They were rough and dry but surprisingly gentle.

'Look, this isn't very easy for me to say,' he looked at the ground, 'but you're right. I have been an absolute brute to you. To be honest you irritated the fuck out of me, then you excited the fuck out of me, which was even more irritating.' He smiled apologetically. 'I feel a complete shit. And I'm . . . that is, I . . . er . . . what I'm trying to say is . . .'

'Sorry?' she volunteered.

'And so you should be.' He looked at her again, a wicked smile playing on his lips.

Tash laughed.

Then, quite unexpectedly, Hugo stood up, pulling her with him. And wrapping his long arms round her, he hugged Tash tightly, rucking up her green jacket and plastering her face into his bare chest.

'You know, I've never really *liked* a woman before,' he said over her shoulder.

'Er, Hugo . . .' Tash edged fractionally away, aware that most of her bottom was being displayed to the revellers on the balcony.

'What I'm trying to say, you stupid cow,' he sighed irritably, 'is that I respect you, if you want me to get all feminist about it.'

'What a nineties New Man you are, Hugo.' Tash smiled, ridiculously touched.

Disengaging herself, she pulled her jacket back over her bottom.

'Friends?' Hugo held out his hand.

Amazed, Tash nodded and shook it.

It was strange, she reflected as she watched Hugo pull on his braces, but in the whole time she had known him, the idea that they would ever become friends hadn't even occurred to her. Now it seemed ridiculously right.

'Here.' She stooped to retrieve one of Hugo's gold cuff-links.

'Thanks.'

Hugo gave her a strange look. Tash supposed it must be his affable expression; friendly gratitude from him was so unfamiliar.

'I'll be holding hands and skipping with Michael Hennessy next,' she muttered, shaking her head.

'What?' Hugo looked up from fixing his cuffs and watched her through his hair. His innocent expression totally belied the fact that he had just glimpsed the most glorious expanse of smooth, round buttock.

'I said I think I need an enormous drink.'

'Touché.' Smiling, Hugo walked towards her. 'But first I need to ask you a favour.'

'Sure.'

'Can I kiss you again?'

'What?' Tash froze. 'But I thought . . .'

'It's just that Sophia's been watching us from behind a pillar for the past five minutes,' Hugo lied, 'and I can't resist winding her up.'

Tash raised her eyes. 'Hugo, I—'

'And since you were so critical of my technique,' Hugo looked the burlesque of hurt pride, 'I need a few pointers to brush up on my Lingua Franca.'

He caught a strand of her hair between his fingers and smiled.

'You mean Francalingus?'

'Exactly,' Hugo started to laugh.

'Hugo, you are *so* predictable.'

Niall must be psychic, Tash thought happily. I've exorcised my crush as surely as a teenager rips down posters of pop idols, puts up Monet prints and starts listening to Debussy. If he were at the party, she'd tear away from Hugo and dash up to him excitedly, gasping her news. Instead, she began to laugh too.

It was as if all the raw, sparking electricity between them had been earthed, discharged into the ground. They leaned against each other and laughed until they were gulping for air. They giggled and hooted like teenagers, wiping away tears and clutching cramped stomachs.

And then, before Tash knew what was happening, Hugo's mouth had found hers.

No longer laughing, Hugo kissed Tash frantically, like a lover united after weeks of separation, trying to compress a hundred, a thousand kisses into one.

'Da mi basia mille,' Tash joked uneasily as he came up for breath.

'Stop speaking French,' mumbled Hugo, running his lips down her neck and into the hollow of her throat.

'I thought you needed to brush up on your Lingua Franca?' Tash tried to buy time, her mind racing. She was beginning seriously to doubt Hugo's dubious concept of friendship.

'God, I want you.' He started to kiss the cleft between her breasts.

Glancing away, Tash stiffened. 'You realise why we're doing this, don't you?'

'Because we want to,' Hugo said simply, beginning to kiss his way back to her face.

'Because Sophia's supposedly watching from behind that pillar,' Tash corrected, nodding to the left. 'And since I can see her dress billowing like an America's Cup leader over there,' she slid her eyes to the right, 'I have doubts about your eyesight.'

'Oh.' Hugo pulled back with a wolfish grin.

'Hugo,' Tash didn't find the situation remotely funny any more, 'you did mean it about being friends, didn't you?'

'Yes,' lied Hugo, smiling at her. 'Exactly my feelings. Totally agree.'

Hugo wanted to marry this girl. He wanted her to move into Haydown, bear his babies, cook his meals, share his nags and lie waiting warm and beautiful in his bed every night. He imagined her smiling at the door of the crumbling house, dogs at her feet, welcoming him back after a long, gruelling weekend away competing. He imagined her helping him school his youngsters, diligently listening to his advice and nodding in agreement. He imagined her waking him in the morning with a tray of croissants, coffee and flowers, her silk dressing-gown falling open to show her beautiful, firm breasts as she bent over. He imagined her wanting him every day for the rest of his life and could think of nothing more complete.

'Good.' Tash gazed into his eyes and Hugo, for the first time ever, felt his heart physically shift in his chest.

'But as Sophia really *is* watching now . . .' Hugo grinned.

Letting out an incredulous half-sigh, half-laugh, Tash rolled her eyes at him.

'No.' She turned to leave.

'Please?' Hugo caught her sleeve.

'*No*, Hugo. I mean it.'

Tash was shocked to find herself wishing he were Niall. The thought made her almost giddy. She closed her eyes.

'Huuuugoooo!' Sophia quacked at them from the balcony.

'Now,' Hugo whispered. 'Now, angel.'

Hugo drew breath as Tash bent her long neck and started to cover his bare torso with tiny kisses, at first slow and light then faster and harder until he could barely breathe with lust. As she found his nipple with her lips, he whistled and laughed.

'Christ, I love you!'

Tash threw back her head in shock, her eyes as wide and bright with surprise as a stag caught by a bullet.

At the same moment, Hugo let out a deafening howl and clutched his chest, his eyes smarting in pain.

'You bit my nipple, you bitch!' he hissed.

'Oh Christ, I'm sorry!' Tash's hand flew to her mouth. 'It's just I thought I heard you say—'

'Oh, there you are.' Sophia, looking surprisingly dishevelled and jaded, bore down on them from the steps.

Then she noticed Hugo's bare chest and stopped. She took in the startled expression on Tash's face and went pale.

'Oh!' Looking furiously embarrassed and even more shocked, Sophia turned her head away and spoke over her shoulder. 'I came to tell you some friends of yours have arrived, Hugo. The Moncrieffs.'

'Gus and Penny? What on earth are they doing in France?' Hugo, fighting to look normal, wiped a damp eye with his thumb.

'Apparently, they're staying in the area,' sniffed Sophia, turning slightly. 'Heard you were here and thought they'd pop in after a nearby dinner party – no idea we had a do on.' Her eyes were very red from crying but they still managed to glare beadily at Tash's jeans. 'They're wearing *cords* of all things. He's got his arm in some sort of sling.'

'That explains it.' Hugo, suddenly buoyant again, looked at Tash as if she was supposed to understand too. 'Poor sod must have had a fall. He was top of the leader board too, short-listed for the World Championships. Must be gutted.'

He had a wild, excited expression on his face which made Sophia back off a little. She had no idea what he'd been doing to poor Tash – who looked rather disgusted, Sophia thought – but knowing Hugo it was bound to be lewd. Probably jumped out at her from the bushes. She'd never understood his sense of humour.

'Must press on and drum up some coffee,' she announced, starting back towards the steps, 'far too many squiffy guests. It's all Pascal's fault for providing so much booze.'

'Come on,' Hugo lifted his jacket and tie from the ground, hooking the latter round his neck and putting his arm around Tash's shoulders, 'I want you to meet two of the nicest people in eventing. You'll love them, I promise. And they're going to adore you.' He started to steer her towards the house.

Tash reluctantly climbed the steps with Hugo's arm heavy on her shoulder, making her stumble as he bounded up them two at a time.

42

Todd woke with a start, his head pounding. The room looked totally unfamiliar.

Reaching out to rub his throbbing brow, he found to his horror that he couldn't. His arm appeared to be trapped by the wrist.

'Shit creek,' he groaned, suddenly recalling the moment he'd excitedly handcuffed himself to the bed in anticipation of Alexandra's night-nurse ministrations.

'Hello there,' a voice greeted cheerfully.

'What the fuck?' Lifting his head as far as he could, Todd gazed along the length of his naked body and spotted Olly Hennessy perched on the windowsill, smoking a Sobranie. 'Oh, Christ.'

Olly was wearing his cycling courier outfit – lycra shorts bulging in very Tom of Finland fashion, leather waistcoat over nothing but a Remy Martin tan, Georgie-girl cap tipped chicly over one eye.

Todd was terrified.

'Like what – what are you planning, mate?' he bleated nervously. 'And why are you wearing my cack-catchers?'

Not answering, Olly grinned and narrowed his eyes as he exhaled a Tonto autobiography-worth of smoke rings.

'I mean – I really love you guys and all that,' Todd rabbited on. 'Like a lot of the boys in cycling are queer and they're a great laugh. But you know, I'm really a man's man – that is a woman's man. Straight. This is all a terrible mistake.'

Flicking his ash out of the window, Olly laughed and stood up, his sixteen-hole Doc Martens squeaking as he moved. Todd cringed back against the bed-head and pulled at the handcuffs. It was a brass bed – solidly welded. He was totally trapped. Closing his eyes, he started to pray.

Still laughing, Olly walked across the room and stood over him.

'Sweetheart,' he purred, making Todd squirm into a pillow. 'I have no intention of taking advantage of this opportunity – although you are very pretty and I must say I'm flattered.'

Todd blinked up at him, like a child realising the bogyeman is humming a lullaby.

'Only, you were having such a lovely sleep, I didn't like to wake you.' Olly perched on the side of the bed, shooting Todd on to the opposite edge, tethered only by his wrists. 'But I just *had* to wait for you to wake up.'

'Yeah?' Todd shifted awkwardly, stiff with embarrassment. 'Why?'

'I need to know where the key is to unlock you, darling,' Olly smiled. 'Because I'd quite like to use this bed later – and I think my lover might have a few awkward questions to ask if he found you chained to it, don't you?'

Todd wanted to cry. 'Er – I haven't got the key, mate.'

'What?' Olly snapped.

'I said I haven't got the key.' Todd swallowed nervously. 'I got the cuffs from that drawer.' He indicated it with his eyes.

'Shit!' Olly covered his face with his hand. 'They're Ginger's. Fuck!'

'What is it, mate?'

'He keeps the key with all his others.'

'Where's that?'

'On a chain around his gorgeous neck,' Olly groaned.

In the barn, Marcus was experiencing the beat as never before, now certain that he was reliving his experience in the womb, with his mother's heartbeat crashing rhythmically around him.

He gyrated and stamped on the crushed, sweaty dance floor, feeling like the most pukka embryo ever.

Wasn't that a huge haemoglobin swigging from a Heineken can to his right? he noticed excitedly. Crucial! He blew his whistle with renewed vigour.

Across the dance floor, a grungy hippy-chick Sloane had her cheek superglued to Rory Wiltsher's Joe Bloggs hooded sweat-shirt. She watched Marcus going into his foot-stamping, Vogue-dancing routine with deep admiration.

'Your friend's like a mondo crucial mover, man,' she shouted into Wiltsher's ear, taking another gulp of Evian and pouring the remainder of the small bottle over her hot, stringy hair.

'Huh?' Wiltsher removed his hand from inside her tie-dyed smock top and gazed at his friend Marcus, who looked as if he was trying to divest his boxers of red ants.

The grunge waif rearranged her string leggings and dragged Wiltsher through flailing arms and rotating helicopter blade hairdos to Marcus's side.

'Hi, Marcus, man,' she yelled. 'Remember me? Cressida Chadwyck-Williams – we like met at the Aldershot Easter rave?' She touched his shoulder, but he flinched away, staring at her with terrified eyes.

'Get away from me!' he screamed. 'You're an anti-Christ antibody. I know what you want to do but I'm telling you now, you don't have a chance! This dood is coming out XY chromosome or not at all!'

His eyes flashed crazily and he noticed Wiltsher.

'Pukka dood!' he wailed deliriously, slapping his friend on the back so hard that Wiltsher head-butted a passing gorilla.

'Thank God you're here, man!' Marcus looked at Cressida in triumph. 'Like, this raver here is my placenta, man. And if you come anywhere near me, he's gonna squirt you with white blood cells, y'know. Be warned, man.' And giving her a meaningful, mad stare he started arm-flailing to the beat again.

Straightening up, Wiltsher groggily rubbed his brow and gave Cressida an apologetic shrug.

'Oh, you poor thing.' She reached up to touch his sore head and encountered what felt like rotting iceberg lettuce. 'Yeuch!'

'It's slick-look gel,' Wiltsher explained limply.

'Really?' Cressida trilled in a strangled voice, starting to back away. 'I think I've just spotted Bruiser de Cadenet!' Flashing a weak smile, she disappeared into the crowd.

Extracting herself from a group of braying hoorays, Amanda grabbed another glass of champagne and, holding it to her burning cheek, stalked outside.

After tonight, she decided sourly, she had no more ambitions to find Mr Conjugal Rights. Just seeing how screwed up Lisette O'Shaughnessy had become was enough to put her off commitment for at least another ten advertising campaigns.

Resting her elbows on the balustrade rail and watching a few drunks plunging naked into the fluorescent pool, Amanda cradled her champagne flute in her palms and slyly elbowed a geranium pot off the ledge to make herself feel better.

At the other end of the balcony, feeling suicidally depressed, Todd hid behind a pair of very dark glasses and shrank behind a potted bay tree as two teenage ravers with Bardot hairstyles giggled past in search of their Australian peddle pusher.

He calculated that he must have lost several thousand francs' worth of merchandise in his attempt to seduce Tash French. And now, despite the plethora of female talent milling around the manoir, he felt uncharacteristically low in libido. He rubbed his sore wrists and shuddered afresh as he remembered Ginger Harcourt, fetched by a distraught Olly, freeing him from the brass bed. The redhead had then calmly upended a vase of lilies and a full ashtray over Todd, slapped Olly across the face and stormed from the room, shouting, 'I'm going to get you for all the Mummy you have!'

Todd didn't quite understand that, but he was beginning to relate. He was broke both in heart and purse. What I need, he thought glumly, is a rich sugar mummy.

As he turned to go, he spotted a narrow velvet body undulating languorously down the steps towards the pool.

Despite his black gloom, Todd bit his tongue with his sweet tooth and smiled roguishly.

As they swayed their way through another medieval funeral dirge, Cass stared dreamily up at Ginger's stubbly chin and sighed.

He was so attentive, she mused, so courteous, so well mannered, so dishy and *so* unlike Michael. He had a way of looking at one which made one's tummy feel feather-light.

'Cass!'

A sharp summons momentarily punctured her enchanted bubble. The tuneless twanging from a thoroughly sloshed medieval band came into crisp focus and she saw a red-eyed Sophia glowering over Ginger's broad shoulder.

'Mmm?' Cass stopped shuffling and gazed at her niece through a mist of contentment.

'I think you should try and sort out Marcus,' Sophia clucked like a ruffled bantam, 'apparently he's making a bit of a nuisance of himself in the barn. He keeps mistaking people for food and then tries to eat them. Sebastian Kelly's in a terrible state. Marcus thought he was a choc ice and tried to lick him to death.'

'Oh.' Cass looked at Sophia's fraught face and started to giggle.

'Can't Michael handle it?' Ginger asked, a protective arm still wrapped firmly around Cass, a smug grin wrinkling his azure blue eyes.

'He seems to have disappeared . . .' Sophia admitted with a rigid chin, refusing to look at him.

'Good!' cheered Cass.

'. . . with Valérie,' Sophia added.

Cass chewed Ginger's lapel in mirth, tears sliding from her eyes. Finally, she sighed happily, exchanging a childish smirk with Ginger.

Sophia shook her head with a resigned tut and gave up trying.

She left Cass leaning at forty-five degrees on to Ginger's make-up covered shirt and marched back to Ben, who was trying to negotiate with the harassed caterers.

Rooter had gone quite mad with greedy excitement and was galloping about the house with his tongue hanging out, tripping up guests. Having polished off most of the contents of the pantry – including a jug of mead – he was now intent on having post-prandial intercourse.

Several waiters had already thrown down their stained liveries and piled into a Renault van to roar angrily off into the night. More were threatening to.

Panic rose as Todd couldn't be found and Rooter became more experimental with his sexual favours. Until this point unconcerned, the spaniels suddenly decided this looked like fun and joined in with panting, howling aplomb.

A well-known opera diva, who'd just arrived from giving a performance of *Tosca* in Paris, was standing on a chair and screaming hysterically in perfect top B flat as the youngest spaniel did perverted canine things to her fur coat. Rooter, meanwhile, had cornered a terrified baroness and was licking his lips.

Ben returned from the irate catering manager and shrugged to Sophia.

'Think I've pacified him a bit. Offered a thousand francs to the man who could catch the dogs and bung them back in the dining room.'

He wiped his forehead with a handkerchief.

'It's all gone so horribly, horribly wrong,' Sophia muttered, close to tears again.

Ben thought this wasn't perhaps the moment to mention that he'd just seen Amanda and Todd stripping by the pool or that in the absence of toilet paper someone had appropriated the leather-bound works of André Gide and was systematically tearing sheets out for distribution. Instead, he gave her an encouraging squeeze.

'Lot of people have told me it's the best party they've been to in ages,' he said truthfully.

'Have they?' She looked up at him with doleful, liquid eyes.

'Absolutely.' Ben smiled, resting his chin on his wife's head and watching Michael staggering from the direction of the lodge supported entirely by Valérie, who was wearing fluffy house slippers.

As Lisette fell ominously silent, Sally tried to come to terms with what she'd just heard.

Some revellers had spilled outside on to the lawns. She could see them through the window, holding their skirts up from the wet grass as they played drunken chase, standing in gossiping groups or staring up at the house, lost in intoxicated wonder. One couple was necking openly. Sally wondered for the thousandth time if Matty had arrived and was wandering about searching for him.

'Well?' Lisette was up and pacing the room like a caged tiger on a starvation diet, pausing by objects as if about to pounce and rip them to shreds.

'Er, sorry?' Sally didn't take her eyes from the window.

Outside, she had spotted Matty standing in the shadows with his back to the house, talking with a rumpled, sexy blonde.

'What do you think I should *do*, Sally?' Lisette collapsed back in a chair and lit another cigarette with the butt of the one she'd just smoked.

'It's not really for me to tell you—' Sally started, her eyes fixed on Matty.

'If you were me, then!' snapped Lisette, tossing the spent butt out into the night air.

The man with the blonde looked towards the window, revealing a large, roman nose and a neck brace. Awash with glowing relief, Sally turned back to Lisette. Then the smile dropped from her face.

Lisette was staring at her impatiently, eyes burning, nostrils flared, long nails tapping on a table like an advancing army of cockroaches in high heels. Deciding she looked like Medusa with PMT, Sally took a deep breath and assessed the distance to the door, before saying in a low voice; 'I think you should leave.

Now. For your own sake as well as Niall's. Three weeks ago he was desperate, frantic to have you back – whatever you'd done. Even if you'd told him what you've just told me I don't think he would've cared. You all but destroyed him, Lis. I've never seen him so – so—' she stopped abruptly as she looked out of the window again.

The man whom she'd mistaken for Matty had been joined by Hugo and a tall girl. Even standing in the shadow of the tree, the girl was unmistakably Tash. Sally stared in disbelief as Hugo dropped his arm from Tash's shoulders and ran his hand slowly down her back, letting it rest just under her buttock.

Oh poor, poor Niall, she thought miserably. What an absolute mess.

'It's that bitch Amanda he's hung up on now, isn't it?' Lisette hissed. The acid in her voice made Sally spin round. 'She has a fucking lot to answer for.'

'No.' Sally shook her head, suddenly filled with an aching sadness. 'It isn't Amanda. They were never really together – only a couple of days, no more.'

Tash adored Hugo, she reflected sadly, like a battered collie still answering only to her master. The more the animal is ill-treated, the more servile it becomes. Eventually, something will snap and nothing can repair the decimated trust. But, unlike Niall with Lisette, Tash still hugged to Hugo's heels.

'Who is it?' Lisette repeated in an arctic voice.

Sally looked at her and shook her head, too abstracted to speak.

'*You?*' It was like a whip cracking.

'What?' Sally recoiled in disbelief.

She still found it barely conceivable how deeply Lisette could misunderstand a man she had lived with for almost a decade – albeit mostly days at a time between busy shooting schedules. In the chilling monologue Sally had just been sole party to, Lisette had described how she'd destroyed his baby because it would get in the way of her career.

Niall, being occasionally prone to Catholic hang-ups, wasn't keen on birth control and had encouraged Lisette to adopt the unreliable rhythm method. Niall, also being occasionally prone to one too many, had not been too reliable himself. The result was Lisette discovering she was missing periods for quite another reason than the excitement of meeting and falling in love with the young American rich kid, Colt Shapiro, who was taking Hollywood by storm.

She hadn't told Niall that she was pregnant. Instead, she'd jetted off with Colt, pretending that she was attending a preliminary interview for a job in the States.

Two weeks later, Lisette had sent a fax to Niall's agent. Niall was away filming in Rome at the time. The two sheets which came spluttering through Bob Hudson's fax late one night consisted of a confirmation of termination from an exclusive Beverly Hills abortion clinic and a hastily scribbled note saying, in the most blowsy, blasé terms possible, that she wasn't a wet nurse but a producer and next time he wanted a kid to ask first.

Sally didn't know anyone was capable of being as cruel as Lisette had been at that moment.

She thought about the baby now growing inside her, the tiny creation she and Matty had mistakenly conceived between them. The unthinking brutality of Lisette's actions was detestable. The fact she now seemed determined to try and patch it up with Niall was even more illogical.

'Do you still love Niall, Lisette?' Sally asked quietly.

'Do *you*?' Lisette snarled.

'Of course I do – but I'm not *in* love with him,' Sally sighed, 'that's just ridiculous. I love Matty.' The words made her want to weep.

But Lisette was too intent kicking up water to notice any undercurrents.

'Oh for Chrissake, Sally, we all know you and Matty are the perfect fucking couple,' she wailed in exasperation, 'with your dolphin-friendly bog-roll and crappy kids' drawings next to the Greenpeace calendar on the kitchen wall.' Lisette drew deeply on her cigarette. 'Look, yes, I do love Niall. Okay, it screwed me up having to share him with every failed junky actor or friend of his deranged family or single-parent Yugoslavian refugee that he ever met. Okay, I fancied other men – needed to in order to make the great oaf look up from his latest script. But I love him, Sally.'

Her face was so impassive that Sally almost wondered if she was thinking about something else.

'You should try living with a method actor,' Lisette joked listlessly. 'When he was playing Hamlet, he got seriously stroppy about me going to mass and wearing a wimple in bed.'

Sally didn't laugh.

'I want to make it work, I truly do.' Lisette widened her beautifully made-up eyes with measured sincerity. 'I missed him so much when I was in the States, it ate me up. When Colt and I split, all I needed was Niall but I couldn't trace him, and I hadn't the guts to contact you guys. Nothing worked – my career started falling apart, affairs never got beyond one breakfast and a gossip-column inch in a supermarket regazine.'

Can't have tried very hard to find Niall if she didn't even leave America, Sally thought savagely.

'Then I was at this party in Bermuda,' Lisette continued, 'you know the sort – everyone networking their arses off. Colt's has-been father was there – Clay – they haven't spoken since he backed Clinton. Holds his right wrist out like a queer because he's constantly got a line of coke on the back of his hand. He cornered me and started ranting on about this bastard called O'Shaughnessy who's getting all Hollywood's hottest scripts at the moment. Hearing Niall's name, I nearly broke down.' She lit another cigarette, hardly pausing between words. 'Clay doesn't know my married name, you see – can't even remember my first one, come to that. Always calls me Ruthie – that's some bimbo Colt was screwing in high school.'

Laughing hollowly, she grabbed a half-full whisky bottle from the bookcase and started to unscrew the top with shaking hands.

'Afterwards,' she poured three inches into an empty champagne flute, 'I just crawled back to my apartment – until I got thrown out – I'm staying with Paul Monro now.' Even in despair, she couldn't resist name-dropping, 'I couldn't eat, sleep, couldn't even get bombed any more.' She dropped her eyes to the glass, a gelled strand of hair falling across her golden cheekbone. 'All I could think about was Niall and how lousy I'd been to him. When Sophia Meredith invited me here, I bawled for a week. I'd been given the chance I thought I'd never get. To apologise,' she looked up, eyes narrowed. 'What I *didn't* realise was that my oh-so-loyal husband has been spreading his lackadaisical Irish favours further than a moulting thistle in a gale.'

Sally swallowed hard, fighting down the urge to slap Lisette's sparkling bronze cheek.

'And Clot?' she asked tersely. 'How do you feel about him now?'

'*Colt*,' hissed Lisette, suddenly shaking with venomous rage, 'is the biggest fucking swine that ever breathed.'

She stood up and began pacing again, tugging on her cigarette like an asthmatic at an oxygen mask.

'You know, I loathe him, abhor everything he poisons.' She stabbed the air with her dying butt. 'He's so selfish, evil and twisted he can lick his own fucking balls.'

She was sobbing between words now. Loud, frenzied hiccups wracked her emaciated body, tears coursed her cheeks, drawing with them layers of thick black kohl and fake tan. It was like watching the Mona Lisa doused in acid.

'He's like a little kid that gets bored of toys,' she raged. 'When he doesn't want you any more, you feel so goddamn ugly, like some sort of freak. It was him that made me send that fax to Bob.' She looked at Sally, her face a contorted mask of agony. 'I was so looped I couldn't even spell my name. He has this terrible, almost voodoo hold over people – some of the things I did when we were together appalled me. When he dumped me I thought I'd self-destruct. He didn't even say he was going – just got his new girlfriend to send a postcard from St Lucia asking for his house-keys back.' Tears fell from her chin as she gazed up at the ceiling in despair.

'And you still love him?'

Lisette's face crumpled and she sank down beside Sally,

whisky spilling on to her dress as she buried her head in her hands and leaned her fragile, heaving body against Sally's frozen one.

The saddest thing, reflected Sally, was that Niall had never mentioned what Lisette had done to him. Both she and Matty had assumed his almost deranged misery was a result of Lisette's departure alone. They had been too wrapped up in their own problems to delve further. Amanda, waiting all too willingly in the ring corner to administer first aid, hadn't really cared.

Only Tash had realised there was something else behind Niall's haunting unhappiness. She had questioned Sally briefly about it once, only to receive a castigating lecture on how much he had adored Lisette. Tash had shut up, totally squashed. Sally now felt like a general who had given orders to retreat and leave the injured to die.

Lisette, no longer crying, was staring out of the window beyond Sally.

'Isn't that Hugo Beauchamp?' she asked, straightening up, her frenzied tears forgotten.

'Yes.' Sally got up to leave, too angry to trust herself a moment longer. 'He's a house guest.'

On her way out, she followed Lisette's gaze and glanced into the garden below. Hugo was laughing with his friends, his right arm exploring underneath Tash's crumpled jacket. Tash's face was hidden in the shadows, but Sally could guess how she was reacting. When Niall comes back, he mustn't see them, she vowed.

'Really?' Lisette dragged eight syllables out of the word.

But Sally had gone.

Shrugging, Lisette extracted a pill from a phial in her clutch bag and, downing it with a swig of whisky straight from the bottle neck, she thought briefly and painfully about Colt before settling down to repair her face.

'I'm afraid,' she told her reflection as she attacked it with a tissue, 'that whatever female charity case my husband has taken under his benevolent wing, is going to find the punt's sunk.'

* * *

Amanda wasn't the sort of woman who went skinny-dipping at parties. That was for hoorays and air-heads. But something about the way tonight was working out had made her feel reckless. Still seething from her argument with Lisette O'Shaughnessy, she slithered out of her velvet dress with the instinctive abandonment of a snake shedding its skin.

The pool was the same temperature as her naked body when she slipped into it, resulting in a luxurious feeling of weightlessness, almost non-being. She shut her eyes and floated on her back, being gently brushed by paper flowers before colliding with a seat cushion.

After a few seconds of letting the warm water lap between her legs, she felt a pair of strong hands grab her from behind and pull her against a long, hard body.

Two smooth, muscular legs wrapped themselves around her.

Amanda sighed and leaned her head back against the sleek chest until she was being supported totally. They didn't speak, letting the gently rolling water wash over their warm bodies as they drifted across the pool. The sensation made a pulse pound between her legs.

Then a hoarse whisper tickled Amanda's ear.

'G'day, Amelia.'

She groaned and opened her eyes, about to roll away and swim as fast as she could towards the steps. But something about Todd's skilled breast stroke made her change her mind.

Other couples had come outside and were undressing excitedly with eager whoops of laughter. Some didn't wait, simply jumping in fully clothed, pushing each other's heads underwater and splashing riotously.

Someone had located a chewed-looking football and was kicking off a game of water polo in the deep end.

A divorced duchess, in saturated silk undies, marked her polo player friend ferociously, despite the fact he was on her own team. The referee, distracted by a glorious full frontage belonging to a member of a highly renowned English family, lost count of the goals, but nobody seemed to mind. A Sloaney all-girl pop group were syncro-swimming in the middle of the game, an overweight drunk had annexed Lotty's fluorescent arm-bands and the seat cushion and was bobbing like a radioactive whale in the shallow end.

One of the spaniels ran around the edge of the pool barking frantically at everyone before losing control completely and peeing on a discarded black velvet dress.

In the shadow of the empty swing-chair an uninvited photographer adjusting his aperture couldn't believe his luck.

The flash went off with a whir of automatic wind-on. Breaking from their conversation for a split second, Alexandra, Pascal and Anton turned to beam at the blinding light before immediately resuming their merry banter. Jean remained snoring beside the buxom redhead with his mouth open and a half-empty punch glass in his hand, much as he had been for the past half-hour. The redhead reached across and pinched his nose for a second or two so that Jean spluttered and gasped in his sleep, reducing his snores to a subdued wheeze.

'Works every time, honey,' she smiled at Alexandra, then gazed wistfully back at Jean. 'You know, he doesn't look a bit like his brother.'

'But, sweetheart, he and Claude are identical twins.' Alexandra smiled and then glanced at her watch. 'You know I'm rather worried, darlings,' she dropped her voice and looked up at her companions almost tearfully, 'this party was supposed to be for my brother, Eddie. And he hasn't turned up.'

'Wonderful thrash, Lex,' a drunk lurched into Alexandra's cheek, spitting peanut fragments, 'you and Pastel must come to Bermont sometime.' Shaking Anton's hand so vigorously that a cuff-link flew out and hit Jean on the nose, he lurched away.

Seeing Pascal's shocked face, Anton coughed noisily to hide his giggles.

Then, like an ancient mower on its first cut since autumn, Jean spluttered and coughed his way back into cognisance. He slowly surfaced from the redhead's lap and blinked around wonderingly before gazing at Pascal in a panic.

'Où est ma femme?' he coughed, glancing around nervously.

Pascal shrugged sulkily. 'Sais pas.'

'Ah bon.' Jean sucked his gums contentedly as the redhead popped a gold-tipped pink cocktail cigarette into his mouth and patted his head.

'There you go, Monsieur Gainsbourg,' she giggled. '*Je t'aime*, oui? Comprenez?'

'Hein?' Jean eyed her excitedly. 'Oui, je comprends.'

Out on the front lawn, whipped by a fresh breeze, Tash's head was clearing as if she'd sniffed a Karvol capsule. And the more she sobered up, the increasingly aware she became of Hugo's unexpectedly adoring gaze and caressing hands. It was like discovering that Freddy Kruger secretly made Blue Peter gifts for Mothering Sunday, the change was so unexpected and difficult to accept. Plugged into the wet ground by her heels so that she couldn't move, she tried to ignore his warm hand creeping around inside her jacket as if trying to find the light switch.

The Moncrieffs, as Hugo had promised, were lovely, with an infectious enthusiasm for life and weather-beaten, healthy faces. Embarrassed that they'd stumbled into such a grand party, they were cowering under a tree in their workday clothes, continually saying they wouldn't stay, before launching into another piece of juicy eventing gossip.

They were an attractive couple in an understated way, thought Tash. Penny wore no make-up and had scraped her naturally blonde hair back from her face as though she werc tying a hay bale. She had small, deliberate features and a snub nose set on a round face, a bit like an appealing mink. Despite her narrow, fragile appearance she was startlingly wiry.

Gus was quite the opposite, built like an anorexic rugby player – all bone and no blub – he had a huge beaky nose, downturned eyes and a wide toothy smile. He could have been a huge man – his shoulders were like a Jumbo Jet's wing-span – if he weren't so thin. His clothes hung from him like loose covers on an ancient armchair. He looked as if he needed re-stuffing.

'Pen and I were originally going to stay with Marie-Claire – she's one of the top French event riders – for a month in November, taking in a couple of European comps,' Gus explained to Tash, 'but when I knocked up my collarbone we brought the trip forward. She's out of action herself with a bust knee. So we're drowning our sorrows in the local vineyards and watching jealously while Penny here gets all the rides and benefits from our mutual expertise.'

'Some luck!' Penny laughed. 'They're both plastered by midday – and you try getting Gus out of bed when he doesn't have to. This morning I did an entire dressage test in front of Marie-Claire in the pouring rain before I realised she'd fallen asleep in her car.'

Tash laughed, her teeth chattering with cold.

'To be honest, I'm grateful to be out of the saddle,' Gus told her. 'My break gave me a well-earned break. Riding fourteen hours a day makes you open a can of dog food with relish at times.' He grinned, fingering the stiff surgical collar.

'Which is what most of your nags should have been years ago,' Hugo laughed, pulling Tash closer to warm her up. 'What's been happening in England?'

As Gus and Penny regaled Hugo with all the latest results and hearsay in their unfamiliar world, Tash became totally absorbed. She found it extraordinary that, in his absence, Gus had lent his horses to another rider whose top two animals had been plagued with lameness. Yet these people were in direct competition. The thought of Edberg handing his racquets over to Sampras or Prost tossing Mansell his car keys in similar circumstances was inconceivable.

'I popped into your place the other day on my way to Rawlin's,' Gus told Hugo.

'Everything okay?' Hugo inquired in a detached voice. 'Gus and Penny live about five miles from my yard,' he explained to Tash, his eyes skipping between hers lovingly. 'I'm told they keep a pair of binoculars constantly trained south-west in the hope of picking up a few tips.'

'Don't believe a word he says,' Gus winked at Tash, 'the only tips I've ever got from Beauchamp have three legs and run backwards at Newbury.' He turned back to Hugo. 'Everything's fine. Fran's doing a bloody good job. She even got your mother to help out when they were short-staffed.'

'Good God!' Hugo rolled his eyes in amazement. He turned to Tash. 'Franny's my head girl. Cross between Cleo Rochas and Thatcher – terrifying. To get my mother away from the telephone would normally take weeks of planning and a full box of Belgian chocolates. To get her into the yard would take three strong men and a straitjacket. You'll see what I mean when you meet her.' He slipped one hand to her waist and gave it a squeeze, touching her chin with the other.

Tash swallowed what felt like a cricket ball in her throat.

'Er – Hugo.' Penny looked at him speculatively for a moment and then at Gus, raising her eyebrows. Gus nodded – as far as his neck brace allowed – so Penny carried on. 'I don't suppose you're free tomorrow, are you?'

'Depends what for,' Hugo hedged, looking at Tash and smiling kindly.

'Well, actually, it's the reason we called in tonight.' Penny smiled at him diplomatically, unsure of what his reaction would be; he'd been off the circuit for a couple of months, after all. 'There's a comp tomorrow the other side of Saumur—'

'I know.' Hugo looked at Tash again, who went pale.

'Oh – good.' Penny looked at them both as if that settled it. 'Marie-Claire's entered a few of her novices – I'm riding a couple – but it looks like the other will have to be scratched because all M-C's girls are committed to ride the top horses there. How do you fancy deputising?'

She and Gus both glowed at him.

'What do you think?' Hugo asked Tash, his hand slipping idly into her jeans.

'Me?' Tash croaked nervously, the thought of tomorrow's competition suddenly punching her in the temples. Then suddenly seeing her chance to dilute the fawning, devoted Hugo, she urged, 'I think you should do it.'

Gus and Penny turned to glow at her instead.

'You must be missing riding after so long in France,' Tash added carefully, watching Hugo's guarded face.

'Terrific!' Gus patted them both on the back and grinned. 'I'll get M-C to phone up first thing tomorrow and square it with the organisers. It might be an idea if you kip down with us, Hugo, so that you can at least ride the nag once before we set off.'

Hugo looked at him in horror. 'I don't think—'

'Don't worry, M-C will be delighted, she was asking about you only yesterday,' Penny giggled, 'said something about Le Lion d'Angers last year – oh, sorry!' She looked at Tash and covered her mouth in horror.

Smiling broadly and trying to hide her relief, Tash shook her head. 'What class will Hugo be riding in?'

'Er – which one is it, Gus?' Penny turned to her husband, who was adjusting his collar awkwardly.

'That big bay cow,' he grimaced and looked at Hugo. 'She's only a baby so she might need nurse-maiding a little. The class is the frog equivalent of a pre-novice. That's a point – the dressage test is different. We'll go through it tonight.'

'Don't worry.' Hugo let go his grip on Tash and looked at her with a glint of the old Hugo malice in his blue eyes. 'I already know it.'

Gus and Penny exchanged bemused glances.

Tash, glancing up at Hugo, found he'd almost instantly regained some of his original sex appeal.

43

By one the champagne had almost run out, the punch was more laced than an eighteenth-century christening robe and the mead was mostly coating the polished floors, giving them a subtly sticky surface and a genuine beeswax aroma.

Sophia had lost Ben again, and was trapped by Larry Saltzman, who had mistaken her for a current starlet. Stuffing his face with foie gras, he was endeavouring to get an angle on her.

'So, tell me, honey,' he coaxed between mouthfuls, squinting at her cleavage, 'when did you get the plastic pyramid inserts? Nice. Rumour has it a certain Dane had to have her left one done on credit.' He gave her a beady look and washed down the last of the pâté with a hefty slug of punch.

As Sophia opened her mouth to deliver something suitably disdainful, she was distracted by a naked man whooping his way through the house from the direction of the pool terrace, pursued by what looked like a certain Argentinian not unconnected with a famous London department store. The latter was carrying Lotty's beloved inflatable hippo dinghy under one arm and waving Tom's snorkelling kit above his head with the other. He also appeared to be wearing Cass's bathing dress, which was far too small and exposed a surly amount of hairy chest.

Sophia closed her eyes in horror and envisaged her dress covering itself in stains, her hair falling lank around her head and three boils popping up on her nose, yellow-tipped and shiny. It was years since she'd suffered one of her panic attacks.

When she opened her eyes again, the two men were gone. Perhaps she had been hallucinating. The little American had got bored of her and moved on to shriek at an ageing singer.

In a daze, she watched Valérie lugging Michael towards the door to the barn. She had him firmly stapled to her side by one burly arm, like Bluto carting Popeye towards a shark-infested pit and inevitable doom.

Totally oblivious of her husband's lurching progress, Cass was staring up into Ginger's aquiline jaw. Meanwhile the red-haired boy feasted his twinkling sapphire eyes on a nearby male bottom.

Unable to bear it any longer, Sophia stifled a dismayed sob with her hand (which had now grown in her imagination to the size of a baseball glove) and charged upstairs.

As soon as she had found the spare key to the bedroom, dispatched the naked couple from her and Ben's four-poster, stripped the sheets into the laundry basket and remade it, scrubbed the carpet in the bathroom where she had come across some dubious-looking blots of yellow, sprayed a liberal amount of Crabtree and Evelyn room scent around and opened the window for good measure, Sophia threw herself on to the bed and gave way to tears.

A little lucidity was beginning to re-enter Michael's somnolent, groggy head. He was gradually getting his bearings.

He was aware of stumbling outside gripped by a muscular bicep. His ears were being unblocked by a deafening thudding from the building they were rapidly approaching.

There were people everywhere. Not the respectable dinner-jacket and ball-dress crowd that he expected, but dangerous-looking delinquent types. The sort of terrifying sub-culture drop-outs with pierced noses and syringe tracks up their arms that appeared in the awful videos his younger son watched.

It was like some fearful fictional inner-city slum: dogs ran around sniffing piles of rubble, clusters of belligerent youths shared odd-shaped cigarettes and cast Michael scornful looks, couples were doing things to each other which he had never seen done standing up before. Dry-ice smoke from the shaking, noisy building ahead of them drifted out and clung to the cobbles like a steaming swamp. Through the slats of the doors, the building itself seemed to throb with evil energy, teeming with the subversive element like savage, depraved animals.

Letting out an outraged wail, Michael broke free and stumbled towards the house. From behind him came a torrent of French expletives and something else, another more familiar voice. But Michael was not about to hang around and find out whose.

It was only when he was safely inside the manoir, leaning against the door and panting with horrified exhaustion that the words he had heard drifted back into his mind to worry him.

'Look, man! It's a raisin smoking a pipe!'

Michael took out his trusty friend and patted down the unlit tobacco with his thumb, scratching his spinning head pensively. He was almost certain that it had been his younger son, Marcus, shrieking.

Tottering around the kitchen, his eyes rolling like Rudolph Valentino in a love scene, his mouth drooling like Bela Lugosi after a binge, Rooter was beginning to feel sick.

Penny Moncrieff glanced at her watch.

'We should go soon,' she looked from Hugo to Gus. 'You might be able to compete on three hours' sleep and a monumental hangover, Hugo, but I sure can't. Do you mind?' She shrugged at Tash apologetically.

'No, not at all,' Tash assured her, smiling broadly. Freezing cold now, she'd already tried to excuse herself from the group once, only to feel Hugo's grip tighten like a manacle on her wrist.

Now he looked at her meditatively before turning to the others.

'Where does Marie-Claire live? Give me the address and I'll follow on later.' He shot a sly smile at Tash. 'I don't feel like turning in yet.'

Tash swallowed in panic. It was plain that this was exactly what he felt like.

Taking in Tash's reaction, Penny nudged Gus.

'You can stay up and have a night-cap with me, Hugo,' Gus urged, then patted Tash on the shoulder. 'This gorgeous girl needs a good night's sleep too. Rule number one in Gus's advice book.'

'Rule number two being vestal purity,' muttered Hugo, gathering Tash into his arms and planting a long, hard kiss on her mouth. As he reluctantly released her, he slipped his hands up to her face and cupped it, his blue gaze guarded and speculative again.

'Come on.' Penny hooked her arm through Hugo's and started to lead him away, calling over her shoulder to Tash, 'See you tomorrow!'

Gus lingered a little longer and shook Tash by the hand.

'Lovely to meet you,' he grinned. 'Actually, rule number two is to take care of beautiful Beauchamp. I love the old sod; he's done me a hell of a lot of favours. I know he has a lousy reputation with women but you're far sweeter than his usual type,' the grin turned to a warm smile, 'and I must confess that I don't think I've ever seen him as smitten, kitten.' He dropped a kiss on her cheek. 'Now go to bed and we'll see you in the morning. They're walking the course from eight.'

And he was gone. Tash stood alone for a while, staring up at the brightest star she could find in the sky. She wanted to wish for something but she no longer knew what. After coveting Hugo for so long, her feelings for him were horribly mixed. She now knew she didn't love him but she couldn't bring herself to hate him either. Friendship seemed the only answer but it was miles away. She briefly thought about Max but it was like trying to remember a favourite tune one hadn't heard for years. There was something else, someone else she should wish for, but her thoughts were too muddled to elucidate.

'Please,' she lost the star behind a cloud for a moment and waited for it to reappear. She could feel the squally wind bite at her exposed bits again.

'Please,' she wished as the star winked its way back into clear air, 'make Hugo Beauchamp a friend.'

She turned to walk back to the house but paused, and looked up again, adding as an afterthought, 'And let me beat him tomorrow.'

Sitting in a transport café ten miles out of La Flêche, Niall was systematically ripping a polystyrene cup into shreds, oblivious of the fact that it was still half-full of gritty black coffee. He stared through his reflection in the plate-glass window beside him and out into the night. Yellow headlights from the road zipped past, belonging to cars which actually worked, any one of which could take him to Saumur, to Champegny and Tash. His mind flicked somewhat wildly over a brief image of hijacking one. But it was only supposition. By now he was quite certain they'd left it too late.

'Damn bloody fucking Audrey!' he hissed.

An English couple with two runny-nosed toddlers who had been frantically leafing through a pristine copy of *Logis de France* for somewhere to stay at such a late hour, looked at him accusingly for a moment. Then their faces clamped over with surprised recognition and, after nudging each other like Hinge and Brackett on a sofa, they looked away and pretended they hadn't a clue who he was.

Niall groped for a cigarette but his packet was empty. He walked over to the counter to buy another and found he only had a couple of francs rattling in his pocket. Running his hands through his hair in despair, he stood stock-still in the middle of the empty café and laughed.

'I've got the old love started again.' Matty came in through the swing doors. He was wiping his hands on an oily rag and had a dark streak running across his forehead and left cheek. 'But I can't guarantee she'll go all the way.'

At this Niall laughed even more. He shook his head and leaned against the counter in a fit of giggles.

The greasy-haired French girl in a food-splattered uniform who'd been sitting by the till watching the overhead TV jumped up and backed away nervously.

Matty scratched his head and patted Niall on the back.

'Come on, mate, I'll drive the rest of the way. You should have let me after that puncture in Luigny. Too much time at the wheel stresses anyone out.'

The English couple took a surreptitious snapshot as Matty helped the stupefied Niall from the brightly lit café.

Searching for his wife, Ben kept being waylaid by long, painted fingernails clutching at his arm – and sometimes ankle if the owner was particularly sloshed – and high-pitched voices congratulating him on the wonderful night he'd laid on, thrusting invitations or telephone numbers into his already overflowing pockets.

'You must come to Mustique next week, darling!'

'Tell Shophia she'sh a miracle. Here's a shtiffy to our little bash in Augusht. Very modesht – not up to your shtandard, I'm afraid.'

'Sweetheart! Marvellous! Terrific crowd! Come to Monte Carlo!'

Ben couldn't find Sophia anywhere. He climbed over a bald man who had fallen asleep in the doorway to the long gallery, but the room was almost empty. The medieval band had deserted their instruments and were drinking the last of the punch straight from the bowl. The snake-charmer, close to tears, was crawling around on the floor looking under table-cloths and inside flower arrangements, calling frantically. A small gaggle of men were still playing medieval cricket, surrounded by smashed china and glass.

Ben climbed back over the cat-napping drunk and looked around the hall. The pop star was still playing the harpsichord, by now taking requests – as long as they were for his own hits. An Argentinian wearing goggles was sitting in a faintly familiar hippo dinghy and singing the Eton Boating Song. A shrieking blonde poured a jug of mead over his head and ran shrilly off into the garden.

In the ballroom, Ben found the last of the food being demolished with barbarian relish. Sitting around the long tables, bellowing with Tudor ferocity, sat an assortment of Sophia's more illustrious guests. They ripped at a whole roast piglet with greasy fingers, gnawed it from the bone, tore hunks of bread from long baguettes to throw at each other, drank soup from the wooden bowls and mead from metal goblets until it ran down their chins and on to their designer outfits.

Ben shrugged and walked out. The Argentinian, still dripping mead, was now crowing 'Row Row Row Your Boat'. Ben popped his head round the door of the China Room.

With amazement, he noticed Alexandra and Pascal crammed into the sofa with Anton, a comely redhead, Jean and Véronique Délon. Jean was wearing a lampshade on his head, Pascal had a geranium bloom behind his ear and the redhead, in tears of laughter, was trying to take her bra off from underneath her dress, her huge freckled bust rising like baking bread. Véronique, wearing a tinted plastic sun-peak and smoking one of Anton's cigars, was dealing out a round of cards.

Alexandra, eyes shining like melting ice, spotted Ben by the door and stretched out a jangling arm for him to come closer.

'Darling! Are you having a nice time?' she beamed up at him.

With her hair falling across her face and her lipstick worn away on several glasses, she looked no older than Sophia.

Ben grinned down at her awkwardly.

'Wonderful, thanks. What are you playing?' He watched as the players went through a complicated ceremony of fetching objects from the room and placing them on the table as they would bets.

'Actually, it's gin rummy,' Alexandra confessed in a whisper. 'I couldn't remember the rules to anything else – but we've spiced it up a little.'

Véronique, having some trouble dealing straight, had dropped half the pack down her neighbour's ample cleavage. Pascal and Anton were helping out and the redhead giggled helplessly as she watched them fumble to extract the battered cards. Jean's lampshade slipped over his eyes and he waved his arms around like King Lear in a storm.

'Coupure de courant!' he bellowed.

As they played the round, what Ben had thought was a pile of coats next to Véronique stirred and yawned. It turned out to be her husband, Henri. He snuggled closer to his wife, stuck his thumb in his mouth and fell back to sleep.

Alexandra and Ben both started speaking at the same time.

'Have you see—'

'I don't supp—'

'You go on,' Ben urged, watching in amazement as the redhead won the round and donned a fruit bowl.

'It's Eddie.' Alexandra stood up and moved Ben to one side. 'It's quite awful. People are beginning to leave and there's been no word from him. I'm starting to get worried. You don't think his plane . . .' Tears began to brim in her eyes.

'Absolutely not.' Ben put his arm around her. 'Bound to be a perfectly simple explanation. I'll make a few inquiries.'

'Oh, thank you, Ben, you are a sweetheart.' Alexandra gave him a kiss on the cheek as Jean, suddenly realising he'd lost the round, let out a croaky whoop and started to remove his trousers. 'What were you going to ask me?'

Ben coughed awkwardly, averting his gaze from Jean's waist-to-knee Airtex underpants. 'You haven't seen Sophia, have you?'

'No, darling, 'fraid not.' Alexandra watched as the redhead, doubled up with giggles, began to slide down her chair and on to the floor.

Chewing his lip, Ben wandered off in search of his errant wife.

Cass applied the last subtle coating of pressed powder to her now matt nose and stuck her overheated lipstick together just long enough to give her lips a dash of Happy Hyacinth. Washing the ends of her fingers under the tap, she glanced up at her glowing reflection and meditated on the fact that she was really a remarkably well-preserved woman.

'You're not looking at the mother of two beautiful, talented, fully-grown children,' she breathed, 'but a woman desired by someone as bright and mature for his age as Ginger Harcourt.'

Ignoring the bemused stares of two women reapplying make-up, she made her way dreamily back to where he was waiting for her, passing the window to the pool terrace and pausing to quickly double-check her reflection in it.

She gawped in horror as she saw tens of nude bodies frolicking in the glossy turquoise pool.

Was that sort of thing legal? she wondered. Surely Sophia had no idea this was going on?

Cass furtively whipped out her specs from her clutch bag and had a closer peek. There was that dreadful Amanda hussy, she noticed, with that awful whiffy Australian. Although, as she craned forward for a better view, she noticed that he did appear to have a remarkably good body.

Whisking away before anyone caught her peeping, Cass headed towards Ginger.

She was greatly relieved to find him talking to Olly. At least my impressionable, artistic son hasn't been affected by this corrupt crowd, she thought hazily. Then she stopped in her tracks as she took in what Olly was wearing. He was dressed like one of Marcus's girlfriends.

As Cass drew closer, she paused beside a wrought-iron candelabrum. They seemed to be arguing about something.

Olly was holding Ginger by the collar while Ginger laughed at him.

'Leave my mother alone!' Olly was screaming. 'She's sacred.'

Ginger carried on laughing. 'And you think flirting with your aunt's pretty little Australian help justifies such obloquy?' he mocked.

Cass looked at her son and his flatmate in puzzlement.

'Look, I wasn't flirting, Gin,' Olly howled. 'I told you, he just chained himself to the bed by mistake while I was in the shower listening to Speedy Eedy.'

Cass blinked in horror.

'You think I'm going to believe that?' Ginger stopped laughing and looked hurt and dejected. 'Why else would you dress so provocatively? You never dress like that for me and you know how much I love it.'

'I'm wearing this for you, you great pansy,' Olly explained sulkily. 'I want you to stop trying to adulterate my mother, so I thought I'd give you a dressing down.'

'You silly fool, Hennessy,' Ginger purred, and Cass watched in alarm as the red-haired boy kissed her son's neck, 'don't you know I'd far rather adulterate her son?'

Cass whimpered and stumbled away, blind with tears.

Please God, let it be a phase, she prayed desperately as she ricocheted off the furniture.

'I'm going mad,' she moaned as a swarthy man dashed past wearing armbands, 'that's my bathing dress!'

'Yo – Mum, man! Over 'ere!'

'Oh, Marcus!' Cass wiped her tears and spotted her younger son, leaning against a pillar and smoking one of his horrible rollies. He'd lost his baseball cap and his flies were undone, but apart from that he seemed remarkably sober.

'Thank God you're all right!' She rushed over to give him a hug.

'Sure, man!' Marcus wriggled out of her grip and squinted at her, a goofy grin glued to his mouth.

Then his eyes started to glaze over.

'Shit city, man!' He leapt back in terror and stared at her with wide-open, frightened eyes. 'What are you doing disguised as my mother, you bastard? No goddamn pickled herring can get away with dressing up as my effing Ma. Come out of there, you vinegar-breathed, scale-faced Danish fish! Show yourself, man!'

He started to rip frantically at Cass's blue satin.

Appalled, Cass fought him off with her clutch bag and screamed for help. They grappled for what seemed like minutes when Marcus suddenly stopped and burst into noisy tears.

'Mummy, mummy . . . for—' hic '– give me? Please, Mummy?' He'd reverted to his old accent, putrid and whiny.

'Marcus dear, what is it? Tell Mummy.' Cass enveloped him in her arms but he slid down her, clutching hold of her legs.

People were beginning to look at them. Cass smiled across apologetically and patted Marcus on the head. He was sniffing wimpishly into her shoes now.

'Marcus, pull yourself together and tell Mummy what's the matter.' She could feel his damp nose against her feet.

'Let me back in, Mummy. I promise I'll be ever so quiet.' He suddenly lifted up her skirt and disappeared underneath.

Cass jumped away in horror but he held firmly on, using a rugger tackle Michael had taught him.

'Marcus, get OFF!' Cass screamed, frantically kicking her legs in an attempt to remove him.

Still whimpering, Marcus held on to Cass's support stockings with superhuman strength. All that could be seen of him underneath her voluminous sapphire skirt was a pair of chunky, unlaced trainers poking out of the bottom.

When Michael staggered into the far end of the hall, clutching his head and glancing furtively around for Valérie's lurking bulk, he saw his wife and thought she was having some sort of fit. The old girl appeared to be thrashing at her frock with her handbag and wailing like a thing possessed. Michael stopped and watched, scratching his bald patch and puffing on his pipe, totally perplexed.

Cass spotted him and screamed, 'Michael, do something!' before tumbling into a pile of crumpled blue fabric on the floor.

Michael watched in surprise as his younger son emerged from the wreckage like a D-Day parachutist.

Marcus then stood up, shook himself down, muttered, 'Must stop the Clangers eating all the Bakewell tarts,' and wandered off in the direction of the barn.

By now Cass was quite hysterical. Michael bent over and examined her closely. The old thing must have shipped too much bloody pop, he thought sympathetically. He'd felt pretty tipsy himself earlier. She was mumbling something about pansies having a swim with Danish herrings now, staring up at him with tear-filled eyes and a runny nose.

'There, there, old girl. Let's get you to bloody bed.' Michael helped to lift her from the floor.

'And then they *kissed*, Michael!' Cass cried, 'in front of everyone. It was like that dreadful film – *Maurice*. He kept going on about Speedy Eedy. I think it's some sort of perverted sex act they perform.'

'Yes, old girl, course it bloody is.'

A few bystanders, thinking this was one of the elaborate side shows Sophia had laid on for their entertainment, gave them a weak round of applause as Michael supported his sobbing wife towards the stairs.

44

Sally was sitting in the children's bedroom, trying unsuccessfully to read an old copy of the *Daily Mail* by the dim orange light of the mushroom-shaped night-lamp.

From outside the half-open door she could hear the occasional sucking and squelching noises of Paola and her long-haired friend kissing.

When Sally had first come up to check the kids, she'd thought her sister-in-law's Italian nanny was in the midst of a passionate lesbian affair. Paola had been attached by various parts of the body to an androgynous figure with a flowery shirt and long glossy dark hair in a pony-tail. But it transpired that these scandalous items belonged to a gawky boy with cotton wool in his ears who introduced himself as 'Algy, man. Peace and Karma.'

Paola, abashed at being caught mid-grope by Sally, had made a big fuss of heating up a bottle for Josh in the little ante-room to the nursery, humming 'The Lord's My Shepherd'.

Sally threw the paper down on the moth-eaten carpet and looked across at Tom, who'd hogged the top bunk for the night. One thin little arm was hanging out, like a still pendulum weighed down by his huge digital wrist watch which told the time all over the world, calculated growth assets to the nearest tenth digit and played the theme to *Terminator* at the flick of a switch. Sally could make out the luminous shape of the Honey Monster sticker Tom had fixed to the strap at breakfast the morning they'd left for France.

She stood up and rearranged his bedding, which he'd flung away from him and pummelled with his feet in his sleep just as his father did. Tucking his arm back underneath the eiderdown and kissing his warm nose, Sally then checked Polly, who was buried completely by her blankets and was just a sleeping lump. Lotty and Tor were also fast asleep, the former pressing her Noo Noo to her cheek with white knuckles, the latter having crawled to the wrong end of her bed, where her tufty hair and a small hand clutching a one-armed teddy poked out from the place her feet should be. Sally tucked in all their bedding rather listlessly and knocked her head on every aeroplane, parrot and cloud mobile in the room.

The suction seemed to have increased outside. Sally popped her head around the door and cleared her throat. Paola and Algy disengaged themselves and looked up.

'Why don't you two go down for a drink and some grub?' she suggested. 'You must be starving, Paola. It can't have been much fun for you cooped up here, you poor thing. I can take over here for a bit, they're all sound asleep at the moment.' She smiled at them brightly.

As Paola and Algy creaked hastily down the turret stairs, Sally made herself a coffee in the little ante-room and stared at her drained reflection in the mirror on the rickety table. She looked grey and tired. Hope was trickling out of her like a slow puncture. It had been all night.

'You silly old fool,' she sighed at her reflection, 'you used to be pretty once.'

'You still are.'

Sally turned so quickly she cricked her neck.

Standing in the doorway, covered in grime like a camouflaged commando, was Matty. His clothes were creased and his face shadowed with exhaustion, but to Sally he had never looked brighter or more welcoming. She blinked and held her sore neck.

'Hello.' He didn't look her in the eyes, but stared at the top of her head as if working out if she was wearing a wig.

'Hello,' Sally muttered.

'You okay?' Matty stared at her shoulders now, presumably checking for dandruff.

He shifted his weight hesitantly and sucked at his finger joint, spitting as he got a mouthful of oil.

'Fine,' she sighed.

'That's good.' He was fiddling with the carton of disposable nappies Paola had left on one surface.

There was a sticky pause which Matty filled by reading the instructions on the side of the packet. He seemed almost relieved when he heard Josh crying.

'I'll go!' He grabbed the top nappy and dashed out.

Sally put her head in her hands and groaned. This was dreadful, she thought in despair. Ten times worse than she could have imagined.

She walked over to the tiny circular turret window and opened it. Outside, the air was damp and cool, smelling of wet leaves and fresh tarmac. Even though this was the opposite side of the house to the barn, a low, muffled thudding filled the tiny room. Sally could hear people immediately below laughing and squealing. Further out on the lawn, a trouserless man was running around with a lampshade on his head.

As the night air chilled her cheeks, Sally felt Matty's arms close around her and his head rest on her shoulder. For a moment she became rigid and unyielding like an irritable cat unwilling to be picked up. Then Matty nuzzled closer and she gave way to the overpowering sense of security and comfort she'd craved over the past few days.

'You idiot.' She turned round and cradled his hopeful, soppy face in her hands. 'Where did you go?'

'Home – at least I think it was. Hard to tell under the dust-sheets.'

Ignoring him, Sally put her nose against his. 'What made you do it?'

Matty shrugged. 'Staying here made me feel about twelve.' His mouth twisted into a wry smile. 'My mother terrifies me, you know. The family's so chaotic – so many feuds. I used to be so bloody insecure.'

'The kids and I are your family,' Sally needled, tugging at his hair.

'And what can I offer you, huh?' Matty pulled away and gazed out of the window. 'I'm hardly one of the industry's success stories.'

'Have I ever asked you to be?' Sally sighed. 'You're the one with the vaulting ambition and the bull-headed principles.' She tugged at his collar. 'I fell in love with you because you could play "American Pie" on the harmonica, quote Nietzsche in German and wear platforms without looking queer, remember?'

Matty shifted uncomfortably. 'You do spend an awful lot of money, though, Sals . . .'

'I am trying.' Sally hung her head. 'I cut up all my credit cards yesterday. But you could have talked to me about it – that's what I needed. Instead, you just buggered off.'

'I know, I know.' Matty dropped his eyes. 'Forgive me . . . please?'

'What's to forgive?' Sally said simply. 'It's both our stupid faults – I guess being here did make me revoltingly resentful.'

'And me paranoid. It's my family's fault – they've always been obsessed by luxury,' Matty hissed bitterly. 'You'll never guess what Niall confessed in the car. He—'

'Lisette's here,' Sally interrupted.

Raising two huge amber eyes, Matty looked at her for a long time. Then, quite unexpectedly, he laughed. Shaking his head, he started to cover her face in wet kisses.

'I'm not joking, Matty,' Sally howled in exasperation. 'She turned up early on and has been prowling round spitting feathers ever since.'

'Really?' murmured Matty and carried on kissing her.

'Matty!' she pulled away. 'Look, she's done some unforgivable things. In his state he might agree to take her back and she doesn't want him. She just wants to get back at—'

Matty covered her mouth with his hand and smiled at her. 'He won't,' he said gently. 'I finally got the idiot to open up a little in the last hour. If what he told me is true, he'll hardly bother to say hello.'

'But that's even worse!' Sally gasped, remembering Tash and Hugo earlier. 'You don't know what's happened—'

'And I don't care,' Matty laughed and kissed her again. 'Right now, I just want to talk to you about *us*, no one else. Niall's old enough to look after himself. And once we've talked – even if it takes all night for me to convince you that you simply have to spend the rest of your life with me, *then* – and only then – I'm going to ask my damned mother what she's done to our house.'

Heading miserably to bed, Tash was making frustratingly slow progress as she lilted and keeled through gaggles of guests, pitching between screeched conversations. Her head felt as if she were sporting a crown of thorns, her stomach heaved as if she'd eaten the berries as well. A feeling of leaden exhaustion seemed to have knocked the air from her body.

She'd been trapped in the banqueting hall for almost an hour now, continually swooped upon by people who thought she was someone else. Apart from Hugo, she'd hardly seen a familiar face all night. As she edged towards the door, her eyes continually scanned across the lurching masses in the hope that Niall had arrived. But even if he had, Tash guessed she wouldn't be able to get at him for the dozens of old chums that would no doubt crowd eagerly around him. The thought made her feel even more sick. She tried to creep away from the group who'd just hailed her over to bitch about Sophia.

'Is it true she's doing a vox pop soap powder ad with Danny Baker, darling?'

Stomach heaving, Tash shrugged and backed into a pair of open arms which closed around her like a safety cage on a fairground ride.

'Hi, remember me? Raoul.'

She twisted round to see a mouth smudged with someone's red lipstick grinning at her. He pushed one of the glasses of punch he was holding into her hand. The fumes alone made Tash's head reel.

'Champagne has run out,' Raoul explained, steering her away

from the cackling masses, pulling a blonde with a slipping beehive along too. 'This is Brigitta.'

The blonde, who looked about sixteen, uncrossed her eyes and smiled vapidly.

'Do you want to go somewhere quieter?' Raoul purred into Tash's ear.

'Actually, I'm going to bed,' Tash said groggily, taking a slug of punch out of embarrassment and gagging, the taste of vomit filling her nose.

Raoul's dark eyes glinted.

'Good idea.' He leaned forward and pressed his mouth to her ear. 'We'll join you.'

'No!' yelped Tash, pulling away and spilling her drink as she ricocheted out of the room.

The hall was even more crowded. Faces turned to her with interest. She was pressed up against scratchy fabric and naked flesh as she scrambled to get through. She knocked someone's drink out of their hand and was burnt by another's cigarette as she squeezed and shoved. A hand grabbed her, someone she'd met earlier dying to introduce her to a group of rich hyenas. Tash whimpered and pulled free. The room was beginning to spin.

'Saw your concert in Rotterdam last October!' a voice screamed over the din. 'Any chance of a backstage pass later?'

His companions shrieked with laughter.

Tash stumbled on. They revolted her with their asinine, unashamed narcissism and pursuit of the ultimate prurient kick. Bile rose in her throat and her stomach heaved in disgust.

And then suddenly a protective arm enveloped her shoulders and she was being steered roughly through the hall and into the dining room, empty except for the spaniels, quivering nervously in their baskets.

It was Niall, still wearing the battered oilskin and old jeans he'd set out in that morning, his dark eyes black and unreadable.

He looked down at her for a long time before wiping away a huge smudge of eyeliner on her cheek.

Tash hung her head and fought tears. A queasy chemical reaction was taking place somewhere near her colon.

How could he find her like this? she thought in dismay. Her green face matched her jacket, her hands shook so much that when she thrust them in her pockets she started to vibrate too. She had to swallow frantically to fight nausea. She felt childish and silly, acutely embarrassed and very drunk.

'Shanks-hic,' she mumbled, gratitude mixing with a huge hiccup. She was shaking uncontrollably now.

The pause stretched on achingly. Tash felt black spots clouding her vision and a cold moisture close around her.

And then, just as she felt her tenuous grip on cognisance finally slip, Niall gave her a sudden, awkward hug. Tash, pitching dangerously to the left, leaned heavily on him and told herself not to faint. She had to keep some fragment of dignity, some tiny iota of self-control. If she gave in to biological demand, she'd never be able to look him in the face again.

He stroked her hair gently. With her face against the heavy waxed cotton, still cold from outside, and that calm, soothing voice in her ears, she found herself wishing the moment could go on for ever. Blood started to circulate again and her head spun for quite another reason. Nausea was being replaced by desire. She sighed dreamily and allowed her mind to ramble into a quick bedroom fantasy.

'My God – if that's not my jacket!' Niall laughed in amazement.

Not quite taking this in, but realising how pissed she was to be leaning against him like a soppy, besotted fan, Tash dragged herself away and swayed a little.

'W-what?'

'That jacket. It's mine. Lisette had it made for me last year. She never thought I was trendy enough.'

Speaking her name, Niall waited for the delayed pain to shoot through his chest and sting the backs of his eyes but for the first time nothing happened.

Tash was looking horrified. 'But – but Ginger gave it to me. I thought it was his. If I'd known, I'd never have – oh dear!'

Flustered, she pushed back her hair with her hands and Niall noticed the earrings. They lit up her incredible face and the tears that were beginning to glaze her eyes. He felt choked and foggy-headed with lust.

'You must have it back,' she muttered, beginning to shrug off the green jacket with drunken clumsiness.

Niall watched the slim brown shoulders and long arched neck appear as she pulled off one sleeve. He couldn't bear it. She had no idea what she was doing to him. He felt like a dirty old man unable to drag his eyes away.

'Stop!' It sounded more desperate than he would have liked. She looked up at him, nervous of his anger. 'You can wear it tonight, Tash.' He hastily pulled the jacket back over her shoulders and even fastened it at the front for her as if buttoning a child's coat. 'I'd like you to.'

'Oh.' Tash wondered if he'd got the wrong idea. Thought she was trying on some corny seduction routine. Her large intestine started to slosh around again at this thought. He'd sounded so embarrassed and appalled. Now the room was swaying gently. She looked down at her hands, her face burning. 'Thanks.'

Niall wanted to get out fast. He couldn't be responsible for his actions at the moment. He needed to grab some self-control around him before he could talk to her. Right now, wearing these sweaty, nicotine-stinking clothes with an unshaven face, he felt old and weak. He'd been totally unprepared for the desirable, dishevelled, Bacchanal radiance of Tash.

'Look,' he glanced towards the door as if reassuring himself of its presence, 'were you all right out there? You looked a bit panicked. Hugo not been bothering you now, has he?'

'Hugo?' Tash resurfaced from concentrating on keeping the room still and realised with a start that Hugo had been out of her rather muddled thoughts for the first time that night.

'Er – no – I've hardly seen him,' she lied.

She contemplated telling him that his theory had worked, but somehow couldn't bring herself to. She simply wasn't up to constructing such a complicated sentence. And, more importantly, it seemed to her that the longer she pretended she was still strung up on Hugo, the less likely Niall was to find out that she'd actually fallen for him.

'Good.' Niall looked at the door again. 'Well, I'd better be getting changed.'

'Yes.'

But instead of leaving he stood motionless, staring out of the window.

He does that a lot, thought Tash in a moment of sudden lucidity. She pondered on the reason for his abstraction, but it remained a mystery. Alcohol had plugged her thinking processes with road blocks. She'd get so far and then be forced to brake suddenly. Everything was being diverted into a cul-de-sac somewhere in her cerebellum.

She considered putting this abstruse observation to Niall but couldn't remember it a second time. Instead, she started humming 'House of the Rising Sun' but it went horribly flat.

Of course! Tash looked up with a jolt. He'd been to collect Matty. Something must have happened to him.

'Is Matty back?' she tried to ask. It came out as: 'Ishmattibshat?'

With the interpreting skills of a dentist, Niall nodded. 'He's with Sally now.'

So that wasn't it. Tash went to scratch her head but ended up thumping herself on the nose. She wanted another drink. And a cigarette. And more than anything, another hug. Instead, she collapsed into a chair at the long table and started to pick at the flower arrangement on it.

The pause was interminable before Niall finally cleared his throat and went out. Tash sat humming to herself for a few minutes, letting the spinning room slow down a little and her feet gain contact with the rest of her body. Christ, she felt sick.

She looked down at one of the spaniels. Even it gave her a slightly withering look with mournful, speckled brown eyes. She considered booting it out of its basket and curling up in there herself for the night. Instead, she scratched its greying muzzle before venturing out into the heaving, noisy masses again to find a cup of coffee.

'Why don't you look where you're fucking going?' howled a furious voice.

'Christ, sorry!' Tash tried ineffectually to mop whisky from priceless silk chiffon.

Glancing up, she saw that the woman she'd crashed into was on the verge of tears, her huge eyes brimming.

'Oh Lord, I'm such a clumsy idiot,' Tash repeated. 'Look, are you all right?'

'I'm soaked in pissing scotch!' the woman snarled.

Tash recoiled as if stung by venom.

'All right, that was mean.' The woman shrugged without remorse, soaking up the damp patch with a tissue, clearly fighting to stop herself crying.

She was truly stunning, thought Tash. She looked like a delicate blue glaze painting of a heron on a Ming vase.

'I don't suppose you know if Niall O'Shaughnessy's arrived yet?' the woman asked, eyeing Tash's jacket with vague suspicion.

Tash opened her mouth and shut it again.

'He's kind of tall and craggy,' the woman grinned. 'I'm his wife, Lisette.'

Shaking her head as though watching a tennis match, Tash backed away and then turned on her heel and bolted to the loo.

When she emerged ten minutes later, her head clearer, her stomach and throat stinging and hollow, Lisette had gone.

Shimmying from the direction of the pool, wrapped in a squashy white towelling robe and towing Todd like an Afghan hound in Hyde Park, came Amanda.

She paused briefly by Tash, who was swaying in the loo door.

'Hi,' she purred with a foxy smile. 'Enjoying yourself? I hear you've been playing with Hugo – so nice for him to find someone else with the same IQ as mental age.'

'Oh go and swivel on your mobile phone,' Tash muttered.

'Sure.' Amanda didn't look remotely fazed. 'But first I must tell you the most exciting gossip – Niall's wife has turned up. It looks as though they're set for a reconciliation.'

'How lovely,' Tash replied evenly.

As soon as Amanda had gone, Tash retraced her steps to the loo and threw up again.

Although his trousers still lay on a threadbare silk sofa in the China Room, Jean had disappeared. Through the tall French windows, Véronique Délon was supervising Henri being sick into a bay tree tub.

Collecting empty glasses between each finger, Pascal yawned and kissed his distracted wife on the cheek before fighting his way through the hall to try and gently persuade a few people to leave.

Left pacing the deserted room, Alexandra was on the phone to JFK airport.

'Yes, Edward *Buckingham* – B-U-C-K-I-N—' She paused by the windows, staring past her friends in amazement. In the floodlit garden, one of the oldest yews had suddenly assumed the most extraordinary shape.

At the end of a weedy lawn, hidden in the topiary, Jean was giggling hysterically to himself, a wicked, triumphant expression on his face and a pair of rusty secateurs in his hands.

Niall walked into the kitchen and almost doubled back on himself.

A chef in a deflated soufflé hat was having what looked like a nervous breakdown over a set of copper pans in the corner. A waitress in medieval garb was fast asleep on Rooter's sag-bag with Rooter sitting beside her looking distinctly put out. And beside him were several revolting piles of what looked like regurgitated 'apples of the ground puree' (mashed potato).

The kitchen was covered in food. Sacks of flour were overflowing near the range. Boxes, bags and crates of fruit and vegetables shrivelled next to the door. Cheese sweated on boards and once neat stacks of pre-prepared dishes which had been salvaged from Rooter's raid had toppled, crumbled or been squashed on to every surface. Empty champagne bottles littered the floor, some in ordered ranks, some on their sides, like a half-felled forest. Even the walls seemed to have been given a liberal coating of William of Canard de l'Orange Soup (Sophia's own recipe). Several manic-depressive caterers were composing resignation letters at the large scrubbed table.

Niall's heart lifted like a hot air balloon given a spurt of gas when he saw Tash at the other end, staring forlornly into a cup of coffee.

'Blank cheque for your thoughts.' He pulled a chair across and sat down beside her. Another chef, trying to chat her up, looked miffed and started on a tearful waitress who was struggling to mend the rips in her buxom wench costume with Sellotape.

'Not worth the paper.' Tash looked up at him with huge, doleful eyes. Then she smiled sadly. 'You look lovely.' She took a swig of coffee, dripping most of it on the table.

Niall ran an anxious finger around his dress-shirt collar. Whatever she did, even blowing her nose on a soggy napkin as she was now, it inevitably made his heart flip over like a burning omelette.

'Is it Hugo?' Niall covered her hand with his and tried not to let the cramps in his chest take hold.

Tash nodded, then shook her head, then nodded, then shrugged and blew her nose again.

'I see.' Niall wondered where the insolent bugger was now. Perhaps he'd staged a walk-out with someone else.

Tash was looking at her hands gloomily.

'He's in the same competition as me tomorrow.' She smiled up at him sadly, not without self-irony. 'Some friends of his have given him a chance ride.'

'Oh, now there's a thing.'

Niall thanked God. I might not say my Our Fathers but there's faith in there somewhere, he thought to himself happily.

'Come outside with me.' Her eyes seemed to be brimming with tears but her chin was set in a stubborn *don't ask me, all right?*

'Okay.' Niall crossed his fingers under the table before standing up. Here was his God-given chance.

They went outside into the courtyard but the music from the barn was still deafening, its ravers spilling out on to the cobbles for a boogie, so Tash led Niall towards the paddock. They spotted Marcus, who was still stamping his rubber heels and flagellating the air with his skinny arms.

'Hi, Marcus.' Tash waved at him as they passed.

'Yo, Pukka!' Marcus jiggled his hips and writhed a bit to the beat. 'What's with the potted shrimp, like y'know?' He raised his eyebrows at Tash and looked at Niall critically.

Tash nodded at him nervously and climbed over the gate to the paddock.

Behind her, Niall nearly passed out. Through a huge rip in the seat of her jeans he could clearly see the tidemark where her tan ended and her knickers should begin. The dirty-old-man feeling returned and he had to take several deep, self-controlling breaths before he could follow.

Tash was waiting for him in the dark field.

'Niall, there's something I have to tell you—'

'Oh yes?' As Niall dropped beside her, his arm creeping around her shoulders, she spun around.

'Lisette's here!' she blurted out.

Tash bit her lip as Niall's hand froze and his head, in shadows, became ominously still.

'I'm sorry,' she whispered in a low voice, 'I didn't mean to tell you like that but I didn't want you to have to bump into her without knowing. I thought you might need time to react first.'

She could feel the tears starting to run scalding marathons down her face and turned away from the light so that he wouldn't see.

'She's been here all night apparently,' Tash continued. 'I got introduced to her by . . . by . . . a friend just after you went to change.'

'Is she with . . . ?' Niall clearly couldn't bring himself to say the name.

'I think she's alone.'

'Well, wouldn't you just know it?' Niall rubbed his forehead and laughed dryly.

Tash frantically strangled a series of huge, tearful hiccups which gobbled through her like a brood of manic turkeys. She stuffed her fist in her mouth and felt hot tears brush against it.

'Shit, shit, shit, shit, shit!' Niall howled at the sky.

Tash could feel a lump in her throat so big it threatened to jettison her head out into the night.

'I must talk with her,' Niall muttered.

'Yes,' she responded automatically. 'Of course.'

Her vision was so blurred, she couldn't even see if he was still there. She wiped her face furiously with the back of her sleeve. Niall's sleeve. Which Lisette had chosen for him. Tash could almost envisage Lisette quoting his measurements to a Savile Row tailor before prowling Selfridges food hall for the ingredients of a cosy matrimonial meal.

'Right!' Niall was still there. He gathered himself up and rubbed the back of his head, clutching on to his hair and pulling his head back to look at the sky and summon confidence.

Tash wanted him to go now. If he was going back to Lisette, the sooner the better. He'd leave her alone to lick her wounds and utter a satisfying, loud, self-indulgent wail in the solitary paddock. Except that she couldn't look into the sunset and cry, 'Tomorrow is another day!' Because tomorrow was a nightmare: she had to face Snob and Hugo and all that 'character-building'. She'd have an Empire State of character by the end of this holiday, she decided, and still no self-confidence.

'Go for it,' she muttered shakily.

Niall stopped looking at the sky and she could make out that he was nodding.

Tash had read that being the sacrificial martyr was supposed to be the height of self-fulfilment. But it felt pretty lousy from where she was wilting.

She turned to walk away to the far end of the paddock and leave him to go to pieces in peace. She couldn't see a thing now and stumbled haphazardly over the deep pits she and Snob had made on endless gruelling circuits over the past few weeks. She came across a fence earlier than she expected and almost winded herself crashing into it.

Before she had a chance to indulge in a good, purging sob, she realised Niall had followed her. Yet again she had to thrust her now teeth-marked fist into her mouth and bite hard.

This was really too much, she seethed. She spat out her hand for a second and turned to him.

'What now?' she found herself snapping.

If he wanted to talk about Lisette, he could forget it, she decided. Martyrdom only went so far, Joan of Arc was French after all, not *a* French.

Niall looked rather taken aback. He stood looking at her silhouette – that was all he could see – and then he reached out and removed her soggy fist from her mouth.

'Tash, can I kiss you?'

Tash nearly fainted with surprise. She snatched back her clammy paw and resisted a temptation to hit herself over the head with it and check she was still alive.

'What?' Not exactly Elizabeth Barrett-Browning, but she was amazed her larynx was still functioning.

'I really want to kiss you, Tash.'

And then he did.

Pressed back against the post and rail fence, Tash felt the warmth of Niall's body against hers and the softness of his thick hair tickling her wet cheek. As his lips found hers, her heart rattled the bars of her ribcage in desperate longing.

She could feel his stubble sand-papering her chin and his tongue dipping lightly into her mouth with enticing delicacy. Then she began kissing him back – at first tentatively and then, like a guilty housewife with a box of chocolates, more and more hungrily until they were both gasping for air.

Surfacing, Tash realised with a stab of joy that the hammering in her chest was Niall's heart crashing alongside her own. He was so tall and his tawny shoulders so wide that she felt snug and secure in his grasp, yet underneath his clothes he was so pitifully thin that she felt ferociously protective. His touch was so gentle yet so electrifying in its effect, Tash could feel her pelvis turn to liquid.

Niall wrapped his arms around her shoulders tightly and pushed the hair away from her neck so that he could fold his cool hands around its warmth and draw her back to his mouth. He smelt of soap and tasted of toothpaste, whereas Hugo had exuded wine, cigarettes and expensive aftershave.

Suddenly Tash realised how right this was, how comfortable and sensual Niall made her feel. With a huge, heady surge of happiness it occurred to her that this was no crush. This was the real deal: log fires, silk sheets, gold rings, red roses, Satie, turtle doves, Aphrodite, Paris in spring, Venice in autumn and Brighton on a wet weekend.

Then she fell through the fence.

Nothing too dramatic, just a splitting of damp wood and a thud as she and Niall landed in the midst of a hawthorn hedge, feet still suspended on the bottom rail.

Tash felt a searing pain slash its way through her shoulder, quadrupled as Niall landed on top of it. This was followed by the slow awareness that something hot was trickling down her leg. Blood.

Niall wasn't moving.

Fighting grogginess, Tash tried to lift him off her long enough to wriggle out from under him but, despite newly nurtured muscles, he weighed a ton and her shoulder shot burning cramps through her whole body when she moved her arm even fractionally. She was trapped.

Panic started to grip her and she whimpered in fright.

Her leg began to throb as she felt the sharp sting of a deep cut hit by the wind, but that was nothing compared to her shoulder. She shifted slightly and cried out in anguish. Beads of ice-cold sweat were beginning to bubble up on her forehead. If she concentrated very, very hard she wouldn't pass out. She must think about Niall. Concentrate on Niall.

'Please be all right,' she whispered into his hair. 'Please, please don't be hurt, I couldn't bear it.'

Suddenly, he groaned and lifted his head. Spitting out a mouthful of hawthorn blossom, he turned his face to hers.

'What happened?'

'The earth moved, Niall,' Tash said quietly, wincing with pain as her head started to become light and echoing again. 'Now would you mind awfully doing the same?'

Then she passed out.

45

As the last of the caterers packed away their dark green coffee cups with lipstick-stained gold rims, Alexandra flapped around the kitchen, holding the walkabout phone with one hand and making herself a cup of fruit tea with the other.

'What do you mean you're not at liberty to say if any of your planes have crashed, you silly little man?' she snapped, wrapping a tea towel around her hand and picking up the volcanic orange Le Creuset kettle from the hob. 'Do you mean to say that Boeings could be dropping from the sky at regular intervals between New York and Paris? Surely you can let me know what's happened to my brother's flight? Yes, I appreciate you get a lot of calls of this nature but if your bloody planes arrived on time, you wouldn't, would you? No, I don't know the flight number, I'm not an air hostess. Yes, I'll hold.'

She sighed irritably and turned round to Michael, who'd just entered, shivering in a brown and russet striped dressing-gown over beige pyjamas with brown piping.

'Michael, darling, you look just like Mr Rigsby. Cup of herb tea to warm you up?'

Michael shook his head, shooting a dubious look at the bright red liquid she was pouring into two ornate mugs.

'Sorry it's so cold,' Alexandra apologised breezily. 'Pascal's opened most of the windows to try and flush out the last stragglers.'

'Well, there's still lots of bloody drunks wandering around

like a Dickensian bloody madhouse,' Michael muttered, starting to look in cupboards.

The kitchen was a shambles, he noticed. The professional cleaning company weren't due to arrive until the next morning and, until then, Alexandra seemed quite content to exist under a layer of grease, crumbs and icing sugar. If it had been Cass, Michael thought, she'd have set to with a hum and a pair of Marigolds hours ago.

'Got any bloody brandy?' He opened the door to the walk-in larder and immediately shut it again. There was a naked couple in there.

'Blast, I've been cut off. I'm afraid there isn't a drop in the house, Michael.' Alexandra smiled at him, tapping out another number from her diary to the phone. 'But if you're really desperate, Pascal might nip down and fetch you out a bottle of Rosé d'Anjou from the cellar. Ah, hello? Is that Edward Buckingham's answering service?'

'It's not for bloody me, it's for the old girl,' Michael snapped irritably, but Alexandra was chatting happily into her portable phone.

Finding a howling draught whistling around the hall, Michael pulled his dressing-gown around him and shuddered. Guests were still kissing noisy goodbyes at the door. Pascal was trying to coax a distressed flute player out of a cupboard.

'I want to geeve you a teep,' he explained.

'Ahhh!' The cupboard door slammed shut, almost taking Pascal's fingers with it.

Michael decided to try the Mogadons on Cass after all. He'd discovered a bottle lying outside Olly's bedroom of all places, but was unsure of the dosage.

He sighed and climbed over an Argentinian who'd passed out on the stairs, wearing nothing but a snazzy bathing dress, before following the sound of screaming which led to his wife.

'Unlock the door, Sophs, I want to get a jumper. It's freezing out here.'

Ben waited patiently outside his bedroom. Someone had

stolen the suit of armour from the landing, he noticed. All that remained of it was a large metal shoe that had been dropped during a hurried getaway. Like Cinderella's slipper, thought Ben. Perhaps he should tour France with it on a red velvet cushion?

'Let me in, Sophs, please?' he groaned, rattling the door handle.

'Sophs . . . Sophia?'

An unpleasant thought struck him. What if she was in there with someone else?

'Er . . . right . . . come out, whoever you are! I know you're in there and I'm not going until you show yourself-er-s, got it?' He thought about adding 'we've got you surrounded', but decided that was going too far.

There was a sinister silence on the other side of the door, followed by a loud thump. Then slowly, cautiously, there was a scraping of key against lock and the door swung open a fraction.

Ben peered in through the narrow gap and came face to face with what looked like an extra from a Ken Russell movie. Set in a ghoulish white face was a pair of smeared black circles from which peeked two waterlogged red eyes. Tangled ebony hair was matted on top of this Transylvanian apparition and beneath was a long shapeless white nightie falling to a pair of woolly red bedsocks.

'Can I come in?' Ben asked gently.

'Suppose so,' mumbled a small voice and the door creaked open just enough to admit him before being hastily relocked.

Ben turned to speak, but Sophia scuttled back across the room and buried herself back in the floral bedclothes which were liberally littered with crumpled tissues. He followed her and sat next to the small bulge she made in the big bed. As soon as he did, the chintz molehill scattered paper hankies in its wake as it relocated itself at the opposite end.

'Sophs – what's the matter?'

'Isn't it obvious!' came a suffocated moan. 'It was an absolute disaster!'

'Don't be silly, Sophs, people had a terrific time.'

But no amount of persuading would change Sophia's mind or bring her out from her self-imposed duck-down exile.

After a few minutes, Ben took out the stack of small card rectangles and swiftly scribbled notes from his pockets inviting the Merediths to parties all over the world. Lifting the covers, he inserted them roughly where he thought her head might be.

'Look,' he ordered.

There was a long pause. Then the covers were lifted at the far side of the bed to let in some light. Finally, two small hands popped out, clutching the small pile of invitations, and angrily ripped them to shreds.

Ben groaned and rubbed his sore ankle in despair. The bed had started to shake slightly. She must be crying again.

Picking up the box of tissues beside him, Ben thrust them under the eiderdown. They shot back out again, flying past him and hitting the dressing table. The bed vibrated even more violently and he could hear a muffled whimper.

But, as it grew louder, he realised that it wasn't the sound of weeping but a full-bellied, riotous giggle. As the smothered guffaws reached a crescendo, a hand poked out next to him, felt around, grabbed him firmly by the lapel and pulled him under.

'Ben,' Sophia whispered softly into his ear, covering him with kisses and starting to undo his bow tie.

'Yes, Sophs darling?'

'Tell me never ever to organise another medieval banquet as long as I live,' she giggled into his neck. 'And next time we have a party, let's just invite *friends* – people we really like, not horrible, conceited monsters.'

Ben burst out laughing.

'Oh, hello, Matty darling!' Alexandra switched off the phone and gave her son a big kiss. 'I'm so glad you're back – gosh, you look pale, sweetheart. I'm afraid you've missed most of the party but to tell you the truth it was really rather dull.'

'Mother, what have you done to our house?' Matty fumed.

'Yes, frightfully boring actually. Pascal was saying only a few minutes ago, nothing really happened tonight. You'd think with all those celebs and playboys and suchlike that there'd be just a mignon morceau of disgraceful behaviour, wouldn't you?' Alexandra looked disappointed.

'Were you blindfold?' laughed Sally, following Matty into the room and putting her arms around his waist.

'Oh, I had such a lovely chat with Véronique tonight.' Alexandra started to fill the kettle again. 'But first I must tell you *the* most exciting news about Eddie. His plane was delayed, which is a terrible bore, I know, but it turns out he's bringing some old chums and – I can hardly wait – a new lover—'

'I asked you what you've been doing to our house,' Matty repeated coldly.

'Don't be silly, darling,' Alexandra said lightly, fiddling with the kettle lid, 'how can I have done anything? I've been here all the time.'

'Don't be facetious,' snapped Matty. 'Why is the place crawling with builders and decorators? I did nothing but make cups of tea with five sugars for twenty-four hours.'

Alexandra laughed gaily.

'You know, I remember when your father and I had Benedict's roof shored up, there was this wonderful old character called Falstaff. Not his real name, you understand; the other men called him that because he fell off a roof in Staffordshire. Quite witty if you think about it. Anyway, he used to say, "Mrs France, I don't know what it is about your tea, but—"

'Mother!' Matty looked up at the ceiling in despair.

Sally was biting her lip to stop herself from laughing.

'Oh.' Alexandra hung her head and looked guilty. 'Well, I just thought . . . one or two small alterations while you were away . . . a little surprise, you know . . .'

'Small alterations!' howled Matty. 'You'd think they were renovating the Sistine Chapel, there are so many limp-wristed men skipping round with dust sheets. And the outside looks like the Pompidou Centre – you can't see the house for scaffolding. I walked past it three times without recognising it. Kept expecting Jeremy Beadle to pop out from behind a lamp-post.'

'Really?' Alexandra said in a small voice and smiled at him. 'Would you like a cup of tea or are you sick to death of it?'

'I don't believe this!' Matty slapped his forehead with his hand and turned away in defeat.

'Oh, I suppose I should mention something else while we're on the subject.' Alexandra floated towards the range and buried her face in a tea caddy.

'Don't tell me – you've paid off the mortgage!' Matty hissed sarcastically.

'Not exactly,' Alexandra replied slowly. 'That is, not all of it.'

'You *what*?' Matty's eyes flew back to his mother in shock, but then swivelled over her shoulder to stare at something by the door, and he whispered 'Shit!' in a low voice.

Alexandra turned round and gasped.

Staggering in and buckling under the dead weight of the body he was carrying, was Niall. Slung over his shoulder in a precarious fireman's lift, with her bottom hanging out of the rips in her muddy jeans, was Tash.

'Ohmygod!' Alexandra rushed forward and pulled out a chair. 'What happened?'

Niall gently let Tash down on to it, and she plunged towards the left before they grabbed her head and rested it on the floury table. He wiped his forehead with the back of his hand and looked down at her anxiously.

'She passed out,' he glanced up at the others, 'and fell through a fence.'

'Is she drunk?' Sally felt Tash's pulse and her forehead. Her heart seemed to be thumping away healthily and she was cool.

'No. I don't know.' Niall sat down on the chair next to Tash and put his hand over hers.

'She's bleeding!' Sally knelt down to where the fragile fabric of Tash's old jeans had been ripped right down the leg. The exposed brown calf was covered with dark, clotting blood.

'I'll call an ambulance!' Alexandra grabbed for the porta-phone and it promptly fell in the sink.

'I don't think that's necessary, Mother.' Matty noticed Niall's clothes were ripped too and both his and Tash's hair was full of twigs and old blossom. 'Have you got some antiseptic we can clean her up with?' He turned to his mother, who was standing with her hands over her mouth looking stunned.

'I think her shoulder's shot, too,' Niall muttered, stroking Tash's hair gently.

'Shot! You're telling me she's been shot?' Alexandra screamed.

'No, I—'

'Why don't you fetch that antiseptic, Mother, huh?' Matty suggested in a placating voice and started to bustle her out of the room. 'I'll go and see if Pascal and I can rustle up a local doctor or someone sober enough to take her to a casualty department to be checked out.'

'I've not drunk tonight,' Niall said quickly. 'I'll take her.'

Matty stopped and looked round, letting his mother go on ahead.

'I'll take her,' Niall repeated.

'Oh, no you won't,' a strong, high-pitched and painfully familiar voice came from the door to the hall.

Niall looked up abruptly and what he saw took his breath away in one swift, agonising punch to the chest. Standing in front of him, the picture of angry, wanton desire, was Lisette.

There was a horrified silence. Sally swore under her breath.

Matty was the first to recover. He turned on Lisette, so close to her that when he hissed she flinched.

'Get out, you selfish cow!' The words seemed to bounce off her. 'Leave him alone,' he finished in a low, deadly voice.

Lisette gazed at him mockingly. 'I think that's up to Niall, don't you?' she asked lightly, looking across at Niall with a bright, excited challenge in her dark-rimmed eyes. 'You can make your own decisions without Sister Matty's guidance, can't you, darling?'

She looks so beautiful, thought Niall, almost strangled with sadness.

This was something he'd dreamed about, hoped for, prayed for, begged for and schemed for endlessly. Yet now the unlikely event had arrived, he wanted to scream, 'Take it back – I'm not ready!'

Suddenly, Tash groaned and a shaky hand crept towards her head. She lifted her face tentatively. One half of it was covered in flour, making her look like a ghost. Her eyes peeked into the room, failed to focus and shut again as she laid her head back on the table with a sleepy sigh.

'Tash! Angel, are you all right?' Niall asked in a desperate voice.

'Ishtoveyoush,' she mumbled and groaned in pain.

'Well?' Lisette prompted. Her voice was laced with frozen venom but her eyes still sparkled, beckoning him away.

'Oh, for Christ's sake go somewhere and talk, the both of you,' Sally snapped angrily. 'We'll look after Tash.'

Matty opened his mouth to protest but, seeing the look on Sally's face, shut it again.

As Niall stood up, all the colour and strength seemed to have drained out of him. He walked over to her like an old man. At the door, he took one last look over his shoulder at Tash. She had her thumb in her mouth and grass seeds in her hair. She looked about fourteen.

Lisette followed his gaze and blew out through her lips with contempt.

'Come on,' Niall sighed.

Not looking at her, he led the way out of the room.

Tash was vaguely aware that someone was pouring a substance which tasted of boiled and distilled underpants avec formaldehyde down her throat.

She moaned and spat it out as fast as it was shovelled down her.

'I don't think she can swallow.' Her mother's voice came floating through Tash's dream about giant brussels sprouts enslaving the planet earth.

'I think it's your herb tea actually, Mother.' Matty's voice, light and dry, made contact just as Princess Diana was being squashed to death by one of these huge green veg.

Tash opened one eye and discovered she was looking straight at a close-up of Pascal's crotch. She closed it again quickly.

'Hello,' she muttered into the table surface, sending up a cloud of flour.

Pandemonium seemed to break out at this. Tash could hear a lot of air gasped and scuffling of feet.

'Ohmygod, she's awake!' her mother shrieked excitedly. 'Hello – Tash? Can you hear me?' She spoke in a very slow, clear voice as if Tash had lost her grasp of English.

'Yes, Mummy.' Tash sighed and opened her eyes. A crowd of concerned faces gawped back at her as if at a specimen in a jar. She decided she preferred Pascal's crotch.

'What happened?' she asked groggily.

'Good question.' Sally smiled over her wine glass, her eyes troubled.

Matty cleared his throat.

'This is nice Doctor Thiérry, Tash.' Alexandra quickly pointed out an unsavoury-looking character wearing half-moon specs and a Burberry mac who was smoking a Disque Bleu and drinking wine at the table. 'He's going to check you out.'

Tash tried not to scream in pain as the rheumy doctor poked and probed her in a dense cloud of smoke. He muttered the whole time under his breath in French, wagging a nicotine-stained finger or shaking his head at her to emphasise certain points.

Her shoulder stung all over as if someone had plugged it into the mains, but Tash grinned cheerfully at him each time he nearly pulled it out of its socket. All her muddled mind could reason was that if he said she couldn't ride today, Hugo would think she was conceding defeat.

Dr Thiérry looked at her through a screen of smoke with his rather yellowing eyes and murmured thoughtfully before diving into his battered leather bag, retrieving a large roll of elasticated bandage and a pair of scissors. Lighting a fresh cigarette and dangling it between his lips, he started strapping up her shoulder.

'Tell him not to go too mad, Mummy,' Tash pleaded to Alexandra, who was trying to persuade Olly and Ginger into the kitchen for a drink. 'I've got to ride tomor – today.'

Alexandra started to gabble to Dr Thiérry while Olly and Ginger sat down, joining everyone else in staring at Tash. Their room was apparently currently being occupied by two drunks and a hungover spaniel.

'He says it wouldn't be very wise, darling.' Alexandra looked down at her.

'But I must!' Tash wailed in a panic.

'I know how hard you've worked, sweetheart, you're bound to be disappointed, but you mustn't jeopardise your health.' Alexandra took her hand and Dr Thiérry resumed strapping. 'He says you might be concussed.'

'You'll have plenty of other chances, Tash,' Sally pointed out from inside another glass of wine.

'You no ride as well with a pain of the arm, no?' Pascal started uncorking a fresh bottle fetched from the cellars.

Tash looked at the clock. It was past five. She suddenly felt too exhausted to argue.

'Have all the guests gone?' she asked, deciding to change the subject.

'Most of them.' Matty sighed, holding out his glass to Pascal. 'The odd one or two are still wandering round refusing to budge. Some are unaccounted for, Jean and Valérie included. The mess is appalling.'

'Marcus and his gang are still going strong in the barn as you can hear,' said Sally. 'Rory Wiltsher came in just now – you were still out cold – grabbed eight baguettes and pissed off again without saying a word. Pascal thinks he's in pain, ha ha.'

Tash desperately wanted to ask where Niall was, but with all these people around was too shy. Beyond taking him outside to explain that Lisette was at the party, her memory was a blur of fact and fantasy. She had a ridiculous recollection of him kissing her. Beside it stood the black and far more realistic image of him and Lisette together.

The loud, waspish buzz of a helicopter taking off outside made her head throb.

Ginger and Olly had moved in on either side of her, desperate for a gossip.

'What *have* you been up to, Tash?' Olly whistled, examining her shoulder.

Tash mumbled something about falling over.

'No, darling.' Olly cocked his eyebrow. 'I meant fiddling with that lovely look Ginger spent hours creating. What *possessed* you to slip into those string slacks?'

'Not that they seem to have stopped her scoring.' Ginger winked, trying to cheer Tash up. 'I spotted her having the *most* exciting tête-à-poitrine with gorgeous Hugo earlier.'

Alexandra, mindlessly pouring a bottle of tomato juice into a jug, pretended not to listen in.

'Yes, you two were looking very chummy in the garden.' Olly grinned. 'Although you'll never believe who I saw skinny dipping in the pool without a strap-mark in sight.'

'No – the best gossip,' Ginger took up the story, 'has to be that Ol and I just spotted that Irish actor chap and his ravishing wife—'

'Look who it is!' Matty said loudly.

Anton had appeared through the door to the courtyard and, finding a rapt audience, started burbling in his expressive, guttural French accompanied by the usual arm-waving and finger-kissing.

He'd been pulling Mercedes and Rolls out of the field with his tractor, he explained happily. In the past half-hour the strolling players' mini-bus had flattened both gateposts and a flowered Dormobile had been careering round in circles, terrifying waiting chauffeurs.

After sharing a quick half-bottle with Pascal, he shouted something to Tash with a meaningful wink and more finger-kissing before disappearing into the night.

Tash took a sip of herb tea and pulled a face. Dr Thiérry had finished with her shoulder now, leaving it trussed and immobile, and was concentrating his full attention and a mist of dispersing ash on her cut leg.

'Anton, he say he weel pick you this morning at seven to get your 'orse ready,' Pascal waved his glass at Tash. 'If you are well, 'e weel take you to the concours. Now 'e use 'is truck to take 'ome the guests who get too ivre to drive,' he laughed heartily. 'Soon I cook breakfast, but for now you 'ave a glass of wine.'

Tash smiled weakly. 'I think I'd prefer a packet of Alka Seltzer dissolved in strong black coffee, if you don't mind.'

In two hours she'd be embarking on the worst day of her life with a strapped arm, a demon hangover – which was already clutching at her temples and sifting through the contents of her stomach – and no sleep. But she hardly cared any more.

'So Niall and Lisette O'Shaughnessy are together again?' she whispered to Ginger, trying not to sound as if she'd been sucking on a helium balloon.

'I hear they're negotiating a new contract as we speak,' Ginger gossiped happily, checking that Olly wasn't listening. 'Can't say I blame him for taking her back – have you seen her? She's ravishing – like an Eton fag in drag.'

46

As the spaniels pushed their steel bowls around the flagstone floor, noisily snuffling up the last of their breakfast, Pascal fell over Alexandra for the third time and waggled his fish slice irritably.

'I can't help it, darling,' Alexandra protested from her position directly in front of the range with her feet in the bottom plate-warming oven. 'I'm absolutely freezing.'

Pascal ignored her and stretched past to give his undivided attention to the griddle iron.

Over the muffled din of the rave still pounding on the courtyard door, the d'Eblouirs' chief cockerel could be heard furiously announcing daybreak from inside the hen house.

Tash limped upstairs to shower and change.

A strange man was asleep in her bed nose-to-nose with Flumps the badger. He didn't wake as she quietly crawled around the room grabbing clothes and a towel before creeping along the corridor to the bathroom.

While she was battling in the shower not to get any of her dressings wet or whimper too loudly when the pain really got to her, the first grey-green beams of dawn crept over the horizon outside. When she leaned out of the cubicle to fetch her shampoo from on top of the pile of things she'd brought in with her, the small rectangle of sky at the far end of the room had turned from dull to polished pewter. By the time she finally fell out of the dripping booth, her bandages sopping and her hangover threatening to abscond with her brain, the window was letting in the first blanched lemon shafts of a rising sun.

Tash took three aspirin and one of the painkillers Dr Thiérry had left (in a small brown glass bottle which, she suspected, dated back to circa nineteen-fifty). Then, pulling on an old pair of striped leggings and a huge Guernsey sweater, she picked up her carrier bag of brand new gear for the show, and staggered towards the stairs.

Padding slowly along the landing, Tash was too preoccupied with nerves, trepidation and her hangover to notice the shambles the house was in.

Overnight, it had come to resemble a set from *Stig of the Dump*; the staircase was virtually impassable for empty bottles, discarded cigarette packets and scattered items which seemed oddly out of place: a snorkelling kit, three jacket potatoes, a lute and a pair of secateurs amongst them.

The hall was chaos. All the flower arrangements had now wilted or been dispersed around the room so that it looked like the steps of a register office on a Saturday afternoon. The floor was awash with crumbs and spillages, the furniture dappled with rings from damp glass bottoms. A chilly wind swept tissues, petals and dust through the air and whipped the chandelier above into a chorus of tinkling discords.

As Tash passed through the small corridor which led to the kitchen she could hear raised voices coming from a room to her right. One of them, with its mellow Irish familiarity, made her breath catch in her throat. She paused outside.

'I just don't see the point in going on like this!' came a woman's voice, high and trembling. 'You're saying I'm wasting my life but can't you see I've got nothing else to live *for*? You don't want me!' she gave a hollow sob.

Niall sighed. 'I haven't said that now, have I?'

Tash could feel the cold of the corridor gnaw through her jumper and seep into her heart.

'What?' Lisette's voice quavered.

Niall was whispering something now; a low caressing murmur from which Tash could only pick single words. He was talking about pain and unhappiness and something to do with a 'panacea'.

Was that like a pancreas? Tash wondered. Perhaps he *was* ill after all.

She leaned forward and a floorboard let out an almighty groan.

Tash bit her lip and listened as he said:

'. . . renewed my faith. I never thought I could feel that strongly about anyone, it's come as a huge shock. The thing that terrifies me is that I have no idea if—'

Another creak from below, Tash held her breath.

'– feels the same way about me. But I know I need to forgive you, Lisette, for both of our sakes. You see, I'm truly in love again and, Christ, it's really spooked me.'

'I need you, Niall!' Lisette was sobbing now.

There was a long pause.

'But do you love me?' Niall was almost whispering.

At this moment, a washing machine in the laundry to Tash's left which had been happily burbling a set of stained napkins through rinse shuddered its way into a deafening spin.

Tash didn't wait to hear Lisette's reply.

Instead she walked numbly, teeth chattering, away from the closed door.

So he did still love Lisette; he wanted her back despite everything. Tash had never felt so utterly wretched.

She paused beside a row of messily layered jackets strung up on brass pegs, unable to face the babbling voices and cooking smells coming from the kitchen. On the floor beside her were piles of shoes and boots covered with cat hair. Someone had stuffed Todd's flashy cowboy boots full of burnt vol au vents. Next to them, Tash recognised Niall's scuffed and worn old paddock boots. Hastily rifling through her carrier bag, she extracted her lucky farthing which she lugged everywhere with her and dropped it inside one.

If it's what he wants, let him have Lisette, she wished. But please make her put on ten stone and get spots.

The kitchen was a welcome fug, despite her mother's shivering grumbles. Olly and Ginger had been dispatched into the village to fetch baguettes, brioches and croissants hot from the boulangerie. A few more people, none of whom Tash knew, had surfaced and were sagging around the room clutching their heads and looking green. Pascal was running around in a pinny like Keith Floyd, a glass of pungent red wine pressed to his lips at regular intervals. Sally and Matty had clearly gone to bed.

Tash drooped into a chair beside a heavy-boned woman with smudged lipstick and a snood that had slipped over one ear who was frantically trying to locate her husband with the porta-phone, which had been dried out on the range.

'It just keeps crackling and hissing,' she bellowed, as if they were all on the other side of the Grand Canyon.

Just as the frazzled woman was about to try again, the phone rang with a low, warbling and slightly sub-aqua buzz.

'What?' she barked. 'Oh.' She looked up and shouted, 'Is there anyone here called Bash?'

'Er . . . I think that's me,' said Tash, uncovering her ears and waiting for the pounding in her head to subside. She'd need another aspirin in a minute.

The woman grudgingly handed her the phone.

'Hello?' Even Tash's own voice thudded through her head like a resounding backfire.

'At last, we thought your lines were down,' came an unfamiliar voice, 'hang on a minute.'

There was a lot of clunking and Tash could hear dogs barking in the background. Her guts were starting to heave again.

'Hello – still there?'

'Yes.' If she kept her head very still it wasn't quite as bad.

'This is Gus Moncrieff, remember? Hugo's mate – oh, thanks, Pen,' he could be heard slurping something, presumably tea.

'Yes, I remember.'

Rooter came over and rested his head and paw on Tash's leg with imploring brown eyes. He looked as hungover as a dog could get.

'Good,' Gus rambled on. 'Look, Hugo's here, he wants a word in a minute. I didn't get you up, did I?'

'No, don't worry.' Tash thought ruefully of her engaged bed.

Gus wanted to know if she'd like to walk the course with them.

Even the thought of it made Tash's head pound with panic. She quite probably wouldn't be able to stagger beyond the first fence, let alone ride it. She'd forgotten the dressage test already. A choking fear put her larynx on the rack at the thought of Snob's sick sense of humour.

'Yes, thanks, that would be great,' she croaked.

A stab in her shoulder coincided with a monumental groan in her stomach. She held Rooter's paw for support.

They arranged to meet at the start at eight-thirty, and Gus handed the phone over to Hugo.

'Tash?' a familiar drawl crackled down the line.

'Yes?' she replied weakly.

Her belly gave a lurch and groaned again. Pascal, thinking she was hungry, placed a loaded plate of little crêpes in front of her, dripping with butter and honey. The moist, sickly smell wafted upwards.

Hugo was asking her to fetch some stuff from his room. His voice got fainter and fainter and the buzzing interference on the line louder.

Tash shook the receiver. Then she realised it wasn't the phone yodelling tunelessly, it was her head. She looked down at the plate of crêpes and felt bile choke her throat. Taking Hugo with her, she sped from the room to the nearest toilet.

The one by the laundry was locked. Wailing at Hugo to hang on, she ran to the downstairs shower-room beside the gym, with Rooter following, barking excitedly.

It was unlocked but two people seemed to have passed out on the floor. Not caring, Tash ran to the loo and threw up. The relief was bliss.

As she clambered painfully to the sink to wash out her mouth, one of the prostrate figures – dressed in full black tie from the waist up and nothing but baggy grey tea-bag underpants below –

groaned and rolled over. Tash looked round, stopped mid-gargle and swallowed a giggle. Coughing, she spat out the water in the basin and grabbed the towel rail to steady herself.

'Bonjour, Jean,' she greeted cautiously. 'Ça va?'

A hired Renault Espace drew up in the courtyard and four jet-lagged people stared out of the broad windows.

In the retina-slicing early morning sunshine, the shuddering rave barn had lost some of its seedy opium-den look, but none of its decibels. Lights still spun and winked in its depths, bodies still writhed and the beat droned on. To the newcomers, it looked like a shabby, rundown farm building full of rather squalid teenagers.

As the driver of the Espace, a tall rangy man with swept-back peppery hair and the watchful eyes of a wolfhound, heaved himself stiffly out of the seat, a stooping youth wearing a red bomber jacket shuffled over.

'Gotta smoke, man?'

Lucian Merriot gave the Artful Dodger a long, meditative look with his pale eyes before tossing him an almost full packet of St Moritz.

The youth nodded a tacit thanks and loped into a second gloomy outbuilding in which sleeping bags nestled in banks of straw, like brightly coloured caterpillars hiding nocturnal moths.

Eddie Buckingham – shorter, more portly than his friend – had jumped from the passenger seat and was making his way round to the back of the car to open the door for an exquisitely attractive passenger in the rear. Eddie took hold of a beautifully manicured hand as a pair of endless legs swung out and two Italian brogues came to rest on the uneven cobbles. Eddie looked down and smiled.

'How are you feeling?' he asked anxiously, the twinkling amber eyes and deep laughter lines concealing his nerves to all except his ravishing companion.

'I'm feeling fine, honey. It's you who's as jumpy as a cat, Eddie.'

'I just want them to love you as much as I do. Well, almost as much.' He winked, smoothing back his glossy raven hair into its small pony-tail at the nape of his neck.

With his expensive soft leather jacket, black silk shirt and cream chinos, he looked more like the manager of a successful rock band than an art dealer.

'You don't want them to disapprove of me, Eddie,' his companion corrected, a veil of soft ash-blonde hair falling across laughing eyes the colour of speedwell.

'I guess not,' Eddie grinned. 'You've got to remember, Lauren, the last time I saw my sister I was – well – *different*.'

'I know, you took the seventies kinda seriously.' One manicured hand came up and nudged him affectionately on the cheek.

'Sure, you can laugh, but I don't know how they're going to take this. *Us*, I mean.'

'I think we missed the party, Eddie.' Lucian, who'd been inspecting the barn from a safe distance, came back to the Renault, closing his long cashmere coat against the early morning chill.

'Can't say I'm disappointed.' Eddie sighed. 'I could do without a first-night audience.' Lucian smiled a lop-sided but nonetheless distinguished smile and winked at Lauren.

The final passenger had emerged from the car and was staring up at the airbrushed streaks of cloud in a pale blue sky. Lucian left Eddie to hide his nerves unloading the trunk and walked over.

'Still feeling lousy?' he asked, putting an immaculately tailored arm around his son's shoulders.

The younger man shook his head and grinned.

'Great place,' he whistled. 'Tash just told me her mother lived in a crumbling French farmhouse. I never imagined this sort of spread.'

Lucian looked at the beautiful house and nodded silently.

After Eddie had handed them their luggage: a smart monogrammed leather suitcase to Lucian, a tatty old rucksack to his son and two tartan Ralph Lauren cases for himself and his blonde partner, they headed towards the house.

'I'd better go in first,' Eddie explained as he faltered on the steps to the open main door. 'I'm not sure if Alexandra's got my message.'

Alexandra was busy pouring coffee and aspirin down a very sheepish Jean and an almost comatose redhead, who had emerged from their bathroom nocturne looking decidedly ragged.

The door to the courtyard lobby was shut against the noise from the barn. No one had seen the car draw up.

Alexandra was further preoccupied and excited by the fact that Valérie had just walked brazenly through the kitchen with a distressed-looking Hollywood gossip-columnist, fresh from a night of passion in the larder of all places. Jean, cringing behind his bowl of coffee, had turned from green to purple like a weather-detecting crystal, but was clearly too ill to move.

'I hope he doesn't commit a crime of passion with the leaf rake later,' Alexandra whispered, trying to cheer up Tash, who was looking more jaded and woeful than ever.

But her words were lost as the sound of a commotion in the corridor drifted in.

'Xandra!'

Pascal, who'd just popped upstairs for some more paracetamol, appeared through the door with a man under each arm.

'Tell me, chérie, one of zees men 'ees your brozer?' he asked triumphantly. He'd been reading the French translation of *Lace* recently.

Alexandra looked up with a whimper of joy and poured scalding coffee all over the buxom redhead's hand, unnoticed by either of them. Putting down the pot, she dashed over to Eddie and gave him a huge, happy cuddle like an overwhelmed setter.

'Eddie! How wonderful! Gosh!' She wiped the tears away with the back of her hand.

Eddie laughed and extracted himself gently.

'Hi, lovie. You look terrific. I want you to meet—'

'Laurence!' Alexandra turned and kissed Lucian on both cheeks. 'I got Eddie's message through his answering service and I don't mind a *bit* you coming to stay with us – we're all delighted. I've put you both in the top turret – my daughter, Polly, calls it the Rapunzel room, it's wildly romantic.'

So this was Eddie's new lover, she thought with immense relief. He wasn't what she was expecting at all, no Stalin moustache or little leather cap with chains on it. He looked like a very dapper, sophisticated businessman wearing a made-to-measure lovat green suit Pascal would die for and a jazzy silk tie. With his broad shoulders and beautifully cut hair greying over the temples, he was, in fact, divine.

Eddie was muttering something and waving frantically behind him, but Alexandra was too euphoric to listen.

She looked at her brother again. He had changed beyond recognition. No longer the skinny figure sporting off-the-wall clothes with a gaunt, hangdog expression and long, messy hair. He looked fit and well fed, almost chubby. It suited him. With the extra weight on it, his face was made kinder, less challenging. His smoky hair was still long but it was sleekly pulled back from his face like a media mogul not a camp hippy. He had a small gold loop in one ear and smelt deliciously of Ferre.

'You look just like Mummy,' she said dreamily.

'Xandra, chérie. Écoute—' Pascal touched her arm and rapidly explained in French what Eddie had unsuccessfully been trying to communicate in English for more than a minute.

'Ohmygod!' Alexandra clamped her hand over her mouth and started to laugh.

Sipping coffee, Tash had watched her uncle come in as if through a smoke-screen. Her heart was still leaping around like a deranged pocket-watch inside her chest, her thoughts flitting from Niall to the day ahead and back to Niall again with bewildering inconsistency.

She assumed the handsome man with Eddie must be his boyfriend, if you could call someone as rakish as Lucian such a thing. She had an odd feeling she'd seen him before. Perhaps he was famous.

Eddie was beckoning at someone to come in. He looked

much older than she'd imagined him. Her memory of this dark, attractive man was so faint that it was like looking at an old family video.

She gazed away and out of the window. The wind was bending the branches of an old oak beside the paddock into a stooping tarpaulin of leaves and buffeting the corner of a green and white pagoda so that it billowed like a mainsail. A weak sun fought to turn the garden into a mural of tart greens.

Across the valley a misty shimmer promised a scorching day. Beyond the hazy wood, like a clump of broccoli snuggling in the fold of a hollow to the left, Snob was probably snorting irritably in Anton's stable, waiting for his breakfast and a chance to prove his superiority over the human race.

Tash glanced back at her uncle. He was introducing Alexandra and Pascal to an enchanting blonde.

'This,' he announced with a nervous flourish, 'is Lauren.'

Despite her elegant Italian clothes, Lauren looked like a precociously pretty fourteen year old. Tash wondered if she was Eddie's love-child. Perhaps she'd turned up out of the blue to announce she was moving in with her father and his gay lover. Even to Tash this seemed improbable. But there was no denying Eddie's protective arm around her and the bursting pride on his face.

Behind them, someone else was trying to edge his way past the small crowd at the door.

Tash mindlessly took in the thick, donkey-blond hair, bulbous nose and curly lips.

Then she did a double-take which made her head almost fly off her neck.

As her senses reunited, she saw a familiar old baseball jacket worn over a faded denim shirt, unbuttoned to reveal a white t-shirt with 'Freshly Laid' emblazoned on the front. A pair of long, athletic legs in charcoal black jeans and Chelsea boots was heading towards her.

She looked up just in time to see a huge, lop-sided grin and wickedly merry eyes bear down on her face before an enormous kiss was planted on her startled lips.

Breathing in a waft of Chanel Pour Homme and feeling a warm hand against her cheek, Tash broke free and gazed at him in horrified wonder.

'Max!' she gasped.

Max flopped down in the chair beside her and put his feet up on the table with a contented sigh.

''Lo, Tash.' He helped himself to one of her pancakes with a grin. 'Any chance of a coffee?'

47

Hours later, Tash sat in the cab of Anton's decrepit horsebox, sipping coffee from the plastic lid of a thermos flask and wondering if her hands would ever stop shaking. Through the dusty window beside her, a glossy blue horsebox had parked with a hiss of brakes and the loud clattering of hooves on wood told her that its contents were being unloaded.

She felt another uncontrollable shudder course through her and growled at herself in frustration. Anton, handing her one of his corrosively bitter cigarettes, didn't even look up from his paper. Tash, on the verge of throwing up for the third time that morning, thanked him politely and put it behind her ear.

'Oh no!' she groaned, ducking down.

Out of the windscreen, which was almost solid with dead flies, Tash caught sight of her mother, trailing three sick-looking spaniels and picking her way carefully over the scattered spheres of horse dung.

Following behind was Pascal, dashing in strawberry Bermuda shorts, with a video camera, two pairs of binoculars and a light meter slung around his neck, looking like a stray member of the Royal press corps.

Tash slid down beside the dashboard, but it was too late. They'd spotted Anton's wooden crate on wheels amongst the gleaming, fibre-glass equine transport palaces. Alexandra tapped on the window briskly, smiling through it.

Tash closed her eyes. But when she opened them again they were still there beaming at her.

She leaned over and slid the stiff window open.

'Isn't this exciting?' Alexandra gushed enthusiastically. She was wearing a green silk trouser suit which would have made anyone else look like a hefty cucumber. 'I didn't realise it was such a big event.'

'No?' Tash replied weakly.

'We've come to give you moral support. Pascal insisted. He's so excited for you.' Over her shoulder, weighed down by his apparatus, Pascal was looking anything but.

'Where's lovely Max?' Alexandra noticed Tash and Anton were alone in the cab.

'Getting drinks from the bar,' Tash explained gloomily.

The morning was flying past, jammed on fast forward, and somewhere along the line she'd lost the remote control.

Tash had only just had the chance for a rushed, shocked hello to Max before Anton arrived, muttering that her horse had gone quite mad and would she like to come and get him ready.

With Max in tow, she'd found Snob looking indignant and hurt with his foot in his feed bucket and Anton's terrified daughter trapped in the corner of the stable.

The temporary pleasure gleaned from the fact that Snob not only appeared to recognise her but also seemed pleased to see her quickly wore off as he left his teeth-marks in Max's bottom.

'It seems I've got a jealous rival,' Max had joked, remaining teeth-grittingly cheerful as he gave Snob a pat at arm's length.

'Yes?' Tash had piped nervously before realising that he was only talking about the horse.

Getting Snob ready with Max around had been awful. Nicking her fags and Snob's Polos, he'd blithely acted as if the London cold war between them had never happened. While Tash's hangover resonated at fever pitch, Max had hovered nearby, asking if she liked his hairdo, his new boots, his straighter-cut Levis and drilling her about her mother's second marriage.

'Pascal is some kinda guy, huh? He must be seriously loaded.'

Tense with nerves and frustration, Tash had washed and

groomed the fidgeting, squirming stallion in virtual silence while Max sat on a straw bale and told her what a 'dynamite' time he'd had in the States, all the 'crazy' people he'd met and 'phenomenal' job offers he was 'thumbing through'. His empathy was not at its most poignant.

Meanwhile, Snob had squashed Tash's feet to a size twelve and farted at her while she was shampooing his tail.

Max then proceeded to describe, strike for strike, a baseball match he'd watched, even down to the brand of popcorn he'd eaten.

By the time they'd set off to the show with Tash map-reading and Max and Anton singing 'New York, New York', Tash was quietly thinking murderous thoughts about deportation. She knew that she'd totally, irrevocably, gone off him.

In the beer tent, Max winked at the curly-haired girl behind the bar as he downed a swift half.

Since arriving with Tash, he reflected sourly, they'd hardly spoken. The rapprochement wasn't going as smoothly as he'd anticipated. What's more, he loathed horses and found the rules of eventing totally unfathomable.

Where was the ball? he'd ribbed on arrival. Why weren't there any wickets or goalposts?

Tash had ignored him. Max was piqued; Tash always laughed at his jokes, it was one of the things he loved about her.

While they'd walked the course with Hugo Beauchamp and the Moncrieffs, Max had tried to lag behind for a talk, a speech of moving integrity and devotion mapped out in his head.

But Tash had been far too preoccupied with worrying about impending self-preservation to listen. Instead, she'd concentrated on Gus Moncrieff's advice about turns and distances and tips on keeping Snob calm between fences and under control over them.

Max had stomped up the final hill in a very black mood.

Following behind Tash, he'd watched in amazement as she was dragged into a bush by Hugo Beauchamp.

'Who the hell is *he*?' Max had overheard Hugo spit.

'My ex,' Tash had muttered glumly.

On the other side of the bush, Max had stiffened and cleared his throat loudly.

Trotting beside her as she paced towards the horsebox, he'd asked her exactly what she meant by 'ex', and how Hugo fitted into the picture.

Tash had shrugged, swallowed and bolted off to be sick.

On spending ten minutes trying to undo the door-zip after a pee in an already rancid portaloo tent, Max had started to develop a Hurricane Edna depression.

He'd snapped at Tash irritably and festered inside the cab of the lorry, eyeing up female bottoms in tight white breeches while she went with the others to register and collect her number.

It was only later, when he'd spotted – and smelt – the pungent white marquee harbouring a small bar, that he'd cheered up. When he took in that they had bière pression, he'd even smiled and kissed Tash on the cheek.

'God, I've missed you,' he'd ventured, cradling her in his arms despite the fact she smelt of horse, hoof-oil and fly-repellent. 'Your letter was the best. We must talk later. Back in a two with a brandy to calm your nerves.'

And he'd pounded off on his long legs, straight through a pile of what his Aussie chums called road dumplings.

In the shadow of the horsebox, Pascal had been given the spaniels' leads to hold and they were joyfully weaving after smells, treating him as a Bermuda-ed maypole. Beside him, Alexandra gestured for Tash to join them.

Groaning under her breath, Tash clambered out of the cab and stood dutifully while they surveyed the scene.

It was now ten o'clock and the showground was drenched in glassy, blinding sunshine. Gleaming, snorting horses tied to boxes had already broken out into a light, hard-water lather on their necks and under their string-vest sweat sheets, aware that the day ahead would be no ordinary plod around well-worn ménages.

In a roped-off arena to the right, brightly coloured show-jumps, like architects' scale models of proposed bridges for Disneyworld, glistened in the brilliant, searing light. The flowers in the tubs to either side of them were already beginning to wilt and the spruces in white pots marking the start and finish were turning a thirsty golden brown.

Further in the distance, the dressage for one of the more advanced classes was being judged in a long, rectangular ring cordoned off by low, brilliant white barriers, so glossy they looked like illuminated neon strips. At the far end of the arena, the judges peered through the dusty windows of a caravan with bottles of Evian lined up in front of them. Soon it would be like sitting in a kiln.

Anton had joined the little group beside the horsebox and was passing out glasses of warm, acidic rosé from a plastic bottle.

Tash took two more painkillers with her wine and concentrated on keeping them down. She noticed that two ambulances had trundled on to the showground and were positioning themselves ready for a day's trade.

'How's everything at the house?' she asked her mother in a small voice, longing for news of Niall.

'Oh, rather jolly really,' Alexandra said cheerfully.

Over her shoulder Pascal puffed his cheeks in surprise.

'Eddie and Lauren apologise but they're having a quick snooze to get over jet lag. Isn't Lauren divine? I couldn't *believe* it when Eddie said they were married. They might come later if they can find it. Sophia was just surfacing as we left. She was positively *furious.* It seems their nanny – Wowla, isn't it? – has run off with some dreadful acid lout. She left a note in Italian which no one can translate. They're bringing Lucian and the kids at about midday. Oh! I must tell you – Amanda Beauchamp seems to have had a nuit d'amour with . . .'

Tash stopped listening, all hope of a mention of Niall dissolved.

She was worried about Hugo. He'd been absolutely livid when she'd turned up with Max, and even more incensed when Tash confessed that she'd forgotten to collect his breeches and jacket.

As they'd walked the course, Max had forced her to hang back from the others and asked in a sotto hiss why Hugo had kissed her so thoroughly on arrival. Tash muttered vaguely about a gregarious personality.

When she'd caught up with the Moncrieffs at a deathly-looking obstacle called L'Etoile à Briquet, Hugo had cornered her behind a bush and demanded a reason for her turning up with 'that self-satisfied jerk'. Tash, running low on inspiration, had said Max was an unpredictable manic-depressive prone to violence, and severe shocks had to be kept to a minimum. Hugo had looked doubtful but valued his profile too much to risk testing her story.

By then Tash had been so jittery and uneasy that she'd hardly taken in any of the second half of the course. It seemed unlikely to matter; she was quite sure she and Snob wouldn't get that far. The question wasn't if they were going to part company, but where.

The fences on the undulating course were almost all huge and tricky, requiring very accurate riding as well as what Gus called 'popability'. Even Hugo expressed surprise at the level of difficulty expected from what was supposed to be a nursery-slope event.

'Hope you've got international medical insurance,' he'd murmured to Tash as they walked up the long, rock-hard hill towards the finish.

'What did he just say to you?' she'd heard Max whisper accusingly a moment later.

Propping her wine on a wheel arch, Tash closed her eyes. A spell in a French hospital surrounded by grapes, nurses and silence broken occasionally by a bleeping piece of technology, seemed the ideal harbour from Hugo, Max and her despair over Niall.

If he's back with Lisette, she mulled, I might as well die an honourable death riding across country on man's noblest beast; a sort of Kamikaze pilot in a hairnet.

Leaving Alexandra burbling about how sweet she had looked as a chubby, grubby toddler at her first gymkhana, Tash walked around to the back of the box to check on Snob.

He was standing in the shadow of the bulky lorry, scratching his nose on a wooden slat. As Tash approached, he whickered and nudged her sore shoulder reproachfully. Then he let out a shrill whinny to a nearby mare who shrieked back excitedly, kicking up a cloud of dust as she paced the radius of her rope.

The ground worried Tash: an exocet missile would ricochet off it. If Snob got out of control, he could ruin his legs for life. Despite the rain yesterday, it was packed down like cement, cracked and pitted, and speckled with sparse clumps of yellowing grass. Only the wooded parts of the course were covered with a lush emerald carpet. Other competitors they'd met on the course had pointed at the dry ground and shaken their heads pensively. 'Pas bien, pas sain.'

When she'd gone with Hugo to collect her number, quite a few in their dwindling class had already withdrawn, thinking the course too taxing for a young horse or the going too hard. Had it not been for Hugo's goading, Tash would have done the same.

Pride comes before a crashing fall, Tash honey, she reminded herself cheerlessly, and adjusted Snob's checked summer sheet before starting to take off the padded travelling boots from his freshly shampooed legs.

She'd spent all of an hour pricking her fingers, being butted in the ribs and collapsing several plastic buckets in her attempts to plait his mane. Now it was a series of neat auburn bobbles straight out of the BHS manual. But Tash's raw fingers and chewed jumper were a testament to the effort that had been spent.

'I wish you'd walked the course with me,' she told Snob, who was munching her hair thoughtfully.

She glanced at her watch. They weren't due to do their dressage until eleven-thirty. By then, Snob would be thoroughly wound up and utterly mischievous. When she'd first led him down the ramp, his eyes had boggled in amazement and he'd made a great show of snorting and spooking at everything around him, even taking exception to Anton's straw hat, which had to be stashed in the glove compartment before he'd let the stout, jolly man within a six-foot radius. Now he was watching the bustling activity of the showground with the anxious excitement of a schoolboy on his first trip to Lord's, his long red ears twitching with eager interest. He nudged her head with his muzzle and calmly ate the cigarette she had wedged behind her ear.

Just as she was dodging Snob's waggling leg in an attempt to remove a dangling hock boot, a warm hand slipped between her legs.

Jumping a foot in the air in surprise, Tash cannoned into Snob's belly and he let out a furious squeal. The hand instantly transferred to her arm and dragged her out from a mass of flailing chestnut and white legs.

'Sorry.' It was Max, looking far from apologetic.

Grinning broadly, he handed her a glass of brandy.

'I couldn't resist it. You really are looking fit, Tash.'

He leaned forward with twinkling eyes and Tash shoved the plastic brandy glass to her lips before Max could plant anything else there.

'Thanks,' she coughed, her eyes streaming from the burn-back as a decidedly rough vintage sank through her.

'Now,' Max took her hand and pulled her down beside him at a safe distance from Snob, who was looking both put-out and jealous, 'before you go out there and kill yourself on that four-legged Mike Tyson, I must talk to you.'

'Oh.' Tash looked uneasily over her shoulder. Only Pascal and Anton were still standing beside the cab. They appeared to be setting up a wager. Alexandra must have whisked the spaniels off to sift through the trade stands. Tash realised she was trapped.

'Look, Max, a lot has happened since I came here,' she faltered, staring at the ground.

'Oh yes?' There was a slight edge to Max's voice.

Tash pulled her knees up to her chin and started picking at a hole in her leggings. She was getting very clammy in her thick sweater but didn't want to go into the horsebox to change in case he followed. Right now, she needed to distance herself from everything and concentrate on remembering the dressage test. After 'enter at working trot, halt at X, salute', it was all a bit blank.

'Things have changed . . .' she continued, pushing her hair back from her face.

'Oh, for me too, Tash. That's what I'm trying to say.' Max laughed, putting a lengthy black denim leg either side of her and taking her hands in his. 'I guess we had a serious communication problem before I left. I did a lot of thinking in the States. They're much more upfront about their feelings over there, less verbally challenged, far more in touch with emotional pulses.'

Tash couldn't believe her ears. The Max she remembered couldn't struggle through a sentence without at least one sporting reference, and thought talking about one's feelings meant one was a vegan rambler.

'I came to realise how vexatious I'd been to you, shutting you out because I was feeling low, not explaining what was bugging me.'

'But I was the same—' Tash started.

Max covered her mouth with his hand and smiled compassionately. He looked horribly like Dr Hilary Jones all of a sudden.

'I got to thinking that I'd really screwed,' he explained. 'You were the most important, exciting thing that had happened to me and I'd blown it by walking out without really thinking. I aired it with Dad a lot. He was great; I guess it kind of brought us back together. He told me to fly straight over to you, even offered to buy the ticket. But I just couldn't get up the nerve. Every time I phoned United, I flunked and pretended it was the wrong number. I thought you'd really hate me for being such a bum.'

He shrugged and dusted some red hairs from his knee. Tash quashed an ungrateful feeling that he was trying to remember his lines.

'Then I got your letter and went ape,' he continued, suddenly grinning. 'Dad had to give me a Quaalude to bring me down.'

Tash wondered if this was some sort of Oriental massage Lucian Merriot was proficient in.

Max wrapped his arms around her legs and rested his chin on her knees, looking up at her through smoky lashes. 'By then I'd met Eddie and Lauren,' he went on. 'The coincidence was *bizarre*. Like it was meant to be, y'know?'

Tash shrugged and nodded.

'Er, Max . . .' she hesitated under his steady, sincere gaze. 'You haven't been born again or anything, have you? Only, I don't think I can cope with Bible readings and "Kumbiya" round the camp-fire. I never was very good at playing the tambourine.'

'Oh, Tash.' Max laughed and shook his head, a tear in his eye.

This worried Tash even more. The only time she'd ever seen Max weep openly – when England was beaten by France in the Five Nations – he'd insisted crossly that it was the start of conjunctivitis.

Snob was stamping irritably behind her.

Tash wished she could do the same, but Max had her legs in a heavy clinch. His timing, she reflected sadly, was lousy. She wanted to run around and panic, tear her hair out and live on her nerves without any dignity. The glow inside her Guernsey was turning into a minor inferno, but it wasn't the heat of passion so much as claustrophobia.

'Tash,' Max gazed at her seriously. 'I love you.'

Tash blinked and looked at him, opening her mouth to speak. But no words came, so she quickly finished off the dregs of her brandy for something to do.

Sweat had started to trickle down her sides and she could feel the sun beating a blistering tattoo on her woolly back.

'Tash?' Max's voice was choked with expectation and worry.

She suddenly found she couldn't look him in the eyes. He was so comfortable and familiar, she knew so much about him: how he'd been bullied at school, adored at university. How, while watching a test match, he could eat a plate of food she'd slaved over for hours only to ask half an hour later what was for dinner. Or, on a night when Graham and Mikey were out, he would be content just to sit across the room watching for hours while she sketched.

'Tash?'

She realised that whatever she did she must never hurt him.

'I love you too,' she whispered, adding quickly, 'you're my best friend.'

That made it seem better. It was, after all, possible to love lots of people, Tash told herself. But she was only in love with one. And with an unbearable sadness lying like lead shot in her heart, she knew it wasn't Max. Not any more.

She glanced at his face and what she saw squeezed her lungs like a vice. He looked so happy, the lop-sided grin crinkling the edges of his roe-grey eyes.

Sitting up, he took her face lightly in his hands and kissed her nose.

Tash felt a tear slide down her dusty cheeks and on to her neck. She couldn't pull away. She had simply no idea how to explain how she felt without shattering his new-found confidence. She *did* love him, he *was* her best friend. So she kissed him back on the cheek as platonically as she could.

Max laughed and hugged her tight, burying his face in her hair, which was full of Snob's grassy slobber.

'Marry me,' he breathed.

'What?' yelped Tash, her nose pressed uncomfortably to his t-shirt, her neck garrotted by her own knees.

'Please. Marry me, Tash. Make me the happiest, if most undeserving, sod ever.'

'I—' Tash quailed. She simply couldn't believe this: she was due to die nobly in an hour and she'd just been proposed to by the nicest, gentlest man she could possibly not be in love with.

'What's the matter, Tash?' Max asked, gently extracting her damp red face with its dribbling nose from his clothing.

'It's just that I—'

'I know, I'm a bit over the top myself at the moment,' Max smiled, wiping her face with the corner of Snob's stable rubber. Tash didn't like to tell him it had just been dipped in coat shine. Her eyes began to smart afresh.

'I really—'

'I guess it's the relief,' he went on, rubbing the back of her neck.

'I need time to think, Max,' she blurted, the urgency in her voice making her sound high-pitched and desperate.

Max looked devastated. All the happiness started to drain from his face.

'Why?' he whispered.

'Um . . .' The coat shine was giving her a twitch. She glanced around and noticed Pascal was watching them indulgently. She mouthed 'buzz off' and he nodded, smiled and carried on gawping.

'Well?' Max hung his head even lower, fiddling with the frays on the hem of his jeans.

Tash stroked his leg reassuringly but it was disturbingly hard and brawny so she transferred to his hair.

'Marriage is a big, bad, dangerous sortofthing, Max,' she explained, frantically casting round for eloquent excuses. But the most articulated thing around was Anton's lorry. 'It wouldn't be like before, everything would change.'

'How?'

God, he would be pedantic about it, she thought tetchily.

An announcement for 'tous concurrents' was crackling over the public address tannoys but Tash couldn't translate more than 'is beginning'.

'We're both looking for work, both broke,' she floundered.

'You see how much we've got in common!' Max laughed nervously.

Oh God, he's really hurt, she thought.

The announcement was being repeated with more urgency. Tash started to panic.

She wondered if she could think up some elaborate lie about being vehemently against marriage. It might seem odd that she'd never mentioned it before, but it was worth a try.

'My parents divorced, Max,' she improvised, nervily twiddling his hair into egg-white peaks. 'Your father's been remarried so often they give him a discount at the drive-in chapel. Marriage can be the most agonising, painful mistake if you're not ready.'

'You once said that made you all the more determined to

make a good marriage,' Max reminded her quietly, brushing her hand away and irritably flattening his hair. 'If I'm your best friend and we love one another surely that's the greatest of all reasons?'

Drat, Tash stewed. She'd forgotten she'd said that. She just had to be brave and honest and explain in the most simple, least painful way possible. She took a deep breath.

'Max, I – Christ, I wish there were an easier way of saying this – the thing is I've met, well no, that's not strictly true. What I'm trying to say is I don't think I can—' She stopped as she caught sight of Hugo and Gus laughing and chatting as they walked over from the direction of Marie-Claire's super-stretch, des res horsebox.

Hugo was looking revoltingly pleased with himself in borrowed breeches and long boots. His stock was tied and pinned above a white t-shirt, advertising an equine supplement, which would later be hidden by his jacket. Gus was wearing a bush hat and baggy Union Jack shorts. They were heading her way.

Following her gaze, Max abruptly let go of her and stood up, rubbing his forehead as if summing up will-power.

'Don't worry, I'll clear off.' He looked down at her, then smiled sadly.

Squinting against the sun, Tash felt her hangover push pins through her temples.

'It's him, isn't it?' Max jerked his head towards Hugo, who had paused to talk to a pretty French rider. 'I couldn't even begin to compete with someone that rich – he's got it all, hasn't he? He'd crush both of us.' He looked at her for a long time as if committing every feature to memory.

''Bye, Tash.' He bent down and kissed her lightly on the forehead before turning to leave.

Tash buried her head in her hands and stifled a sob. The thought of losing one of her greatest friends, of never seeing him again, was crippling. Without thinking, she leapt up.

'Max, wait!'

He stopped, not turning round, his back hunched.

'It isn't Hugo.' Tash wavered a few feet from him.

Max looked at her over his shoulder and shrugged.

'But there is someone else, Tash. Isn't there?'

Tash thought of her hopeless crush on Niall and found she couldn't answer. Tears welled in her eyes.

Turning away again, Max strode towards the main gates.

'Max, wait!'

Hugo and Gus were almost within earshot, Pascal was still hovering, but Tash didn't care. She caught Max up and grabbed hold of his denim sleeve. The stitching ripped and he stopped.

'Oh, sorry.' Tash tried hopelessly to put the torn fabric together again but it kept flopping back. She gave up. There were more urgent things at stake.

'Tash!' Hugo called from ten metres away.

'Look,' Tash looked at Max, lowering her voice, 'I have to get ready but—'

'Oi, Tash!' Gus bellowed from eight metres.

' – but I do love you, Max and—'

'Tash! Hurry up – the class is about to start!' Hugo barked, now less than five metres away and closing fast.

'– and if I win today, I'll marry you!' Tash finished quickly.

Whooping loudly, Max pulled her against him and grinned with delight.

Tash, her painful shoulder crushed in the embrace, winced, totally horrified by what she'd just heard herself say.

She realised that Hugo and Gus were standing beside them. Gus looked embarrassed, Hugo looked both livid and unpleasantly calculating.

'I hate to interrupt love's young dream,' he drawled with barely shrouded anger, 'but they're running half an hour early. Quite remarkable for the French, but there you are.'

'It might be a good idea if you changed and started to warm Snob up,' suggested Gus, clearing his throat awkwardly. 'He'll be pretty hot with just half an hour's work, I'm afraid, but it can't be helped. So many people have withdrawn from the first novice class, it's been halved.'

48

As soon as she mounted, Tash knew that her dressage test would be a disaster. Snob was about as settled as a recently shaken bottle of home-made beer.

While she waited for her number to be called, sweating under her new black jacket, Sophia and Ben turned up, squeezing the Merc in between two dusty Citroëns facing the show-jumping ring. With dark glasses covering their hangovers, they bore the children in various carrying devices or on elastic reins straight over to Alexandra.

'Here, darling.' Sophia attached Lotty to her mother by a long coiled lead. 'You're going to watch the dressage with Granny.'

Lotty, welcomed with huge spaniel kisses, immediately started crying.

Instead of stopping to wish Tash luck, the Merediths then hurried to Hugo's camp, where he was warming up Marie-Claire's stunning dark bay mare.

They'd brought Max's father with them, looking like a dapper sand dune in fawn casuals from head to Guccied foot. He was carrying a borrowed shooting stick and high-tech binoculars and wearing a battered felt stetson.

'Hello again, Tash.' He wandered over. 'Looking forward to it?'

Before Tash could answer, Snob took one poppy-eyed look at Lucian's hat and bolted.

By the time Tash had tugged him back from the opposite end

of the field, the dressage judges were waiting for her to start, glaring menacingly from behind their glinting, dusty window.

'Good luck,' Max called out as Snob jogged into the arena, snatching at his bit. 'I love you. You're doing this for us, remember.'

The last thing Tash saw before she halted at X, was Max talking excitedly to his father.

'Royaume-Uni, nil points,' Max hissed as she thundered out of the arena five minutes later in what was supposed to be long-rein walk.

Tash, puce in the face from frustration and exhaustion, wasn't able to stop Snob long enough to tell him to shut up.

At least, she reflected wryly, after the performance they had just given, the likelihood of her having to honour her bet was non-existent.

Snob carted her unceremoniously back to Anton's horsebox, where he skidded to an abrupt halt on top of Max's jacket and turned his head to chew her new – agonisingly tight – leather boots. He looked up at her sweetly, as violet-eyed as Ermintrude the cow. In reality, he'd just behaved like a Minotaur in a huff.

Tash slid off stiffly, nearly pronging her bottom on a ramp bracket, and leaned against him, burying her burning, mortified face in his saddle. If not the most embarrassing, then the past few minutes had certainly proved the most publicly entertaining feat she had ever achieved in her life.

As if she needed proof, Gus appeared behind her positively creased up with laughter. His small, alert eyes were moist with tears, his eyebrows at forty-five degrees with disbelief.

'Darling, darling Tash.' He put his good arm around her bad shoulder and leaned on her for support. 'You were so gorgeous. Pen and I have just voted you rears of the year – I've never seen a horse perform so much of a test on two legs.'

'My half pass was more of a by-pass,' muttered Tash, loosening Snob's girths. The glossy arena barriers had taken some heavy mangling during that particular battle of wills. 'And my twenty-metre circles took in most of the showground.'

'The horse was over-fresh,' shrugged Gus, wiping his eyes. 'Not your fault considering the number of scratched entries. Hugo said it was a bloody brave bit of riding, says the animal is a complete bugger with anyone.'

'Did he?' Tash looked up, unbelieving.

Gus nodded and flinched at the pain from his collarbone, tactfully not adding Hugo's more scathing comments.

'Oh God,' Tash groaned. 'Here comes the depress corps.'

Alexandra and Pascal had caught them up, knee-deep in children and spaniels respectively. Behind them trotted Polly, the red light of her father's camcorder winking as she videoed their bottoms. Gus quickly wished Tash luck in the next phase and loped off on long, thin legs to carry on helping Hugo and Marie-Claire's other riders.

'You were absolutely terrific, sweetheart!' Alexandra gave Snob's hindquarters a good six feet and came round to hug her. 'So gutsy. Much more elaborate and peppy than those other boring duos.'

'I don't think that's quite what they're looking for, Mummy,' Tash explained, catching sight of a sympathetic look from Pascal.

'Well, I thought you looked simply smashing.' Alexandra extracted Josh's pushchair from a pile of droppings and glowed at Pascal for an auxiliary quote.

'Très bien,' Pascal faltered, looking evasive.

'Anton and Ben are absolute rotters.' Alexandra busied herself tucking back the unruly wisps which had started to stray from Tash's hairnet. 'They've taken Lucian and sloped off to the beer tent. But they told me to pass on their congratulations.'

Polly, her lens trained on Tash's face, giggled.

'Lucky-hen, he say "I cannot bear to watch" and go off to get piss-up.' She grinned up at Tash from behind her optic eye. 'Now you have finish your monter à cheval, will you help me make up a dance routine to show Eddie and Lorry ce soir, *please*, Tash?'

'How would you like a nice, big ice cream, chérie?' Alexandra smiled at her daughter's zoom lens through gritted teeth and towed her off to the refreshments tent, leaving Josh wailing in his buggy and Lotty attached to the horsebox by her elastic harness.

Pascal cleared his throat and feigned fascination over something one of the spaniels was chewing. 'I think thees ees yours, chérie.' He held a rubber curry comb up to Tash.

'Thanks.'

Snob was eyeing Lotty with a mischievous glint in his velvet eye. Tash unhooked his headcollar from the back of the box and slung it over his bridle. She knew she should be popping him over a few practice fences in preparation for the show jumping which came next. But a masochistic voice inside her head made her lead him back to the dressage ring to watch Hugo's test.

Pascal, left with the dogs and Sophia's children, gathered up as many leads as he could handle and tripped over a tattered baseball jacket someone had left on the grass in his haste to bolt to the beer tent.

Hugo's test was predictably sublime.

Gus sat with Penny on the bonnet of a friend's car. Despite his jealously, he had to admit that watching Hugo was one of the all-time joys of the sport.

The mare was jumping out of her skin with primed vitality. Enclosed in Hugo's almost motionless legs, she was as supple as warm wax, smoothly responding to his abbreviated commands like a computer. To the ringside, Hugo hardly seemed to move, his aids barely perceptible, his lean behind apparently glued to the saddle. But in fact every muscle in his body was shifting and adjusting with pin-point dexterity to keep the mare tactile, balanced and flowing, yet bursting with controlled impulsion.

'Christ, he's good,' Gus whistled to Penny. 'One almost forgets. He's been off the circuit for two months but you'd think he'd never been out of the saddle.'

'Perhaps he hasn't,' Penny said smoothly, looking across at Tash's frozen face watching furtively from behind an Opel, where she thought no one would spot her, mechanically stroking Snob's bobbing head.

Penny looked back at Hugo, who was performing a perfect half circle at medium walk.

'I only hope he's learnt from the monumental cock-up he made of Badminton,' she sighed, glancing down at one of the three watches strapped to her wrist. 'I'd better shift it if I'm going to make my start time.'

Penny was competing in a different section from Tash and Hugo, with a much bigger entry and stiffer competition. She was already wearing one of Gus's green and red rugger shirts in preparation for the cross-country section. Nearby, Marie-Claire's long-suffering groom, Simone, was leading round the compact little iron-grey gelding Penny was riding.

Marie-Claire, sitting pillion on a clapped-out moped with her knee heavily strapped, dusty and sunburnt from watching the first rider round the course, was conducting a heated conversation with the tall boy who was walking his liver chestnut around with Simone. She turned to Penny as she approached, and sighed, fanning herself with the schedule.

'The course, it is a bitch,' she announced angrily, her black eyes flashing from Penny to Gus.

M-C (or Master Class), as she was known in the eventing world, was an attractive woman in her early thirties with unkempt short dark hair and a wide sensual mouth which seldom smiled.

'If you ride, the horse will be in jeopardy. If not, my sponsors, they will go insane at me. I need their money – if they withdraw support, I give up. Le pire est toujours certain,' she shrugged, looking up at the little gelding thoughtfully. 'He's tough. His legs, they are like a truck's shock absorbers: uncomfortable, but robust.'

She laughed raucously and tapped on the shoulder of the man in front of her, who started up the moped with a machine-gun splutter.

'What about my shock absorbers?' asked Penny wistfully, thinking about Gus's collarbone and M-C's knee.

'I no hear you!' shouted M-C over the din of the rattling moped. 'You take all the slow options – don't worry about time, no?' And with another tap on the shoulder in front, she was roaring off in a cloud of dust and petrol fumes which made the liver chestnut rear in terror as it tried to set off on the course ten minutes early.

As Penny despondently tightened the jiggling grey's girths, Hugo rode up, lolling with self-congratulatory ease on the dark mare, feet dangling from the pedals, an unlit cigarette in his insolent mouth.

'As mon hôte would say, fuckeeng impresseeve, n'est-pas?' He dropped the mare's reins and jumped off by swinging his leg over her neck, landing by Gus. 'Piece of gâteau, in fact.'

'Don't count your poulets, sunshine. Here, let me.' Gus gave his wife a leg-up and nearly ruptured his neck brace before Simone grabbed the dangling Penny and hauled her the rest of the way.

'Good luck, love.' Gus turned back to Hugo. 'Young Tash might just finish on the bit while you're still admiring your reflection in the last furlong marker, Beauchamp.'

Hugo laughed and threw the mare's reins to Simone. There was a terrible sound of splitting poles from the jumping ring behind the beer tent.

'Talking of which,' he grinned, 'do I hear my beloved starting phase two already? Best of luck, darling!' he called to Pen who was riding off to the start, looking pensive. 'Come on,' he started walking towards the tent, 'this should be good for a laugh.'

Gus followed, casting an anxious glance over his shoulder to his retreating wife.

'Considering you supposedly fancy this girl, you're pretty bloody disparaging about her.' He caught up with Hugo.

'She likes it. Her family are so bloody beastly to her it's what she expects,' Hugo said idly, and walked straight past Max without acknowledging his presence.

Max was in deep dudgeon as he headed gloomily into the beer tent again.

Tash, he decided, was behaving very oddly. Come to that, everyone was behaving pretty oddly. He thought the French *ate* horses – hadn't he had a Burger de Cheval at Orly that very morning? So why were these maniacs all running round dressed as Sibermen on horseback, jumping piles of sticks or just ambling round in circles in front of a caravan?

Max thought ruefully of the Old Boys' Saturday afternoon cricket match which would no doubt be taking place in just a couple of hours in England, a friendly before the big play-off tomorrow. Now that was sport. It would be an away this week; Graham and Mikey were probably zooming too fast down the M3 or M4 in the Golf right now to some sleepy Shires village, anticipating a lazy pub lunch if they were batting first. The cans of Fosters would be rattling in the ice box in the boot and Graham would no doubt be howling along to Van Morrison. In honour of his absence, Max's pads would be brought out and buckled to the Golf's wing mirrors during the match. That was loyalty.

The sooner he got Tash back there the better, he decided. Impressed as he was by the d'Eblouirs' opulent lifestyle, they were too wired for Max to feel comfortable. He liked to think he lived on the edge, pulling the odd spliff and sitting through *The Cook, the Thief, his Wife and her Lover* without giggling, but this was too much.

He was also deeply concerned about the change in Tash. He'd relied on her reacting to his return with the usual delirious gratitude. Instead, she looked tired and thin and hadn't reacted to his proposal at all as he'd anticipated. The idea of a bet appealed to his sportsman's heart – but now he was mulling it over during his third beer, it wasn't the most flattering response. She'd been actively avoiding him and, even to Max's untrained eye, her dressage test was a shambles.

At the far end of the beer tent, scores were being scribbled up on a blackboard as they came in. Two spaniels, their leads winding around ankles and shooting sticks, were frolicking beside it, wolfing down discarded baguettes, sending drinks flying and flirting noisily with the barman's panting, wall-eyed mastiff.

Positioning himself behind Anton and Ben – whom Max thought a terrific chap and knew loads about rugger – Max was pleasantly surprised when a remarkably high score appeared beside Tash's name. His spirits were even more lifted when the shuffling character who kept muddling his chalk with his fag wrote up Hugo Beauchamp's score as by far the lowest.

Pascal let out a tutting sigh and, hooking Lotty's reins to a bar stool, bought everyone a large round of drinks to commiserate.

'Why?' Max accepted a fourth litre of carbonated gnat's piss and thought about another expedition to the impenetrable loo tent. 'Shouldn't we be celebrating?'

'Bit premature, doncha think?' Ben scratched his neck where his polo shirt was too tight and nodded at the result board, where the scorer was happily puffing on his chalk. 'Those are penalties.'

Max choked on his beer and watched his father chatting up Sophia Meredith through unseeing, troubled eyes.

'Did you know,' Sophia was saying as Lucian gazed in unshrouded admiration at her beautiful face, 'someone attacked Mummy's yews last night?'

'I didn't know your mother kept sheep.' Lucian admired her slender ankles, unaffected by the heat. 'Were they hurt?'

'Not ewes, silly, *yews*,' giggled Sophia. 'The vandals – we suspect friends of Marcus, actually, but one doesn't like to point the finger too hastily – have tried a bit of amateur topiary. Awfully primitive, but if you look closely they appear to have been trying to shape a—' she giggled and glanced around, dropping her voice, '– a, you know, a *thing*.'

Lucian raised a perfectly shaped eyebrow and asked what a thing was.

Pascal was now arguing with Anton about politics, cheese and when to harvest that year, simultaneously.

Max turned to watch them with interest. They both spoke with their entire bodies. Anton kept pulling his right eye downwards by the cheek until Max expected a glass eyeball to roll out at any moment. Pascal puffed and 'poofed' with his cheeks, rubbed his fingertips together and continually mimed throwing someone over his shoulder. It was fascinating, like watching two mime artists describing a wild night out. Finally, an exasperated Anton flung both palms out to his side, depositing half a glass of watered pastis over Max's crotch.

Now totally fed up and rapidly going off the French, Max walked out, leaving Ben mid-way into an educational speech on the FEI rulebook.

In the show-jumping ring, the sound of splitting poles actually had nothing to do with Tash.

The competitor immediately before her had been approaching the last fence at a beautifully balanced canter when a frenzied, tail-wagging dog rushed out in front of them, causing the horse to panic straight into the oxer.

The unharmed dog disappeared before anyone could catch it and reprimand the irresponsible owner. In fact, it moved so fast that very few got a clear look at it. Those that did were almost certain it had been a rather overweight spaniel trailing a long lead.

Then Tash pounded into the ring on an overexcited, erratic Snob, her stomach in her mouth.

The jump judges, thoroughly rattled by the dog episode, were barely concentrating as she and Snob ground to a shaky halt, forgetting to salute. The commentator had nipped into the refreshment tent for a quick shot of brandy, leaving the PA system eerily silent. The crowd, drawn to the more exciting prospect of death and serious injury on the cross-country circuit, started to drift away.

Trying frantically to hold Snob, who was so ecstatic at the sight of jumps that he didn't know which one to attack first, Tash had two hesitations and a technical refusal which passed unnoticed. They then careered round the course so fast that Tash's stock flew up in her face, rendering her blind. They took the final fence in the wrong direction at a gallop, leaving the ring to the hollow booming sound of dropping poles.

As Tash slid off Snob in the collecting ring, she waited for the announcement that she'd been eliminated. Beside her, Gus was in the inevitable giggles and Hugo looked incredibly smug.

'Natasha . . . er . . . Franch et Le Fossy Nob,' the loudspeaker crackled into life. 'Cinq pénalités.

'Christ!' Gus hooted in disbelief. 'They must have had their eyes shut.'

'You should cinq your lucky stars,' snapped Hugo, and stalked off to the practice ring.

Back at the horsebox, Max was waiting for her, pint in hand.

He was sitting on the ramp chatting with Ben, who was cuddling a wailing Josh. The fat little baby had been left behind by Pascal during his hasty flight to the beer tent. Later, a stray spaniel had joined him in his carry-cot and eaten his beloved fluffy glo-worm.

Booted out by Ben, the spaniel now cringed under a wheel-arch, stump gyrating with guilt. As Ben and Max greeted Tash with a loud round of applause, it backed away, welding its chin to the dusty ground, eyes imploring.

'Brought you this.' Ben popped his beer on the ground and, passing Josh to Max, produced a shrivelled four-leaf clover.

'Thanks.' Tash took it, feeling touched.

'It's a shamrock from Niall,' Ben explained, heaving himself up with the help of Max's shoulder. 'Apologises for not coming; has a few things to sort out.'

Trying to listen in, Max was holding Josh at arm's length as if he were a pulled grenade. Beside him, tied to the box by her reins again, Lotty waddled forwards and picked up her father's pint before tottering away to ram it under the cowering spaniel's nose.

'Should bring you the luck of the Irish across-country.' Ben grinned sleepily and gazed around for his beer, not hearing the quiet sound of lapping which was now coming from under the lorry.

Tash turned the shamrock over in her hand and bit her lip. Niall must still be talking to Lisette, she realised. God, she hoped he was all right. Despite the gift, he seemed further out of her reach than ever.

Josh let out a peevish bellow and Max nearly dropped him, his face grimacing in horror.

'Little bugger's crabby after last night.' Ben took him back again. 'Bit like his mother.'

He cradled the runny-nosed baby in his arms but Josh wailed even more determinedly. Ben sniffed, pulled a face and swiftly rammed a dummy into the baby's mouth before plonking him back in his carry-cot.

'Damn Paola for pushing off like that.' He unhooked Lotty from the horsebox. 'You know she and that hippy chap loaded that bloody Dormobile with all the fur coats and designer jackets from the beds upstairs? The phone's been ringing non-stop this morning with irate messages about mislaid togs. It's like Lost Luggage at Victoria.'

He sighed, scratched his head and limped off Pamper-wards with Josh's carry-cot held at arm's length and the whining Lotty waddling behind, trailing her Noo Noo on the parched, manure-spread ground.

Emerging nervously from underneath the horsebox, the spaniel rolled its eyes, hiccuped and, lifting its leg on the wheel-arch, fell over. Looking surprised, it picked itself up and reeled towards a hot-dog stand.

Tash, left alone with Max, suddenly felt edgy.

'We have to talk . . .' Max followed her into the stuffy little groom's compartment in the horsebox where she'd left her cross-country kit.

'I thought we had talked,' sighed Tash, still thinking about the shamrock. 'Could you just lift your leg a sec, you're standing on my shirt – ta.'

'Are you deliberately doing badly?' Max pressed himself against the wall so she could bend over.

'Thanks for the vote of no confidence.' Tash got trapped in a corner with her shirt over her head and had to back out slowly. 'I'm doing the best I – sorry—' she cannoned into him before head-butting a feed bucket on the rebound '– can.'

'Look.' Max helped her out of the shirt and threw it over a pile of rugs. As he turned back to her, he tripped over a set of reins. 'Shit – look, I really am sorry for the way I was acting in London, I just—'

'Ouch!' Tash shrieked as he caught her shoulder.

'– I just got – damn!' Scrambling up, he knocked his head on a tack rack and collapsed on the rubber floor again.

A shaft of white midday sunlight abruptly fell across the little compartment, illuminating the hundreds of dust particles disturbed by Tash and Max crashing around.

'Oh – gosh – sorry!' Alexandra yelped as she swung open the groom's door.

Taking in Tash in her bra and Max spreadeagled beneath her, she turned her back on them and called brightly over her shoulder, 'I won't interrupt. I just wondered if you'd seen Ben? Sophia thinks Josh has been abducted – we haven't seen him for ages and the dogs are running loose.'

'He's gone to get a nappy,' Tash explained, ignoring Polly, who was frantically videoing everything, her camera lens coated in ice cream.

When her mother and Polly finally wandered off, leaving the door wide open for interested spectators, Tash struggled into the back protector, which was several sizes too large and had a crotch strap which defied human logic. In it she looked like a cross between Michelin Man and an upright freezer; with the strap done up, she just looked in pain.

'That's a bit of a passion-killer.' Max sat up, rubbing his head and watched her struggling to do up her breeches zip over the foam-filled shell. 'Are you trying out for the New York Giants?'

Tash ignored him and pulled on her black rugby shirt. It stretched to capacity over the back protector, now lop-sided because of her strapped shoulder, so she resembled Quasimodo playing prop forward.

'Whoever this guy is you've got the hots for is in for a shock,' Max said sulkily.

'I have not got the hots for anyone!' snapped Tash, pulling her crash-skull on back to front.

Max stared at her petulantly as if about to cross-examine, but at that moment the box shook and a furious whinny sounded from the far end.

Snob was standing looking annoyed and indignant, with his leg over his lead rope and Polly's ice-cream carton wedged over the end of his nose.

By the time Tash calmed him down, Max had changed tactics. He apologised for being nasty and trotted glumly off to check her score and fetch another brandy to kill the mounting pain in her shoulder; Tash now felt as if someone was giving her a constant half-nelson.

Even Snob was unusually respectful, slobbering gratefully over her clean shirt and only nipping her bum twice when she swapped his tendon boots for brushing ones.

Tash longed more than ever for Niall. She needed his calm reassurance, the way he'd gently rubbed her neck and given her a bolstering hug when she'd got upset about Samion.

She took out the battered shamrock, suddenly feeling horribly selfish. It was so typically generous of him to think of her while he was trying to patch things up with Lisette; he must be horribly preoccupied. She would treasure the little green leaf more than anything. It was probably the last contact they'd ever have – a withered green memento mori. Her eyes filled with her reserve stock of scalding tears as she thought about his kind, craggy-handsome face and soft lilting voice.

Through blurred eyes, she didn't see the approaching pink and red muzzle, sniffing with equine interest, until it was too late. Feeling the brush of coarse whiskers against her hand, she blinked and looked down to see her fingers, now covered with grass slobber, were just clutching a stalk. Meanwhile Snob was chewing contentedly, his long red lashes half obscuring dreamy Bournville eyes.

'The bad news is that Beaumont – or whatever he's called – is leading by nearly twenty runs.' Max had returned and was thrusting a brandy under her nose. 'The good news is – thanks to a quite remarkable pole-vaulting score – you're now eighth out of twelve.'

'Show-jumping,' sniffed Tash, downing the drink in one.

'The other bit of good news,' Max added very casually, lighting two cigarettes the wrong way round without noticing, 'is that your stepfather said he'd be delighted to fork out for us getting hitched.'

He handed her a smouldering foam filter.

'You what?' Tash yelped in horror.

49

No one at the manoir was appreciating the gloriously tropical day. Outside, the overgrown garden, choked with burnished grasses, was polka-dotted like an ornate sari by poppies, field mustard and the last of the lamb's lettuce which Valérie hadn't raided for cold lunches. The bobbing heads of ribwort, like fat beetles wearing lace bonnets, thrust themselves butchly above grey-haired dandelion clocks which leaned on the hedges for support.

The contract cleaners had whisked round the sleeping, staggering or still raving members of the household with startling professionalism. Now every ashtray gleamed afresh, the floors were like ice rinks with polish and rubbish was stacked neatly into huge, industrial wheely bins in the courtyard. The stale smell of spilled drinks and cigarette smoke had been replaced by a sweet, heady blend of beeswax, carpet shampoo and lemon surface cleaner.

Rooter sat forlornly in a cool shadow in the courtyard rubbing his tufted ears with a big back paw and sneezing miserably. The artificial chemicals invading the house had put paid to a well-deserved snooze and irritated his sensitive nose. Worse still, his master was shacked up with a dogist.

Amanda sat on the loo with her feet up against the bath, painting her toenails Morello Cherry and watching Todd through the obscured, steamy glass of the shower.

He was an unexpected treat really, she mused. Vain, selfish and thick, granted – but so was Hugo. And, for all the emotional whirlpool he inspired, Amanda had to admit she found Niall's mind unfathomable and even intimidating at times.

Amanda Austin, she wrote thoughtfully in the steam on the mirror, then pulled a face. *AA* would *not* look good on the luggage, she decided. Drunks and car mechanics. She wiped it off. She'd keep her maiden name. Having a house-husband meant one maintained independence without being labelled unfeminine, or even – horrors – designer dyke. Toy-boys who stayed at home were currently all the vogue among her female chums whom she lunched with at the Groucho Club. And for some of the men, too.

She returned to her toenails, wiping a smudge of red away with the back of her finger, enjoying her idle conjecture.

So – it meant she had to work another few years, she speculated. So what? She wasn't ready for motherhood yet and there was a limit to the number of high-fibre, low-cholesterol, fishitarian recipes one could try out, or wrinkle phone-in daytime TV one could stomach, before marital bliss started leaving stains on your conscience when washed at forty degrees. Two tarts in a kitchen was all very well on a story-board, but ironing-board, draining-board, chopping-board, Electricity Board? Bored, bored, boring.

The countryside alienated her, bringing out the worst of her latent snobbery, and London was horribly lonely if one didn't work. At least the high-stress eighties were a thing of the past. Her office was currently more concerned with setting up a stationery recycling unit than high-flyer-or-fire deadlines.

Todd was, as she had just discovered for the fourth time in eight hours' interrupted sleep, a terrific lover. He was easier on the eye than a bucketful of Optrex and bound to be cheaper than Hugo, who had recently been touching her for cash more than sex. And he hated horses. Dateline couldn't have done better.

When Todd came out of the shower, he admired his reflection in the recently wiped mirror. Remnants of *Amanda Austin* were showing through the new layer of steam but he was too intent on flossing his teeth to care. Shaving with Amanda's Silkipil had made him look as if he'd applied a muscle-rub face-mask, he noticed irritably.

He felt on edge. Soon the guy he'd done the deal with over the gear for the party would be pumping for his share of the profits. Todd didn't suppose he'd had them insured for flood damage.

'When are you planning on going back to Pomgolia, Mand?' He stroked Amanda's short hair back from her head. His wet hand made it stick up in angry spikes. 'Only I was thinking of taking a short trip over there myself.'

'Don't you ever call me Mand!' Amanda snarled, flattening down her hair. Then she smiled brightly, looking about twenty and deliciously wanton again. 'You want somewhere to stay in London?'

'Not really.' Todd shrugged nonchalantly and enjoyed watching her face fall. 'But a few hundred hours in bed with you would be better than a can of Fosters in a heatwave, I can tell you.' He grinned wickedly. 'So I guess, as you insist, I'd be a fool to refuse. As long as there's somewhere to store my bikes and photography clobber.'

'I've got a lock-up in Chelsea. But you can only stay for a few days,' Amanda insisted, hiding her delight. 'I might as well go back to England today. But I need a car – the Peugeot's in Hugo's name – and I doubt you can hire one in the village.'

'No worries.' Todd dropped his considerable chest down to her level and flexed his pecs.

'I've got my bikes here. Tellya what – we'll cycle to Saumur and take it from there.'

He kissed her on the nose.

Amanda sighed. 'Look – there's a couple of clauses I've got to attach to my offer, Todd.' She took out a Dunhill International, lit it, and blew the smoke into his face.

'You mean about using your lock-up for my bikes and studio?' Todd flashed his teeth boyishly.

'I *mean* about my putting you up in London.' Amanda rubbed her chin with the first two fingers of her right hand and looked up at the trompe-l'oeil ceiling in disbelief. Two fat cherubs stared back down at her capriciously. They looked like her boss and his secretary.

'Oh, yeah, that.' Todd leaned forward and kissed her on the chest very slowly, reaching up and tossing her fag into the bath. 'I'll do all the housework.' He crossed his fingers behind her back and kissed his way down to an erect nipple. She really did have sensational skin, he decided, like warm, scented apricots.

'That . . . and . . .' Amanda's voice wavered momentarily before she regained control. 'There's Rooter—'

'Rooter's fired.' Todd moved across to the other nipple.

He'd be sad to see his old friend go, but Isaac had to be snuffed for Abraham in the Bible, didn't he? Todd wasn't sure; he'd only ever read the synopsis. Besides, he reflected, Rooter had got a bit out of hand of late.

'. . . and the nylon cycling shorts have to go. I'm sorry, but they do. Then there's the – right a bit – matter of driving. While you stay, I want—' Amanda gasped as he edged his way lower, 'you to run me to the office and pick me up. You get full use – not so fast! – of my car in between.'

'What is it?' Todd enquired from her belly-button.

'A BMW convertible.'

'Sure,' Todd agreed, his voice muffled. Then he lifted her up and carried her through to the bedroom.

'Finally,' Amanda smiled guilefully as he threw her down on the crumpled bed. 'You cook.'

'What—?' Todd looked down at her in amazement.

The bloody woman wanted a maid, not a potent Aussie lover, he fumed. Then he looked down at her narrow, writhing body, as tanned as Ayers Rock, and up again to those cool, emotionless eyes. He thought briefly about all the money he owed around France; sooner or later it'd start catching up with him.

'No worries,' he grinned, sliding with effortless expertise on top of her. 'Call me Raymond Blanc cheque.'

Cass had amnesia. She also had a blinding headache and a pair of ripped support stockings hanging over the towel-rail upstairs in the bedroom.

So far, she reflected irritably, Michael had failed to come up with a satisfactory explanation for any of these things.

'Michael, dear,' she poured out two cups of beige tea into Alexandra's chipped, translucent bone-china cups, 'surely you can remember what time we got to bed, at least?'

Michael had a bone-dry throat to match the crockery. As with all hypochondriacs, he was terrified that this time it was the Final Gathering. He tied his cravat a little closer and coughed conspicuously.

'Early,' he wheezed quietly. 'We both went to bloody bed early, old girl. Lot of old queens running round in posh frocks.'

'Oh.' Cass wished she could remember something about the night before. It seemed such a shame to have been present at what was doubtless one of the most talked-about and cherished social gatherings of Europe's élite, only to find one had forgotten it all the very next morning.

Cass took another Codis. She hadn't felt this rough since she'd misread the instructions on a Benylin bottle when Marcus was still in short trousers. 'What about Olly and his friend? Did they meet any nice girls?'

'No bloody idea, old girl.' Michael had another coughing fit.

'Well, at least Marcus seems to be behaving himself with some modicum of upbringing.' Cass sighed happily and watched her husband choke on his tea. 'I've just seen him and nice young Rory Wiltsher tidying up the courtyard. So conscientious.'

Michael suspected that the moment he had finally parted company with his voice was bawling Marcus out earlier that morning, having unearthed him in a crumpled sleeping bag with a naked girl. Michael might have turned a blind eye to this natural youthful research, had Marcus not claimed in all seriousness that she was Jeremy Paxman. As the girl looked about sixteen, with a peroxide bob and chain-mail braces on her teeth, Michael had his doubts.

He felt ordering Marcus to have the barn, courtyard and Volvo spotless and shipshape by the afternoon or forfeit his allowance, driving lessons and year in Australia after his A levels was letting the boy off lightly. Michael was, after all, empathic in matters of the heart; he had been quite a confirmed rake when he met Cass and was glad Marcus had got off his starting blocks at long last. It was the delusion element he abhorred. If his son had thought it was Anna Ford, he could have understood.

Sitting on the long chair in the hall, Olly was broodily flipping through an interior decorating magazine.

Ginger had recently announced that he had a huge crush on Olly's ravishing aunt, Alexandra. The romantic redhead was now in the study composing a sonnet to her, as he always did when he fell in love, which was often. Olly wouldn't mind too much, but the sonnets were so interminably dreary and iambically incorrect.

He decided to have a swim and cool off, then possibly drip water all over Ginger's love-poem afterwards whilst wearing the black g-string trunks Ginger coveted.

The wind had dropped so much that even the rustling creepers, which had sounded like belly-dancers in raffia skirts on an all-night dance-athon, were still. The music from the barn had finally done its rapping funk-groove swan-song, and now a hot, dry silence was only occasionally interrupted by the power-drill buzzing of nectar-collecting insects raiding the last of the salvaged flower arrangements. With most of the windows still open, the heat hung like dusty net curtains around them, and two elderly, battle-scarred farm cats, seeking asylum from Rooter in the courtyard, heaved themselves from one sunny square of floor to another, occasionally pausing to watch motionlessly over a promising hole in the skirting.

Olly was allergic to cats. Particularly smelly old rat-catchers like these. He pulled a face at them. One could almost see the fleas trampolining off them, he thought in revulsion, darting past and out on to the pool balcony. The pagoda was still up, providing blissfully cool concrete underfoot. And an awful lot of cigarette butts.

The cleaners obviously hadn't ventured out here, he sniffed. It reeked of a DOM's pub. Sweating food was gathering flies on plates which the caterers had missed, stuffed under seats and on windowsills.

Wrinkling his nose, Olly started down the steps to the pool.

Drat! He stopped in his tracks. Pool cleaners.

Two beer-gutted men in nothing but dirty white shorts were skimming the cluttered surface of the swimming pool and exclaiming with what Olly supposed was typical French ostentation about their discoveries.

One, who sported thick sideburns, was holding up a pair of soggy lace knickers as if he'd just hooked a ten-pound trout. Olly almost expected a photographer to pop out from under the diving board and snap the catch.

Clutching his fluffy red towel around his g-string trunks, Olly silently retreated and hovered behind the balcony balustrades.

The taller of the two men, who had a receding crew-cut and a tattoo on his forearm, was obviously the boss. He simply watched the other one work, occasionally passing comment. Wandering away from the pool, he'd just discovered a nearly full bottle of champagne under a sunlounger.

Olly held his breath. *No, no, no,* he willed.

Beckoning his stooge over, Crew-cut waggled the bottle with more vocal bonhomie and indicated for Sideburns to sit down on a nearby stool. Then, reclining on the lounger, he poured out an inch of champagne into a discarded glass and passed it over, keeping the bottle for himself. Sideburns looked ecstatic.

Olly was furious. As he stalked inside, they spotted his bottom and let out a fanfare of wolf whistles. He thrust his chin in the air and fell over the cats. Even more annoyed, he flounced into the gym and attacked the weight machine. Finding he couldn't lift it at all, he sulkily took off a couple of lead discs.

Twenty minutes later, he was covered in sweat, pumping the heavy weights up and down, fantasising that he was working the bellows to a giant incinerator containing Ginger's collected poetic works. The sinews in his neck strained with each lift, his biceps rose like hills running with thick veined rivers, his quilted stomach glistened, hard and moguled.

Ginger appeared at the door and, resting his upper arm against the frame, started to watch.

Ignoring him, Olly threw a towel around his neck and transferred to the exercise bike.

'You look great,' Ginger whistled.

Olly pretended he hadn't heard.

'Stop doing that and come here,' Ginger ordered with a lazy grin.

Olly still ignored him, crouching like a Tour de France competitor on the finishing straight, bottom waggling.

Sauntering over, Ginger leaned down and turned the tension on the bike up to full, nearly shooting Olly over the handle-bars as the pedals ground to a halt.

Gasping for breath, still furious, Olly looked across at his laughing lover and blinked the sweat from his eyes.

'Put the yellow jumper on, sweetheart.' Ginger waved a piece of paper under Olly's gaze and then slowly ripped it up. 'And that was my best poem yet – I'm going upstairs to pack.' He kissed Olly on the nose.

Sitting back on the bike, Olly grinned.

'But,' strolling out of the door, Ginger gazed coyly over his shoulder, 'if you don't agree to those turquoise borders, I'm going to burn all your Piaf tapes.'

Howling with rage, Olly threw his towel at the door.

Popping his head back round it, unscathed, Ginger winked and disappeared again.

Marcus and his merry band of acid munchkins were busy throwing every bit of rubbish from the barn, including the broken furniture and a loudspeaker which Seb Kelly had fallen through in a drunken stupor, over the thick hedge to one of the oak woods by the tall back gate.

Seb had also thrown up on the computerised DJ's console, but Marcus thought they'd salvaged that. The stained, burned parachute silk had to go, though. Marcus squashed it into empty feed bins in the hayloft, where it steamed in the slanting, mealy sunlight let in by the unshuttered hatch.

'C'ya!' he called out through the hatch as another gang of weary but sated comrades in regulation two-tone baggy jeans, crocheted hats and tatty suede jackets loped off through the gates carrying back-packs, heading for the main road where they could hitch a lift.

Sitting down with his skinny legs hanging out of the hatch, he gazed at the bobbing bobbed heads in the courtyard below, dutifully picking up broken bottles, crunched cans and empty Durex packets, spliff ends, record sleeves and discarded king-size Rizlas.

It really had been a truly mojo crucial rave, pondered Marcus happily. He'd been right telling everyone it was now an annual event. He'd square it with his aunt sometime later in the year, she was cool.

The shady copse at the far end of the garden was heating up under its leafy awning. Tom dashed in and out of rich green glades bursting with wild flowers, pretending that he was a paramilitary commando looking for booby traps. Matty was in Eden, having discovered a fly orchid in the centre of a dry clearing. He only just stopped Tom checking it out for bugs.

Pushing Tor in the buggy behind, Sally struggled with the undergrowth, her bare legs – already covered with a Braille rash of nettle stings – now laced in barbed brambles. She watched Matty excitedly taking photographs of the orchid whilst being dive-bombed by Tom.

She'd only seen Matty through the wrong end of a shutter that morning and was becoming more familiar with his Nikon filters than his face, but she didn't mind; he was happy. Matty only took photographs when he was truly content – he said they were a barometer for his emotions. What was the point, he'd moan when passing photo opportunities in one of his black glooms, of taking a shot only for it to remind you later of a time you were miserable?

Although they'd gone to bed earlier, it was more for Matty to get away from his mother than to sleep. After making love very slowly and indulgently, they had talked until interrupted by

Tom trotting in minus his pyjama bottoms claiming he was hungry and that Tor had just shut herself in the toy trunk.

Matty was furious about what he saw as his mother's charity donation. Sally tried to explain that Alexandra was trying to help in the most peculiar, indirect and typically Alexandra way possible. Matty might like his house messy, draughty and falling about round his ears but Alexandra couldn't see it that way. She didn't give out of ostentation or desire for gratitude, she gave because she thought it would make those she loved happier. Matty gently dismissed this as a lot of psychological jargonese and complained that she'd done it because she wanted to control his life, she always had.

But even Matty had to admit – eventually – that the gift was one huge baling bucket for a sinking ship. It gave him a break – a chance to work for what he believed in again and not just to pay the bills. More importantly, it gave them more chance to be a family and escape the emotional – as well as financial – mess they'd been in until now. Sure, he felt mercenary about it – but, he'd smiled wryly, he was a liberal; weren't they supposed to feel guilty?

A macro Pentax appeared with Matty's body attached to it and started snapping her face.

Sally pulled a girn and hid behind a tree trunk, aware that she was looking decidedly rough with no make-up on and lack of sleep packaged up under her buggy eyes.

But to Matty there was no more glorious woman on earth, except possibly . . .

'Say fromage.' He finished the reel on Tor, who, hair standing on end, had a huge jam stain on her cheek and a mouthful of old leaves. Tor flashed her knickers at him and giggled.

'I'm warning you now, brat.' Matty looked at her in mock remonstration. 'You do page three and . . . I'll expect at least half of your earnings.'

'One thing.' He turned to Sally as they headed back to the house. He was now doing his stint with the buggy and being rewarded by Tor getting out and crawling in protest at his appalling driving.

'Niall . . .' he trailed off and stopped, looking at the beautiful tawny house, bleached in the bright sunlight so that it looked as if it had been whitewashed by the cleaning squad.

Sally shrugged. 'I think our help's been pretty misguided,' she said truthfully. 'Perhaps we should let him sort this one out himself.'

'But she's become such a bitch,' Matty sighed. 'I mean I liked her because she's got guts – she was so sharp and scathing about everything, it made me laugh. And when I saw through her I still bloody forgave her because Niall loved her. But Christ, he put her on such a high pedestal it's hardly surprising she flipped. She's had vertigo for years.'

'Lack of oxygen, low air pressure,' nodded Sally. 'Pedestal envy, too, I should imagine.'

'This is serious.'

'And so am I.' Sally touched his arm. 'Leave them to it, Matty.'

'They've been talking for hours.'

'No, they haven't,' Sally bit her lip as Matty looked at her sharply. 'I met Niall in the kitchen earlier when I was making coffee,' she confessed. 'He said she was asleep but he couldn't leave her for long. He was talking to Ben about something.'

'Why didn't you tell me?' wailed Matty, 'I could've spoken with him.'

'It wouldn't have helped. He's got to make up his own mind.'

Matty nodded and pulled her into a colossal hug. 'How did he look?'

Her cheek on his shoulder, Sally watched a startled magpie, disturbed by Tom's martial patrol, sweep screeching and chattering out of a nearby thicket. She desperately searched for another but it swooped towards the long stretch of garden alone.

'Ashen,' she said quietly.

Turning, ready to start walking again, they looked ahead and saw the magpie was joining a mate.

* * *

Lauren Buckingham curled her smooth, shapely legs around her husband's hairy ones and traced his sleeping jaw with her fingernails. Stubble was now shadowed around his mouth; in sleep, the full lower lip was even more prominent. Eddie resembled a pouting Pre-Raphaelite with his straight nose and wide long-lashed eyes. She couldn't imagine being married to a more exotic-looking man.

She stroked his hair with the back of her hand and he opened one lazy eye and smiled.

'Do you think they like me?' she asked in a low voice, suddenly young and uncertain.

Eddie shifted slightly, putting one arm behind his head and looking down at her.

Christ, he was a lucky sod, he told himself. He still kept expecting to wake up.

He nodded. 'It's funny,' he pondered, 'after all the noise that was made to get me – us – over here, no one seems particularly interested. One of my nephews even mistook me for the drains man on the way to the john.'

Lauren blinked and smiled but she still looked uncertain.

Eddie cradled her face in his hands, 'Don't worry, everything'll be fine. Alexandra thinks you're gorgeous – while you were asleep, I had to ban her from bringing the entire family in here to be introduced.' He laughed, touching her cheek with his broad thumb.

Lauren smiled and cleaved to his touch like a cat.

'I'm afraid my sister, Cass, will probably be the frosty one. Sophia – my elder niece – might get a bit moral, too. They'll accuse me of being a disgusting old lecher taking advantage of a sweet young thing,' he sighed.

'I was hardly sweet when you found me,' giggled Lauren. 'I stank like a polecat and spat nothing but punk abuse. I even bit you! And those clothes needed incinerating. I'm surprised you weren't repulsed.'

'You were pretty odious.' Eddie grinned. 'I seem to recall I tried to get the porter to chuck you out of my apartment when you started going cold turkey locked in my closet. I only took you in because you told me you were pregnant and starving and needed to phone your shrink. The next thing I know my phone bill hits four figures, my refrigerator's empty, the liquor store no longer gives me credit and Warhol sketches start mysteriously disappearing from my walls.'

'Eddie,' Lauren cuddled up to him and smiled mischievously. 'Take advantage of me just one more time. Please?'

'Don't leave me!' Lisette whimpered as Niall tried to creep from the room. Half shielded by the blanket she was clutching in small, shaking hands, her face smeared with make-up and blotched from crying, she was unrecognisable as the ferocious, carnal beauty who had beckoned him forth just a few hours earlier.

Niall stopped and looked at her. She had the glum, self-pitying expression of a child who had just recovered from a tantrum and was meekly waiting to be absolved. Niall could give comfort, could wipe her tears and calm her tattered emotions, but he was finding forgiveness harder to muster.

'Where were you going?' she asked in a small voice.

'Just to fetch a drink,' he lied. 'It's stifling in here.'

Despite the stale stuffiness in the little room, Lisette was shivering. She thrust her chin forward and demanded a vodka and cranberry.

'None left.' Niall sighed, noticing the jug of grapefruit juice he'd fetched earlier was still untouched on the sill. 'For the first time in history, this is a dry house. I was getting coffee.'

'Oh, that'll do. Black without.' Lisette stood up slowly, wrapping the blanket round her like a shawl, and walked hunch-backed to her bag.

Niall didn't move. He watched her crouch over to light a cigarette with a shaking hand before examining her reflection in the mirror of a silver compact.

Pois'nous bunch-back'd toad, he thought savagely, then recoiled at his acrimony.

Contradictory emotions were battling inside him. When she'd been on the verge of breakdown, raving suicidally, he'd suspended all loathing and cared for her with all the tenderness and devotion he'd once lavished so profligately. Yet the moment she gained any grip, he hated her again.

What she had told him during the past few hours made his flesh creep and his throat clench his breath into a tight ball. But still he was bound to her, a crippling, emasculating weight of commitment dragging him under suffocating mud.

'Shit – I look rough,' she scowled, trying to wipe the mascara stains from her cheeks, but they were dried on. Snapping the compact shut, she collapsed back on the chair and sighed irritably. 'Well?' she looked up at him.

Niall sat down beside her and took her hand in his. 'Lisette – what you said before you fell asleep. About us. I don't know if—'

'I meant it!' Lisette's voice rose shrilly. 'So help me God, I meant every word.'

'Lisette, you don't . . . love me,' Niall sighed quietly. He looked at his watch. Nearly midday. Tash might have finished by now.

'How do you know? You're not me!' Lisette said almost hysterically, the self-possession vanished. She clutched his hand till his fingers reddened, her eyes darting. 'I need you, Niall. To get over Colt.'

It sounded so farcical – like one of those prurient, gushy daytime soaps she'd worked on when first in the States. Niall had to resist a dreadful temptation to laugh.

'Lisette, I don't know if I can help you any more,' he whispered. 'I tried to explain—'

'And I told you,' Lisette snarled, 'Christ – how many times? – that drip feels nothing for you. I saw her with Hugo Beauchamp last night, outside in the garden. They were virtually attached by the hip. She's besotted with him, honey, crazy about him. Any fool could see it. Sally did – ask Sally.'

The pain sliced through Niall's chest like a sharpened sabre, but he merely stared at her sneering, venomous features, disfigured with hatred and determination.

Characteristically, she chose this moment to change tack.

It was a pattern she'd set up during the hours she'd paced the room, switching with disorientating velocity from a scourging, feral bitterness to ranting grief, ferocious tantrums and latterly, like a butterfly emerging from a putrid chrysalis, a deathly serenity.

Suddenly her face changed from a mask of malice to one of complete compassion.

'She has no idea how you feel, you realise that, don't you?' she asked softly. 'This girl you're fixated on,' she couldn't bring herself to say Tash's name, 'this child.'

Niall looked up sharply. 'She is not a child!'

'To a thirty-two-year-old she is, Niall.' Lisette looked at him wisely. 'When she was pooping her terry-towellings in abject luxury you were out there desperately tying to foist your virginity on some Dublin tart.'

'Hardly!' Niall was too worked up for mental arithmetic but thought it was unlikely. 'Anyway, as I told you before – there's nothing between us. She's got a boyfriend over here. By Christ, we haven't even kissed!'

Then he looked away, remembering the disastrous fumble in the paddock when Tash had been so desperate to escape she'd knocked herself out.

'Niall.' Lisette laid her hand on his arm, her voice laced with almost hypnotising kindness. 'One of the things that drove me potty when we were together was your crushes—'

Niall opened his mouth in surprise, about to protest.

'No, let me go on – please?' Lisette's eyes were full of tears.

Niall shut his mouth again.

'I'm not saying you were unfaithful sexually – God no, Fidelity on the Roof that was you – but all those lame ducks, one after the other, trooping through the house whenever we got a break together. If it wasn't some actor whose girlfriend had just pushed off, it was a troop of impoverished dancers from Warsaw or your poor uncle from Connemara who'd gambled his last bottle of whiskey away. I virtually had to book an appointment at the Citizens Advice Bureau to be alone with you.'

Niall hung his head and gazed across at the small portrait of Sophia as a child which was hanging on the far wall. It was becoming as familiar to him as a curvy reproduction Renoir in a hotel room.

His eyes were drawn to his watch like a magnet. Ten past twelve. Surely Tash would have finished? He hoped to God she was all right.

'They were my friends, Lisette.'

'And I was your wife, Niall!'

'I thought,' he sighed, 'they were your friends as well.'

'Sure, I liked them – but not all the time, invading our marriage, abusing your hospitality like grabbing leeches. You couldn't see how much they used you, fed off you and then despised you for it.'

'That's not true!' Niall whispered.

'Oh, yes it is,' Lisette persisted, her voice shrill but controlled. 'They used to talk, help themselves to your whiskey, food and cigarettes, laugh behind your back. They used you, Niall, and despised you for it.'

'Lisette, stop it!' Niall covered his ears.

'But it was worse than that!' She pulled back his hands and stared him in the face. 'You got sort of sophomoric crushes on your lame ducks, you were so obsessed with looking after them. You'd get so abstracted I need hardly have been there; you walked, talked, ate, breathed your latest casualty, until even they got so sick of it they pushed off. Look at Gregor and Liam Ochterlony, Quinlan, Sacha – even Matty moved to Richmond without telling you, didn't he? Probably dreaded the thought of you dropping in with a Cantonese and a crate of stout.'

Niall couldn't move or speak. His eyes – wide, black, tortured, brimming with pain, stared at her in silent suffering.

He knew how bitter, how vindictive she was capable of being but the painful truth was that there was an element of accuracy in what she'd said. And he'd thought he loved her to the point of idolatry; all the time she'd felt left out and ignored while he pushed himself on unworthy causes.

Niall rubbed his brow. No wonder she hadn't wanted to carry his child. He covered his eyes in desolation.

Was that how Tash was feeling now? he wondered. A revolted contempt at all his pathetic attempts to foster *her* cause?

'I know those were horrible things to say, Niall,' that hypnotising tenderness again, 'but you must understand that I did – I *do* still – love you but I wasn't capable of sharing you.' Her hand – warm, soft and dry – touched his cheek.

The old enchantment was working again. She had always had this effect on him – the ability to make him feel paralysingly inadequate, totally indebted to her wordly wisdom. He felt his stomach churn with sickening, uncontrollable longing.

Incapable of stopping himself, Niall leaned forward and kissed her. As he felt the soft cushion on his mouth opening like a ripe bud to his touch, he waited for the fireworks to go off in his head and his heart to compress into a tight pip of pleasure. But he merely tasted cigarettes and the sweet sugar coating on the pills she'd been knocking back.

He stretched out and felt her warm, narrow body and anticipated with a shiver the roar of lust soon to uncoil from inside him. Nothing happened.

As he pulled back for air, Lisette was staring at him with the cat-like, intoxicated expression she always assumed when she was turned on, her eyes half shut, her mascara-stained cheeks flushed. It had driven him to distraction with elated victory once. Now all he could think about was how thin she'd become – her delicate features in high relief against a hollow, emaciated face.

He felt a great rush of pity rinsing away his guilt.

'What have we settled, Lizzy?' He hadn't called her Lizzy since they'd met up again; now it hung in the room like a wretched lie, taunting him.

'I'm coming back, Niall.' She snuggled up against him, brushing his chest under his shirt, eager to be kissed again. 'We need each other. I'm a junkie and you're my safe-house.'

Niall sighed. He hadn't agreed, hadn't been capable of making any sort of judgment or reaction to her. He wasn't at all sure if he wanted her back.

It seemed they had talked for hours and settled nothing. He was only certain of one thing – that he needed Tash's calming presence right now almost as much as he wanted Lisette to disappear back where she'd come from in a great puff of sulphur.

'I'm going for a drive.' He stood up, desperate to get away from the poky little prison Lisette had set up as his judgment chamber.

'I'm coming too!'

Niall paused by the door, willing himself to refuse.

'Okay, come on then,' he said finally.

'I'm not going anywhere looking like this!' yelped Lisette, grabbing her bag.

Niall sighed. Tash wasn't vain. It was what made her so beautiful – the fact that she could look gloriously dishevelled without caring.

'Well, take a shower and meet me outside in ten minutes,' Niall ordered, suddenly feeling in control again. 'And for Christ's sake put a pair of trousers on yourself, now.'

After he'd changed into jeans and an old denim shirt, Niall pounded downstairs in socked feet and along the small corridor beside the silent kitchen, bending to extract his paddock boots from the pile of footwear on the floor.

An old English farthing unaccountably dropped from one of his boots.

50

'Pen should've been here by now.' Gus glanced at his watch as he stood with Ben and Sophia at the penultimate fence on the cross-country course.

They were trying to get some shade from a scraggy field maple but the sun, now overhead, was so punishingly hot that it pierced through the parched leaves, toasting their sticky backs. Heat hazes danced on the horizon as Gus squinted against the white light, searching desperately for a glimpse of his wife.

'Number sixty-two's only just gone past.' Ben looked down at his schedule. 'Penny's not until sixty-seven.'

'That means nothing.' Gus was pacing around nervously now. 'A lot of entries have scratched – Pen's one of the last on the course in her class. That last chap had a fall and a couple of refusals; she should have caught him up. Where the hell is she?'

He stared at the gloomy wood from which competitors had sporadically emerged, blinking as their eyes adjusted to the searing sunshine before the long climb to the finish, but the only movement was from a curly-tailed French dog stretching a retractable lead to capacity as it strained to sniff something unpalatable in a hedgerow. Then its owner's whistle was drowned by those of the fence stewards warning of another approaching horse.

Gus tensed and craned his stiff neck to get the earliest possible view of the horse and rider, who could currently be heard crashing through the woods with a fast, hollow thudding.

A sturdy-looking, but obviously exhausted bay appeared, ridden by a French girl who was whooping her sweaty, blowing mount on with loud encouraging cries as they scrambled over the pile of logs out of the wood, stumbled heavily on landing and headed unsteadily towards Gus and the Merediths.

'Is that Penny?' asked Sophia, who was bored rigid.

Badminton and Burghley were far more exciting, she'd decided, with bigger fences, lots of yummy trade stands and the chance to brush shoulders with royalty. This trial, as far as Sophia was concerned, was pony-clubber stuff – a poxy little affair by any stretch. Ben's border collie had jumped bigger sticks in Pedigree Chum Agility classes. And how was one supposed to follow the goings-on when the entire crackled commentary was in a foreign language? No one bothered answering her question as the PA proved her point by hissing into life again and spluttering something incomprehensible.

'You understand that?' asked Ben, hoping Gus hadn't noticed that the girl who was currently getting fairly well ensconced in the bullfinch beside them was number sixty-eight.

Gus shook his head, looking pale.

'Look – isn't that Tash about to start?' Sophia pointed out a pirouetting chestnut, with a flaxen tail and black leather boots covering his white socks, terrifying a couple of stewards fifty metres away. On top, like a daddy-long-legs on a gyrating Belisha beacon, sat Tash, looking pessimistic but controlled.

Sophia and Ben rushed towards the start, leaving an increasingly panic-stricken Gus staring vacantly into the woods. Sophia reached Tash first, just as the starter was beginning to count her down. Ben, limping behind, had got entangled with a loose spaniel.

Alexandra was bouncing around beside Tash, waving a programme excitedly. She'd positioned Josh's carry-cot dangerously close to Snob's glinting hooves, and had linked Lotty and Polly together by Lotty's toddler reins. Polly, videoing her sister's start, almost raised her little niece off the ground each time she lifted her camera to the huge chestnut's rider. Standing behind them, deliberately aloof, gloriously sulky, was Max.

Sophia couldn't quite sum this newcomer up. On the one hand he seemed amenable enough, was attractive and had a *very* successful father. On the other, he was obviously extremely smitten with Tash and didn't seem too bothered who knew it. To Sophia's mind that put him top of her Dubious Characters list.

Hugo, changed into a snazzy red body protector which was worn over his t-shirt and made him look even more demonically roguish and dashing, was standing on Tash's other side, holding his jockey skull and issuing brisk final instructions.

'Make sure you've got bags of impulsion going into the water. Ride him on aggressively if you have to . . .' He held on to a rein to steady the snapping Snob. Tash hardly seemed to be listening.

'Trente secondes.' The starter put away his hip flask and looked at his watch.

'Don't forget to turn hard right after the elephant-trap to get your line for the second ditch – it'll be on you before you know it,' Hugo instructed, checking Snob's girth. It was as if all the animosity and conflict he'd built up during the day was temporarily under wraps, like a shaky Eastern European cease-fire. After an effortless clear show-jumping, he could afford to be magnanimous; his victory was almost guaranteed.

'Gosh, isn't this such fun?' Alexandra jumped up and down breathlessly.

'– to give him a breather,' Hugo was still lecturing, 'then make sure you put in a couple of half halts before the first hill climb—'

The starter appeared to be having some difficulty locating his flag. In the end he gave up and simply held up his arm as he counted Tash down from ten.

'Dix, neuf, huit—'

'Oh, good luck darling!' squealed Alexandra, nearly shooting Snob into the Milky Way.

'Six, cinq—'

'Remember to take two strides between—'

'This is it, darling.' Tash ignored them all and whispered into Snob's long, frantically twitching ears.

'– deux, un, *allez*! Bonne chance!' The starter reached for his baguette.

Tash loosened her grip on the rubbered reins and Snob surged forward in his magnificent, ground-eating stride. They bounded off at a near gallop, perfectly out of control and obviously not asking one another's opinion as to the direction.

'Ohmygod!' Tash closed her eyes as the first fence – a relatively easy straw and telegraph pole affair – loomed large.

'Well, that's that, then.' Hugo turned on his heel and headed towards Simone and the bay mare. 'I suggest you go and wait for her by the ambulance, Alexandra. They might have forms they want you to sign later.'

'What is he going on about?' Alexandra didn't turn from watching Tash and Snob career over fence one, narrowly missing mowing down a few bystanders before thundering off in the general direction of the course.

'Take no notice, Mummy,' breezed Sophia. 'He's just nervous. Last time out, he made an utter prat of himself, didn't he, Ben?'

Ben cleared his throat and said nothing, raising his eyebrows to Sophia meaningfully; he'd made her promise not to mention it. Mercifully, Alexandra wasn't at all interested and started talking to Sophia about a replacement nanny.

'There's a girl in the village who's an utter poppet.' Collecting the children, she led Sophia away from the start. 'A little slow, granted, and the eczema's a touch off-putting at times but she's all heart – oh look! There's one of the boys with a flag in his mouth, how sweet.' She pointed out a deviant spaniel frolicking amongst a picnicking family. 'Do go and catch him for me, Ben.'

Hanging behind them, Max watched as Tash and her big red horse disappeared behind a group of spiny aspen – trembling despite the stillness of the day – on the outskirts of a copse.

He would have liked to buy another beer, but he was running short of French francs and doubted that he'd be able to change dollars on the showground. Not that he had many of those, he reflected glumly. Having expected his father to give him a fat cheque in America, Max had been alarmed to find himself almost begging for money. But Lucian rather pompously refused, saying that Max was old enough to earn his own crust. Explaining about losing his job in England had cut no ground with his father either. Lucian, with his uncanny sixth sense for corporate mismanagement, seemed to know that Max had been instrumental in causing his company's liquidation and Henry's bankruptcy.

Scratching his chin, Max idly wondered exactly how much his potential in-laws were worth.

'You speak French?' the lofty man with the neck brace who'd walked the course with Tash earlier appeared beside him, chewing a thumbnail anxiously. His blond hair – the colour of straw in winter – was dirty and full of dust and he had his t-shirt on inside out. He reminded Max of Graham after a team pub-crawl.

'A bit.' Max shrugged, trying to remember the bloke's name.

'Can you translate that?' he asked, as the tannoy again crackled the message it had been putting out repeatedly.

'Um – I think they're asking for a tractor.' Max listened. 'Something about an ambulance breaking down. I don't know what "remorquer" means.'

'Christ!' Gus spun round and clutched his neck. 'Ouch!'

'Something wrong, Giles?' Max asked, but the tall man's answer was drowned out by the firing-squad explosions of an approaching moped.

'Gus – Vite! Viens ici!' screamed an attractive brunette from the back of the bike.

Gus dashed over and then dodged sideways as the moped almost ran over him with a groan of worn-down brakes.

'Penny, she is fall.' M-C climbed off the bike painfully. 'You go wiz Didier, I find a vehicle pour remorquer – er – to tow.'

'What's happened?' Gus swung his leg over the bike so quickly he kicked Didier in the shins. Didier spat some dark blue abuse over his shoulder.

'She lose 'er line in ze woods – ze markers are sheet – and the 'orse, he knock 'er out on a branche. She 'as commotion cérébrale, I sink.'

'Concussion,' Max translated to a terrified Gus before he roared off, putting up a cloud of dust.

'The foutu ambulance, he weel not start,' explained M-C, limping beside Max as he supported her towards the horse-boxes. 'The drivers, they 'ave been listening to the putain pop music all day and the battery, he is flat. You can believe it? When they get the jump start, they drive straight into a deetch!'

Admiring her sultry mouth and gazelle-like figure, Max flashed his most winning smile.

'Can I help at all?'

Heading towards fence three, La Fosse Boueuse, Tash was blissfully ignorant of the commotion taking place further on in the course. She was only conscious of the rhythmic thudding of Snob's hooves and the thrilling surge of excitement that rippled through him every time he saw a fence.

The first few stewards' whistles to warn of their approach had sent Snob spooking into a hedge but, like Pavlov's dog, he was beginning to associate it with fun and games. Now his long red ears pricked as they blasted shrilly just ahead.

La Fosse Boueuse was a wide, dirty ditch marking a small gladed ha ha in the copse. Spotting it through the trees, Snob put in an alarming surge of speed.

Not managing to apply the brakes at all, Tash closed her eyes as Snob almost slid into the gaping, reedy mud before launching himself upwards. The feeling of pure, unleashed power was electrifying.

He stumbled slightly on landing and Tash's blistered hands got a fresh grip on the reins.

Her arms ached as he grabbed for the bit, shaking his head in frustration because she wouldn't let him take off at breakneck speed. Her face was burning with effort and concentration, her shoulder almost numb with pain, but she didn't care. She'd dreaded this moment, lost sleep, torn her hair out and cried over it. Never in a million years had she anticipated actually enjoying it.

She was aware that they were thundering along on a knife-edge of control. She was using more brute force than skill, and Snob was obeying simply because he realised that she knew the way to more jumps. But his enthusiasm was infectious.

'Slow down, you bully,' Tash coaxed, hardly managing to check him at all as they slid with reckless velocity and a flurry of dust and snapping twigs down the steep bank towards the gully fence, Le Ravin – a solid-looking tree-trunk suspended without a ground-line over a ditch in a shady hollow.

Suddenly, with an impatient snort, Snob thrust his head in the air so that Tash couldn't see the fence below them.

'Steady!' she warned, fighting to check him.

But Snob wasn't listening. Snatching the bit so forcefully that she could feel her arms straining from their sockets, he charged, plunging towards the ditch. It was like pitching, free-fall out of a plane. As Snob dived, Tash was thrown back, the reins slipping through her gloved hands, her stomach leaping into her chest.

She heard a fence-judge shout.

Then, with an almighty effort, Snob jerked up to take off, bashing Tash's nose squarely with his poll.

He'd taken off far too early. Tash, eyes streaming, frantically threw her weight forward to help him, but he was already landing as the jump was underneath them. With a horrible resounding whack, his hind legs crashed into the thick trunk and Tash was propelled out of the saddle on to his neck.

Snob, his front legs over the fence, his hind ones dangling behind, let out a panic-stricken whinny and struggled to free himself. Tash was hanging round his jarred neck. Soothing him with her voice, she tried to get off, but one of her new boots was firmly wedged in a stirrup and her stop-watch was trapped in his martingale. As she wriggled back on to the saddle, Snob dragged one leg over the fence and seemed to pitch sideways. Waiting for the ground to come up, Tash let out a scream and closed her eyes.

Thinking she must have passed out, she opened them again slowly, expecting to see a crowd of eager faces. Instead, she saw

Snob's quivering ears and felt him shaking with fright underneath her. He'd somehow freed the other leg and was standing in the ditch, frozen with shock.

A nervous-looking steward peered out at them from behind a bush.

'Avez-vous mal?'

Hearing the voice, Snob threw up his head and started backing furiously away, rising up on to his hind legs in a series of half-rears until he hit his hocks on the far bank and shot forwards again, panic rising, desperate to escape the ditch. His state of jittery, jolted alarm was seconds away from detonating a flurry of lashing hooves.

Trying to stay on board, Tash shook her head at the fence-judge, knowing that at any moment Snob would explode into a bucking, bolting frenzy.

Not putting any pressure on his mouth, she unhurriedly gathered up the dangling reins. She could feel Snob quaking underneath her, front end rising ready to take off, but she eased him down with her voice. It was like cutting the wires on an active time-bomb.

A second jump-judge was gabbling away at her in French from the other side of the fence, wanting to know if she was all right. Was she retiring or going on? Another competitor was due to set off, didn't she know?

Tash hadn't a clue what the whiskery old goat was going on about so she told him to shut up.

He looked furious and started to rabbit into his walkie-talkie irritably.

She'd never known Snob so rattled. His snorting subsided but he began to fidget uneasily, moving precariously in the narrow ditch, its banks high and pitted with hoof marks. Unpleasantly aware that if she fell off now, she faced being puréed under his studded shoes, Tash steered him away from the fence to give him more room.

Snatching away her grip, he tried to clamber out by the bush the first steward was hiding behind and instantly fell back, nearly bringing himself and Tash down in a heap.

Tash pulled him up, soothing him by talking nonsense, running her hand along his mane – curled like a footballer's perm from the earlier plaits – and giving him a bolstering pat.

Encouraging him with lots of tongue-clicking, she set him at the lowest piece of bank and urged him on.

Snob's confidence was in tatters. His head rose in panic as he reared up so high he nearly fell over backwards, startling him yet further.

'Trust me. Go on, my love,' Tash coaxed.

Snob's long ears trembled, but as she kept on talking, one twitched back and listened.

Gradually he stopped shaking, and with a sigh that seemed to say, 'Well, if you really think it's safe, Mum,' he clambered inelegantly but safely out of the ditch and stood placidly on the bank.

Tash was euphoric. She patted him until her hand went numb and struggled with the zip of her breeches' pocket for a Polo mint.

The fence-judges were both up in arms now, pointing at their watches and then to the corner from which the next competitor would appear.

'Okay, okay – keep your cheveux on. Je continue – d'accord?' Tash yelled at them, laughing with glee as she pulled Snob round and sent him off into his lovely loping canter – much more controlled this time – towards the farmyard complex at fence four.

'Little madam,' the second fence-judge sniffed in French.

'Very brave, though. I would have dismounted,' replied the first, watching Tash and Snob clear the trough with a huge, green leap and bound towards Les Gerbes. The girl had a very nice bottom, he noted.

'What shall we call that?' asked the second fence-judge, pausing to blow his whistle as news came over his walkie-talkie that the next combination were already past fence two La Niche. 'Two refusals, no?'

'They were through the flags by the time the horse reared.' The first steward looked at his companion critically. 'They will get lots of time penalties. It is a small class – why give her unnecessary jumping errors simply because she is English?'

The second man spat into the roots of a huge beech and grimaced. They could hear the next horse's thunderous approach.

'Well?'

The second fence-judge pressed the button on his walkie-talkie. 'Number eighty-one – the *English* person – clear through fence three, first attempt.' He then blew his whistle again, so loudly he nearly split his companion's eardrum.

Gus found Penny strapped to a stretcher in the middle of a deeply-grooved track, which ran through the woods. It was some way from the course so had consequently not been cleared to allow an ambulance through. Even the moped found the going too tough as long grasses clogged up its spokes. As Gus ran along it he had to duck to avoid overhanging branches weighed down by their midsummer foliage.

The leafy avenue was dense with nettles and brambles growing over the pitted gouges made by occasional passing tractors. Some way off a high-tech ambulance, courtesy of a French private health firm, was sticking out from a grassy ditch at forty-five degrees. Two red-faced uniforms were trying to shoulder it out without success.

The jump-judges who'd helped catch the little grey gelding had returned to their posts. He was being held close to Penny by a teenager who was feeding him cherry-flavoured Hollywood chewing-gum, which made his lips curl up and wobble in confusion as his teeth welded together. The girl's parents – obviously spectators, wearing stylish Parisian summer clothes and impractical open-toed shoes – were standing over Penny's stretcher fanning her with a straw hat and chastising their small pug for making sexual advances towards her motionless foot.

'Shit!' Gus ran forward and crouched down by his wife, taking her limp hand in his.

Her eyes were closed and a mint-green stain from the tree

she'd hit mingled with blood on her brow just below her helmet.

'Poor luvvie.' Gus touched her face and turned to scream at the ambulance men. 'Shouldn't one of you idiots be looking after her?'

Too far away to hear properly, they looked around and shrugged.

'Nous ne parlons pas anglais, comprenez?' one yelled back.

Gus twisted back to Pen and started to remove her crash-skull.

'Non!' The teenager's father put his hand on Gus's shoulder. 'I am doctor. It no good to – er – put off the hat.'

Gus felt totally hopeless. If only they were in England he could do something, he thought illogically.

A whistle blew in the distance and he heard a horse pounding through the wood further away, followed by a pause as it took off and cleared a fence then thudded on.

They'd walked the course so thoroughly, Gus remembered. Penny knew that she had to turn right after the ramshackle barn with a tree growing out of it. Why had she carried on? The stewards must have shouted at her but she wouldn't have understood them.

'They should have roped the bloody route out properly,' he fumed under his breath.

Penny groaned and he felt her hand clutch at his, but she didn't come round.

A dull chugging noise had started to build up from the opposite end of the track. It grew to a steady roar, and Gus looked up to see the four-by-four he and Penny had been using earlier as a shooting stick bumping up the track, followed by a tractor so old and dilapidated it seemed held together by binder twine and diesel fumes alone.

As the four-by-four drew up, M-C climbed out, followed by, Gus noticed, Tash's boyfriend, of all people.

'Don't worry, Giles – we'll take Jenny to another blood wagon while the tractor pulls out that one,' Max explained, taking control. 'The show secretary lent it to us – it's totally illegal on the roads, which is why he made us virtually divert by Calais. Here, let's get her inside the Daihatsu.' He stooped beside them and grinned. 'And I thought rugby was dangerous! Has Tash gone past yet?'

'What? Er – no, I don't know.' Gus couldn't take anything in. He was too worried about Penny.

But as they lifted her into the back of the four-by-four, she opened her eyes and looked around blearily.

'Hello, everyone.' She smiled and winced. 'I'm afraid a loose dog made him bolt, M-C. It came out – ow! that hurts – from behind a barn.' She tentatively touched her head. 'I think I have got a hangover after all.'

Max looked at her thoughtfully. 'This dog – it wasn't a spaniel, by any chance?'

But Penny had closed her eyes.

51

Hugo circled the mare again and tried to clear his mind, but it was like clearing Oxford Circus of shoppers three days before Christmas. Again and again the memory of his humiliation earlier in the year came back into unpleasantly sharp focus.

He'd taken off his spurs and discarded his crop just in case, but even so he'd never felt so nervous before a cross-country.

'Raring to go, eh?' Ben limped up, slopping half a litre of beer over the parched soil as he patted the mare. 'Sophs wishes you luck. She and her mother are up to the old neck in gossip from last night.'

He looked up at Hugo's pinched face. 'I say, are you all right?'

'Fine,' Hugo snapped. 'Got a fag I could tug at?'

Ben handed him one.

'Any news of Penny Moncrieff?' Hugo lit it with shaking hands while the opportunist mare threw her head down to snatch at the sparse grass.

'Apparently they're picking her up now – it's a pretty hairy part of the course to get to. The local riding club DC – or whatever they call them over here – has gone to ground in embarrassment; her husband's the chairman of the board of this health lot who own the ambulance. Frightful cock-up.'

'What do you expect from a two-bit operation like this?' snarled Hugo, dragging the bay mare's head up with a piqued yank.

'Er, quite.' Ben hoped operations wouldn't come into it.

Hugo looked back down and asked casually, 'Has Tash

finished yet?' He threw away the barely smoked cigarette at Ben's feet, where it promptly set light to a crisp packet.

'No.' Ben was concentrating on stubbing the little blaze out with his shoe.

Hugo smiled to himself in satisfaction. Tash needed to learn her lesson. Might put that boyfriend off too, he mused. Rugger buggers didn't go for failures, in his experience.

'But she's over half-way round, according to Alexandra's running tannoy translation,' Ben continued. 'Clear so far, too.'

Hugo scowled. The rest of the class had been collecting penalties like bridge scores. One poor soul had fallen off twice in the starting box before being eliminated at the second fence. Three more combinations had scratched after the show jumping. The course was just too demanding. Hugo found the idea of Tash going clear across country preposterous. It was her first competition, for Christ's sake, he thought furiously.

'Quatre-vingt douze? Préparez-vous. Une minute.' The starter – now thoroughly plastered – waved at him vaguely.

Hugo's throat tightened.

Ben thumped his friend's leather boot amiably. 'Not thinking about—?'

'No!' Hugo kicked the mare into action and moved closer to the start box, away from Ben, who scratched his head and watched the tottering starter miss his chewed flag and pick up a half-eaten baguette instead.

'Trente secondes.' The starter held up the baguette and a piece of jambon fumée fell out.

Hugo tensed yet further. The mare, picking up on his nerves, started to nap. Irritably, Hugo slapped her over the neck with the loose end of the reins.

Oh no, thought Ben, the stupid bugger's going to do it again.

The tannoy hissed into life once more and burbled out a course update. Only a few words stood out but they were as clear as the rest were gobbledygook. 'Tash French et Le Fossy Nooob.'

From the grim tone in the commentator's voice it was obvious she was doing well. He only sounded cheerful if someone had fallen or retired.

Hugo frowned and tugged at the mare's mouth so hard she whinnied in alarm. Ben swallowed.

'– quatre, trois, deux, un, allez!' The baguette came down and Hugo's mare sprang forward. 'Bonne chance!'

The starter choked on the haze of dust that was kicked up as the duo streaked away towards the fence.

'You are going to be checked over,' Gus ordered as he helped Penny out of the Daihatsu.

'I am not!' wailed Penny, snatching her hand away and having to grab the tailgate to steady herself as her head spun. 'I'm perfectly all right. It was just a beump on ze 'ead. I want to see how the others are getting on.'

On hard ground she staggered slightly and clutched her temples. Gus sighed and started steering her towards the ambulance nearby, this time provided by voluntary services.

'Will you be all right, Giles?' Max called to the retreating couple as he helped M-C out of the passenger seat.

'Sure – you go and watch Tash finish.' Gus turned.

Max seemed a good bloke, he reflected gratefully. Lousy at names, but willing to muck in. Poor Hugo. Gus couldn't help feeling sorry for him. For a man who normally played harder to get than soap dropped in a bath, Hugo seemed to be getting a delightfully large game-sized dose of his own medicine, from Tash French.

'Tell her there's a supply of water in M-C's box she can use to cool the horse's legs,' he added.

'I'll come too,' Penny announced quite normally, then headed vaguely in the opposite direction towards a trade stand hung with every conceivable item of couture rugging for the discerning equine.

'You're coming with me.' Gus took her firmly by the arm and steered her towards the aspirant first-aid volunteers waiting with menacing enthusiasm, and a huge pile of bandages, splints and first-aid books, by their shining vehicle.

* * *

Snob smartly changed legs as he and Tash swung right by a crumbling barn and headed towards the black shadow of woodland.

Tash's face was so grimy she felt as if she was wearing a drying mud-pack, and she could barely see through the grit on her new contact lenses. Her shoulder was by now a humming pulse of constant agony, her feet were paralysed by cramps in the tight boots and the nappy strap of the body protector had tightened to the extent of rendering the likelihood of future childbirth questionable. But it didn't stop her laughing out loud as Snob cruised over the saw-mill fence on the outskirts of the wood, barely breaking his fluid, gambolling stride.

They then struck a right once more, up a steep bank thick with peat to soften the tightly packed ground, popping over a low brush to land neatly on deep pillows of wood-shavings in the copse.

Tash blinked in the sudden shadowy gloom. It was like jumping into a crypt. There was a still, almost reverent hush. Staves of yellow light, dancing with dust and pollen, fell through the cracks in the canopy of trees above, dazing her as she desperately stared around, trying to recollect the course.

Snob shook his head in fury as she checked him almost to a halt but he did her bidding, trusting her now.

Tash stared at the three tracks which led off through the brindled undergrowth, dingy brown paths like tortoiseshell veins set in verd antique. There seemed to be hoof-marks on all of them. She hadn't been concentrating when they'd walked this bit of the course; she simply couldn't remember where to go.

Behind her, a fence-judge was clambering stiffly over a laddered style to come and give directions, but Tash had made up her mind. They were seriously behind on time already. She'd trust to luck. Plumping for the most pitted track in the middle, she kicked Snob on, and soon they were crackling over mildewing twigs at a Fastnet rate of knots, heading towards the red and white flags Tash had spotted through the trees.

Strange, thought Tash, she couldn't remember that big zig-zag fence at all. Odder still, there was no whistle to warn of her approach and no stewards clutching clipboards and sipping coffee from a thermos.

Snob stiffened with excitement at the sight of the looming jump, and Tash drew him together, checking his stride and gathering his hocks underneath him.

'Christ alive!' she whispered through clenched teeth.

It was a far bigger fence than the others and required a line of draughtsman's accuracy. As she summed it up, Tash could feel Snob falter. Then, setting her eyes on a suitable point ahead between two chunky beech-trunks, she drove him on and they soared over. The exhilaration took her breath away.

The course now became even more confusing, with tracks to the left and right, both leading deeper into the woods to more flagged jumps.

Hardly checking, Tash elected for the right, and they flew over an angled log followed by a sunken road, skirted with an avenue of young lime the colour of mint lozenges. She was almost certain there hadn't been this many fences in the wood when they'd walked it.

On another part of the course, Hugo had a battle on his hands. The mare might be a dream in all other respects, but she was also a closet hydrophobic, absolutely terrified of water.

Ramming on the brakes at the last possible moment, she refused the open ditch which only had a trickle running through its pebbly depths.

His face burning with effort, Hugo cajoled her over on the second attempt with the aid of shouts, kicks, rein-flapping and a sharp smack on the rump with his hand. Hardly professional technique, he realised, but he was too worked up himself to muster the patience he knew he needed to nurse-maid the highly strung youngster.

Now thoroughly wound up, she was goggling at everything in sight, and taking fences with huge, unseating cat-jumps.

They only just scraped over the first element of the farmyard complex, totally wrecking a straw construction by misjudging the stride and thrashing through the middle of it. Thankfully, there was no woodwork built in to bring them up short, but the episode did nothing for the mare's confidence or her trust in her rider. Leaving a leg at the angled gate out of the complex, she almost brought herself down.

Hugo leaned back in the saddle to recover, reins slipping through his hands. Her mouth free, the mare found her feet and tried to bolt.

Snatching the reins back like an angler fiercely pulling in a deep-water pike, Hugo bruised her gentle mouth accustomed only to the softest of aids from M-C. She let out a furious, frightened buck and fought him for freedom.

As they battled their way, tail-twitching, head-shaking and cantering sideways like a frenzied crab, towards a low bank and rails that acted as a 'stocking filler' to the tougher fences, Hugo struggled even harder to control her. At this rate, they were never going to make it round. He had to do something fast; the next but one fence was L'Étang de Moulin, the mill pond.

'You can lead a horse to water,' muttered Hugo grimly under his breath, 'but you can't make it jump.'

Tash sped on through the woods. The trees were thinning out now to become a scant, twiggy coppice filled with pools of blinding light which only served to amplify the dusky gloom of the shadows.

Snob was going so obediently, Tash couldn't help but feel slightly suspicious. Surely any minute he was going to plough into a tree trunk, dropping his shoulder of old?

They whizzed over a set of rails with a tricky, bumpy take-off and steep drop on the landing side, where three jump-judges, loading their folding stools into a dilapidated Citroën, gave them an odd look and consulted half-packed-away score sheets.

At last a bright white gap appeared in the trees ahead, arching over a pile of logs. She remembered that fence, at least. 'It'll be hard for the horse, as well as you, to see what he's taking,' Gus had warned her. 'He'll be unnerved, so give him plenty of confidence and let him have a good look if he wants, without losing impulsion.'

'Right, my lovely – spectacles on, second gear,' Tash murmured, changing Snob on to the left leg and sitting deep into the saddle.

As she drove him on amidst the frantic blowing of whistles, another rider shot out of an overgrown path to the left just behind her and started riding his huge grey at the same fence.

'Get out of the way, you stupid idiot!' Tash screamed, as Snob's head shot up in surprise.

The other rider, wielding his crop like a Bayeux tapestry soldier, yelled something twice as angry and considerably cruder, but mercifully the language barrier prevented Tash comprehending.

Snob, however, French from tête to sabot, got the gist and accelerated like a Lotus in a straight country lane. The grey, lathered to a dull pewter in sweat and blowing out great gasps of air, fell behind.

Tash knew they had to jump clean or there would be a horrific collision. But, without warning, the other rider, still shouting, kicked on furiously, and his poor, tiring horse laboured its way up to Snob's rump just three strides from the fence.

'Fucking moron!' hissed Tash through gritted teeth. He was going to kill them both.

As Snob engaged his powerful hindquarters under him for take-off, Tash screamed in alarm as a whip lashed down on them, catching her elbow. Snob, reeling with surprise, slid almost to the base of the fence, his fore legs still thrashing in the air.

For an awful moment Tash thought they'd had it; envisaged the ambulance, the humane destroyer, her mother's tears and Hugo's 'I knew it would come to this' expression. Then, with a groan of effort, Snob heaved himself over the log-pile and they were out in the blistering, dazzling light of an open field.

'There she is!' shrieked Alexandra, jumping up and down beside Max. 'Look – how sweet, she was giving someone a lead over that fence. Oh dear – he seems to've fallen off. Isn't Tash doing well?'

Max nodded and watched as Tash, grinning from ear to ear, coursed up the hill beside the wood and flew through the bullfinch as if it wasn't there. Throwing up great showers of dry earth, they stormed up to the last fence, a triple made from telegraph poles hung with tyres, and rocketed over it.

Max stood back as she galloped whooping through the finish, overshooting their halt by a mile.

Barely blowing, Snob proudly carted Tash half-way round the field before he would allow himself to be pulled up, jogging back towards the French family and friends with a smug, content expression on his intelligent red face which matched the elated one of his mistress.

'Wasn't he utterly, utterly brilliant?' Tash laughed, covering his neck with pats and hugs as she slid sorely off.

Springing forward, Max made to kiss her grimy cheek, but Alexandra got there first. Bursting with indulgent delight, she hugged her daughter tightly.

'You were so wonderful, sweetheart. Ben, Anton and I stood on top of Pascal's jeep with Lucian's binoculars to watch you. Ben's been calling you the next Ginny Leng and Pascal actually came out of the beer tent to watch you go over that flint star thing – oh, Max, darling, do go and see if Tash's score's up yet – Anton says—'

Tash caught Max's eye over her mother's shoulders and laughed.

'I love you,' he mouthed.

Feeling this high, she could only feel huge great buckets of love for everyone. 'Me too,' she mouthed back and grinned, then rather regretted it as Max, swaggering away to check her score, punched the air like Gazza scoring the clinching goal.

Tash couldn't remember being this happy in years. She knew that she wouldn't win – they had taken far too long to complete the course, and besides, Hugo was streaks ahead of everybody – but her victory was far greater than that.

Turning back to Snob, who was looking peeved that he didn't

seem to be getting any of the congratulations which were being bandied about, she gave his pink nose a great sloppy kiss.

He pulled away indignantly, like a small boy kissed by a great-aunt. Then his huge, purply brown eyes, like pansies dipped in espresso coffee, softened and he chewed the peak off her hat silk. Tash could almost have sworn he winked as, lips snapping, he nudged her boastfully.

'Oh, listen.' Alexandra cocked her head and stopped talking for once, concentrating on the commentary spluttering from two loud-hailers on a pole nearby. 'I think Hugo's in trouble.'

Hugo's bay mare had taken one look at L'Étang de Moulin and decided to head for the Swiss border.

Spitting curses under his breath, Hugo hauled her round and made for the fence again.

It was only a small jump – built like an upturned boat – but the fairly fast-moving mill-stream the other side was a red rag to the nervous, rattled mare. The stream was clear, shallow and sure-bottomed, but the jump took one straight into it without a chance to dip a toe in first.

In the searing sunlight, the water glittered like a sheet of pitted silver.

She approached it like a ten-ton tank up a one-in-four hill and this time, instead of ducking out, she merely ground to a mulish halt a foot away and refused to budge.

Hugo pushed and goaded, clicking his tongue, then making encouraging noises and finally shouting, 'Get over, you stupid bitch!'

The mare could have been superglued to the sawdust take-off. Hugo shivered as a memory bit at his back. He hoped to God history wasn't repeating itself. This time he refused to concede.

He dragged her round once more. Another refusal and they'd be eliminated. No way was he going to let a temperamental, mareish nag with the guts of one violin string embarrass him like this, he decided angrily. If she wouldn't be coaxed then she'd have to put up with steam-rollering.

Once in the water, she would realise it wasn't as bad as she'd feared. She would, in fact, be grateful for the refreshing cool of the stream on her hot legs, splashing up on to her steaming belly, neck and flanks as she moved through it. Hugo had seen plenty of stubborn horses experience the same pleasant surprise on a hot day. If one judged it right, it could cure them of their hang-up altogether.

He took the mare so far away from the fence that one of the stewards asked him if he was retiring. After the man had repeated the question several times, Hugo understood and shook his head.

He trotted her to the right, where the stream would be hidden until the very last moment by a row of cushion-plump elder covered with ageing blossom which had started to scatter like a burst sag-bag on the grass below. Stroking the mare's hot, damp neck, he gave her a quick pat and relaxed in the saddle. This confused her, accustomed to his bad-tempered, overbearing grip, and after a few seconds the tension seemed to seep like a slow puncture from her back and neck. Gathering up the reins, Hugo felt her start, but again he soothed her. Gradually, hesitantly, she unwound.

Then, taking her by surprise, Hugo kicked her into a canter.

The mare sprang into wild action, bolting forward as if she'd been stung on the tail, her hooves suddenly eating up ground, totally unaware that she was careering towards the mill chase.

As Hugo had anticipated, by the time she saw it she was going too fast to stop. She swerved violently to the left but momentum carried her forwards and she was forced to leap with a corkscrew twist of her hindquarters into the sparkling stream.

Hugo felt a surge of pure, exalted victory as he took off with her. A split-second later, this changed to total horror as he realised he wasn't landing with her.

Nicknamed Gluego Hugo in the sport because of his almost cat-like balance, which kept him stuck firm to the saddle even through the most hairy of moments, Hugo seldom fell off. He hadn't come off at a water complex for years. But, as the mare crumpled under him, he saw a clear, sparkling sheet of water fast approaching.

Then Hugo felt the initial cold sting of impact, heard a rush of water in his ears and swallowed more eau minérale than he'd had all holiday.

Landing in the drink is one of the most unpleasant possible falls to have in eventing. First, a messy, chaotic tangle of hooves, wet leather and thrashing water, then – after hopefully discovering everything is still functioning and St Peter or Uncle Nick aren't staring one in the face – the reality of cold, muddy, sopping clothes, waterlogged boots and a saddle that's slippier than black ice under tap shoes.

Sitting on the stony base of the stream, Hugo realised with relief that he was still in one piece. He slowly stood up to see the shuddering mare climbing to her feet a few yards away. She shook herself so violently that Hugo was blinded by yet more drips. Flattening her ears against her head, she then trotted, saddle slipping, with the high-stepping action of a Hackney over to the far bank.

Cursing with every four-, five- and six-letter word he could think of, Hugo waded over to where she had been caught and was being held by a well-meaning, whiskery old bat.

The woman started commiserating with Hugo. Stony-faced, he ignored her and snatched back the bay's sodden reins.

The mare threw up her head and backed off, her eyes rolling to show terrified white rims. As Hugo approached, she snorted nervously and sprang round so that her quarters were away from him, thwarting his attempt to get a foot in the stirrup. Every time he edged forward, she side-stepped, blowing through red-veined nostrils. She was shivering now, her dripping sides heaving, her wet tail just a thin, straggly black rope.

'Come here, you silly cow!' Hugo snapped, tugging harshly at her mouth, cold, humiliated ire stiffening his spine.

She jerked back and reared, spinning round again, but this time she came up against the wall of the little derelict stone mill and was trapped. Quickly blocking her from darting forward,

Hugo swiftly pushed the saddle back to the centre of her withers and sprang back on.

'Right, it's time to teach you a lesson, you old bag,' he snarled, snatching up the reins with such haste that she started to back into the stream again.

'Monsieur!' A magenta-faced jump-judge rushed forward, looking anxious.

'Have I been eliminated?' Hugo snapped abruptly, before he could speak.

The mare gyrated underneath him.

'Monsieur?'

'Moi. *Eliminate.* E-LIM-I-NATE. Comprenez?' He wiped the sweat and stream-water leaking from his crash-skull out of his eyes. 'Christ, is everyone here a moron?'

'Aaaah, non, monsieur. Continuez si vous voulez,' the jump-judge smiled nervously. 'Mais, je pense—'

'*Thank* you,' Hugo said tersely and squeezed the mare so hard with his legs that she groaned.

Hugo thought of his disgrace at Badminton and didn't care. He'd been leading the competition there, too. But he hadn't done anything as fundamental as falling off and getting his breeches wet.

He would never forget the buzz of pleasure he'd felt when riding towards the final sponsor's fence, seconds away from the optimum time and a faultless round. He'd ridden the horse hard, pushing for every last ounce of effort and taking outlandish risks. But that had always been the secret of his success, why the press and crowds found him irresistible. The danger of the sport excited him.

But that day, the unthinkable had happened. To the amazement of fellow-competitors and the laughter of spectators, his horse had simply ground to a halt in front of the final fence and refused to continue. Contrary to rumours in the press afterwards, the animal hadn't been exhausted to the point of collapse. It had simply chosen the most publicly humiliating moment to lose its trust and confidence once and for all. Like all Hugo's rides, the horse had the courage of a lion. But being ridden around the world's most taxing course with the devil crouched on its back had shattered its spirit.

At the time, Hugo had retired with a bemused, disappointed shrug and a sympathetic pat on his mount's neck. Later, away from the glare of cameras, he'd lost his temper and his head. The horse would never event again.

It was a fit of rage that Hugo couldn't forgive himself for, one that had made him re-evaluate his career and consider giving up the sport completely.

But now he felt rational and in control. There was no hot fury, no wild, blazing tantrum. His blood was chilled with icy calm.

Wrenching the mare to the right, he pushed her into a jagged canter towards the next fence.

But the mare had other ideas. She was fed up with the spiteful force of the man on her back, his harsh hands, drumming heels and vice-like, muscular legs. She had one thought in her brain, which – although it might only be the size of a walnut in a Waldorf salad – was working fast. Looking with rolling eyes, she spotted the gleaming, Dinky-car roofs of the horseboxes beyond a field full of sunflowers to her left. There Simone would be waiting with a stuffed haynet and pockets full of mints. Her walnut was made up. Tossing her head down so fiercely that Hugo was thrown on to her neck, she bolted, plunging into the tall, crow's foot yellow blooms.

Hugo let out a bellow of disbelief and pulled himself back into the saddle. Before he had time to think, they were travelling at breakneck speed through the densely packed sunflowers.

Thick, bristled stems lashed at Hugo's legs, club-like blooms bludgeoned his arms. He'd lost a stirrup. The wet reins ran through his fingers like greased ribbons as he frantically tried to gather them up. He was sliding about on the sopping saddle like a dinghy in a force ten.

In a desperate attempt to pull up the rocketing, manic animal, Hugo tried something he knew was a complete jackaroo manoeuvre. Leaning out of the slimy saddle on his one intact pedal like a polo player stretching for a distant ball, he grabbed hold of the side of the mare's bit and tugged with all his off-balance energy.

For a split second the mare swung violently to the left, almost stopping in her tracks. Then the cheek-strap of her bridle snapped and the loosened snaffle came right through her mouth and lay heavy and ineffectual in Hugo's grasp. The mare launched into turbo boost again, propelling Hugo even further towards the racing terra firma below.

He grabbed a hank of mane to stop himself disappearing between those pounding front legs.

Before Hugo could take in what was happening, the saddle slipped perilously to one side, leaving him dangling, battered by passing sunflowers, one arm clutching the martingale neck-strap for dear life.

'Shit!'

The field of horseboxes was approaching fast. Hugo tried to ease his foot out of the stirrup – now at the horse's knee level – so that he could throw himself clear, but, due to his earlier move, it was firmly wedged in. He hooked his other leg further over the mare's back and pushed hard at the saddle but that refused to budge, too.

The dangling reins had snapped and were trailing under the mare's legs. Any minute her pelting hooves might get caught on them and she'd come crashing down on top of him. Sunflower heads were beating a tattoo on Hugo's backside like a QC's mistress. One wedged itself into his flapping number vest and stayed put, another was trapped between his boot and stirrup leather. Petals were everywhere.

Hugo whimpered, close to tears. He was about to thunder through an audience of fellow-competitors like a mutilated harvest float and there was absolutely nothing he could do to stop it.

Tash left the others to listen gleefully to the tannoy and walked Snob back to Anton's box. One girl was crying forlornly by a little trailer as her unfortunate horse held up a puffy fetlock – swollen to the size of a rugby ball – for the course vet to examine. Nearby, a boy with a freshly strapped wrist was shouting at his groom as if his elimination were all her fault. A season's hopes down the drain for both of them. But despite this, Tash couldn't come down. She still couldn't remember ever feeling this exhilarated.

'It's all thanks to you, Fossy Nooob.' She scratched Snob's moist red neck and pulled at his long, loping ears. The chestnut sighed appreciatively and nipped her elbow.

Tash listened with only half an ear as the PA continued to splutter a delighted observation of Hugo's misfortunes. Instead, she concentrated on untacking her Herculean quad, sponging down his tired legs and scraping the worst of the sweat and dust from his auburn coat.

Snob, as if aware of her aching shoulder and throbbing head, hardly played up at all, standing like a rock and only shifting to help her along or silently chew the buckle off his sweat sheet.

Soon the resurfacing pain was too much for Tash. She slumped on to the ramp of the horsebox. In a few minutes, Max would be back from checking the score and this delirious happiness would be punctured like a bike wheel on hedge clippings. Her head throbbed.

Then Tash realised the pounding was not coming from her brandy-pickled head but from behind.

Craning round, she saw a loose horse thundering out of the nearby sunflower field at a deadly gallop. Its coat was black with sweat, its bridle hanging like a massacred stick insect from its terrified face.

As the horse pounded rapidly closer, Tash realised that a rider was hanging precariously from the side further away from her. Clinging on for dear life, helmet pushed over his nose and sunflower heads dangling from every corner, the mystery figure sliding downwards was hard to identify.

Tash stood up stiffly, shrouding her eyes from the sun with her hand. Grooms and riders were running forward but the mare was too quick for them. Ducking away to avoid being caught, she charged between two trailers, scattering buckets and battering her floral load on a wing mirror. The floral load wailed. Tash blinked in amazement. She recognised that indignant bellow – she'd been on the receiving end once too often.

The mare tore through a human chain of stewards and circled sharply round the sagging loo tent, almost depositing Hugo on top of its less than savoury downpipe. She then faced them all playfully, summed up the opposition, and tore towards Anton's box and the whinnying Snob, who was thoroughly overexcited by such a fantastic display of equine superiority.

'I hope to Christ she's not in season,' muttered Hugo, peeping underneath his slipping helmet and desperately trying to kick his foot out of the pedal.

But, despite some hot looks from Snob, the mare cavorted on. Bolting past, she hooked sharply round to the left, let out a series of whiplash bucks and hurled her rider through the air like a scud missile aimed at Saudi Arabia.

Hugo didn't get that far. He landed squarely at Tash's aching feet.

Looking up at her shocked face, Hugo determinedly stopped himself from crying, firmly prevented himself shouting and stoically held back a scream. Instead, he smiled up at the beautiful girl above, and laughed.

'I can't help it, Tash.' He pushed back his crash-skull and grinned, his thick lashes wet with tears. 'I just seem to have fallen for you.'

52

'You took your bloody time!' Niall was sitting astride Marcus's red moped, revving the one Shetland-power, paraffin-injected engine to a furious, waspish whine.

'I'm not getting on that!' snapped a sullen Lisette.

She'd virtually had to Brillo-pad her cheeks to remove Estée's run-proof mascara and was not about to risk her green powder blowing off as she played pillion to a high-rise Sinclair C5.

'Well, don't come then.' Niall flipped up the balance bar with his heel. 'It's the only damn contraption in this place that appears to be working. What do you suppose this knob does?' Scattering straw, the moped jolted forward three feet and cut out with a bronchial cough.

'Wait!' Lisette smoothed down the exquisite suede trousers she'd borrowed from a wardrobe and tied the tails of an expensive silk shirt before climbing sulkily behind Niall.

She'd forgotten how gloriously broad his shoulders were. Perhaps she wouldn't behave quite so crabbily. After all, this was supposed to be their Big Reconciliation, even if she had just taken a quarter-hour cold shower without soap, only to realise that a collection of spotty teenagers had been treating themselves to a peep show from a hayloft opposite. Perhaps Niall was going to whizz her off into a nearby melon field and ravish her, she wondered idly.

On the other side of the courtyard, loading their bags into a jaunty yellow sports car, Olly and Ginger were watching with interest. Lisette waved at them cheerfully.

'Ready?' Niall sighed as she wrapped her slim arms around his waist, letting her hands flop on his crotch.

'Mmmm.' Lisette laid her cheek against his smooth, denim back.

Niall rested his foot on the pedal and kick-started the moped with a roar of strained engine and a shriek of panicked chickens. He didn't see Sally looking out of the kitchen window with a sad and troubled expression on her pretty, sunburnt face.

Lisette did, however, and she stuck out her tongue in glee.

As they passed the lodge house, the sound of hurled saucepans and Gallic abuse almost drowned out the moped's spluttering drone.

Clutching his head, more from a desire not to be recognised than injury, Hugo was led towards the ambulance beside the stewards' tent, an area which was now teeming with casualties. Behind him, he could hear Tash and M-C's groom, Simone, rattling a bucket and calling the bay mare, who was now frolicking amongst the motley collection of trade stands.

'I can manage!' Hugo snapped, pulling away from the jolly-faced steward who'd been propping him up as they walked.

Mustering dignity, he skulked up to the ambulance, shrouding his face.

At the centre of the small gathering, two very overexcited volunteer ambulance men were mummifying a middle-aged woman in crêpe bandages. Inside the blood wagon, propped-up with two musty chintz cushions appropriated from the stewards' enclosure, was Penny. She looked pale and faintly tinged with green, but still radiated plenty of her usual élan.

'Hugo!' She waved frantically over the heads of the crouched officials. 'It's like the Red Cross mission hut at the Battle of Flanders here.'

Hugo cleared his throat nervously, glanced around and crept furtively over.

'How are you feeling?' He climbed over a prostrate body

belonging to a girl who was being fitted with splints for what appeared to be nothing more than a stubbed toe.

'She's feeling terrible,' Gus put a protective hand over Penny's, 'and these bloody Frogs won't take her to hospital until they've finished pratting around doing a Florence Nightingale act on every passing verucca – ouch!' He bumped his head on the low ceiling as he stood up to allow a zealous medic to grab an oxygen cylinder.

'Better get that seen to, old boy.' Hugo smiled as Gus rubbed his head. He tried to sit down but his backside was agony from the floral beating he had taken.

Penny was looking at him oddly. He couldn't work out if it was because he had his flies undone or just that she was still feeling slightly concussed.

'I don't mean to be rude but did you know you had a sunflower wedged into the back of your stock?' she asked politely.

Hugo groaned and ripped off the offending bloom.

'Christ – yes – what a prat!' Gus looked at him suddenly. 'I completely forgot to ask – how did your round go?'

'Ah.' Hugo fiddled with what appeared to be an inflatable leg. 'Interesting question.'

Outside the ambulance, Alexandra had gathered her brood to see if the news that was currently floating around the ground was correct. Rumour had it that Hugo was at this very moment unconscious inside the ambulance, needing immediate major surgery – consensus had it down to be an on-spec tracheotomy – following a crashing fall on top of a local actor-cum-vigneron's Great Dane.

'I really don't think it's right to pry,' she murmured, craning to get a better look inside the ambulance.

'Well, I don't know what all the fuss is about.' Sophia, who had donned her weird sun-specs and a beastly collection of midge bites, was trying to persuade Ben back into the beer tent to escape the heat and flies. Josh was really getting far too whiffy for this sort of heat and Lotty was bawling because her dung-infested Noo Noo had been confiscated and placed in the glove compartment of the Merc.

But Ben was deeply concerned about his old friend and wouldn't be moved.

'Supposing he can never ride again?' He turned to Pascal, horrified at the idea. 'The thought would kill him.'

'Do not worry.' Pascal smiled and hiccuped as he swayed against Anton, now very drunk. He patted Ben's shoulder encouragingly. 'It might be that eet has already, mon ami, no? After all the boy, 'e could be dead now.'

At this Anton staggered sideways, muttered a few sacred French oaths, and ended up in a litter bin.

Tash tried to explain to M-C what had happened to Hugo, but the Frenchwoman was too incensed to listen. Not one of her entries had completed the course – the tall boy having retired after Le Ravin. Her flashing black eyes and whiplash tongue terrified Tash, who beat a hasty retreat back to the sanctuary of Snob's teeth.

Inside the top-oven heat of the groom's compartment, Tash removed the knicker-garrotting body protector and her grimy stock and put on a long red t-shirt. There was no mirror but she was pretty certain it would match her burning, sticky, boiled-sweet face.

Wearing a crash-skull had made her hair mat itself to her head like a hot-washed balaclava and her new boots stubbornly refused to come off. Tash wondered if her feet were now irreversibly deformed like an ancient Chinese noblewoman's.

As she stepped back out into the simmering blaze there was only Snob's irritated whicker to welcome her begrudgingly. Competitors from early classes who knew they had absolutely no chance of winning were starting to pack away tack, rugs and haynets, heave up ramps and climb dejectedly into cabs and four-wheel drives.

Tash sat back against a scorching wheel-hub and wondered briefly where everyone was.

Closing her eyes, she tried to relive every thrilling second out on the course, but instead she found herself out in the paddock earlier that morning, shivering slightly from the cold, frenziedly trying to hide her tears as she talked with Niall. Then beginning to shake for quite another reason as he leaned forward, his handsome, honest face creeping towards hers . . .

'Your shoulder okay?'

It was Max, squinting down at her with a curiously elated expression on his face, sunburnt nose crinkling. Tash had seen it before when his team had won at cricket or he'd scored the crucial try in the last five minutes.

She nodded, unable to speak. The contrast between her moonlit mind's eye image of Niall and Max's crooked smile, hooded eyes and slightly bulbous nose couldn't be more acute. She was stabbed through with pity. For Max because she had treated him so badly, for Hugo because he had been so publicly humiliated and for herself because she'd never have Niall.

'Sorry I didn't win,' she said gloomily.

'Are you really?' Max flopped down beside her and took her hand.

Tash stared at their hands and said nothing. Hers was dry and callused from so much riding.

What did a great big whopping lie matter now? she reflected. Yet she couldn't bring herself to say it. She told herself to be honest for once. Lies always piled on top of her like a flock of dead albatrosses.

In the end she said 'Mmmm,' which didn't seem too cruel.

'I mean, if, say for argument's sake, you had won right now – would you be happy to marry me?' Max persisted.

Tash took a deep breath, let it out, coughed and took another one.

'I don't know – I think it's all too sudden, I mean our relationship was in injury time when you went to the States,' she faltered, cringing at the sporting cliché; it was so easy to pick up the way he spoke, to fall into step with him. 'We need to do a lot of talking rather than make bets – it was silly of me. I apologise.'

'Oh.' Max let go of her hand and looked away.

Something about the sagging line of his back and drooping

shoulders told Tash that the last thing she needed to do right now was be honest. Max had always been infuriatingly adept at being shamelessly self-pitying.

'But I might have done – just for the hell of it.' She stroked the bristling, clipped hair at the back of his neck with crossed fingers.

Max's grin had never been more lop-sided and smug.

'Well, whatd'yaknow,' he laughed, spinning round and giving her a huge hug. 'As top of the leader board and new cup-holder, Miss French, I think you might just have agreed to change nationality. Now givvus a French kiss.'

Oh Christ, what have I done? thought Tash as she was pressed up against the lorry, enveloped in a familiar waft of Chanel pour Homme and given some heavy-goods-vehicle petting.

Niall's moped ran out of gas at the gateway to the show. As the engine died, Lisette's indignant shrieking became clearly audible.

'What the fuck do you think you're doing bringing me here?' she screamed into his ear as Niall resorted to laboured pedal power. 'You know I hate horses.'

The Big Reconciliation was not going according to plan, Lisette decided bitterly. They had passed plenty of likely-looking fields, even the odd tumbledown ruin in seductive honeyed tuffeau, but had ended up on a flattened, smelly stretch of dust and horse manure, being waved at by excited tourists who recognised Niall.

'I just want to apologise to her,' explained Niall through gritted teeth, 'for crowding her.'

'Who?'

'Tash French.'

For a while this didn't register. Then Lisette let out a howl of irritation.

'Surely it could have waited?' she snarled, fighting to control her anger. 'Look, we need to rap this thing out.'

'I'm not bloody M.C. Hammer.' Niall crashed his feet against the pedals in an attempt to move the bike faster. They were being caught up by some old French cavalry fossil with two walking sticks.

'What are you doing now?' wailed Lisette.

'Dumping the fucking moped, now, that's what I'm doing. We're walking.' He threw down the steaming wreck and stalked towards the main collection of drooping white tents.

'Well, that's just great!' Lisette angrily picked her way through the dung piles after him, tripping as her borrowed boots – two sizes too big – caught in a divot. 'If we divorce, I'm bloody citing this – and that moped. Metal cruelty, that's what this is.'

But Niall wasn't listening. He'd spotted some familiar faces by an ambulance. Too many familiar faces.

He scoured them for Tash but she seemed to be the only one missing. People were backing off as two uniformed officials closed the rear doors.

There was Alexandra, looking concerned and talking to a tall, sophisticated man. Perhaps he was a doctor, Niall wondered, starting to panic. And there was Hugo looking very subdued, almost ashen, whispering with Ben.

'Oh God, no!' Niall stopped in his tracks.

It must be Tash, he thought in horror – she'd been knocked out last night, after all, told not to ride, trussed up in bandages.

Niall broke into a run, feeling his feet turn to concrete blocks and the dry ground underneath to treacle.

The group turned in amazement as he raced up to them.

'Where is she – is she all right?' His throat was so dry he could hardly speak as he slid to a halt in front of Sophia.

'What? Oh—' Sophia gave Niall an odd look and glanced at the ambulance, which was choking into life. 'Well, she's conscious again but definitely not all there – it was a nasty fall. They're taking her to hospital. She'll probably be in overnight.'

'Christ!' Niall rubbed his hand over his face and looked around urgently. Tash had been knocked out! Overnight, she said. There might be complications, blood clots, tumours. He had to speak with her.

'Wait!' he screamed as the white blood wagon started to bump slowly away over the pitted earth, taking most of the stewards' tent guy ropes with it. 'Wait!' he croaked hoarsely, setting off in pursuit.

But a firm hand grabbed hold of his arm, pulling him up.

'It's all right, Niall.' Ben held tightly on to him as he struggled to get free. 'She's being looked after. Lots of people take tumbles at this sort of thing.' He smiled awkwardly and avoided looking at Sophia who was mouthing 'drugs' like a loquacious goldfish.

Niall looked at him in amazement. Then something occurred to him and he stared around at the assorted faces who were mostly gaping back at him in bewilderment.

'Hasn't anyone even fucking gone with her?' he shouted furiously.

'There, there.' Ben patted his shoulder ineffectually, obviously thinking he was going through some sort of deluded withdrawal. 'It's all right, Niall.'

'Gus has gone with her, of course,' Hugo snapped.

'Who the fuck is Gus?' moaned Niall.

But no one had time to answer because at the same moment as Lisette staggered up, spitting abuse and carrying her kid boots which had pronged more manure than a market gardener's pitchfork, Max towed a reluctant, positively Glacier mint-white Tash in from the opposite direction.

'Tash!' gasped Niall in disbelief.

'Those are my boots!' shrieked Sophia, narrowing her eyes at Lisette.

But Tash could take nothing in except Niall's excited relief at seeing her. His craggy, curly Irish mouth broke into a wild, amazed smile and he stared at her across the myriad cluster of house guests. Tash didn't even notice Lisette fuming by his side; she just gazed back, her heart suddenly trying to bludgeon its way out of her chest. Frantically embarrassed, she tried to look away and found that she couldn't tear her eyes from his.

Max cleared his throat.

Tash jumped nervously and glanced round. But he was still

looking as if he'd scored a deciding six off the last ball. Her gaze fled hopelessly back towards Niall, catching Lisette's eye en route. The hostility made her flinch.

'I've – sorry – *we've* got some news for you all,' Max grinned from ear to ear as everyone talked at once. 'If you'll just be quiet for a minute.'

Everyone ignored him and carried on chattering, babbling and exclaiming. Sophia started accusing Lisette of stealing her clothes. Only Niall and Tash were silent.

'*Offside!*' yelled Max, so loudly that a nearby spaniel who was slinking guiltily back to her mistress, ran off yelping.

Everyone shut up.

'As I said, Tash and I have some news.' He squeezed her hand fondly.

Tash quailed.

'We've been together for over a year now – as most of you know,' Max grinned at all of them, 'and we've ridden out some pretty rough times – England's monumental cricketing losses amongst them,' he chuckled, nudging Tash. 'On a recent visit to the States, I came to realise that Tash French means more to me than that humble bird who cooks my grub and lets me rest my pints on her head in a crowded bar.'

He paused for laughter. None came.

The group were beginning to fidget; Alexandra had surreptitiously got out her compact, Hugo was pretending to read the schedule and even Lucian was regarding his son with something close to irritated distrust.

'Get on with it, Max,' muttered Tash, having caught a glimpse of Hugo's white-knuckled fist clenched at his side and – much, much worse – Niall's stricken face.

He had no idea who Max was, she realised; Niall had been with Lisette when the American contingent had arrived.

'Er – yes – well,' Max cleared his throat.

Used to making hour-long speeches at sports' dinners full of blue jokes and annual gossip, he wasn't really accustomed to this sort of thing. He was further thrown by the fact that Niall O'Shaughnessy – one of his all-time idols and a tremendous cricketer – had recently arrived with his stunning wife. Max had no idea Tash moved in such high-flying circles.

He knew now for certain that he'd been right to persist. Marrying into the Frenches was a very wise investment. He ignored his father's scornful gaze and cleared his throat again.

'It's like this,' he spluttered on, before they all started moving away. 'Tash and I are going to get hitched.'

'Married,' muttered Tash in a strangled voice.

'Yes – er – married as well.'

There was a totally stunned, nine months pregnant pause while everyone reeled round in surprise.

Only Pascal, having been warned of the possibility earlier, didn't look shocked. Muttering happily, he quickly opened a soggy cardboard box behind him, full of melting ice, and started handing round cool, slippery bottles of champagne.

'C'est merveilleux, étonnant!' Pascal gave them both sloppy kisses as the corks started to pop.

Blinking in astonishment, Alexandra was, for once, totally lost for words. She opened her bag and fumbled inside for a tissue and – extracting the soiled Noo Noo, which she had secretly appropriated to hand back to her wailing granddaughter – blew her nose loudly.

'I'm so pleased for you, Tash darling,' she sobbed, and burst into tears.

Sophia, looking smug, moved forward and kissed the air beside Tash's cheek, saying something about 'if that was what she wanted . . .'

No! Tash wanted to shout. It's not! – it's a terrible, foolish mistake.

But congratulations were already raining down like a first night party. Max started cracking riotous jokes with Lucian and Pascal, kissed Sophia five times, Lisette twice and exchanged a high five hand-slap with Polly, who was still videoing like mad. Several spaniels, taking advantage of the ad hoc party, crept back unnoticed.

Tash, feeling as if she were in a plastic bubble, looked up from being hugged by Anton and the accompanying waft of wine fumes, to see Niall stumble away towards the bar. She felt her throat catch. If it hadn't been for Anton's solid grip, she was sure her legs would have given way under her.

'You weel remember zees day forevehr, no?' Anton breathed a fruity red vintage over her.

Tash nodded, tears streaming down her face.

Then she felt a cool hand on her arm and looked down to see the slight, ballerina-like form of Lisette. Her urchin face with its gleaming, bright eyes and perfect, cherub mouth was now smiling with winning integrity. She had an incredible, chameleon-like ability to switch casts.

'We haven't been properly introduced. I'm Lisette O'Shaughnessy,' she drawled in a ringing, confident voice. That name sliced through Tash's heart. 'I won't intrude on your family gathering but I just want to say both Niall and I are very, *very* pleased for you.'

Tash felt a smile crack slowly through her cheeks and shatter like glass into her soul. Lisette winked sweetly and breezed dutifully off after Niall.

She's never doubted winning him back, thought Tash miserably; she plays him like a chess master shuffles an inconsequential pawn around his board.

She could hear Max talking to her mother and Sophia: 'I hear Tash's father's a keen sportsman, sounds a terrific chap. I can't wait to meet him – businessman, isn't he?'

'Banker,' Sophia quacked proudly.

'With a W,' Alexandra added into her champagne, glancing across at Hugo.

He and Ben stood a little away, in silence. Ben was staidly supporting his friend despite frantic hand signals from Sophia to do his duty. Hugo's hands were shaking slightly, a muscle was sledge-hammering his cheek and his blue eyes had gone strangely opaque. But this passed unnoticed. He looked to the world like the old Hugo: distanced, disdainful and above all – when he wasn't being hugely amused – hugely bored.

Then, just as Tash was trying to prise Anton off after the fourth congratulatory kiss, Hugo walked purposefully forward.

Oh Christ, he's going to bawl me out, thought Tash, taking in his set face and that cruel, curling mouth.

Hugo studied her, eyes narrowed, as if trying to decipher a code.

He's so beautiful, Tash thought sadly, trying to shrink into a nearby tent. I loved him so much.

She flinched, waiting for the inevitable torrent of abuse. But instead of spitting venom, Hugo put a warm hand on her shoulder, kissed her on the cheek and gave her a hug.

'Congratulations,' he said loudly before dropping his voice, 'on winning the class. You worked bloody hard and you deserve it. You know,' Hugo pulled away and looked at her incredulously, 'I really *like* you.' He sounded incredibly surprised.

Gazing back, Tash tried to put all her gratitude and admiration into her face and transmit it to him. If she concentrated very hard, she figured, he'd understand the unspoken feelings in her eyes.

Wondering why she was screwing up her face and squinting like a crone with cataracts, Hugo gave her a quizzical look. Then, pulling himself together, he turned to Max and held out his hand.

'Congratulations,' he smiled. 'You're a lucky bastard.'

Max laughed and shook hands.

'Don't I know it?' He smiled indulgently at Tash, topping up her untouched beaker with the bottle from which he'd been swigging so that the froth ran over her wrist.

Tash gulped, swallowed and wondered if she could muster another smile. Mercifully, she was saved by Ben, who had limped up to peck her on the cheek.

'Jolly good stuff.' He shook her hand awkwardly, uncomfortable as ever with physical contact. 'Well done in the trial, too, by the way. Funny,' he added in an undertone, checking that Max was still talking to Hugo, 'I thought you were having a bit of a walk out with old Niall. Must've been mistaken. What a hoot,' he laughed heartily at such a ludicrous assumption.

Glancing down, Tash realised that she'd taken a great bite out of her polystyrene beaker and swallowed it.

53

There was a mysterious, repetitive noise in the room. An alien, ghostly wheeze, a little like a watch thrumming each second or the wind sleepily lifting heavy curtains.

With her eyes closed and her mind still half attempting to get back into a gloriously gloopy, slothful dream of bobbing along the Thames in a punt with Niall, Tash was not certain where the noise was coming from. Nor was she too bothered. She was blissfully content under the soft, downy whisper of her sheets with the warm, comforting arm resting in the crook of her neck.

She wondered groggily exactly whose arm it was. It must be her own, she concluded eventually, numbed by the weight of her head.

Wriggling against it, Tash decided that she really must shave them. Terribly hairy, and muscled like a marathon runner's thighs after so much riding.

There was that noise again. It was getting louder and was now more like a grandfather clock or a force ten gale.

Tash stiffened. It sounded like someone being slowly suffocated to death. Alternatively, it could be that a wild boar once shot by Pascal was haunting the house and by some fatal error of piggy map-reading had got into the wrong room.

There was a slight silence, then it sounded again. A low snuffling followed by an agonising grunt, a high-pitched squeak and then a long sigh. It was oddly familiar.

Tash opened one exploratory eye, peeked out and contorted her eyeball until it watered.

Someone had forgotten to close the shutters. The room was toasted in sunlight, revealing dusty mirrors and a cobweb like a goal net on the far wall.

As she shut her eye again, the image of a pair of crumpled boxer shorts hanging like a furled flag from the bedpost remained firmly imprinted on Tash's mind. She only knew one person who possessed a pair of underpants with pink elephants frolicking over them. And she was almost certain that the matching socks were currently sharing the bed with her, poking out of the duvet on the end of two hairy legs.

Aware that the arm behind her neck was starting to twitch ominously, Tash kept her eyes clamped shut and started to piece together the happenings of the day before. The party, Niall kissing her, passing out, Max turning up, the trials, her foolish bet. At first it was like a horrific jigsaw puzzle, given to one by a decaying great-aunt, where the thousands of segments are mostly sky, and a pretty stormy one at that. But slowly, painfully, a picture started to form.

She fought through a dense, befuddled fog to gauge the heartache rate of the night before. Locked deep in her mental night-safe was an experience so laden with strained smiles and shaky subterfuge it took a long time to prise out of its subconscious hiding place.

The celebratory dinner had been purgatory. It had seemed to Tash that the more people who knew about her engagement, the harder it would be to tell Max the whole thing was a ghastly mistake. And by ten o'clock the previous night even Alexandra's distant cousin in Scotland had telephoned to offer congratulations. Sophia had spent an hour ringing Hong Kong to break the news to their father and have a bitch about the party at Pascal's expense.

Just as Tash was recollecting with unnerving clarity that Max had made a second speech littered with excerpts from *The World's 1000 Best One-line Jokes* and the occasional quote from *American Psycho*, the snoring beside her reached a fever pitch of nasal rumbles and Max rolled over on to his side, pushing her to the edge of the bed and on to what appeared to be a half-eaten bag of crisps.

Now totally devoid of both duvet and protective arms, Tash gave up dredging out her Painful Memory Bank and quietly slipped off the bed.

As she grabbed her towel and started to creep from the room, she turned to glance at Max. He was still slumbering under the crumpled, sunlit duvet, covered in biscuit crumbs. An open box of liqueur chocolates nestled by his right leg. She'd almost forgotten what it was like to share her bed with half the contents of a well-stocked larder.

He looked rumpled and desirable as he slept. Sooty gold hair, caught in the citric early morning light, fell over his thick black lashes; stubble darkened his chin; his thumb was wedged firmly between his lips.

Tash sighed and escaped on to the landing, heading towards the loo.

She walked through the half-open door and collided with a stooped figure washing his face in the basin. Clutching her nose as she recoiled, eyes beginning to smart, Tash realised the back belonged to Niall.

'Oh, sorry!' she muttered in horror.

He was wearing nothing but an ancient t-shirt with 'The lazy slob's put this on back to front again' written on the back. His long, muscular brown legs and pale, naked bottom taunted her with their feral beauty.

Her face burning and her appendix where her tonsils should be, Tash backed out of the small room as Niall glanced groggily over his shoulder.

'Tash, wait!' he called.

But, totally mortified, Tash dashed along the landing, into a turret, and leaned against the back of another bathroom door. Her cheeks were absolutely fiery with shame and her heart crashed round like an escaped lunatic in her chest.

She hadn't seen Niall since Max's awful announcement at the show ground yesterday. His absence at dinner had been barely commented upon, Lisette joking breezily that he'd been detained by the local gendarmerie, accused of stealing a hired moped. It was, she'd said with a malicious smile, a crime he'd apparently committed before. It turned out that Niall had eaten with Matty and Sally, who'd booked a table at La Filamre, away from the manoir's revelry. Tash found it odd that he should choose to stick with his friends when his cherished, flighty wife had just returned. Odder still when Lisette described how ecstatic he'd been at her return.

Collapsing on to the loo seat, Tash buried her head in her hands.

While the house guests ate, toasted and guzzled the night before, Tash had longed more than anything to talk to him. She'd been utterly appalled that Lisette, despite crowing earlier that evening of their passionate reconciliation, had flirted outrageously with Lucian Merriot all night. Opposite them, Tash had watched her charm Max's father like a hypnotist swinging a gold watch.

Yet when Marcus had returned from a prolonged trip to the bathroom, smelling like a bonfire and announcing that he'd 'just bumped into that weird Irish dood', Lisette's mouth had curled into a coy smile. Shooting a wink at Tash, she promptly whisked upstairs, leaving her dessert untouched and not returning.

The others had all been far too preoccupied with Eddie and his new wife, Lauren, to notice her disappearance.

Everyone had fallen in love with Lauren. She was clever enough to get away with being wildly precocious. With a wicked glint in her open blue eyes, she'd kept them all in stitches over brandy with grossly slanted stories of Eddie's scandalous past. Tash found her snorting, giggly laugh and pampered perfection grating.

'Isn't she wonderful?' Max had whispered as the pretty blonde shrieked at one of her own jokes.

Not following his gaze, Tash had watched Max's face instead. He'd had the same rapt expression he wore when glued to a Madonna video. With a strange feeling of jealousy and relief, Tash had been perplexed.

She'd barely listened as Eddie had revenged himself on Lauren with the gory, similarly embellished, tale of their courtship.

'It was more of a courtorpedo,' Eddie had explained. 'She serenaded me with Public Enemy and flirted over fast-food. The first time we kissed, she refused to take her Walkman off.'

'When we had our first row, I Tipp-Exed out the signature on the Kostabi painting in Eddie's office,' Lauren laughed.

Eddie had grinned. 'The value trebled, so I married her.'

It was a relief, Tash realised afterwards, that the night had belonged more to Lauren and Eddie than it did to herself and Max.

Standing up, she gulped some water from the cold tap and her hair glued itself to the soap.

As she wiped it off, she wished again that the whole, shambling mess with Max would sort itself out by magic. But the longer she left it to go on, praying for a miracle, the more entwined it became, like trying to pull apart a tangle of freshly washed tights.

She had now given up the faint, laughable hope that she would be able to confide in Niall. He was obviously having problems of his own persuading the mercurial Lisette to come back. Tash doubted she would ever be able to look him in the beautiful, craggy face again. Not that she'd get much chance: Sally, Matty and the kids were due to travel back to England that afternoon. Niall was supposed to be going with them.

Where did that leave Lisette? Tash wondered. Would she go too, squashed between Tom's Nintendo and the buggy in Audrey's boot?

She was suddenly aware of the shallow, confined fragility of her relationship with Niall. She remembered him telling her Lisette was the only woman he had ever wanted. Tash, in her madder, badder fantasies, had tried to forget it. Now she found she couldn't. She also recalled, with painful clarity, that he liked women with short hair and Japanese-slim bodies.

Tash straightened up from the sink and let the towel slip.

Standing on tip-toes, she could just see her body down to the belly button in the heavy, gilt-framed mirror on the wall.

If Niall was looking into it, it would be guilt-framed, she thought sadly.

Her reflection stared back like a stranger. Messy hair, sleep in the corners of her odd eyes, wide head girl shoulders tapering to a waist which was admittedly narrower than usual, but would never be as slim as Lisette or Amanda's. The only Japanese she would ever resemble wore his hair in a pony-tail and fought opponents in a circular clay ring.

As she had fallen in love with Niall, she had started to envisage herself as somehow different. Not icy and sophisticated like Lisette or Amanda, but delicate and nymph-like. A mythical sylph that drifted in an enchanted world. A world where evil ogres and hobgoblins stalked around clutching drinks, but which was occasionally lit up by the appearance of her Odin. Except Odin wasn't hers. And the fantasy was really a bit far-fetched even by her standards.

Looking back in the mirror there was no Freyja, no unearthly, seraphic faery. Just Tash. Tall, gawky, hesitant Tash. The same girl who had left the keys in the door of her Hampstead home and nearly missed her plane several weeks earlier. But one thing *had* changed. Max's girlfriend had departed on another flight.

He was still asleep when she stole back across the landing and into her room. He'd moved on to his back again and was letting out a timpani of somnolent snorts.

Padding across the carpet towards him, Tash noticed her winner's trophy from the day before was on the bedside table; Max had used it as a post-prandial ashtray. He'd also left two empty cans of Heineken beside it.

He might have learnt some new-man jargon in the States, she reflected, but it would take more than bandying about phrases like Interactive, Duo-symmetrically Parallel Responsibility Relationships to make him change his socks more than once a month.

I've got to tell him right now, Tash decided firmly.

On cue, Max half opened his smoky grey eyes and sighed.

Then a wide, prodigal grin spread across his face like the sun rising to find it's in the north and the view's better.

'I thought I'd dreamed it,' he said in his low, slightly gruff voice. 'It really is you.'

'Was when I last looked.' Tash smiled awkwardly.

Perhaps she'd tell him later, she thought in a panic. When he was more awake.

'Come here,' Max yawned lazily, not moving. 'You can't tell me you're too drunk now.' Gone was the attentive puppy; the master had returned.

Tash fiddled with a loose strand in her towel and perched on the edge of the bed. Still studying her, Max picked up his heavy Tag Hauer from the bedside table and held it up in front of his face, squinting against the sun.

'When do they have breakfast around here?'

'Knowing my mother, I'd say lunchtime is a safe bet.' Tash looked out of the window, although all she could see was a heavy coating of dried, grubby raindrops.

'You seem to have picked up a lot of admirers while you've been here,' Max mused, stroking her bare shoulder with his finger.

'Yes?' Tash gulped, trying to sound casual.

'Mmmm.' Max steered her closer to him.

Deciding to assert some control over the situation, Tash clambered on to the bed and, finding there was no room to sit down, straddled his legs. Unfortunately, the towel didn't, and now covered about as much as a face flannel.

'Yes.' Amused, Max watched her trying to pull the hopelessly rucked towel around her. 'I noticed Hugo Beach-bum casting veritably wanton beadies in your direction last night.'

'Oh, Hugo's a terrible flirt,' muttered Tash, feeling flustered.

She was appalled to find herself hoping he might mention Niall. Her hypocrisy was dreadful.

'And your sister told me there was a thick Australian who was pretty keen.'

'How poetically you describe your rivals.' Tash gave up on the towel and looked across at him with her head on one side.

There was something unspeakably smug about his manner which was beginning to rile her. 'He was called Todd, he wasn't particularly thick and he tried it on with practically everybody.'

'Must've been thick, then.' Max started removing the bits of towel she had so exhaustively rearranged. 'Only one girl I'd try it on with here.'

'What do you think of Lisette O'Shaughnessy?' Tash blurted, wriggling back and hitting a bedpost.

'Not bad.' Max sat up and started kissing her ribcage, his hair brushing against her nipples. 'Could do with putting on some meat, though. And she's a bit past it.'

'You make her sound like she's got a zimmer frame and zip-up sheepskin boots.' Tash could smell Max's body, warm and sweet; a heady mix of honey and wild garlic. 'Don't you think she's beautiful?'

'Very.' Max surfaced and studied her face so intently he could have been counting freckles.

Tash cleared her throat and picked up the towel again.

'You're jealous!' he teased, looking even more conceited.

Tash shrugged, stunned by her duplicity.

'She's kind of slinky,' Max continued smugly. 'You know – someone who's openly sensual. But she's a bitch as well. O'Shaughnessy's obviously exceptionally cut up about getting her back, and she's holding herself at arm's length.' He shot Tash a pointed look, but she was too stricken to notice. 'Dad's far too long in the tooth to cope with the sort of come-on she was giving him last night.'

Tash wanted to cry into Max's cosy, welcoming chest. He thought Niall wanted Lisette back too. It was screaming her in the face and she wouldn't take the cotton wool out of her ears.

'So you don't fancy her as a wicked stepmother?' she asked in an artificially high voice. She knew she had to keep Max talking; if he touched her again she'd crack up.

'Wouldn't mind.' Max's eyes flashed with excitement for a moment.

Then, seeing her frozen face, he put his hand on her cheek. 'But right now,' he murmured, 'I'm far more concerned with acquiring a mother-in-law – although I have a faint suspicion your mother would rather you hitched up with Beach-bum. But I'm oh-so-glad you've chosen me.' He brushed her ear with his thumb.

Tash felt the golf ball in her throat switch allegiance to lawn tennis. She quickly covered Max's hand with her own to stop it wandering.

'Mummy's not a bad old thing,' she mumbled, desperate to get off the subject of marriage. 'She worries because, living in France, she hardly gets to see her children or grandchildren any more.'

'Did she marry Pascal for his money?' Max asked idly, stroking her thigh.

Tash looked up at him in surprise.

The languid Cheshire cat smile widened, his eyes taunting hers for a reaction.

'Is that why you want to marry me?' Tash asked, wavering between fury and total relief.

His gaze didn't flicker.

'I want to marry you because I love you,' he replied evenly, his hand slipping round to the back of her head. 'And, Christ, I've been looking forward to doing this all week.'

Pulling her forwards, Max kissed her hard on the mouth.

Tash felt nothing but an aching sadness. Her throat decided to take up football. This was definitely the point to burst into tears, she realised with relief.

But when she gave in to the surge of waterworks, none came. She found to her horror that she had finally run out of reserves; she was totally numb.

Max pulled her down beside him and Tash felt his weight shifting on top of her like a hundred stones used to torture medieval traitors. She closed her eyes.

'I've brought you both a nice cup of tea!' chimed a bright voice, accompanied by the sound of the door knocking over the towel rail as it swung open.

'Christ!' Max hissed into Tash's ear.

They twisted round to see Alexandra beaming from the

gaping door. Behind her, Polly – dressed as a Ninja turtle – was peeking into the room with reptilian interest.

'Hello, Mummy.' Tash beamed back at her mother with intense gratitude. 'Hi, Pol – come in and show me your webbed feet.'

Flopping back on the pillow with a wounded sigh, Max rolled his eyes up to the ceiling. Polly perched beside him on the bed and pointed her plastic machine gun between his eyes.

'Were you mating my sister?' she inquired politely.

54

'Do you think he's all right, darling?' Alexandra glanced dubiously in the direction of the kitchen range.

'Oui, maman,' Polly sighed, looking at the hunched figure with his chin propped up on a swing bin. 'I'm going to shoot Max again.' She started bounding towards the door.

'Darling, I don't think they . . .' Alexandra's voice trailed away as her small green daughter squelched out of earshot.

Shaking her head, she returned her attentions to the swing bin. Two sad brown eyes peeked back.

Alexandra felt absurdly sorry for Rooter. Since his master's hasty departure the previous day, the scraggy, noble Briard had gone into a decline. His bowed tail was flying at half mast, his big, woolly head hung mournfully from hunched shoulders the colour of Dijon mustard.

As Alexandra prepared breakfast, he flopped down in front of the range with a forlorn sigh, his huge chocolate brown paws either side of maudlin, cinnamon-speckled eyes. He looked the picture of acute canine melancholy.

Alexandra tried to cheer him up with a biscuit, but apart from lifting his head a fraction of an inch and looking at her wisely, he showed no interest. The spaniels, shut on the other side of the kitchen door, were going mad with snuffling curiosity as they tried to inhale Alexandra's offering from under the crack.

Alexandra decided Rooter was pining to death. His heroic loyalty made her heart want to break.

In fact, Rooter still had a churning stomach and a demon hangover from his Friday night binge. He was also highly anti-humans since Pascal had done a Capulet with a bucket of water during a very promising relationship with the veteran spaniel.

Giving up on the dour dog, Alexandra braced herself to unearth the various bills she'd hidden in the larder.

Her house guests had started to rise and she could hear the boiler gurgling like a turkey on Christmas Eve in its attempts to keep up with all the baths and showers around the maze of unclad pipes which laced up the house; in winter it was like trying to defrost spaghetti.

To ensure complete privacy, Alexandra took out the huge casserole of last night's chicken bones and tossed in some old green bacon rashers, a pile of vine leaves, the lemon slices from twelve unwashed G & T tumblers and half a pot of Valérie's home-made quince jelly. Nipping outside to the dank store cupboard beside the courtyard door, she groped around in the earthy gloom for what felt like small onions and green tomatoes. She was astonished to find a pair of lace pants and a laddered stocking discarded on the potato shelf.

Two minutes later, Alexandra returned to throw the veg into her cauldron, adding a vat of chicken stock and white wine before pushing the whole lot on the hob to simmer. As suspected, the smell was putrid.

But not quite revolting enough, Alexandra decided.

Humming to herself, she filled another pan and put the dishcloths on to boil as well.

Soon the kitchen ponged like a farmer's gumboot and Alexandra was absorbed in fishing invoices out of pots, tins and Kilner jars in the garde-manger.

'Good Lord!'

Covering her mouth with her hand, she sat down on a flour-bin in the larder and reread them.

She had no idea quite how expensive employing one of London's top interior designers could be. And Matty's mortgage seemed to increase tenfold when it was translated into francs. Then there were the caterers for the party, who seemed to have included a huge damages expense on their bill and a florist's invoice which looked more like a landscape gardener's. There were contract chefs and cleaners to be paid, the pagoda hire company, the entertainers, Pascal's wine merchant and a host of others.

Why had they needed a fireworks consultant? Alexandra wondered giddily. There hadn't been any fireworks. Not in the literal sense at least.

She stiffened as she heard the tinny click of court shoes on the kitchen's flag tiles. Stuffing the bills into a box of dates, she grabbed a nearby jar and walked out.

'What were you doing in there – fetching air freshener, I hope,' Cass sniffed pointedly and put the lid on the waffy casserole.

'No, I was just getting some – er,' Alexandra looked at the label, '– mincemeat. Yes.'

'Whatever for?' Cass looked up from edging the dishcloths off the hot plate with the huge orange kettle.

'I thought Rooter might like some,' Alexandra improvised feebly, sitting down at the table. 'He isn't eating, you see.'

Cass ignored her.

Last night, somewhere between her first and second brandies, the black spots in Cass's memory had disappeared. Her groggy amnesia about the party had lifted like a heavy dust sheet, revealing that what she'd once thought a beautiful George III commode was in fact riddled with rot and woodworm.

A sleepless night recalling the dreadful behaviour of her husband and children had left her drained and light-headed, but no less certain whether to face the embarrassment of confiding in someone, or bear the weight of silence.

'I've banished Michael from the house,' she told Alexandra stiffly. 'He's been told to take Marcus and Rory Wiltsher fishing. Thought I'd get some of the men out of our hair.'

'I've got some Vosene you can borrow,' Alexandra replied vacantly, still clutching the mincemeat.

'Um. Yes. Quite.' Cass busied herself making coffee. 'Must have come as a shock to you, Tash and her boyfriend announcing they're getting married,' she twittered mindlessly. 'Turns up out of the blue and the next thing you know you're phoning Peter Jones with a wedding list.' She spooned out the grounds. 'Sophia told me last week that they'd had a tiff; I'd assumed it was all off.'

'Yes, quite extraordinary.' Alexandra snapped out of her daze. On the verge of confessing her real feelings, she caught sight of Cass's legs and looked up at her sister in amazement. 'Cass, are you feeling all right?'

'Wonderful, rather chipper in fact,' lied Cass. 'Why?'

'Well – it's just that,' Alexandra paused, not wanting to hurt her feelings, 'you're wearing *jeans*.'

'Mmmm.' Cass didn't quite match her gaze. 'Rather fun, aren't they? I've had them years but you know how it is – don't want the children laughing at one.' She stirred the water and grounds with a wooden spoon. 'I thought it was time I took a leaf out of your book and went a bit more *casual*. After all, we are on holiday.'

She smiled nervily.

Alexandra didn't like to suggest that matching the jeans with a ruffle-collared shirt, a blackwatch waistcoat, pearls, Hèrmes scarf and court shoes was far from casual. Instead, she suggested they took the coffee on to the terrace. The smell of soup à la dishcloth was starting to strip paint from the walls.

'I say, your mother's having a terrific chin-wag with old Cass out there.' Ben craned out of the window to get a better view and sent a pot of geraniums crashing on to the cobbles below.

'Please don't spy, Ben, it's frightfully rude,' Sophia reproached gently, determined not to snap at him while they were getting on so well. 'Come and do up my necklace please, darling?'

She turned her long throat to him and held up the ends of a gold rope.

'Just can't believe Amanda pushing off like that,' Ben mused for the hundredth time, shaking his head as he fiddled with the clasp.

'Quite,' Sophia sighed.

'Terribly sudden. Poor chap must be damned choked about it,' Ben said, letting the necklace fall on to the back of Sophia's smooth, downy neck. He had always been a little bit in love with Amanda.

Sophia said nothing. She'd begun to harbour an ominous suspicion that Hugo, far from mourning Amanda cycling off into the sunset with Todd, was too preoccupied with Tash to care. The thought made her feel slightly sick.

'Damned upset,' Ben repeated, searching for his cigarettes, which Sophia had hidden again.

'I think Hugo's got other things on his mind, quite honestly,' muttered Sophia. 'He's thinking of giving up the sport, you know.'

'Think it's because he's upset about Amanda?' Ben searched through a drawer.

'Don't be silly, Ben.' Sophia gave in to a quick snap. 'Hugo had an absolutely awful ride yesterday. Dreadfully demoralising to be beaten by Tash. His nerve's probably gone.' She started to separate her eyelashes with a pin. 'And do you mind telling me what you're doing in my undies drawer?'

'Er . . . nothing.' Ben started on the waste-paper basket.

'Actually, I've always thought Amanda was really a little too fierce for Hugo—' Sophia removed some mascara from the pin with an irritable flick. 'She was so much brighter than him for a start. I'm amazed it lasted as long as it did, actually. Of course, there's no hope now.'

Ben started having a loud coughing fit behind her.

Sophia assumed he'd found his fags and continued thoughtfully, 'It was just a sex thing, wasn't it, basically? She was quite wrong for him long term. Hugo needs a—' at this point she nearly pronged her eyeball on the pin as Hugo appeared, smiling over her shoulder in the mirror.

'Yes, I thought we'd start by getting Mummy to phone some of her friends,' Sophia squeaked in a fast, shrill voice. 'It's Sunday so none of the nanny agencies will be op—'

'Oh, don't be a spoilsport, Sophs,' Hugo laughed, walking over to the bed and sitting down.

Despite his amusement, he had a drawn, unslept face. His eyes were propped up by great shadows.

'Tell me what you were about to say,' he demanded lightly. '*I need . . .*'

'A holiday!' lied Sophia. 'I was going to say you need a holiday.'

'You're right. I'll need another bloody holiday to get over this one,' sighed Hugo, lying back on the bed. 'Does anyone fancy coming to see the Cadre Noir in Saumur? Thought I'd visit Penny Moncrieff in hospital afterwards.'

'Terrific idea—' started Ben.

'Actually, Ben and I will be busy all day,' Sophia piped up quickly. 'We're trying to find a replacement nanny, you know.'

Ben, who'd been trying to think of excuses all morning, shot Sophia a furious look. He clearly thought Hugo needed a heart-to-heart about Amanda.

'Don't blame you wanting to be in on the search, Meredith,' Hugo said to the ceiling. 'Don't want some hairy old boot hogging your kitchen all day, dunking nappies in Vanish. Might frighten the dogs.'

'Why not ask old Tash to go with you? Just her sort of thing, isn't it?' Ben suggested, receiving a volley of black looks as return fire from Sophia.

'I thought of that,' Hugo replied smoothly, 'but I'm afraid her fiendancé might sing "Here We Go" and swing a football rattle during the carousel.'

'Thought he was a rugby man.' Ben scratched his head and laughed, still cheerfully oblivious of Hugo's transfer of affections from Amanda to his shy sister-in-law. 'More likely to chant "Swing Low Sweet Chariot" and try to place a bet on the three-fifteen.'

'What do you rate their chances?' Hugo asked idly.

'Pretty slim,' Ben confessed, lighting a cigarette. 'Seems like a nice chap, but Tash is a funny girl, isn't she, Sophs? And if you ask me, she's not as keen as he is. Thought she looked jolly cheesed off last night, actually.'

'Really?' Hugo was trying hard not to look interested.

Ben nodded, assuming Sophia's Maori facial contortions from the dressing-table mirror were a register of disapproval at his smoking.

'Neither of them has got proper jobs, from what I hear,' Ben continued, beginning to sound like his mother. 'And I can't see Tash wanting to stay in London much longer. For a start, where's she going to keep that big chestnut fellow? Costs a bomb to stable a nag there.'

'True.' His face no longer remotely sullen, Hugo stood up and smiled at them both. 'Well, I'm off, then. Thanks so much for the advice, Sophia. Truth is, one of the only things I'll miss about Amanda is her ability to bitch you up.'

Turning on his heel, he walked out, leaving Sophia stabbing the flawless marquetry on her dressing table with the pin.

Beside her, Ben shook his head, tutting and muttering 'damned upset', over and over again.

'You get on very well with your children, don't you, Alex?' Cass asked casually after a quarter of an hour of skimming through a few effusive adjectives on what a good Wimbledon year it had been, how to bake croissants and Alexandra's plans for the garden, which amounted to roughly none.

'My dear, I don't know.' Alexandra hesitated. Quite often she felt that she loved her children far more than they did her. 'Polly seems to put up with me most of the time,' she sighed, gazing over her shoulder as a red Peugeot sped away down the long drive.

Aware that she was turning very pink, Cass removed her waistcoat. 'It's just that I think Olly and Ginger are rather more than . . .' Blushing furiously, she couldn't go on.

'More than what, darling?' Alexandra asked kindly, knowing exactly what Cass was going to say.

But Cass couldn't bear to lose face, tinged with a menopausal flush as it was.

'Oh, nothing,' she shrugged vaguely. 'I was just going to say that I think they're more than grateful to you for letting them stay.'

'Thank you, darling.' Alexandra touched her sister's hand. 'Actually, Ginger left a frightfully sweet thank-you poem yesterday. They're both lovely chaps.'

Cass cleared her throat and smiled bravely.

As the sun peeped over the oak wood, the long shadows started to slip away from the terrace, leaving it basking in clear, deceptively warm morning rays.

Jeans were horribly hot and restrictive, Cass reflected. She wondered how the younger generation managed to wear them dancing all night without rendering themselves barren and then fainting.

'Do you think Tash might be making a terrible mistake?' Alexandra asked suddenly, turning to look at her sister with huge, troubled eyes.

Cass froze for a minute, a curt reply about beggars not being choosers balancing precariously on the tip of her tongue. But something about the way Alexandra was shakily clutching her cup, her wide mouth trembling, made her swallow her words and put a protective arm round her sister's slim shoulders.

'Poor darling.' She stroked her hair gently. 'It has all been rather sudden, hasn't it? One's children can be *so* capricious. Tell me what you think.'

55

Niall dragged himself out of the button-backed chair by his bedroom window, which was now letting in a sharp angle of dusty sunlight, and looked around for some clothes. The energy seemed to have drained out of him, as if he had taps in his toes. His back and neck ached from sleeping on the floor.

Last night, he'd foolishly imagined he wouldn't be able to sleep at all; envisaged himself stalking about the magical house like a lost poetic soul, burying his misery in scotch and drunken misquotes. Instead, he'd conked out like a light, a night's missed sleep catching up with him like a stealthy murderer in a dark wood.

Later, when Lisette had crawled into his bed, he'd barely summoned the energy to shrug her off. Reeking of Fidgi and French cigarettes, she had slithered up on him expecting, no doubt, a night of ecstatic gratification for her prodigal return. Instead, she had received a shoulder, then a back and finally a husband crawling out of bed and on to the floor, clutching a pillow and his pride like a frightened virgin. Mercifully, an exhausted virgin, too; sleep had almost instantly suffocated Niall's misery into drowsy indifference.

When he'd woken ten hours later, his body covered with shivering cramps and a hole where his heart should have been, he'd not felt thankful at all. Not even that Matty – full of pompous integrity – had yesterday dragged him out of a bar in a tiny village, where Niall had been trying without success to pay for a bottle of brandy and a cheese baguette with an Amex card.

They'd moved on to a restaurant set in a converted mill. Niall had eaten nothing, spoken less and blotted out the ache which bit at his temples by drinking carafe after carafe of cheap wine. Sally and Matty's quiet rapport, their sudden, joyful belief that they could make things work out, had propelled him into uncharted fathoms of suffering.

On the way back, Niall had slumped in the rear of Audrey the Audi, drunkenly staring out of the windows as Sally yakked nervously in the front.

He'd known then what was reality now. He hadn't the courage to tell Lisette they were finally washed up, and he hadn't the conviction to be honest with Tash about how he felt.

He vaguely remembered quizzing Matty and Sally about Tash's boyfriend, Max. He'd been too plastered to fully digest the answers, but had the feeling they'd made him miserable.

This morning's encounter with Tash had done nothing to lift his mood. Hungover to the point of sensory obliteration, Niall could still recall her horrified expression as she drew away from him.

Tugging on yesterday's jeans – the day before's jeans – Niall didn't even bother with socks as he crept away from the sleeping shape of Lisette without a backward glance.

He found Matty shovelling a cement-coloured mixture into a gurgling Tor, who seemed to be expelling most of it before it even reached her tongue.

'Christ, you look rough.' Matty shifted Tor to his other knee and looked up. Meanwhile, Tor spat out a large amount of edible Blue Circle on to her father's denim shirt.

'Thanks.' Niall collapsed on to one of the children's beds. It had Hamley's soldiers marching all over the cover. Niall wished he could don a red jacket and hide in amongst them. 'My agent always gives me scripts where I have to lose weight, stop shaving and sweat like Becker in a fifth set. Now I won't even have to go through make-up.'

Matty noticed Niall was shaking like a shell-shocked fusilier. He badly wanted to talk to him, but knew that he would end up lecturing. Lisette was clearly doing a demolition job on the marriage. Yet Niall held such a fragile opinion of himself, the last person he would think to blame for his murder would be the one holding the smoking gun.

'Are you coming back with us this afternoon?' he asked carefully. 'Audrey's sounding a bit rough, but Pascal seems to think he and Jean can fix her.'

Niall shrugged. The possibility of only ever seeing Tash's name in the Forthcoming Engagements columns of one of the broadsheets worked like an ice-pack on his skin. He was still terrified of the outside world – it beckoned him with gnarled, peeling gilt fingers, tipped by razor-sharp, glinting poignards. Yet he knew if he didn't secure some work for the rest of the year, he'd run out of money within weeks.

'I guess I should be taking Lisette somewhere,' he sighed, not meaning it. He couldn't afford to for a start. 'I shouldn't think your mother would be too pleased to have me rattling round here, now. Not with her brother staying.'

'Bring Lisette back with us,' suggested Matty, then instantly regretted it.

But Niall was already shaking his head. There wouldn't be room. The thought of being confined in a car with Lisette for hours on end unnerved him. And the intolerable truth was that he couldn't bear to tear himself away from Tash, even if it was just sharing the same house, catching the odd glimpse, suffering purgatory for it.

He put his head in his hands.

Matty stared at Niall for a long time, a moral battle waging inside him as Tor systematically bashed him on the ear with her plastic spoon.

'It's Tash, isn't it?' Matty asked finally.

Niall linked his fingers at the back of his neck, as if wrenching his head from his shoulders to remove the pain there.

In the ghostly pause that followed, Matty made a mental apology to Sally. When she had first suggested that there was a magical frisson between Niall and Matty's younger sister, he'd dismissed it with amazed laughter. Now it seemed blindingly obvious; Niall hadn't mentioned Lisette at all last night. He could, however, have been sitting for his degree on the history of Tash.

Then Niall released his neck, freeing his constricted body as if removing some long-suffered bandaging, and looked up at him with a strange sort of amusement in his eyes so that Matty was suddenly terrified he'd totally misjudged it.

Still smiling, Niall slowly rubbed his mouth, looked at the wall and ran his hand through his hair so that it stood up on end like an Afghan hound in a gale. Finally, staring back down at his bare feet again, he gave a sad laugh.

'It's a dumb sort of dream, really. A Niall-dealisation. Holy Mother, I'm a fool, am I not, Matty?' He looked up, shook his head and carried on. 'The girl's just got engaged to this – this boy she's lived with for a year, she loves, understands, breathes with. And here's this crazy Irish actor who thinks he's got something going with her after about three conversations. Christ, I live in this fake, sycophantic world where everyone tells you you're God's gift, where women want to sleep with you before you've even asked them their name. Tash comes from a totally different planet; to her I'm some fool who's tried to help her in order to help himself.'

'I don't think Tash would see it that way, somehow.' Matty smiled ruefully, wiping solidifying cement from his ear. 'Her planet, as you put it, is pretty unique: only one or two inhabitants.'

But Niall wasn't listening. 'My wife has just turned up; a woman I was killing myself over in Nîmes – impossibly screwed up, cracking apart in front of my eyes, clinging to me like some sort of ark to protect her from her own bile, and all I can think about is this poor, blissfully unaware kid.'

He dropped his head into his hands again. 'I hate myself for it, but I just want Lisette to go away and leave me alone. Yet, I know that if she did, I'd never stop feeling culpable for our marriage failing.'

As Matty stifled a howl of frustration, Sally appeared at the door in an ancient sailor dress, with Tom swinging on her arm.

Sally started to back away, mouthing 'sorry' to Matty. Beside her, Tom refused to budge.

'Sally's just been sea-sick,' he piped brightly, 'because of the baby in her tummy.'

'Christ!' Matty hissed through his teeth.

His knuckles white against the dirty black of his hair, Niall didn't look up.

Clutching Sally's hand and his ancient teddy, Mr Noops, Tom surveyed the scene with excited interest. His father was obviously about to give a sermon, his sister was covered with grey gunk and trying to eat a plastic spoon, Nilly looked like he always did when he was practising his lines and, Tom personally thought, being intensely embarrassing. Then he realised it was real.

As Sally wavered in the doorway, trying to leave them to it, Tom marched purposefully across the room and, along with Noops, gave Niall a big hug.

'It's all right, Nilly.' He pulled away and gave his father's friend a manly pat on the back. 'I cry sometimes, too. Mashy says it's a very adult thing to do.'

'Today,' sighed Niall as Sally came across too and stroked his hair as she would one of the children, 'I touched for the rip-cord to slow my plunging insanity and found it wasn't there.'

'Oh, stop being so fucking self-pitying and tell the girl how you feel!' snapped Matty, storming from the room.

Sally sighed and sat down beside Niall, putting her arm around his shoulders. 'You know, Matty's not as good as you at being an agony aunt, but I think he's right. You have to tell her, Niall.'

Later that morning, wandering hopelessly around the house, Niall bumped into Pascal, looking ridiculous in an oily boiler-suit.

'You must to stay 'ere, Niyel.' He took Niall's hand and squeezed it between both his as if he were trying to crack a stubborn almond. 'You and your beautifool wife. Alexandra, she ees ver' upset that everybody they are leaving so soon.' At least, that was what Pascal assumed she was upset about; she refused to tell him.

'Thank you,' Niall nodded, feeling his fingers turning blue.

'Bon!' Pascal beamed toothily as if that settled it. 'Now, Niyel. Do you know anysink about mending cars, no?'

Niall shook his head, shot through with intense relief that he would have more time to choose the right moment to speak with Tash. Yet, given this breathing space, he found himself desperate to talk with her straight away. With a sudden sense of purpose, he urgently scoured the house.

He spotted her outside, turning Snob into the paddock for a well-earned roll and rest.

Tash was leaning on the gate, a headcollar over her shoulder, watching the showy stallion cavort around the small field and let off a stream of excited bucks before thundering up to the far end to roll. Niall felt his heart rear up in his chest with excited fear as he walked towards her.

She didn't hear him approach. He paused a few paces off and looked at her, feeling doubt chilling his skin, stiffening his joints. She was looking glorious: freshly washed hair falling in a damp, shiny cloud around her unmade-up face, her cheeks glowing, ruddy with health. In just a cropped red vest top, sawn-off black jeans and gumboots, her skin shimmered the colour of lustrously polished walnut. In Niall's experience, people only looked good when they were truly happy. Tash seemed to be radiating happiness from every pore.

He was suddenly churning with uncertainty. In the baking sun, he was amazed to find himself drenched in absolutely freezing sweat. He simply couldn't go through with it.

Then, before he could creep away, the most junior of the spaniels came bounding up, enthusiastically bearing a stick which it deposited at Niall's feet. Bowing on to its front legs, bottom gyrating in the air, it barked pleadingly for it to be thrown.

As Niall stooped for the stick, Tash turned to see who was there. Smiling, she shaded her eyes and squinted against the sun. Niall felt his heart plummet as, recognising the gawping figure in the middle of the courtyard, her face froze.

Niall tried to call her name, but his voice was a hoarse, soundless croak.

There was a good ten metres between them and neither tried to bridge it. Tash clung firmly on to the gate for support, Niall cowered behind his dark glasses to hide the emotion in his eyes. The stick the spaniel had dropped snapped in his hands.

'Well, hullo there!' came a gruff, hearty voice to the left: confident, very British, slightly arrogant. Niall recoiled from it as he would a gloating critic at a première.

Max came over to him and pumped the hand already pulverised by Pascal. He had mischievous grey eyes and a big, broad smile; the sort stitched on to teddy bears.

'I'm sorry I didn't get a chance to speak with you last night.' He grinned with easy charm. 'I'm sure I sound appallingly cheesy but I have to say I really admire your work. We were all addicted to *Last Train*. Tash cried for days. Mikey – one of our house-mates – still hasn't taken *The Wine Cellar* back to the vid shop. We must owe them a bomb, huh, Tash?' he called over his shoulder, beckoning her towards them.

Oh, those simply conjured images of relaxed, slightly slovenly domestic bliss. Niall felt physically sick with jealousy.

'Thanks,' he croaked humbly, better at taking criticism than praise.

'I think Graham – that's another Derrin Roadie – became a bit of a wannabe after *Galway*. He started wearing Aran sweaters and a Barbour around the house, trying to sing Irish folk songs, which when you're used to him screaming along to INXS from the shower is agony. When he went out and bought a fiddle with the rent, Tash and I hid his Aran and bought earplugs, didn't we?'

With a strange, rubberised thud of dragging gumboots, Tash had reluctantly trailed over to them and was anxiously redoing the buckles of the headcollar, unable to look either Niall or Max in the eyes.

As Max swung a brawny arm around her shoulders, faded rugby shirt sleeve rolled to the elbow, Niall fought a terrible urge to thump him in the amiable face. He was the archetypal bloke; mothers adored them because they always asked for seconds, fathers encouraged them to watch the Sunday afternoon rugby, little sisters fell in love with them. They'd have a huge white wedding with hundreds of relatives, lots of small chocolate-box bridesmaids and one of his rugby chums making an obscene best man's speech. In ten years' time he'd probably run to fat and have an affair with his secretary. But right now, Niall felt like a crotchety, flea-bitten mongrel looking at a pedigree Labrador puppy.

Max was asking him when he was finally going to be lured to Hollywood to join other Irish ex-patriots like Liam Neeson and Gabriel Byrne. Niall tried to concentrate on his face, to listen, but with Tash so close it was as if one whole side of his body had been paralysed with longing.

Having muttered an answer which he hoped made more sense to Max than it did to himself, Niall made a lame excuse and loped unsteadily back to the house.

Behind him, he heard Max complaining in a low voice, 'Not exactly friendly, is he? Got a huge luvvie complex, I suppose. Must be worth a packet, though.'

Niall didn't wait to hear Tash's reply.

He planned to go straight to Pascal, thank him for the offer, but explain that his agent wanted him to return to England immediately. That afternoon, he'd travel back to London with Matty, with or without Lisette.

But instead, Niall found himself back in the gloomy little library where he'd once cried alone about Lisette. Despite being tidied and brightened with flowers for the party, it remained austere and cheerless.

Niall collapsed on to the hard, lumpy armchair, which let out a cloud of dust around him.

Tash was going to get married. He should leave today; he knew he should leave today. But he couldn't. Instead, he rested his forehead on his palms and recited all the great Shakespearean soliloquies he could remember, tears creeping down his face.

56

'Hello, darlings!' Alexandra beamed at Tash and then at Max as she waved eagerly from the terrace. 'Do come and join us – we're all up here.'

Tash, still faint and limp from seeing Niall, didn't relish the idea of more small talk.

Following Max through the gate to the garden and up the crumbling, mossy steps to the terrace, she tried hard to be realistic and rap her foolish imagination's knuckles. Instead, she found herself fantasising that Niall was waiting for her there, having raced through the house, dodging furniture and spaniels, to declare his undying love and challenge Max to a duel after lunch.

He wasn't. Cass was, looking quite extraordinary in jeans and a hot flush, exchanging meaningful glances with her sister. Eddie and Lauren were too, dressed in identical Ralph Lauren silk kimonos with matching smug grins. Pascal was standing behind them, fiddling about creating Kir Royale with his usual Gallic aplomb. Polly, still dressed as a Ninja turtle, was trying to help him by emptying an entire bottle of cassis into the icy depths of a champagne cooler.

Ben and Sophia had just arrived on the terrace with the children, who were fearsomely truculent because they were missing Paola. Ben, looking frazzled, accepted two large drinks from Pascal and forgot to hand one on to Sophia. Instead, he downed the first and started to sip the second. A tight-lipped

Sophia deposited Josh's wailing carry-cot on the table in front of Cass and turned away.

'Want Wowla!' whined Lotty.

'Well, you can't have her. Here – have a sweetie instead.' Sophia stealthily thrust a gob-stopper the size of a squash ball into her daughter's mouth.

Paola had telephoned from Southampton that morning to apologise. Lucian, the only person up early enough to take the call, had talked to her in Italian for an hour about opera. Apparently, Algy was quite besotted with her and was going to ask his father to arrange a record contract to turn her into the biggest thing since Dannii Minogue.

Lucian, who hadn't a clue who she was, found the entire thing highly amusing.

Sophia didn't.

When Lucian had relayed the message, she'd been livid, screaming that she refused, on any grounds, to accept the Italian girl back into her employ. Paola was always sloping off to aerobics classes in the village or parking Josh outside the Spar – so that if Sophia drove by she'd assume groceries were usefully being picked up – while she nipped into the hairdresser next door for a quick session in their solarium. Lucian had been too well mannered to point out that Paola didn't actually *want* her job back.

Oozing charm, Lucian put them all to shame. He'd already read the papers in two languages, squeezed oranges and mixed a muesli for anyone who wanted it, talked to Michael about sailing, Hugo about racing and Pascal about wines, impressing them all with his knowledge. He could currently be heard executing rapid lengths of the pool, having jogged ten kilometres that morning, picking up the bread en route.

Tash noticed subtle changes in Max since he'd been to America, which she was certain owed a lot to his father's presence. He was more domineering and possessive, tried harder to manipulate and sulked like a small boy if he didn't get his own way. Yet his new, attentive charm was hard to resist.

Even now, he was resting an easy hand on her thigh,

occasionally letting his thumb rub absent-mindedly against it. Tash was curiously aware of the gesture; it was strangely insolent and demonstrative for Max. She tried to stop his fingers curling into hers, scrunching her hand into a ball, but he just covered her fist and pulled her hand on to his lap, stapling it against his groin with a loving grin.

'Have you decided on a date yet, Natasha?' Lauren asked Tash, leaning across to help herself to more Kir so that they were almost nose-to-nose.

'What?' Tash found herself whipping her hand away from Max.

'For the wedding.' She twinkled her big baby eyes from Tash to Max. 'I know I can't wait – I just *love* weddings.' She squeezed Eddie's knee affectionately, nuzzling his shoulder.

'I hope that doesn't mean you're planning to have any more.' Eddie smiled lazily, closing his eyes and holding his face up to the sun, his hand stroking Lauren's smooth brown arm as if it were a cat.

'We thought sometime next year,' Tash mumbled vaguely. 'Perhaps.'

'Wow, you're patient.' Lauren stretched her eyes, raking her shiny blonde mane back from her forehead in surprise. 'If someone as divine as Max gave me a ring, honey, I'd drive him straight to Las Vegas.' One blue eye disappeared behind long, sooty lashes and she grinned at Max. 'Saving up, I suppose? I know Max hasn't got a dime to his na—'

'Oh, I'm sure you can plug Daddy for a few grand,' Sophia chipped in lightly, disliking Lauren's showy attitude, 'and Mummy and Pascal will help out, won't you?'

Shrugging vaguely, Alexandra cleared her throat with a stiff smile.

Max looked delighted.

Leaning down to rake at a mosquito bite, Cass tried to exchange another glance with her sister, but found herself nose-to-barrel with Polly's plastic machine gun. Smiling sweetly, she resurfaced and was hit on the nose by Josh's flailing Hamley's keys.

'I say.' Ben, dispensing Kir liberally to anyone who didn't cover their glasses in time, was rapidly getting tight. 'I think poor old Hugo's jolly upset over Amanda pushing off like that,' he announced to no one in particular as he refilled his own glass.

There was a polite silence. Max looked even more delighted. Unnoticed by the others, Cass whipped Josh's keys out of his sticky grasp and dropped them into a nearby lavender bush.

'It really was the funniest sight,' Lauren giggled, twiddling a glossy strand of hair coyly, 'her cycling off with that gorgeous Australian guy. He sped into the distance while she was wobbling all over the drive in a pair of *the* grossest purple cycling shorts.'

'Did these shorts have black piping?' Sophia arched an eyebrow.

'I'm not sure. I think so, yeah.'

'Then they were mine.'

Sophia, absolutely fuming, unthinkingly prevented her mother cornering Tash for a quiet word in amongst the shrubbery by earmarking her for a long-winded gas about nannies.

Instead, Ben sank into the chair beside Tash and nicked one of her cigarettes. By now his haughty cheeks were high with colour and dishevelled blond hair tickled his eyelashes. A spaniel was hoovering up the crumbs in his turn-ups.

'Don't s'pose you'd think about dropping in on Penny Moncrieff while she's banged up?' he asked, shoving a scribbled hospital address under Tash's nose and making it clear she was expected to.

'Er – well – that is . . .' Tash thought that the last person Penny Moncrieff was expecting to 'drop in' was herself. 'I hadn't really thought about it.'

Ben checked that Sophia was still heavily into Pampers with her mother and ploughed on. 'Think you should, y'know. Damned rude not to, after all her help.' He gave Tash a remarkably demanding, beady look. 'As soon as possible, in fact.'

'Well, yes, I suppose you're right,' Tash said quickly. She wondered if walking around the course with her amounted to 'all her help'. The more she racked her brain, the more it seemed to.

'I don't really know how I'd get there, though,' she faltered. 'I suppose Max could come with me and map-read.'

'Nonsense,' Ben improvised quickly. 'Max and I are – um – playing croquet this afternoon.' That didn't sound too challenging for his ankle. 'Can't you find your way to Saumur on your own, huh? Hardly far. Roads not too busy on a Sunday. 'Bout lunchtime's the best time to do these things I always say.' Another pressing stare.

Tash, totally unnerved by Ben's uncharacteristic assertiveness, didn't have the heart to tell him that not only had she never driven a car in France before, but that her mother didn't possess a croquet set. She just nodded rather ambiguously and hoped it would pass over.

At this point, distraction came in the form of Lisette, sweeping on to the terrace, absurdly enticing and waif-like in Niall's old dressing-gown. She yawned, stretched and entranced them all with a wicked smile, an apology for looking so rough (which she didn't) and sleeping so late but, she claimed with a conspiratorial wink to Tash, she hadn't 'had such a magnificent night's sleep for weeks'.

Pascal went into a frenzy of overexcited Kir-pouring, urging her to sit down on his chair while he fetched another and saying that she was – as he had told her lucky husband earlier – a most welcome guest in his home and had made many friends already.

On cue, also in a dressing-gown but this one far better cut and with an inconspicuous monogram, Lucian dripped water on to the terrace as he energetically towelled his still plentiful peppery hair and flexed toned brown leg muscles in front of Cass (who coloured from cream of tomato to spicy Mediterranean in a flash) and Lisette, who looked away with amused lack of interest.

'So where is old Niall?' Ben asked Lisette cheerfully. 'Hardly seen him for two days.'

Everyone's conversations dropped to a sotto whisper so that they could listen in to Lisette's answer.

'He's taking a long bath,' Lisette improvised smoothly, flashing a minxy smile. 'He's a bit stiff, poor darling – backache, I think.'

Tash decided that perhaps visiting Penny Moncrieff wasn't such a bad idea after all. Across the table, Lisette draped herself to best advantage and started extolling the virtues of her talented and saintly other half.

'Of course he's terribly tired,' she purred. 'We spent so much time just talking and talk—'

'Lauren got married in pink,' Max told Tash, pulling her attention back to him. 'I saw the shots – looked really great.' He and Lauren exchanged another warm smile.

'Really?' Tash took a huge gulp of Kir and closed her eyes.

'Did you get married in one of those funny Las Vegas drive-ins?' Cass asked her brother.

Eddie didn't open his eyes.

'He's asleep,' Lauren giggled. 'Isn't he just cute like that?'

Max had turned to talk to his father.

Tash wanted to scream. She needed time alone to think what, if anything, she could say to Max to end her deception. The more she put it off, the harder it was getting to think up an excuse which wouldn't hurt his feelings and humiliate him in front of her family.

'Of course, Niall lives and breathes drama,' Lisette was gushing to Ben, 'he gets exceptionally wound up during filming – if one of the sparks drops a spanner, he can literally blow. He can't switch off, you see. Lives a part twenty-four hours. That's what makes our home life so exciting. Every time he takes on a new role, I'm going to bed with a different man.'

'Ironic,' muttered Tash under her breath.

'But even during his most demanding theatre work, he's marvellously considerate.' Her voice caressed the words like oil, soft enough to be seductively 'off the record', loud enough for Tash to hear without wanting to. 'He once said to me, "Darling, if you ever think I've let acting become my mistress. I'll give it up." That's why he junked *The Cornishman*, not that I asked him. He just said he wanted to be with me. He's the only man I know,' her light drawl became so intimate that Ben loosened his collar with rolling eyes, 'who's content just to sit for hours brushing my hair if I'm tense or massaging my feet and reciting all those funny little folk tales he knows.' She smiled at Tash, her cat's eyes gleaming.

And the only tales you tell him are ten feet tall, thought Tash savagely. She's trying to wind me up. She knows I love him and she's got him, so she's letting me know how unattainable he is. He's probably told her that I've got a honking great crush and he's hugely embarrassed by it. That's why he dashed off from the courtyard, why he's hiding now.

Tash tried to listen to Sophia, who had moved on to the relative merits of Venetian lace christening robes as opposed to Welsh, but that reminded her too painfully of weddings and thinking what to say to Max. Instead, she turned to Lauren and asked her how she got her hair so shiny. The answer was so terminally boring that Lisette's voice kept drifting in and out of her ears like Claudius's leperous distilment. Niall was so 'deep' so 'loving', so 'constant'. Ben, excited and guilty at the intimacy of her confidence, looked as if he was in a steam box. Tash couldn't stand it any longer.

But just as she was about to creep away, Max grabbed her hand.

'Tash – hear this,' he crowed in a voice loud enough for most of them to turn with interest. 'Dad's offered me a job in the States.'

'Oh yes?' Tash replied in a strangled voice.

'A really good one, working on the set of a movie he's financing. It would mean about six months on the West Coast.' He covered Tash's hand tenderly with his. 'I think we should go, baby.'

'That's just great!' Lauren clapped her hands excitedly, tossing her hair so that it whipped Cass across the face.

'I'm just pleased to help a young couple who are so much in love,' Lucian beamed benevolently, his voice laced with heavy sarcasm. Despite just mentioning the project, he had offered Max no such thing.

Everyone was looking very excited for them. In a panic, Tash glanced at her mother. Alexandra, still trapped in the shrubbery with Sophia and yet another list, stared back helplessly.

She knows what I'm thinking, Tash realised with painful relief.

Oblivious of her frozen face, Max had started droning on about getting into the movie business, the American dream and grasping nettles.

'Of course, we'll need some money to get a place out there,' he told them airily, batting his eyes towards Alexandra for a split-second to gauge her reaction. 'But I guess just being together is the most important thing,' he added quickly, squeezing Tash's hand. 'All we need is our green cards, a decent condo and each other.'

Tash listened to him in appalled silence. It was as if her tongue was covered in peanut butter, gluing it to the roof of her mouth.

It was this 'Born again Max' she couldn't understand; the Max who made embarrassing public announcements about his life, loves and honourable intentions. In England, although able to keep an entire room in stitches with below-the-belt anecdotes, he had been almost paranoiacally secretive about his extant private life. So much so that even Tash had never known what their relationship meant to him. Now he was airing his emotions like a guest on the Oprah Winfrey Show. Panic rose in her throat.

'I don't think I want to go to the States, Max,' she announced, surprising even herself with her low, decisive tone.

'Sorry?' Max looked as if she'd told him that she'd joined the Flat Earth Society.

'I said I don't want to go to the States,' she repeated calmly. 'I don't think I could cope with all those Americans, to be quite honest,' she smiled apologetically. 'But as it's only for six months, it doesn't really matter, does it? I can write out the invites, run Graham and Mikey's page boy kilts up on the Singer and train the cats to hold a bouquet. You can airmail your socks to be darned if you like and I'll fax you messages about your dinner being in the oven.'

Winking politely at Lisette, she tripped gracefully away from the astounded, open-mouthed group.

There was an air-drawing silence, during which Alexandra found she was in tears of laughter.

'Drunk,' muttered Max, dashing after her.

'Quite a character, your daughter, isn't she?' Lucian turned to her with a wry smile.

Inside the house, Tash hid in the larder until she could hear Max claiming that she seemed to have disappeared. While trying to hold her breath in the dim, cool little room, she felt the age-old pang for a snack nudging at the sides of her tongue.

Spotting a promising-looking box of dates, she prepared to tuck in only to find it full of paper with only a couple of wizened-looking black seeds buried underneath. Hoping she had discovered the secret love letters from Sean Connery to her mother, she was disappointed that the crumpled leaves transpired only to be a few bills and invoices. She squashed them back and helped herself to a hunk of brioche, eventually creeping out to look for any handy car keys.

She froze with fright as a step came from just inside the lobby, but it was only a short, machine gun-wielding Ninja turtle clutching a dog-chewed rag doll and whizzing past to another door without seeing Tash.

Pascal had left the keys to his jeep hanging on their hook in the lobby. Tash took them, trying not to clink too audibly, and slid furtively through the house towards the turret door that led to the side of the courtyard which couldn't be seen from the terrace.

Almost there, she passed a half-open door to the right and paused as she thought she heard a faint whisper.

'*I have had a most rare vision*,' Niall laughed under his breath. '*I have had a dream, past the wit of man to say what dream it was;*

man is but an ass,' he chuckled bitterly and paused to light a cigarette, '*if he go about to expound this dream.*'

Niall stopped suddenly and listened intently, thinking he'd heard a noise, hoping wildly.

Tash pressed herself back behind the door and held her breath. He mustn't see her.

There was a long pause.

Barely daring to breathe, Tash digested the fact that Niall, if he was laughing as he quoted, must be happy. He had Lisette back. She was fooling herself if she thought he had reason to be anything but jubilant.

She breathed out as he started reciting again. She knew she should creep away, escape before anyone saw her. But the sound of his melodious, husky voice hypnotised her feet into disobedience. She couldn't tear herself away.

'*Methought I was – there is no man can tell what.*' Niall plucked at his cigarette and looked out of the window. '*Methought I was, – and methought I had, – but man is but a patched fool, if he will offer to say what methought I had.*' He shrugged more as Shylock than Bottom and started to pace the room again.

'*The eye of man hath not heard, the ear of man hath not seen,*' he stabbed each point earnestly out to a sombre-looking portrait on the wall, '*man's hand is not able to taste, his tongue to conceive,*' he gave the portrait a Dolittle wink and turned to play to an audience of disapproving Grecian busts, '*nor his heart to report what my dream was.*'

There was another movement outside the door. Niall went as still as a pointer who's just sniffed a rabbit on the other side of a hedge.

This time, Tash knew she'd hung around too long. Someone was coming. Apart from two very inadequate pillars from which she would protrude like a shrew hiding behind a matchstick, there was nowhere to dive for cover. Except . . .

As the voices grew louder and the still air crackled with

movement, she stealthily edged a wilting flower arrangement forward and clambered behind it. At exactly the same moment, Niall's head appeared from the door.

Tash could see him through some dense wisps of drying gypsophilia. Having not been able to look him square in the face for twenty-four hours, she was horrified at how burnt out and haggard he looked. Dirty hair flopped over tired, reddened eyes.

Serves him right for bonking Lisette all night, she decided. But she couldn't really feel vindictive. Her heart went out to him; he was obviously still distrustful, unable to believe his luck, wary that Lisette's longed-for reappearance might cause him even more pain.

It seemed it already had. Two seconds later, Tash's heart redoubled its pity as Lisette, even more slinky with Niall's dressing-gown undone to reveal a scant chiffon teddy, wound her way through the echoing hall pursued by Lucian. The latter would have looked ridiculous if it weren't for his dapper beauty. His thick, peppery hair – now almost dry – framed his handsome, bronzed face and his lean, still splendid body reared out of the scant towelling robe. He looked like a Joan Collins side-kick: mature, intelligent, intriguingly foreign and extremely beddable.

Tash couldn't bear to look at Niall's face as they walked slowly and companionably upstairs.

There could be nothing in it, she thought. Probably wasn't; Lisette had no interest in flirting with Lucian when Niall wasn't around to see, and she clearly had no idea he was watching her now or she would have milked the moment further. She was simply going upstairs to dress, as was Lucian. Why not go together?

But that was no consolation to Niall who, thinking he'd just got her back, must be crucified to see her up to her old tricks again. Tash wanted to burst out from the pollen-decanting tiger lilies and nose-tickling ferns to tell him it wasn't as he thought. Dislike Lisette as she might, Niall's sanity was more important. But, like a Venus fly-trap in a florist, she stayed rigid and unbreathing, nose to nose with a ladybird.

Just for a second, as he turned to go back into the library, Tash could see right into Niall's eyes and thought he must have spotted her floral lair. But he disappeared into the room without a word.

She crawled out, her face yellow with pollen, and bolted to Pascal's jeep. Niall had looked literally desolate. She was appalled that she felt so jealous.

Gibbering with guilty self-loathing for not trying to comfort him, she crunched the gears into a squealing heap and narrowly avoided running over a chicken. She was out on the main road veering from left to right with highway code confusion before she realised she'd left the address of the hospital behind. She didn't even have any money to buy Penny some flowers.

Niall rested his chin on the top of one of the disapproving busts and closed his eyes.

It utterly appalled him. When he had seen Tash with Max that morning he had felt physically ill, chewed inside by the burning arsenic of jealousy. Seeing Lisette with Lucian Merriott just now left him cold and inert. The passionless reaction of a cuckold flame. In a strange way, he realised, he'd resented them – no, really *hated* them – for not being Tash creeping like a shadow through the house regretting her hasty decision.

He felt monumentally depressed that he couldn't drum up the nerve to speak to her.

Listening to the shrill, laughing voices and clinking of glass eeking a muffled passage through the closed window, he could imagine her sitting out there, making plans, listening with rapt interest to Max's sporting mundanities, smiling through those odd eyes of hers.

He couldn't face them all. Sally and Matty were packing upstairs. He could stuff his battered case in five minutes and announce he was joining them. But even as he decided that absolutely, finally, irrevocably he was going to leave, he knew he wouldn't.

57

'So what d'you think?'

'It's a totally hare-brained idea and you know it,' Gus muttered in exasperated tones, staring at Hugo, who was helping himself to Penny's grapes and looking both calculating and excited at the same time, like a schoolboy who's got hold of two hundred soft-pack Marlboros.

'I don't know.' Penny, annoyed at being talked across like a corpse, adjusted the pillows behind her head and winced. 'I could see it working.'

Hugo shot Gus a victorious look and sucked up to Penny by plumping her pillows and laying off the grapes. Instead, he surreptitiously took a handful of cherries; skipping breakfast was catching up with him.

'The balance of her mind's affected, isn't it, duck?' Gus tried to get Penny's allegiance back by tucking her in so tightly that her face started to redden like a trapped finger. 'She's had a nasty fall – concussion, derangement . . .'

'Oh, Gus, do shut up,' sighed Penny, freeing an arm to wave Hugo's proffered water jug away. 'Weren't you saying only last week that now Sasha's leaving to drop a sprog, we'll have to take on someone else?'

'Did I?' Gus looked shifty. 'Well, that must have been before I did the quarterly returns. The livery side runs itself but the stud's barely covering the feed merchant's bills. We simply can't afford it.'

Penny fell silent, unable to disagree.

Gus and Hugo had been bickering for half an hour now, making her head pound. The smell of disinfectant and the echoing distortions which shrilled down the artificially lit corridors to her small, yellow-painted room made Penny feel sicker than ever. Hospitals always had this effect on her. Every time she saw a white coat and a stethoscope her kidneys kicked her in the back or her hands developed sudden rheumatism. As soon as the consultant tipped the wink – they'd said 'any minute now' over an hour ago – she would be free to go.

She stared at the door longingly but all that passed was a tired nurse holding a bedpan at arm's length. The sound of her rubber soles squeaking against the linoleum floor resounded like tortured mice in Penny's head.

Hugo, who had sulkily taken up with the grapes again, suddenly looked animated and asked cagily, 'How about if I took a financial interest?'

'What exactly do you mean by that?' Gus tried hard to look indifferent.

Permanently scraping for cash and searching for sponsors, he would be quite happy to unburden the odd financial interest on to Hugo. But knowing how devious Hugo was, he realised that there'd be more loopholes and catches than in one of Pen's home-knitted sweaters.

'You know you offered me that share in the yard a couple of years back?' Hugo spat a cherry pip into the metal bin with a ping.

'When you told me you preferred to set light to your money because at least that was more fun and kept the dogs warm, if I recall.' Gus smiled philosophically.

'He did give us the old horsebox, Gus,' Penny corrected gently, winking at Hugo.

'Which conked out with uncanny regularity on the way to almost every competition Hugo was also competing in. I think it was programmed.' Gus laughed. 'I had more scratched entries that year than a shaved tart.'

Penny hit him with a chrysanthemum. Gus was very good at

feeling hard done by. He would give in to Hugo's idea eventually; he always did. But they had to get through the statutory ribaldry first.

'Ah well, Augustus dear boy,' Hugo looked even more wily. 'A lot of water's passed under Father's bridge-work since then. For one, as you know, the old bugger's snuffed it.' He grinned callously.

Penny and Gus tried and failed to look shocked. Hugo's father had been a tyrant and a sadist, threatening to cut his eldest son out of his will so many times that Hugo had been sure he was doing it a piece of Spode at a time. Hugo's early equestrian career had been governed by Beauchamp senior with a crop of iron.

'Not only have I now got a lovely fat sponsorship deal,' Hugo continued, munching cherries as he spoke, 'but also lots of surplus lolly since the old man checked hounds for the last time. Unfortunately I also inherited his accountant – a reactionary haw-haw bore who's such a raging snob,' he waved a cherry stalk in contempt, 'that he even wore his Stowe tie to the funeral – wouldn't mind but Stoics are such non-entities. I quite fancy getting up his nose by bedding down a few of your nags in paper money.'

'Hmm.' Gus looked both sceptical and hurt – Hugo had forgotten he was at Stowe. He rubbed his chin pensively.

'You want the same deal again?' he asked as Hugo pinged some more pips.

Hugo shrugged; he plainly didn't remember the specifics. Gus remembered every bitter detail – staying up all night with Penny to draw up a last-ditch plan which might save them from a quagmire of debt. He'd been utterly desperate and Hugo had been as flip as ever, promising to lend him the proceeds of a huge bet he had on the 12.15 at Sandown. The horse had romped in last and Hugo had gone skiing to cheer himself up. Gus had been forced to take out a crippling loan, secured against the house, which they were still paying off now. While he had actually forgiven Hugo far more quickly than Penny had, he'd never truly trusted him again, knowing his power to devastate for pleasure.

Gus knew that he'd be mad to agree to what Hugo was suggesting. It was Hugo at his most spoilt and it made Gus feel unpleasantly like a pawn. But he also knew that if he turned the offer down, he'd be sticking a pin in a financial life-jacket. It was a question of being a pawn or pawning the horses.

'Well?' Hugo was asking, having sketched out the rough outline of a deal.

Gus realised he hadn't been listening. He glanced at Penny, and from her excited, breathless face it was obvious Hugo was offering a lot of money.

'All that for her?' Gus stared at him.

Hugo nodded, unblinking. He still looked as unbothered as ever but there was something odd in his eyes; Gus could almost have sworn he was pleading.

Penny reached for Gus's hand and gave it a squeeze.

'Please, Gus,' she encouraged gently, 'I think we should. She's good enough. You saw yourself yesterday.'

Gus raised a derisive eyebrow and smiled ruefully. 'Well, we both missed her dramatic detour,' he shrugged. Then he looked from Penny's beseeching face to Hugo's visored one and laughed in defeat.

'I want it to be known I have grave reservations,' he moaned over their whoops. 'Not over her talent – but I really can't tell if she's dedicated enough and, supposing she is, she'd be totally shattered if she finds out she's been bought.'

'She won't.' Hugo insisted so forcibly that Penny shrank into the bedclothes.

'The only reason I'm agreeing is because I'm quite sure she'll turn us down.'

'She won't,' repeated Hugo, this time transforming Penny into a blanket-covered lump.

'And if you've given Penny a relapse I'll kill you,' finished Gus.

'Never felt better,' came a muffled squeak from deep inside the bed.

'Good, that's settled.' Hugo rubbed his hands together and grinned as of old. 'Now, where does one get a drink around here?'

Suddenly they all froze at the sound of a husky, slightly tentative voice.

'Er . . . sorry to barge in like this, but I was just passing a sample.'

It was Tash, wavering in the door, absolutely strawberry coloured over her feeble joke. In one hand she clutched a very battered bunch of wild flowers. The other was heavily bandaged and hooked to her neck with a rubber sling. The strapping on her shoulder had been reapplied and protruded like a strange, old-fashioned undergarment from her vest top. In addition to the cut on her leg, which had been freshly treated with a narrow translucent plastic strip that acted as an alternative to stitches, her knees were covered in schoolboy grazes and she had a large black bruise on her forehead.

Penny emerged slowly from her covers, like a mole who knows an irate gardener is waiting for her with a shovel. All three of them stared at Tash in disbelief, quite sure that she'd overheard everything.

Tash went from strawberry to damson. She didn't expect sympathy, but a polite inquiry would be nice. Instead they were regarding her much as they would a stray loon who's just wandered out of the 'highly contagious' ward covered with purple warts.

'How are you?' she asked in a flustered voice, thrusting the flowers shyly under Penny's nose.

'Spoiled,' smiled Penny, frantically gathering her thoughts. 'It's really sweet of you to pop in. I'm actually just waiting to be demobbed.'

'What happened? Did you get thrown this morning?' Hugo's voice, rough with emotion, sounded harsh and cutting.

'What? Er . . . oh this.' Tash looked as though she'd been cornered by an angry headmaster giving her an earful about wearing the incorrect uniform. 'No, I did it just now, actually. On my way here. Nothing serious. I've been in a cubicle downstairs for ages being discussed by a group of French medical students. Because I was so battered already, they sent for a sort of French social worker to check I wasn't being beaten up by a lover or something. But she didn't speak English so we had to talk in German and since I only know how to talk about the weather and say "Mein Name ist Tash und ich bin zwölf" – I stopped learning German at twelve, you see – she wrote me down as completely deranged and I'm being investigated further.' She finished in an embarrassed flurry, aware that she was babbling out of nerves.

Penny had started coughing to hide the fact she was giggling, Gus was covering his mouth in an attempt to look serious, but Hugo was still the picture of appalled concern.

'You poor child.' He sprang up. 'Here, take my seat. Let me take those for you. How are you feeling? Do you want a window open? You weren't trying to drive here alone, were you? Is that how you did it?'

Penny, recovering from her giggles, hid a smile behind her flowers. All Hugo had said to her when he'd sauntered in earlier was 'I'd've given you some Anadin if you'd told me you had a headache yesterday, Pen'. Now he was fussing around Tash like a New Man waiting for his son and heir to appear in an adjacent birthing tank.

'How did you do it?' Hugo asked again when he'd settled Tash on his chair and given her Penny's grapes, which were now more stalk than grape, like a broken molecular model. 'Did you crash? Was anyone else . . . ?'

'No, just me,' said Tash, amazingly brightly. It was such a relief to escape from the crone with the clipboard that her embarrassing accident seemed insignificant. 'I drove Pascal's jeep here and, although I did have to ask "ou on se trouve" at every junction, I just about made it in one piece, but I realised I hadn't brought any money with me to buy Penny a present.' She looked slightly sheepish, remembering her hurried and undetected exit.

'So what happened when you got here?' Gus noticed her elbow was badly scraped, too. Perhaps she'd been run over by an ambulance.

'Well,' Tash's face could have heated a draughty church, 'when I was looking for a parking space in the forecourt outside,

I saw this beautiful clump of flowers growing wild out of the side of an archway so I sort of left the jeep for a minute and nipped out to pick some.' She chewed her thumbnail awkwardly. 'Just as I was bending over to get the most exquisite Maiden Pink, I heard someone shout and felt this huge thing crash against my backside, literally turning me upside down and squishing me against the wall.'

'What was it?' gasped Penny.

'Yes, well . . .' Tash dropped her eyes. 'You see, I'd left the brakes off in the jeep – I didn't realise it was on a slope.'

They looked at her in amazement and then Penny started to giggle. Gus looked out of the window and went as red as Tash in an effort not to.

'You're saying the jeep ran into you?' Hugo shrouded a smile.

Tash nodded.

'And the jeep?' Gus coughed.

'Well, it's more of a Mini Moke now,' Tash explained. 'You see, after a couple of orderlies had backed it up to free me, a lorry, which was delivering swabs or something, came straight out of the archway and ran into it.'

Gus let out a howl and gave in to laughter. Tash looked at Hugo and found she was laughing too. Penny had disappeared under the covers again, which were shaking visibly.

'Oh dear.' Tash chewed her lip and tried to stop laughing. 'Do you think Pascal will be terribly, terribly angry?'

'Terribly,' nodded Hugo. 'But it seems, after your interview with the French social services, that he won't have too much trouble getting you committed.'

He reached forward and gave her cheek a playful nudge just beneath a neat gauze dressing. Tash hung her head.

Hugo looked from Tash to Gus, who was wiping his eyes and sighing with delight. The message in Hugo's eyes was clear.

'Well,' Gus cleared his throat and sounded more purposeful than he felt, 'it's jolly nice to see you. Very sweet to make the effort.'

Tash smiled humbly, remembering that she'd only really come to escape from Max.

'We were just talking about you, actually.' Gus smiled stiffly.

'Oh yes?' Tash looked genuinely surprised and the others relaxed, realising that she hadn't overheard them earlier.

'What are you planning to do when you get back to England, Tash?' asked Penny, emerging yet again from the sheets. She was pink from the heat, her blonde hair standing on end with static electricity.

'Take a bath and a week off,' Tash sighed. Then, realising she was serious and that the others were looking at her like a panel of judges, she felt ruffled. She had no idea what she was going to do. She looked desperately at Hugo, who was smiling like a kindly schoolmistress now.

'Well, Max has just—' Tash started.

'Have I told you about the Cadre Noir?' Hugo suddenly butted in, realising she was about to bring up her ludicrous engagement, which he deliberately hadn't mentioned to the Moncrieffs. Desperate to distract, he started rabbiting quickly about the Saumur cavalry officers' magnificent, almost telekinetic powers of horsemanship, until Gus noisily cleared his throat.

'Weren't you going to get us all a cuppa, Hugo?' He raised his eyebrows with a little telekinesis of his own.

Hugo grudgingly departed after giving Tash's good shoulder a firm squeeze and saying cryptically, 'Think about it.'

Five minutes later, Tash was thinking about nothing else.

'You want me to come and work for you?' she asked in total disbelief.

Penny nodded enthusiastically. Gus looked serious.

'We wouldn't really be your employers – you'd be more of a working pupil. No real wage – just pocket money,' he explained, still trying hard to put her off. 'You'd live in with us, the other three grooms, four dogs, two cats, no central heating and the chance to skate on third lot bath-water in winter. Plus Penny's sister Zoe's cooking, which is one way to sharpen your teeth and strip your stomach lining for life.'

'She does a lovely banana curry,' assured Penny, smiling blithely.

'You'd have to muck in with the rest of us – up at dawn, in the saddle all day when you're not skipping out or helping with maintenance, spending every weekend cramped in a lorry arguing over who can take the only shower. It's truly exhausting – sometimes you wonder why you do it.' Gus frowned. 'When I bust my collarbone, you know I was actually grateful? I felt my arse for the first time in weeks.'

'What you'd be getting,' Penny explained far more eagerly, 'is the chance to compete in the sport, not only with your chestnut chap – who'd be stabled with us and run to stud if you wanted – but with other youngsters. If you're as good as you looked yesterday – no, don't argue – you could end up competing through the grades and really getting a foot-hold in the sport. If not, you'll have an enormous amount of fun, meet the nicest people in the world and be dog-tired but satisfied. Honest.' She grinned warmly, her fieldmouse eyes as bright as wet berries.

It was as if a nurse had nipped into the room and covered her heart with muscle-rub. Tash could feel a hot, excited burning in her chest.

'Gosh, I'm incredibly flattered,' Tash laughed. 'I mean, incredibly. But the thing is . . .' On the verge of dumping about Max and the mess she was in, she changed her mind.

I really want to do this, she realised with growing excitement. Leaving Snob behind had been too painful a prospect to face up to, yet it was always lurking at the back of her mind like a black shadow. Crazily, the thought of losing Niall, who had never really been hers, had been easier to cry and grieve over than abandoning her brave, bolshy red horse. Hard work wouldn't stop her heart aching, but it might make her too busy to mourn Niall or worry about Max. Best of all, it was a wonderful excuse to postpone the wedding. There simply wouldn't be time.

'Come and stay for a few weeks, if you like – see if it's what you want to do,' Penny urged. 'You see, I have a confession to make – there's an ulterior motive to all this.'

Gus turned pale.

'I hear you're a wonderful artist,' Penny went on with a huge grin, 'and what I've always wanted is some really good paintings of the horses. You could be a sort of Stubbs in residence.'

Tash went pink with happiness.

'Well?' Gus looked at her thoughtfully. 'Would you like to give it a go?'

'Why me?' she asked, suddenly uncertain.

'You come very highly recommended.' Penny smiled at her encouragingly.

'So Hugo put you up to this?' Tash felt her heart sink.

Gus, having been set against the idea from the start and having tried his best to dissuade Tash, suddenly found he really did want her to work with them. She had guts and raw determination without any of the usual conceit that accompanied them. The course the day before had been incredibly tough and she'd battled through like an old hand on a very difficult horse. What's more, Hugo would never speak to him again if he didn't get her.

Crossing his fingers behind his back, he shook his head. Penny shook her head too and wished she hadn't; the room spun.

'It was Penny's idea,' Gus said, which was, in part, true. Hugo had told them he was going to ask her to work for him at first, but Penny had pointed out that Tash would never trust his motives. 'And I agree with her,' he added.

Tash noticed that they weren't quite looking her in the eye, but it didn't stop happiness gurgling through her veins.

'I'll have to think about it,' she said finally. That was yet more things to think about. At this rate she'd have to employ a second brain. 'I'm sorry – I know you want a decision now but there's . . . er . . . people I've got to talk to first.'

Gus shrugged. 'Fine.'

'I'll phone you tonight,' promised Tash, taking M-C's number as Hugo returned with a bottle of champagne and four plastic medicine beakers.

Only Hugo, Gus pointed out, could find champagne in a hospital.

'Maternity ward,' Hugo grinned, not taking his eyes from Tash's face. 'I swapped it for twenty Camels and a lighter.'

After saying good-bye and promising to think about it long and hard (perhaps she should book an appointment with her conscience, Tash wondered, *18.00 Max; 18.30 Niall; 19.00 Job offer?*) Tash got a lift home with Hugo, who gave her a sales pitch the entire way.

'You'll never meet two more genuine, fun and loyal people than Gus and Pen. Everyone in the sport adores them and they have the most raucous parties in Berkshire.'

'Sounds like my mother,' grumbled Tash. But she was getting more and more sold on the idea.

They passed a drunken tramp peeing at the side of the road as he swigged simultaneously from a plastic bottle of wine.

'Looks a bit like Niall,' Hugo said idly, glancing into his wing mirror.

Tash felt a sharp pain stab through her sprained wrist and sat upright with a jolt.

When she'd told the Moncrieffs that she needed to talk the offer over, she hadn't meant with Max or her family, she realised. The only person she longed to tell was Niall. But Lisette's crowing earlier had stripped away her childish day-dreams and laid bare the idiocy of her crush.

Furious with herself for being so feeble, Tash ate her way through half a bar of Galaxy she found in Hugo's glove compartment and decided she'd definitely have it out with Max the moment she got back.

'You're not really going to marry that rugby player, are you?' Hugo asked casually, as if echoing her thoughts.

Too preoccupied to notice that they were veering dangerously to the left, Tash shook her head.

'Thank you for asking the Moncrieffs to offer me a job,' she murmured.

Hugo paused a fraction too long. 'It was their idea.'

Tash looked out of the window at an ugly blue fence surrounding a nuclear power plant.

'There's another bar of chocolate in the door,' Hugo laughed.

58

Matty and Sally were just cramming the last bag of dirty washing between suitcases in the car boot like a laundry of mortar between bricks when Audrey finally spluttered into life.

'Thank you, Jean.' Matty shook the old man's oily hand as he emerged from beneath the bonnet, a Gitane hanging as ever between his drooping lips.

Jean was sporting a huge black eye which made him look like a whiskery, battle-worn Jack Russell. According to Pascal, Valérie was off work totally with crushed knuckles and an identical shiner, in mirror-image to her husband's. Nodding at Matty, Jean scratched his head, shrugged, tutted and shambled off towards the lodge for his long-awaited Sunday afternoon nap.

'Bye, Jean!' Sally called after him.

He waved dismissively over his shoulder but didn't look round.

'Charming,' Matty laughed.

'Oh, look.' Sally extracted a long string of peaty onions from the front seat. 'He's left us these. They must be from his garden. How kind.' Her voice went strangely taut.

'You're not going to cry again, are you?' Matty looked at her intently.

Sally shook her head, smiled bravely and started strapping Tor into her harness on the back seat to hide the tears that were welling up in her eyes.

'Better let them know we're off.' Matty patted her on the back and loped into the house.

Sally straightened up and took a long look at the beautiful building, letting two loose tears slide down to her nose. It was a magical place. They had dreaded coming so much and yet it had brought them back together again.

As she wiped the drying tears away and busied herself gathering together Tom and his Nintendo, she heard a car roar into the courtyard. There was a quick crashing of doors and the sound of arguing male voices retreating into the house.

'I've got like a heavy date with Jeremy this afternoon, man,' wailed one. 'I have no idea how you can be so like totally unhappening and mondo scuzz.'

'I've just about bloody had *enough*,' snapped the other. 'You're a bloody little twerp, my boy, and can spend all bloody afternoon in your bloody room, gottit?'

Looking up, Sally caught sight of Michael following a heavily slouching Marcus through the kitchen door at the far side of the house. Beside the Volvo, Wiltsher, absolutely loaded down with fishing tackle, caught her eye and smiled apologetically.

'Are you, like, going, yeah?' he called, dropping a maggot tin.

'Yes. Any minute,' Sally called back.

'Well, like, stay def and keep rapping y'know.' Wiltsher bent down to pick up the maggot tin and dropped three folding stools. As he straightened up, a circular net slipped from his grasp. Dropping the lot, he wandered towards the kitchen, stroking his rats' tails.

Sally shook her head and turned back to Tom. He was standing beside the humming, rattling car talking to Niall about pregnancy.

'And then, you see, you attach the probe to the woman's tummy button and a whole lot of people shout "Shut up" and there's this fuzzy picture on the telly and Sally cries a lot,' Tom explained patiently.

'Does she now?' Niall smiled and gave Sally the ghost of a wink.

'Yes. It's called an ultrascum.' Tom nodded gravely.

Polly had joined them and was listening with interest.

'Sally let me look at Tor,' Tom carried on, 'but she was just a big blob.' He giggled feverishly at the thought.

'My godson has yet again been endowing the fruits of his enlightened upbringing upon me,' Niall laughed to Sally.

'Is that Shakespeare again, Nilly?' Tom tried to look learned.

'Papa says Shakespeare was the most boring anglais to ever live,' Polly announced pompously. 'He says Monsieur Shakespeare wrote très long books because the English do not have sex.'

Tom went into more fits of giggles and awarded Polly a go with his Nintendo for her supreme wit.

A large family troop was advancing towards them from the house, led by Alexandra carrying an absolutely huge disc of Saint Paulin.

Touching Niall's sleeve and dropping her voice, Sally muttered urgently, 'Matty will absolutely kill me for this but, as you insist on staying, I think you should know that Tash is mad about you.'

Niall stopped laughing and shook his head, starting to protest.

'Shut up,' hissed Sally, catching sight of Lisette shimmying towards them with Lucian and Pascal on either side. 'If you've got any sense of self-preservation *talk* to her – level with her, for Christ's sake. Medallion Max seems to think they're returning to London tomorrow.'

'What?' Niall looked appalled, but it was too late for Sally to do anything but raise her eyebrows urgently. Alexandra was already upon them waving the Saint Paulin round like a pizza base.

'I don't know where Tash has got to, I'm afraid,' she apologised, pushing away Rooter, who, appetite recovered, was drawn to the idea of a mild cheese entrée followed by chicken à la courtyard. 'She's still missing and Pascal's discovered his jeep's gone too. But we'll say good-bye without her.'

Niall looked even more worried. Hugo wasn't around either, he noticed anxiously.

'Cass and Michael are inside. They send their love but can't come out because Michael is – er – talking to the boys.'

'Your poor bloody mother is bloody upset about your appalling bloody behaviour on Friday night,' Michael stormed. 'I've told you you're too bloody young to drink.'

Marcus, slouching on a window-seat beside Wiltsher, squinted blankly up at his father.

'Turn that bloody thing off, Marcus!' Michael bellowed.

Rapping out a beat against his skinny leg, Marcus stayed firmly plugged into his Walkman.

'Can't hear you, man.'

'You bloody little twe—'

'Michael,' Cass quacked sharply, 'I think we need to talk about this alone first. After all, your behaviour was hardly without sully or stain.'

'You bloody what?'

Cass pulled her chin back into her neck and narrowed her reddened eyes. 'I'm talking about Valérie, Michael.'

Michael went pale.

Wiltsher began to snigger. Beside him, Marcus offered him a Marlboro. This was better than *Neighbours*.

'You boys better go upstairs and have bloody showers or something,' Michael barked, lighting his pipe with a shaking hand. 'And put those bloody disgusting things out – do you want cancer at twenty?'

'And,' Cass said shrilly, her voice wobbling with emotion, 'we must talk about Olly, Michael.' She pulled out a handkerchief from her sleeve. 'You see, I think he and Ginger—'

'Bloody nice chap, Harcourt,' Michael muttered, clearing his throat in his anxiety to get the topic of conversation away from his drunken antics with the dreadful Valérie.

'. . . are homosexuals!' Cass finished with a whimper.

'You bloody what?' Michael's pipe shot straight out of his mouth as Marcus and Wiltsher started to shriek in their whooping, cackly laughs.

* * *

'Must come and stay with us sometime,' Ben told Matty and Sally while Sophia was out of earshot. 'Can't have these sprogs growing up without knowing their cousins.' He smiled stiffly as Sally unplugged Tor's teeth from his ankle and strapped her back in her car seat.

Tor promptly fell asleep.

'Wonderful little character,' Ben laughed, loping towards Sophia.

'Oh do look,' Sally giggled, gazing in the direction of the manoir's steps, 'it's Chic-to-Chic.'

Matty groaned and rolled his eyes. Saying good-bye was taking for ever.

Eddie and Lauren – looking gloriously trendy in silk casuals – made up for the fact they had barely seen their nephew and family by insisting on taking several reels of photographs.

Everyone posed crabbily in front of the house. Too much wine at lunch meant they now felt sick in the unshaded heat. Tor, grouchy at being woken and unharnessed yet again, bawled throughout. Tom and Polly then disappeared completely and had to be dug out of the vegetable cupboard, where they were re-enacting an 'ultrascum'.

Lauren, who was nose-to-nose with Max about Vegas weddings, turned to Sally.

'Role-playing has a very powerful integrating effect for children trying to relate to modern society.'

'And it has a very grating effect on women relating to modern children,' muttered Sally, hauling them out.

Sophia, sulking heavily because she'd had her photograph taken with no make-up and babyfood drying on her Caroline Charles shirt, admired the way Sally handled the children without any help.

'I suppose it must be bliss not having to look beautiful every morning,' she said enviously.

Sally, realising this was actually Sophia's idea of bridging the social moat, hid how hurt she was and smiled bravely.

'You're lucky as Punch that you always do,' she told her, feeling sick at her sycophancy but aware that now wasn't the time to bitch.

Sophia was so delighted that she actually gave Sally a hug and rashly repeated Ben's invitation to come and stay, quickly adding that she'd phone about dates, to give herself time to think of something awful coming up.

Matty was giving out distress signals. He'd been cornered by Max doing his born again brother-in-law bit – lots of hand-pumping, number-swapping, 'must meet up for a jar when we're all back in London' and tips on the best Indians in Hampstead.

Moving into rescue position, Sally kissed Pascal good-bye. He gave her a huge, very Gallic hug and trapped her under a watery grey gaze.

'Thank you ver' much for coming 'ere,' he said gratefully. 'It means so much to Xandra, you know?'

Sally nodded and looked across to Alexandra, who was frantically trying to hide her tears and blow her nose behind the shield of Saint Paulin.

Almost beside Matty now, Sally hugged Niall once more and let Lisette, who'd shot to Niall's side as soon as she saw him, kiss the air a foot from her cheek.

'I expect we'll see each other soon,' Lisette breezed.

Sally nodded. 'Soon as Cliff Richard loses his virginity,' she muttered under her breath as she turned to detach Matty from Max, who had moved on to the wonders of Twickenham.

'If Tash marries that boy,' Matty hissed, 'I'm going to throttle her great long neck.'

At last they were climbing into Audrey, who had been kept running throughout in case she wouldn't start again and was now beginning to overheat dangerously.

'One last thing.' Matty – standing outside the car and leaning in through the driver's door – buckled Sally's safety belt then extracted something from the glove compartment before turning back to the assembled group.

Walking over to his mother, he handed her a small rectangular package wrapped in tissue paper.

Alexandra gasped and looked up at him through streaming eyes. Matty, so close to, towered over her like a great pine that has shot up past a statuesque juniper without really noticing it. She suddenly struck him as very small and fragile.

'Don't open it now,' he muttered, placing it in her hand and covering it with his own, curiously awkward with her. He cleared his throat. 'Just to say thank you. Thank you for everything.'

He bent down and kissed her cheek. It was soft, warm and smelt comfortingly of fading Arpège.

'Oh darling!' Alexandra sniffed. He hadn't done anything like that in years. Overwhelmed with joy, she enveloped him in a tight cuddle, frantically keeping a grip on the parcel and the cheese.

Matty extracted himself gently and, squeezing her free hand, dashed back to the car.

As they clattered out of the courtyard to a series of hearty waves, 'Bye!'s, 'Safe journey!'s and 'Did you remember your socks were in my room?'s, Audrey nearly collided with a red Peugeot coming the other way. The two cars stopped side by side in the gateway for a few seconds and a cloud of exhaust fumes floated up before Audrey groaned away once more – tanned arms waving out of the windows – and the red Peugeot cruised into the courtyard, coming to a halt beside the Volvo.

Ignoring it, the family started to mill back towards the cool of the house.

'Oh no!' wailed Alexandra in horror. 'I've forgotten to give them their cheese.'

'I shouldn't worry.' Max smiled kindly. 'That ugly rug,' he nodded at Rooter, 'took a bite out of it about ten minutes ago. Look.'

But they both stopped caring about the cheese as Tash, looking like the returning wounded from some terrible Resistance bombing that had gone wrong, climbed stiffly from the Peugeot. With a smile curling his mouth, Hugo was walking round from the driver's side to help her.

But Max was too fast for him. Dashing to the Peugeot, he nearly swept both Tash and himself back inside, he was travelling so fast.

'What the Christ . . . ?'

'I went to visit Penny Moncrieff in hospital,' shrugged Tash, hating being back.

'So, what went wrong?'

If only Max was angry, thought Tash. He just sounded pitifully protective and caring.

'It's a long story, Max,' she sighed. It had somehow been fun telling Hugo and the Moncrieffs. She knew recounting her disastrous parking to Max would just make her appear irresponsible, scatter-brained and foolish, and since he had worryingly called her his 'dizzy little fluffball' already that morning, this was not something she wanted to encourage.

'All right, all right – let's get you inside.' He was sounding like a psychiatric nurse now.

Tash looked helplessly at Hugo, but he just shrugged irritably and moved over to Ben and Sophia, who were talking to the Buckinghams. Instinctively, her gaze searched for Niall.

'Come on, darling,' Max coaxed caringly.

'I want to see Snob,' she snapped back, turning to her mother, who was illogically clutching a parcel and a large cheese, looking aghast. 'It's okay, Mummy, nothing serious happened. Only a broken heart.'

As she limped to the paddock gate, pursued by Max, Tash didn't notice a craggy shadow watching them from beneath the eaves of the hayloft.

His throat dry with dust, Niall threw his barely smoked cigarette into a sand-bucket and almost immediately lit another.

Lisette wavered behind the others in the courtyard – uncertain whether to stick with Niall, who had been in a silent black gloom throughout lunch, or go inside to find Lucian. Flirting with him was getting dangerously moreish.

But, while Lucian was as easy to make as cheese on toast, Lisette reflected, he was also about as bland. Niall was a five-course meal prepared by Marco Pierre White in comparison. Lucian would make her laugh and tell her she was beautiful. Niall just had to laugh and she *was* beautiful.

A cool shadow fell across her face and she looked up, eyes deliberately wide, like a silent movie heroine, to see Niall's silhouette against the sun.

Lisette couldn't see the expression on his face, but he was standing so close she could smell him – the faintest tang of sweat mixing headily with a trace of Floris from an earlier bath. It was the closest Niall had voluntarily come since Saturday morning. He was shaking slightly, running his fingers through his hair, his wide shoulders set in a tense, agitated line.

Lisette felt blissfully cool-headed. Reaching out with a delicate hand, she covered his heart and felt it slamming against his chest. Gotcha. She smiled foxily and dropped her eyes. Lucian could go on hold.

'Let's walk.' His voice was deep and anxious.

Nodding meekly, aware that her vulnerability twisted at his heart, Lisette followed him down the narrow, overgrown path which led past the paddock into the topiary.

Voices floated across the hedge as they passed.

'I want to take it – it means a lot to me.'

'And this job on the West Coast means a lot to me, Tash.'

Niall had slowed to a snail's pace so that he was barely shuffling forward and Lisette cannoned into him. Sighing loudly, she took advantage of walking slowly behind him to neaten her hair and rub the smudges from under her eyes.

'I know – I would never, never dream of stopping you from doing it – but can't you see it goes both ways?'

'I told you about my job first.'

'Oh Max, that's unbelievably childish. Why can't we both do what we want?'

'But it means being apart.'

'I've already told you I don't want to go to America.'

'You'd really prefer swanning around the Home Counties in green wellies pulling lesser spotted bogwort from some paddock?'

'Ouch!'

There was a terrible silence from the field as, on the other side of the fence, Lisette walked into a clump of nettles and Tash and Max realised they were being overheard.

Niall – who was by now barely moving and taking an intense, feigned interest in a very ordinary cluster of betony – shot her a purple glower over his shoulder.

'Max, listen,' Tash carried on in a hissed whisper. 'I think we need to talk seriously about whether this—'

'I'm allergic to pastoral pursuits, you know that.' Max sniffed sulkily, pretending his hay fever had suddenly become far worse. 'I'd be so drugged up with antihistamine, our sex life would be lousier than it was in London.'

'About whether,' Tash squeaked nervously, 'this marriage idea wasn't a bit hasty and—'

'Not that it's got much better.' Not listening, Max swatted a fly irritably. 'We haven't made love once since I got here.'

Across the rails, Lisette almost broke her nose as Niall froze to the spot.

'You were always jumping on me in London,' Max badgered. 'Don't tell me you've gone all virginal and want to wait until the honeymoon.'

'No, I don't want to wait!' Tash wailed helplessly.

'Good.' A broad, lop-sided grin stretched across Max's face.

Realising she could have phrased that better, Tash swallowed hard.

In the agonising silence which followed, Snob, with characteristic diplomacy, could be heard taking a long pee. Niall moved along the fence a fraction, shadowed by a loudly sighing Lisette, and started closely to examine a dusty clump of cat's ear.

On the other side of the hedge, Max knew exactly what Tash was trying to say to him. And he was utterly determined not to let her do it. Sensing she was weakening, he moved forward, catching the ends of her fingers in his.

'Come here,' he murmured.

Tash didn't move, her face loaded with guilt and worry, summoning the nerve to blurt out the truth. But, as she opened her mouth, Max swiftly pulled her into his arms, pushing her head into his shoulder before she could speak.

'You really trust me, don't you?' he breathed into her hair, squeezing her lovingly. 'So help me, I'll never, ever, abuse it. That you're willing to wait for me while I go to the States is the greatest show of love and trust I could ask for. I'm just selfish to want you to come too. It might be difficult financially,' he cleared his throat, 'but we'll fight through it. I love you.'

'Oh Max,' Tash moaned into his t-shirt. 'Max, I—'

There was a sudden loud crash on the other side of the hedge and Snob, who was grazing next to it, threw up his head and shied away in fright, flying to the other end of the small field with his tail streaming.

Pulling gratefully away from Max, Tash dashed over to investigate but, standing on the bottom rail of the fence to look over the hedge, all she could see was a flattened patch of long grass and cat's ear, as if someone had been lying on it. She turned back and shrugged.

Slowly twisting a piece of hay between finger and thumb, Max walked towards her.

'What were you going to say?' he asked softly, hooking his arm around her neck and nuzzling her under her ear.

'Max, don't do that!' Tash yelped. 'You know that's one of my Roger-me zones.'

'What were you going to say?' persisted Max, still nuzzling.

Tash groaned, feeling like a stray having its tummy rubbed by the dog catcher. Over the last two days she'd started to think of Max as a sort of plimsolls and anorak twitcher because he was so keen. Now she shivered deliciously and felt every part of her stomach start to melt very slowly towards the parched soil below. She no longer fancied him as she once had, but they still shared so much: the goofy humour, numerous friends, two cats, endless good, bad and downright raunchy memories. Slipping back into the old routine would be as easy as laughing at an old Tony Hancock show you thought you'd seen to death.

'Just that you really are my best friend,' she wriggled away, opening her mouth for the 'but—'

'*And?*'

Momentarily nonplussed, Tash wavered. 'And what?'

'Ends in "you", begins with "I", four-letter word in the middle?' His face was cheerful and expectant, fingers reaching up to nuzzle again.

'I need you?' Tash joked feebly.

'Close.'

'Want you?'

'Mmm, nice, but no.'

'Love you?'

'Good.' Max pulled her towards the gate. 'Now, as you missed lunch, I'm going to take you down to the village and buy you *the* most enormous liquid one – er,' he paused, one hand on the latch, 'you couldn't lend me a couple of hundred francs could you?'

Gasping to catch his breath, Niall was fuming.

Lisette had pushed him into the hedge out of spite. Although she vehemently denied it, Niall remembered feeling a small heeled foot tugging at his leg before he was sent flying, totally off balance, head-first into the long grass beside the paddock rails. They had only just made it into the topiary without being seen.

'Oh come on, Niall,' she laughed breathlessly. 'You've got to see the funny side.'

It was the same Lisette as ever – a charming, capricious child who wriggled away if you got too close and turned into a whining brat if she didn't get what she wanted. Niall couldn't deny she was bewitchingly complex, but it was like solving a Rubik's cube – once done, the formula was known and the interest gone for ever. Like a shell-shocked soldier going through trauma therapy, he'd started to realise that the guns were no longer exploding all around him.

'Boy, this place is so heavenly.' Lisette flopped down under a sprawling, overgrown box, sure of his love for her, waiting for him to tell her all the things she wanted to hear. Running a slim hand through her cropped mane, she leaned back on her elbows, smiling at him through sun-narrowed eyes, deliberately provocative. She patted the ground beside her, cocking her face imploringly.

Sighing, Niall shook his head. Ironically, her certainty made his task easier.

Dropping on to his haunches, forearms resting on his knees, he took a deep breath.

He then told her in the simplest, most painless way he knew how, that he didn't think they could ever make a go of it and that she had given him the greatest joy and the hardest lessons of his life for which he'd be for ever grateful, but that he simply couldn't carry on living with her after the agony she had put him through. The only thing he would ask of her was to divorce him because his Catholic family would kick up a tremendous stink if he issued her with the papers.

Lisette listened to him with extraordinary calm, her still head on one side, a strange little smile playing on her lips. When he'd finished, she looked at him for a full minute, showing absolutely no emotion beyond mild amusement.

Niall had to admire her cool. She must be hurting, he thought sadly, it was a crippling blow to her pride.

Finally, she licked her lips, slicked back her hair with a steady hand and looked him square in the face.

'So you don't love me any more, huh, Niall?' It was a seductive, mocking question secure in its own superiority.

Niall just stared back at her in silence, refusing to be run around any more.

'Well, touché,' Lisette went on quietly, without bitterness, the smile still dancing. 'I guess that finally puts us on an even par.'

She stood up and made to go with quiet dignity but, pausing by the mangled yew, she turned and looked at him again as if struck by a trivial afterthought.

'One thing – I'm not divorcing you. You can do the honours as you're such a gent.' She flashed that foxy, enchanting smile. 'I'd recommend sooner rather than later – because when you do, I'm going to bleed you so dry you'll crumble into dust.'

After she'd gone, Niall lay back in the shadow of a yew with a sigh of relief and stared through the stretched, out-thrown branches, past their coarse green needles and ripening berries faintly tinged with red, out to the almost artificial blue overhead.

He longed for Tash so much the ache was palpable. He supposed it was a predestined part of his character; he'd finally purged one agony only to find another had crept up and curled into place while his back was turned.

He closed his eyes to the endless blue.

> 'I dream of a Ledaean body, bent
> Above a sinking fire, a tale that she
> Told of a harsh reproof, or trivial event
> That changed some childish day to tragedy—
> Told, and it seemed that our two natures blent
> Into a sphere from youthful sympathy.
> Or else, to alter Plato's parable,
> Into the yolk and white of the one shell.'

Oh Lord in Heaven! Niall sat up with a shock – if he quoted Yeats then it really did mean he was in love.

59

It was a breathtaking evening. The sultry air was rich with heady fragrances from the rampaging garden, like rival scent counters in Selfridges trying to eclipse each other. Insects impersonated Grand Prix drivers angling for pole position or hung in speckled heat shimmers under the awning of the decadently lustrous rhododendrons which had turned the paths into labyrinthine tunnels. The creamy house was as warm, humid and golden as fresh brioche.

Tash trailed from the pool to the paddock. She'd lazily pulled on some old shorts (Edwardian bloomers picked up at a Camden thrift shop) over Sophia's still unreturned bikini and donned her regulation gumboots. Already she could feel her feet parboil and her shoulder itch with heat under its bandages. Scratching under her rubber sling, she paused dreamily by the broken garden gate and stared back across the valley.

It glowed under the yellow-tinted halogen light of a dropping sun, saturating the bosky greens – which folded into one another like half-mixed spinach mousse – with gold and sepia glaze. To Tash, it was as if the landscape was beaten from copper, just starting to wear its chiffon jacket of patina. A streak of white fluff from a jet seamed the sky into two, like sheep's wool caught on a barbed-wire fence. It was the only white on the otherwise unbroken Gauloise-blue canopy.

Tash formed a mental artist's palette. She'd hardly had time to sketch at all. Apart from Matty and Sally's portrait, she reflected, the only things she'd painted since she arrived were her toenails.

The valley, in all its haunting, centuries-old pulchritude, had suffered perpetual cataloguing; hundreds of soft pencils had captured the straight regiments of Lombardy poplars whose lengthening shadows seemed to be pointing scores of accusing fingers at her. Oils, watercolours, pastels and charcoals had recorded the plush corduroy of the distant vines. Masters and amateurs alike had held endless brushes in front of bloodshot eyes, measuring up the statuesque beeches with trunks like smelting chimneys and portly cedars with their sumptuous cloche hats.

Tash tried hard to commit its abundance to memory, but it was like memorising Eliot's *The Waste Land* in one reading.

'I must say, you've got the most extraordinarily odd wardrobe, Tash.'

Tash dragged her eyes away from the hypnotising pull of the view and turned to Ben. He was looking very Raj in buff Bermudas and shirt with a cricket sweater over his shoulders and a hideous flower-pot hat pulled down over his sleepy eyes. He had a pair of binoculars and a battered bird identification book as a feeble excuse to escape from Sophia's current nanny obsession for half an hour.

'Did you have a nice game of croquet earlier?' Tash asked lightly.

'What – oh – ended up playing boules with Pascal. Cheeky bugger kept changing the rules.' He looked at Tash and grimaced – a fresh batch of bruises had started to form diluted inky potato prints on her arms and legs. 'Look, I'm sorry about this morning. Didn't mean you to charge off like that. Had no idea you hadn't driven over here before. How're you feeling?'

'Soggy,' smiled Tash, holding up her dripping white wrist. 'I was paddling in the shallow end when Lauren pushed Max in.'

'Good, good.' Ben wasn't listening. He wore his stiff, preoccupied look, which told her he was working hard on saying something.

'Hear the Moncrieffs have offered you a job,' he finally spat out.

Tash nodded.

'Good people,' Ben said firmly. 'Very flattering to be asked. Snap it up if I were you.'

Tash didn't reply. She still hadn't phoned them.

'Well, s'pose I'll see you later – we're all eating out again, tonight, I hear.' Ben coughed awkwardly. 'Think I can hear a reed warbler.' He nodded meditatively and beat a hasty retreat into the copse.

Tash stared mindlessly at a gnarled medlar. Its craggy, drooping beauty made her think of Niall.

He hadn't appeared since lunchtime. Lisette, pale and subdued – which hatefully just added to her loveliness – had stayed beside the pool all afternoon, speaking to Lucian in her 'confidential' voice, laughing at Max's bawdy jokes, drinking just mineral water. Yet all the time she'd remained strangely aloof. Like a dog who's aware that her master is about to bear down at any minute in a foul temper, she'd let her eyes wander over and over again beyond those she was with to scan the horizon. Max clearly thought she was awesome, but Tash still couldn't bring herself to talk to her.

'Had a siesta, kids?' she'd winked when Tash and Max had arrived.

'Village bar.' Max had plopped into the pool beside Lauren's Lilo with an appreciative glance at her narrow midriff. 'Fantastic game of poker with le patron. Helluva player.'

'i.e. you lost,' Lauren had screeched with laughter, flipping them with water.

Yes, all my money, Tash fumed. While I was braced to confess all, he posted me in the corner with a Diet Coke and a croque madame.

The evening heat was making her sluggish. If she stood staring at the medlar any longer, it would uproot itself and shuffle off to get some privacy. Spurring herself into stiff action, she caught Snob, who was very stroppy about her bloomers and walked to the stalls ten paces behind her, eyes popping, like a teenage son unwilling to be seen with his mother in the high street.

'You poor darling, you must have been eaten to death by flies out there.' Tash noticed he was covered in brown-edged elder blossom from scratching on a bush.

She let Snob chew the rim of her gumboot while she banked up the woodshaving at the sides of his stall. He got so attached to the gumboot that she left it with him and hopped through to the feed store to fetch his supper, hopping back to deliver it.

Snob was a very possessive eater with legs and teeth flying out if she got too close. Tash gave up all hope of extracting the chomped boot until after he'd finished. Standing at a safe distance, she listened to his satisfied, noisy chewing, broken sporadically as he blew loudly into his bucket like a hot air balloon burner.

'Wish I was you,' she sighed enviously, leaning back against the partition. 'Then I could bunk up in here all night instead of having to go to some poxy restaurant to talk about the brides-maids of Dracula and who did Helen Windsor's flowers.'

She scuffed at a stray woodshaving and rubbed her sore shoulder.

'Tash darling, are you in there?'

Tash thought quickly about hiding but, realising she had to talk to someone, sighed again and shouted, 'Here, Mummy.'

'Oh good.' Alexandra blinked in the mealy dark before walking towards her holding out a mug of tea.

'Brought you this, sweetheart. I thought you could use it.'

'Thanks,' Tash smiled. She'd had three mugs of tea by the pool and this one was stone cold. Her mother had obviously donned it as a ruse and been looking for her for some time.

'We're leaving in about an hour.' Alexandra looked at her daughter's one bare foot. Tash was getting odder, if anything, she reflected. 'Eddie and Lauren say they'll ferry you and Max. We've got the entire restaurant to ourselves – Cass's idea. I told her I'd already made tonight's chicken soup, but she got quite wound up about it, insisting that Michael will foot the bill this time. I just hope she's right.'

Tash stared at her mother. That wasn't like her at all. Then she remembered the bills in the date box and bit her lip.

'I'm terribly, terribly sorry about Pascal's jeep.' She looked at the stone flags below. 'I'll try and get the money for the repairs.'

'Don't be silly,' Alexandra dismissed her slightly too sharply. 'Pascal accepts that it was an accident, darling. And he did tell you to borrow a car whenever you wanted.'

Tash fell silent and turned to watch Snob again. He was hoovering up the last of his feed from the floor beside his bucket.

Alexandra followed her gaze and, with a nervous little hum, started tapping her nails on the dusty wood.

'It looks like it might be a bit strained tonight, I'm afraid, darling,' she said apologetically. 'Cass and Michael aren't speaking and poor old Marcus seems to think he'll be made to go fishing with his father every day for the rest of the week in penance for getting a bit tipsy at the party.' She let out an edgy laugh.

Tash seemed hardly to be listening. Suddenly, she spun round with illuminated eyes and looked Alexandra in the face.

'I've been offered a job,' she blurted.

'Oh.' Alexandra looked stunned. 'Not in America with Max?' she asked in a panic.

Tash shook her head and explained about the Moncrieffs' invitation and Max not wanting her to take it.

'What means more to you,' Alexandra asked slowly, looking Tash steadily in the eyes. 'Taking this job or being with Max?'

'The job,' Tash said honestly. 'But it's not as simple as that.' Her bottom lip trembled and she looked away, trying hard to control herself.

'You don't really love Max, do you, darling?' Alexandra asked gently.

'Yes, I do,' Tash croaked, turning back to her mother with her eyes full of tears. 'That's the t-terrible thing. I didn't think you could love – that is, I l-love . . . oh, Mummy.'

'You love someone else more?'

Tash nodded, stifling a sob.

Alexandra held out her arms and Tash went gratefully into

them, desperate for reassurance. The mug she was holding slipped as she moved and smashed on to the flags below, covering her bare foot with tea.

'And now I've broken your mug!' she wailed, sobbing even louder.

'Oh, my poor, sweet Tash.' Alexandra stroked her hair gently. Tash was so much taller than her she had to reach up. 'I guessed as much. Tell me, sweetheart, why did you agree to marry Max in the first place?'

'Oh, it was a s-silly, foolish bet,' Tash sniffed regretfully and explained. It was such utter bliss telling someone and her mother was so warm and sympathetic and didn't lecture or dictate.

'Do you think Max has any idea how you're feeling?'

Tash shook her head. 'It's very easy to fall back in step with him – you've seen how easy-going he is. I love him so much as a friend, I could never hurt him. I almost start to think that maybe, when we're back in London, away from . . . away from . . .' she covered her mouth with her hand.

'This other man?'

Tash nodded. 'That it might all work out for the best and I'll be glad it's happened. Is that a t-terribly selfish way of looking at things?' She blinked at her mother tearfully.

Alexandra looked at her daughter's wet cheeks, runny nose, dishevelled hair and quivering mouth. You're the least selfish of all my children, she thought. But that would be a terribly disloyal thing to say, so she just shook her head.

'You see,' Tash rubbed her cheeks so forcefully with the back of her good hand that they went as red as her nose, 'this other man,' she looked away shamefaced, 'he doesn't love me or anything.'

'No?' Alexandra tried to keep the surprise out of her voice. Tash mustn't realise she knew who it was, she told herself.

Tash shook her head violently. 'He's been very kind to me but he has a lot of problems of his own. He doesn't even really know how I feel, or if he does, he's very embarrassed by it.' The tears of mortification started to swell again.

Alexandra forced herself to keep quiet. She wanted to tell Tash, to sing to the rooftops, that she was wrong. That he did love her – it was so obvious it could have been tattooed on his nose whenever they were together. But she was terrified of bullying Tash. She liked Max and his friendly gung-ho, but harboured a frightful terror that Tash would be throwing herself away on him to a life of cricket teas, shopping in Marks and Sparks and crying over *Thirtysomething*. There was also something ominous about the way Max picked up pieces of china and examined the bottoms when he thought Alexandra wasn't looking.

'I feel such a total fool,' Tash sobbed. 'To have ever thought I stood a chance with someone like him.'

That did it, Alexandra decided. If she *did* say something to Tash, wasn't she only evening up the stakes?

'Tash, sweetheart,' she smiled, 'you have such a dreadfully low opinion of yourself, I'm surprised you don't wear a paper bag and carry a bell. Anybody can see he's in love with you.'

'Oh Mummy, don't,' Tash muttered, knowing Alexandra's bolstering tactics of old.

'Please, please listen to me, darling.' Alexandra bent her knees so that she could look under Tash's hair to catch her eye. 'I had a very long chat with him in the kitchen last night and, after his third brandy, he more or less confessed it. Believe me, darling, he's totally head over heels.'

Tash looked at her mother in disbelief. Niall had been out with Matty and Sally almost until the moment he shot up to bed. And why he should start treating her mother as a confessional was even more mysterious. Everyone knew that, after just one glass of wine, anything told in confidence to Alexandra went straight to Pascal and consequently on to general release.

But she wanted to believe it so much.

'What did he say?' she asked tentatively.

'Well, lots of things, darling.' Alexandra had actually forgotten a lot of the specifics with her hangover. 'One thing does come to mind, because I remember it made me laugh. He said the reason he took a dunk at the trials yesterday was because he needed to cool off after smelling the trail of perfume you'd left behind you on the cross-country course.' She looked at her with delighted expectation.

Tash felt very brave. She took a deep breath and looked across at Snob, who had finished his supper and returned to the gumboot. He was holding it in his teeth like a fat cigar, chewing squeakily.

'You mean Hugo said that?' she finally managed to ask in a high, strained voice.

Alexandra nodded proudly. Please let me have done the right thing, she prayed. I haven't told her what to do, I haven't said I prefer Hugo, I haven't cried or told her how much I love her. Tash's reactions were so unpredictable.

'Thank you, Mummy,' Tash said after a long pause, 'for telling me.' She gave her mother a ghost of a smile. 'You'd better go and change.'

'Of course, darling.' Alexandra beamed with relief and gave her another hug. 'It'll all be all right, you'll see.'

Tash started to count down from ten to stop herself crying.

As Alexandra was making her way from the stalls, she paused beside an old piece of farm machinery shaped like a huge garlic press and turned around, fishing in her pocket for something. 'I almost forgot – I found this sticking out behind the dresser. It's addressed to you, darling. Pascal seems to think Todd left it behind.' She handed Tash an envelope.

'Thanks.' Tash had got to seven. She stuffed the letter in the waistband of her bloomers.

'Do you really have to go tomorrow?' Alexandra hovered.

Tash, at four, shrugged and nodded.

'Oh dear.' Alexandra turned sadly away again and said almost to herself, 'Everybody's leaving.' Before walking out just as Tash reached one.

As soon as her mother was out of earshot, she gave way to bursting into tears, crying into Snob's warm red neck as he irritably jiggled the gumboot around in his teeth, totally unsympathetic.

'It's all so dreadful,' she sobbed. 'First Max and now poor,

poor Hugo. I think,' she wailed even louder as Snob started banging the gumboot against the stall partition in disgust, 'that one of my dreams has just come true.'

Emerging ten minutes later with a raw nose and tight eyes from crying, Tash stood in the courtyard wearing just a bikini, bloomers, tear-stained face and one gumboot.

There were no longer sounds of splashing revelry coming from the poolside of the house. Everyone must have gone inside to bury themselves in gin and tonics and their wardrobes.

Tash couldn't face changing. Maybe if she went dressed as she was, Max would go off her, she thought hopefully.

The evening was still balmy and exquisite. An old biplane puttered overhead as she wandered unevenly into the garden to think about phoning the Moncrieffs.

I'll have to do it sooner or later, she told herself firmly. Why did later always seem the better option?

Hop-scotching across a patch of gravel, she remembered the envelope her mother had handed her and took it from her waistband. The gummed strip was coming apart where Cass had tried to steam it open. Totally engrossed, Tash walked into a low mulberry branch and nearly knocked herself out.

Staggering back from the blow, she trod on a thistle with her bare foot.

'Blast and bloody four-letter fucking words!' she hissed, 'I will *not* cry.'

As she bent down to extract the sharp needles from her heel, she froze. A pair of hairy legs was sticking out from under a nearby yew.

Very slowly and quietly, because she didn't want to be seen if it was a clandestine couple, she stuffed the letter back and flattened herself against an escallonia, staring out through the foliage. Amateur botany seemed to be becoming something of a habit.

The legs were very still. There appeared to be only one pair, putting paid to her Lady Chatterley theory. Jean would have made a hopeless Mellors anyway, Tash reflected nervously.

It could be some mad French flasher lurking with intent, she speculated, or even a drunk left over from Friday night. But somehow Tash knew these limp limbs belonged to Niall. A battered Sartre and adjacent can of draught Beamish helped her deduction. She gazed lovingly at the grubby soles of his feet.

When a wood pigeon flapped and crashed out of a nearby pine, they didn't move.

The flesh of Tash's neck suddenly tightened. What if he'd topped himself, unable to cope with the reality of having Lisette back?

It seemed unlikely (why not do it when unable to cope with the reality of Lisette leaving?) but there was something curiously deathlike about them. And doing himself in under a yew would fit with Niall's sense of dramatic staging perfectly.

It was as if Jack Frost, hiding like a serpent in the escallonia, had crept through the branches to enfold her in his chilly arms and caress the hairs on her spine; Tash was instantly shivering, rooted to the spot with fear.

Jack Frost might not have been in the pink-flowered bush, but something else was. As she carried on gazing at the motionless legs, her scalp creeping, she became aware of an angry buzzing in her ears. She put up her hand and shook her head slightly.

It was like opening the sound-proof door to a deafening factory. The buzzing rose to an angry, whining shriek and she realised her hair was full of wasps.

Screaming in horror, Tash leapt away from the bush, but the wasps stuck with her, like awful tinnitus in her ears, darting in front of her eyes, weaving through her hair. She shook her head violently and felt the first acid sting in her neck. The buzzing rose angrily; she could feel them colliding with her hand as she desperately tried to whip them away.

But the more she leapt around, flailing at the surging insects with her stiff, sprained arms, the more incensed they became. Soon she was going to be raw with stings. She started to sob.

'Run for the pool!' a voice shouted urgently. Niall's legs had come to life.

Tash was shaking her head so much that her sense of direction was shot to pieces. Her rubber sling had trapped itself in the tree. Tearing free from it, she started towards where she imagined the pool to be and felt a strong hand grab her and yank her the opposite way.

Stumbling over divots, brambles lashing her legs and her waspy hair in her eyes, Tash was dragged forcibly along by Niall to the deserted swimming pool. The next minute the furious buzzing was replaced by a loud whoosh as she threw herself in, gumboot and all.

It was hardly with Venus-like serenity that she emerged shortly afterwards. She'd jumped in the shallow end and sunk only four feet to lie spreadeagled on the pool bottom for a few seconds before floating back up again. Her bloomers were full of trapped air and looked like some sort of home-made haemorrhoid comforter, her hair plastered across her face, her nose streaming, bandages peeling. But at least the wasps had gone.

'Are you badly stung?' Niall helped her up the steps.

Tash shook her head as she climbed, coming eye to nipple with the most glorious expanse of masculine brown chest she had ever seen. Niall was wearing nothing but a pair of old, cut-off jeans; he looked very alive and utterly, totally moreish.

Tash stared at his feet, her face burning. 'Just a couple on my neck.'

'Let me see.' He sounded terribly normal and matter-of-fact compared to her gulping agitation.

She obediently turned around and held up her dripping hair. Feeling him breathe on the back of her neck as he examined the stings, she nearly fainted.

'To be sure, they'll be painful but it could have been a lot worse,' he told her, gently easing her back round to face him. 'I'd be wearing your hair up tonight, though. Keep it from irritating them.'

Tash nodded at his knees.

'Besides, it'd suit you that way,' he said with a wisp of a smile.

Of course, he likes short hair, thought Tash miserably. He's just being nice. He's got one nipple higher than the other. *Stop looking, Tash.*

She fought a terrible, burning temptation to reach out and touch that lightly downed, deeply tanned chest. Her heart was pumping so fast she felt seriously light-headed. Any minute now she'd be back in the pool.

Niall didn't move.

Now was his chance to ask her to keep quiet about the kiss at the party, she thought in a panic. She'd kissed so many men that night she was quite sure, in her cloudy recollections, that she must have pounced on him in a deranged moment of totally wired sex-mania. It was all so embarrassing. Laying her crush open like that.

Please don't let him be too nice about it or I'll cry, she prayed. I'll tell him it's quite all right. I'm a respectable engaged woman now. I won't sell my story to the *Sun*: *Naughty Night I Nefariously Necked Niall, superstar's saucy snogging and tantalising tongue technique revealed, by temptress Tash French, 23, a hot-lipped horse-lover from Hampstead.*

'Tash,' Niall faltered finally, mustering his low lilt into action. 'Angel, look at me.'

Tash pulled her lips between her teeth with the effort of looking up into his heartbreaking brown eyes. Then, realising she must look like a toothless crone, she put her lips back to normal and started biting her thumbnail instead.

'Tash, there's something I simply have to say to you,' he went on, looking at her so kindly she had to start to count again, 'and I'm pretty certain it may be the last thing you want to hear, for which I'm truly sorry.'

Tash chewed her nail right off and now had to try to spit it out without his noticing.

Niall cleared his throat awkwardly.

'Lisette coming back like that – it was so unexpected it turned me upside down. I had no idea what to do. I'm sorry I didn't tell you this on Saturday morning, Angel, I realise I must have seemed a complete sod just cosseting myself up with her like that – but we had to do a lot of raking over old ground.

Rapping, Lisette calls it. She was terribly upset.' He looked up at the sky. The biplane was still puttering in the distance. 'I know I should have talked to you sooner – I wanted to – but I'm a terrible coward.'

Tash knew what he was getting at. Her mouth had gone completely dry with humiliation. She swallowed nervously and felt the thumbnail scratch along the length of her throat.

'Then Max appeared on the scene,' Niall cleared his throat again, dropping his eyes, 'and—'

'It's all right,' Tash blurted, unable to let him go on, needing to speak to preserve her self-esteem. 'I've totally forgotten it. Nothing happened. It was all my fault in the first place and you were just terribly kind. This sort of thing must happen to you all the time, I should imagine. People jumping on you and falling in love without even meeting you sometimes, getting women's knickers thrown at you everywhere you go,' she was babbling now and seeing his look of horror pulled herself up short. 'I won't tell Lisette. Never. I promise,' she finished quickly.

'What?' he looked at her incredulously.

'I won't tell her about Friday night,' Tash repeated, feeling her cheeks starting to burn even more. He obviously thought she was mad. A crackpot fan with a crush and a screw loose looking for a loose screw. She felt incredibly silly.

'You can buy a megaphone and tell her on the hour if you like,' Niall said icily. 'Be my guest. Lisette can go to hell and be damned for all I care.'

Biting her lip in confusion, Tash looked at his beautiful chest and listened to the drips falling off her on to the stones below.

Niall nearly jumped out of his skin as he felt a cool hand touch him lightly just below the nipple.

'OhgodI'msorry!' Tash yelped, nearly falling back into the pool.

'Don't be,' Niall breathed, staring at her in amazement.

Tash was acutely embarrassed that she could have let herself go like that. Escape was the only answer, she decided in a panic. Not looking up, she started to stumble away, her single gumboot pouring out water and making obscene raspberries.

But once again a firm hand caught her arm, this time spinning her round so that she was looking him straight in the lovely, craggy face.

'Oh!' Tash squeaked.

He just gazed at her, which was incredibly disturbing; she could bury herself in those soft brown eyes, snuggle up to the beaky, tragedian's nose and eat strawberries off the curling mouth. She was weak with lust and, what the hell, she had nothing to lose. Her pride had been jettisoned on Friday night.

Slipping her fingers through his belt loops, Tash brushed his mouth with the lightest of kisses. His lips tasted of Beamish and were soft pillows between the roughness of his stubble. She could feel the warmth of his breath on her nose. His grip tightened on her arm.

But he didn't kiss her back.

She felt the reckless impulse shrivel into guilt. What do you expect if you try to drink chilled champagne in hell? she told herself, pulling away.

And then Niall slipped his other hand behind her neck, drawing her back towards him and into the most delicious kiss she had ever experienced. No amount of excited Merriot fumblings had prepared her for the explosion of lust it triggered off.

As the length of his body touched against hers, Tash felt a drum-roll of aching desire pummel her in the groin. She kissed him back so excitedly, she almost suffocated from forgetting to breathe. Then, feeling his hands slip down her backbone to brush against the clinging wet shorts, she was pitched into free-fall lust. He was so measured, so delicate, so skilled and so stomach-dissolving that she didn't even notice that he was pressing his hand on her wasp stings.

'Crucial!' a voice whooped sleepily from not ten feet away. 'Y'know, like anyone looking out of a window could see you, man?'

Tash and Niall spun round to see Marcus wearing a wildly fashionable 'Ego Trip Stripper' t-shirt matched with absurdly baggy black denim shorts, and clutching a d'Eblouir family-sized whisky. Lolling behind him, clutching a can of coke, was Wiltsher, looking very pink. They'd obviously escaped to the pool to smoke an illicit spliff before they all set off.

'Bit, like, risky business, that, y'know.' Marcus readjusted his baseball cap, taking a swig of whisky and spluttering. He held out the glass to Wiltsher, who, not taking his eyes from Tash, topped it up to brimming with coke.

'Why don't you both just fuck off?' snapped Niall, looking furious.

He had a protective arm wrapped around Tash who – a second ago gasping with lust – was now as puce as Wiltsher with flustered humiliation.

'Suppose you like an audience, don't you, Niall, man?' Marcus asked, sounding not in the least sarcastic, just genuinely interested. Smiling inanely, he sagged against the frame of the swing-seat and squinted as he lit his smoke.

Tash looked up at the house, envisaged Max watching her buckling under Niall's utterly magical kiss, and burst into tears.

'Oh God!' Tearing herself free of Niall's arm she ran, squelching loudly, into the house.

'Tash!' Niall bounded after her and then slid to a halt by the balcony steps. He slammed his palms against a pillar, absolutely furious with himself.

'Fantastic dress-sense, man.' Wiltsher, his tongue suddenly unstuck, edged closer. 'Lucky Max.' He took the spliff from Marcus and took a deep drag to steady his nerves.

'What?' Niall turned to him like a tumultuous bolt of thunder.

Wiltsher swallowed nervously. Niall was very butch.

'Marrying a goer like that,' he coughed, switching from contralto to bass in an attempt to talk man to man. 'These open relationships are, like, really happening now. Totally nineties, man.' He held out the spliff. 'Want a pull?'

Niall closed his eyes and covered his face with his hands. The world had gone mad, and he'd always thought he'd get there first. Tash had given him a quick peck and, like the slobbering idiot he was, he'd swooped. Now he was just much more confused and almost blinded with useless hope. He groped for his cigarettes, then searched his pockets for a light.

'Don't worry, man.' Marcus tossed Niall his matches. 'I mean, we like promise to keep stum about you and my cuz, man. But, like,' he polished off his drink with a grimace, 'we'd really appreciate a few invites to star-studded parties and stuff in return, y'know? Anyfink where we'll get to meet, like, Catherine Zeta Jones and Sharon Stone and—'

'Shut up.'

Niall's quiet, deathly tone absolutely terrified Marcus. He shut up.

'Look, sorry. Can you make my apologies tonight?' Niall ran his fingers through his hair despairingly, not noticing the cigarette sizzling off several locks. 'I don't feel up to it.'

Marcus and Wiltsher watched him wander unsteadily back into the garden.

'Weird guy, man.' Marcus whipped the spliff back from his friend and tugged at the last half inch of Rizla before chucking the pip in the pool. 'Reckon we'll get those invites?'

'Nrrr.' Wiltsher swilled his coke thoughtfully.

'And he nicked my matches,' Marcus moaned, starting to lope back towards the house.

'Hennessy . . .' Wiltsher asked shyly, shuffling behind his friend.

'Yeah, man?'

Wiltsher cleared his throat nervously. 'Fink I, like, stand a chance wiv your cousin, man?'

Marcus stopped and squinted at his friend. 'You'd have to, like, lose your hairdo.'

60

By the time Tash got back from the restaurant, Todd's letter, which had been drying out on her dressing table, had crisped from papier mâché to parchment.

She picked it up and collapsed on to the bed, feeling ill. Because she was miserable, she'd drunk far too much.

Horrid, boring, crappy night, she thought wretchedly. No Niall; stewing with guilt about Max, who'd yet again been sweet; feeling beastly about Hugo. Across the table, Marcus had winked at her more often than a pervert with a facial tic. Every song blasting out of the radio in the car or sad strain of Chopin in the restaurant had made tears well in her eyes. But if she closed them all she'd seen was Niall's shocked face before that heavenly, intoxicating and utterly forbidden kiss.

The whole dinner had taken years off her life and all she'd managed to eat was half a king prawn and the parsley on her Jambon Fumé aux Abricots. The Hennessys – who had suggested eating out in the first place – had been more divided than the new Soviet Commonwealth. Despite Cass's goading, Michael had yet again failed to get out his well-guarded plastic. Only after Pascal had paid did Michael loudly offer to settle for his 'brood'. With typical generosity, Pascal had shrugged him away. Michael didn't offer twice.

Tash watched the ceiling twirl around the light-fitting and held up Todd's letter in front of her face. It was no good, she couldn't even concentrate on *Dear Tash*. She kept reading and rereading it like a long Pinter sentence.

Max, who had followed her into the room, started to undress by the window. Tash flopped her head to the side and looked at all three of him. Shirt over the head, shoes prised off at the heel and tossed away, trousers dropped, socks peeled, boxers down the flagpole. It all took about fifteen seconds.

'Why do you always undress so quickly?' she asked, uncrossing her eyes to look him in the face.

'Because I'm not paid for it,' said Max and, wrapping a towel around his hips, wandered off to find a spare bathroom.

Tash thought about the comment for a long time, completely failed to get to grips with it, burped loudly and shakily tried to stand up. It was hard going but eventually she found herself swaying in the middle of the room. Three seconds later her brain rejoined her head.

Max had brought up some pumpernickel and pâté, the biscuit tin and several peaches, she noted. They were clearly in for a rollicking night.

Staggering over to the window, Tash tried to cool her face on the glass and, finding it wasn't there, almost fell out. The window was wide open.

She gaped at the drop below, relieved that she wasn't facing the prospect of visiting hospital for the second time in a day.

'I'd probably be grilled by a French social worker about my attempted suicide this time,' she mused, squinting at the stars and trying to find the Plough.

Christ! The hospital! The Moncrieffs! She hadn't phoned them.

Crashing into the doorpost, she left Todd's letter on the bed and tottered on to the landing. Having returned twice to fetch her shoes and then M-C's number, she stumbled downstairs and towards the phone.

'Y'know, Wilt, man.'

'Yeah, dood?' Wiltsher's head popped out of his sleeping bag.

'Like, if we're gonna stop these totally mindblowingly unhappening fishing trips we're gonna have to, like, er . . .'

'Come up with a seriously wicked plan?'

'Yeah.'

'Awesome idea, Hennessy.' There was a long pause, and in the darkness Marcus could be heard picking at the dry skin on his feet.

'Er . . . what sort of plan did you have in mind, man?' Wiltsher asked eventually.

'Oh, yeah.' Marcus thought, pulling a pillow under his armpit. 'Like, we're gonna have to get the old girl talking to my crumbly Pa again, y'know.'

'You mean play crucial Cupid, man?'

'Yougottit, child.'

'Pukka and rad idea, homeboy!' Wiltsher enthused. 'Like, howee gonna do it, chill dood?'

'Er . . . yeah, like I haven't had time to y'know work that one out,' Marcus said feebly.

'Oh.'

There was another long silence.

'Like, Pa's planning a scuzzy eight hours fly-casting tomorrow, man,' Marcus pointed out through the gloom. 'We'll have to get the dusty doods hip-hopping and chucking cheesies like Adam addicts before then, man. Otherwise it's raasclaat rod dipping, y'know.'

'Sorry, I don't understand what you're saying, Marcus.' Wiltsher sat up and squinted across the unlit room.

'Get my wrinklies talking again tomorrow,' hissed Marcus. 'Otherwise Ma will needle Pa to death and basically we'll be throwing back minnows and hooking the old boy's maggots for the next two weeks.'

'Oh, yeah, happening.' Wiltsher nodded. 'Now I'm reading your tag, def rapper.'

'Tubular.' Marcus sighed with relief. 'Like, we'll crash out on it tonight, man, and work out a happening POA in the morning, y'know.'

'Er – yeah.'

'Like, we'll have to get up seriously previous tomorrow, man.'

'What time, dood?' Wiltsher picked up his alarm clock and

stared at the luminous figures. Mickey was bashing Pluto over the head with his long hand.

'It'll have to be half nine, man.' Marcus sighed heavily at the sacrifice.

Wiltsher set his clock and wriggled back into his sleeping bag.

'Night, dood.'

'C'ya, man.'

When Tash reeled back into the bedroom, Max was well ensconced in the biscuit tin, chuckling over something he was reading.

She froze in horror as she saw it was Todd's letter and sidled towards her towel in case she had to make a quick exit to the shower. In her drunken haste, she picked up Max's chinos and wrapped them around her neck by mistake.

'This is hysterical, have you read it?' Max laughed, holding up the letter and starting on a Garibaldi.

Tash shook her head nervously, wondering what terrible indiscretions Todd could have made. Had he mentioned drugging her on Friday night? That was another of her memory's rather vague blurs.

Max paused as he noticed she was wearing his trousers as a muffler, shrugged and carried on. 'This guy, Todd – was he staying here? He wants you to look after his dog. He's got the most amazing literary style.' He looked at the note again. 'He says you always struck him as a doggy woman, that Rooter – is that the dog? – has some rorty habits, chunders if he eats tinned meat, gets scungy if he doesn't have regular hose-downs, likes the chilled article at least once a week and is a ripper cobber if you treat him right.'

'Oh yes?' Tash was weak with relief. 'Anything else?'

'Yeah.' Max swallowed some more Garibaldi. 'There's a postscript. Hang on – here it is. *When you go back home to Pongolia, Tash, don't worry about putting Rooter in quarrie, he'll just love it. Only tell them to make sure he gets a bitch or two in his pen cos, like his master, he's a corking sack artist and goes into a moodie if he hasn't dipped his snorker for a while.* Is this guy for real? He sounds like one of Mikey's family.'

Tash smiled stiffly and started to woozily pull off her clothes. Thank God, he hadn't mentioned any of her Friday night activities. Then she stopped dead and turned to look at Max.

'You mean to say Todd wants me to dogsit Rooter?'

Max was making himself a pâté sandwich. Since he'd eaten her meal that night as well as his, Tash thought this was a bit excessive.

'Seems to,' he nodded, his mouth still full of biscuit. 'He says that Rooter's a thank-you present for cleaning up his act – what on earth did you do to him? – and if you ever want to rack down or rage all night in London, to ring someone called Amanda's number. It's here at the top.' He held out the letter to show her. 'Bloody stupid seeing as you already live in London. At least till we go to the States.'

'Er, Max, I've got something to tell—' Tash fell over sideways trying to take off her leggings.

'Strikes me,' Max ignored her and started on the sandwich, 'that this Todd character's got a bloody nerve.' He munched on a tough bit of pumpernickel, so Tash tried again.

'Max, forget the dog for a minute, I—' She was having difficulty getting up off the floor.

'I mean, dogs are really expensive to keep,' Max went on emphatically, 'and I can't see the cats taking to one much – Rooter's not that big rug on legs, is he?'

'Forget the bloody dog!' Tash snapped, finally standing up before tripping over the towel stand.

'Are you drunk?' Max regarded her critically as she groped for support and stumbled into the wall.

Mustering dignity, Tash disentangled herself from a lamp cable.

'Max, I've taken the job with the Moncrieffs,' she blurted.

The patronising smile on Max's face slid away. He very slowly dropped the remainder of his sandwich in the biscuit tin and carefully shut the lid.

Tash rubbed her chin nervously. She'd told him over her fifth or sixth glass of wine that night that she wouldn't take it. But Gus had made her laugh so much on the phone with Penny shouting messages in the background, and they'd been so kind about being woken up, that she'd suddenly wanted it again more than anything.

'Max, I think we really need to talk about us,' Tash faltered, perching on the end of the bed.

'I just can't *believe* you could do that to me!' Max exploded. 'I really need you right now and you're pissing off to bloody Berkshire!'

'Max, this isn't working—'

'Don't you love me at all?' he went on, not listening. 'Because I love you. Really *love* you – and believe me, it took a lot for me to come over here and say that. You really hurt me in London – so I go away to try and put myself together. Then I get this letter that says you're sorry, that you love me. I fly here, I sacrifice my pride, I open my heart to you and what do you do?'

'Max—' Tash was beginning to feel sick.

'*What* do you do?' Max's eyebrows were ramming against his hairline. 'You throw it back in my pissing face. You say you love me, agree to marry me. Then two seconds later, you're doing this. Do you like totally fucking me up?' He blinked at her. 'Have you and Lisette O'Shaughnessy been swapping notes on how to make a man cry? Rumour has it, Niall was falling apart tonight because that cow's chasing Dad. Is that what you want me to do, huh?'

Biting back tears, Tash couldn't answer.

'You'd better take your shower.' Max pulled the sheet up to his neck and turned towards the wall. 'We'll talk about it when you can see straight. I've ordered a cab for four tomorrow. We're booked on the afternoon train to Paris.' The tight ball of his back showed that this was his last word till he'd 'fugged it out', his phrase for a long, simmering sulk.

'I'm so sorry,' she whispered, almost to herself, as she crept away. 'It's all my fault.'

She only got as far as the landing side of the door before she broke down. Leaning against it, she slid to the floor and sobbed into her knees.

When Michael tried to get into bed, he found Cass face-down, spread out like a starfish with each limb reaching to a far corner of their double bed, determinedly pretending to be asleep.

Propping his pipe on the bedside table beside his Le Carré, he sighed loudly and scratched his bald pate.

'Er, Cass, old girl?'

She didn't answer, her eyes clamped tightly shut like a small child during a scary moment in *Dr Who*.

'Budge up a bit, old thing.' Michael tucked in his striped pyjama top and tried to edge under the duvet.

Growling slightly, Cass clenched her fingers round the corners of the mattress and refused to move, clamped firmly to the bed.

'Come on, old girl,' Michael puffed impatiently, 'don't be bloody childish, huh?'

He made another faltering attempt to clamber in, but Cass was clinging on tightly, still muttering under her breath like a bush-tailed cat.

'What?' Michael blinked, not believing his ears.

'The chaise, Michael,' Cass repeated, not opening her eyes. 'The *chaise*.'

Michael scratched his head and glanced behind him at the old chintz chaise-longue that he'd been thus far draping his trousers over each night. Then he blinked. It was made up with typical Cass care – the pillow plumped, neat hospital corners in the sheets, a small striped beige pile folded at one end.

'And put on those clean pyjamas,' Cass hissed, reaching out a hand and snapping off the bedside light.

Wiping her tear-stained face, Tash crawled along the corridor to have a shower. As she passed Niall's door she saw that the light was on under it and nearly broke down again by the skirting board. Was he in there fugging out far, far more important things than poor, unwanted Rooter and taking a job with the Moncrieffs?

Suddenly Tash froze, wondering if Lisette was in there too. At the restaurant it had been clear to all that the flirtation between Lisette and Max's father was hotting up. But creeping back from calling the Moncrieffs, Tash had seen Lucian making himself a single mug of hot chocolate in the kitchen.

She remembered Max saying that Niall was falling apart with jealousy. The kiss by the pool was just a way to pay Lisette back, she realised hopelessly.

She listened very quietly outside the door, but heard nothing. Realising that if anyone walked past she would look pretty odd crouching in nothing but an old shirt and make-up stained towel outside Niall's door, she resumed crawling to the bathroom, so tired and low she could hardly see straight.

'Here,' Lucian kicked the door shut with the back of his heel and carried the mug over to Lisette. 'One cocoa. I can't believe you drink the stuff – it's packed with cholesterol.'

'Thanks.' Pointedly picking the skin off the surface, Lisette put it down on the windowsill untouched. 'It helps me sleep. I'm out of pills.'

'They're even lousier for you,' Lucian smiled. 'You should treat yourself better. I would. Goodnight, then.' He pecked her on the cheek and turned to leave.

'Lucian?'

'Mmm?' Pausing at the door, he glanced over his shoulder. His face gave nothing away.

Lisette drifted forwards and ran her nails lightly through the grey wings of hair above his ears. Stretching up, she kissed him on the mouth. 'Goodnight.'

After he'd gone, she lit a cigarette and tipped the cocoa down the sink. She didn't know who had occupied the little attic room before her, but it reeked of aftershave. The bed had been stripped and a pile of folded sheets left on top, ready to be made up. Tossing them on to the floor, Lisette kicked off her shoes and sat down.

The previous occupier had also positioned the cracked, dusty mirror so that they could watch themselves in bed.

She wriggled further towards the unmade-up pillows and admired her reflection. Closing her eyes, she lay back and waited for the knock on the door.

Niall slept unsoundly alone in his own bed. He had violent dreams of turning up at Tash's wedding just as the vicar was asking if there was any just impediment, only to find when he screamed out 'yes', that underneath the veil stood Lisette, grinning foxily in Tash's place.

He struggled out of bed and poured himself a glass of Badoit.

Someone was having a shower next door, singing 'House of the Rising Sun' in the most appallingly flat alto.

The fizzy water was lukewarm. Holding back from retching, Niall pulled open the window and looked out at the night sky. It was literally jumbled with stars, like a Paul McCartney crowd in Wembley Stadium holding up lighters during 'Hey Jude'. They certainly weren't there to support the shower crooner, who had moved on to Zadoc the Priest in a strangled cat wail.

A light breeze lifted his hair and chilled his eyes. The pots of flowers on his sill, dried out in the recent heat, were providing an impromptu maraca accompaniment to Handel. Niall edged himself on to the sill and sat between them, one knee drawn up to his chin.

Lighting his last cigarette and inhaling so deeply that the sparks flew back in his face, he began to wish on each individual star that Tash loved him.

The pelting water had cleared Tash's head. She stalked back across the landing positively spitting with indignation about Max's attitude.

She'd just spent the best part of her shower, teeth-cleaning, face-washing and spot-examining routine thinking up absolutely brilliant things to say to him about how unreasonable he was being. Pressurising her into marrying him, expecting her to drop everything and go to the States, borrowing all her money and refusing to talk about the shambles their relationship was in. She would try not to hurt him – she'd say how much he meant to her – but he was being whiney and manipulative and she wasn't going to stand for it any longer.

Tash paused by the landing mirror to practise a couple of facial expressions and amazingly witty put-downs.

Full of invigorated, inebriated enthusiasm she burst back through the door and opened her mouth for the first of her great one-liners.

He was asleep, his snoring not yet at fever pitch but a gentle comforting hum. His thumb was firmly between his lips, clean hair tousled, one arm flung to the side as if to welcome her. Beside him, on her pillow, was a note scribbled in her eyeliner on the back of Todd's letter.

Forgive me for being a resentful sod. I love you.

Instead of spinning me tails, make me a horsehair shirt with all the fluff you rake from your nags in Berkshire.

Wake me up.

Tash felt her anger start to evaporate.

She didn't have the heart to wake him purposely but, still chewing over the odd really genius comment, she heaved herself cumbersomely into bed with a very loud sigh just in case. Max didn't wake, so she moved his outstretched arm to one side and let it drop from a fair height. Still he snoozed.

She spent a long time plumping her pillows, nicking the entire sheet to bundle herself in, pummelling down into the mattress and waving her legs about to find the most comfortable aspect.

Max sighed contentedly, ground his teeth and, with a great shedding of biscuit crumbs, rolled over to put a warm, heavy arm around her before starting to snore more vibrantly, a funny little smile on his sleeping face.

Tash breathed out sulkily through her nose, turned her back on him, knocked three books off her bedside table, rammed him hard with her bottom and waited.

Nothing. And now she'd forgotten what she was going to say.

I'll go back over it and then push him totally off the bed, she decided.

While she was polishing up the sharper points of her home-hitting quips, Tash was irritated to find herself sinking in and out of sleep. In the peaceful cocoon of the dark, snoring room, drowsiness crept away with her conscious thoughts tucked under its arm. The dry mouth and temple-nudging of a hang-over had already started to loom large. Nestling back into Max's warmth, she decided to tell him tomorrow.

61

'Wiltsher . . . ?'

'Leave me alone, Mum.'

'No, man – it's me, Hennessy. What time is it?'

'Er, hang on . . . eeuch, one of your socks is on my pillow, Hennessy man . . . er, about ten, I think.'

'Raaschit, man! We like overslept, y'know.'

Marcus jumped out of bed and searched around for yesterday's Y-fronts, crashing into the wardrobe door and treading on the surfacing Wiltsher in his wake.

'Keep your feet off the, like, equipment, y'know.' Wiltsher groaned, rubbing his head so that the rats-tails stuck up on end.

'Get up, you grody,' Marcus demanded, dragging on his two-tone baggy jeans back to front. 'We've, like, gotta think up a plan, man. We've gotta reconcile my parents, y'know. 'Cos if we like don't, y'know what it means, man?'

'Hmmph?'

Marcus put a hairbrush in his mouth to look like his father's pipe. 'Let the bloody rod do the bloody work, boy. Right – question sixteen: who scored the most number of bloody sixes in the 1986 one-day against Sri Lanka at Headingley?'

'Yeah?' Wiltsher contemplated staying in the comfort of his chrysalis sleeping bag for a few more hours. Fishing wasn't such a bad hobby, he mused, even if Pa Hennessy was ranting on throughout about the social benefits of a stint in a good regiment. In fact, a lifetime of reading J.R. Hartley in between parasailing with the Marines seemed totally happening to Wiltsher compared with getting out of bed right now.

'I think I'll, like, pass on this one, man,' he sighed, settling back into his nylon pod.

Marcus stood on Wiltsher's neck.

'Okay, like . . . eiigh . . . I was just . . . heeuch . . .'

'Joking?' suggested Marcus.

Wiltsher, rapidly turning Marlboro red, nodded.

Marcus smiled and removed his foot to pull on his trainers.

'Like, now for the plan. Fwor!' Marcus sniffed his trainers and elected for a pair of wedge-heeled DMs. 'The M.C. Hennessy crucial groove mix to, like, sweeten my wrinklies and stop the fishing expeditions.' He started to throw clothes at Wiltsher. 'I call it the TACKLE, man: The Angling Cupids Kindling Love Ecstasy.'

'That's, like, heavy and serious shit, man,' Wiltsher gasped admiringly.

'I know.' Marcus looked smug. 'Now, like, hear the action. We're going to forge a relationship, man. What we do is . . .'

Later that morning, Hugo walked away from phoning Gus Moncrieff with a very satisfied grin pulling at his cheeks. He sauntered on to the balcony overlooking the pool and leaned his palms against the stone ledge, staring out at the faded haze of quilted hills beyond the house.

So Tash had accepted the job, he mused happily. His long shot had landed the bird right at his loader's paws.

Hugo laughed out loud, throwing his head back with glee and punching the air in a victorious high five before checking over his shoulder in case anyone was watching.

Tash was leaving for London that afternoon. Hugo had deliberately planned to spend the day away from the manoir, looking at some horses with M-C. He knew he must sit tight and wait until she came to Berkshire. With Max hovering like an eager wicketkeeper, he hadn't been able to have a word alone with her in twenty-four hours. But Alexandra had assured him that the engagement was a terrible mistake and that Tash was far keener on him than he'd dared imagine.

'Darling, she's been in love with you for years,' she'd encouraged. 'Just wait for all this business with Max to wash over. She loathes being crowded. Why not write her a letter or something? Make it jokey, but pepper it with romantic quotes. I promise you, she'll adore it.'

The only poetry Hugo knew involved 'A young lady from Pinge', had five lines and was as blue as one of Lady Thatcher's twin-sets, so Alexandra had kindly jotted down a few apt lines.

Hugo glanced at his watch and winced. He was meeting M-C in ten minutes. He'd better get a move on.

Taking out a pen from the pocket of his navy Musto, he wandered through the double doors to the China Room and settled down in front of Alexandra's scruffy walnut writing desk.

How odd, someone seemed to have been trying out a bit of forging on all the scrap paper, he noticed.

Hugo examined the practised signatures closely. There were two distinct words. Lots of repetitive, mean little scrawls ending with an extravagant loop, which were totally illegible. The other was a clear, round, schoolgirl's hand. *Cass.*

Shrugging without interest, Hugo pushed the jottings to one side and, extracting a clean sheet of thick cream paper, began to write *Darling Tash.*

'Have you worked with children for long?' Sophia glanced from the clipboard notes in front of her to the interviewee's long red nails.

'Oui, madame.'

'And you also cook, I believe?' Sophia eyed the girl's fluffy blonde hair and wide blue eyes, jotting *no bra* on to her list.

'Oui, madame.' The girl was staring out of the study window at Hugo, who was climbing into the Peugeot wearing the blackest of dark glasses.

'And experience with horses?'

'Oui, madame.'

'Good.' Sophia noticed the fashionable pink suede mules showing slender brown ankles. 'And what about your English?'

'Oui, madame.'

'No,' Sophia sighed. 'I mean to what level have you learnt it?'

'Oui, madame.'

Growling through her teeth, Sophia looked at the ceiling after she'd gone.

'Oh, God!'

'Thought she was rather charming.' Ben had gone very pink.

Sophia shot him a withering glance. 'Ben, if you're going to think then please do so quietly.'

'Bien sûr, Lisette must stay wiz us.' Pascal beamed at Lucian cheerfully over the debris of breakfast preparations. 'I say to 'er yesterday that she and Niyall, they are ower guests for as long as they want for eet.'

'Ah.' Lucian wrinkled his grey eyes awkwardly and ruffled his hair, wet from swimming, aware that he would have to approach the subject slightly more subtly.

Alexandra, who was searching for her shoes to go and buy bread in the village, groaned weakly into the coat stand. More guests, more money. While she hated her family leaving so soon, she was equally unwilling to put up all their peculiar friends indefinitely.

'Er – I think – perhaps – there could be a bit of a problem there, Pascal—' Lucian faltered as he towelled his head.

'Eh?' Pascal was giving his all to beating some eggs.

'You see, I don't think Lisette is exactly keen to stick around in close proximity to Niall.'

Pascal laughed. 'Oui, oui. I know what she means. The man would be ver' good company if 'e wash quelquefois, comprenez?'

Lucian smiled weakly and ploughed on. 'I spoke to Lisette last night and she mentioned that she'd find it extremely uncomfortable spending any more time under the same roof as Niall. It seems they've been unable to reconcile their differences.'

'Oh, poor Niall.' Alexandra stopped her search and looked up. 'What a desperate shame.'

'Yes, quite.' Lucian, not matching her gaze, started frantically towelling his ears. 'But you see the awkwardness of the situation.'

'Bien sûr,' Pascal nodded sadly, still concentrating on the eggs.

'We can't just boot Niall out,' Alexandra insisted, turning to Pascal, who was now reading the paper upside down without noticing that he was depositing beaten egg straight into Rooter's enthusiastically gaping mouth.

'He's going through a very rough patch at the moment,' she explained to Lucian, adding, 'I promised Matty I'd look after him.' She fingered the pendant Matty had given her on leaving: a fat, grimacing effigy of a rain forest god carved in stone by endangered Brazilian tribesmen. Although Pascal claimed it looked just like his first wife, Alexandra valued it immensely.

'Oui, chérie.' Pascal looked apologetically at Lucian over his half-moon specs.

'Lisette's in a crisis, too,' Lucian urged. 'All her possessions are tied up in the States with a crook called Colt Shapiro.' He pulled the towel round his neck. 'She came to the party attached to a very jet-set rabble who've promptly pushed off and left her here. She's got no money, clothes, legal representation, noth—'

'She's got herself out of worse plights than that, now,' said a mild voice.

The three of them looked up in alarm to see Niall wandering out of the laundry and across the lobby, clutching two odd socks and a very creased shirt which had been dyed baby pink in the wash. Lisette still had his towelling robe so he was sporting a faded t-shirt and some very jazzy boxer shorts.

'It's all right,' he smiled kindly, trying to ease their embarrassment. 'I'll not be hanging around longer than today. If I don't get back to London soon, I'll never work again.' He rubbed his unwashed hair back from his face, showing red eyes sunken behind huge black circles and more stubble than a cornfield in autumn.

Pascal cleared his throat and busied himself with what was left of the eggs. Desperate to fill the pause, Alexandra asked Niall how he had slept and then regretted it – he looked as though he hadn't slept in weeks.

But Niall just smiled. 'Fine, thanks. You've been very good to me Alexandra – Pascal.' He helped himself to a bowl of coffee and moved slowly towards the door, pausing beside Lucian. 'You know, if you could be looking after Lisette, I think she needs it; she's been through a rough time in the States. Although my guess is she'll land on her feet soon enough.' He looked at Lucian and lifted his eyebrows cryptically.

Lucian fought a terrible urge to apologise. After what Lisette had told him last night, he should be preparing to duff Niall up. But he couldn't help feeling there was a terrible sadness in Niall which didn't quite accord with Lisette's side of the story.

He was strongly attracted to Lisette – she had just the sort of oiled-back confidence he loved in ambitious women – but he didn't entirely trust her, and certainly wasn't planning to make any serious move on her until he was sure she wasn't flirting out of spite. Despite her flattering interest, he'd done no more than peck her on the cheek yesterday, burying himself in paperwork once he got to bed. He valued being a single man in New York far too highly to respond instantly to a desirable woman coming on strong. It would be like stealing coal in France to pay excess baggage on when travelling to Newcastle. He needed the chance to examine the coal closely and see if it really did, as he hoped, shelter a diamond.

'I can help her get back to the States, but I've got some business to wrap up here first,' he told Niall, trying to sound practical and uninterested. Keen to switch quickly to a less volatile topic, he ploughed on, 'Besides, I want to get to know my son's future in-laws some more. Since the happy couple are about to leave to sort themselves out in England, someone's got to stick around and tell Alexandra how happy Max is going to make her daughter.' He smiled at Alexandra and Pascal, anxious to ingratiate himself after causing such a sticky gaffe.

Niall winced and nodded. He'd gone so pale he almost blended into the whitewashed wall.

'I'm sure Lisette will be grateful. Thanks,' was all he said, his voice taut with emotion. Leaving his socks on the table, he left the room almost at the run.

'Oh shit,' Lucian muttered.

He looked up at the d'Eblouirs. Pascal had returned cheerfully to cooking, whistling through his teeth as he worked. But Alexandra was staring at the door Niall had just shot through. She had a perplexed expression on her face.

'You don't think,' Lucian looked up at her, flashing his charming smile, which lacked sincerity when he was nervous, 'that I've upset him?'

Alexandra nodded and his smile dropped with an almost audible clank.

She gave a funny half-laugh. 'But not, I somehow think, for the reasons you're imagining.' She looked at Pascal and, for once, he twigged too.

'Tash, I say eet before, she ees funny girl.' He put his arm around his wife's shoulders and touched her sleek hair comfortingly.

'Yes, terrific sense of humour,' Lucian agreed enthusiastically, glad to be off the subject of Niall O'Shaughnessy – whom he thought dangerously unbalanced. 'She's a stunner – you know I'm amazed and delighted Max has gone for such a sassy, independent girl. According to his mother – my first wife, Barbara, you'll probably meet her soon – he normally dates such drippy types. Babs told me the last one was a complete wet mute – some photographer, I think. Tash is so wonderfully lively and fun, isn't she?'

Alexandra and Pascal hardly appeared to be listening. Pascal seemed very amused about something. Alexandra looked pensive.

Rooter, having polished off the beaten eggs, had both huge front paws up on the table and was starting on the smoked ham with greedy, chomping jaws.

'Max is happier than I've ever known him.' Lucian carried on giving a summary of Tash's extraordinary effect on his son.

He omitted mentioning that he and Max hadn't spoken for the two years leading up to his last visit. Not, in fact, since

Lucian had discovered that while he was secretly slipping Max the odd thousand (to help him pay off a crippling overdraft dating back to his university days) without letting Babs find out and up her claim for alimony, Babs was doing exactly the same in reverse, trying to avoid Lucian cottoning on to the fact she was shacked up with a wealthy sports promoter. Discreet enquiries had also revealed that Max did not have an overdraft at all; he'd cleared it all in his final term by putting his hall fees on an accumulator at Epsom. He, in fact, used the money his parents provided to bum around Australia and bring back two freeloading friends whom Babs loathed.

Lucian also failed to mention that Max was now in such dire financial straits that he'd upturned three tables and punched a wall when Lucian refused to lend him money in the States. Or that he hadn't even mentioned Tash until they'd met up with Eddie and heard the description of Alexandra's idyllic house in the Loire.

All this Lucian left out as he told the d'Eblouirs just what a loving and well-adjusted lad he was, and how strung out on Tash he'd become. He felt a degree of guilt, but figured he owed his son some loyalty. He was also unwilling to relinquish Pascal – and possibly James French – as potentially fruitful business contacts.

'Max simply adores Tash, you know,' he finished.

'Yes, Eddie told me that last night,' Alexandra said faintly, beginning to realise just how difficult things must have been for her haphazard daughter. 'I am a stupid woman,' she sighed to no one in particular, blanching at the memory of how encouraging she'd been to Hugo.

Lucian, moving on to Max's sporting achievements, promptly shut up. In the silence that followed, Rooter could be heard polishing off his pilfered ham.

Fortunately, at that moment Marcus and Wiltsher came whooping along the little corridor which ran from the China Room, ready to fall on breakfast.

'You're up early, boys,' Alexandra greeted them with feigned jollity.

'Yeah, man. We're celebrating our new-found independence, man,' smiled Wiltsher, searching the chaotic table for something edible. 'These are seriously wicked.' He picked up a pair of bobbing antennae on a plastic alice band discarded by Polly.

'Like, we can safely say, Aunt Lex,' Marcus cackled throatily, 'that, like, y'know, the only angling that'll go on this savvy'll be Ma fishing for compliments.'

Wiltsher giggled over his orange juice, showering a slavering spaniel. 'And Hennessy's old man *casting* aspersions on Ginger Harcourt's manhood.' He tried on the antennae.

'And Ma laying *bait* for Valérie.'

Alexandra looked at them blankly.

'Is there any bread, man?' Wiltsher asked brightly.

'Oh Lord, I forgot!' Alexandra sat down, totally drained of energy. Tash, money, Eddie's new wife whom no one had time to speak to properly, Sophia's nanny, weddings, Matty's confused friend and now Cass and Michael. What was happening to her lovely family reunion?

'I'll go to the village,' offered Lucian, desperate to get away from the madhouse.

'You're so cool putting everyone up like this,' Marcus smiled sweetly at Alexandra and then Pascal. 'We've had, like a, y'know, mondo def and crucial time, man. Haven't we, Wiltsher, dood?'

'What?' Wiltsher looked up from spooning jam into his mouth, saw Marcus winking, and nodded vigorously, his antennae bobbing. 'Totally wicked.'

Alexandra brightened. 'Have you really?'

They both nodded in unison, like plastic dogs in the back of a Ford Capri. Wiltsher had jam all over his chin, Marcus had ink-stains on his hands.

'Thank you, boys,' beamed Alexandra, feeling choked.

'Er – Aunt Lex, man,' Marcus started speaking with loaded sincerity. 'I've been meaning to, like, ask you something.'

'Ah ha!' Pascal, who'd been listening in, turned back to a new batch of eggs with a knowing smile.

'Anything you want, Marcus,' offered Alexandra, hoping it wasn't going to be a very expensive question.

'Well, like, y'see the doods – that is, guys from school and that – they, like, enjoyed the rave – that is, party – so much that I kind of, like, thought you wouldn't mind, man, seeing as Ma says you're so rich and that, if – er – like, next year . . .'

In the lobby, Niall stopped listening and turned away with hunched shoulders. They obviously weren't going to mention Tash again.

Back in his room, he unearthed his old black jeans from a Himalayan pile of clothes. Firmly hooked to the fly button by a tangled tassel was the slinky black dress Lisette had been wearing on Friday night.

How typical, she always led me by the groin, he thought with a rueful smile.

Niall sighed as he unpicked the knot, careful not to tear the dress, which had probably cost more than the contents, fittings and coat-hangers of his own wardrobe at home. Great wafts of Fidgi kept floating up and assailing him, sending his senses reeling into orbit.

He couldn't bear Lisette in his sight but certain things had a Pavlovian effect on him, triggering off great pangs of longing. Slim necks clear of hair, tiny, snaky waists, tortoiseshell-rimmed glasses, glossy tights, tulip-bud lips. It was so shallow, but it had been the sum total of his attraction to Amanda.

Yet while he could analyse his fascination with Lisette, almost turn it around in his hand and examine it like a flawed gem, his understanding of his feelings for Tash was as impossible to hold in one palm as the unmined depths of a South African hillside.

He'd totally failed to follow Matty's advice and speak to her. By hanging around yesterday, all he'd succeeded in doing was pushing her in a pool and groping her when she climbed out. And he knew he would be crucified to stick around and watch her leave with Max. No one wanted him to stay on at the manoir, anyway.

Totally dispirited, he started loading his strewn clothes into a couple of dog-eared bags. He'd have to hitch back. Lisette had left him with crippling debts when she'd walked out. It was one of the reasons he had taken a tacky US backed no-brain spinner in Nîmes instead of the worthy George Eliot adaptation offered him by the Beeb. Triple the money, one hundredth of the concentration required. He could burst into tears on set, roll up drunk and act as though he had an urgent appointment to get to without much haranguing. Or so he had thought before he was fired. His fees from that had doubtless done an about-turn on the way to his statement. All his money was tied up with creditors in England. He had no travellers' cheques left, his plastic was full up, he'd even borrowed from Sally to buy Tash's books.

He looked in the mirror. At least no one would recognise him now.

'Oh, Shaughnessy.

> 'O, never give the heart outright,
> For they, for all smooth lips can say,
> Have given their hearts up to the play.
> And who could play it well enough
> If deaf and dumb and blind with love?
> He that made this knows all the cost,
> For he gave all his heart and lost.'

London had never seemed so unattractive. He didn't think he could bear to be in the same city as Tash. Let her have it all for her home-making, cake-baking, 'gainst all others forsaking, domesticity, he mused. He was going to Ireland to visit his mum.

62

Cass couldn't help noticing the note peeping out of Michael's sports jacket. It was so difficult not to. He would leave the damn thing hanging over the back of her dressing-table chair. And the piece of paper was virtually falling out of the inside pocket. Especially after Cass had prodded it. In fact, it did fall out when she shook the jacket vigorously. So did Michael's keys, lighter, pipe tobacco and three furry Extra Strong Mints. Another dubious sign. When did Michael last want to freshen his breath?

Hastily shoving the scattered contents back, Cass lingered over the note.

Splashing sounds and strains of 'I Vow To Thee My Country' were echoing through the bathroom door, indicating that Michael was still laboriously soaping between his toes. Cass flipped open the note, quite sure it was an inordinately boring fishing itinerary or similar.

It was a letter. Cass froze and reached for her reading glasses, which were hanging on a chain around her neck. Michael's handwriting was still ridiculously difficult to decipher even after years of marriage. With middle-age spread and hardening of the arteries had come compression of the copperplate. Cass pronged herself in the eye with her specs before starting to read.

What she saw made her clutch her chest in shock and lean on the dressing table for support.

Valérie! Of all the women he could possibly choose to pen a

mot d'amour to, that bulbous, blousy, buxom Belial! So it *was* true. While her own world was falling apart on Friday night, he was buried in the unfathomable bulk of Valérie's bosom.

She quickly reread some of the sentences.

> *. . . the most exciting, invigorating and totally bloody mind-blowing moment of my life . . . my bloody rocket exploded in ecstasy . . . my old girl doesn't bloody understand me . . .*

Cass bit her lip and fought tears. It was so unlike him. He'd never told her about his wild side. These words weren't ones ever used by the Michael she knew. He must have hidden his true self for all these years.

She started to read the bit that really hurt. The sentences that made it totally impossible to confront him with this.

> *. . . cannot happen again. You must understand that, although she often makes my life a bloody misery, I will love my wife unswervingly to the grave. What happened on Friday night was bloody heaven in a marriage of cold shoulders and migraines night after night. But it was also one hell of a mistake. Cassandra is my main woman, my numero bloody uno in perpertuity. You, my sweet, were just a weak man's sojourn.*
>
> *With regards,*
>
> *Michael Hennessy, FREconS, VD.*

'So unlike him,' Cass sobbed quietly, crumpling the note in her hands. 'He wouldn't spell perpetuity wrong unless he were terribly upset. Oh, poor, poor Michael. How lonely he must feel. I never realised I was so cold.'

She looked down at the note and realised she couldn't put the creased, tear-stained paper back in his jacket. Stuffing it in her dressing-gown pocket, she swore to bring him back from Coventry to a hero's welcome. If she was loving enough, he might forget all about the letter.

In the bathroom, Michael Hennessy was forming a plan of action second only in complexity to the Dunkirk landings. He vowed not to tell Cass that he'd found the letter she was planning to send to Ginger Harcourt, thanking him for his impassioned poetry, gently rebuffing his advances yet suggesting they perhaps meet up for lunch next time she was in London; she would tell Michael that she was meeting a girlfriend to do another wing of the National Portrait Gallery.

'She will bloody not,' muttered Michael to his reflection, carefully steering his razor around his pipe. He'd ripped the letter into tiny shreds and fed it down the loo before his bath.

The thing that hurt, he fumed, was that she was so bloody honourable and gracious about it, explaining that she wouldn't dream of embarking on an affair with a boy like Ginger, however beautiful, gentle and besotted he were. That not only would it be unfair to Ginger but that it would be doubly cruel to Michael and her children.

Marcus, the letter had claimed, *is a talented, brave and intelligent boy who, missing out on love and attention from his crusty old father, would be devastated if I let him down with such reckless self-indulgence.* There followed a long and hurtful reference to Michael's refusal to buy his younger son the car he so deserved. *Michael himself wouldn't care much*, the letter went on, *but he needs me to polish his trophies and run his baths, which are the only tasks I feel I can still perform for him without being bullied away.*

'Bloody ouch!' Michael cut himself for the third time. He was beginning to accumulate a Santa Claus beard of white antiseptic. He had to cool off or she would guess that he'd cottoned on to her little façade.

Cass had hardly mentioned herself. Her selfless cares lay only with her husband and offspring. Especially, for some reason, Marcus and his acute hatred of fishing.

Michael despised himself for thinking her such a selfish, society-driven snob of late; for sulking at her unreasonable demands instead of seeing that they were the last desperate pitches for attention. He resolved to correct that before she did anything silly.

She might take her bloody sister's example and start casting around for attractive, passionate Frogs, he reflected anxiously. Anton had been hovering with intent just recently.

But what did one do if one was going to be romantic? Michael stared at his steamy reflection, perplexed. Roses and chocolates, he supposed. But those were also adulterers' guilt presents. Expensive jewellery was an option Michael dismissed; that was for flash nouveaux who didn't have an exorbitant crammer to pay for. Then he hit upon an idea.

Lisette moved over to the light of the window to put in her contact lenses. She hadn't brought any saline solution with her so had whipped someone else's from the bathroom. The change in chemicals stung at her eyes.

She suspected that the general consensus of opinion would place her in bed with Lucian last night. But when, after an hour, he hadn't knocked on the door, Lisette had sulkily grabbed her clothes and decided to swap rooms. If he had stolen upstairs later, he wouldn't have found her there. The thought made Lisette smile. Like most people who prided themselves on being monumentally late on all occasions, she hated being kept waiting herself.

So, overpowered by the smell of Kouros, she had been driven downstairs in the early hours to the bedroom recently vacated by Matty and Sally. It hadn't been tidied since they'd left and last night she'd shared a duvet with a grey bra, two pen lids, a broken-spined David Lodge paperback and a leaflet on ante-natal clinics in Richmond. Lisette was feeling very anti-natal at the moment.

That was another reason for making a pitch at Lucian Merriot, she mulled. Men of his age, although bent on rediscovering their sexual drive, seldom wanted the nappy-changing, teething and broken nights to go with it.

The more she got to know him, the more she liked the idea of sticking close to this debonair, off pat ex-pat. He might not be the most exciting of prospects but he was secure, dependable, rich and consequently far better qualified to get her rocky career back on line than Niall, who was absurdly talented and in demand but monumentally unbalanced. She needed security and back-up now.

Niall's defection hurt – her pride was more shattered than she cared to admit when her old, unwanted faithful had finally turned and bitten her on the nose. But she'd learnt to reason with failure; a wildly pre-eminent female producer had once told her, 'Honey, you're trying to walk in size fifteen footsteps – it's a bitch eat dog industry. You pause for emotion, for family, for relationships, you watch your future in this business go up in boardroom cigar smoke, capeesh?'

Lisette knew if she let herself mourn for Niall, for their lost child, for gorgeous, feckless Colt, she'd cry until the only thing left in the world was a lone dove desperately searching for an olive twig. And crying ruined your looks. From now on she was planning to eat, drink and make Merriot.

Someone was warbling a deep bass rendition of 'New York, New York' in the bathroom across the landing.

'They're playing our opportunism, darling,' she smiled to herself.

With one lens in, she watched in fascination as Niall appeared out of a side turret carrying two holdalls, wavered by an overgrown flower bed, turned as if to go back into the house, paused, scratched his head, walked into the flower bed, fought his way out, scratched his head again and started walking unsteadily towards the drive.

When he reached the newly laid tarmac, he stopped and gazed over his shoulder, still seemingly undecided. His shirt was on inside out, cuffs undone, jeans roe-grey with dust. Lisette had never seen him look such a mess.

Then he shook himself and set off, almost running, between the tall poplars towards the gate.

'Bye bye,' she whispered cynically, slapping her fingers against her palm in a mock wave.

She'd win him back one day, just to prove she could, she told herself. But he was too pathetic to want right now. And Lisette had a sly idea why. Reaching for her kid boots, she determined to put one of them into his little side-kick once and for all.

* * *

'Oh Michael!' Cass came rushing out of the bathroom, pink in the face with excitement.

'Yes, my love?' Michael, for once pipeless, looked up from arranging some wild flowers on his wife's bedside table, looking furtive because he was afraid she might think he was being cissy.

Cass noticed what he was doing and looked even more delighted.

'What you wrote on the mirror – it's just come up in the steam from my bath – did you mean it?'

''Course I bloody meant it,' Michael croaked and then smiled. 'Thanks for laying out my clothes. Bloody decent of you considering I've been so—'

'No, darling – it's me that's been beastly. Sending you out fishing like that just because I had a hangover and booting you out of bed last night over some silly argument about picking up the tab at the restaurant. I was going to apologise as soon as I'd – er—' she couldn't really say she was waiting until she'd put her make-up on, which sounded terribly vain '– as soon as I'd had time to think up exactly the right way to say how much I love you and how sorry I am that I've been so horribly resentful all this holiday.'

'Think you just bloody have,' Michael grinned. 'And I'm sorry I've been a bit off, too, old gir – I mean, dear child. I – er I,' he coughed, 'love you too, of course.'

'Oh Michael.' Cass burst into tears with relief as he gave her a stiff hug, which she knew was his ultimate gesture of affection. She was nearly popping with happiness.

Michael was terribly relieved. The steamy mirror idea had been inspired and very cost-effective. Pity all he could remember to quote was P.G. Wodehouse, but it seemed to have done the trick.

Eddie came out of the bathroom still humming Sinatra hits. Lauren followed behind, wrapped in a sheet because there didn't seem to be a clean, dry towel left in the house.

'Sweetie, you've still got your shower cap on,' she pointed out.

'I'm starting a trend.' Eddie padded, naked except for his plastic head-dress, along the landing.

'Yeah, a downward one – shit!' Lauren's sheet had got caught in some splintered skirting and refused to budge.

'Rip it,' Eddie suggested, standing with his hands on his hips, watching her.

'I can't, it's Bruges,' cried Lauren, frantically trying to free the shredding fabric. She turned and noticed Eddie laughing at her. 'Honey, get into the room,' she giggled, 'you look like a Central Park pervert.'

'Ah ha!' Eddie pulled a lascivious face, made doubly revolting by the shower cap, and crept towards her with his arms outstretched. 'I'm gonna pull you into the bushes, little girl. Cumun see my puppies.'

'Eddie!' Lauren shrieked in fits of giggles as he pulled her away from the sheet.

A shrill voice came floating up the stairs, speaking very slowly and clearly as if imparting instructions to the village idiot.

'It's very good – *très bon* – of you to come for an interview at such short notice. The children – les *enfins* – are – *sont* – up here – *ici*. I am sure you will get on with them – *ils aimer* – very well. Just along here on the left – is that *gauche* or *drat*, I never remember?'

'Pardon, madame?' came a little voice.

'Christ!' Eddie started towards the bedroom, Lauren backed in the direction of the bathroom. They were still holding hands and came to a jitterbug halt.

'This way!' hissed Eddie.

'No, in here!' urged Lauren.

'We are a very respectable family – *notre famille est très respectaaabelle*,' the voice crowed in an appalling accent, 'so we expect our staff – *les domestiques* – to behave decorously at all—'

Sophia rounded the corner to come face to face with a nude couple. The Blonde Bimb-aunt, as Ben had nicknamed Lauren, was being carried in a distressed damsel clinch across the landing by Sophia's weirdo uncle Eddie wearing an absurd flowered shower cap. *Her* shower cap, which had disappeared weeks ago.

'Disgusting!' she spat in a horrified voice, turning to bustle the little French nanny, who had come so highly recommended and was so gloriously plain, away.

But the girl had already seen the worst. Screaming at the top of her voice that she was a good Catholic, madame, and could under no circumstances work amid such debauchery, she shot down the stairs and out of the house faster than Seb Coe being pursued by a following wind.

Breathing deeply, Sophia slowly regained her composure.

'You'll catch your death of cold standing in a draught like that,' she told them archly and, turning on her Louis heel, flounced downstairs.

In a bid to escape from Max, Tash staggered outside in her nightie, still clutching a mug of tea, to let Snob out. Squinting myopically around the courtyard, she noticed with relief that no one was around. Hugo's red Peugeot had disappeared, leaving a snail's trail of hot rubber sticking chicken feathers to the cobblestones.

After another failed attempt at seduction, Max had spent all morning trying to get some Test results on the BBC World Service, rendering him speechless with concentration. Typically, he was acting as if last night's argument hadn't happened. Having tried and failed to wrest his attention and thrash things through, Tash was now waiting for her hangover to subside before resuming any attempts at communication.

As Tash led Snob from the stalls to the paddock gate, he lifted her nightie with his teeth. Pulling it back down, she almost jumped out of her skin as a piercing wolf whistle screeched from the kitchen door.

'I'd recognise that tush anywhere. How come you let him do that and not me?' Max shouted jokily. 'Pascal's cooked some great sausages and stuff for breakfast. Come inside.'

Tash watched his bleary outline disappear back into the house. She hadn't eaten properly for days and her stomach heaved unpleasantly at the thought of Pascal's winy, herbed blood-red sausages. Lingering to marvel as Snob took a thundering, pipe-opening circuit of the paddock, she then crawled back upstairs to pack.

Again, Tash hesitated by Niall's door. Again, she was too cowardly to knock.

Instead, she started disconsolately throwing her things into Mikey's rucksack. Everything was full of dust and covered in dry green stains from Snob's slobber.

She had a lot more to take back than she'd brought. She'd need her skull cap and the crippling boots for the new job, so she left out a woolly jumper and an old striped blazer she'd bought in Oxfam and never got the smell of armpit out of. There still wasn't enough room, so she turfed two seedy sweatshirts and a copy of *Relax and Gain Confidence.*

She lingered sadly over the sultry black bustier Ginger had given her. Tash had no idea who it really belonged to. Had she really worn it on Friday night? she wondered. In London she would never have the nerve. Perhaps she should put *Relax and Gain Confidence* back?

'Oh, God.' Tash covered her mouth and sat down on the bed with a heavy thud. 'What am I doing? I can't possibly go back with Max.'

With total horror, she realised that in just two days she'd let herself regress into the meek, romantic invertebrate again. If she let the slide continue unchecked, then within twenty-four hours she would be in Derrin Road, tripping over beer cans, drying socks, irregular girlfriends and cricket pads.

Tash knew for certain that she didn't want to go back, even if it was just for a few weeks before setting off for Gus and Penny's yard. If the 'wedding' was announced to the lads, it would be totally impossible to retract. And, most horrifying of all, if she left the manoir today, she would quite probably never see Niall again. She had to say something to him.

Heading towards the door, she stopped in her tracks and pretended to be collecting her damp bikini from the towel rail.

For, standing watching her from just outside on the landing, was a petite, foxy figure.

Tash had mislaid her contact lens solution and could only see clearly to the end of her nose. For a terrible moment, she thought it was Amanda, back from her cycling tour with fresh vitriol. Then her heart plummeted even further when she realised that it was Lisette.

'Hello there, how are you getting on?' Lisette shimmied lithely into the room surrounded by an ambrosial cloud of scent. Her enchanting smile was beaming out a thousand watts. 'I hate packing, don't you?'

'Er . . . quite.' Tash fumblingly folded up the bikini, then, remembering it was Sophia's, unfolded it again.

Lisette perched herself beside Tash's case and watched while the tall girl stuffed in embarrassingly grotty underwear, matted combs and leaking bottles of shampoo.

'You're so lucky having such a lot of close family,' she enthused. 'I'm an only child – and both my parents are dead now.'

Tash looked up at her. 'Oh, how awful for you. Don't you have any relatives?'

Lisette shook her head untruthfully. 'Niall finds my reliance on his family difficult to understand sometimes.' She watched Tash's expression. 'He's like you – brothers, sisters and cousins all over the place. He takes the security for granted.'

Biting her lip, Tash looked away. She fought a desire to pick up the catering-sized jar of pickled onions on Max's side of the bed and empty it over Lisette's short, glossy hair.

'Oh, I know you must think that's a terrible lie, considering I left Niall for a bit,' Lisette went on blithely. 'But believe me, there was far more to it than that.' Her voice was confiding, but the 'you-wouldn't-understand' message came through clearly.

'Actually, my family hardly ever gather together like this,' Tash babbled, desperate to change the subject. 'Only for christenings and weddings and things.'

'In that case,' Lisette picked up smoothly. 'You'll all be meeting again very soon.'

'What?' Tash fingered a denim shirt.

'You and Max,' Lisette prompted.

'Oh – yes.'

'Seems to me it's been a holiday of romances,' she added carefully, trapping Tash under her hypnotising sylphine gaze.

Not answering, Tash folded the shirt into a smaller and smaller bundle.

'I think your uncle Eddie's pure gold,' Lisette suddenly grinned, picking up Tash's crash-skull and trying it on, 'he's like a terribly wicked Pacino with a Bloomsbury mind. And Lauren is so beautiful. One feels like a faded familiar sitting next to her. Do you wear this in bed?' She knocked the outside of the crash-skull with her fist enquiringly.

Looking at her, Tash found it impossible to imagine Lisette feeling overshadowed. She was quite simply one of the most astonishing-looking women she'd ever met. She even looked bewitching swamped by the jockey's skull, in which Tash looked like Biggles.

'So when's the wedding?' Lisette's smile was sweet enough to take the edge off battery acid.

Tash mumbled something about next year.

'Take my advice, grab something as gorgeous as Max fast, or someone else will.' Lisette took off the skull and casually cast it aside, picking up one of the silk shirts Alexandra had given Tash instead. 'Mmm, this is nice. Where is Max in a million, by the way?'

'Eating breakfast.' Tash didn't want to talk about him to Lisette; she had a feeling Lisette had a way of worming doubts out of people without them noticing.

But thankfully Lisette, who was now trying on the shirt, didn't pursue her line of questioning. Instead she admired her reflection in the mirror – the deep amber gave her skin a tawny glow and made her blonde hair appear burnished.

Suddenly, she turned to Tash with a ravishing smile, her eyes full of sparkling mischief.

'I almost forgot, Niall said to pass on his farewells. And to Max.'

Tash was folding her t-shirts, her hands moving slower and slower.

'You mean . . . ?' she couldn't finish, aware that she sounded as if she'd swallowed road chippings.

'Didn't he tell you? Of course, no, he wouldn't . . .' Lisette let caustic insinuation weigh her words like roofing lead on to Tash's conscience. 'He went this morning – back to clear up the house for me – so sweet. He says it's a complete dump because he threw so much around after I left.' Lisette idly let the knife spin deeper and deeper.

Tash shuffled over to a chair to fetch a pile of leggings. She came back with a pair of Max's trunks and a cushion instead, calmly packing them into a loose corner of her rucksack with the jar of pickled onions.

'The trouble is – oh God, I feel such a bitch for saying this – but I'm not sure if I want him back.' Lisette strangled a little sob and sank down on the scarves Tash was about to pack. She looked up at her with wide eyes. 'Look, I'm sorry. Do you mind if I dump on you like this?'

Tash shook her head, mindlessly packing two pillow slips.

'You see, he's so amatorial and demanding,' Lisette confessed. 'So completely obsessive . . .'

Tash packed a full ashtray and a sopping towel.

'. . . he never lets me breathe because he does absolutely everything for me.' Lisette tried on the diamond earrings which Tash had put on the dressing table ready to give back to her mother. 'I go to shave my armpits – I find he's already got there. I go to phone my mother,' she looked at herself in the mirror again and stroked her neck with a smile – then, remembering she'd just said that her mother was dead, hurried on, '– she – er – says she'd had a lovely chat with Niall earlier and – aren't these divine? – has heard all our gossip, thanks. If I ask him to back off, he only speaks when he's spoken to and creeps around like Mrs Danvers, lurking behind doors with a feather duster and leaving meals under cellophane.'

Tash vacantly packed a pot plant, carefully inserting its leaves between two shoes so that it wouldn't get battered.

'Can't you see how impossible it is being married to someone so totally strung up on one?' Lisette looked up imploringly. 'I just don't think I can take any more of his slavish adoration. It's like being hitched to Igor. These earrings are truly lovely. Can I borrow them?'

Tash stared at her in amazement, a small lamp wavering between the bedside table and her rucksack.

Lisette laughed lightly. 'Oh, I know it must seem absolute heaven to *you*.' The stress was slightly too laboured. 'The big star, living and breathing under your own roof. But, honestly, darling – you simply can't imagine what it's like having someone love you so much they lick the ground you walk on.'

The lamp fell to the ground with a very ineffectual thud. Tash grimaced. Something more dramatic was definitely in order here. What was it she'd thought of earlier?

'But I'm sure . . .' she replied slowly, digging out the jar of pickled onions. Half-full, she noticed. It would have to do. '. . . that you've licked the ground first.'

'What?' Lisette was so perplexed she didn't notice Tash unscrewing the jar.

'It strikes me,' Tash explained, smiling at Lisette with what she hoped was frank, if unloved, sincerity, 'that Niall has a rival in love – you. You love yourself far more than he ever could.'

Upending the jar, she watched with unhampered pleasure as vinegar soaked Lisette's beautiful hair, followed by the little highly perfumed balls ricocheting off her head and shoulders.

Lisette yelped in horror.

'That,' Tash screwed the lid back on the jar with care and put it in her rucksack as a keepsake, 'was for Niall, because he's too cowardly, stupid and kind to do it himself. He might want to come and eat them off you later, but at least he'll taste how sour you've become.'

Lisette had jumped up and was spitting vinegar from her mouth, dripping and dropping so many onions she should have been wearing a beret and whistling 'Frère Jacques'. She pulled the earrings from her lobes and tore off the sodden shirt, depositing them at Tash's feet before silently stalking to the door. There, she turned around with a look of pure acid.

'Niall told me that you were a twitched-up little freak,' she snarled, 'and now I know why. I can't believe we both felt so sorry for you.'

After she'd gone, Tash collapsed on to the bed and chewed the sheet in frustration. It tasted strongly of pickled onions. She already felt awful about what she'd done. Perhaps Derrin Road wasn't such a bad prospect after all.

'You'll never guess what,' came an excited voice, and Max clomped heavily into the room.

Tash kept her head buried in the bed and grunted.

'Fwor – can't say I go for that scent, Tash. Bit like the one my mother wears.' An abrupt shifting of the bed indicated that he'd sat down on it. 'The latest news is, Dad's just been on the phone to the States about this film he's backing. Turns out Honeyman and the casting agent are dead set on O'Shaughnessy taking the lead – they want him to fly over there this week for a test.' Tash's back got covered in soil as he removed the pot plant from her rucksack. 'You'll get done by Customs for this – I'm sure it's dope. The fee they're offering for this movie is literally in millions. Trouble is no one here knows where he is – he's just pushed off.'

Tash howled with remorse.

'Yes, it is a shame.' Max clearly thought her reaction was a bit exaggerated. 'Dad's having a screaming match with Lisette through a door right now because she claims she hasn't a clue where he is either, just keeps telling the old man to piss off. At least that seems to put her out of the stepmother stakes,' he laughed cheerfully. 'It rings true, though. Dad says she told him last night that she and Niall were finally declared null and void; Niall broke it to her yesterday. Apparently, he's hung up on one of your mother's house guests who's shacked up with someone else now.'

Tash howled even louder.

Max patted her on the back. 'Are you coming down with something?' he asked cautiously.

Tash made a sort of strangled goat noise.

'Take an aspirin later,' soothed Max, deciding it must be PMT. 'This'll cheer you up. Ben thinks Niall's after that bruiser called Amanda. The dog-man conquered there, I presume. But your ma's being very shifty about it. Says she thinks it's someone else. Polly claims it's her. I'm going to start a book on it. What d'you think to ten to one on for your sister?'

Tash stopped wailing, lifted up her head with a sniff and nodded philosophically.

'What odds am I?' she asked with a tearful tremor.

Max screamed with laughter. That was the best joke he'd ever known Tash tell.

'You, my love, have been withdrawn from the race card.' He kissed her head. 'From now on, you're being retired to stud.'

Tash supposed a brood mare and nightmare must be closely related.

Feeling faint, she shrank away from Max and ate a stray pickled onion as a comforter.

Poor Niall, having his love-life open to scrutiny. John McCririck would be popping out from behind the dresser wearing a jaunty deerstalker soon, letting the watching public know how the fillies were looking in the paddock and what the latest odds were.

But Tash, with a sick churning of excitement and hopeless regret, knew for certain who to put her money on. Only the gates had opened and the field had sped off before she'd had a chance.

'When did he go missing?'

Max was watching her closely now, the muscles of his cheeks quilted like one of Sophia's Chanel handbags.

'Hours ago,' he replied slowly. 'Probably out of the country by now.'

Tash closed her eyes with the effort of not screaming.

'You know,' Max touched her hair, 'if we ever split up again I'd fall totally apart. I even think,' he joked feebly, 'that I love you more than David Gower.'

He leaned forward for a kiss.

Picking another onion off the sheets and ramming it into her mouth, Tash decided that having a dream come true wasn't always as gratifying as it was made out to be.

63

Half an hour before she was due to leave, Tash trailed despondently back along the paddock path from saying goodbye to Snob who, not understanding, had been at his most rumbustious and chewed the dried flowers from her drooping straw hat.

Rooter shadowed her heels as if aware that he was about to be well and truly orphaned. Tash had been guiltily feeding him dog biscuits all morning, so now great strings of drool kept landing on her feet. She'd just found out that the cost of getting him to England and through quarantine would be over eight thousand francs and far, far more than that to transport Snob. She didn't want to ask her mother for the money, but knew that as soon as Alexandra and Pascal returned to Paris, Rooter and Snob would be reduced to sleeping in cardboard boxes. The spaniels stayed with Jean and Valérie when the d'Eblouirs were away but, since Jean – armed with a twelve-bore – had already furiously evicted Rooter from crapping on his vegetable patch for the fifth time, Tash thought it unlikely they would oblige and babysit eight more legs.

It was a dilemma she had yet to solve. As with all her pressing problems, she'd decided to shelve it under *Potential causes of corpse being found in Highgate Ponds wearing lead winkle pickers* until she got back to England and saw her bank manager.

She could see his face now, pale with fear as he reached for the drawer that contained the bottle of Bells and herbal tranquillisers. The listening bank would invest in ear plugs and go on a self-improvement group therapy weekend on 'How To Say No' if it heard about how she intended to pay off a four-figure loan on a wage of thirty pounds a week in deepest Berkshire.

As a concession to her lily-livered weak will, Tash was sporting a long, flowing skirt and cambric shirt over a broiderie anglaise bodice. She felt distinctly odd and kept finding herself humming 'Le Jardin', picking harebells and leaning dreamily on gates, telling Rooter to wear his rue with a difference. Most disturbing of all was the fact that Max, Ben, Pascal and even Michael had all said how lovely she was looking. She was horrified. One didn't compliment someone's funeral shroud. Men had terrible taste, she mulled.

'Tash, darling!' came a deep, sexy drawl. 'May I say how absolutely delightful you look today.'

'Thank you, Lucian.' She turned around and accepted a very civilised kiss on the cheek from Max's father.

Lucian put a broad, suntanned arm around Tash and started to steer her towards the house. Rooter followed jealously, trying to squeeze in between them, snuffling for biscuits.

'I wanted to collar you alone before you go, get *down*, you beast.' Lucian slyly aimed a kick at Rooter but caught Tash on the shin instead. 'Ah – sorry. Yes, I just wanted to say how glad I am the way things have turned out.'

'Oh, yes?' Tash croaked, just stopping herself from swooning penitently by the vegetable cupboard.

'Mmm.' Lucian was pink from a very successful, boozy networking lunch with Pascal. 'You know Max was so worried about coming out here, about asking you. He thought he'd be rushing things,' he stopped and turned to her. 'He honestly thought that – buzz off, you great hound – you'd have got someone else. Kept saying that, since all his friends fell in love with you at least once – like catching measles – out on the open market there would be an epidemic.' Lucian laughed heartily.

'Max's friends . . .' Tash had gone white. She joined in laughing nervously and picked a tiny ivy-leaved toadflax flower from the wall of the house, turning its thin purple stem around between her fingers. As far as she was aware, the only one of Max's friends who had ever taken to her was a little squirt called Geoffrey who wore a kagool, worked in computers and had once sent her a Valentine's card with a fluffy dog covered in glitter looking cow-eyed on the front. He'd only done that because, in a moment of sympathy and in vino, Tash had introduced him to a few people as 'Gorgeous Geoffrey' at a Derrin Road thrash.

'So you can imagine how excited he is.' Lucian put his hands on her shoulders with fatherly assertion. Tash looked down and watched Rooter slobber all over his smart cream trousers. 'And I am too. You're a very special girl, Tash – and I know you're going to make my son very happy.'

It was straight out of *Dynasty*. Blake Carrington couldn't have delivered it better under a blue-rinsed toupée. Tash looked around for a boom operator and someone to powder her nose.

Lucian was in flattering close-up, the pepper and salt wings above his ears neatly groomed, the rest of his glossy mane suspiciously rigid, his Welsh slate eyes sincere.

'And you can rest assured,' he nodded, with a slight catch in his voice, 'that myself, Alexandra – your father, James, I'm certain – and my first wife, Babs,' he gave a faint sigh, 'will make sure you have the best goddamn wedding a couple could want.'

Tash's smile took on a slightly Jack Nicholson intensity. She had to resist cackling like a deranged medium who's just tapped into Lady Macbeth's solar-psychic forcefield. Instead, she thanked him, handed him the squashed toadflax flower and wandered wispily up the steps to the kitchen to find something extremely sweet and calorific which she could wolf to cheer herself up.

Sitting dozily on the back of a thousand-decibel truck which had lost its suspension in the last war, squashed between two crates of cabbages and a regiment of potato sacks, Niall changed his clouded mind.

Ireland would be too beautiful at this time of year, he

realised; it would be impossible to grieve there. His mother would be lost to her trowel and rosary in the garden, his brother almost living at the racetracks, his sister-in-law heavily pregnant and surrounded by beautiful, unruly children. All Niall wanted was Tash. He pulled himself together and decided to turn back.

They thundered past a sign on the other side of the road. Niall twisted around to read it, panic rising in his guts. Through a haze of dust and diesel fumes, he made out that Saumur was eight kilometres in the opposite direction. Tash was leaving at four, he remembered. He had an hour.

He tapped hard on the cab's rear window, trying to get the driver's attention. The man was stone deaf. His mangy piebald dog was outraged, baring its teeth and letting out a frenzy of barks before scrabbling at the window in frustration. But the driver merely thumped it over the head with his arthritically gnarled hand and carried on thundering the laboured truck along the endless, poplar-lined road as if he were on the home straight at Le Mans.

Niall looked down at the tarmac below, but it was moving too fast and looked far too hard to throw himself on to. He groaned in frustration and looked at his watch. Five past three. The stench of vintage cabbage was suffocating.

They passed two sets of traffic lights, each of which turned green as they approached. Niall bellowed in rage and threw three potatoes at passing road signs telling him how much further he was from Saumur. He shook in horror as he realised he could have been at Cherbourg by now had he not spent most of the day drinking with a dejected young cavalry officer in the Hotel Bretagne.

The officer had given Niall a lift as far as Saumur on the back of his huge, cob-like Suzuki, insisting he buy the actor a drink in honour of his fame in France. So much for not being recognised. Niall only wished he could have afforded to buy a drink in return. But after a few glasses that had hardly seemed to matter.

It had been one of those occasions where the formality between strangers is suspended because of an awareness of some sort of united emotion, and a certainty that they will never meet again. Together they had drowned their sorrows in three bottles of Chateau de Montreuil-Bellay; the officer telling Niall about his girlfriend in Limoges who had just run away with a travelling vending-machine salesman, Niall telling the officer in his broken French about Tash. Neither had commented on the other's plight, merely feeling a mutual satisfaction in the telling and listening. The unfledged officer had eventually staggered back to his barracks to sleep off the wine and Niall had reeled, as tight as a wasp in a cider apple, to coax a lift out of the deaf farmer.

Niall snapped out of his trance. Opportunity had suddenly presented itself as the farmer slowed to light a cigarette, both hands off the wheel and veering dangerously towards the right, causing his cowering dog to fall off the passenger seat.

Spotting something that looked vaguely like a soft landing, Niall threw himself off the back of the truck and collided with a dusty verge outside an agricultural machinery warehouse.

As he waited for the air to come back to his lungs, he looked up to see a sign offering him a free bag of chicken feed if he bought a new set of harrow chains. He only knew this because an English family who had chosen to set up their full-dress picnic in this picturesque spot – between a major French industrial road and the corrugated warehouse, overlooking yet another nuclear power station – were busy translating the sign with the aid of *French In Three Months*.

'Look, Brian, that man seems to have fallen out of a lorry.'

'So he has, Ann, so he has.'

'No, *don't* touch, Scott, and come back here at *once*! You don't know where he's been. Charlene, *don't* hit your brother like that. Brian, love – will you go and see if he's dead, *please*?'

'Of course.' Brian squared his shoulders and got up from his floral folding garden chair. 'These Frogs are flaming savages. It's not like in *French Fields*.'

A pair of terry towelling socks in very polished tan Jesus Creeper attached to hairy white legs shuffled up to Niall. Then a shiny red face with an even shinier red nose descended to Niall's level and examined him closely.

'I don't think he's dead, Ann, but he looks a little peaky. Will you pass me the phrase book, please?'

Niall blinked at the face, focused in and hiccuped.

Brian had started leafing through *French In Three Months* for a suitable opener. Niall decided to save him the effort.

'Would you be going to a little village called Champegny, by any chance? Because I could do with a lift, now, if it wouldn't be too much trouble to you.'

'Speaks very good English, doesn't he, Brian love?' squawked Ann, who was out of Niall's sight due to the huge, beaming face of Brian. 'Leave that *alone*, Scott.'

The face moved even closer to Niall's and peered at him with squinting contemplation, as if examining mould smears on a culture dish.

'You know, Ann,' he turned and shouted enthusiastically over his shoulder, 'I think it's that chap from the telly, the one our Lorraine fancies.'

'That scruffy bloke – what's his name, love?' Ann screeched ecstatically, leaping up from the folding Formica trestle table and running over.

'Jimmy Nail!' Brian announced proudly. 'Hey – Jim, mate. Was that a stunt? Where are the cameras? Can I have an autograph for my daughter? These are her kids – hey, Scott, Charlene – come and be introduced to Jim here.'

Niall shut his eyes and smiled. To cap it all, he realised he'd left both his bags on the back of the truck, careering north.

'Au revoir, Bernadette!'

'Au revoir, madame, monsieur. À bientôt et merci beaucoup!'

'Oh, Ben, isn't she sweet!' Sophia squealed, giving her husband a quick hug before dancing back into the house. 'And fancy wanting to start tomorrow. So keen.'

'Hmmph.' Ben limped after her, glancing over his shoulder at the retreating figure of Bernadette: future nanny to his children, devout Catholic, English degree holder with a face like a camel and a bum like a rhino. 'Probably got the hots for you, Sophs.

Better move into the Hall soon, that's all I can say. Don't think the staircase at Home Farm is up to it. D'you think she'll want to use the car? Suspension'll go.'

'Oh, Ben, Ben, Ben.' Sophia's ringing laugh echoed around the hall. 'She's so *cuddly* – you saw how the children took to her.'

'Think Josh'll grow up with a complex,' Ben growled. 'And poor Lots nearly lost her Noo Noo down that – er – décolletage.'

'Mother says she cooks like a dream – just think. We won't have to get horrid Sabrina ffoulkes-watsit's daughter in to do the DPs any more.' Sophia swung round a column in delight. 'And Joan'll be thrilled to bits. She called Paola a "hussy". Said she was known as the Friscatty Filly in the village.'

Ben didn't give a hoot what the housekeeper thought. He just knew he would have nightmares about Bernadette's bulges.

'Oh, Ben.' Sophia crept up to him and kissed him on the nose. 'You don't mind *that* much, do you?' She looked up at him through her lashes and pouted.

How could he mind? It was like the Mona Lisa winking and stretching out a beckoning finger.

He indulged in a deliciously long kiss and sighed.

'As long as you *promise* not to let her read any Fay Weldon,' he smiled.

Sitting on an eight-berth whipped-cream sofa in Chelsea, flipping through some Robert Mapplethorpe photographs in a glossy coffee-table opus, Todd Austin breathed in the sensual tang of freshly ground coffee and smirked.

Amanda was back at the office for the first time today. To Todd, that conjured up instant images of filing cabinets, filing nails, filing for divorce and filing through the bars on the windows; receptionists in floods of tears, sales managers having nervous breakdowns, supervisors sneering behind each other's backs and trying to buy the most shouts in the pub at lunch-time when a promotion was on the cards; lots of little plastic signs saying *you don't have to be mad to work here, but it helps* and *behind every successful woman is a whole pile of unwashed laundry.*

Too true. Todd had spotted a nice Chinese firm just around the corner he would take the holiday cargo around to later. Meanwhile he had a huge stack of Amanda's videos to go through, including the one he'd made earlier with Amanda's camcorder (set up on a tripod in the corner of her sumptuous cream flat) of himself singing the greatest hits of Midnight Oil. But first he'd just slot in this intriguing one marked *Things Getting On Top Of Me.*

Todd reached for the remote control and pressed play before strolling into the kitchen to fetch another chilled article out of the fridge. He was drawn back by a series of very familiar shuddering gasps.

A few seconds later, Todd's smirk had turned into a wide grin. He tilted his head sideways to get a better view of what was happening on screen. Boy, was Amanda photogenic, her slender proportions transferred beautifully into 2D. Which was more than could be said for the drongo with her.

Todd stared at the freckled, heaving torso currently displaying a sexual technique that was about as imaginative as press-ups after a cold shower. The torso's head was cut off the frame but Todd could tell that it wasn't Hugo, who was in far better shape. After a few more groaning jerks the torso let out a great bellow and a huge red face flopped into frame, looking as if it were in the midst of a seizure.

Freezing the picture, Todd examined it closely. He then strolled over to the far wall and extracted a photograph. He held it up beside the screen. The same red face glared from both.

'Bingo, bonzo!' He lifted his can to them and took a large swig before returning to the photograph.

A huge bulldog of a man wearing a garish lime-green suit was accepting an award for Best Television Advertisement from a harassed-looking VIP. Amanda had pointed the photograph out to Todd on their first night.

'My bloody boss,' she'd hissed grimly. 'Makes Stalin seem like Rodney Trotter.'

Todd hadn't got the joke, but now things were starting to add up like an abacus on a downward slope. The shallow but protracted split-sight relationship with Hugo, Amanda surviving the recession so buoyantly, her reluctance to have Todd staying in the flat for more than a couple of weeks.

Todd was surprised and disturbed by how jealous he felt.

'For your own protection, Mand.' Todd removed the tape and put it on the coffee table ready to stow with his stuff.

If her creepy boss was blackmailing her into sleeping with him, then Todd was just the man to help, he mused.

'You're gonna have a house guest for far longer than two weeks, my darling.' He slotted his demon demo tape into the machine. 'But don't worry; this little skippy's gonna take care of you.'

To strains of 'Beds Are Burning', Todd started to gather together the holiday washing and jam it all into Amanda's Meile together with his trainers and half a packet of Persil.

'I always said I wanted to be Newman,' he murmured to himself, selecting the programme. 'I guess I'm just doing the next best thing.'

'You gotta big arse?' demanded six-year-old Scott.

'Er . . .' Niall, fighting nausea in the back of the metallic blue Escort, looked at the small boy in alarm.

'Well, 'ave you?' demanded the recalcitrant Scott.

'Lad wants to know if you've got a large pile,' Brian boomed over his shoulder.

Niall was even more shocked. He was trapped in a car with a bunch of anal retentives with less than half an hour to get back to Tash.

'How many bedrooms has it got, Jimmy?' Ann looked up from her knitting and turned to him.

'Oh – house!' Niall sighed, winding down the window to breathe away from the dense fog of Parma Violets and Tweed. 'Er – three, I've got three.'

'Three houses, Brian,' there was an edge in Ann's voice. 'Think of that. All those homeless people in Debenham's doorway and Jimmy here's got three houses.'

Niall had his head out of the window now, but all he got was a lungful of dung fumes from the sheep lorry in front.

'No, I meant I've got three bedrooms,' he groaned but the wind whipped his words towards the boot.

'Grandad's going to buy me Sindy's fold-away pent-arse for my birfday, aren'cha Grandad?' shrilled Charlene who was tucking into a packet of Monster Munch, offering Niall one by thrusting the packet directly under his nose.

Niall felt his stomach heave afresh. The crisps were whipped away by the wind and Charlene started to cry.

They were passing a solitary café bar now. Three nubile blondes were drinking pastis under a Coke umbrella outside. Niall recognised it; they were only a few kilometres from the manoir. His heart lifted slightly.

The next moment, Brian put his foot on the brake so violently that Niall was nearly garrotted by the window trim.

'Let's all have a nice refreshing drink, shall we?' he suggested in a thick voice, peering into his rear-view mirror at the three blondes.

Ann followed his gaze and her mouth, along with the accompanying Parma Violet pong, disappeared.

'I think Jimmy has an appointment to get to, Bri,' she snapped curtly.

Brian wiped his beef-tomato face with a pink handkerchief and sulkily put the Escort into gear. Then a light bulb lit up like Blackpool illuminations in his turned-down eyes.

'Fancy an ice cream, kids?' he asked cheerfully, shooting Ann a mean look.

The children shrieked in delight.

'There!' Brian started to turn the car around to the furious hoots of oncoming traffic. 'Can't disappoint the kiddies can we, Ann?'

Ann had inadvertently pronged herself in the eye with a knitting needle and was looking daggers.

With the car now at right angles across the road, Niall thanked Brian for the lift and got out. Staggering through the tooting, manoeuvring traffic and almost under a tractor emerging from a field-entrance, he started to reel in the general direction of the manoir.

He realised he was still half-cut. He simply had to get there before Tash left, but each time he tried to run, he fell into a ditch.

'There's a minor rally assembling in the courtyard to say good-bye,' announced Max, coming into the bedroom and gathering up Tash's rucksack and one of his sausage-shaped sports bags.

'Didn't know there were any collieries in Champegny,' muttered Tash despondently, heaving herself up from the bed. 'Is the taxi here yet?'

'Yup,' Max paused by the mirror and coiffed up his donkey-blond hair into whipped cream peaks. 'Ready?'

Tash nodded silently. She donned her pastoral hat and shuffled behind him as they made their way through the house and out into the courtyard.

'Will you stop saying goodbye to everything, it's costing us a fortune,' Max snapped five minutes later as she took one last, doleful look at the valley after kissing each of the spaniels in turn. 'We'll both come back again soon, I promise. Together.'

'When hell needs central heating,' Tash muttered into the senior spaniel's ear.

Where were a big clap of thunder and an earth-splitting streak of lightning when you wanted them? she wondered.

Max shot her an odd look but, before he could say anything too probing, the taxi driver prowled over to accost their bags as hostages, and everyone else fell on them with final farewells.

Tash was astonished to find that the entire household had staggered out into the sunshine wearing smiles and wearing thin.

Lauren and Sophia – having avoided one another since the nanny incident – were horrified to come face to face wearing exactly the same Georgio shirt. Lucian, however, broke the icy cool by diplomatically complimenting them both on their impeccable taste. Sophia simpered warmly and started telling Lauren about her marvellous new nanny.

'The glorious thing is that I'll have so much more time on my hands,' she enthused.

'Whatever you do,' Ben muttered into Eddie's ear, 'don't let Sophs take Lauren out shopping.'

Eddie nodded grimly.

Tash cried a lot during the next ten minutes, especially when Anton rolled up reeking of aftershave and bearing a huge bunch of flowers he had stolen out of Jean and Valérie's garden.

'I no let my favourite angel leave wizout me taking the privilege of a keess,' he said grandly, almost flooring Tash with lips and Paco Rabanne.

Giving Anton a broad berth, Cass wafted up in a rival cloud of Chanel No 5 with Michael's fingers firmly clamped between the gold rings on her own.

'It's been so nice to see you again, dear.' She left a fuchsia lip print on Tash's cheek. 'You're a very sweet girl.'

When Michael gripped her hand, removed his pipe and repeated the statement, Tash almost broke down.

Looking very pink beneath his dreadlocks, Wiltsher loped up with Marcus scuffing the ground behind him.

'Go on, Wilt,' Marcus urged.

'Bye, Tash, man,' Wiltsher mumbled, kissing her shyly on the cheek. Then suddenly Tash found herself enveloped in a clinch.

'Wicked!' Marcus hiccuped in the background as Tash frantically disentangled herself from dreadlocks.

'Like I've wanted to do that all week, man,' Wiltsher murmured happily, reappearing three shades redder. The fuchsia lipstick had transferred on to his forehead and Tash now had a pair of bobbing alien antennae attached to her straw hat.

Even Jean and Valérie, despite the matching black eyes, had turned up to say goodbye, proffering a bag of fennel and six fat melons. Tash completely soaked three paper tissues.

The taxi driver lit up a resigned cigarette and settled down to read his paper.

While Max was enthusiastically swapping addresses, phone

numbers and sporting anecdotes with anyone who wanted them, Tash said goodbye to her sister, Ben and the children. Lotty handed her a drawing of her and Max. Tash was a big, colourful blob covered with bandages splodged on in Tipp-Ex, with long arms holding on to a red horse. Max was a little grey blob added on in the corner, carrying a deflated football.

Tash laughed and wiped away a tear. Lotty must have hidden psychic powers.

As Sophia turned to wipe Josh's dribbly mouth, Ben grabbed Tash and steered her to one side, looking furtive.

'Hugs sends his apologies and says to give you a big kiss.' He pecked her cheek with tightly puckered lips and went pink. 'And to pass on this,' he added, handing Tash an envelope which he'd had to hide from Sophia and Cass all day.

'Thanks.' She quickly thrust it into her pocket.

As Tash drifted away to hug her mother, Pascal and Polly, Ben regarded her incredulously. He couldn't be certain, but he was beginning to suspect that Hugo wasn't nearly so upset about Amanda as at first imagined.

The taxi driver irritably switched on his radio and started to fill in the crossword.

'I'll sort out something for Snob and Rooter,' Tash promised her mother. 'I'm going down to see the Moncrieffs' yard in a week and I'll ask their advice about transportation, don't worry.'

'Oh, we'll arrange something.' Alexandra waved the problem away with a distracted hand. Then she gazed into Tash's eyes enquiringly. 'Is everything all right? Are you sure about what you're doing?' She nodded discreetly towards Max who was back-slapping with his father.

Tash bit her bottom lip and nodded. 'I think we've got it all worked out,' she lied.

'Good.' Alexandra kissed her again. 'You know I'm going to miss you so much,' her voice wobbled.

'Oh, Mummy.' Tash started to cry again.

'You ready?' Max appeared at her side.

Tash nodded and then shook her head with a wail. 'I haven't said goodbye to Rooter!' she sobbed, wandering off to find him.

'Kerist!' Max exchanged an exasperated look with the taxi driver, who nodded at his meter. 'I've heard about the cost of living, but the cost of leaving's beyond my means.'

Niall picked himself up off the verge again and cursed. He was coated in dirt, his shirt-arm ripped and the knees of his trousers black with melting tar from the road. That was the third tree root he'd tripped over in two minutes. He was utterly exhausted and running out of time.

His throat dry with dust, ears pounding with rushing blood, head as light and empty as a helium balloon, Niall broke into a stumbling run again.

64

At last, Tash had said good-bye to everyone at least three times, cried buckets and failed to scream, 'It's all been a horrible, horrible mistake, I love Niall.' She had no excuse not to climb into the back of the taxi with Max and speed towards the train that would take them to the airport.

In her fantasy world, her directory of wild hopes and impossibilities, Niall was supposed miraculously to reappear and claim her as his. In reality, Max was looking twitchily at his watch, Lisette had swanned up appropriately dressed in scarlet and was smiling in a very Baby Jane fashion beside Lucian, and if Tash didn't beat it soon both she and her mother were in serious danger of moving on to a fifth handkerchief.

'I'll write,' she promised Alexandra, scanning the horizon one last time for signs of Niall clanking in on a white horse. Nothing. The only white horses Niall was acquainted with came out of a bottle.

Tash hopped into the car and settled herself on a burning dralon seat. The rear shelf of the taxi was absolutely crammed with furry gonks. 'I Will Always Love You' was blaring out of the stereo. She whipped out another tissue.

To whoops from the family, Max leapt from the cab at the last minute and kissed Alexandra very smarmily on the hand, before bouncing back in beside Tash.

'I think she appreciated that gesture, don't you?' he asked.

Tash wanted to throw up.

They finally started to move off and Tash waved frantically through the rear window, sniffing into a cuddly ape which was suctioned on to the glass by its paws, unaware that if one squeezed it – as she accidentally did – an obscene article popped out of its nether regions. Consequently, as she disappeared down the drive like Scarlett staring at Tara, everyone in the courtyard was being treated to repeated glimpses of a primate's plastic privates.

As all but the manoir's jutting turrets finally disappeared behind the tunnel of trees, Tash fished out Hugo's letter and started to scan it with streaming eyes. What it said made reading almost impossible; she kept having to wipe her eyes and blow her dribbly nose. He was showing such a generous volte face, she felt impossibly moved. She'd expected him to be vindictive and manipulative. Instead, he'd offered to take care of transporting Snob across the Channel and to organise for Rooter to stay with M-C for the time being. There were some very odd poetic quotes jotted on to the end of the letter which Tash didn't quite understand.

He who bends to himself a Joy.
Doth the winged life destroy;
But he who kisses the Joy as it flies
Lives in Eternity's sunrise.

Will Blake certainly understood what he was saying there. I wish I did; Joy sounds like a terrible flirt.
See you in Berkshire – H. xxx

Gorgeous, gallant Hugo, thought Tash with a wail. If she'd read this three weeks ago, she'd have been crying with delight.

'What are you blubbing for now?' Max demanded.

But, shaking her head, Tash didn't answer.

Giving up trying to read the letter over her shoulder, Max grumpily turned to watch the gates looming ahead.

He'd guessed straight away that the good-looking swine, Beauchamp, was smitten. It was the reason for Max's inspired proposal on Saturday morning – a defensive volley which, he prided himself, had miraculously paid off. And would soon, Max hoped, also pay off his overdraft, pay off his debts, pay off the speeding fine he hadn't told Tash about and pay off any competition.

Far more dangerous than Hugo, however, was Niall O'Shaughnessy. He and Tash were both dotty, both susceptible, both ridiculously romantic. They also fancied each other rotten – it hadn't taken Max long to notice that Tash became clumsy, tongue-tied and feverish in his presence, while Niall never took his eyes from her.

Max knew just how tentative his hold on Tash was; how easily she could slip through his stinging fingers like a dropped catch. The realisation irritated him intensely, but also gave him a competitive kick he found incredibly erotic. He'd never fancied Tash so much. It was why he was now bustling her back to London instead of staying on to ingratiate himself more with her jolly, rollicksome and gloriously rich family.

Having stung Pascal for their air fares and finally coaxed a couple of grand out of his father, Max felt flush enough to wine, dine and win Tash back over the next few weeks. He hoped to conduct the entire operation in bed, breaking only for cricket on SkyTV and a pizza delivery. Tash would soon forget Niall, he reasoned. Back in London, the magic of the romantic house and its intangible inhabitants would wear off and she'd settle back into her warm niche like a puppy curling up in the snug fireside basket after playing in its first ever snow.

They were turning the corner out of the labyrinthine manoir drive now and on to the narrow lane which led to the main road. Max waved at two riders hacking past; Tash was too engrossed in her letter to notice. Max eyed it again, but her hair was totally obscuring his view, meaning he'd have to sneak a peek later.

Turning back to the windscreen, he noticed a bedraggled figure standing in the middle of the road, arms outstretched in an air traffic control wave. It was obviously some mad yokel intent on involving them in a difficult breech lambing in a nearby ditch or something. Max sighed crossly.

A second later he sat bolt upright as he realised who it was.

He glanced at Tash. She was still turned to the door, chewing her thumbnail as she reread the letter.

The taxi driver started to brake.

'Drive on,' hissed Max.

'Pardon?' the taxi driver asked in an anxious voice. The waving man was getting closer.

'I said drive *on*,' Max urged. 'Go past him.'

'There ees no room, monsieur.'

'This says there is.' Max waved a two-hundred-franc note under his nose.

'What is it, Max?' Tash looked up.

'Nothing – just a goat in the road.'

The taxi had started to accelerate again. Niall was only a few metres away.

Seeing him, Tash gave a small gasp as she suddenly took in what was happening.

'Stop the car!' she demanded in a shriek.

The driver started to brake again.

'Drive on!' bellowed Max, proffering the money.

The driver wavered.

'Stop!'

'On!'

'Stop!'

By now they were kangaroo-hopping at an alarming rate towards Niall, who was beginning to look mildly concerned.

'Four hundred!' offered Max, 'and fucking drive on!'

As they bumped and crashed over the verge to avoid Niall, Tash tried to wrench open the door.

Leaning past her, Max shut it again.

Tash screamed in fury, crying Niall's name, but Max thrust one of the taxi's furry gonks in her mouth and told her to shut up. The driver turned the radio up to help drown her muffled shouts.

As the car passed, Niall thumped his fist on the roof in anger then wailed because it all but broke every knuckle.

The last he saw of Tash was a small, tearful face staring out of the back windscreen, wearing a chewed straw hat on her head and an electric blue fluffy gonk in her mouth.

His wails turned into the low, mournful moans of despair as he sank down on to the verge and, elbows on knees, put his face in his hands. She'd shouted for him, she'd tried to get out. Her face had said it all. He knew he wasn't wrong.

'Damn it!' He looked up and punched the ground, pulverising his smashed-up hand even more. He was going to move heaven, earth and Birnam Wood to be with her.

Niall heaved himself stiffly up, reeled for a few seconds, and then rubbed his neck. He had no money, no passport, clothes or identification. The manoir was just a few minutes away. But no one there would welcome him; Lisette was no doubt at this moment poisoning them all against him; Tash's future father-in-law was in situ and, along with the rest of them, would be planning the wedding of the decade.

He'd done with free-loading, he told himself.

Gathering his energy and his pride around him, Niall started limping on drained reserves of both towards the main road and the disappearing taxi.

After a few minutes, Tash stopped crying, throwing gonks at Max and screaming at the top of her voice, and turned to stare stonily out of the window, occasionally letting out a shuddering snort or an echoing sinal sniff.

They were speeding along the main road now, the taxi driver obediently keeping his accelerator pedal rammed into the rubber floor mat. Tash gripped the door handle with white knuckles, but the road ahead was an uninterrupted stretch of glistening tarmac. She glanced at the speedometer; they were doing over a hundred and forty kilometres an hour. Tash wasn't very good at conversion, but guessed that was too fast to jump out Dukes of Hazard style.

'I only did it out of love, Tash,' Max pleaded again, 'to stop you being humiliated by this obsessive crush you've got on Niall. He's an emotional wreck. Anyone can see that. He's just grateful for the sympathy from a pretty – no, a truly beautiful – girl. He doesn't feel the same way as I do.'

Max lapsed into an awkward silence, aware that his repeated assurances weren't working. She'd fug it out for a while and come round, he was sure. Niall had looked a mess – dirty, drunk and washed out – not the big star she'd tried to catch when it was only just starting to fall. By the time they were back in Derrin Road they'd be laughing about it with Mikey and Graham over a tinny and a vid.

Still gripping the handle, Tash chewed her lips and narrowed her eyes, her resolve hardening. She'd never felt so white-hot angry in her life; she kept expecting the passing bushes on the side in the road to burst into flames as she looked at them. She'd just realised how like his slick, insidious father Max was. He wasn't the big, cuddly blond teddy bear she didn't want to hurt – he was the spoiled brat who'd stolen it from her. She could remember only too clearly just how beastly he'd been to her in those last few months in London.

They overtook a chicken lorry at high speed. A cloud of dust and feathers whipped through the back of the taxi.

Blowing her nose noisily, Tash listened to a French DJ introduce a record.

As 'I Will Survive' blasted through the system, she sat bolt upright and almost laughed out loud.

A spidery vine tractor was turning out of a field ahead of them, its orange roof light flashing like the Tardis. Coming the other way was a stream of traffic crawling behind an English caravanette.

Of *course* Niall hadn't been on a white charger ready to whisk her away, thought Tash. They were both damsels; it was why she loved him. He was weak too, his fairytale world as bizarre and lop-sided as hers. They'd just have to rescue each other.

Hissing through his teeth, the taxi driver started to brake behind the vine tractor, his eyes darting from the road to Max in the rear-view mirror.

Tash gripped the handle tighter. Max was watching her like a hawk, so she looked out of the window, feigning interest in a lone rider trying to calm a very wild grey. The horse was gaping at the vine tractor with the same expression as Sophia passing Woolworths. Its electrified mane and ground pepper coat were very familiar.

As traffic started whooshing past them in blasts of fresh air, the taxi slowed almost to a halt.

Max stiffened.

Tash was staring at the rider in overjoyed amazement.

'My knightmare in shining amour,' she whispered.

Hugo was astonished and delighted when, trying to pacify the mad grey that had ditched Penny Moncrieff on Saturday, Tash burst from a nearby taxi and raced towards him.

'Can I please, please have a lift?' she gasped as she slid to a dusty halt beside the gelding.

Only just preventing the irascible grey from going into orbit, Hugo took in Tash's stricken face. Then, glancing over her shoulder, he noticed Max charging towards them like a prop sizing up a tackle, and he instantly realised what was happening.

'Hop on.' Hugo felt his heart bursting through the skin of his chest. 'And for Christ's sake hold tight.'

Without hesitation, he reached out a tanned arm and hoisted her up behind him in the saddle, shifting almost on to the pommel to give her room.

Tash scrabbled up, her skirt twisted round her waist to display the red lace knickers Max had given her for Christmas.

'You bitch!' Max wailed, sliding to a halt ten feet away, aware that he hadn't a chance of stopping her now. '*And* you told me you'd never wear those knickers!'

Unable to look at him, Tash closed her eyes, gripped on to Hugo's waist and buried her face in his back.

Then, to the amazement of passing motorists, Hugo dug in his heels and the grey shot off, speeding through a gate and across a field of ancient vines. Tash's hat flew into the wind behind them.

* * *

Half a mile away, dashing out on to the main road, Niall was drenched in sweat, crippled by the stitch and almost torn limb from limb with cramps.

Glancing wildly at the road sign opposite and blinking perspiration from his eyes, he read the distance to Tours and almost wept.

He tried to flag down passing cars, but taking one look at the deranged, dishevelled figure covered in dirt, none of them stopped.

'Oh Christ help me!' he wailed, breaking into a run again.

Then he stopped in his tracks.

Creaking towards him at the pace of an octogenarian monarch on walkabouts, came the spindly outline of an emaciated old crone on a bicycle. Her head swathed in a black headscarf, she was grinning broadly and listing heavily to the left under the weight of a huge stick-pile of French bread stacked under one arm. As she lifted her hand for a friendly wave, the bicycle wobbled dangerously and came to a groaning halt.

'Ça va?' the old woman greeted toothlessly.

'No,' Niall shook his head. 'Not ça va at all, madame. Very un-fucking ça va – Christ, sorry!' he was close to tears.

Not understanding a word, the woman grinned and nodded. Thinking he was a tramp, she offered him a stick of bread.

Gazing at the rickety bicycle, Niall shook his head. If only he had some money, he thought hopelessly. Then he remembered his watch.

Unclipping it with fumbling fingers, he tried to explain the barter, but the old woman still thought he wanted bread and kept shaking her head.

'C'est libre, monsieur.'

'Non – votre bicyclette, madame!' Niall pleaded, waving the watch. 'It's a Rolex – very valuable. Please understand! The bicycle.'

'Ah,' the woman beamed at him and, tutting, shook her head.

'Oh, God.' Dropping the watch, Niall put his head in his hands.

Then he felt a heavy weight lean against him and almost fell over. For a moment, he thought the old woman had collapsed. But looking down, he realised it was the bicycle. In the basket was his watch.

Turning round, he saw the old crone shuffling off, still clutching her bread. She beamed over her shoulder and waved him away with a gnarled hand.

'Merci, madame,' Niall croaked, almost overcome with gratitude.

Hoisting his leg over the rusty old bone-shaker, he started to pedal frantically towards Tours.

Tash and Hugo finally slithered to a halt by the manoir's tuffeau wall on the outskirts of the estate. Supremely fit, the grey was barely short of breath and jiggled nervously, still snatching the bit. His neck was just starting to darken.

Tash, however, had to unglue herself from Hugo's sweaty back. When she slid to the ground, her knees almost buckled under her. Catching her breath, she leaned against a nearby beech for support as Hugo jumped off, his black chaps heavy with dust, grimy face wreathed in smiles.

'Thank you,' she gasped, 'thank you so much.'

Hugo pulled the gelding's reins over his head. She must have read his letter in the taxi, he realised, and changed her mind. He hadn't felt happier in his life; winning gold in the European championships last year, watching his first foal born, sitting beside Selina Scott at a charity dinner. They'd been nothing compared to this rush of heady, asphyxiating pleasure.

'It's me that should be thanking you,' he said truthfully, moving closer to her as the gelding snatched at grass. 'I'd almost given up hope.'

Tash was staring at him, her bottom lip quivering.

'Shh – come here,' Hugo soothed, pulling her against him. He supposed it must be the relief. The feeling of her warm, moist body against his made him shiver with delight. He buried his face in her neck.

'You know,' Tash's voice shook with emotion, 'you really are the kindest man, Hugo. I can't believe I thought you were such a brute once – I'm sorry.' She hung her head. 'That's awful. I don't think so any more.'

'Shh – I know.' Hugo ran his hand down her soft, tousled hair and grinned, remembering what Alexandra had said. 'Did you really fancy me for so long? I had no idea.'

He could feel Tash nodding.

'Horribly, it tore me apart,' she confessed, pulling away slightly. 'It's all right – I don't any more. You don't have to worry about me jumping on you suddenly or anything.'

She didn't notice Hugo's body tensing.

'You see, that's why I think I value your friendship above anything really,' Tash went on, mindlessly brushing burrs off Hugo's t-shirt. 'Because I once thought it so impossible.'

Closing his eyes in pain, Hugo gripped her tighter. The gelding nearly tugged his arms out as it moved on to another patch of grass.

Tash buried her face in his wide, secure shoulder. It smelled of her mother's washing power mixed with the sweet, heady smell of horse. 'Oh, Hugo – I do so wish I'd fallen in love with you instead of Niall.'

Displaying the greatest self-control he'd ever been forced to muster, Hugo patted Tash gently on the shoulder and reluctantly let her go.

'Look.' He took her face between his hands. 'You'd better get that beautiful arse into gear.' He glanced down, unable to bear staring into her funny odd eyes any longer. 'Take that beast,' he nodded towards the grey, '– don't worry, after Snob he'll probably seem like an old hack.'

'But—'

'Don't argue,' Hugo snapped. 'Just take the horse, bugger off,' he looked back up at her with a twist of a grin, 'and find that disconsolate Irish idiot before it's too late.'

Thrusting the reins into Tash's hands, he turned around before she could see the tears brimming in his eyes.

That, he thought in amazement, is the first truly selfless thing I've ever done in my life. He wiped his eyes with the back of his hand and pushed back his hair. And it feels bloody lousy, he decided.

On the crowded, dusty main road, Niall was making agonisingly slow progress. The ancient, groaning bicycle was almost sucked underneath a huge pantechnicon as it thundered past, its load clattering.

Bouncing on and off the verge in a wonky u-turn as he fought to control the bike, Niall wiped the sweat from his face and looked up. He thought he was hallucinating.

An eye-rolling, sweating grey horse was pounding towards him, its racing hooves sending up a cloud of spaghetti western dust from the tinder-dry verge. Flapping behind it, like a torn battle banner, the rider's floral skirt cracked in the wind.

Wobbling precariously, Niall started to laugh, his feet grinding the rusty pedals into furious orbits as he cycled back the way he'd come.

Traffic was beginning to slow in amazement. A group of vine workers in a nearby field took off their hats and scratched their heads as they watched the grey horse racing towards the shuddering bicycle.

'Christ!' the rider wailed, standing up in the stirrups as she careered within metres of Niall. 'I can't stop!'

'Shit.' Niall could see two flame-red nostrils closing fast. The bone-shaker wavered hazardously before toppling into a clanking heap.

Niall leapt clear and into a ditch just as the grey overshot its halt, jumped the debris of bicycle and clattered off.

When he picked himself out, Niall wiped the dust from his eyes and blinked up the road, shielding his face from the sun with his hand. Shimmering in the distance was a girl on a horse. They'd slid to a halt in a haze of dirt twenty metres beyond him. No one could mistake the length of leg, the dishevelled mane or the huge, heart-breaking smile for anyone but Tash.

The traffic had almost come to a standstill. Rival radio stations clashed as windows were wound down for a better view. The vine workers had congregated and were uncapping a plastic bottle of wine.

Twenty metres apart, grinning from ear to ear, dust and emotion smarting their eyes and choking their throats, Tash and Niall stood and stared at one another.

Very slowly, Niall lifted his hand from shielding his eyes and held up his palm.

'Stay there!' he shouted with a choked laugh. 'I'm coming to you. Don't move a muscle.'

Niall looked over his shoulder and saw a high-bodied tractor chugging towards him, its orange light winking. He put out his thumb. Then, to a cacophony of horn-beeping applause from eager spectators on the road and noisy glass-raising cheers from the workers in the fields, he leapt on to the rumbling vine tractor.

Squinting through the haze of dust in disbelief, Tash laughed aloud. Niall's white charger, trundling towards her, was the same vine tractor that Max's taxi had slowed for, still making its sedate progress towards Tours.

Delirious with happiness, she slithered off the grey and patted his wet neck. Pressing her face to his cheek, she turned and watched Niall jump from the tractor. Hot, grimy, scruffy and smiling, he had never looked more desirable.

'Hello,' she croaked, reaching up to touch his throat.

'Hello,' he breathed, blinking dust from his eyes.

A hundred Kleenex were whipped from boxes on parcel shelves as, laughing like children who've found Christmas has come six months early this year, they tumbled into each other's arms.

Epilogue

Alexandra settled back into the swing-chair beside the pool and covered her brother's hand with hers. Together in companionable silence they watched Lauren playing with Lotty in the pool, reducing the normally sombre little girl to shrieks of giggles. Polly swam around them jealously, demanding another game of Marco Polo.

After a while, Alexandra turned her head sideways and smiled at Eddie. He was watching Lauren with such amazed delight as if still not quite believing she was his.

'She's lovely.' Alexandra squeezed his hand and he swivelled his eyes to her. 'I'm sorry we've all been so preoccupied, sweetheart. We hardly seem to have had a chance to welcome both of you or to really take in the fact you're now married,' she sighed sadly. 'This whole holiday – the party – was supposed to be for you, darling, and we've all but ignored you since you arrived.'

'Perhaps it's better that way, Lex.' Eddie patted his sister's knee kindly. 'It's been so long – Lauren is so young – I was frightened you'd all shun me. Having so much going on meant we fitted in without anyone really noticing.' He paused awkwardly and his hooded eyes shone with concern. 'I do love her, you know. People love to say she married me for the money – and I took her in because she flattered my ageing vanity but—'

'I know,' Alexandra laughed. 'I've got a younger husband, remember? You should have heard Matty when I first met

Pascal. And I know she didn't marry you for your money, darling.' She smiled with a knowing wink.

'Ah,' Eddie grinned. 'But I'm as rich as you now, sister dear. My gallery's finally exhibiting something the critics like. Totally overhyped crap,' he winked back wickedly. 'I've discovered this great new psychotic artist called Qued Zap – critics only like work coming out of padded cells at the moment – his *Rip in Canvas III* made one hundred fifty thousand bucks commission last week. The corporate art boys can't buy enough. It's like Kostabi in the eighties, but with a social conscience.'

Alexandra took in this piece of information with a steady gaze, but her heart beat faster. Behind her, she could hear Cass trying to persuade Marcus to transfer from canned five per cent to freshly brewed tea.

'But I've made it in your favourite mug, Marcus. You remember Mr Elephant?'

'Eddie, darling,' Alexandra whispered eventually, glancing nervously at a snoozing Pascal. 'Please say no if you can't do it – but I have a tremendous favour to ask you.'

'Mmm?' Eddie was looking at Lauren again. She was waving at him to join her in the pool. He shook his head.

'Could you possibly lend me some money?' Alexandra turned as red as her bank statement. 'You see, this party was terribly expensive and Pascal doesn't really know yet exactly how much a fully qualified madrigal singer costs to hire and—'

'Of course I will.' Eddie shut her up. 'Christ – I must owe you thousands.'

'Oh, thank you, darling!' Alexandra kissed him on the cheek.

They lapsed into silence once more. Michael was telling Marcus to bloody well drink his mother's tea and enjoy it. On the other side of the pool Sophia, grumbling that Lucian and Lisette had been over half an hour fixing more Pimms, was angling herself to catch the last rays of sun before setting off for Holdham tomorrow. She made Ben move his sunbed so far to one side that he capsized into the pool and emerged, looking surprised, beside Lotty.

Alexandra sighed happily. A sun-drenched tranquillity

seemed to have descended over her beautiful house, and the Hennessys, d'Eblouirs and Merediths were united as never before. Even Rooter, having recently impregnated two flirtatious spaniels and Valérie's shih-tzu, was lazily content. Only Hugo, stomping into the house ten minutes earlier and slamming the door, had broken the peaceful bonhomie of the afternoon.

Flopping her head away from the sun, Alexandra looked up at her house and wondered briefly why the shutters were closed on Lucian's window in the middle of the day.

'Pascal—' she stretched out her hand and rubbed his chest.

'Mmm, chérie?' Yawning, Pascal looked at her over his sunglasses.

'Do you think we should invite my mother to stay next week? Pascal? Hmmm? Oh, bother – Eddie, help. I think he's fainted. Eddie?'